The All-American King

by

Kent Krause

The All-American King

Kodar Publishing
ISBN 13: 978-0615878560
ISBN 10: 0615878563

This is a work of fiction. Though well-known actual people, places, and events are mentioned in this novel, all of the characters, names, and events, as well as all places, organizations, and dialogue in this book are products of the author's imagination or are used fictitiously.

Permissions

For Jill

Other books by Kent Krause:

Men Among Giants

Behind in the Count

Acknowledgements

I express my sincere thanks to the following people:

- Tim Graeve for sharing with me his considerable firsthand knowledge of high school baseball and football.
- Dave Bombela for informing me about evangelical culture in Des Moines and the nation in the 1970s.
- Brenda Cushing for advising me about locations I used as settings, and for introducing this book to many new readers.
- Greg Cushing and Dan Kruse for relating to me their experiences as starting quarterbacks in high school. Thanks also to Greg for allowing me to examine the playbook he now uses as a football coach.
- Ron Krause and Carol Krause for answering my questions about the proper terminology of various items.
- Robert Widhalm, Doug Kruce, and Tania Kruce for reading the manuscript and providing valuable comments.
- Cindy Conger for writing the first published book review of this novel.
- Kevin Burton for introducing Dave King to our East High classmates.
- Jonna LaToure for providing an insightful analysis and many helpful suggestions for this book.
- My wife Jill Krause for everything. She repeatedly read the manuscript, imparting useful suggestions and needed edits; she advised me on numerous character, plot, and wording issues; and from start to finish she continually encouraged me to write and publish this novel. Without her support, *The All-American King* would be a long-abandoned idea in the dustbin of my memory.

Additional Material

All of the major characters and many of the minor characters in *The All-American King* represent individuals included in the Biblical account of King David's life. A **Character Guide** listing these representations is included in the back of the book.

Additionally, there is a **Chapter Guide** matching each chapter of *The All-American King* with its corresponding sections of the Bible.

Finally, a study guide is included at the back of this book with **Discussion Questions** for book clubs or small groups.

"Jesse was the father of Eliab his firstborn; the second son was Abinadab, the third Shimea, the fourth Nethanel, the fifth Raddai, the sixth Ozem and the seventh David. Their sisters were Zeruiah and Abigail. Zeruiah's three sons were Abishai, Joab and Asahel."

1 Chronicles 2:13-16

Chapter 1 – September 1973

"Why don't they like me?"

"Why doesn't who like you?"

"Our brothers and sisters. Why don't they like me?"

Ozzie blinked and leaned forward to better focus on the road. "Well Dave, that's a tough one," he said through a yawn. "I mean, there's so much to not like about you. Where would I begin? Your revolting appearance? Your irritating personality? Your complete lack of coolness? Any one of those topics would take all morning to discuss."

"Forget it." It wasn't easy trying to talk to him about anything important.

"So, what exactly are you talking about?" he asked a few moments later.

I glowered at him. "They ignore me, make me feel stupid, pick on me."

"Pick on you. How?"

I couldn't believe he was so oblivious to my persecution. I wondered if his special cigarettes with the pointy ends had wiped out his memory. "There are hundreds of examples. Remember Father's Day a year ago? Right before we were supposed to leave for the restaurant, Eli and Shane grabbed me and gave me a swirly. I had my coat and tie on and everything."

Snorting laughter shot from Ozzie's nose.

"I'm all wet and disgusting because of them and Dad yells at me for making us late."

"They're just messing with you," he said, still chuckling. "It's what older brothers do."

"No," I snapped, "that was mean. Just like everything they do to me. If they were just messing around they wouldn't have pissed in the damn toilet before dunking my head."

Doubled over the wheel, his body convulsed with amusement. "You're going to send us into the ditch if you don't stop cracking me up."

I stared straight ahead, eyes fixed on the headlight beams slicing through the predawn darkness. As we rode on in silence, he must have felt a twinge of guilt for laughing at me. "Don't worry about them," he said. "They're nothing special." As second youngest, Ozzie had taken his share of sibling abuse too. But when he was picked on, it was more like teasing or joking. With me it was different.

"They treat me like dirt," I blurted in a voice higher than I intended it to be. "Except for you, none of them like me."

"That's not true." He glanced over at me with a wry smile. "I don't like you very much either."

"Fine."

He yawned again. "Dave, you've got to realize that you were number nine. Think about it. That's three ranks lower than Cindy Brady. The whole kid thing had played itself out by the time you were born. When you came along our reaction was pretty much, 'Aw crap, another one?'"

"Uh-huh." I regretted bringing up the subject.

Ozzie's battle-worn '62 Ford pickup rattled up East 38th Street, beyond the Des Moines city limits. We continued north for three more miles as the tall grass and yellow wildflowers in the ditch whizzed by as a barely visible blur. After turning east, he interrupted the mechanical monologue of his beloved four-wheeled steed. "We've all gone through a lot the past decade." He sounded uncharacteristically serious. "Our brothers, sisters, and especially the old man."

"Yeah, I know. But they don't have to take it out on me."

"You have to understand, years ago things were going great for everybody. The restaurant was packed every night. Money was rolling in. Fun vacations every year. We were one big happy family of Kings. You were born in what, March of '58? It was only four years after that when … things changed." He eyed me with a grim look.

Saying nothing, I shifted in my seat.

"Then it was one rotten thing right after another for our family." His words were laced with pain. "Maybe they somehow link you to that bad stuff. They remember how great things were before. Then you come along and soon afterwards the bottom falls out. I'm sure nobody actually blames you—none of what happened was your fault—but maybe on some unconscious level you stir up some hard feelings for them."

I stared ahead to the farthest limit of the headlights' glow. Recalling the string of family calamities that marked my childhood spawned a sick feeling in my gut. Pondering Ozzie's words, I wondered if he was right.

He turned north as we entered the final leg of our trip. Both of us were quiet. A cloud of depression seemed to fill the cab. He took a breath like he planned to speak again. I looked over, anticipating more brotherly wisdom. He instead tilted his body, grimaced, and cut loose a ferocious blast from down low. I jumped at the unexpected noise. It began like a badly-played tuba and then after a few seconds tailed off into something resembling the sound of bacon frying. Such outbursts from my brother were common, though this one was louder and longer than most of his offerings.

"Whoowee—that has some bite to it," he proudly declared.

"I hope you rot in your own stench."

He grinned and started waving his exhaust toward me. Only a second later it hit like a crushing right from George Foreman. "Aaaawww!" I cried as I franticly waved both hands in front of my nose. It was no use. The warm foul air rushed through my nostrils and cascaded down my windpipe. "Ohhhh, that's horrible," I coughed. It was as if someone had taken a dead skunk that had been decaying on the highway for three days and jammed it in my face.

My coughing turned to gagging. I started cranking the handle to roll down the window, but it just spun around and around while the window remained tightly shut. In my panicked quest for fresh air, I'd forgotten that it was broken. I gasped violently as bright-colored spots danced before my eyes.

Meanwhile, Ozzie's villainous laughter grew louder and deeper. "BWA HAH HAH HAH HAH! Bow to my power, young one. Bow to the awesome power of my anus!"

Fumbling with the other handle, I pushed open the passenger door and stuck my head out. Sweet life-giving country air flowed into my lungs. My coughing slowly subsided. After about thirty seconds of deep breaths I leaned back in. The driver's maniacal chortles continued.

Thankfully, we soon reached our destination. As he turned onto a gravel driveway, we passed a metal mailbox labeled "Obadiah King" and between two large pine trees that stood like giant green sentries. The pickup, still reeking of Ozzie, rolled down the long driveway and came to a stop amid a cluster of farm buildings. We dropped out of the cab and approached our grandparents' white two-story farmhouse. Livestock and livestock byproducts had never smelled so good.

"You do realize that you're going to hell," I said.

"Yep." He ran both hands through the brown mane that hung down well past the edge of his shirt collar.

Light from the house spilled through the open front door. Samson, a black, brown, and white shepherd-collie mix, stood inside with his nose pressed against the screen. He greeted us with a couple of crisp barks. Ozzie belched in reply. Samson backed up as my brother pulled open the screen door. The dog gave him a quick sniff before planting two paws on my chest. "Hey boy," I said, scratching behind his ears. His tail swished back and forth. Ozzie and I grabbed our work jackets off a coat tree in the front hallway.

"Good morning boys," an elderly female voice called out from the kitchen.

"Morning Grandma," we replied, almost in unison.

"The pancakes will be waiting for you when you're done."

"Thanks Grandma."

We donned our jackets, which we wore to keep our school clothes reasonably clean of farm residue, and exited the house. Samson followed close behind. If we didn't mess around or face any unexpected problems, we could finish our chores in little more than an hour. That usually left about fifteen minutes for breakfast, before we had to leave for school.

I trudged toward the sheep pen, while Ozzie headed to the cattle barn. Samson padded along at my heels. About twenty paces from the wire fence, the dog slowed and started growling in the direction of the pen. An instant later, he erupted into a torrent of furious barking. I'd never heard him so enraged.

"What's wrong?" I asked, peering intently through the dimness. "What do you see, boy?" My eyes scanned the large shed where Grandpa kept his sheep.

Ozzie jogged over. "What's his problem?" The three of us advanced cautiously. Samson's barking slowed to a steady snarl. As we got closer to the fence, a noise drew our attention to the right. There, at the far end of the pen, I could make out the shapes of a group of sheep crowded into a corner. Their desperate bleating was now discernible over the dog's combative growl.

"That's not good," I said. "How did they get out of the shed?" Scanning left across the pen, my eyes stopped on three dark objects about fifteen feet from the sheep.

Ozzie saw them too. "What the hell?" he whispered.

The largest of the dark shapes—the one in the middle—shifted, creating a recognizable silhouette. My heart pounded as I stared in disbelief. Samson fired off three barks.

"Wolves," Ozzie hissed.

I'd never been that close to a wolf, let alone three wolves, before. The one in the middle was larger than I imagined a wolf could be. The creature turned toward us. His two companions did the same. The lower half of each wolf's face and body was light gray. The fur on top of their heads and backs was dark and barely visible in the early morning gloom. The effect was eerie. Ozzie, Samson, and I stood paralyzed.

After several moments, the large wolf bared its teeth and growled. My brother screeched an expletive and bolted away. Samson raced alongside him. Unmoving, I continued to lock eyes with the predator. The two other wolves turned back to the sheep, no doubt seeking to take care of unfinished business. Tracking their path, I noticed something I hadn't seen before: a casualty from the flock lying on its side. Dark splotches mottled its fleece.

The sight ignited an angry fire within. Springing from my paralysis, I placed both hands on top of a post and jumped the wire fence. Upon landing, I turned quickly to face the wolf. Its red eyes measured me. The sound of my feet hitting the dirt caused the other two animals to turn around. They took up positions on each side of their leader. I'd achieved my first goal—the sheep were safe for the time being. I, however, was standing alone in an enclosed pen with three feral beasts.

Low growls filled the air. The creatures started to advance. My mind raced. *Aren't wolves afraid of people? What if they're rabid? Could just one bite give me rabies? Would punching or kicking be more effective?* Finding a weapon seemed advisable. Glancing to my left, I saw nothing against the shed. I then remembered that we kept a shovel inside. Sidestepping to the entrance, I pushed open the unlatched door. Fortunately the shovel was only a few feet away. I seized it and darted back outside. The wolves were still there, continuing their slow advance. Gripping the handle with both hands I waved the metal blade back and forth in front of me. As they closed, the two smaller animals fanned out to my right and my left. Adrenaline raced through my body. I decided my best chance would be to charge forward and bring the shovel down on the largest one's head. *Hopefully the other two will then scatter. But if they don't ...*

A thunderous explosion shattered the air. I dropped the shovel as dirt sprayed up under the largest wolf. He jumped as if he'd been electrocuted. Wrenching my head toward the sound, I saw Grandpa and Ozzie standing just beyond the fence. Smoke billowed from the barrel of the shotgun Grandpa had leveled at the wolves. He broke open the gun and loaded another shell into the breech. Looking forward again I saw nothing but empty ground. From the opposite side of the shed came the sound of wire rattling. Picking up the shovel, I stalked around the wooden structure. Off in the distance, three dark shapes raced across the pasture toward a clump of trees. Down at my feet was a low sagging fence wire that had served as a gateway into and out of the pen.

I returned to Ozzie and Grandpa. My brother's slender frame appeared even thinner in the shadow of our barrel-chested grandfather. The three of us stood in silence for a few moments while Samson paced about. "Since when do you have wolves around here," Ozzie blurted.

"Haven't seen any for a while," Grandpa said in his usual husky voice. "Been quite a few years, I'd say." He broke open the shotgun and picked out the unspent shell with his thick fingers. He then turned and started back to the house, slightly bent over like always.

My brother and I lingered a bit longer. Staring at the dead sheep, he shook his head. "Unbelievable," he said. "Not real, man." He walked off towards the cattle barn.

I found a spot behind the silo to bury the mangled lamb. Placing her lifeless body into the ground made me realize how attached I'd grown to these stupid animals. Back inside the shed, I filled the water basin and pulled down bales of hay from the lofted storage area. While scooping ground meal out of a barrel, I was startled by a voice.

"You know, I'm sorry you boys have to come up here every day." Spinning around, I saw Grandpa standing at the entrance. His plaid shirt and denim overalls stretched to contain his brawny torso.

"Uh, yeah." I immediately regretted my lame reply.

"I told your father it wasn't necessary, but he insists. You know how stubborn he is." Grandpa's rheumy grey eyes reflected strength and determination. I imagined how they must have blazed with fire when he fought at Belleau Wood over a half century ago.

"It's no problem, Grandpa."

"He doesn't think I can do this anymore. Wants me to give it up." He sighed and stared into one of the corners of the shed. Even with his forward lean, he still towered above me.

I thought back to last May when Dad had first told Ozzie and me that we would be helping with the morning chores at Grandpa's farm. I wasn't happy about it, but I understood. Grandpa was eighty-two. Though most farmers retired long before that age, he just kept on working, year after year. He didn't know any other way—and he was always able to do the job. But last year, Dad noticed that he was slipping a little. Tasks that used to be routine were becoming a struggle. Though Grandpa could have hired more help, Dad wanted family here at the farm to check on his aging parents. After the harvest, he planned to talk to Grandpa again about retiring and moving to the city.

"I reckon it is about time," he said, nodding slowly. My grandfather was bald on top with a band of stubbly white hair that wrapped around the sides and back of his head. Since all the pictures of him as a younger man were black and white, I never knew what color his hair used to be. He drew a deep breath and gazed down at a lamb chomping on some hay. "I feel bad about you boys having to come up here so early, but today, Dave, I'm glad you were here." His eyes shifted to me. "What you did to save those sheep took courage. Real courage."

My jaw was open but no words came out. I could only nod in response. Grandpa turned and ambled away. The realization slowly set in that an older relative had acknowledged, in a positive sense, something I had done. A man who had once charged through machine-gun fire to attack German trenches said that I had courage. For the first time in my life, I felt like a man. My head buzzed as I finished my chores.

Because of the unexpected delay, Ozzie and I had only a few minutes to scarf down Grandma's world-class pancakes. We climbed into the pickup at 7:40 a.m., twenty-five minutes before school started. Covering the eleven miles, four of them in rush hour city traffic, in such a short amount of time was not possible for normal law-abiding drivers. Fortunately—or unfortunately—my brother was nothing of the sort. Flooring it after exiting our grandparents' driveway, he raced south and west across the county roads. Slowing up a bit after entering Des Moines city limits, he weaved his way through traffic to reach Eastridge High School at 8:03. He normally embellished his accelerations and lane changes with whoops and expletives. On this morning's drive, however, he was uncharacteristically quiet. I guessed that he was embarrassed by his reaction to the wolves. Especially since it was witnessed by his younger brother.

We grabbed our books and started jogging from the distant student lot to the limestone school building. Bounding up the concrete stairs, we passed between the large classical-style pillars and through the heavy front doors. "See ya later, sophomore scum," Ozzie said as he veered left down the front hallway. I turned right to head for my first period class. Rapidly traversing the school corridors, I slid into my seat just as the bell rang.

My first three classes—English, Algebra II, and Biology—passed without incident. Like usual, I spent as much time checking out the girls as I did absorbing the fine instruction being bestowed upon me. And, like usual, my unwanted superpower of invisibility remained in force. All objects of my distraction had no idea I was even in the room.

Fourth period was gym. On this day, the boys were separated from the girls. I was actually pleased with that arrangement since several young ladies were still chirping about Billy Jean King's recent straight-set triumph over Bobby Riggs. I too was glad she won, but I didn't need to keep hearing about it.

After changing into our gym clothes, we gentlemen were sent outside to the track. Mr. Anderson started us off with some stretching exercises and light calisthenics. He then divided us into groups of five for the 40-yard dash. My group was the third to run. I easily beat the four running against me, and my time bested that of the other group winners as well.

After the sprint competitions, Mr. Anderson had us all line up for the one mile—four laps around the track. A few of my heavier classmates groaned and cursed. "Just keep up the best you can," the gym teacher said. "Jog slowly or walk if you have to."

He clapped his hands to replicate a starting gun. Pacing myself, I stayed with the pack through the first two circuits. Picking up speed, I grabbed the lead in the third lap and crossed the finish line a full ten seconds ahead of the guy in second place.

"Good run, King," Mr. Anderson announced. Bent over and still panting, I could not reply. "Maybe you'll consider joining the track team in the spring," he said.

"I'll keep that in mind."

"Outstanding!" He then turned to urge on the stragglers, who would continue stumbling across the finish line over the next several minutes.

My fifth period class was World History. I liked history, but since the class immediately followed lunch, I usually struggled to stay awake for the whole hour. Today would be different. Upon taking my seat in the fourth row, I noticed that our teacher, Mr. Barnes, was not at his desk at the front of the classroom. The din of student chatter increased as my classmates sensed fifty-five minutes of freedom. Just then the door opened and a towering presence entered. The noise ceased. With a purposeful stride, the presence crossed the room and stopped behind the teacher's desk. I immediately recognized his leathery face and sandy brown crew cut. Standing six feet six inches tall, he surveyed the class. Like me, the other students sat frozen. They too knew who he was.

My fascination with Sal Benjamin Kishman began at age seven, the same age I became a baseball fan. I had memorized all his statistics and career highlights from his years playing right field for the Philadelphia Phillies. From 1938, his rookie season, to 1942, he was one of the most feared sluggers in the National League. In 1943 he joined the Marines and went off to fight the Japanese. When he came back from the war, however, the keen batting eye had disappeared. Strikeouts and pop ups replaced the monstrous home runs and scorching line drives. His average plummeted. He was in the minors by 1948 and out of organized baseball by 1950.

Iowans never forgot Sal Kishman though. Born and raised on the east side of Des Moines, he remained a local legend. East-siders were ecstatic when he became the head baseball coach at Eastridge in 1957. Though a state title remained elusive, his teams nearly always competed for the conference championship. The many dozens of his former players who went on to play college and professional ball added to his legendary status. For the people of Des Moines, especially those on the east side, Coach Kishman represented true baseball royalty.

And he was standing at the front of my fifth period World History class.

"Mr. Barnes has unexpectedly taken ill this morning," a baritone voice announced from on high. "I will be teaching this class today." In addition to his duties as baseball coach, Mr. Kishman also taught 11th grade American History and Civics. He did not look thrilled to be babysitting a bunch of sophomores during his planning period. Actually he never looked thrilled. The stern look at the head of the class was the same expression I'd seen in numerous sports page photos. On the field, that intense countenance often erupted into a volcano when one of his players didn't hustle or when a questionable call went against the Eastridge High Braves.

He started calling the roll.

Do NOT say anything stupid, I told myself.

"Ackerman." He read the names gruffly, like a Marine drill sergeant.

"Here."

"Allen."

"Here."

As the coach moved down the alphabet my mind inexplicably wandered back to fifth grade when, in a similar circumstance, one of my smart-aleck classmates responded to the calling of his name with, "Yo-ho-ho and a bottle of rum." The words rang through my head.

Do NOT say it. Do NOT say it. Though I fought desperately to evict the silly reply from my mind, it grew louder and louder. My throat tightened at the thought of Kishman's likely response to a sophomore who tried to make a mockery of him. I recalled how Phillies fans used to call each of his home runs a "Kish of Death."

"Hanson … Howell … Jackson." Each name was followed by a "here." He was getting closer. I had to get it together.

"King." Upon hearing the coach bark my name, a grenade of terror exploded in my belly.

"Here." Despite my near nervous breakdown, I'd managed to give a respectable response. I breathed a sigh of relief. My joy, however, was short-lived. Kishman was silent. *Why isn't he saying the next name? Something is wrong. Something is very wrong.* My body trembled as I wondered if I had said something other than "here" and didn't realize it.

"King, huh?" Kishman looked over in my direction. "Which one of you is King?"

Swallowing hard, I meekly raised my hand.

"You wouldn't be related to Eli King, would you?"

The noose of tension loosened. Eli King had been a star first baseman for Eastridge in the late 1950s and was now one of Kishman's assistant coaches.

"Yes sir, he's my brother."

"Brother?" Kishman shot back, his voice a bit higher. "I didn't know there were any more of you King boys left. Just how big is your family, son?"

"I've got six brothers and two sisters. Eli is the oldest. I'm the youngest."

"I should hope so, for your mother's sake." A few laughs escaped from my classmates.

I chose not to tell him about Mom. I also didn't tell him about Nate and Ray.

The coach paused for a couple seconds, seemingly deep in thought. "So, can you hit like Eli and Shane? Or pitch like Adam?" There was the barest hint of a smile on his face. In all the newspaper and magazine pictures I'd seen of Kishman, only one showed him with any kind of levity. An AP photographer caught him grinning as he returned to the dugout after hitting a 450-foot home run off fellow Iowan Bob Feller at Sportsman's Park in St. Louis during the 1940 All-Star Game.

The gears in my head clicked and spun trying to churn out a suitable reply. *Don't be cocky, but show some confidence.* This was my chance to impress Sal Kishman. I wanted to make it count. "I can hit some, and pitch, and play shortstop, or wherever." My voice tailed off. I felt myself slouching in disappointment with my response.

"Is that so?" Kishman asked, raising his eyebrows. "Well then, I hope to see you at sophomore baseball tryouts next spring."

"You will … definitely." I debated telling him that I hoped to make the varsity team as a sophomore, like Eli. I'd hit over .500 every year since my second season of Little League, and I had a better-than-average fastball when I was on the mound. Wisely, I kept my mouth shut.

Kishman's gaze returned to the attendance book. "Kohler."

"Here."

"Kruse."

"Here."

The parade of names continued until Sara Young issued the last "here."

Despite my awe for Sal Kishman, I had to admit the teaching style he displayed in our classroom was uninspired. After finishing the roll, he picked a random name from the attendance book and told the victim to start reading from the textbook chapter we were currently studying. Though hearing my classmates struggle through lengthy passages was in no way engaging, I followed along closely in the book. Fear of Kishman's wrath was a powerful motivator. When he barked my name, the fourth one called, I was ready to go. The transition was nearly seamless.

After about thirty minutes of listening to teenagers drone on about ancient Greece, Kishman got bored. With a halfhearted attempt at using Athenian democracy as a segue, he started lecturing about current events. It did not take long for his heated discourse to awaken the class from its state of near slumber. The bulging veins above his temples further underscored the passion he felt for his opinions.

Though I was quite certain the impromptu lecture would not be on Mr. Barnes's test, I still took notes. At the end of the class period my notebook contained the following: "Nixon—A great man. Strong leader. Keeps order in a nation threatened by hippies. Watergate—A baseless witch-hunt by liberals seeking to weaken our republic. John Dean is a traitor. This whole thing will blow over in a couple months. Will soon become a forgotten footnote in history. Vietnam—Huge mistake for us to leave. Got to start bombing the North again. Get the troops back in there. If we don't the South will fall to the commies. The rest of Asia will follow. The Draft—Need it back. The country is weak without it. Young men need discipline. Israel—Need to support. Important ally. Another war with the Arabs is on the horizon."

The bell rang and I was off to sixth period: Choir. The students were finally starting to sound respectable. Miss Williams seemed pleased. Of course, she could not let the hour pass without cajoling me about joining Concert Choir next semester. "You have the talent right now, Dave. Very few sophomores are invited to join Concert Choir. You would have so much fun." Her words reminded me of hearing my sisters describe how beautifully our mother could sing. Though I liked the idea of further developing any musical ability I may have inherited, spring semester meant baseball tryouts. I did not want the extra time commitment required for Concert Choir to hurt my chances of making varsity, or at least JV.

After the final bell, I visited my locker to collect the books I would need for homework. On the trek to the distant gravel parking lot, I reflected on my day. Though I'd danced with wolves at dawn and raced past my peers in gym class, only one highlight stood out—meeting Sal Kishman. I imagined starring on his baseball team. After each dazzling play, he acknowledged my achievement with a smile and a handshake.

Upon reaching the lot, my baseball fantasies dissipated. Ozzie's truck was nowhere to be seen. *Not again.* His last class occasionally dismissed a couple minutes early. When it did, he and his friends would take off without me. This had happened four times already this month. He always deflected my later protests with a retort about how he had to ride the bus home every day when he was in tenth grade. That may have been true, but it did not make the experience any more pleasant for me.

As I traipsed to the bus stop, my mind conjured wishful visions of Ozzie's pickup running out of gas at a busy intersection. *Or, better yet, maybe a tire could blow out. A speeding ticket would work too. And then the cops could spot a bag of weed on one of his stoner friends.*

My bus arrived after a prolonged wait. As the crow flew, my house was only four miles east of the school. As the bus meandered, this distance took about a half hour to cover. A car accident on the route added another ten minutes to the journey on this particular afternoon. After exiting the bus, I still had to walk another two blocks up the street. I reached my driveway at 3:55 p.m., more than an hour after school had let out. Stupid Ozzie.

I unlocked the back door to an empty house. Dad was at the restaurant. He usually went in around 3:00. Before leaving, he left a note for me on the refrigerator. "Do the laundry."

I grabbed a bottle of RC and plopped on the sofa to watch a rerun of *The Courtship of Eddie's Father*. The house fell dim as the outside light from the overcast sky faded. During a commercial, my gaze shifted to the family picture atop the fireplace mantel. Two parents sat in the center surrounded by nine children of varying ages. Everyone was smiling and seemingly happy. Two years old at the time, I was seated on my mother's lap. As I'd done a thousand times before, I shut my eyes and tried to remember her. A faint presence hovered at the distant reaches of my memory. I eventually returned to the beaming faces in the picture. The image never seemed quite right to me. Maybe it was a depiction of reality at one time, but it was not a reality I had ever known.

At 4:30 Perry Mason replaced Bill Bixby on the screen of the RCA console television. My wandering mind struggled to focus on the courtroom drama. I finally gave up and shut off the TV. The house was quiet. After letting my thoughts drift for a while longer, I started the laundry and ate supper—macaroni and cheese, toast with peanut butter, and canned pears. Homework came next. My brain resisted, but the promise of *Monday Night Football* afterward provided it with the needed incentive to start plowing through the assignments.

Ozzie clattered into the house at a quarter to eight. He stuck his head in my room as he passed by. "Hey Toad." He had been calling me that since seeing *American Graffiti* a couple weeks earlier. I myself had not yet seen the movie, so I could only imagine what the Toad character was like.

"Thanks for the ride home," I said, glancing at him out of the corner of my eye.

"You are so welcome. You know I'm always here for you. If you ever need anything, and I mean anything, you just ask. You're my brother and dammit, I …" At that, he pretended to get choked up with emotion.

After giving him the bird, I returned to my trigonometry problems. Ozzie shuffled down the hall singing one of Judas's songs from *Jesus Christ Superstar*.

I finished my homework around 8:30. With a basket of laundry fresh out of the dryer, I settled on the couch in front of the television. Ozzie lounged in the green La-Z-Boy, already watching the game. "That's a good girl," he said as I started folding the warm clothes. Roger Staubach hit Calvin Hill to drive the Cowboys deeper into Saints territory.

"Crap." Ozzie didn't like Dallas. Neither did I.

At halftime, I went upstairs to practice playing my guitar. The instrument, a Gibson J50 acoustic, had first belonged to my brother Ray. He loaned it to me when he left for the Army four years earlier. It was no longer a loan. Before playing, I always ran my fingers over the R.S.K. he had carved into the back of the guitar's neck. I started strumming the opening notes to "Over the Hills and Far Away." I'd been practicing the song for a month and, for the first time, played it all the way though without any mistakes. Raising my fist in the air, I soaked in the cheers from an imaginary arena crowd.

I retrieved a second load of laundry from the dryer and returned to the couch just in time for the start of the second half. Ozzie remained slouched in Dad's easy chair.

"Not bad, Jimmy Page."

"Thanks."

The Saints were down 12-3 at halftime. Things went from bad to worse for them in the second half. "Come on Manning, get rid of the ball," Ozzie yelled at the TV. Manning didn't get rid of the ball and got planted for an eight-yard loss.

Dad came home a little after ten. Upon hearing the car pull into the driveway, Ozzie scurried over to the sofa. Without a word, Dad clumped across the living room and dropped into his green chair. Though the hefty man in the La-Z-Boy resembled the happy father at the center of the picture on the mantel, the real life version had less hair, thirty more pounds, and no beam in his countenance.

"You get the laundry done?" he asked, without moving his eyes from the RCA.

"Yep."

"Good."

I wanted to tell him about meeting Sal Kishman, but figured he wouldn't care. Ever since my Little League days, he had never showed much interest in my baseball games. I then thought about describing the encounter to my brother, but knew it wouldn't matter to him either. With limited athletic ability, Ozzie was the one King brother who had never played any sports at Eastridge.

On the television, Howard, Frank, and Dandy Don tried in vain to make the Cowboys blowout entertaining. At 10:30 Dad told me to turn the channel so he could watch Carson. A few minutes later I realized there was no reason for me to still be up, especially since an alarm clock would be piercing my ears in about seven hours.

As I lay in bed, my thoughts turned to baseball tryouts. *Once I make varsity next spring, people will have to take notice—my dad, my brothers and sisters, the girls at school. I'll be popular. Everybody will want to hang out with Dave King, star of the Eastridge High Braves.* The roar of the crowd grew louder as I drifted off to sleep.

Chapter 2 – November 1973

With a mischievous grin, Ozzie surveyed our nephews. "So, you little sewer rats want to make a friendly Thanksgiving wager?"

"What's the bet?" Anthony asked.

"If I can eat more turkey than the three of you combined, then you all have to do whatever I tell you to do for a whole day. If you three eat more bird than me, then I will do whatever you tell me to do for an entire day."

The Krieger brothers leaned their red heads together to discuss the proposition. Each glanced over at the competition, a skinny seventeen-year-old of average height. Though younger—Anthony was eleven, Joe was ten, and Asa was nine—my nephews concluded that their numerical advantage would carry the day.

Anthony turned to my brother. "All right, you're on."

"We're gonna bury you," Joe taunted as he gripped his fork. Asa laughed with anticipation.

Ozzie sat back his chair with a look of confidence. "Prepare to be vanquished my rodent nephews. You have fallen into the quagmire of impossibilities, for you now face the hopeless task of trying to defeat the Mighty Wizard of Oz! BWA-HA-HA-HA-HA-HAAAA!"

"More like the Gizzard of Oz," Anthony retorted.

"Chicken gizzard," Joe said.

"Chicken poop!" Asa added. Laughter burst out from all three brothers.

"Boys!" Zoe snapped from across the table. "Settle down." Her sons stifled their mirth and momentarily sat still.

Meanwhile, the wait staff of The Royal Court finished bringing out the food from the kitchen. Our plates were soon covered with mountains of turkey, stuffing, mashed potatoes, green beans, corn, and cranberry sauce. The Thanksgiving feast commenced. Each year on this holiday, the King family gathered for dinner at Dad's restaurant. There were fifteen of us seated around a large rectangular table in the private dining room, plus four children at a nearby kids' table.

Ozzie raced out to an early lead in the fowl-eating competition. Like a vacuum cleaner he sucked down the piles of meat, both white and dark, before him. The Krieger boys also dug into their food with much alacrity. Before finishing their first pieces of turkey, however, all three made the mistake of glancing over at my brother. Eyes wide, they looked on with horror at the rapacious eating machine at the end of the table. My freak-of-nature brother was nearly finished with seconds by the time the boys had recovered from their shock. Asa picked up a roll and was about to take a bite when Joe swatted it out of his hand. The sphere of bread rocketed past my ear and hit the wall behind me.

"Don't fill up on rolls, moron!" Joe scolded. "The bet is for turkey."

The din of King family conversation filled the room as several small discussions broke out around the table. My sister Abby sat to my right. I had yet to see her face though as she was locked in conversation with the person on her right—my other sister, Zoe. Leaning slightly toward the curtain of straight blond hair that draped the back of Abby's head, I tuned in to their chat.

"Soooo, tell me about this new guy," Zoe said. "Did you meet him at Iowa State?"

"Yes," Abby replied, setting down her fork. "His name is Jerry. He's in my psych class. Each week he'd sit closer to me in lecture. And then two weeks ago he sat right next to me. After class we started talking. It was mainly about school stuff at first. Then he started making jokes and being really funny. We flirted for a while and then he asked me out."

"Are you going to keep seeing him?"

"I think so," Abby said with a snicker. "There's definitely potential …"

By that point, I'd heard enough about dreamboat Jerry. If he truly did have potential, I could learn all about him in person next Thanksgiving. Glancing around Abby's head, I noticed that Zoe's face was fuller than I remembered. The crow's feet extending from the corners of her eyes were also recent additions. Nonetheless, her freshly-permed brunette hair and vibrant purple dress suggested that, at thirty, she could still attract her pick of suitors—just like in high school over a decade ago.

To Zoe's right were Katy and Eli. Katy was a tall, thin woman who said little and smoked much. Despite her height, Eli's large head towered above her blond bob. His dark hair was cut short in a butch, the military style resembling that worn by his boss. Eli and Katy's toddler, Benjamin, sat in a highchair between his parents.

My father sat at the head of the table in a regal high-backed mahogany chair. The large wooden throne effectively conveyed the intended monarchical effect. To Dad's right, on the opposite side of the table from me, were my brothers Adam and Shane and their wives, Shannon and Pamela. The three Krieger brothers completed the row. At the opposite end of the table from Dad sat Ozzie. His chair was of regular size to avoid any confusion as to which end was the head of the table.

Though it was difficult, I tried to hear the more distant conversations.

"You really should consider opening a place downtown," Adam told Dad. "That's where the money is going. Look at how well Babe's is doing."

My third oldest sibling, behind Eli and Zoe, Adam wore a thick headdress of flowing brown hair complemented by long furry sideburns and a bushy moustache. He had been a manager at The Royal Court since 1965, the year he dropped out of college. He did this in part because his girlfriend Shannon was pregnant and in part to save the restaurant, which was on the verge of financial collapse. Though he was only nineteen at the time, Adam's energy and administrative skills helped right the ship. By the early 1970s, The Royal Court thrived once again.

"I have considered it," my father replied. "But we're doing fine right here. We don't need a second restaurant."

Since I already knew how Adam and Dad's discussion would turn out, I trained my ears on the other conversation at the far end of the table. "No way Dallas loses today," barked Eli, jabbing his fork in the air.

"Wrong," Shane countered. "Miami is the best team in football, period. They win easily." At twenty-six, a year younger than Adam, Shane was the only adult male not wearing a coat and tie. He instead sported a white double-breasted cook's jacket. He'd been a Royal Court employee since April 1967, a couple months after his release from the state penitentiary. Dad hired him then because no one else wanted an ex-con with a history of drug dealing and aggressive behavior. Few thought he would last at the restaurant, but a desire to avoid returning to prison and an ultimatum from then-girlfriend Pamela proved to be powerful motivators. Soaking in Dad's wisdom, Shane eventually developed the skills to become sous-chef at The Royal Court.

Amplifying giggles from the four youngsters at the kids' table drowned out the rest of Shane's NFL commentary. Ranging in age from seven to four, two of the children belonged to Eli and Katy and two belonged to Adam and Shannon. I returned my attention to the mound of stuffing before me. Ozzie, meanwhile, extended his ingesting lead over our hapless nephews.

A couple minutes later, Monty, the restaurant's assistant manager, entered the room. Looking anxious, he said something to my father. Adam started to get up, but Dad gestured for him to remain seated. My father then stood and exited the room, the prim Monty following close behind. Peering through the dark-tinted window that separated us from the paying customers, I tried to follow their path. But the opaque glass caused the pair to blend in with the shadowy figures in the restaurant's main dining area.

With Dad gone, the family's conversations grew louder and less restrained. I considered trying to join in with one of them, but an opening did not present itself. Nobody was concerned about me anyway. Across the table, two of the three Krieger boys had conceded defeat. They were saving what little room they had left for pumpkin pie. Crimson-faced Joe, however, pressed on. Eyes blazing with determination, he continued to force bits of turkey into his mouth.

"Give it up, Joe," I said. "Ozzie's stomach is a black hole."

"I'm … not … done … yet," he replied through heavy breaths. Head bowed, his face hovered just above his plate.

"You're just gonna make yourself sick."

Ozzie uncorked a vigorous belch. "There, now I've got room for more."

Abby turned and glared at him. "Gross."

"Damn it, Ozzie," Zoe said. "Is it really necessary to teach my boys ALL your disgusting habits?"

"Uh, yeah, actually it is," he replied. "It's important they learn proper technique from a master." He turned to our nephews. "Hey guys, who wants to pull my finger?"

After a few more disdainful remarks, my sisters resumed their conversation. I had just started in on seconds when Dad entered the room and approached my end of the table.

"Dave, I need you to get an apron on and start bussing tables."

"Huh?" I stared up at him not quite comprehending what he'd just said.

"You heard me." His voice was slightly louder. "A couple people called in sick today and we're falling behind out there."

"But we're still eating. We haven't had pie yet."

"Now, Dave," he said, snapping his fingers.

"Dad, it's Thanksgiving." A dizzying sense of disbelief clouded my thoughts.

He positioned his face only a few inches from mine. His eyes glowed with anger. "You listen to me. I won't take any backtalk from you. When I tell you do to something, you DO IT!" Nearly yelling his last words, he punctuated the declaration by slamming his fist on the table. Nearby silverware and plates jumped with a clang.

The room fell silent. I knew that further protests would only increase the humiliation before my inevitable defeat. I slowly pushed my chair away from the table.

Dad stomped off to his throne. "Insolent kid."

I sensed every eye in the room fixed on me, the family outcast banished from Thanksgiving dinner. My head down, I trudged in silence toward the door.

"Stupid little whiner … spoiled brat." Those comments and a few other derisive mutterings came from Eli, Adam, and Shane's end of the table. Fists clenched, my first thought was to charge back and slap one of them hard across the face. Fortunately, my second thought vetoed that idea. Eli was a true giant, nearly as tall as Coach Kishman. Adam, though not as tall or burly as Eli, still towered over me with his six-foot one-inch frame. And Shane, the shortest of the trio, had the thickest torso, the brawniest arms, and the nastiest mean streak. Exiting the room was my only sane move.

I slunk through the noisy kitchen. The steamy air smelled of coffee and cooling pies—pumpkin and apple. Making my way to the dishwashing area, my breaths shuddered. I felt a wave of tears preparing to storm out. "No," I said aloud, struggling against the urge to cry. Amidst the racket of clattering pans and running water, I stopped to take a deep breath. When I reached the clean apron bin, I shook off my navy blazer, wadded it up, and slammed it into a garbage can. I then tied on an apron, grabbed a cart, and pushed through the swinging metal doors.

The main dining room of The Royal Court resembled a castle chamber. Colorful banners and shields with feudal crests adorned the gray stone walls. Suits of armor stood guard at each of the room's doorways, creating the impression that there really were knights inside ready to wield their swords and poleaxes against unruly guests. Large iron candelabras hung from the ceiling, while smaller versions stood on tables and in wall nooks. A stone fountain occupied the center point of the room. A large brick fireplace and thin glazed-glass windows with rounded tops further contributed to the medieval atmosphere.

I scanned the tables and booths before me. Stacks of dirty dishes and other dining refuse were everywhere. Thoughts of Tom Sawyer and a long wooden fence materialized. I decided to start on the side of the dining room that did not have a cloud of smoke hanging over it. As the chatter of conversions and clatter of utensils filled the air, I rolled my cart to a round table, its red tablecloth stained with gravy and other food residue. I glanced over at the dark glass window of the private dining room. Though I couldn't see the people inside, I imagined they were having a great laugh at my expense. It was tempting to break a few dishes and glasses, but I made a conscious decision to do otherwise.

Clearing away the dirty plates and silverware, I recalled all the early mornings I'd spent toiling at my grandparents' farm. That was on top of all the work I had to do at home each day and the hours of low-wage labor I put in at the restaurant. My resentment of my father multiplied. Thinking about school did nothing improve my mood. I had no real friends there and remained a nonentity to the girls in my classes.

Though I tried to avoid looking at any of the diners, I noticed Reverend Samuels at one of the tables. He was the pastor of Faith Community Church, a large nondenominational church on the west side of the city. Seeing him reminded me of the other Des Moines VIPs who frequented The Royal Court. The list included John Ruan, Bill Knapp, Duane Ellett, Sal Kishman, and Governor Robert Ray.

I recalled the story Dad liked to tell local luminaries about the restaurant's establishment. Drafted into the U.S. Army in 1943, my father was sent to France a year later. He spent most of his wartime service stationed near Paris on a quartermaster's staff. Never tasting combat, he did sample the creations of a talented French chef named Pierre. Immediately falling under the Frenchman's spell, Dad developed a fervent ambition to cook. Though it cost him much of his GI's salary, as well as a few crates worth of supplies from a U.S. Army depot (a detail often left out of the story), Dad convinced Pierre to teach him his secrets. After returning home, my father further refined his culinary skills at a downtown French restaurant. Having accumulated the necessary capital and experience, he opened The Royal Court in 1949.

I settled into a routine after clearing the first couple of tables. Working methodically, I swept through the dining room at a brisk pace. After I had shuttled what seemed like my thousandth cartload of dishes to the back, Monty placed a hand on my shoulder. "We're about caught up now, Dave. You can go back to your family." A smile spread below his thin moustache.

"Okay."

"We were really buried for a while. You did yeoman's work out there. I very much appreciate your help."

"No problem," I lied. Dropping my apron into the appropriate bin, I noticed my blazer hanging up nearby. Someone had retrieved it from the garbage and brushed it off. Feeling childish for tossing it away earlier, I slipped the jacket on and exited the kitchen.

As I approached the door to the private dining room, my anger returned. *Forget it, I'm not going in there.* Wheeling around, I stalked toward the front exit. Outside, the chilly November air soothed my heated face. Weaving through the cars in the parking lot, I reached THE ROYAL COURT sign near the street. The sign was actually a stone wall that was four feet high and twelve feet long. The restaurant's name was painted in bright red on the side facing the street. A foot thick, the wall provided a good place to sit and watch the cars go by on Hubbell Avenue. Hopping up onto the cold hard surface, I surveyed the area.

Directly across Hubbell, the East Des Moines National Bank sat dark and empty. Down the street to my right, across University Avenue, Annie stood in front of the Anderson Erickson Dairy. Like me, she was spending her holiday afternoon watching cars and trucks pass by. Unlike me, she didn't have much of a choice. Annie was an inanimate fourteen-foot tall fiberglass cow and thus spent every day watching the traffic on Hubbell and University.

After gazing at her for a while, I imagined the giant bovine springing to life. *Smoke billowing from her nostrils, she stomps into the intersection. Head low, she effortlessly flips several cars off the road. Other drivers crash into each other trying to avoid the enraged beast. She then turns and charges at The Royal Court. Smashing through the stone facade and into the main dining room, she spreads havoc among the panicked diners. With a terrifying "mooooo," the cow again lowers her head and storms through the glass window of the private dining room. Once inside, she—*

"Dave?" A voice from behind snapped me out of my dark daydream. Turning, I saw Reverend Samuels. His overcoat was long and black. His hair was short and white. "Mind if I join you?" he asked with a friendly smile. "My wife and her sisters are engaged in a considerable discussion about quilting, so I thought I'd get some fresh air."

"Uh, sure." I scooted forward to slide off the sign.

"No, no. Stay there. This looks like a fine place to sit." With surprising dexterity, the old man placed both hands on the stone wall and hoisted his thin frame up beside me. "Piece of cake," he said, eyeing me through his spectacles. "It appears that your father put you to work today."

"Yeah." The knot of anger inside my stomach remained tightly wound.

"Well, that's good of you to help out. You're a good man, Dave." The expression on his wrinkled face turned inquisitive. "Say, do you remember me?"

"Sure. We met a few months ago." I gestured back towards the restaurant.

"Indeed we did. And I remember meeting you long before that, when you were just a young lad tagging along behind your father as he greeted patrons."

"Yeah?" I recalled my dad sometimes letting me follow him around the restaurant when I was little, but did not remember any specific customers from that long ago.

After a couple minutes of small talk, the reverend asked, "Does your family still attend that church on the east side?"

"No, we don't go to church." I examined my black shoes dangling below me.

"I see. Wasn't your father an elder there?"

"Yeah, I guess. He quit going after Mom died. I was four, so I don't remember much about that church."

"That was a difficult time for Jesse," Samuels said, his voice trailing off. We sat in silence for a while as a few cars passed by on Hubbell.

"Dave, do you believe in God?" His tone was cheerful and breezy.

Uh oh, this can't be good. The question came as a surprise, though perhaps it shouldn't have. After a brief pause I replied, "Yeah, sure."

"Did you know that God is interested in you?"

"Oh?"

"Yes. God loves you and seeks a relationship with you." He paused. "Something like a father-son relationship."

That's just what I need—another one of those types of relationships. The thought of God was unsettling to me. Whenever I did think of the divine, which wasn't often, I thought of an angry Zeus-like figure randomly unleashing his wrath upon us helpless humans. Having already felt the effects of such wrath, I just wanted to avoid future lashes from the celestial bullwhip.

"Hmmm" was my reply. I tried to think of ways to change the subject.

"I know you and your family have been through a lot, Dave. But you know God was there through it all. He never stopped caring for each of you. Then and now, he seeks to guide you and bring about good in your life."

I remembered Rodney Krieger's funeral three years earlier, when a church elder told Zoe that her husband's death was God's will. If that was the case, then I didn't want anything to do with such a God. My already simmering emotions flashed hotter. "If God is so caring and so good," I blurted, "then why didn't he save Mom from cancer? Why didn't he stop Nate and Ray from getting killed in Vietnam? Why didn't he protect Rodney from that drunk driver?"

"There are no easy answers to those questions, Dave." The pastor's somber eyes matched his voice. "The question of why good people face tragedies has challenged theologians for centuries. But make no mistake, God did not take pleasure in what happened to your mother and your brothers. He was right there with you during those difficult times, weeping alongside you."

"But he's supposed to be God. Couldn't he stop that stuff from happening?"

Samuels looked off in the distance and sighed. "We live in a fallen world, Dave. God created man and gave him the freedom to make his own choices. Man made bad choices. He sinned. Sin in turn brought evil into the world, and evil has brought suffering. That is the world we now live in—a world in which bad things sometimes happen to good people."

Crossing my arms, I contemplated his words. "When Mom died, was God punishing us for something?"

"Oh no, Dave. It's not God's will that we suffer. But he can draw us nearer to him through our sufferings. He knows all about the pain we experience from when his own son died for us. Furthermore, your mother's death was not the end of her existence. It was just the end of her time here on earth. Those who know God—like your mother did—pass from this world into eternal life in heaven."

Samuels then quoted a few verses from the Bible about salvation. "In addition to eternal life," he continued, "God also transforms our earthly lives. Right here, God wants you to be the best person you can be. If you walk with him, you will be a man of strength and character."

"Character?"

"Yes, it's what's inside you. The qualities that make you the person that you are. 'A man's character is his fate.'"

I nodded, though I was a bit confused.

"You see, Dave, life is a series of choices. Some of them are not very significant in the big picture. What will you eat for breakfast? What shirt will you wear today? Other choices have a greater, more lasting, significance. Where will you work? Whom will you marry? And there are a handful of choices that define who we are. These decisions impact our entire lives and maybe even where we spend eternity. I believe that what we decide about God is the most important of these choices."

Staring straight into my eyes, he paused to let his words sink in.

"This is a lot to think about, I know. Especially after eating so much great food. Your father and your brother are splendid chefs." He patted his stomach. "Well, I guess I should return to my wife. It's been wonderful visiting with you."

"Thanks." We shook hands.

The pastor dropped down from his perch, nearly losing his balance when he landed. "Guess I'm a little old for gymnastics," he said, steadying himself. He turned to face me. "Do you have a Bible at home?"

"Yeah." I knew we had at least a couple of them somewhere in our house.

"If you get the opportunity, you might like to read the Gospel of John. It's the fourth book of the New Testament."

"Okay."

"It might take you a few days to get through it, but there's no rush. John will teach you more about what we just discussed." Reaching into the pocket of his suit jacket, he pulled out a business card and handed it to me. "This has the church number and my home number. Please call anytime if you'd like to talk about, well, anything." His smile was warm, though his face was pink from the cold. "Goodbye, Dave."

"Bye." I watched the old man walk away.

After several paces, Samuels turned around. "I believe God is going perform mighty works through you, Dave." He smiled again and then continued his trek back to the restaurant. When he disappeared into the building, I examined his card and slid it into a pocket.

A while later, I heard familiar voices behind me. My relatives were leaving the restaurant. Though my butt was numb from sitting on the cold hard stone, I did not move from the sign. Adam's kids, seven-year-old Martin and four-year-old Jane, ran over and stood before me.

"Bye Uncle Dave," Martin said. "We hafta go."

"Bye Unca Dave," Jane added with a wave of her little white mitten.

I dropped down and gave them both a hug. "Bye. Remember to be good so Santa will bring you lots of presents."

"We will," Martin replied. The two children ran off toward their parents who were saying goodbye to Eli and Katy.

I walked slowly through the parking lot. Aside from waves from the three bloated Krieger boys, no one acknowledged my presence. No tearful goodbyes for Dave. Entering the restaurant foyer, I met Ozzie carrying two covered plates of food.

"Where've you been hobbit boy? Ennh—save it, I don't really care. But you are supposed to help me haul food out to the car. So grab some grub. Chop chop."

Uncle Isaac and his family were spending the day with Grandma and Grandpa. Like usual, Dad promised to bring them leftovers from the restaurant. I grabbed a couple of covered bowls from the kitchen.

While driving to the farm, Dad did not say a word to me. I likewise said nothing to him. The enticing aroma from the food in the car reminded me of the seconds and the pumpkin pie that I missed. From the passenger seat, Ozzie must have sensed my bitterness simmering behind him. In true Eddie Haskell fashion, he started rambling about how great the food was, especially the pumpkin pie. "That may have been the best pie ever baked in the history of the world. Gotta eat it fresh out of the oven though. It's just not the same when it's a leftover." He later speculated about the tasks he would assign his nephews during their day of slavery.

We returned home just after 9:00 p.m. The house was chilly. Because of the Arab oil embargo, Dad did not allow the thermostat to be set any higher than 65. Before changing out of my dress clothes, I placed Pastor Samuels's business card on my dresser. The bottom drawer of my nightstand then caught my eye. Clearing away several layers of comic books, old homework assignments, and other debris, I found what I was looking for: a rectangular box with a label that read, *New American Standard Bible*. Removing the lid revealed a black leather book inside. On the cover, near the lower right-hand corner, the name DAVID E. KING was inscribed in gold letters. Tipping the box upside down with one hand, I let the Bible fall into my other hand. The smell of leather danced in my nostrils. On the first page there was handwriting:

> Presented to: Dave King
> By: Grandpa and Grandma King
> On: December 25, 1971

A forgotten Christmas present. I checked the table of contents for the book of John. After placing the bookmark ribbon between the appropriate pages, I set the Bible on the dresser next to the pastor's card.

An uneventful weekend passed. Sunday evening I spied the black leather Bible sitting exactly where I'd left it three days earlier. Out of curiosity I started the Gospel of John, reading the first four chapters. I read a few more chapters each subsequent evening and finished the book Thursday night. It was more interesting than I'd expected, especially the part about Jesus being God's son. Before reading John, all I had known about the Father,

Son, and Holy Ghost was that they had caught the last train for the coast the day the music died.

Friday night I was home alone, as usual. Dad was at the restaurant. Ozzie was out on a date. Before he left, my brother slapped on a generous dose of musk and announced his prediction for the evening. “This bunny’s gonna give it up for the Wizard. Tonight, the yellow-brick road leads right here.” He pointed to his crotch with both hands.

“Yeah right,” I replied. “And then will winged monkeys come flying out of your butt?”

“Maybe, my little munchkin,” he chuckled. “Give me a jumbo beef and bean burrito and who knows what I can conjure up.”

“Where you taking this girl?”

“Vets Auditorium. Bulldog Bob Brown is battling Harley Race in the Main Event.”

“Wrestling?” I laughed. “You’re taking your date to see All-Star Wrestling?”

“Yes, wrestling. She’ll love it. And then later, I’ll give her the Ozzie-driver.” He complemented his statement with a couple of pelvic thrusts.

I tried to think of a suitable reply, but he was out the door before anything came to mind. I knew Ozzie’s dates were anything but charm school graduates, but wrestling seemed to be pushing it. I predicted an evening of disappointment for both him and the unlucky girl.

After supper, I passed on my usual appointments with *Sanford and Son* and *Room 222* to return to my Bible. I reviewed John again before flipping around to some of the other books. A passage in Romans caught my eye: “But God demonstrates His own love toward us, in that while we were yet sinners, Christ died for us.”

I wondered if that was really true. It boggled my mind to think that the creator of the universe cared about me. I returned to John’s gospel to read more about Jesus: “He who believes in the Son has eternal life …”

As my thoughts drifted to my own life, a hollow feeling came over me. What did I have? My mother was gone. I had no real friends. No girlfriend either. Most of my family did not even like me. I imagined myself stuck waist-deep in a vast pit of mud that extended as far as my eyes could see; no other soul was in sight. I had hoped that things would soon change, especially if I made varsity next spring, but sometimes I wondered if my life would always be isolated and empty.

The words of the Bible, on the other hand, seemed to offer something different. Reflecting more about what I'd read created a flicker of anticipation that grew into a surge of energy. It was like what I felt as a kid on Christmas morning, only with more resonance. I sensed that change could indeed happen, that God was closer, that eternal life was within my grasp.

I was unsure about what to do next. Then I remembered Pastor Samuels saying something about a "prayer of salvation." Aside from pastors at funerals and weddings, Grandma and Grandpa King were the only people I'd ever seen praying in person. They just bowed their heads and talked to God, as if he were there listening to them. I figured that must be how you do it.

A 60-watt bulb in a desk lamp provided the only illumination in my dim room. I sat cross-legged on the rug beside my bed. Praying aloud, I started talking to God. My voice was tentative at first, but after a couple sentences the words started rolling out. I told God I wanted to follow him. That I was sorry for my sins. That I believed in Jesus.

Though my rambling prayer lacked eloquence, I had a sense that it was heard. An unfamiliar hope flowed through my body. Wanting to tell someone about my experience, I noticed the business card on the dresser. *Yes, he should be the first to know.* My finger spun the dial on the phone. When Reverend Samuels got on the line, I recounted what I'd been reading in the Bible that evening and the previous week. The old pastor must have been amused at hearing me natter on and on as if I were the first person to uncover these long-lost ancient truths. I finally told him about my prayer.

"Dave, that's wonderful," he said. "I'm so happy that you're now a fellow believer. Tonight, your name was written in the Lamb's Book of Life."

I wasn't sure what that meant, but the pastor's positive tone indicated that it was likely a good thing. We talked for about half an hour about God, the Bible, baptism, and church. Since I didn't have a license yet, he told me about a congregant on the east side who would be happy drive me to Faith Community Church on Sunday mornings.

Upon hanging up the phone, I went into the bathroom and looked in the mirror. I'm not sure what I was expecting—maybe a halo glowing above my head. But I looked exactly the same. If something about me was actually different, it was not a visible alteration. After pacing around the empty house for a while, I returned to my room. Sitting beside my bed again, I asked God to help me understand more about how my life had changed tonight. When finished with my prayer, I flipped on the radio. The song that greeted me was "You've Got a Friend."

Chapter 3 – May 1974

With a sharp CRACK, the ball shot from Eli's bat, bounced over the pitcher's mound, and rocketed toward the open grassland of centerfield. Pressing hard to my left, I launched into a dive with my glove fully extended. The ball slammed into the web of my Larry Bowa Rawlings just before I hit the dirt belly-first behind second base. An instant later, I was on my knees firing a strike to first—just in time to rob the imaginary runner of a base hit.

The other infielders complimented me on my "sweet dive."

"Not bad, Davy-boy," Eli yelled from the batter's box in a tone that somehow mixed praise with condescension. "Alright maggots, that's enough fielding practice. Bring it in."

The fourteen boys on the Eastridge High junior varsity baseball team gathered around Eli near home plate. The roster included thirteen juniors and one sophomore—me. Making this team as a tenth grader wasn't easy. I'd prepared for baseball all winter and spring, jogging three miles every other day, along with a daily regimen of 200 push-ups and 250 sit-ups. I also used the old brick-tied-to-a-broomstick exercise to strengthen my wrists. The twisting motion required to raise and lower that stupid brick over and over brought intense pain, but it was effective. Newfound strength surged through my wrists and forearms. For mental exercise, I studied *The Science of Hitting* by Ted Williams. The book was a Christmas present from Ozzie. Probably the coolest gift he'd ever given me, and the second coolest thing he'd ever done for me.

My hard work paid off. At the end of the tryout sessions in April, Coach Kishman assigned me to the junior varsity team. I was thrilled—playing on JV meant I had a chance to get promoted to varsity sometime during the season. At first the other boys on the JV team gave me a chilly reception. They didn't like a sophomore joining their exclusive club of juniors. To make matters worse, they were sure I would receive special treatment from my brother, the JV coach. I received special treatment all right, but not the kind anybody would want.

"Today ladies," Eli announced, "we're going to close out practice at the track. So haul your asses over there. Let's go! Move it! Move it!" I could tell he missed his days in the Marine Corps.

After the team jogged over to the track surrounding the football field, Eli herded us to the starting line. We didn't know what our coach had planned, but after nearly two hours of practice, none of us was looking forward to it.

"We're going to play catch the rabbit," Eli announced with a sinister smile. I had a sinking feeling I knew who the rabbit was going to be. "Davy-boy," he sang while pointing down the track, "start walking." Though Eli called everyone else on the team by his last name, I was always "Davy-boy." On the first day of practice he explained that I had not yet earned the name, "King." I trudged down the track.

"Listen up, ladies. Davy-boy is the rabbit. He gets a head start on the rest of you hound dogs. You will all run until you catch the rabbit or you go all the way around the track. Everyone who does not catch Davy-boy must not only complete this first lap, but they get to run a second lap as well. If anyone DOES catch the rabbit, then Davy-boy gets to run an extra lap for every dog that catches him. Got it?" Eli turned to me after I'd walked about ten yards. "Okay Davy-boy, stop there."

I glowered at my brother. This was so typical of him. Just as I was starting to win over the other players, he wanted to drive a wedge between the juniors and me. It was a no-win situation. If I avoided getting caught, they would all be mad at me because they had to run an extra lap. If I slowed up to let some of them catch me, then I would have to run a bunch of extra laps.

"Ready? Go!" Eli barked. My legs sprang into action. The pack of dogs behind me howled in pursuit. Some of them started out sprinting to make a quick catch of the rabbit. Once somebody caught me, that person was done running. I on the other hand had to complete the entire lap, regardless. Though my lungs started to simmer, I forced myself to dig harder. The pounding steps behind me rang alarmingly close in my ears.

"Get back here, Davy-boy."

"Slow down, man."

"Come on, King. I ain't running another lap."

About a quarter of the way around the track, my body decided there was no way it could handle any extra laps. The Captain Kirk inside my brain ordered the Scotty inside my engine room to fire up the warp drives. I started to fly, and not a moment too soon. Charlie North, our centerfielder, was closing the gap in a hurry. Sensing that only about three yards separated us, I blazed down the long straight section of the track. We were both fast—I wasn't sure who was faster. Though my lungs burned and my legs ached, I maintained a slim lead. Fortunately, my stamina was superior on this day. After about seventy yards of sprinting, I could hear him fall back. He conceded defeat with a couple of sharp expletives.

Though it took everything I had, the duel with Charlie left me a comfortable distance ahead of the rest of the team. I eased up in the final turn and coasted to the finish line.

Eli greeted me with a cold smile. "The bunny rabbit survives," he said, no doubt pleased that his plan to alienate me was working. Over the next minute, my teammates, heads down and panting, lumbered across the finish line. Eli stood among his players with his hands on his hips. Towering above them, he delivered their sentence. "Since none of you slow hound dogs could catch Davy-rabbit, you've all earned an extra lap. Let's go ladies! Now! Move it!" My brother's shouts and claps set the herd in motion again. Several boys muttered curses in my direction as they plodded forward.

I sat in the grass still catching my breath as I watched my teammates begin their tortured circuit. Eli walked over, his lofty frame blocking out the sun. "Kishman wants to see you in his office after practice."

His words zapped my body with a current of electricity. I sprang to my feet. "Really?"

He nodded, his grim expression shaded under the bill of his cap.

"Did he say why?"

Eli scrunched his face into a puzzled frown. "I think it has something to do with you making passes at the other guys. The coach don't like homos on his teams, you know."

"Damn it, Eli!" I immediately regretted my outburst since I'd planned on witnessing to him about my faith sometime before the season was over.

"Calm down, Dave. I don't know why he wants to see you. He didn't tell me." Eli turned and headed toward the track. After several steps he spun around and glared at me. "Out here, I'm Coach King. You got that?"

I nodded and started pacing back and forth in the grass. *Why does Kishman want to see me? Is he demoting me to the sophomore team?* My head was still swimming with worry several minutes later as Eli gathered his exhausted players together. After the usual disparaging remarks about our masculinity, he said something about the next game and let us go. Though a couple of my teammates were still peeved, most of them didn't seem to be too upset with me about their extra lap. They all would have done the same thing in my spikes. Two of the guys even jokingly called me "The Rabbit." I could barely hear their words, however, since my thoughts had long since gone elsewhere. I jogged on ahead of them toward the school building.

My heart racing, I crept down the hallway to Kishman's office and tapped on the door. No answer. Since the door was ajar, I peered inside. The chair behind the coach's desk was empty. *Now what should I do? Hit the showers?* I quickly dismissed that idea, reasoning that Kishman might be more impressed if he could see evidence of how hard I'd worked during practice. Feeling restless, I didn't want to just stand around in the hall. I then remembered that I needed to pick up my guitar from the music room. That morning, at the Senior Class Day Assembly, the choir students sang "Raindrops Keep Falling on My Head" while the Drama Club performed a skit from *Butch Cassidy and the Sundance Kid.* Miss Williams had asked me to bring my guitar to school to play during the performance. Since the music room was on the near side of the building, I could be back in five minutes. I hoped the walk would dissipate some of my anxiety.

With my black case in tow, I returned to Kishman's office. Taking a deep breath, I rapped the door lightly with my knuckles.

"Yeah," came a gruff reply from within. I stepped into the room. Coach sat at his desk studying a sheet of paper. A trail of smoke ascended to the ceiling from a dying cigarette stub in a nearby ashtray. Steel eyes peered above black rectangular reading glasses to zero in on me.

"Have a seat," he said. His leather face bore no emotion. I slid into one of the two empty wooden chairs in front of his desk and stood my guitar case against the other. Kishman flashed a curious look at the instrument. He then trained his stare on me again. I returned his gaze for as long as I dared. His cobalt eyes were a bit bloodshot.

"You heard about what happened to McDonald?" he asked. Drew McDonald, a junior, was the top reserve infielder on the varsity team. He'd broken his ankle sliding into third base during the last game.

"Yeah, that was too bad." I tried to keep a steady voice to mask my nervousness.

"You probably haven't heard about Celek." Kevin Celek was a senior. Starting shortstop.

"No." I shook my head.

"Seniors just received their final grades. His are in the toilet." He paused to suck the final bit of life from his cigarette stub before smashing its remains into the round black ashtray. "Oh, he'll still graduate, by the skin of his teeth. But the straight Ds he pulled this semester knocked him off the team. School policy."

"That's too bad. Celek is a good ballplayer."

"He's a jackass," Kishman shot back. "We're the top-ranked team in the state and he can't crack open a damn textbook to keep his eligibility. Just like that I'm down two infielders. It's not that Celek could hit that much, but he could field. And he was fast." Coach looked off to the side shaking his head. "Jackass," he said with a bitter chuckle.

"Oh" was all I could say in reply. My nose caught a faint whiff of alcohol through the cigarette stench hanging in the air.

Kishman scanned the sheet of paper in his hand. "The junior varsity team has played three games," he announced. "All wins. In those games, Dave King has gone nine for twelve with three doubles, a triple, and eight RBIs. King also has a walk and three stolen bases." He looked up at me. "Is that right?"

"Yes, sir. I believe it is."

"Your brother says you've got a glove, too. Made some nice plays at shortstop."

My eyes dropped to the front panel of his desk. *Really? Eli has never said anything positive to ME about my play.*

Coach's stare bored through my head. "Here's the deal," he finally said. "Burton's going to play second base the rest of the season. Kishman will move over to shortstop. But that leaves me without any true middle infielders on the bench. Dave King is the best hitter on the JV team and he happens to play shortstop. You see where I'm heading with this, son?"

Gulping hard, I wondered if he could hear the pounding of my heart. "Yes, sir. I think so."

"Good. We've got a game tomorrow at three o'clock, here. There's a varsity uniform for you on the table in the back of the locker room. Take it home with you. It should fit. Here's our schedule of games." He handed me two sheets of paper stapled together.

My head spun as I took the schedule. I couldn't believe it. I was on the Eastridge High varsity baseball team. Sal Kishman was my coach. A tickling excitement spread through my belly.

"Thank you, sir." I couldn't stop a big goofy grin from covering my face.

"Make no mistake, King." He jabbed a long bony finger at me. "You probably won't be starting any games this year. There won't be too many innings for you. But you come to every game prepared. When I need you to pinch hit or pinch run, you'd better be ready. Whether you're playing or not, you keep your head in every game, every inning, every pitch. And at practice you bust your ass. Give me all you got, and then some. Understand?"

I nodded. "Yes, sir. I'll do my best."

"Alright King, that's all."

"Thank you, sir. See you tomorrow."

Kishman grunted as I grabbed my guitar and headed for the door. Just as I was about to exit the office, he barked my name.

Jolted, I spun around. His expression had lightened ever so slightly. "You know in all my years of coaching, I've only had a handful of sophomores make varsity.... Congratulations."

"Thanks, Coach."

He then glanced down to my guitar case. "You any good with that thing or do you just carry it around to impress the girls?"

"I play a little."

He grabbed the pack of Kents sitting on his desk, tapped out a cigarette, and lit up. "Would you mind playing something? My head's been killing me all afternoon. Maybe some music would take my mind off the pain." Placing a giant hand in front of his face, he rubbed his temples with his thumb and middle finger.

"Uh, yeah. Sure." Of all the scenarios I'd imagined before entering Coach's office, this was a possibility I had not considered. "What would you like to hear?"

"Anything. Something pleasant." The gruffness remained in his voice.

My brain scrambled for ideas as I opened the case and removed the guitar. *Something pleasant? What does that mean?* I sat down and strummed the pick across the strings. After a couple panicked seconds, a song popped into my head: "Horse With No Name." I hadn't played it in a while but was confident it would come back to me. The song was basically three chords. Placing the fingers of my left hand on the appropriate frets, I started playing.

Kishman flipped through a stack of paperwork. Every so often he put the cigarette to his mouth for a drag. He worked as if I wasn't there. After I'd played for a while, he looked up. "Don't you know the words?"

I stared at him with wide eyes. "You—you want me to sing?"

"There are words that go with that song aren't there?"

"Uh, yeah." I started over, this time singing along. I always sang while I practiced playing at home, so I was pretty sure I knew all the lyrics. Feelings of awkwardness, however, created hesitancy in my voice. I was terrified one of the other ballplayers would walk by when I got to the "la la" part of the song.

After I'd sung a couple of lines, Kishman nodded and went back to his paperwork. Taking that as a sign of approval, my confidence increased. I hit a groove, both singing and playing.

About halfway through the song, I noticed the family portrait sitting on his desk. Judging by how closely the man in the picture resembled the man behind the desk, I guessed that it was a recent photo. The wife in the portrait looked several years younger than Coach, perhaps in her middle or late forties. Around the couple were the five Kishman offspring, three sons and two daughters. I hadn't met any of them but I knew that the middle three were students at Eastridge. Mary, a senior, looked frumpy. John, a junior, was a starter on the varsity team. I'd meet him soon enough. Michelle was a sophomore, like me. She had caught my eye whenever I saw her in the lunchroom or in the hallways—especially when she wore her cheerleading uniform. She stared at me from the picture with an alluring smile. I could almost hear her say, "Hey Dave, that's so cool you made varsity. Maybe you and I could—"

My wavering focus caused me to botch a chord. It didn't sound horrible, but I could tell that Kishman noticed. Regaining my focus, I completed the song without incident. And my eyes stayed far away from the lovely Michelle.

"Not bad," Kishman said. "You got another one?"

I tried to think of another song he might like—something similar to the last one. My fingers started playing "Heart of Gold." My voice soon followed. Glancing up at the framed picture of President Nixon on the wall, I realized that Coach might not be a fan of Neil Young. Fortunately, he remained fixated on his paperwork and did not seem to mind. At least I wasn't playing "Ohio."

After I finished the second song, Kishman looked pleased. "The head's a little better. You got a good voice, King. Maybe if baseball doesn't work out, you can go on the television and host your own show. Like Johnny Cash a few years ago."

"Thanks."

"That's all, King."

"See you tomorrow, Coach."

Even though I was lugging a guitar case, three schoolbooks, and a baseball uniform, I actually enjoyed the bus ride home. The word "varsity" kept ringing through my ears. I wanted to tell the other passengers about my promotion, but somehow restrained myself. With the warm breeze from an open window blowing through my hair, I offered a silent prayer of thanks to God.

As I trudged up the sidewalk toward my house, I spotted Ozzie and his pudgy stoner friend Randy in the driveway drinking beer. Leaning against my brother's red pickup, they each wore a muscle car T-shirt and bell-bottomed jeans.

"Hey look, its David Cassidy," Randy said, gesturing at my guitar case.

"Nah, that's not Cassidy," Ozzie corrected. "That's Bonaduce right there."

I squinted at him with a look of contempt. My wavy collar-length hair was dark auburn. It looked nothing like the glowing red locks of Danny Partridge.

"Hey Danny," Randy said, chortling, "sing something for us, will ya? How about 'Come on Get Happy?'"

Ignoring the moronic comments, I stopped in front of Ozzie and set down my load. "So they're actually gonna let you graduate, huh?"

"Damn straight, my little hobbit."

He couldn't call me that much longer. I was up to five-seven. Only a couple more inches and I'd be as tall as him. "Principal Peterson is probably tired of you stinking up his hallways," I said. "That's what I think."

"Yeah, well I think you can kiss my ass." Ozzie punctuated his statement with a crisp burst of flatulence. Randy responded with honking laughter.

I snickered. "I'll give you five dollars if you grab the microphone on stage at your graduation, place it over the proper orifice, and let one rip."

"Make it ten and you've got a deal." He grinned. "Remind me to eat something with lots of onions before the ceremony. Those things make me fart like the Fourth of July." He finished his beer and flipped the empty can into the back of his pickup. Randy did likewise.

"Everything makes you fart like the Fourth of July," I said.

"True." He nodded in agreement.

"So what do you got planned for tonight? Probably gonna get an early start on your college reading list, huh?"

"Incorrect, young one. Tonight the Rand-man and me are gonna hit the loop, pick up a couple of lovely ladies, and make them both very happy. How about you? You going to one of those Lunatics for Christ meetings?"

"It's Youth for Christ. And yes, I am going. They're showing *A Thief in the Night* at my church. You guys should stop by and check it out. It's pretty heavy from what I hear."

Ozzie grabbed the final two cans of Coors sitting on the hood of his truck and handed one of them to Randy. They both yanked off the pull-tabs and tossed them in the back of the pickup. The small metal pieces rattled around with several hollow clangs. "Nah, I'll pass," my brother said. "I've heard what that movie's about. I'm not into those end-of-the-world fairy tales. If they were showing something about UFOs, then I'd be there. That stuff's real, man."

"Well, if you change your mind the show starts at eight."

"Not likely. Tonight the Wizard's gonna be showing some lucky babe his tin woodman, if you know what I mean."

Shaking my head, I remembered that I hadn't yet told him my big news. "Hey, you're not gonna believe it. I made varsity today. Coach called me into his office after practice and—"

"No way."

"Yeah! Drew McDonald broke his ankle and Kevin Celek tanked his grades, so I got called up."

"Celek *is* an idiot," Ozzie said. He took another drink from the tall yellow can in his hand. "That's great Dave. I mean that's huge! We should all go out and celebrate tonight and … oh, wait a minute. I just remembered, I don't give a SHIT about baseball!" He then leaned his head back like a wolf howling at the moon and unleashed a thunderous five-second belch.

Caught in the middle of a drink, Randy sprayed beer across our lawn. "Awesome, man," he gasped, doubling over with laughter.

"You need help," I said, gathering my stuff.

"Later, Bilbo," Ozzie called out as I walked towards the house.

"Later, Your Gaseousness."

Once inside, I headed for the full-length mirror on Abby's closet door. There, I held up the uniform in front of me. A surge of energy shot through my body as I beheld the vibrant red "Braves" against the brilliant white background of the shirt. Sewn just below the fancy swoosh that underlined the team name was the number 17. It instantly became my new favorite number. Examining the pants, I imagined the red pinstripes becoming a blur as I blazed around the bases. Tomorrow could not arrive soon enough.

After a quick supper, I hopped on my ten-speed and pedaled over to my grandparents' house. Having sold their farm last winter, Grandpa and Grandma now lived in a two-bedroom house that Dad had found for them in an east side neighborhood about a mile away from our house. Though the move was a big adjustment, I think they knew it was for the best.

Turning onto their street, I saw my grandparents sitting in lawn chairs in front of their garage. They both smiled as I coasted into their driveway. Samson jumped up to greet me as I stepped off my bike. "There's Dave," Grandpa said in his husky voice. "How was school today?"

Unable to contain myself, I launched into a lengthy monologue about making varsity. I included everything: practice, singing in Coach's office, the uniform, and any other detail I could recall. They both appeared to listen intently.

"That's great, Dave," Grandpa said. "Quite an accomplishment."

"Yes, indeed," Grandma said, nodding.

"As I recall," Grandpa continued, raising a shaky finger, "my mama, she got to hold you when you were just a few months old. Oh, you never knew her. She passed not long after that. But she looked at you and said that you were going to grow up to be a great man. That's what she said. I remember it like it was yesterday."

"Mm-hmm," Grandma added.

"Mama thought maybe you were going to be a musician. But it could turn out you'll be a big league ballplayer."

"I hope so," I said, recalling the stories I had heard about my great-grandmother Ruth.

We talked for a while longer. I always enjoyed visiting my grandparents. They were both excellent storytellers. I especially liked hearing Grandpa's accounts of his experiences as a Doughboy in France and Grandma's stories about feeding the hoboes who stopped by their place during the Great Depression. And now that I was a Christian, we shared a new bond. They often asked me about what I was reading in the Bible.

Around seven, as the cicadas started screeching, Grandma asked to go inside. She looked different than the last time I saw her. The silver hair was pulled back like usual, but her wrinkled face now had a grayish tint. Hanging onto my arm as we walked to the house, she moved slowly. Once inside, she said she felt like getting ready for bed. After Grandpa helped her get situated, he said she wanted me to read the Bible to her before she went to sleep.

I went in and sat beside her bed. With her dentures removed, her face was gaunt and sunken. "What would you like me to read, Grandma?"

"How about Philippians 1, dear?"

I opened the Bible and started reading. She had fallen asleep by the time I finished the chapter. In the pale glow of the nightstand lamp, a look of peace blanketed her countenance. I closed the Bible and shut off the light.

After saying goodbye to Grandpa, who was sitting in his rocking chair watching public television, I hopped on my bike and pedaled home. A short time later, Jeff and Terry, a couple upperclassmen football players I'd met through Fellowship of Christian Athletes, rolled into my driveway. I dove into the backseat of Jeff's Plymouth Valiant and we were on our way to Faith Community Church to watch the movie.

Returning home a little before midnight, I crept into a dark house. Ozzie was still out on the town, no doubt failing to attract any positive attention from the opposite sex. Abby, now on summer break from Iowa State, was out with her boyfriend Jerry. Dad's cacophonous snores covered the creaking sounds generated by my skulk up the stairs. Though he never gave me any trouble if I was home before 12:00, I tried not to wake him after he'd gone to bed. Not disturbing a sleeping bear always seemed like a wise policy.

After I crawled into bed, *A Thief in the Night* started replaying in my head. The movie had really grabbed my attention—and not just because it was filmed in Des Moines. I wondered how close we were to the end times. If the rapture were to suddenly occur, I felt confident that I would go to heaven. So too would my grandparents. *But what about the rest of my family and my teammates? Would they be left behind?* I made a mental note to read the book of Revelation, as well as *The Late Great Planet Earth*—a book recommended by the church's youth pastor. As I drifted off to sleep, Larry Norman's "I Wish We'd All Been Ready" provided a soundtrack for the movie images still flashing through my mind.

The next morning my eyes popped open at 7:50, just like every Saturday. Before waking up, I had been in the midst of a disturbing dream. Pursuing UNITE agents were trying brand me with the Mark of the Beast. I shook off the troubling images and stumbled into the hallway. The doors to both Ozzie and Abby's rooms were closed. Shuffling down the stairs, I entered the kitchen to find Dad sitting at the table reading *The Des Moines Register*. He lowered the paper. "Sal Kishman was at the restaurant last night," he said. A tiny smile accompanied his gaze.

I froze. "Oh?"

"Says you're on the varsity team now." Dad rubbed his short graying beard.

"Yeah. Found out after practice yesterday. Surprising, huh?"

"He's showing a lot of faith in you. This is a big honor. Eli was the only one of your brothers to make varsity as a sophomore." His expression stiffened. "Don't let up now. You keep working hard. Don't let the Coach or your new teammates down."

"Yes, sir." I opened the refrigerator wondering if Dad's little speech was his way of congratulating me.

"Your game is at three today?"

"Yeah."

"Do you have a ride?"

I set down the bottle of orange juice in my hand. Surprisingly, I hadn't even thought about how I would get to the game. "No. I don't really know any of the varsity players yet."

"Maybe I'll go in a little early today. I can drop you off."

"Thanks," I said with relief. From that moment until we left, my mind remained fixated on the upcoming game.

Dad steered his dark blue Cadillac into the parking lot near the Eastridge High baseball field. "Good luck," he said.

"Thanks." Exiting the car, I felt ten feet tall in my new uniform. I looked around to see if anyone was noticing me, the newest member of the top-ranked varsity baseball team. But it was still well before game time, so no spectators were there yet. I strutted across the lot toward the field, my spikes crunching the gravel below. Two ballplayers in Braves' uniforms sat on the tailgate of a green Chevy pickup. A few feet away, another Braves player was leaning against his beige Malibu sedan dipping graham crackers into a jar of honey. Recalling the picture on Coach's desk, I recognized him right away as John Kishman.

When I got closer to the pickup, I also recognized the two boys on the tailgate. The tall burly blond kid was Frank Harrison, Eastridge's first baseman and clean-up hitter. The thin guy next to him with the long brown hair and Burt Reynolds mustache was Sean Liotta, a long reliever and spot starter in the Braves rotation.

"Hey guys," I said, extending a hand. "I'm Dave King, your new teammate." Both seniors had been snickering at something one of them had just said. As they looked over at me, the levity disappeared from their faces. Harrison stood and muttered something under his breath. He then swatted my hand aside and jabbed a thick finger into my chest with such force I had to take a step back to keep my balance. Towering above me, he glared into my eyes with grave fury.

"Listen you little prick, you are NOT our teammate. You've done nothing to earn the right to wear this uniform. We're the undefeated number one-ranked team in the state, and we don't need some midget sophomore gettin' in our way. You got it?"

Stunned, I couldn't formulate a response. Liotta then stood at Harrison's side with a look that was even more menacing. "He asked you a question, shithead." He shoved me back another step.

Still not believing what was happening, I struggled to speak. "Guys, listen, I uh …"

"You don't tell us to listen," Harrison interrupted. He grabbed my shirt and lifted me up to my tip-toes. I now had an uncomfortably close view of his raging blue eyes and the blond stubble on his face. "If Coach wants to put useless little mascots on the bench, that's his business. But you get one thing straight. None of us wants you here. You wanna survive this season, you'd better lay low. Don't let me see you, hear you, smell you … or we're gonna have a meeting, you and me, after the game under the bleachers. You dig what I'm saying?" His bulging temples and reddening face crushed any remaining hope I had that this was all part of some good-natured hazing ritual.

"Your brother may have pulled some strings to get you on this team," Liotta added, spitting tobacco juice on my shoes. "But you'd better find a way to get out. Fake an injury. Tell Coach you gotta quit to spend more time with the chess team. I don't care what you come up with, but you'd better think of something quick. Or someone could get messed up." He flipped the bill of my cap so it flopped to the ground behind me.

"Hey guys, leave him alone," John said, appearing to my right.

Harrison's eyes remained fixed on mine. "Stay outta this, Kishman," he warned through gritted teeth. "This ain't any of your business."

"He's not hurting anybody, Frank. Besides, our bench is thin. We might need him to pinch run for Moose sometime."

"We've got NO use for this douche bag," Harrison said, shaking me for emphasis. His grip was so tight, the collar of my shirt dug into the back of my neck.

"Frank, seriously, let him go. Let's get ready for the game."

"I thought he told you to stay out of this," Liotta said, glaring at John.

"Come on, man." John placed a hand on Harrison's shoulder. "There's no time for this."

Harrison finally released his grip on my shirt, adding a shove for good measure. I staggered back, barely keeping my balance. In the process, I stepped on my cap. Harrison meanwhile had turned to face John, who, although taller than me, was still about five inches shorter and fifty pounds lighter than the hulking first baseman.

"You don't tell me what to do, Daddy's boy."

"What the hell is that supposed to mean?" John shot back, standing his ground.

"It's no secret how you got your starting spot, Kishman," Harrison said. "I'm sick of twerps from the Pee Wee leagues using family connections to get on my varsity team."

Clenching his fists, John stepped forward so the bill of his cap slid under the bill of Harrison's cap. "I didn't get any special treatment at tryouts and you know it. I earned my spot, like everyone else!"

"Back off Kishman … before you get hurt."

"Make your move, big man."

Both adversaries tensed up, their eyes locked in a combative stare. Harrison's face grew redder. I'd never heard of anybody brave enough, or crazy enough, to stand up to him. The big senior's mouth started moving but no sounds came out. It was if he was channeling his rage into a silent monologue as a final preparation for battle. Liotta stood nearby, stone-faced. Just then, Ronnie Vasquez showed up.

"Hey dogs, what it is," the Braves third baseman said with a toothy grin. Upon noticing the face-off, his smile vanished. "What? We got a fight here? Come on guys, save that energy for the field."

Still focused on John, Harrison took a breath. "If your daddy wasn't the coach, I'd splatter your ass across this parking lot." John glared back in silence. Vasquez and Liotta then grabbed a shoulder and pried Harrison away. Still smoldering, he snatched his equipment bag from the back of his pickup and slammed shut the tailgate so hard it sounded like a cannon blast. He stormed off toward the field, Liotta and Vasquez following a few paces behind.

I felt like a two-ton boulder had just crushed my biggest dream. The threat of physical violence was bad enough, but even worse was the realization that I was not welcome on the varsity team. The dejection left me barely able to breathe. My first thought was to run home. I then noticed John still watching Harrison stomp away.

"Thanks," I said. "Sorry I caused trouble between you and Harrison."

He turned, revealing an intense expression much like his father's. But whereas Coach's face resembled creased leather, John's freckly face was smooth and youthful. "Not your fault," he said. "Harrison's a jerk. Actually, the team's full of 'em. Sure they can play ball. On the field, they're like a machine. Relentless and unstoppable. But they *are* jerks. They get a number one ranking and a couple articles in the paper and they think they're the Oakland A's." His expression lightened.

"Well, thanks for helping me out back there."

"Forget it. That oaf needs to learn that he can't boss everybody around just because he's big and can hit a baseball." He paused. "Oh, I'm John Kishman."

"Dave King." We shook hands. "Maybe I'll see you next year."

"Huh?" His brow scrunched in a look of puzzlement.

"Since I'm just going to cause problems here, it's probably best if I tell Coach I want to go back to JV."

"The hell it is! Dad would shit bricks if you did that. You know how thin our bench is now?" He picked up my cap, knocked it back in shape, and plopped it on my head. "I was serious about you pinch running for Moose. You ever seen him try to haul his fat ass around the bases? You can time him with a sundial."

A small smile cracked my face, but inside I was still churning.

"Forget about Harrison," John continued. "He'll move on to something else soon enough." He gave my shoulder a light shove. "You earned that uniform. You earned a spot on this team. So get ready to play and help us win ballgames."

He grabbed his glove and walked with me to the field. Like the other players who had already paired off, we played catch to warm up. Nobody else on the team acknowledged my presence. After stretching exercises, John introduced me to a couple of the reserves. The chips on their shoulders weren't as large as the ones carried by the starters. Sid McGee, who'd only had one at-bat so far this year, even shook my hand. He seemed to have a sense of humor—a welcome change from the rage that had greeted me in the parking lot. As for Harrison, he still seemed pissed off. But as three o'clock approached his focus shifted to the game. When the Braves took the field before the top of the first inning, he threw practice grounders to his infielders, including John, like nothing had happened. From his shortstop position, John fired strikes back to Harrison like business as usual.

All of the Braves out on the field looked sharp. Throws blazed around the diamond with pinpoint accuracy. The three outfielders moved like cheetahs that could run down anything hit into their zip code. Each of them had an arm, too. The JV team was good, but these guys appeared ready for the College World Series.

I sat on the bench next to McGee as the contest against Tech High began. Aside from a victory, my main hope for the afternoon was that Harrison would have a good game. *Anything to take his mind off Dave King*. Unfortunately he struck out in his first two at-bats and grounded out his third time up. His fourth trip to the plate came in the bottom of the sixth with two outs. Three fastballs left him down in the count 1-2. Batting from the left side, Harrison stood like a coiled tower of potential energy. The Tech pitcher must have figured he had him set up for an off-speed pitch. Harrison likely had the same thought. He exploded on the changeup, producing a booming crack as wood met ball. The white sphere sailed high in the air, clearing the football bleachers that stood beyond the right field fence.

The mammoth blast capped a stellar day for the Braves offense. Vasquez had three hits. John had a single and a double. Darryl Jones, our fleet-footed leadoff hitter, had two hits, a walk, and three stolen bases. Moose, the hefty catcher, homered in the fourth inning, allowing him to circle the bases at a leisurely pace. On the mound, Al Matzke, the staff ace, did not have his usual dominant stuff. But he still held Tech to three runs over six innings. Not bad for an off day. Matt Loos pitched the seventh to close out a 7-3 Eastridge victory.

The guys on the team were oblivious to my presence after the game. They laughed and chatted about their plans for the evening. Just to be safe, I stayed out of Harrison and Liotta's way. Aside from handing me a practice schedule, Coach didn't pay much attention to me either. Although I'd survived, the first day of my varsity career left me with a nauseous feeling. Mired in the ashes of my scorched dreams, I debated quitting baseball forever.

The Eastridge players piled into their cars. Dad assumed that I'd catch a ride home with one of my new teammates. He didn't figure his son would become a baseball leper so fast. As I started walking home, my mind tried to calculate how long it would take to complete the four-mile trek on foot. Before I reached the edge of the lot, someone called my name. Turning around, I saw John standing beside his car.

"Hey King, need a ride?"

Chapter 4 – July 1974

My eyes popped open at 7:03 a.m. I had gone to bed nine hours earlier, but restless currents of energy had kept me twitching in semi-consciousness through much of the night. Following a visit to the bathroom, I went downstairs and retrieved *The Des Moines Register* from the front stoop. After pouring a glass of orange juice and grabbing a banana, I settled in at the kitchen table with the paper. The front-page headline proclaimed, "SECOND IMPEACH CHARGE VOTED." *Coach is not going to like that. Especially not today.*

I flipped through the pages to find *The Peach*, the newspaper's sports section. At the top of the first page was a bold announcement, "Metro Rivals to Clash in District Final Tonight." Taking a sip of juice, I read the article below.

> Metro Conference champion Eastridge will meet West Des Moines Valley tonight to decide the Class AA district crown. The top-ranked Braves (25-1) feature a lineup that includes five first- and second-team All-State selections: Frank Harrison, Darryl Jones, Ronnie Vasquez, Tim Frazier, and Al Matzke.
>
> Having posted the best record in school history, Eastridge is looking to win its first state baseball championship. The Braves have won eight conference titles under Sal Kishman, but his teams have never advanced to the state tournament during his 17 seasons as the Eastridge coach.
>
> The Valley Tigers (20-6), second place finishers in the conference, have eliminated the Braves from

> postseason play each of the past two summers. Hoping to continue that trend, Coach Tom Acheson sends first-team All-Stater Phil Galbraith to the mound tonight.
>
> The game is scheduled for 8:00 at Roosevelt High School.

Below the article was a box titled “Roaring Tiger” that summarized Galbraith’s season thus far: 15-0 record; 11 shutouts; 6 no-hitters; 105 innings pitched; 241 strikeouts; 0 earned runs. The statistics sent a shudder down my spine. Most devastating was what Galbraith did on July 17th, not quite two weeks earlier. On that day he shut out the mighty Eastridge Braves to hand us our only loss of the year.

My stomach churned. I was more worried for my team though, than for myself. There was little chance I would be facing Galbraith. Thus far I had made only twelve plate appearances for the varsity team. That included two hits in seven official at-bats, with three sacrifice bunts and two walks. I was also used as a pinch runner a few times. During the postseason, however, Coach did not like to play his reserves. As such, my butt had remained nailed to the bench during our district victories over Carlisle and Newton.

And yet, I was still nervous. The Braves were my team and I wanted my team to win. Thanks in large part to John, I’d slowly gained acceptance with the other varsity players. I now felt that we were fellow warriors battling for a common goal. We’d been so dominant. Many of our victories were blowouts. But then, in the last game of the regular season, we ran into *him*. Galbraith made the Eastridge lineup look like a bunch of Little Leaguers. The team managed only two hits and a walk in a 4-0 loss. Though the Braves rebounded to win their first two postseason games, something was different. Galbraith had planted seeds of doubt into our heads. It seemed that nearly all of my teammates had started to wonder, *Are we really that good?*

With elbows on the table, I rested my head in my hands and closed my eyes. Thoughts of God’s awesome power came into my mind. I then recalled several Bible verses that I had memorized. A sense of peace enveloped me. I invited words of praise to flow through my head. Instead, a wet slimy presence entered my ear.

The cold damp sensation shocked me out of my serene state of prayerful contemplation. "Aaaahhh," I cried, shooting out of the chair.

"Wet Willy!" Ozzie announced, snorting with laughter. I was so deep in meditation that I hadn't heard him slither into the kitchen.

"Oh, that is disgusting." I reached for a Kleenex on the kitchen counter. "Don't you ever get tired of acting like a first grader?"

"Actually, no," Ozzie replied, still snickering. "I can't say that I do. I find that acting like a first grader keeps life entertaining."

"You're a very bad man," I said in my best Judy Garland voice as I dried out my ear with a tissue. "What are you doing up this early anyway? Didn't you stay out late last night prowling for naive young females with poor eyesight?"

"Nah, even the Wizard sometimes gets bored turning innocent Dorothys into wicked witches. Randy and me went to see *Blazing Saddles*. Man, I love that campfire scene." He chuckled a couple times. "Afterwards we grabbed some Big Macs and then I was zonked. Hell, I was home and in bed by midnight." His eyes got wide. "Oh no! I just realized something. I'm turning into you! You've been using that voodoo religion of yours against me, haven't you? You and those other Jesus Freaks at Faith Community Coven."

"Yep, that's it," I replied. "You're on to us. Tonight we were all gonna get out our Ozzie dolls and poke needles into them. Then we were planning to cast the conversion spell to turn you into one of us. By the way, can I borrow a strand of your hair?" I reached toward his head.

"Hell no!" he said, slapping my hand away. He then glanced down at the article about tonight's game. "Hey, you know I'm coming to that?"

"Oooohh, I'll alert the media."

"You should. It's big news whenever I make an appearance somewhere. The men bow and the women swoon. Anyway, I heard there's this little hobbit who sits on the Eastridge bench for the entire game. He never moves. All he does is swing his furry feet back and forth. I've just got to see that for myself."

"Very funny. You've got the wit of a Ralph Malph and the coolness of a Potsie."

"Wrong, Shortcake. If I'm anybody on *Happy Days*, then I'm Chuck, the cool older brother. He's the only reason that stupid show is a hit."

"What about the Fonz?"

"Nah, he's just a '50s cliché. People are gonna get tired of him real quick."

"Okay Chuck, why are you really coming to the game tonight?" I asked, peeling a banana.

"Isn't this the district final?"

"Yeah."

"Gonna be a huge crowd?"

"Yep."

"And Valley's got that big ape pitching, right?"

My mouth full of banana, I nodded.

"Well," Ozzie continued, "when he shuts you guys down again, all the Eastridge fans will be crushed. Dozens of chicks from our school will be crying their eyes out. And the Wizard will be right there to console them."

"You're a real prince. On behalf of the team, I thank you for your loyal support."

"On the other hand," he said, stroking his chin, "those Valley fans will be awfully excited after their big win. Maybe I'll slide over to their side and help some sweet young thing celebrate their victory."

"You really should read the Bible," I said. "There's this guy in there called Judas. I think you'd like him."

"I know all about Judas from *Jesus Christ Superstar*. He *is* a cool guy. Got a great voice too." Ozzie pulled a box of Captain Crunch from the cupboard and grabbed a carton of milk from the refrigerator. Moments later, we were both sitting at the table reading the paper.

"You visited Grandma this week?" I asked, after finishing the sports section.

"Nah, I haven't made it over there for a while," he replied, crunching his cereal.

"You might want to do that."

"I know, I know. I'll swing by there."

"When?"

"I don't know," he said defensively. "Soon."

"Good. I think having family around would help her get better sooner."

Nodding once, he returned to the comics page.

"Is there enough gas in the mower?" Dad asked as his Cadillac rolled to a stop in the driveway at his parents' house.

"Yeah."

"You can go in and say hello before you get started." He sighed. "Then, while you're mowing, I've got to have a difficult talk with your grandfather."

Inside the house, we found Grandpa sitting at Grandma's bedside. It was a familiar sight. "Jesse and Dave are here," Grandpa whispered to his wife. The covers on the bed were pulled up to her neck so that only her pale wrinkled face was visible. Grandpa rose from his chair. "I know she'd be pleased if you'd read the Bible some," he said to me in a solemn voice. After gripping my shoulder, he exited the room with my father.

I grabbed the black leather King James on the nightstand and sat down. Grandma had spent most of the past three days in bed. Despite her appearance, I remained hopeful that she would soon rally. She had previously fallen ill like this at the end of May. I spent hours then praying for her recovery. And one morning her color and energy suddenly returned. She was back on her feet wielding her cast iron skillet like nothing had happened. She and Grandpa even came to my baptism at Faith Community Church two weeks later. After Pastor Samuels lifted me up out of the water, I brimmed with joy looking out at the congregation. In the third pew, smiling and clapping along with the rest of the worshippers, were my grandparents. They were the only members of my family who were there.

"Hello Grandma."

Her eyes slitting, she nudged her head in my direction. I read a couple of her favorite Psalms before turning to Chapter 8 of Romans. After finishing the chapter, I recalled the stories she had read to me when I was little—when I stayed at their farm while Mom was in the hospital, and afterward.

"I love you, Grandma." Her eyes remained shut. As I got up to leave, I heard a weak voice.

"Dave."

I leaned my head close to hers. "Yes, Grandma. I'm here."

"Dave … the victory is near." She shut her eyes again.

"Victory?" I waited for her to continue, but she drifted off to sleep. *Did Grandma know about the game tonight?* After thinking about it for a few moments, I concluded that she was talking about her recovery. *She could feel that she was getting better, just like before.* I prayed silently at her bedside and left the room. Dad and Grandpa were sitting at the kitchen table wearing somber expressions. They stopped their conversation as I passed by and went out the back door.

The afternoon sun beat down without mercy. Fortunately, it only took about forty minutes to mow the small dandelion-speckled lawn at my grandparents' house. Though the summer heat wrapped me like a parka, the exercise helped calm my nerves about the game. For a while, anyway.

"I gave Adam and Shane the day off," Dad announced after we had returned home. "They want to go to the game tonight."

I grabbed a bottle of Pepsi out of the refrigerator.

"If you see them, you might let them know that their grandmother is going to have to go to a nursing home. I don't like discussing such matters with them at the restaurant."

I flinched upon hearing his words. "I don't think she has to go to a home yet, Dad. She's gonna get better. Soon. She told me."

"Dave, I just had this same discussion with your grandfather. I'm not going to get into it with you now." He stared at me for a few seconds. "Just tell your brothers to visit their grandparents tomorrow."

"Yeah, okay."

"Oh, and try to find out what Eli is going to be doing after the baseball season ends. Ask him if he has a job lined up yet."

The concerned look on Dad's face told a familiar story. Over the past ten years, Eli had been involved in a number of business ventures. All of them failed. Since his assistant coach position at

Eastridge kept him employed for only five months each year, every August he had to find another job. Though Eli was a lousy cook with no business sense, Dad always offered him a position at the restaurant. Too proud to work under his younger brothers, Eli usually tried to find something else. One year it was roofing. Another year it was painting. Last year he tried selling encyclopedias.

Since Eli was defensive about his career status, I had no intention of asking him about his job prospects. If Dad wanted to know, he could pick up the phone. After finishing my Pepsi, I headed up the stairs for a shower. On the desk in my room was a note.

> Dear Bilbo,
>
> If you somehow get into the game tonight, don't let the pressure get to you. Don't think about how you'll be letting down your teammates and all the fans if you FAIL. And don't worry about STRIKING OUT or making an ERROR to cost your team the game. If you CHOKE, it's no big deal. Nobody will remember your humiliating failure 50 years from now.
>
> Your Superior Brother
>
> p.s. Wizards rule and hobbits drool!

I wadded up the note and tossed it in the garbage.

John's beige Malibu pulled into my driveway a little before seven. I threw my glove in the backseat and crawled in. Matt Loos occupied the passenger seat. As the Braves top relief pitcher, Matt had grown a moustache like that of Rollie Fingers. It looked silly when he first started growing it, but now it wasn't too far off from the original.

"He's got a temper," Matt said, referring to Galbraith. "Last year, he'd get wild sometimes. He lost a few ballgames as a junior. We just need to stir him up and get him riled."

"You think it'll be that easy, huh," John replied.

"Check this out," Matt said, rapping John's arm with the back of his hand. "I heard that after his second baseman made an error to let Hoover score a run, Galbraith cornered him after the game and busted his jaw. And that was a game Valley won six to one."

"Really? I wondered why Valley started using a different second baseman."

"Yeah. Galbraith is a loose cannon, man. We get him rattled and he'll lose it."

"Well, he hasn't lost *anything* yet this year," John said. "What do you think, Dave?"

"After you take him deep in the first, his focus will be shot," I replied. "That big oaf won't last through the second inning."

They both laughed. Galbraith remained the topic of conversation during the rest of the drive across town to Roosevelt High School.

The team was quiet during warm-ups. My teammates usually traded putdowns and witty banter before a game, but not on this occasion. There were even a few uncharacteristic overthrows and miscues. I tried to suppress the ominous feelings budding inside me.

Just before game time, Coach gathered his players around himself and Eli. Kishman's face seemed a shade paler than normal. His gruff voice was soft at first. "I've coached a lot of good teams before, but you men standing right here are the best I've ever seen. You've had one hell of a season. You've played like champions. You *deserve* to be champions." He paused, before continuing in a louder voice. "And you're too damn good to lose twice to anybody. Tonight, you go out on that field and show those bums what greatness is all about. Nothing can stop you! The victory is yours! Claim it!"

After a couple moments, Frank Harrison slapped his hands together. "Hell yeah! Let's do this!" We players then crowded into a huddle and touched our right hands together above our heads. A few seconds later we shouted in unison, "Braves power! HOO-ah!!" Our fans cheered.

Since we were designated as the visitors, the Valley Tigers took the field. Our first three batters donned red helmets and began taking practice cuts. The rest of the team migrated over to the bench. After claiming a spot at the far end next to Sid McGee, I turned to look through the chain-link fence behind me. With the bleachers nearly full by this point, many people were milling about trying to find a place to watch the game. Fans from the rival schools hurled insults at each other. The language was loud and foul. Games between Eastridge and Valley were usually rowdy. The heat, humidity, and high stakes of this contest added gasoline to the fire. The Des Moines Police Department had sent four cars to the game. Scanning the crowd, I saw officers break up an early fistfight between two shirtless young hoodlums.

A sharp noise resembling a gunshot jolted my attention back to the field. Galbraith was warming up. His pitches slammed into the catcher's mitt with violent velocity. Atop the mound he stood like a colossus towering over the infield. The Valley media guide listed him at 6'9" and 265 pounds. He looked bigger in person—much bigger. He even made Kishman and Eli seem average. Galbraith's full beard and long unruly dark hair added to his intimidating presence.

"That guy cannot be eighteen," McGee said.

"Looks more like twenty-five to me," I replied.

Darryl Jones, the Braves centerfielder, stepped to the plate from the left side. The lower half of his Afro rolled out below his batting helmet. Kishman paced in the third base coach's box. Galbraith's first pitch was a white laser that flashed over the plate. Valley fans cheered. Since my team occupied the bench on the third base side of the field, I could see Jones's eyes widen after the ball hit the catcher's mitt.

Another barely visible fastball put Jones in the hole 0-2. I leaned back to check out the bleachers behind home plate. There were five different men with clipboards sitting in the first three rows. One of them held a radar gun as well. He grinned after checking the reading. I figured he must be a scout for the Chicago White Sox, the major league club that had drafted Galbraith in the first round. The other scouts were probably from teams that had selected Eastridge players. Jones flailed helplessly at the next pitch, a fastball he likely never saw. The crowd on the Valley side of the field hollered its approval.

John was up next. Though he fouled the second pitch straight back over the backstop, he too struck out on three pitches. Tim Frazier, the Braves leftfielder, batted third. His .487 batting average led the Metro Conference. Standing in from the left side, Frazier looked a lot like Reggie Jackson. He certainly had Reggie-like power, and he combined that with a Rod Carew batting eye. Galbraith needed only four pitches to finish him off.

Despite the inauspicious start to the game, Coach clapped his hands and tried to rally his troops. “Let’s go men! Shut ’em down!” Eli echoed his sentiments. On the mound for the Braves was our ace, Al Matzke. Though his 12-0 record and 1.96 ERA were overshadowed by Galbraith’s statistics, Matzke too could dominate an opposing lineup. Nobody wanted to say it out loud, but most Braves believed our pitcher needed to throw a shutout for us to have a chance. Matzke sent the Tigers down in order. The Eastridge fans roared.

Leading off the second, Harrison stood at the plate coiled and ready to strike. He hit .392 during the season and led the conference with 14 home runs and 41 RBIs. None of that mattered tonight though. Harrison was way behind on Galbraith’s first two heaters. The Tigers pitcher then followed with a cruel changeup. Harrison, expecting more heat, had started his swing early and was way out in front. The bat flew out of his hands and spun through the air like a detached airplane propeller. Harrison’s thick body corkscrewed into the ground before toppling over. Valley fans howled with laughter. Ronnie Vasquez followed by striking out on three fastballs. Ted Graeve, our right fielder, went down on a nasty curveball that buckled his knees.

McGee leaned over to me. “It’s bad enough that monster throws fastballs over a hundred miles per hour. But when he mixes in those unholy off-speed pitches, it’s just not fair. He should be pitching in the majors this summer, not here.” A sick feeling roiled my stomach. Coach and Eli looked tense as they exhorted their fielders to play tough D.

John made a nice play on a tricky hop to retire Valley’s first batter in the second. The next Tigers hitter smashed a solid line drive to left, the first hit of the game. Matzke shook that off to get the next two batters on a fly out and a pop out.

Between innings I scanned the crowd again. With the bleachers overflowing, fans had spread down both outfield lines. Some sat in lawn chairs, while others just leaned against the chain-link fence that surrounded the field. Many late-arriving spectators claimed spots in the grassy area beyond the outfield fence. An outbreak of applause and shouts drew my attention to the stands nearest our bench. Fans there had just unfurled a banner that proclaimed in large red letters, "LEE TOWNSHIP AGAINST THE WORLD!" Valley supporters responded with boos and one-finger salutes. I then spotted Adam and Shane sitting three rows below the banner. Each wore a faded Eastridge cap.

Moose led off the top of the third. As he stepped into the batter's box, a Tigers fan yelled, "Hey look, it's Haystacks Calhoun!" Laughter cascaded from the Valley bleachers. Several Braves glared over at the twenty-something man who had shouted the comment. Chuckling with the guys around him, he wore orange jeans and a tight white T-shirt with a cigarette pack rolled up in one of the sleeves.

"After the game, that blond pretty-boy is dead," Harrison growled.

"Ignore those idiots," Eli said. "Focus on the game."

Galbraith required just eleven pitches to mow down Moose and the two hitters that followed. Nine up and nine down. The entire Braves lineup had struck out.

The bottom of the third started well enough for Matzke. The first Tigers batter looked at a called third strike. Galbraith then lumbered to the plate. He looked even scarier with a large wooden club in his hands. Though he'd hit some monstrous home runs this season, he had a tendency to chase pitches out of the strike zone. He struck out on a curve that was a foot outside.

After clearing that hurdle, Matzke must have relaxed a bit too much. He walked the next two batters. With Valley's best hitter coming up, Coach strode to the mound to talk to his pitcher. After play resumed, the batter turned Matzke's first pitch into a screaming line drive headed towards right. Les Burton, our second baseman, leapt up with glove extended. The white bullet disappeared with a loud smack. When Burton landed with ball safely in Rawlings, the Braves coaches, players, and fans exhaled a collective gasp of relief.

The run-saving play injected some life back into our bench. All the Eastridge players stood to watch the top of the fourth.

Jones, leading off, bunted Galbraith's second pitch down the third baseline. Anticipating such a move from our speedy centerfielder, Valley's third baseman had crept up to the infield grass. Charging in, he barehanded the ball and threw out Jones by a step. Batting next, John made solid contact with a Galbraith curve ball but grounded it straight to the Tigers second baseman, who threw to first for an easy out. Frazier then went down looking.

"Damn," McGee said. "Tim only struck out twice all season. Now he's done it twice in one game." Frazier slammed his helmet down and yelled a compound expletive as he stalked back to the bench.

"Yeah, let's not tell him about that," Cy Hodges, a reserve outfielder, warned.

Kishman urged his troops to play sharp as the Braves took the field in the bottom of the fourth. The first Valley hitter singled sharply up the middle. The next batter hit a slow roller over to Harrison at first. Thinking about rushing a throw to second, he took his eye off the ball at the last instant. It bounded off the heel of his glove and rolled a few feet away.

"Gimme an EEEE!" someone on the Valley bench yelled. The crowd responded in kind.

"Gimme a threeee!" the player added. The Valley fans again gave him what he wanted.

The next Tigers batter laid down a sacrifice bunt to advance the runners to second and third with only one out. Kishman brought the infield in. We needed a strikeout. But what we got was a chopper that bounced over Matzke's head. Ranging quickly to his left, John made a great play to keep the ball from bounding into centerfield. But he had no chance to get the Valley runner sprinting home. John threw over to first to retire the batter, but the Tigers had scored a run. Their fans exploded. Groans of despair could be heard from more than a few Braves supporters. Though visibly dejected, Maztke collected himself and got the next hitter to pop out to end the inning.

Harrison led off the top of the fifth. Three straight fastballs whizzed past him—each was called a strike.

"Son of a bitch!" Coach roared. He stomped from the coach's box and grabbed the wooden bat from his startled first baseman.

Kishman then held the bat high above his head with both hands and brought it down hard over his knee. After the loud snap, he threw the two pieces of wood at Harrison's feet.

"That's how useless that bat is in your hands," Coach growled. The Valley fans whooped it up. Galbraith grinned. Harrison slunk back to the bench with his head down.

After Vasquez struck out chasing a curveball in the dirt, Coach barked a harsh expletive involving the Savior's name. A long "ooooooohhhh" flowed from the Valley bleachers.

I stood and rattled the fence to encourage our next batter. "Come on Graeve, rip it!" Graeve tapped the ball back to the pitcher, ending the inning.

Galbraith led off the Valley fifth with a towering fly ball to left. He started his home run trot, but the distance of the drive did not match its height. Frazier made the catch with his back to the fence. A groundout, a double, and another groundout followed. The score remained 1-0 with two innings left to play.

Before the top of the sixth, shrill screams diverted our attention over to the area near the main concession stand. Two teenage girls were locked in combat. One had grabbed the other's long hair and was swinging her around in a circle. Several boys stood nearby, transfixed by the action. I wondered if Ozzie was among that noble lot of lads. It took three police officers to extricate the girls from each other and temporarily restore order.

Hoping to frustrate Galbraith and break his rhythm, Kishman told our hitters to stall by calling for time between pitches. Moose tried it first, but struck out to lead off the sixth. When Burton employed the same strategy, the Valley fans started booing. The guy in the orange jeans stood up and grabbed the fence. "You east-side boys should stop stalling so we can get this over with," he shouted. "Your mamas and daddies have to get up early tomorrow so they can come over and scrub our toilets and cut our grass." The comment brought laughter from one side of the field and profanity from the other.

Galbraith grew annoyed with Burton's delaying tactics. "Get in the box you coward!" he yelled from atop the mound. The big man then blew away our second baseman with a white rocket that seemed even faster than his earlier heat.

"Yeah, let's get him mad," McGee said. "That's a good idea."

With two outs, Coach sent in Hodges to pinch hit for Matzke. Hodges was a good contact hitter who batted .362 during the season. Our hopes surged after Galbraith missed with his first two fastballs. Hodges then looked at two bullets that came right down the middle, and struck out swinging at an eye-level fastball.

"Damn it!" Kishman snarled. He stormed over and grabbed the aluminum bat from Hodges's hands. Coach then cocked it back and let loose a mighty swing. The bat smashed into the metal pole at the end of the chain-link fence in front of our bench. The resounding clang of metal crashing into metal echoed across the field and beyond. The crowd noise ceased momentarily before the Valley fans unleashed a round of sardonic cheers. When Coach let go of the bat it remained fused in place, the aluminum barrel bent at a 90-degree angle around the pole.

McGee leaned over. "Coach has lost it," he whispered. "The expectations to win it all this season were just too much. Now that he realizes we're toast, he's finally snapped."

"Can it," I said. "The game's not over yet." I stood and slammed my palms against the fence. "Come on D, let's go!"

Hodges, now shaking, sat down next to McGee. "That's just wrong," he said. "We're in high school. We shouldn't be expected to bat against a guy who throws harder than Nolan Ryan."

"Those pitches coming in a bit fast, are they?" McGee asked.

"They are literally not visible," Hodges replied.

Sean Liotta came in to pitch the sixth and immediately got into trouble. Valley put men at first and third with one out. Kishman paced back and forth along the bench like a caged tiger. His face glowed red and the veins in his temples swelled to the size of fingers. "We're number one the whole damn year," he muttered, "and we can't even win our district." He turned to glare at us on the bench. "We can't even get one damn runner on base! Not one!" He picked up an equipment bag and slammed it to the ground, before stalking back to the other end of the bench. "And now we lose to these bastards again."

"I told you," McGee whispered. Ignoring him, I stared out at the field.

Liotta caught a break when an overanxious Valley hitter popped a fly ball into short right field—not nearly deep enough to score the runner from third. The next batter hit a blooper to left center. Since it was too shallow for an outfielder to catch, it looked like disaster. But John raced back from his shortstop position in a full sprint. Launching into a Superman dive, he made a stunning over-the-shoulder grab.

That brought the top of the seventh—our last chance. The Valley fans were on their feet, taunting and dancing. Galbraith was pumped. After finishing his warm-up tosses, he stomped around the mound slamming the ball into his glove. "Three more outs and these bitches are done," he yelled. His teammates responded with shouts.

Galbraith, however, had jacked himself up too much. His first two fastballs to Jones sailed high and outside. After a conference with his catcher, the big right-hander settled down. He bored his next two pitches through the strike zone as Jones watched. The fifth pitch was low, creating a full count. All of the Braves on the bench stood. This was the first time any of our hitters had a three-ball count. Galbraith took a little extra time before firing in the payoff pitch.

The sickening sound of ball striking flesh preceded the batter's yelping and crumpling to the ground. Galbraith's errant fastball had nailed Jones in the thigh. The umpire removed his mask and knelt down beside our centerfielder. Kishman jogged to home plate. Moose looked over at me. "Start stretching, King. He's going to need a pinch runner." I thought about it for a second. *I'm going in the game!* My mind raced as I bent down to touch my toes. *Maybe I can steal second and then third. I'm the tying run—I've got to score.*

Taking a couple of steps toward the field, I was shocked by what I saw next. Jones was limping down to first and Kishman was walking back to the coach's box. Along with most of my teammates, I stared in disbelief. Granted Jones, with 28 stolen bases in 26 games, was the normally fastest guy on the team. But having just taken a cannonball to the thigh, he didn't look like he could outrun Moose anymore. I returned to the bench.

“Coach’s lost it, man,” McGee said, shaking his head. I was starting to agree.

Nonetheless, the tying run was on first. We had hope. Galbraith paced about, clearly upset about allowing a Brave to reach base. Despite the rage, he quickly regained his focus. He used blazing fastballs to get ahead of our next two hitters, before finishing them off with wicked off-speed pitches. John struck out waving at a changeup. Frazier went down swinging at a curveball that broke low and inside. Harrison, in the on-deck circle, tapped the donut off his bat and took a step toward home plate.

Kishman called time. “Get back here, Harrison.”

“Huh?” The big first baseman had a confused look on his face.

“No way you’re going up there to make the last out.”

Harrison’s jaw dropped.

“Based on what you’ve done tonight,” Coach jeered, “I can’t believe you’ve ever played this game before.” He then turned to the bench with a crimson face. “Have any of you jackasses ever played baseball before?” His voice came out as an anguished yell.

“Coach, please,” Harrison protested.

Kishman turned and yanked the bat from his hands. “Sit down, Harrison. You’ve already done your best to cost my team this game.”

His face pale, our dazed first baseman retreated to the bench where he buried his head in his hands.

“We need a batter, Eastridge,” the home plate umpire announced.

Kishman glared down the bench. “Does anybody on this team know how to hit a damn baseball?”

An uncomfortable silence followed. Before my good sense could stop me, I sprang to my feet. “Coach, I want to bat.” The words came out of my mouth, but I couldn’t believe it was me who was saying them. Kishman stared at me with smoldering eyes. The heads of all my teammates jerked toward me.

After a couple seconds, Eli stood and scowled. “Sit down, Dave, you conceited little bastard. We’re down to our last out. We don’t have time for your stupid games. Let one of the real ballplayers—”

"Shut up, Eli," Coach interrupted, grabbing my brother's shoulder and spinning him around. "Just because you choked in the tournament when you played for me doesn't mean he shouldn't have a chance." The two towering men glared at each other for a few seconds. Eli then lowered himself to the bench, sulking like a five-year-old boy who had just been sent to bed without his supper.

"King," Coach barked at me, "put a helmet on and get up there." I hurried down the bench and grabbed a red batting helmet. "Take this, it's mine," Kishman said, thrusting an enormous caramel-colored bat at me. Emerging from the bench, I took a couple uncomfortable practice cuts with the 42-ounce wooden club.

"Coach, I'm not used to this heavy of a bat," I said. He nodded and took it back.

I then found my favorite aluminum Easton in the rack. It seemed nearly weightless after swinging Kishman's hefty bat. As Coach informed the impatient umpire of the switch, I took a few more swings near the on-deck circle. Murmurs trickled down from the Eastridge bleachers. "Who's that? … Where's Harrison?"

As I approached the batter's box, I heard a familiar voice cutting through the night. "Dave King! The mighty Wizard commands you to get a hit!" Glancing up, I spotted Ozzie standing at the top of the bleachers. He held both hands straight above his head with his fingers pointed at me as if casting a spell. A smile cracked my face before I turned my attention back to the field. Stepping into the batter's box, I tapped my bat on the plate. A flock of butterflies staged a Mardi Gras festival in my stomach.

"Hey look at the scrub Eastridge is sending up to make the last out," Mr. Orange Jeans yelled. Similar taunts followed from his buddies.

Galbraith stared at me with a look of amused contempt. "Have you guys given up?" he asked in booming voice. "Where's Harrison? I wanted to strike out a real hitter to end the game."

"Just pitch, Sasquatch," I replied. The smirk vanished from his hirsute face.

"Watch it, punk," the Valley catcher said. "You make him mad and he'll put you in the hospital … or the morgue."

No longer concerned about the hobbled Jones trying to steal second, Galbraith went into a full windup. Watching his motion reminded me of a trebuchet's movement before it launched a projectile. I told myself to follow the ball out of his hand. It's a good thing I did because Galbraith sent a bazooka round right at my head. *DUCK!!!* Bailing out, I felt a furious rush of air against my face. The Valley fans howled as I hit the ground.

"Told you," the catcher taunted as he tossed the ball back to his pitcher.

I picked myself up, dusted off my uniform, and looked over at Coach to check for signs. He stood unmoving in the coach's box. Piranhas replaced the butterflies in my stomach. Still, I did not want to show any fear. I turned to the mound. "Is that all the harder you can throw, Lurch?" Galbraith's foreboding glare did not change. He went into his windup. My eyes struggled to follow the next pitch—a white flash that smashed into the catcher's mitt with an earsplitting crack. The sound reminded me of a howitzer report.

"Striiiiieeeeee!" the umpire yelled, raising an arm. I stepped out of the batter's box to look at Kishman. No signs. My hands shook. A chilly fright threatened to overwhelm me. I recalled a Bible verse: "I can do all things through Him who strengthens me."

Not feeling so alone, I stepped back into the box. The next pitch blazed past with an angry hiss. "Striiiiieeeeeee!"

As I stepped out, doubt infected my mind. I was down 1-2 and could barely see the fastballs coming at me. *I'm going to strike out to end the game.* The dreadful words echoed through my head. I silently recited another verse: "Be strong and courageous! Do not tremble or be dismayed, for the Lord your God is with you wherever you go." A flicker of confidence returned.

The Bible, however, doesn't say much about how to hit a 102-mph fastball. But *The Science of Hitting* does. I recalled Ted Williams's three rules for hitters: get a good ball to hit, think properly, and be quick with the bat. *I've got to think. Since I'm down in the count, Galbraith might try to get me to chase something out of the strike zone—a curveball maybe. That's how he retired the last batter. Must focus.*

"Get in there and bat you little bitch," Galbraith yelled. The roar of the Valley fans anticipating a game-ending strikeout was deafening. I stepped in and followed the pitcher's motion. After leaving his hand, the ball appeared to be flying towards my head again. Ready for a breaking pitch, I stayed in the box and prepared to swat at the ball when it bent across the plate. The pitch was indeed a curve, but it did not have a sharp break. I held my swing as it whizzed past my nose.

"Ball." The umpire's call brought yells of disapproval from the Valley fans. He was correct though; the pitch was high and inside.

I stepped out of the box. *Okay, think. The count is 2-2.* I reasoned that Galbraith would want to finish me off with the next pitch. *No way he wants the count to go full. A walk puts the tying run at second and the winning run on first.* I guessed that a fastball was coming since that was his most accurate pitch. Though many baseball experts believe that batters should not guess, Ted Williams maintained that anticipating the next pitch is part of proper thinking.

Another Bible verse ran through my head: "In God I have put my trust, I shall not be afraid. What can man do to me?" Armed with the Word of God and the advice of the Splendid Splinter, I felt an empowering calm replace the searing anxiety that had scorched my insides only moments earlier.

"Quit stalling, you little shit," Galbraith yelled. "I've got a victory celebration to get to." I stepped into the box. He went into his windup. Anticipating heat, I started my stride early. If the pitch had been a changeup or a curve, I would have been way out in front. The pitch was in fact a fastball—a white comet blazing toward the outer half of the plate at waist level. Having just seen a couple of his lasers, my eyes were better able to track the ball than before. I strode forward and whipped the bat around.

Aluminum met cowhide with a piercing metallic TONG. It felt like the ball disintegrated upon contact with the barrel. Though the ball did not disintegrate, it shot off the bat so fast I did not see where it went. A fearful thought flashed in my mind. *What if the ball went back up the middle and hit Galbraith in the head? He'd be killed for sure.* Looking out at the mound, I saw the giant leaning over and staggering to his left. But that was normal for him. He threw so much of his body into his pitches that his momentum carried him way off balance in the follow-through.

Running toward first base, I scanned the field for signs of the ball. I soon spotted the Valley centerfielder racing back and looking over his shoulder. High above in the night sky, a small white dot seemed to hover. As I progressed up the line, I could see that the dot was actually moving away from me and starting to descend. I lowered my eyes for a moment so I could make sure I touched first base. Heading toward second, I saw the centerfielder standing at the fence, his eyes focused upwards. I thought he was preparing to make the catch, but I was wrong. His head continued tilting back until he was looking straight above himself. He then turned his back to the infield to face the area beyond the fence. There, I saw a white object fall hard into the grass about twenty feet past where the outfielder stood helplessly. Several children converged on the area of impact.

After I touched second base, a disturbing sensation came over me. A moment earlier, the ballpark had sounded like a prison riot. Now there was complete silence. I wondered if I'd lost my hearing until I discerned the sound of my spikes hitting the dirt below—crunch, crunch, crunch. The effect was eerie. *Am I dreaming? Is Rod Serling going to emerge from the crowd?*

The silence continued as I trotted toward third. Straight ahead in the coach's box, Kishman stood catatonic. He stared out at centerfield, his mouth hanging open. As I neared the base, a single voice echoed from the Eastridge bleachers. It sounded like Frazier's mother. "Oh yeah! That's right!" A thunderous roar then exploded from the stands. Rounding third, past the life-sized statue of Coach, I saw my teammates bounding toward home plate. Jones already stood there with a big grin on his face. When I touched home, the Braves greeted me like a tidal wave. Congratulatory slaps rained down upon my back, helmet, and shoulders. Joyful shouts filled the air. Graeve hit me with a solid chest thump. Moose nearly broke a couple of my ribs while lifting me off the ground in a bear hug. Even Harrison stood nearby clapping.

After a few moments, the umpire broke up our party and herded the team back to the bench. Eastridge fans remained on their feet in a boisterous ovation. The tumult continued even as Vasquez stepped into the batter's box. I made my way down the bench with an entourage of teammates clamoring behind me. I passed Eli, who had remained seated the whole time. His face shrouded in gloom, he nodded at me and then stared out at the field. I finally found my familiar seat at the far end the bench. My teammates' whoops continued.

Galbraith's first pitch to Vasquez sailed five feet over the umpire's head. The next three pitches weren't much closer. Graeve then walked on four pitches the Valley catcher struggled to reach. Coach Acheson visited the mound to try to calm down his pitcher. It didn't work. Fury radiated from the big man's face. Moose stepped up to the plate. Four pitches later, the bases were loaded and a new Valley pitcher was jogging to the mound. Galbraith, meanwhile, was destroying a water cooler on the Tigers bench. His deep curses echoed across the park.

A single and an error plated three more Braves runs. When Jones flew out to end the seventh, we were ahead 5-1.

Coach, having finally returned to his body, told me to play second base in the bottom of the seventh. With Harrison out of the game, Burton shifted over to first. Matt Loos and his Rollie Fingers moustache came in to pitch. Stillness had fallen over the Valley bleachers. Mr. Orange Jeans and dozens of other Tigers fans were already gone. Shoulders slumped, the first Valley batter stepped up to the plate. He grounded out to John. The next hitter sent a routine grounder to me that I threw over to first. The Eastridge fans started chanting my name. "Oh, good grief," John said, unable to contain a smile. "That is so wrong."

"I think it sounds great," I said, floating several feet above the ground.

Loos struck out the next Valley batter to end the game. We celebrated our district title with a dogpile near the pitcher's mound. After several minutes of revelry, Coach gathered the team together. His face ashen, he spoke slowly. "This was a rough one. We went through hell out there, but you boys pulled it out. That's what champions do.... I think we know who this goes to." He handed me the game ball. "Good job, kid." My teammates shouted their approval.

After the game, all of the Braves headed over to Hilltop Restaurant on the east side to celebrate. The owners were big Eastridge fans, so they allowed the festivities to continue way past their usual closing time. Adam, Shane, and Ozzie were among the horde of friends and relatives who joined the players at this impromptu pizza party. Though I drank nothing stronger than Coke, my head spun in delirium the whole time. For once, I was a hero. I wished the night would never end.

The next ten days were a blur. The Eastridge High Braves recovered from their near-death experience with renewed focus and intensity. In our first substate tournament game, we thumped Grinnell 11-2. Reinstated by Coach, Harrison slugged two homers and drove in five runs. In the substate finals, Eastridge beat the previous year's champion, Jefferson of Council Bluffs, 7-3. In the first round of the four-team state tournament, we topped Dubuque Hempstead 6-2. Kishman put me at second base for all three games. Batting eighth, I went five for twelve with two walks and three stolen bases.

The title game was played at Sec Taylor Stadium in Des Moines, home of the AAA Iowa Oaks. I was again in the starting lineup as we faced Burlington for all the marbles. Though both teams had powerful offenses, the game ended up being a pitchers' duel. Matzke and their starter both had good stuff. Leading off the seventh in a tie game, I pulled a hanging knuckle-curve into left field for a single. Two outs later I stole second. John's base hit then drove me home to put the Braves ahead 2-1. In the bottom of the inning, Burlington had two runners on with two outs. The next batter rocketed a line drive to my left. With a quick lunge, I speared the ball to end the game. We were the 1974 state champions.

Though our drive to the championship had kept my head in the clouds, my grandmother's health remained a source of concern. She didn't seem to be getting better, so Dad put her in a nursing home. Nonetheless, I maintained hope that she would recover soon and return home. I prayed for her every night.

Three days after we won the state title, the phone rang an hour after Dad had left for work. It was a lady from the nursing home. Grandma had died. The words hit me like a sledgehammer. *Why didn't she get better? What did I do wrong? Is God mad at me?* After calling the restaurant to break the news to Dad, I sat in silence for about a half hour. I then called Pastor Samuels. Though grief limited my understanding of his wisdom, he patiently talked to me about the temporality of our earthly lives and God's gift of eternal salvation. He also read several passages of scripture.

After I hung up the phone, one of the verses Samuels had read echoed over and over in my head. "For to me, to live is Christ, and to die is gain." A short time later I heard the words Grandma had said to me the afternoon before the Valley game. I finally understood.

Chapter 5 – October 1974

"Come on!" John shouted. "Lift!"

A compressing pain flared through my arms and shoulders as I struggled to push the barbell up and away from my chest. I groaned in agony and desperation.

"It's all you!" he exhorted from above. "I'm not helping!" His fingers approached, but did not touch the bar.

The upward movement of the weights came to a stop—gravity and 185 pounds of metal had matched the force of my aching muscles. I arched my back to get more leverage.

"Don't cheat! You keep that back straight!"

Heeding John's command, I straightened my back. But the tide of battle had turned against me. With my head about to explode, the bar started to inch downward towards my chest. My shaking arms were close to giving out.

John mercifully grabbed the bar with both hands and helped me hoist it into the top barbell holders. "Alright, killer. Good job." The heavy metal dropped into place with a loud clang. "Just about got that eighth rep on the fifth set. Not bad." His face was upside down from my vantage point.

My back flat on the bench, I panted desperately for oxygen. Blood drained from my head as the feeling slowly returned to my throbbing arms, shoulders, and chest. After about a minute, I sat up. "Why? Why do we kill ourselves like this?"

"For the girls, old pal," John replied from the other side of my basement weight room. "It's all for the girls. Gotta get those muscles they love so much." He grabbed a 35-pound dumbbell and started curling. "That's why we do the curls … the curls for girls." A slight smile cracked though his grimace.

"Can't they just love us for our minds and personalities?" I asked, wiping the sweat from my forehead with an old Rat Patrol T-shirt.

"With your mind and personality? Fraid not." He snickered. "Plus, you're a football player now. You need to keep up your strength for the gridiron."

"Yeah, I really need to bulk up to carry that clipboard around each Friday night." My breaths still came hard. "That reminds me, why did I let you talk me into going out for football?"

"Hmmm. That's doesn't sound like the inspiring leadership the Eastridge High Braves need from their second-string quarterback. Remember, you're just a broken ankle from running the show." He switched the dumbbell to his left hand and resumed curling.

"I think we all know that if Duncan goes down, the team is in a heap of trouble. It's different for you. You're a starting cornerback and you get a lot of snaps at wide receiver. I do nothing during the games. For me, this football thing is a waste of time. A pointless, painful waste of time."

"I'll have none of that kind of talk, young man," John said, wagging a finger at me. "You're ignoring all the cool stuff. Think about it. You made varsity even though you hadn't played organized football since flag league in sixth grade. That's damn impressive. Plus, football is keeping you in shape for baseball. All those wind sprints are making you even faster. And look how strong your arm has gotten throwing the pigskin around at practices. You'll be blazing baseballs across the diamond next spring. Once Dad sees your cannon of an arm, he'll probably put you at third base." John lowered the dumbbell to the concrete floor. "And check out those muscles on you, dude. You're gettin' huge!"

I stood before the full-length mirror my brother Nate had hung on the wall years ago when he lifted weights in this unfinished corner of the basement. It was hard not to like what I saw. Defined pectorals pressed against the front of my tank top. My arms bulged with newly developed triceps, biceps, and forearm muscles. And my height had reached five-nine, a full three inches taller than I was a year ago.

"Now who's the hobbit?" I mumbled to myself while flexing in front of the mirror.

John filled a plastic cup with water from a cooler. "Best of all, next year Duncan will be in college. That means you, Dave King, will be the starting quarterback." He downed his drink. "And the team's got a lot of good juniors and sophomores who will be coming back with you. Eastridge is gonna kick some serious ass next season."

"Yeah, maybe."

"Man, you got to get pumped about this." He slapped my chest. "Baseball is cool and all that. I know it's your game. Mine too. But football stars, they are the gods of the high school universe. You lead the Braves to the conference title next year, you'll have your pick of the ladies." A smirk spread across his face. "Then you won't have to settle for my dingbat sister."

"I like Michelle," I said, sitting on the bench to start a set of leg curls. "She's a fox."

"Puh-lease." He rolled his eyes. "That is so wrong."

"She's got a killer smile, sexy eyes, a cute nose, and she's got a great—"

"Stop it! That's my sister. You're grossing me out."

I knew I had him on the ropes. "You know, John, Michelle's really got a lovely set of ..." I cupped my hands under my pecs.

"Ahhhhhh," he cried, charging over to put me in a headlock. I hooked his leg and lifted him off the ground. We tumbled over onto the concrete floor. After about a minute of wrestling, the stench and our aching muscles—both products of a lengthy weightlifting session—compelled us to quit. Lying on our backs, we stared up at the bare light bulb and exposed wooden beams.

"You should be happy I'm dating your sister," I said, catching my breath. "That means I'm not on the market anymore competing with you for girls. Cause you know none of them would go for you, if they thought they had a chance with me."

"Shiiiiit," John scoffed. Sitting up, he grabbed an old shirt-rag and ran it over his hair, face, and neck. "That does remind me of something." He wadded up the shirt and threw it on my face.

Casting the foul garment aside, I propped myself up against the weight bench. "What?"

"Just what the hell were you thinking when you wrote that song for Michelle?"

"Oh, that?" I chuckled. "It was no big deal."

"You wrote her a SONG! We're football players. We don't do that Neil Sedaka crap. Hell, I had to hear about it for two straight weeks." John stood, flicked back his dark collar-length hair, and started talking in a falsetto voice. "We were at the park and Dave played his guitar. Then he sang a song that he wrote just for meeee. It was soooo romantic." Clasping his hands together in front of his chest, he kicked up a leg behind him and batted his eyes.

"Shut up." I couldn't help grinning at his performance.

"But that's not the worst of it, lover-boy. Michelle had to tell all the other cheerleaders about dreamy Dave's love song. So then Betty asks ME why I never do anything romantic like that for HER." He shook his head. "You're making the rest of us dudes look bad."

I shrugged my shoulders. "Uh … oops."

"Yeah, oops. I should bill your ass for the flowers I had to send to Betty the next day."

"How about if I write Michelle a heavy metal song next time? Maybe something with a Black Sabbath flavor."

"How about I set your guitar on fire and we put an end to these homemade love songs?"

After grabbing a couple RC bottles from the old downstairs refrigerator, we migrated into the finished half of the basement. I turned on the Admiral television and we each plopped into a large beanbag chair and waited for the black and white set to warm up.

"Speaking of your sisters," I said, "how's Mary doing? She still mad at me?"

John took a swig of pop. "Gee Dave, I don't know. She gets three different friends to tell you how much she likes you. I mean, the poor girl really laid her heart out there. And you, being the cold-hearted snake that you are, feed her some story about not wanting to date your coach's daughter. THEN, two weeks later you're going out with her little sister. I can't think of any reason why Mary would still be mad at you."

"I know that looked bad, but Mary's not my type. Plus, she's two years older than me and was leaving for college. Michelle is my age. We're a better match."

John scoffed. "Translation: You think Mary is dull and, for some insane reason, you think Michelle is foxy."

"I don't think Mary is dull. It's just …" I was quiet for a few seconds. "What I did was pretty bad, huh?"

"Nah." He leapt to his feet and plucked three darts from the dartboard. "It's actually kinda funny. You reject my annoying older sister so you can date my annoying younger sister."

"Thanks. I feel much better now."

"Don't worry about it. Seriously, Mary's fine. She's forgotten about you. She's got some new boyfriend over at Iowa already. Poor bastard. And she'll start talking to Michelle again, someday." He fired three darts at the round board.

"What about your dad?" I asked. "He's mad about what I did to Mary, isn't he?"

"Doubt it."

"Really?" I got up to adjust the tuning dial on the Admiral, which had finally conjured up a picture. I stopped tweaking when the faces of McMillan and his wife were clearly visible on the screen. "In history class, he's been acting like he's kinda pissed off at me. It's been that way since the start of the semester."

"Dad always acts like he's pissed off." John squinted and sent three more darts into the board. The last one hit the bull's-eye. "Hoo-ah! Check that out."

"So he's okay with me and Michelle, even though you guys are Jewish and I'm a Christian?"

"Hah, that's funny. Dad has NO interest in religion. We never go to temple or observe the Sabbath. And have you seen how many hot dogs he eats? Besides, my dad is only half-Jewish. His mother was a Catholic immigrant from Sicily. Her maiden name was Matrisciano."

"Really?"

"Yep. The story is, her family had ties to the Mafia."

"So there really is something to that Kish of Death thing?"

"You bet," John said with a laugh. He then hummed the theme from *The Godfather*.

"Wow." I dropped into a beanbag. "I'm lucky Mary didn't put a horse's head in my bed."

"There's still time for that. Oops, sorry Ringo." John had sent an errant dart into the fake wood paneling that covered the walls of the basement rec room. It hit only a few inches away from a Beatles poster that my brother Ray had tacked up years ago. "Anyway, my dad couldn't care less that a Gentile is dating his daughter. Although—" The pause was abrupt.

"Although what?" My eyes shifted from Rock Hudson and Susan Saint James over to him.

"Nothing." He pulled the dart from the dark wall panel.

"Come on, John. What were you going to say?"

"It's no big deal." He continued throwing darts. After about a minute, he relented to my stare. "Fine. If you must know, Dad was a *little* pissed at you after the baseball season."

"Why?" My voice raised an octave. "What did I do?"

"It wasn't your fault. It was those newspaper articles about the tournament games. They made it sound like Dad had lost his coaching edge and that you had to save the team from his mistakes."

"I didn't like those articles either," I protested.

"Then there were those chants from the fans praising you. He hated those."

"Yeah, some of them were pretty cheesy."

"So Dad finally gets his state title and it seems like everybody is crediting a sophomore reserve as the real reason for Eastridge's victory. That got to him a little. But he kept it all inside for the most part. I only know about it because I know him. I know how he thinks."

My heart sank. "Oh no. I'm sorry. I didn't mean for that to ..."

"Forget it," he said with a wave of his hand. "Like I said, it's not your fault. He's gotten over it. By next season, he won't even remember that he was mad at you."

"He doesn't hate me?"

"No, he doesn't hate you." John didn't sound as convincing as I would've liked.

An hour later he decided to take off. We walked out to the driveway where his maroon 1970 El Camino sat. “Man, I can’t believe you got your hands on such an awesome car,” I said.

“I know it. This was Steve’s pride and joy. I about shit when he offered to sell it to me. Took all my savings, but it’s totally worth it.”

“You have a cool brother.”

“Well, his new wife had something to do with it. She wanted him to get a practical car.”

“Whatever works.”

“Yeah, there’s nothing like owning your very own chick-magnet.” After firing up the engine, he rolled down the window. “Hey, how’s your grandpa? Maybe we can stop by for a visit later this week.”

“He’s okay,” I replied. “You don’t have to do that.”

“I want to. Those stories he tells about the war are great. I’ve got to find out what happened when he wandered into that deserted French village.”

“Thanks. He’d love the company. How about Wednesday?”

“Sounds good. And I’ll see your sorry ass bright and early tomorrow morning.”

Riding to school in John’s sweet El Camino was the best part of most weekday mornings. Unfortunately, the ride was always followed by a day of education. First period was English. I heard very little of Mr. Farnsworth’s riveting discussion of *The Grapes of Wrath*. My mind was instead consumed by what might transpire the following hour.

My second period class was American History, taught by Mr. Sal Kishman. On this particular Monday, our midterm papers were due. Though mine was finished and ready to turn in, there was still cause for concern. Kishman had threatened to randomly select students to read their papers out loud. I had a sinking feeling that I’d be one of the unlucky winners of that odious lottery. What John had told me the previous night about his father only increased my apprehension.

Though I was expecting it, my heart skipped a beat when Kishman barked my name at the start of class. Upon his surly command I plodded to the front of the room. The assignment was to choose a current event and write about how it was similar to a major event in American history. I wrote about how President Ford's recent pardon of Richard Nixon was similar to the Compromise of 1850. My thesis was that both actions, although intended to unite a divided nation, had the effect of causing further division among Americans.

The eyes of my classmates zeroed in on me. I examined the first page of my paper and took a deep breath. After filling my mind with positive thoughts, I looked at my peers again. Their stares no longer unsettled me. The large presence behind the pine desk to my right, however, was still a bit unnerving.

Though my speech was halting at first, after a couple of paragraphs I fell into a rhythm. Since I had practiced it about a dozen times, I rarely had to look down at my paper. Confidence grew as I expounded upon my points—points that I'd spent much time researching. I had even gone downtown to the Des Moines Public Library to find information. And now, the effort I'd invested was paying off. Seeing that I held the attention of my classmates further energized me.

"All right, King," Kishman interrupted about halfway through my paper. "That's enough." The other students looked puzzled. I too was confused. *Maybe since he knows that this report is so good, he doesn't need to take up any more class time evaluating it.* That was the only thing I could think of as I looked over at him.

"Can anyone tell me what's wrong with King's paper?" he asked, peering out at the class over his black rectangular glasses. "Anyone?" Nobody said a word. Still trying to process what was happening, I gaped at the coach.

"You say that President Ford, similar to Henry Clay, had the noble intention of bringing together a divided nation," Kishman said, now addressing me. "Ford attempted to do this by pardoning his so-called fallen predecessor."

I scanned my paper to find the exact section he was paraphrasing.

"Look at me when I'm talking to you!" he shouted. His amplified words hit like a defibrillator, leaving me with an urge to visit the restroom. He pressed his glare at me for several seconds.

"First off," he finally continued, "Gerald Ford should never be mentioned in the same breath as a great American statesman like Henry Clay. Second, Ford is an accidental president. He's not worthy to carry Richard Nixon's jockstrap."

I fought to keep that image from materializing in my head.

"But even a lightweight like Ford could see that pardoning President Nixon was the correct course of action." Kishman's blistering stare remained fixed on me. "That pardon saved the nation. It started healing the wounds of Watergate. Any idiot can see that. But maybe you think it's better to keep beating a dead horse."

Heat radiated from my face, which I feared was now beet red. Kishman looked out at the class. "King here must think that our country hasn't suffered enough from Watergate." He pointed at me. "He wants the nation to stay divided while hippie lawyers drag Nixon through the muck of an unnecessary trial. Kick a good man while he's down, right King?" He shook his head with contempt.

I wanted to reply, but knew that anything I said could and would be used against me.

"You see, class," Kishman continued, "King is a wannabe athlete. His head is filled with dreams of playing in the pros someday. He's so preoccupied with these pipedreams that he's become a mediocre student who can't even write a decent history paper. Oh, King will make the pros all right. Someday he'll retire from the Golden Arches league with the all-time record for burgers flipped."

A few snickers rolled out from the class. My hands shook as I tried to think of something to defend myself from the unfair attack. Fearing another wave of invectives, I said nothing.

"That's all, King. Sit down. You get an F for this assignment." With that, Kishman added the final injury to his insults. Dumbfounded, I slunk back to my seat. I wanted to yell at him, but knew that a public challenge to his authority would not end well for me. I'd seen his volcanic temper erupt on the baseball field dozens of times. I made a plan to talk to him about my paper in a couple days, when his mood was not so foul.

"Let's hear a good paper now," he said. "From somebody who knows something about history." He called Kelly Lewis, a straight-

A student. Her paper, no doubt the best one in the class, would further bury my much-maligned effort. Hearing very little of Kelly's speech, I spent the rest of the hour staring at my desk, alone in my toxic thoughts.

After class I wanted to sprint down the hallway screaming. Instead I got caught in a herd of slow-moving students. I thought about lowering my head and plowing through the mass of humanity, but decided against it. While plodding along, every so often I'd hear, "Hi Dave," or "Hey man," from a passerby. Unable to speak or even force a smile, I merely nodded my replies. Upon finally reaching my locker, I slammed my palm against the metal door. It then took me three tries to get the combination right.

As I exchanged my books, a miasma of cigarette smoke, marijuana, and body odor wafted into my nostrils. I turned to see Doug Edmonds leaning against the locker next to mine.

"It's Dave the homo boy," he said with a morbid grin. He stood about six feet tall. His long stringy red hair was dark from having not been washed for several days. The acne on his face formed a constellation resembling Ursa Major. A pack of cigarettes peeked out from the front pocket of his worn flannel shirt.

"Doug," I said, looking back into my locker as if that would make him disappear.

"So, I hear your gettin' some action with the Coach's kid this year."

I decided to ignore that comment.

"Yeah, it looks like you and John Kishman are gettin' real cozy nowadays." Standing nearby, Doug's troll-like followers cackled.

As I glared at him, a montage of unpleasant memories replayed in my head. In our junior high years Doug was taller than average and I was shorter than average. So he took it upon himself to regularly torment me. He especially loved to twist the mood ring on his finger so that the hard glass shell faced down on the palm side of his hand. He'd then sneak up from behind and smack the top of my head so the ring cracked against my skull.

After taking his abuse for nearly three years, I finally stood up to him in eighth grade. Unfortunately, my rage and determination did not quite make up for his considerable size advantage. I took a rigorous beating that Friday, but it was Doug who looked more roughed up the following Monday. More importantly, the persecution stopped. I did not know why until a month later when a classmate told me that Ozzie and Randy had visited Doug the day after the fight. My brother never mentioned anything about it. I didn't bring it up either, but I always remembered what he had done for me.

Now that Ozzie was off at college, Doug must have grown nostalgic for the bad old days. "I bet the showers after football practice are real fun for you and Johnny," he said.

"What's that supposed to mean?" I slammed my locker shut.

After glancing over at his buddies, he started singing about me being John's "backdoor man." His henchmen chimed in with the appropriate Led Zeppelin chorus.

"Drop it, Doug. I'm not in the mood for your crap today." I turned to leave.

He stepped forward to block my path. "Come on Dave, aren't you gonna tell us about how you give Johnny a whole lotta love. How every night you give that fairy the hot—"

Doug was unable to finish that last bit of eloquence. I think it had something to do with my fist crashing into the side of his jaw. After impact, his tall wiry body flew backwards and splattered across the floor. A thin line of blood trickled from the corner of his mouth.

The hallway fell silent. I glowered at Doug's cronies. "You got something to say?" I asked impolitely.

Eyes wide and mouths open, they slowly backed away. The bell rang sending the remaining onlookers scurrying to class. I glanced one last time at Doug's corpse and then stalked off to chemistry.

Not surprisingly, I paid little attention to the first-rate teaching provided by Mr. Hudson during third period. Recent events instead consumed my mind. Hitting Doug Edmonds spawned conflicting thoughts. On one hand, I felt guilty for losing my temper and not heeding Christ's command to turn the other cheek. On the other hand, it felt good to drop that creep like a sack of potatoes. One minute I'd say a silent prayer for him. The next minute I'd clinch my fists and imagine belting him again.

After class I returned to my locker. The body had been removed. While placing my chemistry textbook on the top shelf, I felt a firm grip on my shoulder. "I understand you had some trouble this morning," an adult voice boomed from behind.

A shivery fear slithered down my spine. I spun around to see the towering uniformed presence known as Neil. He stared down at me with a grim look on his pale face. "You know it's not nice to leave a mess like that behind," he said. "Just because I'm the head custodian here doesn't mean I enjoy cleaning up the filth you students create."

"Guess I'm busted, huh?"

"I'm afraid so." His thin lips barely moved as he spoke. "I'm going to have to take you to the office. You're probably going to be suspended."

I contemplated those dreadful words for a few seconds. *Dad will be so pleased.* "Okay," I said, shutting my locker. "Let's go."

The crowd parted before us as we started down the hallway. After about twenty paces, Neil slapped my back and chuckled. "Eh, I'm just messin' with you, Dave. Now go on, get to class."

Stunned, I looked up at his beaming face. "Huh? You mean I'm not in trouble?"

"No."

"But what about Edmonds?"

"Oh, I scraped his carcass off the floor last hour. Took him to the nurse's office for some ice. He went to the vice principal and said that you hit him. She didn't believe him or she didn't care. Neither did Principal Peterson. Guess Edmonds shouldn't have keyed their cars last month. Peterson sent the punk home."

"Oh … well, shouldn't I turn myself in?"

"Nooo!" Neil grabbed my arm and led me to a corner. He looked around to make sure no one was eavesdropping. "Everybody here knows that drug-dealing delinquent had it coming," he said in a hushed voice. "Besides, you're a football player and you're the hero of the state champion baseball team. The suits here don't want to bust you. As far as Peterson is concerned, nothing happened. Capisce?"

I felt guilty and relieved. Actually, it was mainly relief. It was hard to feel too much guilt after the morning I'd had. If nobody else was going to make an issue out of the incident with Edmonds, then I wouldn't either. I thanked Neil and headed off to trigonometry class.

Michelle's early lunch period and my late lunch period overlapped by fifteen minutes. With no classes together, we had little other opportunity to talk during the school day. I usually waited for her in the wide hallway outside the cafeteria.

I had just found a spot along the brick wall next to the trophy case when Michelle and her two friends, Liz and Amanda, emerged from the lunchroom. Michelle wore a bright flowery minidress—orange, yellow, and purple were the predominant colors. A generous amount of leg was visible between the bottom of the skirt and the top of her white knee socks. Smiling, she scudded across the hallway with open arms.

"There's my guy," she said. "Did you miss me?"

"Oh yeah." I returned her embrace.

"Did Betty give you my note in trig?"

"Yep."

After a few seconds she planted a kiss on my lips. It was electric, but the audience made me uncomfortable.

"Oh puke! Get a room you two," Liz commanded.

Michelle finished kissing me and leaned her head into my chest. "Leave us alone. My boyfriend's had a rough morning." She then stepped back and grabbed both of my hands. "I heard you got in a fight." She pushed out her bottom lip to create a pouty face.

"It wasn't really a fight."

"Were you defending my honor?" she asked, tilting her head.

I mumbled something about Doug making fun of John and me.

"Oh." Michelle looked disappointed.

"I heard you knocked the guy out with one punch," Amanda said.

"My boyfriend the bad ass," Michelle commented with a smile.

"Guess all that weightlifting is paying off," Liz added.

"Maybe," was all I could say through my embarrassment.

"No complaints here." Michelle hugged me again.

"Young love is so nauseating," Amanda mocked. Liz nodded and poked a finger into her open mouth.

"Quiet," Michelle said, breaking our embrace. "You guys are worse." The three girls then traded teasing insults. After their banter subsided, Michelle turned her attention back to me. "See what I have to put up with?"

"Terrible," I said with mock solemnity.

She straightened out my shirt. "We should get going to class."

"Yeah, and I gotta go figure out what's in today's mystery meat."

"We still on for tonight?"

"Yep."

"Good. I told John to pick you up at six forty-five. Be ready then, okay?"

"Yep."

"Bye," she said softly, kissing my cheek. I couldn't resist watching Michelle and her short dress walk away. *I can't believe I'm dating a girl that hot.* As I continued staring, she turned and waved. Quickly raising my eyes to meet hers, I waved back. Amanda said something causing Liz to laugh. Michelle swatted Amanda on the arm with the back of her hand.

Unfortunately, I now had a problem that initially emerged when Michelle first kissed me. This problem grew more pressing after feeling her hugs, smelling her perfume, and watching her fine form glide away. Unable to walk across the hallway into the crowded lunchroom, I had to turn and face the display case on the wall. While pretending to read the names of the 1952 conference champion basketball team, I shut my eyes and envisioned Klinger from *M*A*S*H* prancing around the tents of the 4077th in a yellow dress. After about a minute with Jamie Farr, the problem subsided and I was able to turn and enter the cafeteria like a gentleman.

John's El Camino appeared in my driveway at 6:45 p.m. on the nose. "Bye," I yelled to my dad, who was somewhere inside the house. I didn't wait for a reply before darting out the front door.

John shook his head at me as I settled into the passenger seat. "Man, you owe me big time," he said with the barest hint of a smile.

"Yeah, I know. I know."

He backed out of the driveway and sped down the road. "Not only do I have to cart you over to my house, oh wheel-less one. But—" He raised his index finger for emphasis. "I also have to take my moron little brother to a movie so you can be alone with my dingbat sister for the evening. AND THEN, I have to drive your sorry ass back home again."

"This is really cool of you," I said. "I've been trying to scrape together enough dough to get my own wheels, but practice has cut into the hours I can work at the restaurant." I could have mentioned that pizza, pinball, and Michelle also slowed the saving process, but didn't want to give him any more ammunition for his rant.

"Hmpf," he said, accelerating past a slow-moving red Opel.

"An opportunity like this doesn't come around very often. Your dad hardly ever lets Michelle out of the house on a school night. And now your parents are finally going to be gone all evening, but it's my dad's night off. So we have to meet at your house."

"Yeah, yeah. I just hate being an accomplice to this. I don't even want to think about all the vile acts you're going to doing with my sister tonight."

"It's not like that," I protested. "We're going to be studying."

"Uh-huh, of course you are."

"See, look at this," I said, holding up a couple of textbooks.

"Yeah, you're not fooling anybody. None of those books are going to be opened tonight." Part of me hoped he was right.

I rolled down the window, slouched back, and let my foot hang outside the car. John pushed *Who's Next* into the eight-track player. "Baba O'Reilly" blared from the speakers as we cruised over to his house in the suburb of Pleasant Hill. My pulse quickened when he pulled into his driveway.

"Alright, Casanova," he said. "Go study. I'm sure you're gonna be covering a lot of human anatomy tonight."

"Stifle it, John-boy." After shutting the car door, I poked my head through the open window. "Thanks man, I really do owe you." He nodded with a feigned look of derision.

John and Michelle's youngest brother, Bosworth, bounded out of the Kishman abode, an impressive two-story house with an attached garage. A tall gangling ninth grader, Bosworth wore a jade green paisley shirt with a huge collar.

"Hey Boz."

"Good luck, Romeo," he replied with a childish smirk.

"Shut up," I said, giving his head a slight shove as we passed on the walkway leading up to the front door.

When I reached the porch, Michelle opened the door. She stood behind the glass wearing her colorful short dress and a coy smile. Her light golden brown hair that barely touched her shoulders appeared to have recently spent some time with a curling iron. She pushed open the storm door and grabbed my hand to pull me into the house. Outside, John's car roared away.

After a brief, but tingling, kiss she stepped back and smiled. "You're here." Her bright amber eyes danced.

"Yes, I am. And your parents are not?" The aroma of Love's Baby Soft tickled my nose.

"Nope. They said they'd be gone 'til midnight. John and Boz won't be back from the movie until ten. So I've got you all to myself for the next three hours."

A surge of nervous anticipation swept through me, followed by a stern voice of conviction. *Stay cool man, you know you're not going to do that.*

We passed through the living room. All was neat, tidy, and in its proper place, much like the times I'd been there when hanging out with John. After Michelle poured us a couple of sodas, we sat at the large dining room table, where she had stacked her textbooks, notebooks, and three-ring binders.

So, we actually are going to study tonight. I felt both disappointment and relief.

"You know our pictures from the Homecoming Dance arrive next week," she said, opening her chemistry textbook.

"Cool." I opened my book.

"You looked so cute in your suit."

"Thanks. You looked great too."

"Your hair looks so boss now that you've let it grow long in back." She reached over and flipped the wavy locks hanging below my neck.

"I'm glad you approve," I said.

"It was so fun that night." A short snicker followed. After a couple seconds, the giggling erupted into full-blown laughter.

"What?"

"But …" It took her a while to compose herself. "You dance like a drunk horse." She put a hand over her mouth in a vain attempt to stifle her laughing.

"Hush." My face reddened as I pretended to review the atomic weights of the non-metallic elements.

She thrust her arms out in front of her and started jerking them around in circular motions. Still snickering, she then awkwardly rotated her torso back and forth.

"I do NOT dance like that," I said in a humorless tone. But soon I was laughing too, as she continued to mimic by groovy dance moves.

For the next hour, she interrupted our study of chemistry with a variety of discussion topics: the unfortunate wardrobe choices of select classmates, the new cheerleading routines, why we weren't selected to be on the Homecoming Court, and possible cars I might consider buying.

Then, out of the blue, she asked, "Want to see my room?"

An alarm blared in my head. *Danger! Danger Will Robinson!* While preparing for an intense mental debate, I caught a glimpse of her enticing smile.

"Okay," I replied. Debate over.

As I followed her up the stairs, my heart rate approached hummingbird levels. She entered her bedroom and flipped on the light. "Here it is," she sang in a girlish voice.

Standing at the doorway, my eyes took in Michelle's room—*the forbidden zone*. There was a definite theme: lavender walls, dark purple shag carpet, mauve bedspread, and various pink accents. A big black teddy bear reclined against a pillow on the bed. Assorted unicorns adorned the walls via paintings, posters, and cross-stitch patterns. There was also an unfortunate picture of

David Cassidy. I took solace in the fact that there was only one Dave actually present, and it wasn't him. *In your face, Keith.*

Michelle took my hand and led me inside. After a minute of forgettable nervous conversation, she looked at me and said, "You have the deepest blue eyes."

Moments later, we were on the bed making out in the dim glow of the nightstand lamp. We had kissed many times before but never with this level of enthusiasm. As our faces remained fused together, my head started buzzing. Thoughts of how to advance our interaction to the next level soon enveloped my mind. An inner voice cried out: *No! You can't do this. You've made a commitment.* I tried to think of a Bible passage to douse the flames of temptation. Frantic, I silently recited the first verse that popped into my head. "And the man and his wife were both naked and were not ashamed." *Okay, that didn't help.*

As Michelle's hands started roaming, a Civil War-style battle broke out in my psyche. On one side of a field, blue-coated soldiers stood in a line. Their commander announced, "Enough Dave King! This action shalt not further progress. Thou shalt desist this very minute!" On the other side of the field a line of soldiers in gray uniforms opposed them. "Hell yes, Dave!" their commander yelled. "We're going ALL the way!" It looked to be an evenly matched fight.

"I love your muscles," Michelle whispered as her hands slid under my shirt and across my pecs. Her sensual touch transformed the Confederate soldiers into Panzer tanks. The Union troops fled in disarray. My shirt flew off and landed on a stack of records across the room.

The next few minutes sizzled. A dress was unzipped and a bra came unlatched. Though Ozzie had shown me a few of his *Playboy* magazines in years past, I'd never seen anything like the vision of twin perfection that was now before me. Already high, the dazzling sight sent me into orbit. My shaking hands crossed into uncharted territory.

Just then I heard a low rumble and felt the house vibrate. *Cool, the earth really does move in these situations.*

Michelle pulled back with wide eyes. "Oh shit!"

"What?"

"That's the garage door opening. My parents are home!"

A bucket of ice-cold water poured over my head. Stunned, I tried to think of an explanation. "We'll tell them we were studying."

"No," she said, refastening her bra. "Daddy will kill you if he finds you here. Zip me up! Hurry!"

After obeying her command, I stood up intending to retrieve my shirt from across the room. But when I tried to take a step, I realized that my feet were bound together. *My jeans are around my ankles. How did that happen?* I hopped a couple times trying to maintain balance, but my forward momentum caused me to topple face first into the thick purple carpet.

"Hurry," Michelle hissed. In what seemed like a single motion, she flashed about the room shutting the door, turning on the overhead light, and tossing my shirt to me. It landed on my head as I sat on the floor zipping up my pants. By the time I'd put my shirt on, Michelle's parents had entered the house.

A look of panic consumed her face as we heard heavy steps coming up the stairs. She pointed down at the bottom of the bed. I dropped to my belly and shimmied underneath. It was a tight fit, but I made it. There was a knock at the door.

"Honey?" The gruff voice was unmistakable. The door opened. I saw two giant black wingtips enter the room.

"Hi Daddy." Michelle's voice, amazingly calm, came from right above me. I didn't breathe.

"Is everything okay?"

"Sure, everything's fine."

The black shoes stepped closer. "Why are you reading in here with the door shut? Aren't your brothers still at the movies?"

"Oh, yeah. Habit I guess. I'm so used to them bugging me, I just shut the door when I came in to read." An agonizing silence followed. "You and Mom are home early," Michelle said in a cheerful voice.

"Yes. The host got sick. It's still not early enough if you ask me. I hate those black tie affairs." There was another pause. "Why is the dining room light on?"

"Oh, I'm sorry, Daddy. I was studying at the table and forgot to shut it off when I came upstairs."

Terror jolted my soul. *Oh no! My books. My shoes. They're still downstairs!*

Kishman grunted disapprovingly. After not moving for what seemed like two eternities, the wingtips turned around and stepped out of the room. The door closed behind them.

Michelle slid off the bed and tiptoed across the carpet. A few seconds later, I slithered out from my hiding place. She moved to the window and turned the latch.

"Are you serious?" I whispered.

"It's the only way," was her barely audible reply. "Hurry. I've got to go get your books."

"What about my shoes?"

"Shit!"

She opened the window. As cool air blew into the room, she flipped the latches holding the screen in place. After a furtive kiss, I squeezed through the opening. Fortunately, her second floor window overlooked the roof of the front porch. Stepping gingerly onto the shingles, I crept down to the edge. Peering over the gutter, I estimated that the ground was about eight or nine feet below. The thought of jumping in socks seemed crazy, but I had no other alternative. Driven by the potential horror of facing Kishman's wrath, down I went. Though I tucked and rolled upon impact, sharp pains shot through my feet, ankles, and lower legs. I rubbed the afflicted areas. Nothing felt broken.

Regaining my bearings, I rose to a crouch and skulked toward the sidewalk. Behind me the front door of the house opened. I froze.

"Pssst."

I turned around to see Anne Kishman in a long red evening gown standing on the dark porch. She waved me over.

Still crouching like a soldier, I scuttled up to her.

"Here," she said, handing my books and shoes to me. "He didn't see them."

"Thank you, Mrs. Kishman," I whispered. "I'm really sorry about—"

"It's okay. Now go."

I scurried away, not stopping to put on my Chuck Taylors until there was a block between me and the Kishman house. Upon checking my watch, I realized that John wouldn't be home for at least an hour. The two-and-a-half-mile trek back to my house would have to be made on foot. Still sore, my feet and ankles protested at first. But I soon forgot about the pain as my thoughts returned to what had happened this evening.

A cloud of guilt settled over me. I once thought that I had built giant stone walls around my chastity. Walls that were fortified by prayer, scripture, sermons, and songs of praise. I now knew that those fortress walls were actually made of balsa wood. *What made me think I could control myself in such a fiery situation?*

I reflected on the commitment I had made last November—my commitment to follow Christ. *I can't let myself fall into such dangerous temptation again.* A terrible thought entered my head that I might have to break up with Michelle to avoid sinning against God. But my lips still buzzed with her kisses and I could still feel her hands sliding across my back. *I love being with Michelle. I don't want to lose her.* My mind desperately grasped for possible resolutions to the quandary. *Marriage? We're only sixteen. We can't get married yet.* The answer seemed no closer than the stars dotting the night sky above.

Feeling the weight of the world on my shoulders, I kept walking.

Chapter 6 – May 1975

“Man, this is one bitchin’ car.”

“Thanks.” I changed lanes and accelerated past an eighteen-wheeler.

“Woo, feel the power of that 289 V8,” Ozzie said. “When you told me you got your hands on a ’67 Mustang, I figured it had to be a rusty old shitbucket.” He ran his fingers across the dash. The meager goatee and thin moustache, both recent additions to the lower half of his face, still looked out of place to me. “But man,” he continued, “this machine rules. How’d you swing it? The old man give you a raise?”

“Nah, I’m getting the same pennies a day I always did. Sid McGee’s dad owns a dealership. You know that one by the bend on Grand Avenue? Well, this guy is big into Eastridge sports. We get to talkin’ baseball and football. Then he tells about this blue Mustang he just got in. Cuts me a deal and here I am, king of the road.”

“I never would’ve guessed that your first hobbitmobile would be this cool.”

Bristling, I thought about pointing out that I was now taller than him. But I decided against it so as not to interrupt his raving about my car.

“Yep,” Ozzie said, inspecting the radio and eight-track unit, “this sweet ride takes out some of the sting of having to waste the day at some snore-fest graduation ceremony.”

“Well, this is kind of a big deal. Abby’s the first one of us to get a college degree. The ceremony won’t be that bad.”

"Easy for you to say. I just carted all my crap home three days ago and now I gotta go back to Ames and sit in Hilton Coliseum for ten hours listening to some gray-haired prune bloviate about how the Class of '75 is at an important crossroads in their lives."

"Bloviate? The college boy is learning some big words."

"And if that's not bad enough," he said, ignoring my comment, "next month I have to blow another Saturday at Abby's stupid wedding."

"Yeah, the nerve of that girl. Graduating from college and then getting married. Who does she think she is, anyway? We should get Dad to have a talk with her."

"Damn straight. Say, who is this guy she's marrying?"

"Jerry? You saw him at Easter six weeks ago … and at Christmas … and at Thanksgiving. And I know you met him last summer at the Fourth of July picnic. Didn't you ever see Abby and him together at Iowa State? They've been dating for a year and a half."

"Jerry, huh? Doesn't ring a bell." Ozzie yawned. "But I gotta be honest with you. Up at school, I drank a lot of beer and smoked a lot of weed. With all the brain cells I've killed, I'm lucky if I can remember your name, Frodo. No wait, that's not right. Merry? Pippin? Mary Poppins? See, I can't even remember what the hell you call yourself anymore."

"Dad would be so pleased with his investment in your education," I said. "What kind of grades you getting this semester?"

"I dunno. I can't remember which classes I took." He grinned.

I shook my head. "Maybe you should go ask Alice, when she's ten feet tall."

"I think she'll know," he sang as my Mustang passed a green Torino station wagon. "Say, while we're on the subject of not remembering, what was that you were talking about when we got in the car?"

"I was telling you about what happened with Mr. Kishman last fall. You really don't remember? I'm sure I told you about it last Christmas."

"Oh, sorry. Sometimes I stop listening when you're going on and on about something."

"Excuse me?"

"Well yeah, Dave. I mean even you gotta admit you can get kinda preachy sometimes. Whenever it sounds like you're going into one of your Billy Graham rants, I just tune you out. It's like meditating. Your voice becomes a faint buzz and then it disappears."

"Shut up," I snapped, barely passing on the urge to swear.

Ozzie laughed for a few seconds. "All right. What were you saying?"

"Forget it."

"Oh come on. Tell me." I drove on in silence. "Tell me, damn it." He leaned over to drive a hard noogie into the side of my skull.

"Fine." I swatted his hand away from my head. "You remember how Kishman trashed my report in front of the class?"

"Okay, yeah, that does sound kinda familiar."

"And then, that night, he almost caught me with Michelle at his house."

"Oh yeah." He cracked up. "That was beautiful, man. My little brother hiding under the bed and then sneaking out the window. If only I had that on film."

"Well, Michelle and I broke up a couple weeks after that. Kishman was putting a lot of pressure on her to stop seeing me. The stress was getting to her. And I'd been having second thoughts about the relationship too. So, it just kind of ended."

"Tough break, man. I remember her. She's a fox. Say, did you ever get to jump those bones?"

I frowned. "You really haven't heard a thing I've said about my faith, have you?

"Take it easy, sweetums. I was just checking. So what happened with Coach Chuckles?"

"After the break up, Kishman stopped picking on me in class so much. But he was still giving me Ds and Fs on my assignments. And I was doing good work too!" I jabbed the air with my index finger. "I thought I might not pass. I considered telling Dad. It wasn't fair. I should've been getting an A or a B-plus at worst."

Ozzie batted the toy rubber lion that hung from my rearview mirror. "Damn."

"Then sometime around Thanksgiving, John got involved. Told his father to lay off."

"Really?"

"I didn't ask him to do it. I didn't even know what he had done until weeks later. I guess he told his dad he wouldn't play baseball anymore unless he started being cool to me. Kishman was pissed but couldn't afford to lose his starting shortstop. All I knew was that my grades started getting better in December. In the end, I got a C for the class."

"Should've been an A though, huh?"

"Yeah. Kishman's grade kept me off the honor roll. But after all I'd been through, I took my C and ran. Funny thing is, I was scheduled to have him again for American History this semester. I got that changed in a hurry. My days in a Kishman classroom are done forever."

"What about baseball? You playing for him again this year?"

"Yeah, well, absence apparently made Coach's heart grow fonder. With me not dating his daughter or sitting in his classroom, he must have forgot why he was mad at me. Plus, a lot of guys from last year's team graduated. Kishman needs all the experienced players he can get. About a month ago, he spots me in the hallway and tells me how much he's looking forward to having me on the team. Says he's counting on me to start at third base. It was like nothing had ever happened between us."

"I wouldn't trust him," Ozzie said. "The man is not stable."

"It gets better. Last week at practice, Coach asked me if I still have my guitar. Says his migraines are back, and that my music really helps ease the pain. He wants me to play songs for him after practice again."

"No way. You're not gonna do it are you?"

"Actually I am. He usually runs his practices like Hitler. If I can do something to bring him down to a Mussolini, then I've got to give it a try."

"Be careful, man. Someday I might be reading about how the police found you in Kishman's freezer all chopped up into a hundred little pieces."

"Yeah, right." I snickered. The Mustang continued racing north past the recently-plowed fields on each side of I-35. The temperate wind whipping through the open windows provided a pleasant ventilation.

Ozzie opened the glove compartment to check out my eight-tracks. "So, is there life after Michelle?"

"I went on a few dates this semester. No big deal."

"Who'd you take to prom?"

"Maggie Talbot."

"Yeah? How'd that go?"

"Fine. She's a nice girl." *But she's not Michelle.* My thoughts drifted back to prom night. Watching Michelle dance with her boyfriend, Paul Lasch, drove a spear through my gut. My grip on the wheel tightened.

"A nice girl, huh? That's too bad. You going to see her again?"

"Yeah. I'm supposed to take her to Riverview next Saturday."

"Cool. Get her on the Wild Mouse before any of the other rides. After the car jerks around that first turn, she'll be clinging to you like a vine the rest of the day."

"I'll keep that in mind," I said, considering ways I could get out of the date. A road sign informed us of our entry into Story County. "So how'd you like your first year of college? You know, when you weren't getting wasted."

"Getting wasted is what college is all about, young one."

"There had to be something at ISU that expanded your mind."

"Hmmm. Well, I discovered some cool bands. The Ramones. A few others." He arched his back into a stretch. "And my mind has been opened to new ideas, I guess. I now have a better understanding of people who are different than me."

"That sounds good."

"Yeah," he continued, "I've even learned to accept you and your situation."

"Really?" I smiled. "You finally accept that I'm a Christian?"

"No, not that. I accept that you're gay."

"Shut up." I nearly gave him the bird.

"Now, don't be that way. You should be proud of who you are. We learned in psych class that homosexuality is not a mental disorder. It was such a relief to learn that my queen brother is not crazy. I accept that your lifestyle is not wrong just because it's different. So what if you're into dudes? That's okay. You're not mentally ill, Dave."

"Too bad I can't say the same for you," I grumbled.

Neither of us spoke for a while. Ozzie then swatted my arm. "Hey, you seen that new Monty Python movie yet?"

"No."

"Aw man, you gotta go see that. I went to it last Saturday. It is so damn funny." He cupped his hands and started clapping in a pattern that sounded something like a horse galloping. I had no idea what he was doing, but he seemed to be amused with himself. "Oh, that reminds me, I need to do something in your general direction."

"Huh?" I glanced over. With one leg lifted, he gritted his teeth and creased his face into a look of intense concentration. It was a sight I'd seen oh so many times before. "No, Ozzie! I go on dates in this car. Girls sit there!"

"Sorry Dave," he grunted. "I've got to break in your new set of wheels."

"Come on, man! You're in college now. You're too old to be doing this—"

My pleading was interrupted by a deep reverberating rip. Fortunately, we both had our windows rolled down.

Angst clouded the air at school on Monday. The recent Mayguez incident sparked concerns about a possible revival of U.S. military action in Southeast Asia. With the frantic American exodus from Saigon still fresh in their minds, many of my classmates worried about the return of the draft. For me, discussions of Vietnam brought back images of the flag-draped caskets at Nate and Ray's funerals. As such, I usually tried to change the subject to something other than foreign policy.

My mind spent much of the day dwelling on baseball practice after school. Or, more specifically, what was going to happen after practice. I wondered which Kishman I would encounter. The affable coach who welcomed me back to his team or the petulant tyrant who pressured his daughter to break up with me and tried to flunk me from his class. I prayed for the best.

After a fairly typical practice, I showered, grabbed my guitar, and headed over to Coach's office. His door was open. "Come in,

King. This head's going to be the death of me." He rubbed his temples.

I sat down and opened the case. "Good practice today," I said. "The team is getting there."

"We'll see," he grumbled, retrieving a half-smoked Kent from the ashtray. His subsequent sigh added a scent of alcohol to the haze of cigarette smoke clouding the room.

As Coach returned to his paperwork, I started playing and singing. The words of "Folsom Prison Blues" flowed out of my mouth while the accompanying chords danced from my guitar. Kishman seemed engrossed in whatever he was reading. That suited me just fine. Near the end of the song, there was a rapping at the door behind me. Abner Kishman entered.

"The kid can sing," he said. A few inches shorter than his cousin, Abner had dark hair that was just long enough for a part. His face was leathery, like Coach's, but it had fewer wrinkles. "Shouldn't you be wearing black if you're going to play that song?" he asked me, flashing a crooked grin.

"Yeah, I guess so," I replied. I'd first met Abner last fall when he was hired as an assistant coach for the Eastridge High football team. But since he coached the defense and I was the seldom-used second-string quarterback, our interactions were limited. This spring Coach asked Abner to fill the opening created when Eli decided not to return as his assistant.

"Here's the report on the sophomore pitchers," Abner said, handing a stack of papers to his cousin.

"Got anything this year?" Coach asked.

"Nah, they're all shit. Bunch of noodle arms that are gonna get lit up like Roman candles when the season starts. But give me some time, I may be able to salvage something."

"Great. Just great." Coach skimmed the papers.

"Yeah, great. Alright Sal, see you tomorrow. Sorry to interrupt your concert, kid." With a clap of my back, Abner exited the room.

As Kishman lit another cigarette and returned to his work, I started the second song in my set: "Desperado" by the Eagles. It was one of Coach's favorites from last year. When I reached the last part of the song, there was another knock.

"Yeah," Kishman barked at the closed door. It squeaked open.

"Daddy, I … oh … I didn't mean to interrupt."

My head turned to the doorway. There, a vision of tan legs, red jogging shorts, and a tight gray t-shirt hit me like a lightning bolt. I almost dropped the guitar at the sight of such alluring female beauty. Amber eyes stared back at me.

"What is it, Michelle?" Kishman asked impatiently.

Mouth agape, she looked over at her father. "Oh, I was, um … I just wanted to know if it would be okay if I went to a movie tonight with Liz and Amanda."

Kishman was quiet for a few seconds. I inspected the floor, my mind flooded with memories. "Fine," he said. "Be home by eleven."

"Thanks Daddy…. Hi Dave," she said to me through a winsome smile.

"Hi," I croaked. She pulled the door shut and disappeared into the hallway. Lost in my thoughts, I gazed at where she had just stood.

"Did I ask you to stop playing?" A harsh voice snapped me out of my stupor.

"Sorry." I dropped my pick. After retrieving it, I took a deep breath and tried to remember the third song I had planned to play. A Confederate flag then popped into my head, causing the opening notes to "Sweet Home Alabama" to leap from my guitar—*turn it up*. I didn't have the song completely mastered but I could get through it okay. Plus, I loved trying to sing like Ronnie Van Zant.

Just as I described how the people in Birmingham felt about their governor, Kishman slammed down his pencil. I glanced into his bloodshot eyes, which were aimed directly at me. Quickly looking away, I continued singing. Coach arose and stepped over to the shelves along the wall to the right of his desk. His hands shook as he scanned the awards, pictures, trophies, and other memorabilia from his playing and coaching days. Seconds passed. Beads of sweat rolled down my back as I tried to stay on key. "I just don't understand," he said.

I stopped playing. "Coach?"

"I just don't understand why you've got it in for me." He slowly turned around to reveal a smoldering countenance. "I saw how you looked at my daughter, you lecherous cur." He thrust his index finger forward like a spear. "You've tried to turn my son against me. You've tried to turn my daughter against me. You've even tried to turn the school against me by taking credit for my state title."

His words crashed down like an anvil. "Coach, no. I haven't tried to do any of those things."

"The hell you haven't," he hissed through bared teeth. "Get out … get out of my office." He turned his back to me.

Trembling, I placed my guitar in its case and snapped shut the lid. As I stood, I caught a glimpse of Kishman. He was facing me again. In his left hand he held a large wooden bat—a relic from his playing days. He was swaying slightly, like a skyscraper in a heavy wind. He mumbled something as he tapped the head of the bat on his desk, the same way a hitter might tap the plate upon stepping into the batter's box.

"Coach?" My eyes remained locked on him as I backed toward the door.

"Damn you, King!" He suddenly raised the bat and slammed it down on his desk. It sounded like a gunshot. Papers scattered; the ashtray flipped upside down; the metal inbox crashed to the floor. Still glaring at me, he cocked back his arm to fling the bat in my direction. I bolted for the door as the massive Louisville Slugger spun past my head, missing by only a couple inches. The impact of bat smashing into wall knocked loose a picture of Coach from his rookie season with the Phillies. The clattering of the bat and the shattering of the picture frame glass created a heavy racket on the floor. I flung open the door and darted out of the office. Knowing that Kishman had several more potential missiles among his memorabilia, I sprinted away as fast as I could while lugging a guitar.

"Stay away from me, you bastard!" Kishman yelled from his doorway. His anger echoed through the empty halls. "Stay away from my family!"

I burst out of the school and hurried to my car. After dumping the guitar in the passenger seat, I peeled out of the parking lot and sped home.

The house was empty. As I paced in the living room, anxious and ominous thoughts multiplied in my head. Finally, my knees hit the floor. I asked God for protection and guidance about what to do. After the "amen" my hand reached for the phone. I wanted desperately to tell someone about what had happened. *Pastor Samuels? No, he's out of town at a retreat.* I decided to call John. His mother answered and said that he'd just left for a date. Since I didn't want to call the Kishman house later that night, I would have to wait until the next morning to talk to my friend.

After a distracted evening of waitering at The Royal Court, I returned home around 10:15. Dad came home a short time after that. I had not told him anything about Kishman and didn't plan to. I doubted that he would believe me. Alone in my room, I read the Bible, prayed, and wrote lyrics for a Christian song I'd been working on. I didn't get to bed until 1:00 a.m. Sleep did not come easily that night.

Tuesday morning before class, I stood in the front hall hanging out with the athlete crowd. That was normal. What was not normal was that John was not with us. An uneasy feeling grew in my stomach. I tried to remain optimistic. *Maybe he's just running late this morning.*

After third period, Michelle appeared at my locker. That too was unusual. We rarely talked anymore, and when we did it was only by chance encounter. "John wants you to meet him in the back parking lot at lunch," she said, looking grave.

"Huh? Where is he now?"

"He's home. He didn't come to school today."

"Why?"

"I don't know. Something happened last night when I was out. The door to his room was shut when I got home and it was still shut when I left for school this morning. Mom wouldn't tell me anything. Neither would Boz. Sometime while I was asleep John slid a note under my door telling me to have you meet him at lunch." A fearful concern rang through her voice.

"Oh." My mind raced.

"Dave, what's going on?"

"I wish I knew."

After fourth period, I hurried through the halls to the back parking lot. I'd only been outside for about thirty seconds when a short squeaky sophomore with red curly hair came up from behind and started chattering away. “Hi Dave! Oh my gosh! You wouldn’t believe who’s going out with …” Paying little attention to her yipping, I scanned the street for a maroon El Camino. It appeared a couple minutes later. Resisting the urge to pat the girl on the head and scratch behind her ears, I excused myself and approached the car.

John said nothing as I got in. I immediately noticed the mirror Aviator sunglasses covering his eyes. Examining the side of his face as the El Camino screeched out of the parking lot, I could partially see what was behind the shades. My heart sank. I continued staring as he turned north onto East 14th Street.

“You waitin’ for a kiss or what?” he asked, keeping his eyes on the road.

“John, what happened?”

“I was going to ask you the same thing.”

I paused for a few seconds. “Yesterday after practice, I was playing songs for your dad. Michelle stops by to ask him something. After she leaves, he flips out yelling and screaming. Then, he throws a bat at me.”

“I figured it was something like that. He said it was you who went berserk and started throwing things around his office. I knew he was lying.”

“Why does he hate me so much? I think he’s going to try to kill me.”

“That’s not going to happen. I won’t let him.”

“What happened between you and your dad last night?”

“We had a little discussion. It took a while, but we finally reached an understanding. He said he’s going to leave you alone from now on.”

“What else happened, besides talking?”

“Nothing else happened.” He accelerated through a yellow light turning red.

“John, I can see your eye.”

“That’s nothing.”

“Your dad did that, didn’t he?”

“Nothing happened, so drop it.”

“You stuck up for me and he hit you.”

"I mean it, Dave! Not another word!"

"That's not right. You need to tell someone."

Spinning the steering wheel, he screeched into a gas station parking lot where he slammed on the brakes. He put a finger in my face. "This is my business, Dave. You don't say a word to nobody. Not your dad. Not your pastor. Not any of your brothers. Got it?"

"He hit you because of me. And it could get worse. I can't let you go through this alone."

"Listen, I'll be fine. I graduate next week. Then it's only three months until I'm out of that house for good. I can take care of myself until then. If you tell someone about the bat or anything, he'll just deny it. Administration will take his side. He's got a lot of clout at school. And then he'd get even angrier. Trust me, it will be better for you and the people who have to live with him if nobody else gets involved. And like I said, he told me he's not going to bother you anymore. Please, let's just leave it at that."

I could see my face in both of his mirrored lenses. "But …"

"But, nothing. This is how it has to be."

Double-dings from cars at the full service pumps provided the only sounds as we both stared straight ahead for the next few minutes. "I'm gonna miss baseball," I finally said.

"Me too."

"What do you mean?"

"I'm quittin' the team," he said with a sigh.

"No way. You've got to keep playing. Your scholarship is at stake."

"I'm not playing for him anymore."

"Don't think of it as playing for *him*," I said. "You've got a full-ride at Iowa. If you sit out your senior season, they're gonna ask questions. They might reconsider."

"I don't care much about my future in baseball anymore. I just want to get out of here."

"Well, I care about your future in baseball. You've got a spot on the Hawkeye roster if you don't screw it up. Then after college, you could make the majors. Don't trash your dreams because of me. I feel bad enough already about what's happened to you."

"We'll see." He rubbed his forehead.

"With me off the team, your dad won't have any reason to flip out anymore, right? I'll stay away from you this summer too. I don't want to put you at risk."

"Never!" John said, facing me. "I'm not going to let him end our friendship. I'm eighteen and nearly out of high school. He doesn't run my life."

"Just be careful, man."

"I'll be fine. And we're gonna hang out like usual, got it?"

"Yes, sir." We were again quiet for a while. "Hey, you ready to get something to eat?" I asked, breaking the silence.

"I'm not hungry. You can get something. Where do you want to go?" He put the car in gear and circled around to exit the parking lot.

"You gotta eat something," I said.

"Nah, I don't feel like it."

When he looked forward, I glimpsed the edge of his darkened eye. A twinge of guilt followed. "I don't want anything either. Just take me back to school or drive around somewhere."

John cruised over some county roads just north of the city. From the stereo speakers, Mick Jagger sang about wild horses. The El Camino eventually found its way back to the Eastridge parking lot. "What are you going to do the rest of the day?" I asked.

"I don't know. Drive around. Hang out. Break your high score on the astronaut pinball machine over at Hilltop."

I laughed. "You don't got enough money for that."

"You working tonight?"

"Nah, I got the night off."

"Wanna hit Thunderbird Lanes and knock down some pins?"

"Sounds good."

As I passed though the school doors, pangs of dread stabbed my insides. I popped into the boys' room and found an empty stall. There, amid the vulgar graffiti, I prayed silently for John and his family.

Crashing a chess club meeting, I hung around school long after the final bell. My plan was to wait until baseball practice was underway so I could slip into the locker room and drop off my uniform for the equipment manager. My head on a swivel, I crept down the hallway past Kishman's dark office. Entering the empty locker room, I said goodbye to my beloved varsity uniform. I ran my hand one last time over the red 17 stitched into the fabric.

The route back to my locker took me past the display cases in the long hall that bisected the first floor of the school. With no one else in sight, I stopped to examine the baseball exhibits. The 1974 state championship team stood out prominently. From a large framed picture, the players, myself included, looked back at me with confidence and pride. Nearby was a ball with all of our signatures and the bat that I'd used to hit the home run off Galbraith. Staring at the images and artifacts carried me back to that game. The roar of the crowd echoed through my head. My body tensed as I visualized the giant pitcher going into his windup. The pitch blazed from his hand and … something gripped my shoulder.

"Gaaaaaa!" I jumped like a startled cat. If only there had been curtains nearby for me to cling to.

"Wow, somebody's jumpy," Neil said, looking pleased with himself.

"I didn't know anybody else was around," I stammered. "How were you able to sneak up on me like that without making a sound? A pin drop would echo through this empty hallway."

"My people have long been masters of stealth," he said, trying to sound like an Indian chief.

"Ahh."

"Yeah, it really freaks out the palefaces, especially the principal. Him nearly crapped pants when I popped out of supply closet last week." A grin crept across his face. "So anyway, what are you doing here so late, Dave?"

"I quit the baseball team. Had to turn in my uniform. Thought I'd reminisce about the good old days for a while." I gestured at the display case.

"I see. I thought I heard Coach's shouts echoing through the school building yesterday afternoon. Was that for you?"

I looked down and nodded.

"What happened? You play a song he didn't like?"

"I actually don't know what happened. The man just started yelling and told me to stay away from him. I think he's losing it."

"Well, he has been drinking a lot more lately."

"Huh? How do you know?"

"After fourteen years of cleaning up this place, not much gets past me. Plus, the old guy isn't so crafty about disposing his empties. You should see all the Jack Daniel's bottles in the back dumpster."

"Really? I didn't know."

Neil reached into the pocket of his dark blue uniform and pulled out a pack of Juicy Fruit. He offered me a stick before taking one for himself. "Thanks," I said.

"You'd think Kishman would show a little gratitude to you for saving the team last season." He surveyed the statuesque gold championship trophy.

I turned to the case and sighed. "Hard to believe that less than a year ago I was starting in the state tournament and now I'm off the team. Didn't even get to play one game this year."

"Tough break, kid. But you're young. You've still got football. You'll get plenty of opportunities to make your mark in life."

I brushed my fingers over the display case glass. "You know, I actually thought I had a chance to play in the majors one day. Second base for the Royals—that was my dream. Pretty stupid, huh?"

Neil put his hand on my shoulder. "It's not stupid. Dreams aren't stupid." A moment later he started fumbling with a heavily populated ring of keys. After jingling them around for a few seconds, he found the one he wanted. He then pushed it into a lock on the display case.

"What are you doing?" I asked.

"They were going to wait, but there's no sense in that now." He slid open the glass and grabbed my home run bat.

"What are you going to do with that?"

"It was supposed to be a surprise," he said. "The principal was going to present it to you at a ceremony before the first game of the season. The entire Eastridge faculty and staff were going to be there." He held up the silver bat to admire the polished aluminum. "Wow, how about that? I can still feel it buzzing from your hit." He winked at me.

"They were going to give it to me?"

"Yeah. But Kishman ruined that, didn't he? Here, take it."

"I can't take this."

"It's yours. The principal has already made the decision. I'll let him know I gave it to you. Better take it now before Kishman tries to steal it."

I grabbed the handle of the bat with both hands. "There's nothing like it," I said.

Neil locked the case. "Well, I'd better get going. I gotta slay a demon that has befouled the boys' room on the second floor. Arrgh, a most hideous creature it is," he said in a pirate voice. "See ya later, kid."

"Thanks, Neil."

Moments after he had walked away, I heard a noise in the stairwell at the far end of the hallway. Spinning around, I caught a glimpse of flannel and red stringy hair disappearing behind a corner. I approached the stairwell, where a faint stench still hung in the air. *Doug Edmonds?* Descending, I scanned the basement hall but saw no one.

My new prize soon reclaimed my attention. It was hard to take my eyes off of it. At home, I stood the beautiful silver bat in a corner in my room. *Kishman may have driven me off the baseball team, but at least I'll always have this bat.*

The next day, my first three classes were about as exciting as they always were on a Wednesday morning. But my blissful ennui was interrupted near the end of third period when a voice cracked from the classroom's intercom speaker. I was to report to the office. After gathering my chemistry books, I started down the hallway as my brain processed possible reasons why I could be in trouble. Nothing came to mind. *Maybe Kishman attacked another student and they want me to testify about what happened to me. Maybe they want to know why I quit the baseball team.*

Upon my arrival in the main office, the secretary picked up her phone and alerted the principal of my presence. She then pointed at the door. "Go on in. They're waiting for you." I took a deep breath and entered the throne room of Eastridge High.

A quick scan of the principal's office revealed multiple rows of books neatly ordered in a tall bookcase, three hanging plants, assorted pictures of Eastridge sports teams, a flag, and two burgundy chairs in front of a large maple desk. A vice principal, Ms. Pierce, occupied one of the chairs. Principal Peterson, with his graying beard, sat behind the desk in a dark three-piece suit. To his right, standing with arms crossed, was HIM! Coach Kishman glowered at me as if he were trying to set my head on fire using only his eyes.

"Dave, come in," Peterson said. "Shut the door, please." He then gestured at the open chair. "Have a seat." My eyes on the floor, I advanced.

"Yes, get in here and have a seat, you thieving son of a bitch," Kishman hissed.

"Sal!" Mr. Peterson and Ms. Pierce said in unison. I sank into the chair, wary of any sudden lunges the towering inferno to my left might make.

"Dave," the principal began, "let me assure you that you have not been summoned here for disciplinary reasons. We just need to ask you a couple of questions."

"Yes, sir." I wiped my sweaty palms on the sides of my jeans.

"We have received information that the head custodian gave you a bat yesterday that he removed from the school's trophy case. Is that correct?"

An arctic blast of fear swept through me. *Maybe Neil wasn't supposed to give me the bat.* Not wanting to answer, I shifted in the chair.

"Answer the question, you thief!" Kishman snapped.

"Sal, I'm warning you," Mr. Peterson said. "One more outburst and you will be excused from these proceedings." He glared at the coach, who aimed his glare directly at me. A few seconds passed.

"Dave, did Mr. Heimlich give you a bat yesterday after school?" Ms. Pierce asked in a firm voice.

I turned toward her. She was an attractive black woman in her mid-forties with a reputation of being able to sniff out any student attempts at deception. Though her face held a staid expression, her eyes offered a hint of understanding. "Yes, ma'am. He did."

"Did he say why?" Mr. Peterson asked. Kishman shifted his weight from one foot to the other.

My mind and my voice raced. “He said you were going to present it to me at a ceremony before the first game, and since I was off the team he thought I should have it now. He said he was going to tell you about it.”

“That’s bullshit and you know it!” Kishman roared. “You bribed that janitor to help you steal the bat. I know how you operate.”

Mr. Peterson slapped the desk. “That is quite enough, Sal!”

“You tried to steal that bat like you tried to steal credit for my state title.”

“You are excused, Sal,” the principal shouted, rising to his feet. “Leave, now!” He pointed at the door.

Kishman scowled at me for several more seconds. “I’m not through with you,” he whispered as he passed by my chair. A slamming door marked his exit.

Mr. Peterson sat down and rolled his shoulders to straighten out his suit jacket. “Dave, there was no ceremony planned. The bat is school property and is to remain in the display case. Mr. Heimlich had no jurisdiction to give it to you. Do you understand?”

“Yes, sir.”

“Would you return the bat to this office tomorrow?”

“Yes. I’m sorry. I didn’t know.”

“It’s okay, Dave,” Ms. Pierce said. “We know you wouldn’t have taken the bat on your own volition.” She sighed as her expression softened. “Mr. Heimlich wants the students to like him. Sometimes, he tries a little too hard. Yesterday, he must have gotten carried away.”

“It’s a shame,” Mr. Peterson added. “He was a fine custodian.”

“Sir?” My eyes widened.

“We’ve suspended Mr. Heimlich and started the paperwork to terminate his employment at Eastridge. We needed your testimony before we could continue with that process.”

His words hit like a punch to the solar plexus. *I’ve provided the rope to hang a good man.* “He’s going to be fired?” I asked in disbelief. “But I’ll return the bat.”

“Unfortunately Dave, we’re left with little choice in this matter. Mr. Kishman is threatening legal action against Mr. Heimlich if we do not act. It seems that Mr. Heimlich made a series of unsubstantiated accusations against Mr. Kishman this morning. The situation could easily spin out of control. Trust me, it is best for all involved if Mr. Heimlich finds employment elsewhere."

On the way back to class, I replayed the events of the previous afternoon. A realization slammed home. *Doug Edmonds—Coach is using him to spy on me. Kishman is trying to get me expelled or even arrested.* I felt sick.

At the start of lunch period, I sought out Neil's son Thor. Like me, he was a junior. He agreed that we should talk. We bought sack lunches and exited the building. After we found a bench, I gave him the Reader's Digest version of my recent history with Kishman. In deference to John, I left out the part about Coach trying to kill me with a bat. I finished my story with, "Thor, I'm really sorry about your dad. I never wanted anything bad to happen to him."

"I know that, King," Thor said with a nod of his large flattopped head. "It's not your fault."

"I feel like it is. I wish I wouldn't have taken that bat. I'm so stupid!"

"King, I've known you for more than a year. We've been at a hundred FCA and Youth for Christ meetings together. I know you wouldn't steal anything and I know you didn't want Pop to get fired." He stuffed a handful of chips into his mouth.

"Thanks, Thor." We ate in silence for a while. "Is your dad gonna be okay?"

"Hope so." A look of concern flashed across his face. "Maybe this is part of God's plan for my family. We'll just have to tighten our belts for a while. I need to drop a few pounds anyway." He patted his ample belly a couple times. "My kid brothers do too."

"Hey, I can talk to my dad. He might have an opening for your dad at The Royal Court."

"No," Thor said with a dismissive wave. "Pop would never go for it. He'd see it as charity. Thanks, though. This is just a trial my family has to go through. It'll make it all the more sweeter when I'm gettin' the big bucks in the NFL. When that happens, the first thing I'm gonna do is buy Mom and Pop a big house. Then neither of them will have to work again." He grinned and finished off his sandwich.

"Wow. That's a cool plan."

"Gotta have faith and stay positive, my friend." He gave my shoulder a light shove. "Dig this, football practice starts in less than three months. This fall we'll be the big bad seniors." He flexed his beefy arms and woofed like a dog. "You'll be the starting quarterback and I'll be the center plowing the way for you."

"Well, I know you'll be the center. You were All-Conference last season. Me, I could be riding the bench again. Ziph has a good arm."

"You'll start at QB," he said, devouring a chocolate chip cookie. "I just know it."

Thor's optimism and faith helped boost my spirits. While walking back to the school building, however, I glimpsed the baseball field off in the distance. Thoughts of Kishman returned. Since becoming the target of his wrath, I'd lost a girlfriend and a chance to pursue my dream of playing baseball. Even worse was the fact that others were getting caught in the crossfire. John was an abuse victim and Neil Heimlich had lost his job. I wondered how many more casualties this war would claim.

Chapter 7 – October 1975

“You all know what’s at stake right now,” Coach Keeler said, nearing the end of his halftime talk. “If we win, we’re in the playoffs. If we lose, we’re not. It’s that simple.” He directed his flinty stare at one player … and then another … and then another. “I don’t want this season to end tonight. I know you don’t either. Now get out there and make sure that doesn’t happen!”

With a shout, we jumped up and funneled toward the locker room exit. “King!” Grabbing my arm, Keeler pulled me away from the pack. He stared into my eyes as if trying to communicate telepathically. Though several inches shorter than me, Coach nonetheless stood as a tower of authority. A worn red Eastridge football cap rested on his thick jowly head, which itself, in the absence of a visible neck, seem to rest directly on his broad torso.

“Yes, Coach.” I returned his gaze.

“This game is what we’ve been working for all season. We haven’t beat Dowling in over a decade—before I started coaching here. Tonight we can do it!” He pumped his fist. “We’re only down 13-7. Our boys are giving it all they’ve got, but they need a fearless leader to guide them on the field of battle.”

I nodded, gripping my helmet tighter.

“You *are* that leader, King. Ever since two-a-days you’ve busted your ass like no other player I ever coached. You never stopped working to make yourself better—running, throwing, thinking. Your determination and leadership have lifted this team. Those men out there respect you. They will follow your lead. Go lead them to victory!” He pounded my shoulder pads with both fists. “Victory, King! Victory!”

"Victory!" I shouted, storming out of the locker room. As I charged down the corridor toward the lights of Williams Stadium, my thoughts drifted to the blazing hot practices of last August. Back then, I never thought anything would replace my love of baseball. But my passion for football steadily increased over the course of the season. I loved the competition. I wanted to win every time we took the field. Against undefeated Dowling, that fervor was boiling over.

My teammates prowled the sideline like caged tigers. I darted about, slapping helmets and shouting encouragements. NASA could have used the adrenaline flowing through my body to fuel its next space flight.

At the start of the second half, Eastridge's Chuck Walker returned the kickoff to our 34-yard line. After Keeler gave me the play, I trotted onto the field. Kneeling in the huddle, I told my teammates what he had called, along with the snap count. Upon taking my position under center, I surveyed the white jerseys arrayed against us. Dowling's granite defense had lined up in a 6-1 formation. The middle linebacker glared at me. "I own you, King," he jeered. "You ain't goin' nowhere."

Thor hiked me the ball and the two lines slammed into each other. Feral grunts and the crash of colliding helmets, pads, and bodies shattered the air. With our tailback, Ricky Clark, shadowing me, I followed my blockers to the right seemingly looking for a hole in the brick wall built by the Dowling defenders. Then suddenly, I faded back three steps. Clark rushed forward to save me from a charging defensive tackle. Scanning left, I spotted Walker open on a post route. I fired the ball to where he was heading. The countless passes I'd thrown through the swinging tire hanging from the large oak in my backyard paid off. The tight spiral went precisely where I wanted it to go. Walker gathered in the pass and ran several more yards before a safety cut out his legs.

After the 21-yard gain, we had the ball at the Dowling 45. My teammates were jacked up. Our fans roared. Two handoffs later, we faced a third and one. I ran an option keeper left to pick up three yards. The middle linebacker, however, made me pay for that first down with a hammering blow. It felt as if my esophagus had shifted six inches to the left. Lying in the grass, I saw a couple of my linemen standing above me silhouetted against the stadium lights. After they hoisted me to my feet, I regained my bearings and was ready to go. Having been hit a thousand times since August, my body was conditioned to take such punishment.

With inspired blocking from Thor and the rest of the powerful Eastridge line, we mixed passing and running plays to advance the ball down the field. But then two short runs and an incomplete pass left us with a fourth and seven at Dowling's 11-yard line. I jogged to the sideline as our field goal unit took the field. Phong Baccam's kick passed just inside the right upright to make the score 13-10. Momentum was ours.

Unfortunately, the Dowling Maroons offense was just as intimidating as their defense. They used an arsenal of weapons—fleet receivers, slashing running backs, and a strong-armed quarterback—to steamroll hapless opponents. Dowling had won games this year by scores of 42-0, 34-0, 54-0, and 72-0. But the Braves defense was fired up to face them. Abner Kishman had worked his troops into a frenzy for this game. "Attack the ball!" he roared from the sideline. "Defend your ground! Don't let them into our backyard!" Our defense bent but did not break during Dowling's first drive of the second half. Facing a fourth and goal at our 6-yard line, they kicked a field goal to push their lead back to six points.

We managed only one first down on our next drive before Dowling's swarming defenders forced us to punt. The Eastridge defense, aided by a holding call against the Maroons, then returned the favor. Getting the ball again, we advanced to midfield before hitting a wall. An excellent punt pinned Dowling at their 5-yard line with just under nine minutes left in the fourth quarter.

Undaunted by the shadow of their own goalposts, our adversaries started moving up the field. As they advanced the ball, the Dowling running backs and receivers stayed inbounds to keep the clock running. I paced the sideline. "Don't worry, King," Thor said. "We'll get the ball back." His pudgy face was flushed with exertion; his red jersey was torn and darkened with sweat. But his blue-gray eyes conveyed an indomitable sense of hope.

"Amen, Brother Heimlich," I said. "And thou and thy blessed linemen shall lead us into the promised land." Thor and some of the other players sitting nearby smiled and shook their heads.

"You crazy, man," Walker said to me, before finishing off a cup of water.

Out on the field Dowling had gained another first down. Time ticked off the clock. Each elapsed second stung like a pinprick. I turned to scan the stands. Football crowds at varsity games were always animated. That this was Halloween night added to the liveliness. Our fans wore an eclectic array of costumes—Indian braves, witches, ghosts, and clowns. Batman, Superman, and the shark from *Jaws* also made an appearance. Most memorable was the guy (or girl) dressed up like Dr. Frank-N-Furter from *The Rocky Horror Picture Show*.

A loud cheer brought my attention back to the field. Our defense had stuffed a Dowling pitchout for a five-yard loss. Gaining only six yards on their next two plays, the Maroons had to punt. Following a fair catch, we had the ball at our 14-yard line. The clock stopped with 3:37 left to play.

Eastridge's offense took the field. Ten sets of eyes looked into mine. "So," I said, "how much time should we leave on the clock after we score this touchdown?" After going over the play Keeler had called, we broke huddle with a clap. "This sure beats trick-or-treating," I yelled as we lined up in an I formation.

"Yeah, but we're still gonna get some candy," Clark added.

Two running plays—a draw and an option pitch—picked up a total of eight yards. Rather than playing it safe and running to get the first down, Keeler called for a flag pass pattern to the tailback. I dropped the ball right in Clark's hands as he raced down the sideline. After he was knocked out of bounds at our 42, there was 2:27 remaining on the clock.

An incompletion and a failed quarterback sweep left us facing a third and ten. Coach called for a reverse. After handing the ball to Clark who ran to his right, I drifted to the left. Clark handed the ball to Walker who blazed across the backfield in my direction. I picked up speed to lead the way for him. A large Dowling linebacker loomed ahead. Pumping hard, I hurled myself into his torso and tried to push him back. He flailed at me with his meat hooks and finally knocked me out of his way. But by that time, Walker had streaked past. A cornerback forced him out of bounds after a 13-yard gain.

"Nice block, King," Walker said back in the huddle.

"Not bad for a quarterback," Thor chimed in.

A pitch to Clark and a slant pass brought us to the Dowling 34. With only 1:05 left in the game, we used our second timeout. Hoping for a quick six, Keeler called a play-action pass for the end zone. Faking a handoff, I dropped back and scanned the field. *Walker is covered. So is—RUN!* The pocket had collapsed. As Maroons closed in, I raced across the backfield in a large semicircle. I looked downfield wanting to throw but the receivers were still covered. I then cradled the ball into my body and sprinted forward, away from the pursuing rushers. A linebacker came up to meet me. I juked left and abruptly shifted right to blow by him toward the middle of the field. My peripheral vision caught a cornerback trying to cut me off, but I accelerated past him and spun around a charging safety with a 360-move. Two converging defenders finally escorted me to the ground at the 10-yard line.

A loud roar erupted from the bleachers behind our sideline. Catching my breath, I corralled my teammates into a huddle. Our tight end brought in the next play—a handoff to the fullback. We picked up only two yards but it gave me a chance to rest. Coach then motioned for a time out. The referee's shrill whistle blew with 25 seconds on the clock.

As my teammates and I gathered on the sideline, Keeler called for a Blue Blazer 17 right. "You've got to be sure you can make it in, King. It's eight yards away. We can't stop the clock anymore. If you don't think it's there, just toss it and we'll try something else." I nodded as my stomach somersaulted with nervous excitement.

"Okay boys, let's get our candy," I said in the huddle. We lined up in an open formation—the receivers wide on the ends; the running backs spread out behind me. Heart pounding, I barked the count. As I dropped back, both receivers and both running backs ran toward the end zone. After they all curled left, I saw what I wanted to see. Bringing the ball back to throw, I pump-faked left and then darted to my right. Sprinting past our right tackle, who had just flattened a defensive end, I charged toward the end zone pylon. Dowling's secondary defenders abruptly abandoned our receivers and raced over to try to cut me off. Two white jerseys closed fast as I neared the goal line. Launching into a dive, I extended the ball in front of me as they hurled themselves at my flying body. The ensuing collision slammed me hard to the ground. Nonetheless, my two-handed grip remained tight on the ball, which was a foot inside the end zone. The ref's hands shot up. After our extra point, the kickoff, and a failed Dowling Hail Mary, the clock expired. The final score: Eastridge 17, Dowling 16.

I didn't drag my carcass out of bed until a quarter to ten the next morning. After spending some time with my old friend Captain Crunch, I grabbed the sports section to verify that last night's game actually happened. The headline, "King leads Eastridge past No. 1 Dowling for Metro Title," provided the desired confirmation. While reading the accompanying article, I heard a car pull into the driveway. A few seconds later the back door opened.

"Well, if it isn't the big hero," a familiar voice announced.

I looked over to see a tall man wearing a thick helmet of brown hair. The smirk that appeared below his shaggy moustache nearly connected one furry sideburn to the other. He wore plaid fuchsia slacks and a black turtleneck. Very few people could pull off that look. Unfortunately, my brother was not one of them. "Hey Adam," I said. "What brings you to the old home place this glorious Saturday morning?"

"This foxy lady came into the restaurant last night and asked if I'd get your autograph."

"Is that so?" I raised my eyebrows.

"Actually, no. I've got some payroll forms for Dad to sign. He slipped out early last night to listen to the second half of some stupid football game."

"Really, he listened to my game?"

"That's what he said he was going to do. So is he here?"

"Downstairs I think. I just got up. Haven't seen him yet."

"You are such a lazy ass." Adam shook head.

"Well, I didn't get home until two. Didn't get to sleep 'til after three."

"Knocking down a few cold ones to celebrate the big win, huh?"

"Nah, I just had a Coke and pizza at Chuck's. Then me and a few of the boys cruised around for a while. They drank a little, but no beer for me."

"Oh, that's right. You're still a teetotaler Christian, aren't you?" he asked with disdain.

"Yes. Is that so bad?"

He sighed and forced a tight-lipped smile. "Dave, you're young and impressionable. I just hate to see you get duped by those kind of people."

"Duped? What's wrong with wanting to serve God, the creator of the universe?"

He rolled his eyes. "Like I've told you before, man created God. Not the other way around. You shouldn't try to serve something that doesn't exist. It's not healthy."

"I know God is real. He is the most real presence in my life."

"Riiight. This imaginary friend of yours, I assume he talks to you."

"God is not imaginary, and he DOES communicate with me. He answers my prayers and he speaks to me and all believers through his Word."

"Ah yes, the Bible," Adam said, glancing up at the ceiling. "The infallible Word of God."

"You should read it sometime."

"I wasted enough time on that book when I was a naive little kid."

"What do you have against the Bible?"

"Well let's see," he said with amused contempt. "It demeans women. It glorifies violence. It condones slavery. It contradicts itself. But perhaps worst of all is the Bible's exclusivity. Any person who's never heard of Jesus Christ, no matter how virtuous, is damned to hell for eternity. Doesn't sound too fair to me. According to the Bible, millions of good people will fry just because they were born into the wrong culture or at the wrong time in history."

"Your misconceptions of the Bible don't make it any less true," I said. "God reveals himself to everybody in some way. He wants all people to seek him and find salvation." I took my cereal bowl to the sink.

Adam shook his head. "I suppose you own a Pet Rock too."

"No, I heard they're too hard to train." I turned to face him. "Won't do any tricks."

He snickered. "Say, you're getting taller, aren't you?" He ran the blade of his hand from the top of his head to just above mine. "You're about six feet now, huh?"

"Pretty much. Just an eighth of an inch shy last time I got measured."

"Damn. You've done some serious growing the past couple of years. If you keep this up, you're going to catch me."

"Maybe."

"You know, Eli and Nate had late growth spurts too. They kept growing until they were nineteen. I was six-one at sixteen. Thought I might top Eli. But that's where I stopped—stayed the same as Dad."

"Whatever God decides," I said with a wink.

"Stop that." He frowned. "Alright, I've got to get these signed and hit the road." He whacked my arm with the forms in his hand and moved toward the door to the basement.

"Hey Adam. I'm headin' over to see Grandpa now. You want to come with?"

He looked surprised. "Oh, I can't today. I've got a lot to do."

"We wouldn't have to stay very long. I'm sure he'd like to see you. I think he gets kinda bored over there sometimes."

"Sorry. Maybe next time." He disappeared down the stairs.

The back door of Grandpa's house was slightly ajar. I tried to remember when somebody had last visited him. Busy with school, football, and work, I myself hadn't been over in four days. Pushing open the door, I crept inside. The air was stale. Samson's water and food bowls sat empty in the middle of the kitchen floor. I crossed the kitchen and stepped into the dark living room. Heavy curtains shut out the sunlight. After my eyes adjusted to the dimness, I saw Grandpa sitting on the davenport. He was leaning forward with his head in his hands. Samson sat on the floor staring at him as if expecting an answer to a question he'd just asked.

"Grandpa?" He didn't move. Samson turned his head causing his tags to jingle. After the dog padded over to me, I heard a faint whine while stroking the fur on his back. Grandpa still didn't move, but I could hear him breathing. A dry tongue licked my hand. Spurred to action, I darted into the kitchen and filled the water dish. Samson immediately lowered his snout into the bowl. His rhythmic lapping continued uninterrupted as I filled his food dish and went back into the living room.

I sat next to my motionless grandfather. One of Grandma's quilts was wadded up in a large ball next to him. "Grandpa?" I placed my hand on his back. A pungent whiff of body odor filled my nostrils and lingered. He lowered his hands and turned to me.

"Dave?"

"Yes, Grandpa."

"Dave … where's Hannah?" His eyes glistened in the gloom.

Words eluded me for an instant. "Grandma's not here."

"Well, where'd she go? When will she be back?"

A lump formed in my throat. I slid off the couch and knelt before him. "Grandma died," I said, gazing into his confused face. "She's in heaven now."

He straightened up and looked past me as if trying to comprehend something. "Oh."

"Grandpa it's daytime. I'm going to open the curtains. Is that okay?"

He nodded. The sunlight flooding the room drove away some of the dreariness but also revealed a layer of dust on nearly every hard surface. "You ready for lunch?" I asked. He again nodded. In the kitchen, Samson's head was now half buried in his food dish. The water bowl had been emptied. "I'm sorry, boy." I filled it again. Still chomping, the dog looked up at me for a couple seconds before returning to his Alpo.

Coffee and food stains marred the avocado stove and beige Formica countertop. Dirty dishes filled the sink. A glance at the clock revealed that it was 11:10. I had plans to meet some teammates at noon for burgers and pool. After a sigh, I made a phone call expressing my regrets.

My new lunch plans consisted of grilled cheese sandwiches and a can of Campbell's Bean with Bacon. As I stirred the orange soup, I thought of Dad preparing his famous *blanquette de veau* at The Royal Court. *Yep, I'm a chip off the old block.* Lucidity slowly returned to Grandpa as we ate. He spoke sparingly at first, but eventually broke into a story about a trip he and Grandma took to Florida in the 1950s. While finishing the chocolate malt I made for dessert, he asked about football. My report of last night's game brought a spark to his eyes.

It took me about an hour to wash the dishes and clean the kitchen. After putting away the last pan, I knew my work had just begun. Though Grandpa said it wasn't necessary, I dragged the old Electrolux out of the closet. While vacuuming and dusting, I was thankful that Grandpa lived in a small two-bedroom house. Samson, meanwhile, was outside ridding the backyard of trespassing squirrels. I next tackled the bathroom, cleaning the sink and scrubbing the toilet. The final task that I knew needed to be done was the one I dreaded most. I prayed fervently that I would not have to be an active participant. After filling the tub, I went into the living room where Grandpa sat in his rocking chair watching a college football game.

I took a breath. "Grandpa, your bath is ready." I spoke with conviction, as if we'd discussed this before—even though we hadn't.

He looked surprised. Wheels turned in his head. "Oh … okay," he finally said. Rising with great effort, he tottered down the hall to get clean clothes out of his bedroom. After making sure the bathroom door was not locked, I sat in the kitchen listening for any signs of trouble. I was exceedingly thankful that Grandpa completed his bath by himself, and without incident.

As I prepared to go, he asked me to take him to a place where neither of us had been since Memorial Day. After helping him to the car, I drove to Laurel Hill Cemetery south of the Fairgrounds. Hanging onto my arm, he made the slow trek to Grandma's familiar black gravestone. We stood silently for several minutes until he was ready to go. When we returned to his house he was somber but alert. He said he planned to read a few chapters of Isaiah that evening.

I drove home knowing that Dad and I would need to keep a closer eye on Grandpa in the future. When I stepped into the kitchen, the clock arms pointed to 4:32 p.m. That left me with just enough time to get dressed for work before my shift began at the restaurant.

An epidemic of football fever gripped the east side of Des Moines the following week. Everywhere I went, people asked me about the playoffs. On those evenings I waited tables at The Royal Court, a dozen or more patrons wished me good luck and asked for my autograph. Tips were better than ever. At school, the varsity starters enjoyed adoration and reverence from most students and even a few teachers. The players were energized. We'd worked hard in practice all season, but the intensity reached new levels during that first week of November. The boys ran faster, hit harder, and scrimmaged with more determination. The excitement surrounding Eastridge football reached a crescendo on Friday—game day.

Undefeated Burlington was our first round opponent. The game would be played on their home field. Though I didn't mind missing school, I dreaded the 180-mile bus ride. The lumpy seats with the torn green vinyl covering did nothing to add to my enthusiasm for this mode of travel. Neither did the exhaust stench that wafted through the bus and into my lungs. To make matters worse, I couldn't sit still. I felt like jumping out and running all the way to the Mississippi River. Fortunately, Thor sat beside me. He quoted inspirational scriptures from the open Bible in his lap. Hearing God's Word helped me to settle down and maintain a spiritual focus … for a while, anyway.

After more than three hours on the road, the bus pulled up to Bracewell Stadium in Burlington. Kickoff was set for 7:05 p.m. That meant two more hours of stewing with anticipation. When it came time to dress for the game, I felt like a medieval knight preparing for battle. Adrenaline surged as I donned my pants, pads, socks, cleats, and jersey. Fully armored, we players did not want to wait anymore. But game time was still over an hour away, so we fidgeted. The clock seemed frozen. A couple guys threw up. Finally, it was time for warm-ups. Excitement burned inside me upon viewing the dazzling white grid freshly painted on the emerald field. The feeling remained as we returned to the locker room. Following Coach Keeler's final pep talk, we charged through a banner back onto the field. I felt like I could fly. The rapid pounding of snare and tenor drums cut through the cool evening air like machine gun fire. The crowd roared. Cheerleaders shouted. Stadium lights blazed high above.

We won the coin toss and elected to receive. Just before kickoff, a feeling of calm came over me. My mind and body readied for action. I prayed silently for victory. After the return, the Eastridge offense lined up at the 27-yard line. I took the snap, dropped back and fired a strike to Walker near the sideline. That first completion brought a rush of exhilaration—the play resulted in a 12-yard gain. Clark then burst through a hole for eight more yards. The following play, I crossed midfield on an option keeper. Our offense advanced with machine-like precision. When throwing, I felt like I could hit a quarter floating in the air thirty yards away. When carrying the ball, I felt fast and powerful, like a racehorse. My teammates radiated a similar confidence.

Three minutes into the game, we were up 7-0. After our second drive, the score was 14-0. It was one of those nights. Nearly everything went our way. With eight minutes left in the fourth quarter, Coach sent in Calvin Ziph, the backup quarterback, to replace me. I walked off the field to a thunderous ovation from our fans.

The ride home was loud and rowdy. The bus echoed with whoops, shouts, and the exclamation, "Dyn-o-mite!" Keeler let us have our fun. He even laughed when a few of the defensive backs cut loose with their rendition of "Jive Talkin" by the Bee Gees. The lumpy seat didn't seem so uncomfortable on the three-hour trip back to Des Moines.

I'd just been seated in a booth at the hilltop Pizza Hut when John arrived a couple minutes past noon. He tried to fight it, but a huge grin stretched across his face as he approached. I stood. We shook hands and traded slaps on the back before sliding into opposite sides of the booth.

"That did NOT really happen last night, did it?" he asked, still smiling. "Eastridge did not beat the top-ranked team in the state 42-7, did they?"

I shrugged. "I'm thinking something like that may have happened."

"Unbelievable." He shook his head. "I was there and I still can't believe it. You sons-of-bitches are gonna win state. Man, I wish I was still on the team!"

"I wouldn't crown us yet. We've got Sioux City Heelan next week in the semifinals. They've got a monster defense. And if we somehow win that game, Dowling will probably be waiting for us in the finals. You know they'll be looking to dish out some revenge."

"Listen to Mr. Humble," John said. "You guys beat Dowling last week when they were the number one-ranked team. Then you beat Burlington last night when they were the number one-ranked team. Face it, the Braves are the real number one 4A team in Iowa."

"Not yet."

"Puh-lease. I'm not listening to you anymore. Last summer all I heard was, 'I don't know if I'll be starting at quarterback. Ziph is really good.'" John used a whiny voice when mocking my words. "Now you're not only starting, but you're one of the top QBs in the state."

"You're definitely exaggerating now, Kishman. You forget the three interceptions I threw in our opening-game loss to Central Waterloo?"

"First game jitters," he said with a dismissive wave. "You were still learning the position. Plus, Central Waterloo has a good team."

"Well, how about the next week against Tech when I fumbled twice and threw two more interceptions and almost blew the game."

"But you didn't blow the game. You kept your cool and led the team to victory."

"We won 14-13 against a team we were favored to beat by two touchdowns."

"Eastridge won. That's all that mattered. Then in week three you got a little better, and you kept improving all season. And last night, what was that? You passed for over two hundred yards and rushed for another hundred. Admit it, man. You're the next Steve Davis."

"Yeah, right," I chuckled. "So you've got me starting for Oklahoma next year, huh?"

"Nah, screw Switzer. You gotta be Hawkeye, man. I can already hear Jim Zabel raving about you on the radio."

"I don't know if Iowa is going to offer me a scholarship." The waitress came over and took our order: one extra-large pizza—half sausage, half pepperoni.

"Don't worry, they'll offer you the full ride," John said. "Especially after they see what you do in these last two playoff games."

"Missouri, Western Iowa, and Drake have showed a lot more interest in me than Iowa."

He took a long draw of Coke. "Aw man, forget about them. You gotta wear the black and the gold, baby!" He straightened out the front of his black sweatshirt so the yellow-lettered IOWA showed more clearly.

"Yeah, that would be cool to play for the Hawks. And we could be roommates."

"Hell yeah," he said, pumping his fist. "With you as the big football star and me as the big baseball star, the chicks will be hanging around our place day and night."

"Sure they will," I said, taking a drink. "So, how's the Hawkeye baseball team looking? You met the other players yet?"

"Yeah. I think we're gonna be good. You know we got Boddicker? After you took down Galbraith, he won Pitcher of the Year honors in '74."

"Is he going to send me a thank you card?"

"No, but he did say that if he were pitching for Valley that night, he would've struck you out with a changeup to end the game."

I laughed. "Funny guy. I like him already."

A husband and wife walked up to our booth with their two young boys. They must have recognized me from the pictures that had recently appeared in *The Register* and *The Tribune*.

"Uh, hi Dave," the father began. "Sorry to interrupt you, but my boys are big fans of yours. Could they get your autograph?"

"Sure," I said, pleased that John had to witness this.

After the family left, he shook his head. "What about me? I'm the one who talked you into playing football. I'm the one who dragged your sorry ass into the weight room. They should be asking for *my* autograph. I birthed you, man." He tried to conceal a smile.

"Uh-huh," I said, feeling good about myself. Our pizza arrived a short while later. After we both inhaled a couple slices, John's expression darkened.

"Has my dad given you any trouble lately?"

"No. It's like he's forgotten about me this semester. I'm glad he has nothing to do with the football team."

"But his cousin does. Has Abner caused any trouble?"

"No problems from him either. We don't have much contact with each other. When we do, he's always been cool. I think Abner's main goal is to win football games. He acts like he doesn't even know about your dad's beef with me."

"Good. I was hoping to hear that." He paused. "You see much of Michelle anymore?"

"No, not really. She cheers at the games, but I force myself not to look at her. Too distracting." I didn't tell him about the hours I still spent thinking about her—wondering if we could try again.

John nodded and devoured another piece. "How's Boz doing on JV?"

"Good. He's really filled out. Gettin' stronger and more accurate. Word is, he'll be starting varsity quarterback next year."

"That's what he was saying. I didn't know if he was bullshitting me or not." After we had focused on our food for a while John looked up and said, "You'd never believe it. I went to church last Sunday."

A slice of pizza fell out of my hand and landed face down on my plate. I stared at him, waiting for the punch line. "It's true," he said, snickering at my mishap.

"Great! What do you think? You want to talk about any spiritual stuff?"

"Well, not really. See, there's this fine-looking honey in my economics class. We've gone out a few times. She's a Christian." He feigned a frown. "Geez, I can't get away from you people.

Anyway, she asked me to go to church with her. So I did. I'm thinking it'll help me get down her pants." He cracked up laughing.

I groaned. "You're as bad as Ozzie. But I guess I should just be thankful that you're going to church, regardless of your motives."

"Yeah, church is alright. It's kinda wild with the music and all. I may go again sometime."

"Cool." We finished our pizza and talked for a while longer. I signed another autograph and received good luck wishes from three other football fans. John and I then rolled a few games at Thunderbird Lanes before driving to the new mall on the south side of town. That evening, we went to a party at Ricky Clark's house. With church the next morning, I left a little before 1:00 a.m. Driving home, I thought about how great it would be to hang out with John at college next year.

Coach took it easy on us at practice on Monday. Tuesday was a different story. Though aching and exhausted, I felt good walking off the field. The offense clicked. I gained confidence that we could move the ball against Heelan. My mind even started considering plays we might use against Dowling in the finals.

Deep in thought, I didn't notice Principal Peterson and Vice Principal Dooley standing just inside the locker room. "Dave, could we speak with you for a moment?" Peterson asked.

"Uh yeah, sure." It was strange seeing two men in suits in this environment. My teammates, dead tired, took little notice of the visitors.

"Perhaps we can talk in Coach Keeler's office," Mr. Dooley said. The overhead lights glared off the top of the small man's bald head. "He'll be arriving shortly, yes?"

I nodded, wondering what this could be about. *Maybe a TV reporter wants to interview me about Eastridge's playoff run.* Peterson and Dooley's faces revealed no clues.

Keeler and his assistant coaches soon arrived. The principal informed Coach of his desire to discuss a matter in private. Keeler dismissed his assistants and then led the way to his office. Coach occupied his usual red leather chair. Peterson motioned for me to sit in one of the two wooden chairs in front of the desk. After shutting the door, Dooley stood beside Peterson. I was a bit unsettled that they both remained looming above me.

"Jim … Dave," Peterson began, looking first at Keeler and then at me. "A disturbing issue has been placed before us—a matter that I'm hoping we can quickly clear up with this meeting." He took a deep breath. "An anonymous party called the school office earlier today and insisted upon speaking with me. Refusing to identify himself, he said only that he was the father of one of the Eastridge football players. This caller proceeded to inform me that Dave King has been selling drugs to his son and other members of the team. He said that he would contact the media with proof unless Dave was suspended from the team." I heard Peterson's words but they did not quite register with me. It was like the principal was talking about another Dave King.

"That's preposterous," Keeler exclaimed. "It's probably some jackass from Sioux City."

"That was our first reaction as well. We normally dismiss anonymous allegations, but given the heightened public interest in our football team, we want to be absolutely certain that our program is clean. So I authorized Vice Principal Dooley to look into the matter." Peterson nodded at the vice principal. "Mr. Dooley."

"Yes." Dooley cleared his throat. "I expected to find nothing, of course. But, uh … I received some testimony that raised concern." Coach and I exchanged a confused glance. Dooley continued in his usual high voice. "I first interviewed Doug Edmonds, a student who unfortunately has an insider's perspective on drug use here at Eastridge. During my interrogation about recent drug trafficking at this school, Mr. Edmonds revealed that Dave King had indeed approached him and others about purchasing amphetamines. Mr. Edmonds then reported that he had witnessed Dave making such a purchase from a dealer near campus."

My head felt like it was being squished. I couldn't speak. "You can't take the word of a doper like that," Keeler interjected.

"Agreed," Dooley said. "So I continued my investigation. After school today, I interviewed Sal Kishman, Dave's former baseball coach." Losing strength, my body slumped in the chair. "Though reluctant to discuss the matter, Mr. Kishman finally revealed that he was forced to dismiss Dave from his team last May for drug use. The coach said he tried to keep this quiet to avoid embarrassing one of the heroes from his state championship team."

Keeler placed his head in his hands. "This can't be right." He looked at me with a pained expression. "That's not true, is it?"

"No!" I said. "Absolutely not. I've never used or sold any drugs." My face grew hot.

"We are, as you might expect, puzzled by these revelations," Peterson said. "Mr. Dooley and I have decided that a search of Dave's locker is the next logical step in our investigation of this matter. Do either of you object?"

"Dave?" Keeler asked.

I thought for a moment. *My football locker is padlocked. Nobody could've planted anything in there. Once they see that my locker is clean, my innocence will be proved.* "No. No objection. That's a great idea."

Peterson decided to wait for the other players to clear out before checking my locker. I fiddled with my pads through the uncomfortable silence. My mind raced. *Why is this happening to me?* Finally, the last of my teammates shuffled out. Sitting on the bench in front of my locker, I grabbed the padlock and spun the dial. I then pulled down on the lock but it clicked unyieldingly. Frustrated, I dialed the combination again. Nothing. I sensed the impatience of the three men standing nearby. A panicked feeling of dread encased me. A third try and then a fourth were unsuccessful. I had to pee. After examining the padlock—a silver Master Lock with a black dial—I figured out the problem. My padlock had a dent on the bottom. The one in my hand had no such dent. It was new.

"Dave, please," Keeler said. "We don't have all day. Open the damn locker."

"I can't, Coach. This isn't my padlock. Somebody replaced my lock with a new one."

I turned to meet skeptical looks. Peterson dispatched Dooley to call a custodian. This delay was even more unnerving than the one in Coach's office. Keeler paced while Peterson stood with his hands clasped behind his back. Both men looked annoyed. Finally Dooley arrived with a janitor. After a loud snap of the bolt cutters, he removed the padlock. Peterson then searched my locker himself. I braced for the worst. Reaching deep in the back, he pulled out a small plastic medicine bottle full of green pills. The principal shook it and then twisted off the lid. Keeler and Dooley huddled over the small container.

"Pep pills," Dooley said.

Coach looked at me with disgust. "Greenies Dave? Is that how you've been doing it this season? Damn it! And you've been selling these to my team!" He slammed my locker door shut, sending a metallic crash echoing around us.

"No, Coach. Those aren't mine. I swear. Somebody planted them." I was telling the truth, yet even I thought my pleadings sounded pathetic.

"We're going to need to check your school locker too," Peterson said grimly. On the long march from the stadium to the school, I felt like a dead man walking. I knew that whoever orchestrated this conspiracy could have easily planted something in my school locker. There were always students hanging around when I was opening it between classes. Anybody could've lifted my combination. Though I'd never used drugs before, it came as no surprise when Peterson found two Ziploc bags full of marijuana in my locker. The principal ordered me to report to his office at ten o'clock the next morning.

Dad came home that evening a little before 10:30. "What are you doing in here?" he asked, upon entering the kitchen. "You just sitting at the table doing nothing?"

I had been there for three hours—trying to think, trying to pray, trying to figure out what I could do to prove my innocence. At the start of the day, I was a big football hero. Now, I felt like the world was conspiring to destroy me. "Dad … I need to talk to you."

The unease that consumed my insides must have been evident in my voice. His forehead wrinkling with concern, he draped his coat over the back of a chair and sat down. "What's wrong? You in some kind of trouble?"

I nodded. "I think I might be off the team. Maybe even expelled." I told him what had happened after practice. And then I told him about my history with Kishman, including why I quit the baseball team last May. Back then, I had to let my father think it was because I couldn't get along with the coach. For the first time, I told someone other than John about how Kishman blew up and threw a bat at me.

Dad remained quiet the whole time I spoke. I wondered if he believed me. When I finished he looked down and rubbed the back of his head. "What do you think happened?" he asked. "How do you think they planted those drugs?"

"I've been thinking about that all night. Kishman has to be the mastermind. Who he's got working for him, I don't know. Definitely Edmonds. They worked together before when Neil got fired. Maybe Kishman's cousin, Abner. Maybe Boz. Maybe some of the varsity players. I don't know who I can trust anymore."

"Why do you think Sal is doing this now? Didn't you say he's left you alone since last summer? You're not back with his daughter again, are you?"

"No, I'm not dating anybody during football season. Kishman has probably seen my picture in the paper or read some of the articles about me. Maybe my success is getting to him. Or maybe he's jealous of all the attention the football team is receiving. After the crappy record his team had last season, nobody's talking much about Eastridge baseball. But everybody is talking about Eastridge football now."

Dad was silent for a while. "That son of a bitch!" He slapped the table. "I always treated him like royalty when he came into the restaurant. Gave him the best table. The best wine. I can't believe he would do this."

I pressed my fingers against my aching temples. "He ended my baseball-playing days and now he's doing the same with football."

"Why didn't you tell me what he did last May, when it happened?" Dad asked with pain in his voice.

"I didn't want to make things worse for John. I didn't think anybody could do anything."

"I'm your father. I would have helped you." His face unraveled for an instant before tightening into a look of defiant resolution.

"I'm sorry, Dad. I didn't know what to do at the time."

"When is your meeting with the principal tomorrow?"

"Ten."

"I'm going with you."

"Mr. Peterson didn't say anything about—"

"I don't care what Peterson said. You don't know who you can trust up there. I'm not going to let you face those wolves by yourself."

The next morning, I got out of second period a few minutes early. I met Dad at the front entrance of the school. He wore a black suit. The meeting took place in a conference room adjacent to the main office. On one side of the long table sat Principal Peterson, Vice Principal Dooley, Vice Principal Pierce, and Coach Keeler. Dad and I sat across from them on the other side. Everyone bore a tense demeanor.

"Mr. King … Dave," Peterson began. "In addition to our review of yesterday's events, we interviewed several members of the football team this morning." He glanced at a sheet of paper. "One of the players, Calvin Ziph, testified that Dave has repeatedly offered to sell narcotics to him and several other players."

I bristled with anger. *That snake. He's never gotten over losing the starting quarterback spot to me.*

"This places us in a very difficult position," Peterson continued. "We all find it hard to believe that Dave is a drug dealer, but we have testimony from multiple witnesses, including a faculty member. And worst of all is the physical evidence found in Dave's lockers." Sighing, he shuffled another sheet to the top of the stack before him. "After careful review of this case, the school administration and the football coaching staff have agreed on what we believe is a fair ruling." Peterson's eyes bored directly into mine before returning to his paper. "Taking into account the student's prior record of good conduct, we have decided that Dave King will not be expelled nor suspended. However, he will be removed, effective immediately, from the football team. The reason will not be made public. Coach Keeler will announce to the media that Dave King's absence from the team is for personal reasons."

Dad and I sat in stunned silence for several seconds. "You say this is a fair ruling," my father said. "Fair to whom? Certainly not my son, whose chances for a college football scholarship will be severely jeopardized. And for what? Because you're scared of some caller who's afraid to give his name."

"Mr. King, please," Peterson said. "Place yourself in our shoes. We've found evidence. We have testimony."

"Yes, let's consider the testimony. Your faculty witness is an unbalanced sociopath who tried to assault my son with a baseball bat." Looks of shock covered all four faces across from us. "One of your student witnesses is a known drug dealer. And the other one, what's his name?" Dad asked me.

"Calvin Ziph," I said. "The second-string quarterback."

"Oh, there's a credible source," he exclaimed. "The one player who stands to gain the most if my son is suspended from the team. Did any other players testify against Dave?"

"Thus far, none of the other players have reported that Dave has sold drugs," Dooley said. "But we must consider that they could be covering for a teammate."

Dad slammed his fist into the table. "And that psychotic baseball coach and those two students could be lying. Did you consider that? They could have planted the drugs. It would've been very easy to do. And what about Dave's character and his participation in those Christian groups? Did you consider that?"

"Mr. King, I assure you we did take into account Dave's past record," Dooley said. "But we also had to consider additional factors."

"Such as?"

"Three years ago, as I'm sure you recall, Mr. King, Dave's brother Oswald received a three-day suspension for smoking marijuana on school grounds. And several years earlier Dave's brother Shane was suspended on four separate occasions for drug possession and fighting."

Dad's face reddened as veins bulged from his neck. "Dave should not be held responsible for his brothers' actions," he said, barely keeping his fury contained.

"Well, then," Dooley said, "perhaps you are familiar with the on-field brawl Dave took part in earlier this season." I remembered the incident. During the Lincoln game, Walker got into a scuffle with one of their safeties. A bunch of players from both teams started shoving each other. I ran into the fray to try to help separate the two sides. It was not a big deal. The so-called brawl lasted less than a minute before order was restored.

"That just proves my son is not a coward. That he stands by his teammates. Which is what you should be doing for him now, when he's being slandered. Have you no backbone?"

My father argued with Dooley and Peterson for at least fifteen more minutes. Keeler looked like he was going to be sick—like he could feel his state championship slipping away. Dad threatened to sue the school. Peterson countered by threatening to expel me. I worried that they might have enough evidence and testimony—though false—to support an expulsion. *At least the administration's first ruling would allow me to graduate next May.* I finally intervened to stop the quarrel. Though clearly reiterating my innocence, I expressed my willingness to accept Peterson's original decision. Dad, no doubt tired of all the fruitless arguing, stood. "You haven't heard the last of me," he snapped at Peterson, before exiting.

I walked with my father to the front doors of the school. Conflicting emotions swirled inside me. "Thanks for coming here today, Dad."

"I'm not done with them," he said wearily. "They won't get away with treating you like this." The lines on his face were more pronounced than usual. I wanted to hug him, but couldn't.

Though I didn't say a word, by the end of lunch period the whole school knew I was off the team. A student office assistant had overheard enough administrative talk to piece together what was going on. She fed the grapevine and the news spread. The roles of Doug Edmonds and Calvin Ziph were included in her reports. Most students, especially my teammates, were dumbfounded and infuriated. Later that afternoon two ambulances rolled up to Eastridge High, thirty minutes apart. The first one carried away Edmonds, who was found stuffed in a restroom stall, bloody and semi-conscious. The second ambulance carried away Ziph, who was found in a similar condition in the boys' shower room. The football team had issued its response to Principal Peterson's ruling.

Dad met with his lawyer the next day. There was not enough time to get my suspension from the team overturned before Friday's game. The attorney said that maybe he could do something to force the school to reinstate me before the championship game the following week, if Eastridge made it that far.

Friday night I was home. Principal Peterson had requested that I stay away from the stadium to avoid inciting more incidents. My football dreams shattered, I was too depressed to eat. Still supporting my teammates though, I turned on the radio just as the game began. With Ziph in the hospital, Boz Kishman, the JV quarterback, was pressed into duty. He and the Eastridge offense faced one of the top defenses in the state. The Braves first possession ended in a fumble. Their next possession ended with an interception. At halftime Heelan led 16-0. Two quarters later, Eastridge's once-promising season came to an inglorious end. I shut off the radio and knelt beside my bed in prayer. "God, you are my refuge. Though enemies surround me, my hope remains in you …"

Chapter 8 – April 1976

My pace slowed as I passed by the long jewelry case. Stopping, I peered through the glass at the bracelets, necklaces, and earrings. Each item greeted me with a glittering wink. I then spotted a brilliant peridot ring. *She would love this! I should buy it!* I tilted my head to read the price tag: $199. *Or not.*

Meandering over to the men's department, I thought about next Sunday. A spasm of nervousness flared in my abdomen. Scanning the selection of dress shirts neatly arranged in their clear packaging, my eyes fixed on an indigo color. *Yes. This will look great under my charcoal blazer.* Having completed my first objective, I strolled over to the ties to find an appropriate match. As I reached toward one with gray paisleys, an unfamiliar voice grabbed my attention.

"Is that Dave King?"

I turned around to see a tan man with an athletic build and slicked-back hair. His closemouthed grin seemed a little cocky, even as it creased the lines on his face. I had seen that look before under the bill of a baseball cap in sports page photos. "Coach Acheson?"

"What brings you to Younkers?" he asked.

"I'm just lookin' for some new clothes for Easter service. I'll be singing this Sunday—my first solo in front of the congregation."

"Ah, I see. Hey, great shirt you got there. I like it. I like it."

"Thanks." I shuffled the shirt from one hand to the other.

Acheson's face scrunched. "You still not playing ball for Eastridge?"

"No, sir. No baseball this summer."

"Well that's too bad. But it makes my job easier though." His grin returned.

"I read that Valley is favored to win the Metro this year."

"Yeah, I think we'll be okay. I'd feel a lot better if my boys would listen to me more. They think they know it all. If we're not careful, Eastridge could take us down. I'm kinda glad you're not playing, you know what I mean? After what you did to Galbraith a couple years ago. Man, that was a tough pill to swallow." Acheson talked fast, like a salesman.

I smiled faintly. "So how's he doing? Still with the White Sox organization?"

"No." His expression fell serious. "You didn't hear? Phil never made it out of Rookie League. That home run you hit really messed him up. Got inside his head. After that, his control was shot. The Sox just cut him loose. I hate to say it, but I think his baseball career is over. It's a shame. He had an atomic arm, that one."

Surprised, all I could say was, "Oh." I looked down. There was a brief moment of silence.

"Say, Dave, I know it's none of my business but … I mean, I can understand why you're not playing baseball. I know a little about Sal Kishman. Enough to understand that his coaching style may not be for everybody. But that football thing last fall, I never figured that one out. You guys were in the semis, ready to take state. And then, boom, you're gone."

"Yeah." My eyes focused on the shirt in my hand.

"The newspaper said, 'Dave King left for personal reasons.' I've been coaching for a long time. I know that personal reasons don't keep a star player out of a big game—unless that personal reason happens to be a death. The player's own death, that is."

I nodded. My mind flashed back to last November when I spent nearly the entire month ducking the press. The whole time my vocabulary consisted of little more than, "No comment."

"The rumor going around Valley was that you were busted for drugs," he said. "I never believed it myself. I can tell when a player is doping and you didn't fit the bill."

"I never took drugs. It was complicated. I can't say anything more."

"I don't mean to pry, Dave. That's your business. It just never made sense to me."

"Yeah." I glanced over at an elderly couple on the other side of the men's department.

"You're still going to play football at college, aren't you? With your talent, you must have received a full ride somewhere." His smile revealed two rows of unusually straight teeth.

"No, nothing. Not after, you know." I wanted to leave. "I'm going to Iowa in the fall. I'm gonna try to make the team as a walk-on."

"A walk-on? I thought I read months ago that you had a bunch of scholarship offers."

"Things changed after I missed our last game. Rumors spread about me. Coaches got concerned." I gripped the shirt tighter, causing the clear plastic to wrinkle audibly.

"Man. What a shame. What a shame. That's a tough break for you, kid." He looked away for a while before returning his gaze to me. "You ever consider playing baseball at Iowa? You could try to walk on next spring. That Kishman kid is there isn't he?"

"Yes, sir. John is on the team. But I haven't played baseball since I was a sophomore. I don't think I'd have much of a chance of cracking the Hawkeye roster."

Wheels seemed to start turning in Acheson's head. "Dave," he finally said, "here's an idea." His tone was like that of a father about to impart wisdom upon his son. "Why don't you come over and work out with my team? You couldn't play in any games, of course. But the practices would keep you sharp. Give you a better chance to make the team at Iowa next year."

My jaw dropped. "You mean practice with the Valley Tigers?"

"Yes. Why not? Can you make it over to our school by three-fifteen?"

"Um, yeah, I guess. But is that legal? Wouldn't somebody at Valley object? What would your players think?"

"I'm the coach. I run the baseball program. If I say Dave King is practicing with us, then that's the way it's going to be. Discussion over."

"Wow." Though it seemed screwball, his proposal did appeal to me. I liked the idea of resuscitating my baseball dreams. "Yeah, okay," I said, though still considering the ramifications. "That sounds great, Coach. Thanks for the opportunity."

"No problem." Acheson smiled. "I look forward to seeing you on the field. You'll be helping my team. It'll do those slackers some good to see a guy who really hustles. Gives a hundred percent all the time. That'll shake things up." He nodded. "Tell you what, I'll give my team a heads-up tomorrow. Then Wednesday, you show up for practice at three-fifteen. Okay?"

"Yes, sir. Three-fifteen, Wednesday."

My head buzzed all the way home. The thought that I might have a chance to play baseball again was too much to keep inside. I had to call John.

"You're gonna do what?" was his first response.

"I'm gonna start practicing with the Valley baseball team," I repeated. "Acheson invited me. It'll help me stay in shape for football tryouts this summer. And if that doesn't work out, maybe I can make the Iowa baseball team next spring. We could be teammates again!"

"Wow … that's just weird. Imagining you in one of those ugly orange uniforms."

"I won't be wearing a Tigers uniform. I'm only going to practice with them. No games."

The line was quiet for a while. "Acheson isn't pissed that you knocked his team out of the tournament two years ago?"

"Nah, I don't think so. He was really friendly. Since I'm not playing for Eastridge anymore, he doesn't think of me as an enemy."

John paused again. "Well, I guess it makes some sense. It's not like your own school is helping your athletic career. Be careful though. Some of those Valley players might want to take a shot at you, the hero who brought down the mighty Galbraith."

"Don't worry. I can take care of myself."

"It would be cool if we could be teammates again. And Iowa could sure use some of that Dave King enthusiasm."

"You guys are doing alright."

"Yeah, sorta. It's been a struggle to stay consistent. An up and down season, you know."

"You're smacking the ball though," I said. "What's your average now?"

"Uh, before the last game it was .353. If I pick it up I may be able to pass Stumpff for the team lead by the end of the season."

"Cool. So how's everything else going?"

"Can't complain, my man." John's voice perked up. "I'm still lovin' the college life. What can I say? Freedom agrees with me."

"When are you coming back?"

"Well, finals are the second week of May. But I'm thinking of staying here this summer. Get a job somewhere in Iowa City after baseball is over."

"Oh, I see." I made little attempt to mask the disappointment in my voice.

"Yeah, I know it sucks we won't get to hang out much this summer. But you'll be out here in August for football practice. That's not that far off. Then we'll have all year to rock and roll."

"I know. But I was looking forward to cruisin' around in the El Camino next month."

"I'd like to move back to Des Moines this summer, but I can't live under his roof again. It's just not gonna happen."

"Still not talking to him?"

"No. Not after our blowup last November. After that shit he pulled on you, I have nothing more to say to him. He doesn't pay my tuition. I don't owe him anything. I have no reason to have any contact with him whatsoever."

"So you won't be back at all this summer?"

"I'll try to make it back for a weekend or two. Visit you, Mom, and my brothers."

"What about Michelle and Mary?" I asked with a laugh.

"Mary I see enough of out here. But I guess I should check up on the dingbat. Make sure your ex is stayin' out of trouble. Your dad doesn't mind when I crash at your place?"

"Not at all. There used to be a small army living here. This summer it'll just be Ozzie, Dad, and me. We've got plenty of space. You can take Abby's old room if you don't mind the cooties."

"Thanks, man. That's cool. So Ozzie will be there, huh? Is he still, uh, Ozzie?"

"Yeah, pretty much."

"Delightful," John said with a dose of sarcasm.

"Tip of the iceberg, my friend. You've only seen the tip of the iceberg. I've been dealing with his twisted humor for eighteen years."

"Be glad you're not going to Iowa State with him."

"Amen Brother John. Oh, uh, speaking of religion …"

"We were speaking of religion?"

"No, but we are now."

"Fine, Preacher Dave. What do you want to discuss this time?"

"You still going to church with Dawn?"

"Yeah. Believe it or not, I am still going to church with her. I've even gone to a few Campus Crusade meetings too."

"Really?"

"Yeah. At the last Crusade meeting, they showed *The Cross and the Switchblade*. Cool flick."

"Great. Dawn must be getting through that thick skull of yours. Or maybe it's God who's speaking to you."

John laughed. "I don't know about God, but Dawn does plenty of talking."

"When I meet her, I'm gonna tell her you said that."

"Yes, please do. Speaking of Dawn, I'd better get going. I told her I'd pick her up at eight. I'll talk to you later this week. I gotta find out how those practices go with Valley."

"Sounds good. So where you taking her tonight?"

"We're gonna see *All the President's Men*. You seen it?"

"Yeah. Inga and I went last Friday. It's pretty good."

"Groovy. Alright man, I'll give you a buzz Thursday or Friday."

Tuesday morning started out like usual. But after a sleepy economics class, I spotted a sheet of notebook paper folded into a square at the bottom of my locker. Someone had apparently slid it through one of the door vents during first period. I pulled it open to read a message written in purple ink: "Meet me at the old farm house tonight. 10:30. We need to talk."

I read the note over and over. The handwriting was sloppy—most likely an attempt to conceal the writer's identity if the note fell into the wrong hands. But I knew who wrote it. Thinking back, I recalled a series of signs suggesting that we might be talking soon. *But why after dark at an abandoned ramshackle house several miles outside of town?* The secretive nature of this proposed rendezvous reminded me of Deep Throat's clandestine meetings with Woodward and Bernstein.

Other events happened at school on Tuesday. My mind, however, made little record of any of them. Driving home, I was finally able to recall sitting with Inga in the lunchroom. The images came back slowly—long red hair, pretty freckled face, bright blue eyes. She was a tennis player, an animated girl with a quirky personality whom I'd met at FCA. Her smile always struck me as a little weird though. Today it was a bit frightening. I think she got mad at me. I vaguely remember hearing, "I feel like I'm talking to a zombie, Dave." She was. And I definitely couldn't tell her why.

Shuffling food and drinks to diners at The Royal Court similarly couldn't wrest my attention from my upcoming encounter. Hopefully everybody got the stuff they ordered. Finally, at 10:10 p.m. I was clear to go. With a snort, my Mustang galloped out of the restaurant parking lot and raced down University Avenue. Then, speeding north on East 14th, I was soon beyond city limits. After turning onto one county road and then another, I drove for a few miles before passing a tottering corn crib that served as an unmarked signpost on the route to the farmhouse. I slowed to try to spot the gravel road that seemingly led to nowhere. I found it, and spent the next mile listening to small stones pelt the undercarriage of my car. I eventually reached my destination: an ominous two-story wooden corpse looming above the narrow road. There was no other car in sight.

I'd only been to this ancient dwelling once before—a couple months earlier with a few football buddies. Last winter the long-abandoned house became an after-dark curiosity to a select few in the athlete-cheerleader crowd at Eastridge. It was something like the haunted houses that kids go through at Halloween, only unsupervised and spookier. After exploring the dilapidated insides, however, most students lost interest. The stench of a rotting raccoon did nothing to encourage repeat visits. For the past several weeks, I hadn't heard of any classmates coming out to the house.

I backed off the gravel road onto the hard grassy strip that had once served as a driveway. I left the engine running in case I needed to make a quick getaway. After killing the headlights, I was enveloped in darkness. I cracked the windows. A fusty breeze blew in, adding to the unsettling effect of my surroundings.

I pressed the light button on my watch to check the time. It was 10:31. A hooting owl and the sound of brush rustling in the wind kept me on edge. *This is not a good idea. Kishman could be behind this. He could've lured you out here to finish you off once and for all. It would be weeks before anyone found your body.* I turned to check the dark structure towering behind my car. My hand gripped the gear stick.

Just then, a glow appeared off in the distance. The light brightened as the noise of tires crunching over gravel grew louder. A car pulled off the road and stopped; its front bumper was only inches away from mine. *I'm trapped!* I shielded my eyes from the blinding headlights, which fell dark an instant later. Still seeing spots as my eyes readjusted, I couldn't discern any recognizable details about the person who got out of the car and approached. Just as I remembered that my passenger door wasn't locked, it opened. A figure wearing a hooded sweatshirt slid into my car and pulled the door shut. My muscles tensed. I stared at the dark silhouette of the person's head, which was still concealed by a hood. After several seconds of silence, I flipped on the dome light. The hood came down.

"Boo!" Michelle said, giggling. I exhaled in relief. A few moments later, the levity faded from her face. "Thanks for meeting me here, Dave."

"Uh, yeah, sure. So, um, why exactly did we need to meet *here*?"

She fluffed her hair with both hands. "You're dating Inga. I'm dating Paul. Everybody knows our cars. We have to protect our reps, you know. And just imagine what Daddy would do if he knew I was talking to you. I didn't know where else we could go without being spotted."

"Oh."

"I know I could've called," she continued, reading my mind. "But I wanted to meet you face to face."

"I see." A whiff of perfume carried me back to the fall of '74. My senses leapt. I tried to remember if there was anything in the backseat.

"Dave," she said, taking a deep breath, "I've been doing a lot of thinking this semester. I mean, we're seniors now. We're gonna be out on our own soon. And I, um …" She turned away, gazing silently out the side window.

"Michelle?" I thought about putting a hand on her shoulder, but didn't. "Michelle?"

"It's just," she sputtered, turning to me with a serious expression. "It wasn't fair. What happened to you last fall. The way the coaches turned on you. The way the principal kicked you off the team." Even filled with concern, her amber eyes hypnotized me.

"I didn't know you felt so strongly about football."

"It's not football I feel strongly about," she snapped. "It's us, Dave. You and me. What happened to you with football reminded me of what happened to us. How we broke up. That wasn't fair either."

Unable to reply, I just stared at her. An army of ghouls could've burst out of the abandoned house and I wouldn't have noticed.

"I let Daddy pressure me. I was younger then. I don't feel like we had a fair chance. And now with high school almost over, I don't want to live my life always wondering what if."

"What if?"

"What if we were meant to be together and we let stupid stuff tear us apart."

The wheels spun in my head. Her words made me excited and dizzy. She wore a look that was somehow angelic and alluring at the same time. A burning hope ignited inside my heart—and somewhere else.

"I've thought about you, too," I said quietly. "But that was so long ago. And you're Paul's girlfriend now."

"Paul and me are just a high school thing. It's not like we're married."

"You two have been together for over a year."

"Not straight through," she said, swatting my arm. "We broke up for a while when he was all caught up with basketball."

"Well, anyway."

"Well, anyway, I'm thinking that we might be breaking up again. Soon. Maybe for good. He just doesn't seem to get me. And sometimes he acts like he owns me. There's only been one guy who I felt really understood me, who cared about the real me. And I let him get away."

My first impulse was to grab her and kiss her, but I fought it off. I knew there were other issues to consider. I looked away and ran both hands through my hair. "Michelle, this is …"

"I know. But I think we owe it to ourselves to think about this."

"Well, what do you want to do? I mean, you're going to prom with Paul and I'm going with Inga. That's less than three weeks away. Plans have been made."

"I've thought about that. We can go to prom with our dates like planned. But we'll play it cool. Won't do anything heavy with them, you know. Then we won't have any physical stuff with other people clouding our judgment."

My mind flashed red as I stared ahead at her barely-visible car. I had heard stories about what she'd already done with Paul. My fists clenched. Mental images of the two of them together made me want to chew barbed wire. I shut my eyes and inhaled. *You won't be doing anything like that with Inga anyway. You might as well agree to this. At least she won't be doing anything MORE with Paul.* "Yeah, okay," I replied. "We'll play it cool with our dates at prom. Then what?"

"Then we'll see how we feel about each other afterwards. Maybe we can go out as friends a few times. That will give us a chance to figure things out."

"Okay," my mouth replied before my mind had finished processing the idea.

"Great." She batted the toy rubber lion hanging from my rearview mirror.

"What about your dad?"

"You're going to Iowa in the fall, aren't you?"

"Yeah."

"So am I. We'll be a hundred miles from here. Daddy won't be able to interfere with us there." She flashed that sweet little smile that always killed me.

I smiled back. "It will be nice to get away from here."

She checked her watch. "Speaking of Daddy, I gotta go. He thinks I'm at Amanda's, doing homework." She looked straight into my eyes. "Dave, what we had was really special, and …" She grabbed my hands and held them through a prolonged gaze.

"Yeah, it was special." My pulse raced.

"Dave," she whispered.

"Yes."

"If you and Inga win king and queen at prom, I'm gonna dump a bucket of pig's blood over both your heads."

"Huh?" My eyes widened. The sweet smile remained frozen on her face. "Why would you say that?" I asked. "Where did you … oh, you're still into those creepy slasher novels, aren't you? Is that where that came from?"

"Yes, nerd." She giggled. "The book with the pig's blood may have been written by one of your relatives. Do you have a crazy cousin named Stephen?" She brushed the back of her fingers across my cheek.

"Uh." Her touch evaporated my ability to answer that last question.

"Okay, I gotta go." She hopped out and glided to her car. The blinding headlights returned as she backed out onto the road. After her taillights disappeared in the distance, I let my car creep forward onto the gravel. My Mustang then rolled away from the ancient farmhouse that now had another secret to keep.

Wednesday afternoon's practice at Valley was promising. It felt good to toss the ball around again, and none of Acheson's players seemed to object to my presence. Racing home afterwards, I had just enough time for a quick shower and a bite to eat, before hopping back in the car to drive to my sister's house.

"You need a haircut," Zoe said, opening the door. "Anthony's downstairs with his brothers. They're playing pool with Jay and Jerry." She slipped into the kitchen while I entered the living room. Abby sat on the sofa holding a half-full glass of iced tea.

"So your husband's hustling our nephews out of their allowance money, huh?"

"No," she said. "Jerry sucks at pool. It's Zoe's future husband who's doing the hustling."

"I heard that," Zoe yelled from the kitchen. "You want any pop, Dave?"

"No thanks." I glanced over at the television. News anchor Paul Rhoades was reporting on the wave of unique patriotic gifts that citizens were sending to President Ford to celebrate the nation's 200th birthday.

A moment later, Zoe appeared with a tray of Girl Scout cookies, which she thrust under my chin. "Here. Have a cookie." After I took a shortbread, she set the tray on the coffee table and joined Abby on the sofa. "First off, Abigail," Zoe said, pointing at her sister, "Jay is not my future husband. We've only been seeing each other for three weeks. Second, if anybody's doing any hustling, it's Joe. You should see that kid play. He keeps asking me to take him to a pool hall to roll some marks. The boy scares me sometimes." She took a sip of tea.

"Yeah, Joe certainly is ambitious," I said. "It's hard to believe he's only twelve. He acts like he's in high school."

"Well, he's not," Zoe said. "They're all still in junior high. And they all look up to their Uncle Dave. You remember that." Her brow furrowed as Abby snickered.

"I've been taking Anthony to church with me."

"Yes, but don't forget about Joe and Asa. They're all competitive with each other. If one of them gets something, the other two want the same thing."

"I ask Joe and Asa to come to church with me too, but they don't want to go."

"They're younger than Anthony, and they're not into religion like he is. But you should do stuff with them too."

"I do."

"I know. But since you've been taking Anthony to church on Wednesdays and Sundays, the other two have gotten jealous."

"Sorry. I'll try to even things out. Maybe we can catch a movie this weekend. Lately, time has been scarce with homework, the restaurant, and Grandpa."

"He's not going to be able to stay at his house much longer, is he?" Zoe asked grimly.

"No, I don't think so. Dad and I have to go over there all the time. We're afraid to leave him alone for even a day anymore."

Both women looked down at their tea. "Has Dad said anything about a home?" Zoe asked.

"Yeah, he's checked out a few places. I think he's gonna move Grandpa sometime this summer. You know, before I go to college in the fall."

"Oh yeah," she said. "You'll be graduating next month, won't you? So where are you going? Iowa?"

"Yep. I'm gonna be a Hawkeye."

Abby groaned. Zoe smiled at her and looked back at me. "Too bad you're not going to Western Iowa or Nebraska. Then you'd be closer to the boys and me. Assuming I get that promotion to the Omaha office."

"That's right," I said, "you might be moving soon. Is that looking likely?"

"According to the company vice president, it is. If he's right, we'll be moving in August."

"And that just sucks," Abby said, setting down her empty glass. "My only sister is going to abandon me."

"Omaha's not that far," I said. "Only a couple hours from here."

Abby squinted at me through her tortoise-shell glasses. "And you," she said. "I'm not even talking to you. Going to Iowa. Ick! Everybody knows Iowa State is better. Why aren't you going there?"

"The Cyclone coaches were never much interested in me. Plus, John is at Iowa."

"And don't forget," Zoe added, "Ozzie's up at ISU. We need to protect Dave from his brother's corrupting influence." The three of us laughed.

At that point, we heard the Krieger boys bounding up the stairs. They tromped across the kitchen and stopped abruptly upon entering the living room.

"There they are!" I said. Their faces flush, they shuffled about.

"Jerry said Joe's a shark," Asa proclaimed.

"Shut up!" Joe retorted, shoving his younger brother.

"Boys behave," Zoe chided. "You ready to go Anthony?" He nodded.

"Joe, Asa, you guys are invited too," I offered. They both shook their heads and examined their socks. "Well, maybe next time," I said.

Anthony sat near the front door to put on his shoes.

"Has your church found a new pastor yet?" Zoe asked me, striding over to brush Anthony's mop hair into place with her hands. He rotated his head trying to get her to stop.

"Yes. Allen Thomas. He was installed three weeks ago." A deep pain returned as my mind flashed back to January when I received the shocking news about Pastor Samuels's heart attack. Three months after his passing, my grief had not abated.

"Good," Zoe said. "You like him?"

"Yes. He's a great preacher. Cares about people. That's what we need, since we're all still kinda hurting over losing Pastor Samuels."

A short time later, Anthony and I were out the door and on our way to Faith Community Church.

On the drive home after the service, Anthony jumped from one topic to the next. "Uncle D, I hafta write a term paper on who I think's gonna win the election this year. Do you know who it'll be?"

"Wow," I said. "That sounds like a tough assignment for eighth grade. The primaries aren't even over."

"I know! Do you think Carter's gonna win the Democrats?"

"Yeah, I think so. I kinda like him. He seems like a strong Christian."

"How about the Republicans? Think Reagan will beat Ford?"

"No. Not likely. It's pretty hard to take the nomination from a president."

"So who will win between Carter and Ford?"

"Got me," I said, raising a palm. "I'd just flip a coin and then write about the reasons why that guy could win."

"Yeah, I could do that," Anthony said, shifting in his seat. "Hey, think you could teach me to play the guitar?"

"Hmmm, that might be possible. What type of music do you like?"

"I dunno." He shrugged. "Anything but disco. That stuff sucks!"

I glanced over at his grinning face. "Such language from my cherubic nephew."

"Sorry."

"Well, you're right. Disco does indeed suck. Hope it doesn't catch on."

He laughed. "Oh, Uncle D, could you show me the baseball field at Eastridge? Since we're gonna be movin' to Omaha this summer, I'll never get to play there."

"I don't know Tony-O. It's after dark. Your mom's expecting you home soon."

"The dark makes it the perfect time. Nobody will see us. We don't hafta stay long. I just want to walk on the field where you played. Pleeeease." His round face radiated with hope.

"Alright, but not for very long."

"Yes!" he said, pumping his fist. He then started singing, "Uncle D is the coolest!"

At the next light, I turned south to head toward the school. A few minutes later I pulled into the lot near the Eastridge High baseball field. Distant street lights cast a faint illumination over the gravel. Exiting the Mustang, I noticed a vehicle at the far end of the dim lot. As we approached, my heart started pounding. It was Coach Kishman's black Oldsmobile. The driver's door was slightly ajar, but no one appeared to be inside.

"Somebody's here," Anthony said quietly.

"Yeah, maybe we better do this another time," I said. A distant moan drew our attention toward the baseball diamond. After standing frozen for a couple seconds, I started heading in that direction. Glass crunched under my loafers. On the ground were the fragmented remains of a Jack Daniel's bottle. With my nephew close behind, I advanced slowly to the field. A large shadowy mass was lying in the grass between the pitcher's mound and home plate. When we neared the chain-link fence, the image became clearer.

"Who's that?" Anthony whispered.

"Coach Kishman."

"You're kidding!"

"Shhh. Keep your voice down." I covered his mouth.

He backed away from my hand. "Uncle D, you've got him. After all he's done to you, this is your chance get him back."

I was still dumbfounded by the sight. "What are you talking about?"

"We can bring him down. I'll run over to that gas station down the street and call the newspaper and tell them to send over a photographer. Kishman's wasted face will be on the front page of *The Register* tomorrow. We can get him fired!"

"Anthony, no." I grabbed his shoulder. "This man has a family. He's the father of my best friend."

"But isn't he the reason you can't play football or baseball?"

"It's not our place to take revenge."

Anthony's face sank with dejection.

"It's up to God to handle whatever happened in the past," I continued. "Our job now is to help that man. Remember, we're supposed to love our enemies. We're supposed to forgive."

"Really? Even people like him?"

"You're a new Christian, Anthony. I know it's not easy to understand. But trust me, it's the right thing to do."

"Well, what are we supposed to do to help him?" he asked with annoyance.

"You wait here. I'm going to try to talk to him. Then we'll move him to my car if we can and take him home."

"Fine," Anthony said, crossing his arms.

I passed through an opening in the fence near the home team's bench and approached the prostrate giant. Face down, he still had on the old jersey and baseball pants he'd worn to practice several hours earlier. An empty whisky bottle lay in the grass a few feet from his head.

"Coach?"

He rolled over and tried to sit up. "Uhhh … who's there," came the gruff reply. His eyes scanned the surrounding dimness.

"Coach, it's Dave King."

"Youuuu," he hissed, directing his gaze at me. "You've come to rob me … you son of a bitch!" He slurred his words.

"No, Coach. I'm here to help you."

"Help me? … All you've ever tried to do is destroy me." He rolled onto his hands and knees.

"Coach. You were my hero. I have your baseball cards. When I was a boy, all I dreamed about was playing ball for you."

He pushed off the ground and staggered to his feet. "Horseshit! You hate me."

"No."

"I'll show you what Dave King did to me." He turned and stumbled onto the mound. With his back to me, he opened his fly and started urinating. "This is what Dave King did to my life," he shouted. "Pissed all over it!" As liquid smacked the dirt below, a dark stream rolled down the mound between his feet. After what seemed like at least a full minute, he zipped up and turned around to face me.

"I've always been loyal to you," I said. "I always busted my butt to please you. I did everything I could to help your team win. Nobody wanted you to win a championship more than me. After we won the title, I always told the reporters what a great coach you were."

He mumbled something incoherent while staggering forward off the mound. He dropped to his knees in the grass about five feet in front of me.

"Coach?"

"Didn't you ever wonder? … Didn't you ever wonder like the rest of them?"

"Wonder what, Coach?"

He breathed heavily. "Didn't you ever wonder what happened to the great Sal Kishman? … Why he never got it back?"

My mind scrambled to process what he was saying. "Got what back?"

"We all went to war," he said, staring into my eyes with a vacant look. "Then, we came back and everybody was a star again. Feller was still great. DiMaggio was great. That bastard Williams … great, great, great." He flung his arms up and then brought them down to steady himself. "But not Sal Kishman … he couldn't hit anything anymore. What's wrong Sal? Are you pressing? Did the war affect you? … Those son-of-a-bitch reporters." He bowed his head.

"Coach, maybe we should get you home."

He looked up, his tormented face streaked with tears. "I still hear his screams."

I couldn't speak for few seconds. "Whose screams?" I asked quietly.

"Okinawa … they hit us at night … Pete and me in a hole … the flares went up … Japs come at us yelling … mortar shells exploding … smoke all over … seemed like they were everywhere … a Jap dropped down on me … fought him hard … finally gutted him … I grabbed the BAR … couldn't see a damn thing … got turned around … saw four of 'em running at me … four dark shapes …" His words trailed off into broken sobs—sounds I never could have imagined coming from him.

"Coach." I knelt in front of him.

"I fired … cut right through 'em … they all dropped." His body shook. He pounded the ground with his fist and then looked up at me in horror, as if he were actually back on Okinawa. "They were ours! … *my* squad … Pete … didn't know 'til I heard him calling my name … begging me to help him … Japs kept coming … had to keep firing … lost track of Pete … heard his distant screams … finally pushed the Japs back … but he was dead … all four Marines dead … murdered by me." His sobs resumed. "I murdered my buddy."

"Coach, it wasn't your fault. You didn't—"

"It WAS my fault! … I should've known better … still heard his screams after the war … couldn't see straight … couldn't hit a damn baseball … wanted to end it … Anne came along … thought she could rescue me … tried to build a new life … kids … coaching … but I can never escape … the screams … Pete calling for me … begging me to help him." Still on his knees, Coach doubled over like someone had kicked him in the stomach. "I'm damned forever," he wailed.

Trying to overcome my shock, I took several deep breaths. "Coach, no matter what you've done, you can be forgiven. Christ died for all our sins, even the ones we think are the most terrible. You can be free of this guilt."

"I've heard that crap before," Kishman shot back with a derisive laugh. "It doesn't work. God left me a long time ago. I'm going to hell, where I belong."

"No, Coach. If you repent—"

"You think it's that easy, huh? … Repent and it all goes away." He fell onto his side. "It's NOT that easy for some of us."

"Dave?" a voice asked from behind me. Startled, I turned around to see Anthony. I'd forgotten he was there. "What are we gonna do? My mom's gonna wonder where I'm at."

"Help me. Let's get him up and try to move him to the car."

With great effort, Anthony and I lifted Kishman to his feet. The stench of alcohol nearly overwhelmed us. Coach mumbled and grunted as we walked him to the parking lot. When we passed a trash barrel, he leaned his head in and vomited. The splattering sounds echoed inside the metal drum. We finally maneuvered him into the passenger seat of my Mustang and buckled him in. After taking Anthony home, I continued on to the Kishman residence in Pleasant Hill.

Though horrified, Anne maintained a brave front. Boz helped me move his father into the house. After an arduous waltz, we finally guided Coach to the living room sofa. "Dave," Kishman whispered hoarsely as we laid him down. "I'm sorry for what I did to you. You didn't deserve it. You're a good man … a good man."

"You are too, Coach."

Anne thanked me and asked if I'd drive Boz out to the school so he could bring her husband's car back. Michelle stood nearby looking shell-shocked. Our eyes locked for a moment before I left with her brother.

Boz was quiet most of the ride back to Eastridge. "Dave," he said as we neared the school, "I didn't have anything to do with that football deal last November. I never testified against you. Dad asked me to, but I didn't do it."

"I didn't think you did, but thanks for telling me."

"Man, he is so messed up. Guess you're gonna have quite a story to tell everybody at school tomorrow."

"I'm not telling anybody."

"Really? After what he did to you?"

"This stays quiet. I told my nephew the same thing. Your dad deserves a second chance. I think he reached a turning point tonight. Maybe now that he's bottomed out, he'll get help and start dealing with his demons."

I dropped off Boz at his father's car. On the drive home, I prayed for Sal Kishman.

Chapter 9 – June 1976

“Michelle and I are getting married.”

“Oh, is that all?” John said. “I thought you had something important to tell me.”

“I’m serious.”

The ensuing silence made me wonder if the phone line had gone dead. “Really?” he finally asked.

“Yes, really.”

“How long have you two been back together? A month?”

“A little more than that.”

“I see. Have you set a date?”

“No. Actually, Michelle doesn’t know yet.”

“What do you mean? You haven’t even asked her?”

“No.”

Rapid-fire laughter burst through the phone. “You dog! You had me going there.”

“No, I’m not kidding about this. I’m going to ask her. Really.”

“You got a ring?” John asked, still chuckling.

“Yes.... Well, no. I don’t actually have it yet. I got one picked out at Joseph’s, but I’m still a couple hundred short. I should have it by the end of the month.”

“So you’re going to start college as a married man? How’s that gonna work?”

“I got it all figured out. We can get married in August—before the semester starts. Dad will help me with tuition and school expenses this fall. Then hopefully I’ll get a football scholarship. If not, maybe I can get a baseball scholarship next spring. And I’ll get a job at a restaurant in Iowa City to pay for our apartment. I got plenty of waitering experience, you know."

"Uh, yeah. So, come September you'll have a full schedule of classes, football practice, a job at a restaurant, and you'll be starting a marriage. Do you really know what you're getting yourself into?"

"Yes," I said defensively, "I can handle it."

"I guess we're not going to be roommates this fall, huh?"

"Yeah, I'm sorry about that. That's why I'm tellin' you now, so you'll have time to ask one of your teammates. But we'll still hang out. All the time."

"Well, okay," he said. "But marriage, Dave? Why are you in such a hurry to get hitched to the dingbat?"

"Here's the deal, John. Your sister is, um, really hot."

"Ugh. So you still have vision problems. A good pair of glasses will clear that up. Then you can drop all this marriage nonsense."

"Hush, John-boy. It's like this. I'm a Christian and I'm committed to not doing it before marriage. Know what I mean?"

"Okaaay."

"Yeah. And Michelle is … man, the other day she had on this halter top and these tight shorts. About knocked me out. When we're alone, I try to stop at second base. But it's killin' me. I'm going crazy—"

"Okay! Stop, please. I don't need any more of these filthy images in my head."

"So you understand what I'm saying?"

"Yeah, I guess. But Dave, this is marriage. You do know that's a lifetime thing?"

"Yes, I know that." With my free hand, I grabbed the long spring cord connecting the phone handset to the wall unit and started twirling it like a jump rope.

"Don't get me wrong," he said. "It would be great to have you as a brother-in-law and all that. But have you really thought this through, with something other than your—"

"Yes," I interrupted. "I've thought it through, over and over. I've prayed about it. I know what I'm doing."

"Well great then. Does my dad know that you and Michelle are so serious?"

"Yeah. He doesn't have a problem with us anymore. Things have changed since that night in April. I think he's getting better. He still doesn't say much to me though. And I'm not gonna ask if I can rejoin the baseball team. Don't want to push it."

"That's probably a good idea," John said in a serious tone.

"What? What's wrong? Is there something I should know?"

The line was silent for a few seconds. "Don't tell anybody this, Dave. Boz called me yesterday. Said he overheard Dad on the phone making an appointment to go see a medium."

"A medium? Why?"

"I guess he wants to talk to someone who's dead."

"I know what mediums claim to do. But who does your dad want to talk to?"

"I dunno. Maybe Pete. Maybe that Pastor Samuels from your church. Mom once told me that they were friends a long time ago. And Boz said he heard Dad asking the medium if it was possible to talk to deceased pastors."

"Oh. I remember one time Pastor Samuels telling me that he knew your dad way back when. He didn't say much else, but he gave the impression they had a falling out."

"So anyway, Dad may have made some progress overcoming his problems with the bottle, but I don't think he's got it all together yet."

"Well, um, that's not the best news."

"He called me earlier this morning."

"Who? Boz? I thought you said he called yesterday."

"Boz did call me yesterday. I'm talking about my dad. He called around seven this morning. Got me out of bed."

"Really?"

"Yeah. Said he wants to see me. Wants to talk."

"That's good, right? You gonna meet him?"

"I wasn't. All the crap he's pulled still pisses me off. But I know he's trying to change. And he said it was really important. He wants to see me as soon as possible. I figure I should go talk to him. Hear what he has to say. Maybe I can find out what's going on with this séance business."

"So you're coming back to Des Moines?" I asked hopefully.

"Yep. Tomorrow, late afternoon. Dad wants to go out for supper. I figure we might be talking for a while, so that could take up all of Friday night. But I was hoping you and me could hang out Saturday. Then I gotta get back here for work on Sunday."

"Cool! Yeah." I sat up in my chair at the kitchen table.

"You're free Saturday? You don't have baseball practice at Valley?"

"No. That ended last week. The Valley players told Acheson they didn't like having me around anymore. They were always cool to me on the field, but I guess they were complaining to their coach behind my back. Said I might me telling your dad about their signals and strategies. Some of the Valley administrators weren't too happy about my presence over there either."

"Oh well," he said. "You practicing with the Tigers was a little weird, you know."

"Yeah. But it was kinda fun to be on the field again. Reminded me how much I love baseball. Helped keep me in shape, too."

"When are you coming out here for football tryouts?"

"About six weeks. It's coming up. Hey, that reminds me. Guess who called yesterday?"

"Wolfman Jack, wantin' you to perform on *The Midnight Special*?"

"No, wise arse. It was Coach McNabb at Western Iowa. He said one of his incoming freshmen just got arrested for armed robbery. Gonna be going to prison instead of college this fall. So the coach has an available scholarship. He offered it to me."

"Wow!" John said. "That's great! Are you, uh …"

"No, I'm not. That did give me a lift, though. It's great to get an offer for a full ride at a Division I football program. But I'm gonna be a Hawkeye."

"Well, I'm glad you're comin' out here. But you'd better think about this. You don't want to miss out on a great opportunity. Thor's going to Western Iowa, isn't he?"

"Yep. He's got a shot at starting there as a freshman. But me, I got other plans. My best friend, my wife, my future is in Iowa City. I'm going to play football at Iowa as a walk-on this fall, and then, God willing, Coach Commings will offer me a scholarship."

"If he's smart he will. Hey man, I just noticed the time. I gotta get going."

"Meetin' Dawn?"

"No, work. Stocking, stocking, and more stocking. I won't be meeting Dawn 'til later this evening, after I'm off."

"Cool. So I'll see you Saturday?"

"Yeah, Saturday. I'll call you sometime in the morning. And I've got some news of my own to tell you when I get back."

"Really? You gettin' married too?"

"No, but it's pretty cool. You'll just have to wait."

"Aw, man. Alright. Goodbye, future brother-in-law."

"Goodbye, Dave."

I walked across the kitchen and hung up the phone. Turning around, I recoiled in horror. Leaning against the wall near the entryway was an unexpected presence.

"Hiiii Daaave," Ozzie sang. He wore a faded Black Sabbath T-shirt, ragged red sweatpants cut off at the knees, and an impish grin that extended almost completely around his head.

"Oh, no," I groaned. "I didn't know you were back there."

"You don't say."

"What are you doing up?" I glanced at the clock. "It's not even eleven yet."

"Thought I'd get up bright and early today. Something about birds and worms, you know."

"I wouldn't call ten-fifty bright and early.... So how much did you hear?"

"Oh, Dave, Dave, Dave. My beloved little brother. Let's just say you made my day. Maybe even my whole year."

"I don't want to hear it." I plopped into a chair at the kitchen table. "You wouldn't understand."

He scooted over to pat the top of my head. "What's not to understand, young one? You want to get laid, and because of your fruity religious beliefs you think you have to get married first."

"Ozzie, you weren't supposed to find out yet." My voice trailed off.

"Maybe not. But we can't stuff that genie back in the bottle, can we?" He tousled my hair before sliding over to the refrigerator. "You know, I was just thinkin' I needed to come up with a new nickname for you. After hearing you talk to Johnny-boy this morning, I figured it out. From now on, you're McMurphy. Ya know why?"

"Because I've flown over the cuckoo's nest," I said reluctantly.

"That's my boy!" He popped the cap off a bottle of Mountain Dew. "To be honest with you, McMurphy, I was gettin' worried that people might start thinkin' of me as the black sheep of the family. You know, with my crappy grades, long hair, and general lack of motivation to do anything work-related? But now, you've let me off the hook. In one fell swoop, you've surpassed all my screwups put together. Please let me be there when you tell the old man your big news."

"I'm not doing anything bad here. Dad will respect my decision."

"He's gonna fill his pants! He'll rant. He'll rave. He'll run around the house screaming, 'Why Dave, why? Why do you mock me, my idiot offspring?' Then he'll call the nice men in the white uniforms to come and take you away to Nurse Ratched."

I leaned back and looked up at the ceiling. "He will not. I've got it all planned out. I'm being responsible."

"You're being a friggin' lunatic, Dave! Less than a month after you escape the prison of high school, you decide to enter the prison of marriage. And you know, this sentence is going to last a helluva lot longer than your time at Eastridge."

"Michelle and I are happy, okay?"

He took a swig of pop. "You're a teenager gettin' hitched to a girl you didn't even knock up. Boys your age should only get married if there's a shotgun pressed into their backs." He ripped open a bag of potato chips and crammed a handful into his mouth.

"I'm an adult."

"No, you're eighteen," he said through his crunching. "And she's seventeen, right?"

"She'll be eighteen in August."

"And you've been dating for how long? A cool five minutes?"

"I know what's right for me." I pointed a thumb at my chest. "For us."

"You don't know shit about what's right for anybody. Man, you got your whole life ahead of you. They'll be plenty of chances to screw it up later." He shoveled in another load of chips.

"Ozzie, just drop it." I glared at him. "I don't need your advice."

"Oh, is that so? That's real nice, Dave. After everything I've done for you." He spread his arms out wide. "What am I to you? Some bit player in the grand drama that is your life? Whenever you've got something important going on, I'm supposed to shut up and stay out of the way. Right?"

His tone was just serious enough to create a twinge of guilt. "It's not like that," I said.

"Sure it is. You're about to make the biggest decision of your life, and do you ask Ozzie for advice? Nooooo. Can't do that. You even try to keep it a secret from him. Admit it, you think of me as an older sibling in one of those TV shows who takes a backseat the younger star. To you I'm Mary Ingalls, and you're Laura."

"Oh, please." I rested my head in my hands.

"Melissa Sue Anderson has a voice, damn it."

"Actually, I think you're more of a Nellie Oleson."

"Melissa ... Sue ... Anderson ... has ... a ... voice!" He punctuated each word with a wild gesticulation of his arms.

"Okay, Mary. Speak."

He paused to gather himself. "Forget it. You won't listen to reason. Go ahead and get married so your imaginary god won't punish you for gettin' a little action. Fine with me."

"It is fine," I said defiantly. "And I'm so thrilled to have your blessing."

He started making himself a peanut butter and jelly sandwich while I skimmed an article in the paper about the American Freedom Train's recent stop in Indiana. After a couple minutes he piped up again. "So Laura, where's our pa, Michael Landon?"

I paused to imagine our balding father with a full head of flowing brown hair. "He's over at Grandpa's." I drifted to another article while Ozzie devoured his sandwich. "What are you doing this afternoon?" I asked a while later.

"Headin' over to Back Door Tavern at two."

"Isn't that a little early to start drinking?"

"Of course not. But this time I'm not going there to drink. Randy's brother is meetin' me there. Got a couple of Kiss tickets he's gonna sell me."

"Kiss? I didn't know they were coming to town."

"They're not. They're in Kansas City on July 26th. The Wizard's goin' on a road trip to see his buddies Gene, Paul, Ace, and Peter." He stuck out his tongue and kicked his foot into the air.

"Sounds like a lovely evening."

"You betcha." He tore open a Ho-Ho wrapper. "Say, how come I never hear you playing any Kiss songs on your guitar?"

I chuckled. "'Detroit Rock City' just doesn't have the same punch on an acoustic."

"You could play 'Beth.'"

"Yeah, maybe," I said, turning to the comics page.

"Oh come on, man. You gotta start learning some Kiss songs. I could even get you some paint to cover your face. Tell me that wouldn't be an improvement. Plus, I think you and the band have similar religious views. I hear that Kiss stands for Kids in Satan's Service."

"Wow. Sounds great. Where do I sign up?"

"I'll bring you back a membership form from the concert." He walked away. A few seconds later, he returned to the kitchen. "I almost forgot, Dave," he said, standing behind me. "I never congratulated you on your impending nuptials." Before I could respond, he grabbed the elastic band on my underwear and yanked it up to the back collar of my shirt. I yelped as my Fruit of the Looms wedged high and tight.

"You are so dead," I said, pushing my chair out. But as I struggled to my feet, the pain of cotton lodged deep inside my rectum made rapid movement impossible. The cackling Ozzie scurried up the stairs. Fuming, I dropped my pants and began to extricate.

After the restaurant closed that evening, I slunk back into the kitchen at The Royal Court. Finding a stool near the apron bin, I kicked off my shoes and began rubbing my feet.

"What's wrong, bub?" Shane asked. "Feet hurt?" His voice, like the man himself, was thick and tough.

"Man, that was one brutal night. And this is a Thursday. Where'd everybody come from?"

"Don't knock it," he said, drying his hands with a towel. "That's money in the bank, my friend. Money to pay your wages."

"Yeah? So what you're saying is, Dad can afford to give me a raise now?"

"No, missy. That dough goes to me." He jabbed a sausage-like thumb into his expansive chest. "Since the old man had tonight off, we can assume all them folks was coming for MY cooking. Plus, baby needs a new pair of shoes."

"How is baby Jonny?"

"Just turned two. How do you think he is? The little monster gets into everything. I gotta come here for my sanity." He flung the towel into a bin.

"I bet Pam appreciates that."

"Eh, she deserves it. The kid gets all his bad traits from her."

"Uh-huh. I'm sure she would agree with that assessment."

"Damn right." He spun around to bark at two cooks who were racing wheeled garbage barrels around the salad-prep table. Shane started his lecture with, "Hey lunkheads!" and ended it with, "Now, quit lollygagging and get back to work. The sooner this place is clean, the sooner we're outta here." He offered a similar encouragement to the dishwashers.

I put my shoes on. Shane turned back to me, his face pink from yelling and a night of toil in the steamy kitchen. "Pam knows I love the little crap master. I keep tellin' her we gotta get busy and have two more so I can start a baby juggling act."

I laughed. "Well, you do get good elevation on your Jonny tosses."

"The kid loves to fly. I think he's gonna be an astronaut some—"

A scream from the front of the restaurant cut him off. He burst though the swinging metal doors into the dining room. I was right behind him. "What the hell?" he yelled across the empty room. Two waitresses were behind the cash register. As we advanced, I could see that one of them was consoling the other.

"We got robbed," Tania said. She had her arm around Heidi, who was crying. "A guy just held a knife to Heidi's throat and cleaned us out."

"What?" Shane demanded. "What did he look like?"

"He had a ski mask on. Dave, where were you?" Tania asked me. "You should've been out here to help us. We could've been killed."

Dumbfounded, I could not think of anything to say. "Damn it!" Shane yelled. He punched a wall, before turning back to the girls. "Did you see what he was driving?"

"No!" Tania replied indignantly. "I'm going out there to get stabbed."

"I–I didn't hear a car take off," Heidi stammered, wiping tears from her face.

"Really? Let's go." My brother grabbed my shirt and yanked me toward the front doors. I felt like I'd been hitched to a tow truck. We stormed out into the parking lot. Heads spinning in all directions, we made our way to the curb. "There!" He pointed down Hubbell Avenue. About three blocks distant, on the other side of the street, was a man walking away at a brisk pace. When he passed under a streetlight, it looked like he was carrying a bag. "You're fast, get 'em," Shane said, pushing me forward. "Keep him busy 'til I can catch up."

Without thinking, I darted across the street. My feet throbbed as my Dexters pounded the pavement. Though not designed as running footwear, at least they weren't the platform shoes that Adam had tried to convince all the waiters to wear. After crossing the railroad tracks I hit my stride and was rapidly covering ground. Then I started thinking. *What if this guy isn't the robber? What if he is? Didn't Tania say he had a knife?* I prayed for strength and protection.

After I'd closed the gap to about a block, the man heard the clopping of my shoes and looked back at me. He immediately broke into a run. Feeling the night breeze against my face, I raced after my quarry. He wore a dark loose-fitting shirt and striped bell-bottomed pants. His stride seemed uneven at times.

There was a bend in the road at 18th Street, where Hubbell turns into Grand Avenue. The man continued running west, toward downtown. A honking car screeched to a halt to avoid hitting him as he crossed 17th Street. After veering around that same car, I had narrowed his lead to less than twenty feet. Adrenaline surged, driving away the pain and fatigue I should have been feeling after an extended sprint and a night of waitering. The man slowed to a jog after crossing 16th Street. Near the entrance to the adult movie theater at 1536 Grand, he stopped, dropped the duffel bag, and spun around. A glint flashed off the blade in his right hand. I tried to slow down but my momentum carried me towards him. Swerving to the side as he lunged at me, I threw up my arms and sucked in my stomach. The sweeping blade narrowly missed catching my shirt as I flew by.

Planting my feet on the concrete, I whirled around, ready for combat in the dimly lit sidewalk arena. Both of us crouching, we sized each other up like gladiators at the Colosseum in Rome. His face was dark. His hair darker. The charcoal eyes trained on me were bloodshot and foreboding. "Come on boy, come on," he said though heavy breaths. The blade in front of him waved ominously back and forth. Deciding not to wait for the inevitable charge, I faked a move to the right and then shifted left, knocking his arm away and planting a fist into his ribs. He groaned and stepped back, flailing wildly with the knife to keep me from advancing.

"You're dead now, boy," he hissed. We resumed our face-off, each moving sideways in a slow circle. Finally, he lunged at me with the blade. Sidestepping, I grabbed his wrist and forearm with both hands. He then nailed me in the face with a stinging left jab. The blow shook my senses and filled my mouth with the taste of blood. I nonetheless maintained my grip. He hit me again, though I managed to tilt my head to limit the punch to a glancing blow. Bending my knees and leaning back for leverage, I rotated my body to swing him around in a semicircle. After building up speed, I released his wrist and forearm to fling him against the theater wall. His face smacked into a busty poster promoting the currently featured film. Though staggered, he hung onto the knife, which he swung blindly as he turned around.

After the blade swept past, I stepped forward to throw a right hook. He ducked back from the blow and then lunged at my thigh. I jumped to the side just in time to avoid getting stabbed. I fired a left jab that caught him squarely on the jaw. He stumbled back a couple steps, but maintained his balance and his grip on the knife. Our eyes locked as we faced off for another round.

My adversary then suddenly flew sideways and skidded across the sidewalk. Shane had rumbled in and nailed him with a sledgehammer blow backed by every ounce of his considerable girth. The man's knife sailed through the air and bounced across the pavement with a series of dull clacks. Still in his white cook's jacket, Shane stood over the motionless robber crumpled on the ground. My brother nudged him with a foot. No movement. I retrieved the duffel bag, unzipped it, and looked inside.

"The money's here," I said.

"Good," Shane replied, still trying to catch his breath. His eyes remained focused on the unconscious man below. "Good job, Dave." He clapped my shoulder.

The rest of the evening included a slow walk back to The Royal Court, a conversation with two police officers, and a lecture from Dad, who had raced up to the restaurant after Tania had called him. I finally got home about twelve-thirty. As I lay on the sofa holding an ice pack to my mouth, Dad entered the living room and dropped a stack of paper-clipped bills on the coffee table. "That's two hundred and fifty dollars," he said. "You've earned a bonus. And not for what you did tonight. Like I said earlier, that was reckless, dangerous, and unnecessary." His stern look then softened. "The money is to show my appreciation for all your hard work the past three years. You're a good waiter. Now you'll have some extra cash for when you go off to college."

"Thanks, Dad." Crawling into bed a half hour later, I was still unaware that I had just reached my primary financial goal.

Friday morning, I woke up fully aware of that which I did not realize the night before. So powerful was my excitement, the previous evening's battle seemed like a nearly-forgotten movie I'd watched ten years ago. Less than an hour after getting out of bed, I was in the car. After a stop at the bank, I headed downtown. On this occasion, speed limits did little to restrain the gallop of my Mustang. The clerks at Joseph's Jewelers were happy to see me. I made the purchase. They wished me luck.

Back home, I hid the ring in a shoebox full of baseball cards under my bed. I chuckled at the thought that the player on one of the cards was now guarding the ring that would soon be on his daughter's finger. Whenever I returned to my room throughout the day—after lunch, after visiting Grandpa, after playing basketball with Ozzie—I retrieved the small beige ring box from its hiding place. Each time I popped open the lid, a one-half carat diamond gleamed back at me in all its glory. I held it up to the light and tilted it at different angles. The rock sparkled as if it contained a constellation of tiny stars. "That one's got a lot of fire," the salesman told me. "It's going to dazzle that special girl of yours."

A little after five, I left to go pick up Michelle for our date. I had relocated the ring box to the glove compartment under a stack of eight tracks. I wasn't sure if tonight would be THE night, but wanted to have the ring close by just in case the time and place seemed right.

I pulled into the Kishman driveway and parked next to the black Oldsmobile. It was surprising that Coach's car was there and the El Camino was not. I figured that Coach would have taken his vehicle when he and John went out. *It doesn't matter which car they took. The important thing is that John and his dad are now talking to each other again.*

I walked up to the house and rang the doorbell. Boz answered with an expression that changed everything. I had seen the look before. Not from him, but from Dad years ago when he found out that Nate had died. And then a few months later when Ray had died. The dazed countenance. The shattered aspect. The red eyes radiating hurt and disbelief. Without a word, Boz turned and moved back into the living room.

A cold fear swept through me. *No, this is not what you think.* Fighting to remain calm, I stepped into the house. Anne and Michelle sat huddled on the couch. A faded memory of Zoe and Abby sitting that same way flashed by. The sound of my girlfriend and her mother crying spawned a thick dreadful pain. They both looked up at me with anguished faces, but were unable to speak any words.

"The highway patrol just left," Boz said in a hollow voice.

I started to shake, terrified at what he would say next.

"John was in an accident on the interstate. He died on the way to the hospital."

I felt like I'd been dragged under water and couldn't breathe. As my soul recoiled, Boz described the details of what had happened. I processed the information in bits and pieces. The words "never regained consciousness" replayed over and over in my head.

No! It's not true. They got the wrong person. It wasn't John. It can't be. I dropped to the floor and buried my face in my hands.

The sound of a car starting in the driveway jolted me out of my desperate struggle to will this all away. Anne stepped over to the window. "Sal."

"Where's he going?" Boz asked her.

"I don't know." She turned to me. "After the officers told us the news, Sal left the room. He didn't say a word. I'm afraid he …" She stopped herself after a quick glance at Michelle. Desperation filled Anne's eyes.

Pushing away the grief, I shot to my feet. "I'll go after him."

"I'll go too," Boz said.

"No!" Anne said, embracing her son. "I want you here. Dave will bring him back. Right?"

I nodded. An instant later I was starting my car. The Oldsmobile was not in sight when I hit the road, but I had an idea where Coach was going. Tires squealing, I weaved through traffic and floored it as yellow lights turned red. The Mustang left several honking horns and angry shouts in its wake. As my car raced, so too did my mind, trying to stay ahead of the dark realization that pursued me.

There were a handful of vehicles in the parking lots near the Eastridge High ball fields. Most were in the lot nearest the softball diamond. A game was scheduled to be played there later in the evening. I slowed down to scan the baseball field. Seeing nothing, I continued on toward the parking lot at the rear of the school building. What I saw there brought relief and fear. The Oldsmobile sat alone. I pulled up next to the empty car.

The school's doors would normally have been locked at this time of day during the summer. I hoped that Coach had forgotten to relock the door behind him. He did. Ahead of me was the long hallway that led past the entrances to the gymnasium and the swimming pool. I sprinted down the corridor, which ended in a T intersection with another hallway. Taking a left, I hurried toward the coaches' offices. I knocked on Kishman's door. No response. I twisted the knob but it was locked. No light glowed behind the opaque frosted window in the door. I looked both ways down the hall for any signs that Coach had gone somewhere else in the building. A stabbing dread reminded me that there might not be much time. I made my decision.

After taking two steps back, I threw my full weight into a kick that struck near the knob. With a sharp crack, the door broke free of the latch and swung open. The pale hallway light did little to illuminate the dark office. My eyes staring straight ahead, I could barely make out the silhouette of a large figure behind the desk. My trepidation increased as I remembered the last time I was in this room.

"Coach?" No answer. "Coach, your family is worried about you. I'm going to turn on the light, okay?" With my eyes fixed on the dark shape in front of me, my hand groped the wall to locate the switch. When the light came on, I blinked at the sudden brightness. Kishman was sitting in his chair, his head tilted back as if he were studying something on the ceiling. I stepped forward.

"Coach, I …" My brain processed the details. The hazy white smoke. The unfamiliar acrid smell. The blood trickling from the corner of Coach's mouth. The pistol clutched in his left hand. And the grotesque red halo splattered on the wall above his head.

My senses overwhelmed, I staggered back out of the office. After stumbling several paces down the hallway, I knelt down and vomited. My breaths came out in halting, painful gasps. The long corridor started rotating around me. Barely remaining conscious, I clutched the wall and struggled toward the exit.

The bright sunlight outside hurt my eyes. Dropping down to the pavement, I leaned against the side of my car. There I sat coughing and crying—and fighting to comprehend the incomprehensible.

I did not want to talk to anyone the next few days, not even Michelle. My mind could not focus on anything but John. Thoughts of him rolled in like waves. Sometimes I'd even expect him to call or stop by. But then, moments later, reality would come crashing down. A torturous ache settled upon my soul.

The double funeral was Tuesday at Merle Hay Funeral Home. Anne asked if I would speak during the service. I agreed, not knowing if I could get through even a single sentence. The funeral home was packed with Kishman's relatives, old Phillies teammates, veterans who had served with him in the Marines, former players he had coached, and teachers and administrators from school. More than a hundred of John's friends from Eastridge and Iowa were also there. When the time came, I took the podium.

"I became a fan of Sal Kishman when I was a young boy first learning about the game of baseball. As a Little Leaguer I dreamed of playing for him on that big field at Eastridge High. He seemed larger than life. A mighty warrior on the diamond. I'll always remember when he promoted me to his varsity team. It was one of the happiest days of my life.

"Coach led his teams with a fire and determination that spread to those of us who were blessed to play for him. He inspired us to greatness. In teaching us how to excel on the baseball field, he instilled a discipline in us that impacted every area of our lives. Though a mighty man has fallen, Coach Kishman will live on in all his former players."

Fighting to maintain composure, I was careful to avoid meeting anyone's eyes in the crowd. Tightening my grip on the podium, I continued speaking. "John Kishman reflected all the best qualities of his father. John was a great athlete and a selfless teammate. He made everyone around him better. When faced with a battle, on or off the field, he had the courage of a lion. And yet, his sense of humor never failed to crack me up. John was my best friend. He was always in my corner, no matter what.

"I could tell you a hundred stories about John, but there is one that stands out to me. Last August, before the start of my senior year, he knew I was trying to make starting quarterback at Eastridge. It was a Sunday—the day he had to leave for college. It was over a hundred degrees outside. Everyone with an ounce of sanity was inside in the air conditioning. But John dragged me over to the park to work on passing drills. He ran route after route while

I threw the ball to him. I thought I was suffering but it was fifty times worse for him running those routes over and over in the blazing sun. And if you know John, you know he ran hard every time. I begged him to stop, but he kept running the routes until I got the passes right. He put himself through hours of torture, just to help me get better. That was John. That's who he was. My friend forever."

After laying John's glove on his casket, I sat in a daze through the rest of the funeral. Following the graveside service, I drove alone to a spot along the Des Moines River outside town. My leather Bible lay in the passenger seat. The diamond ring was still in the glove compartment. I grabbed both and walked to a small grassy area down by the bank that was almost completely surrounded by trees. Before my world turned upside down, I had been thinking of proposing to Michelle at this spot. Sitting in the grass, I popped open the lid to the small ring box and watched the stone sparkle in the sunlight. After a few minutes, I closed the box and set it down beside me.

I tried to pray, but felt alone and unheard. I opened the Bible and turned to passages about eternal life, hope, victory, and faith. My mind wandered. No matter which verses I tried to read, I could not focus. The words all jumbled together. They did not make sense. Not against the dark circumstances that now surrounded me. Efforts to keep reading just led to frustration and eventually, anger.

I slammed the book shut and looked up at the sky. "It wasn't enough to take Mom and two of my brothers, was it?" I said aloud. "What did I do? Tell me, what did I do?" The white clouds floating across the cerulean sky offered no response. I shot to my feet, drew the Bible into my body like a Frisbee, and flung it out over the river. The book rotated round and round through the air before a gust of wind caused it to open and hover for an instant. Then, pages flapping wildly, it dropped into the water with a deep splash.

Tears crawled down each of my cheeks. I brushed them off and glanced at the ring box in the grass below. I grabbed it and looked up at the sky again. "Who's next? Who are you going to take from me tomorrow?" I squeezed the soft box so tightly, pain shot through my hand. "Is it Michelle?" In a sudden motion I hurled the box out over the river. It sailed through the air in a high arc before hitting the surface of the water. "Is that what you wanted?" I yelled at the sky. "Now are you happy?"

Back home in my room, I noticed a University of Iowa schedule of classes on my desk. I gripped the booklet with both hands and ripped it in half. After sitting on my bed and staring out the window for what could have been an hour or more, I started rummaging through the papers scattered across my desk. Finding the sheet I was looking for, I dialed a phone number that I'd written at the bottom. After a brief conversation with a secretary, my call was transferred to the person who had given me the number a week earlier.

"Coach McNabb, this is Dave King. If that scholarship offer still stands, I'd like to go to Western Iowa this fall."

Chapter 10 – March 1977

The clock mercifully reached 2:00 p.m. Along with the other eighty-plus prisoners of Political Science 155, I filed out of the classroom, down the stone steps of Voorhis Hall, and into the refreshing spring air. Walking among the masses, I spotted the ancient oak in central campus unoccupied. Heeding its call, I veered off the sidewalk and ambled toward the tree. Sitting against its large trunk, I watched the droves of students passing by. Robins chirped from the branches above. After a couple minutes, I started to fade. I had forced my brain to stay alert for the past hour and now it demanded a reward. My heavy eyelids fell.

"The King is asleep." A deep voice jolted me from a nascent dream. "Awaken, O monarch." My eyes opened to a squint. A mountainous presence in a green letter jacket stood before me. At the top of the mountain was a grin.

"Hey, Thor," I said. "What's going on?"

"Nothing much. Haven't talked to you in a while. What you been up to?"

"Eh, you know. Weights. Classes. The usual."

"Cool. You mind if I park here for a while?" He gestured at the spot beside me. I grabbed my backpack and slung it a few feet away. He lowered himself to the ground and leaned back against the tree. "Spring practice is just a week away," he said. "Ain't that grand?"

"Grand isn't quite the word I'd use."

"Aw, come on, King. It's football! We haven't played in four months. Aren't you ready to get back into the action again?"

"Action? Easy for you to say. You played every game last season. Even started the last three. All I did every Saturday was stand on the sideline."

"You held for some PATs after Seitzer got hurt. And you ran the scout team offense each week. Your contributions there were huge."

"Oh boy, wasn't that exciting? The glory of being a third-string quarterback. I didn't take one snap in a real game. Zero."

A Frisbee landed a few feet in front of us. A skinny frat boy in a short-sleeved yellow sweatshirt and white painter's pants ran over to retrieve it. "Hey, it's The Hammer!" he said, grinning at Thor. He then looked at me. "Hey, it's uh … hey man!" He flung the Frisbee in the direction of a distant buddy and darted away.

"See," I said. "That's exactly what I'm talkin' about."

"Your time will come, King. You're part of a big dog football program. You gotta pay your dues and climb the ladder. We got a great quarterback here. You can learn a lot from Patton this fall. Then he'll be gone and you'll be leading the offense our junior year. Dave King, starting QB for the University of Western Iowa Falcons!" He backhanded my chest.

"What about Henderson? He's got *two* years left. He'll be starting quarterback when I'm a junior. I'll have to be his backup."

"Nah, I don't think so. If you work your butt off next season, you'll pass him. You're the better player. Shoot, you're already one of the best natural athletes on the team. That's why you need to get excited about spring practice. This is your time to dazzle the coaches with your hustle and on-field instincts." His voice danced with enthusiasm. "Come on man, you got to start preparing for the awesome future you're going to have here."

"Shit, like that's gonna happen." Glancing over at Thor, I saw a veiled look of disappointment. We were both quiet for a while.

"So," he finally said, "I've been going to this cool church in town. You might want to check it out. I think you'd like it. Got great music."

I tensed. *Oh crap. Here we go again.* "I'll think about it."

"Hey, you heard of BSU?"

"Is that a Baptist group or something?" I asked, watching the campus traffic subside.

"Baptist Student Union. It's an awesome Christian group. Meets over at Noble Hall on Thursday nights. There's music and food. The leaders are really cool. They also got these Bible studies that students host. Real laid-back fellowship. The one I go to meets tonight at Chuck Gaston's room. Wanna go?"

"Nah, sorry. My roommate Perry and me are hittin' the town tonight."

"Oh, gotcha," he said in a subdued tone. I checked my watch and tried to think of a parting comment. Before I could speak, he asked me another question. "So, uh, you and that volleyball player still going together?"

I tensed again, wondering how much he knew. "Yeah, Amy. We're still dating."

"Pretty girl. Tall."

"Yeah, six feet. I'm not used to going out with girls who are about as tall as me."

Thor chuckled and scratched his crew cut. "Dave, you doin' alright?"

Crud! I should have gotten out of here when I had the chance. "Yeah. Of course I am. Why wouldn't I be?"

"Well, it just um … it seems like you've changed a lot since high school."

"A lot of dudes change when they get to college. Change is good."

"Sometimes. But it can also be bad."

"What's that supposed to mean?"

He shifted his body to face me. "I know you went through a lot last summer. What happened to John and Coach Kishman shook me up too. But I'm worried it started you down a different path. One that—"

"You don't need to worry about me," I said with irritation.

"You're a brother in the faith. I'm just concerned about you. In high school you were on fire for God. You were a leader. On and off the field. And now …"

"And now, what?" I stood. "You don't approve of me now because I don't do everything you do? I don't have time for all that stuff anymore."

"I think you're struggling." He squinted his pudgy face. "You don't want to go to church or be around other believers. It's like you're running from God. Like maybe you blame him for what happened."

"Thor, save it!" I jabbed a finger down at him. "I'm an adult. I don't need some fat ass Sunday School teacher checking up on me all the time. Just mind your own damn business, alright?" On the football field, Thor could flatten monstrous defensive linemen. In pads and a helmet, he seemed invincible. My last statement, however, really seemed to wound him. A childlike sadness glistened in the eyes of the 260-pound man. I grabbed my backpack and stalked away.

After about ten paces, my conscience flickered. *Thor did not deserve that.* I stopped. A few seconds later, I walked back. The hurt expression remained frozen on his face. "Thor, I'm sorry. I didn't mean that." I looked off in the distance at nothing in particular. "Last year was shit, you know. Pastor Samuels died. Then I lost my best friend. And Coach, that image is still burned into my head." My body shuddered. "Michelle and me broke up. Before everything happened, I was about to ask her to marry me."

"Really?" Surprise replaced the hurt in his eyes.

"Yeah. Even had a ring." I glanced up at the bell tower. "Then I get out here for football and I'm treated like the water boy. Got pounded on the scout team and rode the bench all season. And my jackass advisor signed me into a bunch of puff jock courses. Had to fight just to get a decent schedule. Of course, when I finally did get into some good classes, I immediately fell behind. Having to learn a different opponent's offense every week didn't help. So I barely survived the fall semester with a C average. This semester, I'll be lucky to get that."

"Yeah." He nodded. "My grades aren't much better."

"Back in Des Moines, my grandpa had to go into a nursing home." I paused to maintain composure. "My dad had his dog put to sleep. Didn't even ask me. I loved that stupid dog. I would have found him a home."

"I'm sorry, man."

My chest heaved with a substantial sigh. "I appreciate your concern for me, but I can't go back to church and all that stuff. It would just remind me of high school. Things I'd rather forget."

"You've gone through a rough stretch." He shifted his body to get up. I held out a hand to help hoist him to his feet. "I can dig that you don't want to go back to church," he said. "But you know God is on your side. Always has been. Even through all that stuff last year. Gotta keep walking with him and he'll lead you out of the valley. Remember, the Lord's got some big dog plans for you." He woofed, though with less exuberance than when in uniform.

I nodded, though not really accepting his words. "Yeah."

"Hey, you let me know if want to hang out. Playing cards, studying, a movie, whatever. You know where I live. Just one floor above you. Stop by anytime."

"Thanks." We parted with a handshake. As I trudged to my dorm, painful memories from the past year lingered in my head. Increasing my pace, I tried to think of something else.

My Monday evening dining experience at the training table included the usual enlightened conversation with Perry and a half-dozen other freshman football players. Ozzie would have been pleased with the etiquette and discourse of my dinner companions. I took in hearty amounts of meatloaf and mashed potatoes to prepare myself for what was to follow later. Just as we all returned to our dorm floor, the payphone in the hall started ringing. Perry answered and said it was for me. Upon taking the phone, I was greeted with an adolescent rendition of "Happy Birthday to You" from my three Krieger nephews. Anthony's voice cracked like Peter Brady's. Each boy tried to ham it up more than the others as they neared the end of the song.

"Great job, guys," I said after they had finished. "Thank you. I'm touched. Huey, Dewey, and Louie couldn't have sung it any better." Boyish laughter and a few cracks about me being Donald Duck followed. After some unintelligible comments, I heard rustling and Zoe asking for the phone.

"Hello," she said. "Happy Birthday."

"Thanks, Z. Your boys are sounding lovely."

"Aren't they, though? It was a miracle to get them to sit still long enough for one song."

"I bet."

"So birthday boy, do you have big plans for tonight?"

"Some of the guys are taking me out on the town. They're talkin' like it's gonna be some grandiose evening. But knowing them we'll just be sittin' around Mayfair Club or some other bar, drinking beers and looking at each other. Hopefully we won't stay out too late. I got a midterm tomorrow."

"In what?"

"Astronomy. I'm not ready for it. I really should stay in and study, but that won't fly with the crew."

"Astronomy? Sounds exciting."

"I don't know about that, but it fills a science requirement."

"Do you have a major yet?"

"Just declared at the start of this semester. History."

"History?" She chuckled. "So you're planning to keep working as a waiter after you graduate. That's sweet. Dad will appreciate that."

"Very funny, beloved sister."

"Damn right, I'm beloved. After all I've done for you. Speaking of my many kindnesses, I need to ask you something. The boys and I aren't going to make it back to Des Moines for Easter. So I'm going to have dinner here. Would you like to join us or are you going home that weekend?"

"I won't be going home that weekend. Don't have that much time. So, yeah, I could pop over to your place for Easter dinner. Sounds great."

"Good. The boys keep asking me why you don't visit more often. We're not that far, you know. How long does it take to get here? Twenty minutes?"

"Yeah, I know, I know. It's been crazy here with classes, weight training, and a bunch of other crap."

"Well, I knew it couldn't have been the dazzling cultural wonders of Council Bluffs."

"Hey now, don't make fun of the Bluffs. It may not be a bustling metropolis like your precious Omaha, but the town has character. I like it here."

"Whatever you say, little Davey."

"Can't call me that anymore, Z. As of today, I'm nineteen."

She sighed. "That can't be right. Seems like just last week I was helping Mom change your stinky diapers. Now I feel old."

"Oh, come on. What are you? Thirty-four? That's not that old."

"Gee, thanks. Actually, some days these kids make me feel like I'm sixty-four. Of course, I still tell people I'm twenty-nine." She then covered the phone and yelled something. "I should go. I think Anthony and Joe are trying to shave Asa's head. It's always something with these animals." I heard laughing and shouting in the background.

"Okay. Thanks for calling and for the invite. See you at Easter."

"Yeah, sure. Have fun tonight. But not too much fun."

After hanging up, I headed to my room and started reading my astronomy book. While I was on the phone, Perry had gone to the floor lounge to play foosball. I estimated that I had an hour, maybe two, to study—a woefully short amount of time to cram six weeks of galaxy information into my head. Looking for any advantage, logical or not, I ate a Milky Way. Though it didn't increase my knowledge of the subject matter in any appreciable way, it tasted good. Around eight o'clock, Perry burst into the room with a posse of six rowdy freshman behind him. "Alright, Einstein," he said, shutting my book. "Time to celebrate you becoming an old man. Grab your walker and let's go." He and a cornerback named Ted pulled me up and hustled me out the door.

We stumbled back to the dorm a little after 3:00 a.m. I did not remember crawling up into my lofted bed, but somehow I made it there. My alarm, which I had fortunately remembered to set before going out, went off at 9:00. Upon awakening, a jackhammer started boring into my skull. The noisy pounding continued as I swayed across campus to my 9:30 Astro exam. After exiting the science hall ninety minutes later, I could count on one hand the number of answers I gave that were definitely correct.

I had two more exams the following day. Though not at all confident in my performance on either, I was upbeat heading back to the dorm. My midterms were finally over. So were Amy's. And we were getting together that night. Perry's price to vacate the room that evening was two six-packs of bottled Budweiser. I gladly obliged. Everything was set.

The first stage of the date consisted of burgers at Sid's All-American and *Rocky* at a drive-in. "Did you like the movie?" I asked afterwards, pulling out of the gravel parking lot.

"It was okay," Amy said, her voice flat.

"Well, thanks for going. I know boxing isn't your thing, but that movie really gives me a lift. I've seen it three times now. I wanted you to see it at least once. Thought maybe it would inspire you when volleyball practice starts up. Next time you can pick the flick, okay?"

"Alright." She stared out the passenger window.

"Everything okay?" I asked. "You've been kinda quiet all night."

"Yeah, I'm fine," she said with a forced smile.

I tried to think of something I might have said or done to upset her. Nothing specific came to mind. *Maybe I should have planned a more romantic evening.* I hoped her mood would change during the second stage of our date. We held hands walking from the student parking lot on the edge of campus to the athletic dorms. Cool evening gusts slapped against our faces.

We climbed the stairs to the second floor of the five-story brick structure known as Stander Hall. Shouts from a spirited wrestling match in the lounge echoed down the hallway. Accompanying that racket was a discordant blend of Boston, Hank Williams Jr., Bob Dylan, and Funkadelic emanating from various open doors. The cacophony was partially muted when we entered my room and I shut the door. Amy draped her tan coat over the back of my desk chair and drifted to the window. Her straight blond hair hung down to the center of her back. I paused to admire the rear view of her lithe form.

Spurred to action, I slid a Captain and Tennille album from its jacket and placed it on the turntable. "Love Will Keep us Together" soon bounced from the speakers. Before meeting Amy, I hated that song. It now produced a near Pavlovian response. Past memories mingled with sultry anticipation. I slid over and wrapped my arms around her from behind. The fresh herbal fragrance of her hair stoked a fire growing inside me. I pushed back her blond locks and started nibbling on the exposed ear. My hands began to explore.

"Dave."

"Hmm?"

"I'm pregnant."

With jarring violence, those two words plunged me into the Arctic Ocean. I stepped back. "Huh? … uh … you are?"

"Yes." She turned around to face me. Solemnity filled her dark blue eyes.

"Are you sure? I mean … I wore … um … we used protection."

"Not every time. Remember that party at Delta Upsilon? We were both so buzzed afterwards we didn't use anything."

"We didn't?" I tried to recall the fuzzy details of that evening.

"And I'll save you the trouble of asking. You're the father. There's been no one else."

"I wasn't going to ask." I said slowly. "But are you sure you're pregnant?"

She sighed. "Three weeks ago I was late. At first I didn't think it was a big deal. But then another week passed. Nothing. Then another. Nothing. So I went to the doctor yesterday. I'm definitely pregnant."

"Oh." My head spun. I understood the words, but I struggled to comprehend their implications. I backed away and sat on my desk. Amy stood by the window with her arms folded in front of her like she was trying to stay warm. We stared at each other. Tennille continued singing. The Captain continued playing.

"Dave, we're freshman." Her soft face started to unravel. "This isn't supposed to happen."

I walked over and took her in my arms. "It's gonna be okay," I said, not sure if I believed myself.

A short time later, Amy pulled away and wiped a couple stray tears from her cheeks. "There's only one thing to do," she said in a firm voice. "I called a clinic in Omaha. They can get me in Friday morning. I don't want anyone to know, okay?"

I stared at her in bewilderment.

"Don't tell anybody. None of your friends, alright?" Her tone was sharper.

"Okay." My head continued spinning.

"I don't expect you to go with me, but would you help pay for it? They want the money that day."

"Amy, I um, of course I'll help. We're in this together. But shouldn't we talk about it first?"

"What's there to talk about?"

"The options. This is all so sudden. I mean, Friday. That's soon."

"Options, Dave? We're nineteen-year-old college students with no income. We don't have any options."

"But do you have to do this so soon? I just found out. It all seems so rushed. I'd like some time to—"

"If you don't want to help, just say so!" she snapped. "I'll take care of this myself. You just get on with your life like nothing happened." She whisked her coat off the chair.

"Amy, it's not like that." I grabbed her arm. "I'm with you. I'll help you. But can't we wait a few days before making such a permanent decision?"

She jerked her arm away from my hand. "Dave, you don't get it. I can't talk to you right now. I've got to get out of here." She unlocked the door.

"Wait. I'll walk you home."

"No! I live a hundred feet away. I don't need your help getting home." She shot an angry glance at me. "I need to be away from you. We'll talk tomorrow, okay?" The door slammed behind her.

I lifted the needle off the record and looked out the window. Down below, Amy strode across a commons area and disappeared into the women's athletic dorm that mirrored Stander Hall. Crawling up to my bed, I stared at the ceiling. For the next several hours my brain sunk deeper and deeper into a sea of fretful disbelief.

Perry's noisy entrance to the room a little after 10:00 the next morning startled me out of a depressing dream. "Still in bed, lazy ass? Damn. You must have done some major spiking on that volleyball girl of yours." He pushed open the frayed yellow curtains, forcing me to squint at the sudden infusion of light.

"Uhhhhh," was my semi-coherent reply. He did not stick around for long. After a few more remarks about what he thought I did the previous night, he changed his clothes, grabbed his backpack, and left. Moving in slow motion, I struggled down to food service at a quarter after eleven. I scanned the crowded dining hall for Amy, but she was not there. At 1:00 p.m., out of habit, I went to biology class. There was really no point though, since my mind did not accompany my body. My notes for the day's lecture consisted of a single word: "photosynthesis." All through class, like every other part of the day, one issue consumed my thoughts. *What should I do?* I tried to take comfort that this would all be over tomorrow. But peace would not come. The thought of Amy lying on her back with her feet elevated in metal stirrups sent a shivery chill down my spine.

After class, I wandered aimlessly. Among the campus flora there were a few signs of spring's impending arrival, though most trees remained leafless. Their brown, naked branches reached out like skeletal fingers to the blue sky above. My mind drifted to my brother Adam. The summer after his freshman year at Iowa State his girlfriend Shannon found out she was pregnant. So Adam dropped out of school, took a job at The Royal Court, and married her. She gave birth to Martin the following February. He just turned eleven. *But I don't want to quit school; I don't want to marry Amy; I don't want to be a father yet*. I shut my eyes, wishing I could go back in time.

I eventually found myself milling about the semi-wooded hilly area near the Student Union. There, among the trees, I tried to think of someone I could talk to about this. A memory of John returned. My pain intensified. "Why did you have to leave me, man?" I asked aloud. "Look at the mess I got myself into."

I meandered back to a cement walkway where a woman approached pushing a stroller. Skipping a few feet ahead of her was a little girl, probably about four or five years old. The pink ribbon in her hair matched her coat and the flowery pattern on the rolled up cuffs of her jeans. "Hi, mister!" she said with a bright smile. After I returned her greeting, the girl resumed skipping. In the stroller, a bundled baby seemed amazed by each new sight taken in by his darting eyes. He looked up at me and squirmed.

"Nice day, isn't it?" the woman said.

"Yes, it is."

She continued on her way. I started back to my dorm. A cold fear swept through me as I thought about the conversation I would be having later that evening.

Spiders gnawed at my insides as I knocked on the door. Staring at the cork message board, I tried to think of what to say. *I don't even know what I want to happen.* Amy's roommate Joan answered. After some cursory small talk, she announced that she was going to the library to study. Her demeanor seemed normal, but she obviously knew something was up between Amy and me. Glancing around, I was struck by how neat and orderly they kept their dorm room. The space Perry and I shared was a dump by the second week of the fall semester.

"Hi," Amy said softly. She looked tired.

"Hi." I tried to smile. We stared at each other for a few seconds.

"I'm sorry about last night," she finally said. "I just couldn't stand talking about it anymore."

"It's okay. I'm sorry, too."

She settled into an old brown loveseat. "Have a seat," she said, gesturing across the room. I pulled the chair out from her desk and sat facing her. We were both quiet for a while. "At least this will be over soon," she sighed.

"The abortion?"

"Yes. It's almost three hundred dollars. Could you pay half?"

"Amy, can't we talk about this first?"

An impatient look draped her face. "What's left to say?"

Queasiness coated my stomach. "I don't like the idea of being a parent, but it's hard to feel good about what we're planning. I mean, that's a kid we're talking about. Our kid. What if you go through with this and we both regret it afterwards?"

"Dave, we don't have any choice."

From the confusion swirling around my head, a crazy thought emerged. "What if we get married?"

The derisive laugh that followed was like a slap in the face. "Marriage? We don't even like each other."

It took me several seconds to recover from that blow. "I like you. You don't like me?"

"Okay, I'm sorry. I like you, Dave. What I meant was, we hardly even know each other."

"We've been dating for almost two months."

"No, we've been screwing for almost two months. That's our relationship. We have fun together, but that's it."

"That's not true," I said. "Our relationship is more than just physical."

"Oh really? Aside from details about my body, what do you know about me? And don't even mention how I like Captain and Tennille music while we're … you know."

"Uh …" My mind frantically searched for something appropriate.

"What's my middle name?"

"Did you ever tell me?"

"Yes. And I can see how much it meant to you. Where am I from?"

"Wisconsin," I said with relief. "See, I know things about you."

"Oh yeah? Where in Wisconsin? I told you that, too. More than once."

Struggling, I just couldn't pull it in. "Um … it starts with a J, right?"

"Janesville."

"I would've gotten it. So we don't know everything about each other yet. We can learn. We'll grow closer after we get married."

She approached and put her palms on my cheeks, before sliding them down to my shoulders and upper arms. "Dave, so strong, so beautiful … and so naive. Marriage is hard, even for a couple that's in love. We're not even close to that. Plus, you're on a scholarship and don't have a job. Same with me. What would we do for income? Where would we live? The dorms?"

"I can quit school and find a job." I wasn't even sure I wanted to do what I was proposing. "I know my dad would hire me full-time at his restaurant."

She turned and stepped away. "And where would we be six months from now after our marriage falls apart? Out of school, divorced, and making minimum wage. It would be irresponsible to bring a kid into something like that just because of an accident."

"My brother and his girlfriend dropped out of college after their freshman year to get married. They're still together after eleven years. Got two great kids."

She spun around, glaring. "I don't care about your brother. This is us. This is our lives!"

"And the baby's." Upon hearing myself speak those words, my conscience surged. "I don't know if I can live with myself if we take a human life."

A thick crease formed between her eyebrows. "Don't you dare say that. It's not a human life. It's not anything yet."

I stood and put a hand on her shoulder. "Amy."

"Don't." She retreated to the other side of the room.

"Whether we admit it or not, there's a person inside of you and—"

"I'm not going to marry you, Dave! Not ever! Just drop it!"

Another thought materialized as I stared into the storm raging across her face. "We can give up the baby for adoption."

"No! I'm going to the clinic tomorrow."

"The baby would go to loving parents. And we wouldn't have the guilt of ending a life."

"That would be a great deal for you, wouldn't it? You wouldn't have to do anything. Me? I'd have to carry someone else's baby for nine months while getting fat and throwing up every morning. Then I'd fall behind in school and have to quit the volleyball team. All so you can have a clear conscience and get on with your life like nothing happened."

"I know it would be hard, but it would be the right thing to do."

"Since when did you start caring about what's right and wrong?"

Her words stung. "I know I haven't been a saint." My eyes dropped to the floor. "But I'm trying to avoid doing something worse. I don't want us to make a mistake that can't be undone. We need to consider what's best for the child."

"But what about what's best for me? Don't you care about that? Don't I matter? It's my body, Dave. I should have a say in what happens."

"I do care about you. I just don't want you to do something you'll feel guilty about the rest of your life. Don't you wonder how an abortion might affect you? Don't you think you'll wonder about the baby afterwards?"

"It's not a baby! It's not anything yet," she said, starting to cry. "Thousands of women get abortions and are just fine. Why can't I? I'm not breaking any laws."

"I don't care what other women do. I care about us, what we do. Listen, if you choose adoption, I'll do everything I can to help you. During the pregnancy and after. I'll help you financially for as long as you want."

"Great, now you're trying to bribe me." She dabbed her eyes with a Kleenex.

"No. I just want you to know how important this is to me. Please don't go to that clinic tomorrow." My voice cracked. "Won't you at least take a couple days to think about adoption?"

"Adoption won't work."

"Why?"

"After carrying a baby inside me for nine months, I'd love it too much after I saw it. I wouldn't be able to give it away."

"So even though you know you'd love your baby, you've decided to kill it?"

"Damn you, Dave!" she screamed. "Stop saying that! It's not a life! It's a mistake! A mistake you made!" She grabbed a textbook off her desk and hurled it at me. I deflected it away with my hands. "Why can't you be an adult?" she yelled. "What can't you accept the decision I've made?"

"Amy, please. I—"

"Shut up! Just shut up and get out! I never want to see you again!" She grabbed a desk lamp and jerked the cord from the wall.

"Okay." I moved to the door as she cocked back her arm. "I'm going." Outside in the hallway, a dozen girls stood in their doorways staring at me. None of them looked happy. Embarrassment and shame joined the frustration and despondency

I'd felt in Amy's room. My head down, I walked the gauntlet of scorn before exiting to the stairwell.

I trudged across the dark campus. My scrambled thoughts eventually settled on one realization: *The baby is going to die. Tomorrow, the baby you fathered is going to die*. A wave of nausea came suddenly. I ducked behind a bush and vomited. A vile bitter taste filled my mouth.

Some students passed by. "Damn dude, loaded already?" one of them asked. The others laughed. I stayed on my knees and did not turn around. Eventually, I wandered over to the trees near the Student Union. I found a concrete bench and sat down. Bowing my head, I started talking silently to God. It had been months since I'd prayed about anything. Now, caught in a nightmare of my own creation, I begged God to provide a way out. I prayed over and over for him to change Amy's mind—unlikely as that seemed. When I finally looked at my watch, it was after midnight. I'd lost all sense of the passing hours. Back at Stander Hall, I crept into my room.

I wallowed in bed until 10:30 the next morning. Wanting a distraction from the guilt and grief weighing on my heart, I decided to go to my 11:00 American History class. Despite Professor Kauffman's riveting lecture on the "businessman's government" of Calvin Coolidge, my mind remained clouded with depression. Midway through class, I had to get out of there. As I skulked up the aisle toward the rear exit of the lecture hall, Kauffman stopped talking in mid-sentence. "You there, walking out," he bellowed at me. "I hate you. You son of a bitch." I kept walking, certain that all eyes in the room were now on me. A few students snickered. "I've told you all many times," the professor continued in an unctuous tone, "I do not like it when malingerers walk out during one of my brilliant lectures. I am casting pearls of wisdom before you and …" The lecture hall's doors closing behind me finally blocked out Kauffman's voice.

Once outside, I kept walking. Exiting the university grounds, I trekked through blocks of residential neighborhoods and eventually ended up in downtown Council Bluffs. Hours later, I found myself back on campus next to Looft Lake, the man-made body of water north of the Student Union. Sitting in the grass on the bank, I tossed sticks into the water and watched them float away. After another hour, the sun began to set.

"You're hard to find." The female voice startled me. I turned around. Amy was there. "Mind if I sit down?" she asked. I gestured to the ground next to me. She sat, wrapping her arms around her knees. The rays of the setting sun illuminated her blond hair, which contrasted beautifully with her dark green windbreaker. We both looked out at the water.

"Did it hurt?" I asked. "Are you okay?"

"I didn't do it."

I looked over at her. "You didn't?"

"No."

"You're still pregnant?"

"Yes."

I wanted to say a lot of things, but nothing came out of my open mouth.

"I didn't get to sleep at all last night," she said, still gazing at the lake. "I drove to the clinic this morning. Started filling out the forms. Then I was crying. I couldn't go through with it."

"Amy." I put my hand on hers.

"I've been thinking all day about what to do. Finally, I called my mom. Had a long talk. I was surprised at how cool she was after hearing everything. She helped me get a better perspective on all this. Dad doesn't know yet. I'll tell him when I go home next weekend. That'll be a fun conversation."

"Oh." I was hanging on her every word.

She sighed. "I've decided to have the baby and give it up for adoption. There's a Lutheran social services agency back home Mom told me about. I'm going to contact them."

"You're moving back to Wisconsin?"

"Eventually. I'll finish out the semester here. I'll be four months along by finals week. Hopefully, I won't be showing too much. Then I'll stay in Janesville in the fall and have the baby there. Next January I'll start classes at Wisconsin. Most of my credits should transfer. Maybe I can get back in shape and make the Badger volleyball team."

"How can I help? I'll do whatever you want."

"I don't need you to do anything. Just don't tell anybody here, okay?"

"Of course, but I want to help. I'll send you money, like I said last night."

"That's not necessary. I'm not going on welfare. I'll just be skipping a semester of college. I'll be fine." She tossed a twig into the water. "Adoptive parents pay the agencies to cover the mother's expenses. Money won't be an issue."

"Will I need to sign something?"

"Probably. I'll let you know. Aside from that, it's best if you're not involved. It'll be less complicated for all of us."

"Okay." I continued holding her hand, processing all that she had said. "Thank you, Amy."

"I'm not doing it for you. This is my choice. I'm at peace with the decision."

"I'm sorry about everything," I said. "I never meant to put you through this."

"I know. We did this together. We had fun. Just got careless. You're a sweet guy, Dave. I'll miss you." She squeezed my hand. "Guess you're the first guy who asked me to marry him, sort of." Her lips formed a languid smile.

"I would have done everything I could to make it work," I said. She nodded and looked across the lake. A while later, she stood. I did too. After a long embrace, she walked away. I watched her until she disappeared behind the administration building. Her decision had brought profound relief to my soul, but it also marked the end of our relationship. Though in my heart I knew we weren't right for each other, it still hurt.

Thankful for the answer to my desperate prayers, I resolved to change my ways. Instead of partying late and sleeping in, I arose early to read Scripture and write songs of praise. I also started attending church and Bible studies. Over the following weeks, my faith grew stronger, along with my relationship with God. I felt like a prodigal son returning home.

My newfound fervor and discipline extended to the other areas of my life as well. Instead of lounging around playing cards and watching television, I diligently studied my textbooks and the team playbook. Out on the field, I stormed each football practice with nuclear energy. The coaches noticed. They started giving me more snaps at quarterback during scrimmages. I even threw a touchdown pass in the annual Green-White spring game.

Occasionally I ran into Amy on campus. We never talked. Just a quick greeting and a fleeting smile was all we shared. Finals week I stopped by her room several times to say goodbye, but she was never in. When I showed up on Thursday, her roommate said she had already left for Wisconsin. A hollow feeling came over me as I scanned the half-empty room.

During summer break in Des Moines, I worked nearly full-time at The Royal Court and was active again in the music ministry at Faith Community Church. My resolution to avoid dating while Amy was pregnant left me with a quiet social life, though I did watch *Star Wars* four times that summer. I told no one about my big secret. Nobody knew I was sending money to a pregnant girl in another state. Nobody noticed when I received mail from a social services agency. Nobody watched me as I signed the enclosed forms, sealed them in an envelope, and mailed them back.

I welcomed the start of football practice in August. My enthusiasm and intensity continued to impress the coaches and my teammates. Though Sid Patton remained the starting quarterback and Rollie Henderson his backup, Coach McNabb increased my playing time. I lined up as a flanker for a couple plays in each of the first three games of the season. The ball never came my way, but it was exciting just to be on the field in front of the screaming fans. But then, the first week of October, one of our linebackers accidentally rolled over my ankle during a scrimmage. The resulting fracture was small, but it ended my sophomore season.

A few days later, as I sat studying in my dorm room, a teammate told me I had a call. Still adjusting to life with crutches and a cast, it took me a while to hobble out to the payphone in the hallway.

"It's over," Amy said. "Everything went okay. I'm fine. So is the baby."

"That's great," I stammered through my shock at hearing her voice. "I've been praying for you." Even though the hallway was empty, I kept my voice down to avoid being overheard.

"Thanks. It's a boy. He has your mouth and cheeks."

"What are the adopting parents like? Did you talk to them much?"

"Not at all. It's a closed adoption. I don't know them and they don't know me. They don't know who you are either. That's the way it's supposed to be. I'm not even sure if I should be telling you about this."

"Well, I'm glad you did! I've been thinking about you all the time. Wondering."

"Now you know…. Thanks for the money, but I told you not to send anything."

"I wanted to help."

"I know, but everything's covered. Please don't send any more."

"Okay. Let me know if you need anything. Ever."

"I'm tired, Dave. I should go."

After I hung up the phone, dizzying thoughts about the baby flooded my mind. I tried to imagine what he looked like. What his family would be like. *I'm part of him, but he will never know me.* After hobbling back to my room, the realization sank in that I would probably never see Amy again. The goodbyes we just said were possibly the last words we would ever speak to each other. Memories of our time together floated by. I wondered what the future would hold for her. I pulled a picture out of my wallet. It was her senior portrait from high school. A tear rolled off my cheek and just missed landing on the smiling face I held in my hand. Moments later I heard my roommate's voice out in the hallway. I quickly slid the picture back into my wallet.

"Hello!" Perry said, imitating Squiggy from *Laverne and Shirley* as he flung open the door. Rick Wilkerson, a sturdy tight end, followed him into the room.

"What's goin' on guys?" I asked, trying to act like everything was normal.

"Me and the Wilk was just wondering where you went to high school?"

"Eastridge in Des Moines."

"See, I told ya," Perry said, swatting Rick's arm. They exchanged knowing smiles.

"What?" I asked.

"You might want to take a look at the newspaper, King," Rick said. "Let's just say, you're gonna have some company here next fall. Might be a familiar face."

Chapter 11 – September 1978

I examined the shadows cast by the iron bars of Gate A as the morning sun ascended above Falcons Stadium. A faint buzzing sound grew louder. My eyes scanned the distance to locate the source of the noise—a green blur racing down Stadium Drive. Tires wailing, the automobile skidded into the vast empty parking lot and sped straight toward me. The vehicle's size expanded along with its proximity. Just as I prepared to dive out of its path, a piercing wail shot from four screeching tires. In a cloud of white smoke, the Dodge Dart burned to a halt only ten feet away.

Three teenage boys, all wearing shades, piled out. Approaching, they swayed their torsos like Tony Manero in *Saturday Night Fever*. After a brief stare down, a grin broke across the freckled face of the smallest of the three. "Uncle D!" Asa exclaimed, removing his sunglasses. The other two followed suit.

"You nut cases." I mussed the red hair atop their heads. "Look at how light these mops are now. You guys go inside at all this summer?"

The three boys simultaneously retrieved combs from their back pockets to restore order to the chaos I had wrought. Joe organized his locks into a side part, while Anthony and Asa divided their tresses down the middle.

"And you," I said, putting Anthony in a headlock. "How'd you get a license driving like that? Your mom know how insane you are?"

"Who do you think taught him to drive?" Joe quipped.

"Hey, I just like to make a strong entrance," Anthony said, wriggling free from my grip.

I sighed. "Anthony Krieger with a car. That don't seem right."

"The world is a scarier place," Joe said.

"Shut up, nimrod," the oldest brother retorted, adding a shove. Joe shoved back.

"Alright boys, let's go." I led my nephews through the iron gate for a stadium tour that included the locker rooms, the weight room, the rehab room, and the press box. Since it was early morning on Labor Day, we pretty much had the run of the place. I saved the best for last.

The "whoas" and "wows" accelerated as we stepped onto the sacred green grass of the football field. The three boys roamed about looking up in all directions at the empty seats. I threw passes to each of them as they ran routes across the field. Imagining thousands of screaming fans all around them, they imitated television announcers describing their catches.

"Man, I can't wait for Saturday!" Asa said, tossing the ball back to me. "That is so cool of you to get us tickets. We get to see Uncle D out on this field, leading the Falcons."

"Where will our seats be?" Anthony asked.

"Fifth Row, Section 6," I said, pointing to the spot. "Right on the forty-yard line."

"Oh man! Too cool! I bet this place gets loud."

"Has Coach McNabb made the official announcement that you'll be starting?" Joe asked.

"No. Not yet. Starting assignments will be posted tomorrow before practice."

"It's going to be you at quarterback, right? You're a junior. The other guy's a freshman."

"I hope so, but it's Coach's call."

"Boz Kishman can't carry your jockstrap!" Joe snapped.

"Joseph! None of that. Boz is a great QB. Got a strong arm."

"Your arm is better," Anthony said. "And can he run a 4.4 forty like you? I don't think so!"

"The only reason Boz even has a chance is because he's related to the quarterback coach," Joe said, punting the football. "Was that legal, hiring a recruit's uncle?"

"Abner Kishman isn't Boz's uncle. He was his dad's cousin. And yes, hiring him was legal. Western Iowa needed a quarterback coach. Abner knows his stuff. He won a lot of games as head coach at Eastridge the last two years. Helped Boz become the top high school quarterback in the state. Coach McNabb and the staff here believed Abner was the best man for the job." I fired a long pass to Asa who was running down the sideline.

"It's a bunch of bullshit if you ask me," Joe said. "You should be starting, period."

Though I felt the same way, I thought it better to maintain team unity in front of the boys. "Watch the language, Joe. Here's the deal. A lot of schools wanted Boz. Good ones, too. UCLA, Purdue, Florida State. Did hiring Abner Kishman give Western Iowa an edge in the recruiting battle? Probably. But no rules were broken. And now Coach McNabb has a top-notch quarterback for the next four years. Sure, I hope Boz is my backup while I'm here. But that's not my decision. If Boz is the starter, I'll just have to accept that and help the team as a reserve."

"That'll really stink if you don't play Saturday," Anthony said. "I've already told everybody at school my uncle is gonna be starting quarterback for the Falcons."

"I'm not even going to the game if that wannabe starts instead of you," Joe said.

"Me neither," Anthony agreed.

"Don't worry about it, men. The world's not going to end if I'm not the starter. I'll just have to work harder. Alright, who wants to race? Hundred yards, let's see what you've got!"

We lined up at the goal line and took off. I had planned to sprint ahead and then let the boys catch up for a close finish. Asa, however, stayed right on my heels. I had to run full speed just to keep my slight lead. He was only two steps behind when I crossed the other goal line. Anthony and Joe, running neck and neck, reached the end zone a few seconds later.

"Man, you're fast," I told Asa. "You a freshman at Omaha Central now?"

"Yeah," he said, panting.

"Going out for the freshman track team?"

"Coach wants me on varsity."

"I bet."

"King!" A booming voice echoed through the stadium. My nephews and I snapped our heads around. Abner Kishman stood at the entrance to the tunnel that led to the home locker room. He wore a gray Falcons T-shirt and green shorts. "What the hell are you doing out there?"

"Just showing my nephews the stadium. I cleared it with Coach."

"Well, I'm unclearing it. That field is not a playground. Get those kids out of here. Then report to my office. I'll see if I can find something more productive for you to do with all this free time you seem to have."

"Yes, sir."

"What a jerk," Joe said under his breath.

"Easy, Joe," I whispered. "Sorry, boys. Guess that's it for today."

I made sure I was in front as we walked off the field so they could not see my red face. Behind me, I heard Anthony and Joe muttering about Abner. I silently agreed with nearly all their comments. As we neared Gate A, Asa jumped on my back for a piggyback ride.

"Alright boys, see you Saturday," I said, lowering Asa to the pavement beside Anthony's car. "I'll keep an eye out for you guys in the stands. Be sure to wear green." Anthony and Joe nodded, before donning their sunglasses.

"Bye, Uncle D," Asa said. "Thanks for showing us around." His grin suggested that he had already forgotten about the rude eviction.

The Dodge Dart squealed away. I went back inside to face Abner Kishman.

The next morning I lost track of time and accidentally arrived at my Spanish class several minutes early. Grabbing a copy of *The Falconer* off one of the desks, I skimmed an article about President Carter's upcoming peace talks with Anwar Sadat and Menachem Begin. I then flipped to the college newspaper's sports page, where a column headline caught my eye: "Falcons QB Controversy Actually a No-Brainer." I had no choice but to read what followed.

With the season opener less than a week away, the question of who will start at quarterback looms over Falcons Stadium like a dark monolith. Should it be the junior who has warmed the bench for two years waiting to get his chance? Or should it be the gunslinging freshman who spurned several powerhouse football programs to come to Western Iowa?

Falcons faithful are evenly divided on this issue. But really, I ask, should there even be a debate? An examination of the facts suggests otherwise.

Consider their high school records. At Des Moines Eastridge, Boz Kishman led the state in passing yards and touchdowns two years in a row. With Western Iowa's fortuitous hiring of his prep mentor, Abner Kishman, as quarterback coach, there is every reason to believe Boz will soar to new heights as a Falcon.

In contrast, the most notable aspect of Dave King's high school record was his dismissal from his team for "personal reasons." Can you say bong hit?

But what about the tail of the tape? The towering Kishman is 6'4" and 230 lbs., while King is listed at 6'1" and 205 lbs. The taller Kishman has a clear advantage peering over the line to find an open receiver. Moreover, with 25 extra pounds of beef, Boz will also prove more durable.

College experience? As a junior, King should have an advantage here. Wrong. All he has done at UWI is break his ankle and twiddle his thumbs on the bench. Boz, on the other hand, graduated early from high school so he could attend spring practice with the Falcons. His performance in the Green-White game last April was so dazzling that QB candidate Rollie Henderson saw the handwriting on the wall and transferred away.

Too bad Mr. King did not do the same. It doesn't matter. He will get the message loud and clear on Saturday when the Boz Kishman era officially begins at Western Iowa.

My eyes crawled to the top of the article to read the byline: "Caleb Nagel, senior." The accompanying photo showed a chubby face with an arrogant smirk. I felt a hand on my shoulder.

"Hola, Dave. Ready to become bi? Bilingual that is." Wesley Carr slid his rail-thin frame into the desk next to mine. His voice was high and nasal, like usual.

"Hey, Wes." Steam continued to build inside my head. "Ever heard of Caleb Nagel?"

"Read the article, huh? Forget about it. It's rubbish, like everything else in that rag."

"What do you know about him?"

"Not going to let it go? Honestly, you football players need to think about something other than, well, football."

I glared at him.

"Fine. I don't know much. Nagel usually writes a weekly opinion column. Strictly bourgeoisie drivel. They must have demoted him to the sports page. Oops. Sorry big guy. No offense. Oh, almost forgot, he's a frat president too. Alpha Lambda Phi, I think."

I calmly folded the paper and placed it under my desk. Over the next hour I should have been learning how to conjugate Spanish verbs, but Nagel's words kept boring into my head. I told myself to let it go. *Take a deep breath; count to ten; just forget about it.* That stuff actually worked—for about two minutes. The flames returned. At the end of class, I sprang out of my seat.

The furnace inside me grew hotter as I stomped across campus. Whenever I saw students laughing, I assumed they had read the article and were making fun of me. I burst into the Student Union. I knew *The Falconer* offices were downstairs somewhere. I debated whether to fling open the office door or just kick it in. *Caleb Nagel is so dead!* Storming down the basement hallway, I spotted my destination. Just before I reached the door, a woman appeared in front of me.

"Hi, Dave. Could I please speak with you for a minute?"

Though I barely gave her a glance, I noticed that she was about three or four inches shorter than me. "Sorry. I have business to take care of." I sidestepped around her.

"I think I know your business. I'm the editor of *The Falconer.* That's why I want to talk."

Stopping in my tracks, I finally looked at her. Vivid green eyes gazed back at me. Dark chestnut hair flowed down below the collar of her yellow and purple blouse. Other details slowly came into focus—clear tan skin, lilac eye shadow, and a slight smile that was warm but serious. The sight overwhelmed me, even more so when a faint whiff of enchanting perfume hit my nose. She spoke again. Staring hopelessly, I heard the voice but did not comprehend the words. I think it was a question. Something about the cafeteria. "Okay," I said, not knowing what I had just agreed to. By that point, I'd already forgotten why I was there.

"Good," she said, extending a hand. "I'm Abigail Taylor. Nice to meet you."

"Dave King," I stammered, grasping her hand. Her grip was soft, yet firm. My arm tingled.

"Like coffee? I'll buy."

"Sure. Okay." I hated coffee. Didn't matter. I was prepared to down a quart of motor oil to keep this encounter going.

A group of students heading down to the basement forced me to fall behind Abigail as we climbed the stairs. I ordered my eyes not to check her out. They disobeyed. The glance they stole sent high voltage through my body. By the time we reached the cafeteria register, I had yet to regain all my senses. She paid for the coffee and bought us each a donut too. We found an empty table.

"Dave, let me express my profound apologies for this morning's column. As editor, I take full responsibility."

I nodded, still hypnotized by her eyes.

"Due to a scheduling conflict, I left an assistant editor in charge of the final edit for today's edition. This guy and Caleb Nagel are friends. So Caleb was able to slip in his sports piece without my knowledge. I would never have approved the column had I read it."

Oh yeah, the column. That's why I'm here. "I see. I didn't realize that a newspaper columnist could get away with slipping something past his editor."

"Normally he can't." She sighed. "But Caleb is also my boyfriend. He sometimes uses that to try to take certain liberties at the paper."

A bloodcurdling scream ripped through my head. *Nooooooooo!! Please, no! Oh the humanity! Oh the horror! Why? Whyyyyyy?* Externally, my expression remained unchanged. "Oh," was all that came out of my mouth.

"He won't get away with it. I'm planning to suspend his column from the opinion page for two weeks. That's his pride and joy. He doesn't usually write sports pieces. But this Boz Kishman is a pledge at his fraternity. Caleb thinks it'll boost the prestige of his house if Boz is the starting quarterback. He can be such an idiot, sometimes."

"No argument here."

"Don't get me wrong, Caleb has his good qualities. But his parents are rich. Filthy rich. He has always had things handed to him. Because of that, he can get a little arrogant. Thinks he's smarter than other people. The guys in his house call him the 'jackass of all trades' because he thinks he knows so much about everything."

"And he's *your* boyfriend?"

She ruffled her brow into a stern expression. "That's my business, isn't it?"

"Sorry. I didn't mean anything by that."

She looked down at her coffee. "It's okay," she mumbled. "I'm used to it."

I thought about making another comment but took a sip of coffee instead.

"So, Dave, please accept my personal apology and my apology on behalf of *The Falconer* staff. And please don't hunt down Caleb. Beating him up would just create trouble for you with the university and the Nagel family lawyers. Besides, once you're named starting quarterback, no one is going to remember that inane column." Warmth returned to her face.

I did not speak for a few seconds. "I'm glad you got to me before I found Caleb," I said. "I'm ashamed to admit that I was planning on having a not so civil discussion with him. You saved me a lot of trouble. Thank you, Abigail."

"Please, call me Gail. And you're welcome. Maybe now you'll remember me at the end of the season after you've led the team to a big win in a bowl game. Perhaps I could even get an exclusive interview with the star quarterback of the Falcons."

"Sure." A big smile crossed my face.

She left a short time later. I remained at the table pretending to study Spanish vocabulary. *Caliente!* I finally floated away from the Union about ten minutes later. For the rest of the morning, my mind remained blissfully detached from any hint of a quarterback controversy.

That afternoon, Thor and I walked to the stadium. "This is it, King. Zero hour. You ready?"

"Yeah. I'm tired of all the waiting. The waiting and debating. Whichever way this goes, I'll be glad to see an end to all this speculation."

"I hear that. You, uh, read *The Falconer* today?"

"Yeah, I saw it. Guess somebody's not a fan, huh?"

"It's nothing. Just a bunch of garbage from an ignoramus. You'll be the starter."

"You really think so, or are you just being a friend?" I asked.

"Of course I think so! I spent a whole season snapping you the ball in high school. I've seen what you can do on a football field. Man, no one could stop the Eastridge offense our senior year. That state title would've been ours if you hadn't been railroaded off the team. Boz may have put up a lot of big numbers when he started, but his teams never even made it to the playoffs."

"Well, Eastridge had a great line when I played. You guys opened some huge doors for me."

"I'm ready to do it again. All us big dogs on the O-line are ready to steamroll everything in front of us." He tilted back his head and woofed a couple times. "And with you back there tossing the pigskin and running through the holes we make, there's not a defense in the nation that can stop us. I bet we average thirty-five points a game this season. Definitely get to bowl."

"And I might be watching it all from the sidelines. Boz has looked great in practice so far. A lot of people like him. And he has the same last name as the quarterback coach."

"Have faith, King. It's Coach McNabb's decision. He'll make the right call."

We waited for a car to pass by before we crossed Stadium Drive. "Thor, you ever wonder why Abner and Boz came here? I mean, after his success in high school he could have gone anywhere."

"Sure, I wondered. Western Iowa has a strong program and Coach McNabb is a big name, but it does seem like something else may have drawn them here."

"Yeah, me. Seems like they've both been on some kind of vendetta since they arrived on campus. Boz has ignored me and Abner has been on my case nonstop. Neither treated me like that in high school."

"I noticed." Thor sighed.

"It's like they blame me for what happened to John and Coach."

He grunted. We reached the doors that led to the field house at the south end of the stadium. "Hey, you go on in and check out the starting assignments," Thor said. "I'm going to stay here and pray. Talk to the Big Man about all this."

"Oh … uh, thanks."

"Dave, whatever happens remember that God is working in your life. If you're the starter, praise him. If not, praise him. You're under his awesome grace, either way."

"Thanks, man." We slapped hands. Despite Thor's words, butterflies built a thriving metropolis in my stomach as I traversed the long corridor. A few of the other players were already milling about the locker room. Their faces provided no clues about my fate. I approached Coach McNabb's office. Taking a deep breath, I scanned the depth chart posted on the wall beside his door. My jaw dropped. My name was not on the list. Neither was Boz's. The first two spots below Quarterback were blank. Only the third stringer's name was posted. "See me" was written off to the side of the blank spaces.

Swallowing hard, I knocked on the coach's door.

"Yeah, come in," a southern accent announced from inside. I entered. "Ah, yes, Dave. Come in, now. Shut that door, if ya would. Grab a seat."

"Thanks, Coach." I was normally awed by the enormity and polish of his office. This time, I was just nervous.

"Dave, I'm gonna cut ta the chase. This quarterback thing has been blowed all outta sorts. I thought it best if I first talked to you and Boz directly." He removed his steel-framed reading glasses and examined me with hazel eyes. The sharp points formed by his nose and jutting chin drew my eye away from the roadmap of wrinkles on his face and neck. The layer of hair covering his head reminded me of freshly fallen snow. Though he seemed physically small sitting behind his aircraft carrier-sized mahogany desk, the coach exuded an aura of authority.

"Yes, sir."

"Not since Elvis died last year has an issue regarding a king got me so tied up in knots," he said. I stared at him, blankly. "That was supposed ta be a joke, son. Guess I'm losing my touch."

"Sorry. I'm just so focused on football right now that I missed it. It's a good joke, sir."

"Well, maybe not." He glanced over at the wall displaying old photos of him during his playing days at the University of South Carolina. "Dave, it's like this. I voted one way. Blaine and Abner voted another." He looked back at me. "I know I'm the boss, but I take the advice of my offensive coordinator and quarterback coach seriously. So what I'm sayin' is, we're gonna start Boz on Saturday."

Not a muscle moved as I maintained eye contact.

"Now make no mistake, son. This was a tight decision. You're just a nose behind in that number two position. You'll get playin' time, I guarantee ya that." He pointed a bony finger across the desk at me. "I know you're a thoroughbred, and we'll get ya out there ta run. Yes, sir. You'll get into the action. Some kickoff and punt returns. Some plays as flanker. And if anything happens to Boz, yer in."

For the second time this day, a bloodcurdling scream ripped through my head while the person across from me heard nothing. My fingertips dug into my thighs, but I uttered no sound. I saw no point in words. I had spent my first two years at college hearing that I was the quarterback of the future. Now I was the quarterback of the never would be. What was there to say?

Coach shuffled in his leather chair. "Aren't ya gonna say something, son?"

"Thank you, sir." My voice was calm. "Is that all?"

"Uh … I guess it is, for now."

I stood. "I'll see you at practice." Saying nothing to any of the other players, I slunk to my locker. Finally, Thor came over.

"Well?"

I looked up and shook my head. His face deflated. "Dave, I'm sorry." He put a hand on my shoulder. "It's not right. Hey, Coach might listen to me and some of the other starters. We can go talk to him."

"No. The decision has been made. All that's left is for us to do our jobs in whatever role we've been given.… Praise him, right?" My heart, however, was not in my words. Thoughts of quitting spread like tentacles around my brain. I did not have my best practice that day.

News of Coach's decision was on the 6:00 news that evening. My humiliation mushroomed. Teammates and other students did not say much to me about it, but I knew a lot of them had jumped over to the Boz bandwagon. Reporters from *The Daily Nonpareil* and the *Omaha World-Herald* cornered me Wednesday morning for interviews. I fed them the standard crap about respecting Coach's decision and being eager to help the team in my role as a backup.

The nadir came Saturday. Running out of the tunnel at the back of the pack with the other reserves, I felt the full impact of being benched in favor of a freshman who had never played a down of college football. I might as well have been wearing a pink dress in front of the 45,000 fans crowded into Falcons Stadium for our game against the Iowa Hawkeyes. To make matters worse, the black and gold worn by the opposing players and fans unleashed a flood of memories about John. Sadness mixed with humiliation.

The Hawkeyes had not had a winning season since 1961, a trend that did not seem likely to change this year. Western Iowa was a two-touchdown favorite. Watching Boz jog onto the field with the other starters for the first series hit like a punch in the gut. He was nervous and the Falcons offense struggled. Part of me delighted in the fumble he lost and the three interceptions he threw. Fighting that attitude, I forced myself to pray for the team to succeed. It was like swallowing nails. Despite Boz's subpar performance, Coach never told me to get ready to go in. Not one single play. The Falcons won 24-21, thanks to a strong running game and a late interception by my former roommate Perry Arbuckle.

For the rest of the weekend, the flames of the quarterback controversy blazed hotter in the media and on the sports call-in shows. Monday after practice, Coach McNabb stated emphatically to the press that Boz would be the starting quarterback for next Saturday's game at Iowa State. I skipped supper at the training table that evening and went to the library for a while. The sun was setting as I trudged back to the off-campus house I shared with Thor and two other Christian teammates. It was a two-story, four-bedroom shanty that fit right in with the other run-down structures in the student slums west of campus. The only thing upscale about my new abode was the rent. None of us were particularly diligent about picking up the place. When visitors commented about the mess, we quoted Jesus' story in Matthew 12 about demons being attracted to an orderly house that was swept clean.

My housemate Tank was sitting on our carroty sofa tossing a SuperBall up into the ceiling fan. Whenever a rotating blade hit the ball, it shot around the living room like a pinball. The big man responded each time with a torrent of honking goose laughter. Tank Garber's name may never have appeared on a dean's list, but football experts ranked him as one of the top five right tackles in the nation. "Man, this is great!" he said. "Ya want to give it a try?" I politely declined and entered the kitchen. A couple slices of pepperoni pizza were in the refrigerator's normally abandoned vegetable crisper, just where I had hidden them a day earlier. *Jackpot!* I made short work of my culinary treasure and started rummaging for a dessert.

There was a knock at the front door. Moments later, Tank yelled, "Yo, King. You got company." After a swig, I set my capless bottle of Mountain Dew back in the refrigerator door. As I made my way out of the kitchen, the 280-pound Tank nearly ran me over.

"You gotta girl?" he whispered.

"No. You know that."

"This may be your lucky day then. That chick out there is a twentieth century fox! I'll give you some privacy, dude." He clapped my shoulder and lumbered up the stairs. One thought flashed before my eyes in bold neon: *ABIGAIL!* I hastily ran my fingers through my hair and dragged a napkin across my mouth. Strutting into the living room, I tried to think of a witty opening line. Three steps in, I froze.

My eyes told me that Michelle was standing just inside our front door, but my brain could not quite process the image. "You look like you've seen a ghost," she said, forcing a smile. "It's okay. I'm not going to yell at you. I come in peace."

"Oh." I flashed back to our last conversation two years ago when I told her I was going to Western Iowa. She did not take the news well.

"Your hair is shorter," she said.

"Yeah. I had to get it cut so my helmet would fit right."

"I like it."

"Thanks."

"I know I should've called first, but …"

"Not a problem. Would you like to sit down?" Since the two stuffed chairs in the room were buried under textbooks, papers, empty pop bottles, and various clothing items, we sat at opposite ends of the antiquated couch. After a lengthy glance, I pried my eyes away from her tight violet sweater.

"I wanted to tell you earlier," she said, "but I got so busy. There's always a million things to do at the start of the semester, you know."

"Tell me?" My brows rose.

"Yeah. I, um, transferred to Western Iowa. I'm a student here."

"You are? I've never seen you on campus."

"The semester just started two weeks ago and there are over 12,000 students here. You could go the whole year without seeing someone."

"Yeah, I guess so." Her amber eyes drew me in. Memories returned.

"After Mary graduated last year, I kinda felt alone out there in Iowa City. Plus, it was always tough going to school where John went. I understand why you didn't want to go there. Just walking past buildings where I knew he had classes bummed me out. I had to get away. Western Iowa has a good business program, so I came here."

"And you have family here."

"Yeah. Having Boz and Abner around is kinda nice." She paused. "I'm sorry about this whole quarterback thing. It's nothing personal with Boz."

I nodded, though I didn't believe her last statement. "Worked out well for him that a relative got hired as the quarterback coach."

"It hasn't been easy for either of them, Dave. They've both been raked over the coals since Boz was announced as the starter. Abner has been getting prank calls and threatening letters. Someone even egged his house Saturday night."

"Really?"

"Yeah. Don't tell anybody, okay? I don't think he wants anyone on the team to know."

"Fine."

"Last night Boz and I were over at Abner's house for supper. I can tell that all this stuff is bothering him. He's even called the police."

"I'm sorry to hear that," I said. "Some people take this football stuff too seriously."

"Yeah, it's the same way at Iowa. And they have a sucky team." We then talked about the differences between her old school and her new one. After several minutes, she checked her watch. "I should go. I just wanted to pop in and say 'hi.' Let you know I'm out here now."

"Thanks for stopping by. It's great to see you." Without thinking I then blurted, "Want to go get some ice cream?"

Her expression fell serious. "Oh, Dave, I can't. I'm on a diet, and Paul's expecting me at his place pretty soon."

"Paul Lasch? You two are, uh … he's out here too?"

"Yeah. We started seeing each other again at Iowa. He transferred here when I did."

"Oh." I tried to mask my disappointment.

"See you around, Dave."

From the front window, I watched her walk away on the sidewalk. Trying to study afterwards was pointless. Giving my brain the night off, I turned on *Three's Company* and then joined Tank for a few rounds of ceiling fan pinball. For once, I enjoyed watching the SuperBall rocket around our living room even more than he did.

Thoughts of quitting the team orbited my head all day Tuesday. I'd swat them away, but like gnats they kept coming back. After a grueling three-hour afternoon practice, the gnats transformed into hornets. The sound of their buzzing coalesced into one big question: *Why am I still putting myself through all this torture?* I wondered if my benching was God's punishment for my carnal past with Amy. After reading several Psalms and praying that evening, a flicker of encouragement returned. I resolved to stick it out a while longer.

Around midnight, Thor, Tank, and our other housemate, the Rooster, wanted to play cards. The Rooster was an undersized linebacker who was so named because of his bright red Mohawk and scrappy tenacity on the field. The game we played was 500. Just after my partner Tank blew a nullo hand, the phone rang. I was closest.

The tone of Zoe's voice told me immediately that something was wrong. So deep was her anguish, I could barely understand her words. "There was an accident … Asa died … my little boy is gone." In the agonizing conversation that followed, I learned that all three of her sons were riding together when the crash occurred. Anthony and Joe escaped with minor injuries. They were taken to Methodist Hospital. I said I'd get there as fast as I could. Just before hanging up, Zoe told me one more detail—Abner Kishman was also involved in the accident.

Asa's funeral was Friday at Trinity Church in Omaha. The whole King family was there. We had not all been together since Grandpa's funeral the previous January. Though somber, that occasion was not unexpected. Grandpa had been ill for several months. His service celebrated the long life of a noble man of God.

Asa's funeral was different. It took place under a dark cloud of tragedy. Everyone in the church sat shocked and numb. It was beyond comprehension that Asa—fourteen and full of life only a few days ago—now lay in a casket. Zoe was inconsolable. Her piercing sorrow rang through the church. The sounds tore my heart out. I fought to keep it together.

After the burial service at Forest Lawn Cemetery, I broke away from the crowd to walk in solitude among the gravestones. I read dozens of names and dates. Ozzie approached. With short hair, a neatly-trimmed goatee, and a new black suit, he barely resembled the brother I grew up with. "Hey man," he said.

"Oz."

"I can't believe this. It is not real. It can't be."

"I know." I brushed my fingers across the top of a gray stone.

"What exactly happened with the accident? Zoe can't talk about it. Nobody else seems to know very much. Do you?"

"Anthony told me a little. I talked to Abner Kishman too. I guess the boys took it pretty hard that I wasn't starting at quarterback. They blamed Abner. Started prank calling him. Sent anonymous threatening letters. Even egged his house one night."

"Zoe didn't know about any of this?"

"Guess not. Those kids are clever. I'm sure they covered their tracks. Anyway, one night they decided to follow Abner home from practice. Wanted to scare him. He sees a strange car tailing him and floors it. He's already spooked by everything else, you know. So he goes flying down the interstate over the bridge into Omaha. Joe stays right on his bumper."

"Joe? He's got a license?"

"Learner's Permit. He wasn't supposed to be driving without an adult, but I guess he talked Anthony into letting him drive that night. You know Joe. Anyway, they were going about eighty or ninety, I guess. At some point, Abner changes lanes. Joe tries to do the same and loses control. Rolls the car. He and Anthony had their seatbelts on. Asa did not."

"Damn."

"Abner feels terrible. He had no idea it was my nephews chasing him. I told him it wasn't his fault. I feel like it's mine."

"No," Ozzie said. "Blaming yourself for something that wasn't your fault won't help. Won't bring Asa back." He grabbed a twig and flung it through the air. We continued walking under the overcast sky.

"How's school?" I asked.

"Cruddy. But a little less cruddy than before. I may even make it outta there next May."

"That's too bad. I was hoping you'd stay at ISU long enough for us to graduate at the same time."

"Wiseass." He punched my arm. "I gotta finish next spring. Dad said he's cutting me off after my fifth year."

"That's no good. Then you'll have to get a job."

"Tell me about it. It sucks. I already had to get my hair chopped for interviews. I guess accounting firms aren't interested in hiring guys with the Alice Cooper look. Who knew?"

"You can grow it back after you land a job."

"Oh, I will. Trust me.... So, are you still traveling with the team to Ames tomorrow?"

"No. Coach said I don't have to dress for the ISU game. I'll be staying in Council Bluffs. I'm glad. I'm not in the mood for football." We walked back to the line of parked cars that snaked through the cemetery. Some were starting to clear out. Ozzie veered off to talk to Eli and Shane, who were standing near a black limousine. I noticed Joe lingering alone under the canopy at the burial site. His arm was in a sling. I walked over to him.

"Hey, Joe," I said quietly. "You want to ride with me back to your house?" Staring down at his brother's casket, he said nothing. He had been silent since the accident.

"Joe, I know this hurts. I know what you're going through. I've lost two brothers. We'll get through this together. I'm here for all of you. You, Anthony, your mom. We'll press on. I'll help you."

He looked up at me. His eyes were dead, as if his soul had vacated his body. He finally spoke in a distant, empty voice. "No. I will do this alone." He then turned and drifted into the endless rows of gravestones.

Chapter 12 – November 1978

The roar of the crowd grew louder. The opposing lines collided. Boz dropped back in the pocket. Though his protection held, he shuffled his feet and hurried a pass into coverage. A Louisville linebacker plucked the ball from the air. The roar diminished into a collective groan. The linebacker charged past would-be tacklers into Falcons territory. A tight end finally brought him down at the 27-yard line. Curses rained down from the stands. More than a few spectators shouted my name.

As our defense trotted onto the field, I sat on the bench and bowed my head. In what had become a familiar prayer, I asked God to help my teammates overcome the adversity they faced. An outbreak of shouting not far to my left brought an abrupt end to my supplication. Abner Kishman screamed at Boz. "Why the hell didn't you look for the safety valve?" was among the many questions the quarterback coach yelled. Boz shouted back. The air was blue. Louisville kicked a field goal. We trailed 20-0 with 12:37 left in the third quarter. Boz slammed down his helmet and stormed off.

Abner stalked over to Coach McNabb. After a brief discussion, Coach scanned the bench until his glare locked on me. "King! Git over here!" Helmet in hand, I obeyed. "Yer in, boy. Now move that ball! I'm sick of what I'm seein' out there." His eyes burned. The lines on his face darkened into deep crevices. I nodded and hustled over to where the offense was gathered.

During the kickoff, Abner reviewed several plays with me that were likely to be called during the next series. I remembered them all as if I were actually looking at the playbook. My confidence soared. This would be my first meaningful action this season. I had taken a few snaps in some earlier games, but the outcome of each contest had already been decided when I came in.

This time the starters were still in the game and there was nearly a full half left to play. I ran out onto the field. The PA announcer sent my name echoing through the stadium. The crowd roared. My adrenaline flowed. "Alright boys," I said in the huddle, "let's have some fun. Bishop 7 right on three." We clapped and lined up at our own 22-yard line. Barking the snap count, I felt ten feet tall. Thor hiked me the ball. I moved right and handed it to Rich Bryant, our speedy tailback. He burst through a hole, adding six yards to the 1,000-plus he had already gained this season.

The next play came in. I took the snap. After a three-step drop I fired a laser that hit flanker Sammy Jones between the numbers. He bolted forward for a pickup of eleven yards. First down. Our fans yelled their approval. I felt like the power of God was surging through me.

We marched down the field. On each play, the offensive line, led by Thor and Tank, exploded into the Louisville defenders. Rich raced through the open holes. When I dropped back to pass, I had all day to find a target. My deliveries were smooth and easy, just like in practice. On the ninth play of the drive, I found tight end Rick Wilkerson open in the end zone. The stadium erupted. Falcons players hollered as they bounded off the field. Coach McNabb greeted me on the sideline. "Good job, King. You keep it up, ya hear? I know we can move the ball against those people." After the PAT, we trailed 20-7.

Buoyed by the shifting momentum, the Falcons defense held Louisville to only one first down. After the punt, our offense took the field. My teammates had hungry looks in their eyes. I felt like the commander of an elite group of warriors. We again advanced the ball. But after crossing midfield, the Louisville defense stiffened. Facing a third and seven at the Cardinals 46, I faded back to pass. My receivers were blanketed. Ducking away from the outstretched paw of a defensive end, I cut left and raced downfield. I picked up seventeen yards and another first down before a cornerback forced me out of bounds. Several defenders hung their heads as they trudged into position for the next play. Rich then broke free for a 29-yard touchdown run. We had closed to within six points.

The ensuing Louisville possession ate up several minutes and resulted in a field goal. Penalties killed our next drive. Fortunately, the Cardinals offense then suffered the same fate. After the Louisville punt, we took over at our own 32-yard line with 5:41 left in the fourth quarter. With the Falcons down 23-14, our fans grew audibly restless.

Coach McNabb called a reverse to start the drive. Thanks to wide receiver Preston Coleman's speed, the run netted 23 yards. A draw play and two completed passes brought us to the Louisville 18-yard line. Hoping to surprise the Cardinals, Coach called an option. It was a play the Falcons had rarely used this season. Taking the snap, I kept the ball and turned the corner. Seven yards later, I was buried by a 250-pound linebacker. My whole body hurting, I could barely talk in the huddle. I was most pleased that the next play, a fullback trap, did not involve any running or throwing on my part. It proved to be a perfect call. Ed Korbelik rumbled through the confused defense and into the end zone. We trailed 23-21 with 3:14 on the clock.

Abner, greatly animated, shouted exhortations to me as I caught my breath on the bench. "Helluva job, King! That's three TD drives. They can't stop you. Hell no! Next time you get out there, it'll be for the ballgame. Two-minute offense. No mistakes. Field goal is all we'll need."

After Abner had finished his encouragements, I walked over to Burhan Mak, our placekicker. He stood near his practice net shifting his weight from one foot to the other.

"You ready to kick the game-winner, Big Mak?"

"Goo-wad, King!" he said in his Malaysian accent, "I hit ten for twelve this year. What do you think?"

"Sorry, man. Just making sure you're ready."

"King, you stupid oaf! You remember the Air Force game? You know why we win? Because I kick a damn field goal with no time left. That's why we win! Just get me in range and I save your asses again." His brown face cracked into a broad grin. The accompanying snickers he emitted reminded me of the sound of teeth being brushed.

The Falcons defense meanwhile had forced a punt. The kick bounced into the end zone. We had the ball at our 20-yard line, but only 53 seconds remained and we had no timeouts left. Our defense had to use them all during Louisville's last possession. Out on the field, I scanned the ten faces around me. "Alright men, let's win this game. We're going to run Nuclear Red Series C. No huddle."

On the first play, I found Rich in the flat. He scampered out of bounds after an eight-yard gain. The next play, I overthrew Sammy running down the sideline. On third down I could not find an open receiver, so I tucked the ball and ran. I juked past one linebacker and broke the tackle of another before a cornerback knocked my legs out from under me at our 43. The clock paused at 32 seconds while the chains were moved.

A dropped ball and a deflected pass left us with a third and ten. Coach signaled an option keeper for the next play. Expecting another pass, the Cardinals were caught off guard. Racing hard, I rounded the right corner and picked up 13 yards to reach the Louisville 44. Only 12 seconds remained in the game. My heart pounded. The teams hurried into position as the chain-bearers hustled down the sideline. With the snap, the Falcons receivers bolted forward. Preston and Sammy sprinted hard down opposite sides of the field. Rick charged down the middle, while Rich ran a crossing pattern. Looking right, I fired behind Preston, hoping he remembered the route. Just as the ball rolled off my fingertips, he planted and curved back toward the sideline. He and the spiral arrived at the same place at the same time. Cradling the ball, he stepped out of bounds at the 29-yard line. Five seconds were left on the clock.

I leaped in the air and pumped my fist. The crowd exploded in cheers. The Falcons field goal unit scampered onto the field. On the sideline, coaches and players congratulated me with slaps on the back. We then held our breath as the teams lined up. Louisville called a timeout. A collective exhale followed. Tension hung thick all around us. Burhan paced in a figure eight pattern muttering to himself before shooting a practice kick into the net. He was facing a 46-yard attempt, one yard longer than his career best.

The teams lined up again. I stood at the edge of the field, fists clenched in anticipation. Some of guys around me could not watch.

It happened in an instant. The snap. The hold. The kick. Barely missing the outstretched arms of the leaping defenders, the ball sailed through the air in a low arc. A hush came over the stadium. Our coaches and players leaned forward to gauge if the ball was on target. The brown projectile floated down, clearing the yellow crossbar by no more than a foot. The referees' hands shot up. A gun sounded. The scoreboard confirmed our victory: Falcons 24, Cardinals 23.

Huge linemen hoisted the 165-pound Malaysian kicker onto their shoulders and carried him off the field. Beaming, he thrust his green helmet into the air. "You see, King," Burhan shouted as his procession passed by, "I'm always ready! Now we're both heroes!" A thousand hands patted my shoulder pads as I pushed through the throng of fans toward the locker room tunnel.

My exuberance continued the next morning at church. Worshipping stirred deep waves of joy that I hadn't felt since high school. After lunch I reported to the stadium along with the other first- and second-teamers. Most of the guys were upbeat from our big win, though some were dragging from hangovers. After running a few laps and forty-yard dashes, the team filed into the field house to watch game film. Each position coach led his players into a separate office. Like usual, Coach McNabb joined Boz and me in Abner's office.

The projector chattered away as black and white images of the game danced across the portable tripod screen. While watching the first half, Boz slouched in his chair. He leaned his head on one fist and then the other. Abner occasionally pointed out mistakes he had made. With more restraint than usual, the quarterback coach offered brief suggestions on what Boz should do differently in future games. McNabb remained quiet.

Finally it was time to watch the second half. My ego jumped at the sight of me, Number 17, racing past defenders and firing strikes to receivers. Both Abner and McNabb complimented me on my poise in directing the offense. Watching the end of the game gave me goose bumps. After Abner shut off the projector and flipped on the light, we all sat around his desk. He and McNabb were on one side; Boz and I sat on the other side. The two coaches then summarized what worked and what did not work during the game. Then everybody was quiet. I wondered if we would soon be dismissed.

"Boys, I'm gonna cut ta the chase," McNabb finally drawled. "Dave is gonna start at quarterback next Saturday." His eyes shifted back and forth between Boz and me. Silence again filled the room. Though rumors of such a move had been spreading, it was still a shock to hear him say the actual words. "Now Boz, don't you go frettin' about this, ya hear? We still believe in you. We're prouda what ya done this year. Gained some valuable experience. You know yer the quarterback of the future at Western Iowa. We just—"

"Screw that!" Boz said. "One bad half and you bench me. That's crap! I'm outta here." He stood and turned to leave.

Abner shot to his feet. "Bosworth!" His voice hit like a thunderclap. "You watch your mouth when you address the coach. No one has dismissed you. Now sit down and shut up!" The rage in his voice reminded me of facing his cousin's wrath back at Eastridge. The crew cut that Abner now wore added to the effect.

With a sullen glare, Boz sunk back into his chair.

"You are not being benched because of one bad half," Abner continued. "You've struggled all season, and you're just not getting any better. Coach Vanderlinden and Coach McNabb agree with me on this."

"Going into yesterday's game we were five and three with me as starting quarterback," Boz protested. "That doesn't sound like struggling."

"Four of those wins came against teams with losing records. And the scores were closer than they should have been. Our passing attack has been sorely lacking all year. The running backs and the defense have had to carry the team. We won those five games in spite of your quarterbacking, not because if it."

"That's bullshit."

"You want to know what's bullshit?" Abner asked. "How about the eighteen interceptions you've thrown this year? Five of them run back for touchdowns. Hell, you've only thrown five touchdown passes to your own receivers. That means you've thrown as many touchdowns for our opponents as you have for us. *That's* bullshit."

"Gentlemen please," McNabb said in a soothing voice. "Let's all simmer down. Now Boz, we know yer workin' hard out there. But ya got ta be patient. Remember, yer a freshman goin' against defenses loaded with juniors and seniors. Some of them boys been startin' for three years now. Yer time will come, I guarantee it. In a couple a years, you'll be one of the top collegiate quarterbacks."

"So I have to sit the rest of this season and all of next year?" Boz said. "I'm not waiting that long to start again. I'll transfer."

"Don't you threaten us, boy!" Abner shot back. "We make the decisions around here. Not you! You understand me?" After Boz grunted contemptuously, Abner lunged across the table and grabbed the freshman's shirt, pulling him forward. "You answer me when I ask you a question!"

"Abner, please," McNabb said, rising and placing both hands on the quarterback coach's shoulders. "Unhand the boy." A couple seconds later, Abner released his grip. "I think it's best if Boz and me go talk about this in my office," McNabb continued. "We all need to cool down some. Come on, son. Let's go."

Coach patted my shoulder on his way to the door. Boz glared at Abner for a few more seconds before stomping out of the room. McNabb quietly closed the door behind them. I examined the tabletop as Abner paced behind his desk. He finally sat down.

"King, I owe you an apology. We should've started you a lot earlier. Definitely after the loss to Notre Dame. Hell, we should've gone with you to start the season. Now we're already nine games in."

I suppressed a flash of anger. "We can't worry about that," I said. "What's done is done. We've just got to focus on winning our last two games. We need those to get to a bowl."

Abner stared at me. "King, you've got a great attitude. You're a mature kid. A leader. Damn it, why didn't we start you sooner? We could be eight and one right now, and ranked. Instead, we get blown out by Iowa State and struggle to beat Drake."

"That's in the past. We've got Memphis next Saturday. That's all I'm thinking about."

"Yeah, Memphis." He shut his eyes and tilted back his head. "King, I wasn't fair to you. I just wanted Boz to succeed so bad. After what happened to his daddy and Johnny, I tried to look out for him. Devoted my coaching career to him. At Eastridge I put everything into making him a great quarterback. We lost ourselves in football. It helped ease the pain. I wanted the kid to be a big star in college. When Western Iowa offered me this position, we jumped. Gave us the chance to stay together. I thought he was ready this season." Abner shook his head. "He wasn't."

"He'll still have his day." I tried not to think about Asa.

"I don't know." He frowned. "Not with that attitude of his."

"He'll cool down. He's a good kid."

Abner tapped a cigarette out of a box of Kents and lit up. "You know, you played a helluva game yesterday. Really saved our bacon. That could've have been our fourth defeat. Would've killed any chance we had for a bowl."

"Thanks. We've got a great team. They really stepped up." The smell of burning tobacco carried me back to the days of playing guitar in Sal Kishman's office.

"Damn right they did." He jabbed his Kent toward me. A wisp of white smoke swirled up to the ceiling. "And they're young. We only lose two starters on offense. You, Bryant, Jones, Coleman, and four-fifths of the line are coming back. Man, they're good. And they're still getting better. With you playing like you did yesterday, we're gonna score some points next year."

"Yeah. The defense is improving too."

"You bet." He leaned back and seemed to drift into a daydream. I silently thanked God that I did not quit the team back in September.

Monday morning during American Literature a familiar feeling returned. The sensation always started in my stomach, as if I'd just downed a cocktail of excitement, queasiness, and longing. It then spread through my body. Though the feeling hit at random times, it was always sharpest on Monday-Wednesday-Friday mornings. It was on those occasions I went to the Student Union after my lit class for a hit of that which would make me feel better, and worse.

After buying a coffee, I found a table in the cafeteria that allowed me to sit with my back to the wall. The regulars were present—the brooding Goth couple, the trio of science geeks, the mousy loner, and the bearded professors in their tweed jackets with the elbow patches. Other campus miscellany were scattered about at various tables. Pretending to review my European history textbook, I waited. My ever-vigilant eyes monitored the front of the room.

A couple underclassmen recognized me and said something about a nice game Saturday. I nodded, trying to look studious. Fortunately, they did not linger. At 9:15 *she* appeared at the cash register. Hair in a ponytail, she wore a pink turtleneck and a long maroon floral-print skirt. Her radiance transfixed me. It was as if she was in color and everything else in the world was black and white. Her usual companions, the short redhead and the dowdy brunette, were not with her. *Maybe this would be a good chance to go talk to her*. She glided through the tables and took a seat on the other side of the cafeteria. My courage evaporated. I buried my face in my book.

My thoughts churned for the next several minutes. I was then electrocuted by the sound of my own name. "… mind if I join you?" It was her! She stood right there before me, smiling. I gestured awkwardly at a chair. She placed her notebooks and coffee on the table and sat down. A lilac fragrance tickled my nostrils. "How are you?" she asked. "I haven't talked to you in forever."

"Uh, Abigail, hi, um, yeah. I think it was the homecoming rally about a month ago." Having just glanced at my watch, I knew that it was precisely 29 days, 12 hours, and 23 minutes since I'd last talked to her.

"Wow, that's right. I see you in here all the time. But you always look so busy studying, I don't want to bother you. And you never stop by to say hi to me."

Damn it! "Oh, um, yeah. I just come in here to review my notes for my ten o'clock history class. No big deal. Now that you mention it, I have seen you here a couple times. You're usually with friends. I didn't think *you* wanted to be bothered."

"Don't be silly, Dave! I'd love for you to come over and join us. Then I could impress Suzi and Christine. They're reporters for *The Falconer*. They'd be so jealous that I know the starting quarterback of the football team."

"How did you find out about that? It wasn't going to be announced until this afternoon."

"Ooh, I just got a scoop." She giggled. "Actually, it's no big secret. After Saturday's game, the students would riot if you weren't named starter. Jim, our sports editor, was stomping around the office this morning yelling, 'King better be starting. I'm going to start a petition to get rid of that old man if King isn't starting.' He just went on and on."

"Takes his football seriously, huh?"

"Oh yeah. Just like everyone else on campus." Her nose wrinkled playfully. "So, congratulations. Aren't you excited?" She touched my arm.

"Yes, definitely." *Because you just touched my arm.*

"I bet." She took a sip of coffee. I did likewise. "How is everything else with you? Are Anthony and Joe doing okay?"

"You know my nephews?"

"No, but I read the articles about the accident. That was heartbreaking."

"Oh. Well, it hasn't been easy for them. Anthony is finally talking more. I think he'll be okay, eventually. His faith is strong. Joe is still in a shell. He only talks if you ask him a direct question. And then he usually just responds with single word answers. It's going to take time for him to get over what happened."

"That would be rough. How's your sister?"

"Zoe is okay. It's been hell for her, but she's a tough girl. She's been strong for her boys. Everything life throws at her, she fights through it. We lost our mom when I was four. A few years after that we lost two brothers in Vietnam. Then Zoe's husband was killed by a drunk driver. And this year, Asa."

"That poor woman. Dave, I'm so sorry for what your family has gone through." Her green eyes glistened with compassion.

"Thanks." I looked down at my coffee. "Would you believe she got robbed last month? Someone cleaned out all her jewelry and a bunch of cash she had stashed away."

"Oh my gosh. That's terrible. Was anybody home at the time?"

"No. The boys were over at a friend's house and Zoe was working late. She found out when she got home from work."

"That is so sad. I'll be praying for her."

"Thanks," I said with surprise. "You're a Christian?"

"Yes. How about you?"

I nodded. She then proceeded to tell me about when she accepted Christ in sixth grade. She also described her churches in Carmi, Illinois, where she grew up, and Lincoln, Nebraska, where her family moved when she was sixteen. I told her about FCA, BSU, and the weekly Bible study I attended with several other football players. The conversation was both wonderful and torturous. I loved hearing about her faith, but that made the fact that she was with someone else even more agonizing. I felt like yelling, "God, why do you torment me?" But I instead prayed silently for the strength to accept his will.

I would need every ounce of that strength when she mentioned Caleb Nagel, an odious reminder of the brick wall that stood between us. She lamented his reluctance to go to church with her. Hearing her talk about Caleb as her boyfriend made me want to retch. Nonetheless, I nodded politely at the right moments. She then asked me if I was dating anyone.

"No, Abigail, I am not."

"Dave King!" she said with a frown. "That's the second time you've done that. No more!"

"Huh? What?" I was so depressed hearing about Caleb that I did not know what I had done. *Did I curse him out loud? I thought I was just doing that in my head.*

She tried to maintain an indignant demeanor, but her beautiful lips stretched into a smile. "It's Gail. My friends call me Gail. I've told you that before."

"Oh, uh, sorry. I don't know why I do that." My scrambling brain then provided my mouth with a response that made no sense. "I've got a sister named Abigail. We call her Abby."

"Sister! Are you saying you think of me as your sister?" she demanded with a trace of amusement.

"No, of course not," I blurted. "I was just sayin' I've got a sister named Abby. That's all. Gail's a pretty name. I won't forget it from now on."

She coyly raised a brow before glancing at her watch. "Oh my gosh! It's a quarter past ten. We've been talking for an hour. Didn't you say you had a ten o'clock class?"

"Yeah. European History. It's cancelled for today."

"Really?"

"It is now." I grinned.

She laughed. "I'm sorry. I just lost track of time."

"Don't worry about it. It was fun talking to you."

"Yeah, it was fun," she said with a smile that rocketed my heart rate. "But I've got to get going." She stood and gathered her notebooks and empty coffee cup. "I've got a 10:15 meeting at *The Falconer* office with the general manager and the department heads. Good thing they can't start without me." She tilted her head. "Say, Dave, can I ask you a question?"

"Uh, sure."

"Do you like coffee?"

"Yeah, of course I do. Who doesn't like coffee? Gotta have my cup of Joe every morning. Can't get going without it."

"Oh. I noticed that your cup is still half full, and whenever you take a drink you make a face like you're taking medicine or something."

Busted! "Oh, um, I didn't know. That's just how we football players take our coffee—strong and bitter. Helps us stay focused."

"Hmm, interesting." She nodded. "Well, I should go. Bye Dave," she said sweetly. Not wanting to get busted again, I did not watch her walk away. My eyes nearly seceded from my head in protest. For the next several minutes, I reflected on the conversation. *She really didn't want me to think of her as a sister? That's good, right? You can't date your sister.* I was in high spirits the rest of the morning.

Practice that afternoon was actually enjoyable. I finally got to wear the red jersey that protected the starting quarterback from hits during scrimmages. The team was also unusually upbeat for a Monday practice—the starters looked especially sharp. Boz, however, moped around. I tried to encourage him, but he ignored me. After practice, McNabb addressed a gathering of reporters at the edge of the field. I quickly escaped to the field house.

After a short weightlifting session and a shower, I donned my brown leather jacket and ventured out into the crisp autumn evening. I was part of a convoy of players heading to the training table at Crookham Hall. My former roommate Perry walked alongside me.

"You heard what's for supper tonight?" I asked.

"Dung," he replied. "Steaming vats of monkey dung. Succulent brown goodness in every heaping spoonful." He had a crazy look in his eye.

"So glad I asked."

"Dave! Dave!" A frantic female voice jerked our heads to the left. Charging straight toward me was a pack of reporters. "Could we ask you a few questions?"

Sighing, I veered over to face the phalanx of microphones.

"I'll save you a big pile of supper," Perry called out as he continued walking.

The interview lasted about ten minutes before Abner exited the field house and shooed the reporters away. Given the topic—me starting—I did not mind answering their questions.

The last player to arrive at Crookham Hall, I brought up the rear of the supper line. Though starters routinely cut to the front, I passed on that unwritten training table privilege. Cutting always struck me as juvenile and bad for team morale. Plus, there were plenty of T-bones and mashed potatoes for everyone.

Following supper, I walked home alone. It was well after sunset. The flickering streetlights above provided a sparse illumination of my street. I passed two cute girls on the sidewalk. "Hi Dave," one of them said. I had never seen either of them before. *I think I'm going to like this starting quarterback thing.* Feeling good about myself as I approached the house, I wondered if any adoring coeds would be waiting on my porch.

Instead, a fist came flying out of the darkness to greet my jaw. It was attached to a tall lanky figure that had been crouching behind an unkempt evergreen bush at the front of the house. The punch stung, but the surprise was worse. My assailant wrapped his arms around my torso and tried to drag me down. I rotated away as if trying to escape the grasp of a defensive lineman, but he hooked my leg and lifted it up. I started hopping in an attempt to keep my balance. The man, his face hidden behind a ski mask, stepped forward to push me to the ground. I grabbed his shoulders and took him with me.

We rolled over each other in the grass. He ended up on top of me. I gripped under his armpits and flung him off—an easier task than I thought it would be. For the first time, I truly appreciated the persistence of the Falcons strength coach in helping me to increase my bench press to 300 pounds. After the man hit the ground, I sprung up and pounced on him. As he flailed at me, I ripped off his ski mask. Grabbing his wrists, I pinned his arms to the ground. He struggled in vain to break my grip. I recognized his face.

"Paul? What the … what are you doing?"

"Get off me!" He twisted his body in a desperate attempt to escape, but my knees pressed his shoulders firmly to the earth.

"Why? So you can attack me again?"

After a series of futile writhing motions, he let out an exasperated groan. "Stop trying to take her away." He started to cry.

My anger dissolved into pity. I released his wrists and stood up. "Here," I said, extending a hand.

He remained on his back, rubbing his eyes. "You don't love her. I do. Stop trying to take her from me."

"I'm not trying to take her from you." The past semester flashed through my memory. Michelle had stopped by "just to say hi" quite a few times. It happened at least once, sometimes twice, a week. She often hugged me when she left. One time she even gave me a peck on the cheek. I didn't discourage her. Having not dated much since Amy left campus, I liked the female attention. But Michelle's visits ignited fires inside me that were not easily doused. When she was around, I often imagined what it would be like to go all the way with her. The thoughts posed a growing challenge to my renewed commitment to wait until marriage. After each visit, my mind became a battleground.

"You're not, huh?" Paul sat up and brushed the grass from his disheveled hair. "I know she comes over here. She still likes you. She's even called me 'Dave' a couple times."

"I don't ask her to come over. She just stops by. All we do is talk."

He looked away and started sobbing again. "Now you're the starting quarterback. I can't compete with that. I've lost her."

"You haven't lost her. I don't like Michelle that way anymore."

"Well, how do you like her?"

"As a friend. We went through a lot together. When John died, she lost a brother and I lost a best friend. I care about her and her family."

"You can have anybody. Why do you have to take *her*?"

"I'm not taking Michelle."

"Please let her go." He sniffled. "She's all I've got, and she's hung up on you."

"Listen, I have let her go. I don't want her. I know we're not meant to be together. I'm sorry she's been coming over here. I'll tell her not to do that anymore. I'll put a stop to it."

"Really?"

"Yes. Michelle is your girl. I promise I'm not going to get back with her."

After sitting quietly for a while, he stood. "Sorry about jumping you. She's got me all screwed up. Please don't tell her or anybody else about this."

"Tell her about what? Nothing happened here." I brushed some lawn debris off his shoulder.

"Thanks, Dave."

I asked if he wanted to hang out inside for a while. He declined.

When I went in the house, Tank was watching Monday Night Football with a big bowl of popcorn in his lap. "You missed the kickoff," he said with a full mouth. "Where you been?"

I plopped into a chair. "Just ran into an old friend from high school."

Tuesday was Election Day. The plaza east of the Student Union bustled with activity. On one side was a group of students promoting the campaigns of Dick Clark and Tom Harkin. Some of them waved posters featuring red, white, and blue donkeys. On the other side of the plaza was a gathering of students brandishing signs hailing Roger Jepsen and Julian Garrett. Patriotic elephants graced their posters. Shouts rang back and forth between the two groups. The elephant people yelled about inflation, abortion, and Panama. The donkeys responded with Watergate, peace in the Middle East, and a woman's right to choose. I passed swiftly through the gauntlet of democracy on my way to Spanish class.

After lunch, I voted and walked over to the field house for practice. Ned, the head trainer, stood at the door to the locker room. He told us to wait inside in our street clothes. The players buzzed with optimism that practice would be cancelled—a reward for our hard work the previous day. One of the defensive linemen entertained us by playing the Star-Spangled Banner with his armpit.

After about ten minutes, Coach McNabb entered. His assistant coaches fanned out on each side of him. The players hushed. It was then I noticed that Boz had not yet arrived.

"Take a knee, boys," Coach said, looking haggard. We complied. "I've had alotta ups and downs in my years of coaching. Today is the worst of it. I don't know how to tell y'all, so I'm just gonna say it." The tone of his voice caused an ill feeling to germinate in my gut. It was an all too familiar sensation.

"Last night," McNabb continued, "there was a fire at Coach Kishman's place. He got his wife and daughters out of the house. Doctors say they're gonna be okay. But Abner took it pretty bad. Burns. Smoke. He didn't make it."

The whole team was paralyzed. Not believing what I had just heard, I scanned the row of assistant coaches for Abner. He was not there. Beads of sweat rolled down my back.

McNabb looked down and shook his head. "I'm so sorry ta hafta tell ya this, boys. Abner was a good man. A fine coach. Gave his all for the Big Green." Coach's mouth quivered. A few moments later, he turned toward the exit.

After a painful silence, Blaine Vanderlinden, the offensive coordinator, stepped forward to address the team. "Funeral arrangements haven't been made yet. We'll let you know. There will be no practice today, gentlemen. Coach Jackson will lead us in prayer, and then you can all go on home. Remember to keep the Kishman family in your thoughts and prayers."

Before we left, several players asked about the details of the fire. Vanderlinden told us that it started between 2:00 and 3:00 a.m. "The authorities think it was arson," he said.

That last word rang violently through my head to spawn a terrifying thought. *Please God, no!* I rushed out of the locker room and sprinted home. Bursting into the house, I grabbed the phone and dialed.

"Zoe Krieger."

"Zoe," I wheezed, struggling to catch my breath.

"Dave? What's wrong? You sound like you're trying to make an obscene call."

"Where were the boys last night?"

"My boys? They were home with me. Watching television and doing homework."

"Are you sure they were there all night? Could they have slipped out after you went to bed?"

"Slipped out? No. I'm a light sleeper. I would have heard them if they tried to leave. Why are you asking me all this? Is someone trying to pin something on them?"

"No, it's … I just wanted to make sure they were home last night."

"Yes, they were home. Satisfied? Now can I go? I've got a lot of work to do."

"Yeah, okay. Sorry. I'll call you at home later tonight."

I paced around the house. *Arson*. The word haunted me. A man had died. *That makes it murder*. I sat down and tried to focus. Thinking about my nephews made me nauseous. *Who else could have done it?* I then remembered that Boz did not show up for practice today. He and Abner had been on the outs since the game Saturday. *Maybe getting benched pushed him over the edge.* I tried to think of other possibilities. Caleb Nagel came to mind. *As Boz's fraternity brother, maybe he wanted revenge against Abner.*

Thor, Tank, and the Rooster came home. All of us depressed, we discussed the possibilities. They speculated that it was probably a crazy fan who did it. Nonetheless, the thought that my family could be involved would not go away. By four o'clock, I could not take it anymore. I jumped in my car and drove to Omaha.

"Hey, Uncle D," Anthony said, opening the door. "Whatcha doin' here?"

"I was in the neighborhood." Inside, Joe sat at the dining room table surveying a chessboard. He said nothing. Anthony slid into the chair across from him.

"Check it out," the older brother said. "I finally got him on the ropes." Though in no mood to analyze a game, I glanced at the board. Anthony's white pieces outnumbered Joe's black pieces.

"Boys, Abner Kishman is dead. He was killed in a fire at his house last night."

Anthony looked up with a grave expression. "Oh, that's terrible, Uncle D." Joe, continuing to examine the board, did not move.

"The police think it was arson."

"Oh."

Joe moved a piece and stared at me with gray eyes. "I'm sorry to hear that, Dave. No one should have to die like that." His voice lacked inflection.

Anthony moved a piece. "Yes! I got his queen! I think I'm actually gonna beat him." Joe's mouth formed a faint grin. He turned to study the board.

"It was arson," I repeated in a firm voice. "You know what that means? Given what happened two months ago, the police are going to want to talk to you. Probably tonight."

"You think we're suspects?" Anthony asked. "We were here all last night. Ate supper here and didn't leave the house 'til this morning, when we went to school."

Joe captured the white bishop with his rook. "All night," he said, "right here."

"Mom knows we were here," Anthony continued. "Once the police talk to her, they'll know we couldn't have done it. Don't worry, Uncle D." He moved a piece. My eyes bounced back and forth between them.

Joe captured a pawn with his knight. "Check."

"Oh, nooo," Anthony said. "Look at this. He's gonna do it again."

"I'm afraid so," Joe said. "Once you took the queen, your fate was sealed."

"Crap." Anthony moved his king.

Joe moved a bishop. "Check."

"I want you both to go to Abner's funeral," I said with irritation.

"What?" Anthony said, jerking his head towards me. "I ain't gonna—"

"No, he's right," Joe interrupted. "We should go pay our final respects to Mr. Kishman. Let us know when the funeral is, Dave. We'll be there. Maybe we could ride with you."

"Fine," Anthony said. He tipped over his king with a look of disgust.

"Not quite the Game of the Century," Joe said. "But I think Fischer would have been impressed with my queen sac. Want to play?" he asked me. He smiled wide enough to reveal teeth. It was not a comforting sight.

"I've got to get back to campus. How about if we go to church tomorrow night, Anthony? We haven't been to a Wednesday service for a while." He nodded. "I think you should go too, Joe."

"That will be great, Dave," Joe replied. "See you tomorrow."

My stomach twisted as I drove back to my house. I tried to pray at the wheel, but the words came out in a jumble. My unease increased after I got home. The house was empty. Pacing alone in my room, I wanted to punch a hole in the wall. Time passed and my housemates still did not return. I then remembered that it was Tuesday night. They were at a Bible study in the athletic dorm. Really needing someone to talk to, I made a decision. *I don't care about her boyfriend. I'm going to call.*

She was home and agreed to meet. By the time I reached the fountain by the Student Union, she was already there. Though she faced the opposite direction, I recognized her tan down jacket. Her hair danced in the breeze. Remnants of banners, posters, buttons, and other campaign debris littered the plaza. I stopped about five feet behind her. "Hi." When she turned around, I gasped in horror. "Oh, Gail!"

"You don't like my new look?" she asked with a wan smile.

"Does it hurt?" I could not help staring at the apple-sized bruise around her left eye.

"Not too bad. Not anymore."

"What happened?"

"Let's walk." She led me to the sidewalk that crossed central campus. "First, you have to promise me that you won't freak out."

"What? I don't like the sound of that."

"Now Dave, it's okay. Just listen."

"Fine."

We passed by the bell tower. "Somebody from Alpha Lambda Phi saw us talking in the Union yesterday. He told Caleb we were together all morning. Said we were flirting and holding hands, and a bunch of other stuff he made up." She sighed. "Caleb, of course, believed him. He came over to my sorority last night during supper. Called me a bitch and a whore in front of everybody, then stormed off. I let him cool down for an hour and then went over to his house. I get there and he's drunk. Completely trashed. I tried to explain that he had it all wrong. He just sat there in the den, not moving. It's like he was a statue. Then all of a sudden, he leaps up and hits me. Got me good, as you can see. Knocked me halfway across the room."

I stopped in my tracks. "He is dead. He is beyond dead. I'm going to gut him and grind his bones into fertilizer." I turned to head back to fraternity row. Everything in front of me was red.

"Dave, where are you going?" I felt Gail's hand on my shoulder.

"I'll give you three guesses. Don't try to talk me out of it."

"You can't see him now. Visiting hours are over."

"Huh?"

"Caleb is currently residing in the Pottawattamie County Jail. Three of his frat brothers saw him hit me. They called the police and turned him in. That makes four witnesses, plus the physical evidence." She pointed to her eye. "His father is furious. He said he's going to let Caleb rot in jail for a while before he posts bail."

"Good. And when he does get out, I'll be waiting for him." I cracked my knuckles.

"No Dave, you won't. First off, beating up Caleb would land *you* in jail. Second, he isn't going to be around here anymore. After his arrest, six pledges at his fraternity reported him to university administration. They accused him of some nasty hazing violations. Have you ever heard the rumors about the carrot and peanut butter rituals?"

"Those stories are true? Ewww."

"Apparently. And my boyfriend was the ringleader. I had no idea. I am such an idiot."

"No you're not. You were just trying so hard to see the good in him that you missed some things. I can understand that."

"Maybe." She flicked her hair back from her face. "Anyway, Caleb has already been kicked out of his frat and the university is in the process of removing him as a student. After he serves his jail sentence, I doubt that he'll stick around here. Especially since so many people want to take a shot at him."

"Are you okay?"

"I'm fine. The eye looks worse than it is. This is actually a blessing. I'd been wanting to break up with Caleb for several weeks. I didn't know how to do it without hurting him." We started walking again. "But enough about me. You sounded upset when you called. What did you want to talk about?"

I told her about Abner, the fire, and my conversation with my nephews. I recounted pretty much every related detail I could think of, including my history with Sal Kishman. My mouth must have been running for a half hour straight as we wandered around campus. We ended up sitting on a bench next to Looft Lake. The moonlight shimmered off the surface of the water.

"That is so sad," she said with sympathy in her eyes. "I'm sorry, Dave. It's terrible what you've had to go through this year." She brushed her fingers over my arm. "I know you're worried about Joe and Anthony, but maybe it's best if you step back and wait for the investigation to be completed. It's a police matter now. They'll figure out who set the fire. And even though your nephews were acting a little strange today, it doesn't mean they're guilty of anything. You said they're still getting over losing Asa. That could have been why they acted the way they did. Hearing about Abner probably stirred up a lot of emotions for them. It's not easy for boys their age to deal with stuff like that."

"Maybe that's it." I looked up at the moon. "Either way, you're right. I'm just going to have to wait."

"I'll be praying for you."

"Thanks. Thanks for listening." I glanced at my watch. "It's getting late. I should let you get home." We walked to her sorority. At the front door she turned to face me.

"Dave, I'm glad you called. You can come to me whenever you want to talk about anything, okay?" Her eyes sparkled.

"Thanks, Gail. Maybe I'll see you tomorrow at the Union." My inner voice piped up. *Just tell her, you wimp!*

"Yeah, I hope so."

"Bye," I said nervously, before turning to walk away. *Come on, nancy boy, grow a pair. How long do you think a girl like that is going to stay single?* I stopped and spun around. "Gail."

My heart rattling against my ribcage, I walked back to her. A time bomb that had been ticking for two months finally went off. "I know you've got a lot going on in your life right now—my timing is probably crap. But I have to tell you something." I shoved my trembling hands into the pockets of my jacket. "I, uh, don't really like coffee."

She looked confused. "Okay."

What I said next was like jumping out of an airplane, and I wasn't sure if I had a parachute. "All those mornings at the Union, I go there just to see you. Even if it's only for a few glimpses. What I'm saying is … I'm crazy about you, Gail. I can't get you out of my mind. When I'm in class, at practice, eating, trying to sleep, you're there. I've never seen a woman as beautiful as you. I lose my breath every time you walk in the cafeteria. And you're so smart and caring. When we talked yesterday, I wanted to stay there all day with you. I'd call you my dream girl, but you're far beyond anything I could ever imagine. You're so unbelievable, I … I'm uh, going to stop now. I'm sorry about this. I just couldn't keep it bottled up anymore." My last words came out in a mumble.

She gaped at me in shock. My inner voice returned. *Idiot!! What was that? All you had to do was ask her to a movie. Was that so hard? Instead you become a gushing fountain of sappy drivel. Have you ever talked to a girl before?*

As she continued staring, I tried to think of a parting comment that would salvage my last shred of dignity. Then suddenly, the statue came to life. Without a word, she grabbed me. The tight hug was voltaic—not some "you're a good friend" embrace. My senses boiled over until I was floating witless high above the earth. After what could have been minutes or hours, she whispered in my ear. "I feel the same way about you."

My burgeoning romance with Gail kept me soaring the next couple of weeks. It kindled an ardor unlike anything I had ever felt. My past feelings for Michelle and Amy may have been strong, but they were primarily fueled by lust. Though physical attraction was a powerful part of my relationship with Gail, we also shared a friendship and a spiritual bond that I had not experienced with a girlfriend before. It was great just to be in her presence. As long as I was with her, I was happy.

But the dark shadows cast by Abner Kishman's death still lingered. The arson mystery gnawed away at me. It hit Boz even worse. Unable to finish even a single practice, he quit football and dropped out of school. Less than a week after the funeral, he was back home in Pleasant Hill living with his mother. The rest of the team rallied together. Maintaining our focus and discipline on the field, we won our last two games to finish the season at eight and three. That earned us a bid to play in the Garden State Bowl in New Jersey in December. Though it was not Miami or New Orleans, the players and our fans were still excited. Western Iowa had not been to a bowl game since 1973.

The Monday before Thanksgiving, there was a break in the arson investigation. Coach McNabb announced to the team that police had found the body of a street thug named Daggar in an alley in downtown Omaha. He had been robbed and stabbed to death. Bar patrons and transients who knew him reported that Daggar had been bragging recently about burning down a house. His boots matched the footprints found in Abner's yard the night of the fire. Daggar also matched the description given by a neighbor of a man lurking around Kishman's neighborhood that evening.

I was greatly relieved by the news. Then, Coach revealed one more piece of information. Prior to his death, Daggar had been seen at the bars flashing a large wad of bills. Wheels spun in my head. I raised my hand.

"Didn't the police say that Coach Kishman's house was not robbed that night?"

"Yes, that's right."

"So where did Daggar get all that money?"

McNabb sighed. "Investigators think he was hired. They reckon someone paid him ta burn down Abner's house."

"Do they know who?"

"No, Dave … they do not."

Chapter 13 – October 1979

The menacing lens protruding from the large mounted box reminded me of an alien ray gun. It was only a slight comfort that the personage behind the contraption looked human. Bright lights blazed down from above. I glanced up at the black mike boom and fidgeted with the gold buttons on the cuff of my green blazer. A red light on top of the box came on.

"Welcome back to *Falcons Football Wrap-Up*," said a man a few feet to my left. "I'm Bret Slater." He sat facing the camera in an olive swivel chair identical to the one I was in. His thick sandy brown moustache was the same color as the curly sphere of hair covering his head. He wore a lime sports jacket with wide lapels and a yellow tie that matched his plaid polyester slacks.

"Tonight we are joined by senior quarterback Dave King." Slater swiveled to face me. "Welcome to the program, Dave." He spoke in his usual punchy on-air cadence.

"Thanks, Bret. It's great to be here."

"Now, Dave, this has to be an exciting time for you. You're co-captain of a team that is undefeated and ranked 12th in both the AP and UPI polls."

"Absolutely. This is a very exciting time for my teammates and me. But we know there's still a lot of work to do."

"This season, of course, is a big contrast from your first three years at Western Iowa." He wrinkled his forehead to convey a more serious look. "In fact, a year ago at this time you were still riding the bench, a backup to freshman Boz Kishman. How frustrating was that?"

"Well uh, sure, I was disappointed I wasn't playing. But I tried to remain positive and use that time to study the playbook, work hard in practice, and continue to get better as a football player. More importantly, I can see now that God used that experience to teach me perseverance and how to be content in difficult circumstances. So even though my junior season was frustrating, God used it to strengthen my faith in …"

"That's super," Slater interrupted. "And then came the Louisville game last November. I'm sure all Falcons fans remember that day. Taking over in the third quarter, you led the team to a thrilling comeback victory. Then, with you at the helm, Western Iowa defeated Memphis and Navy, before closing out the season with an impressive win over Arizona State in the Garden State Bowl. The Falcons finished with a nine and three record and a top twenty ranking for the first time in nearly a decade." The forehead wrinkled again. "Dave, how important was last season's finish to the returning players?"

"Closing out last year with a winning streak and a bowl victory provided a major boost for the team. It really helped our confidence, especially with so many starters coming back. Even at winter conditioning I could see the excitement in my teammates' eyes. We all had high hopes heading into this season."

"Western Iowa has certainly lived up to those expectations, bursting out of the gate with five straight victories. That includes an upset of Penn State, a team that contended for the national championship last year. Are you surprised at the Falcons' success thus far?"

I shifted in my chair. "No, not really. I know that if we play the way we're capable of playing, we have a chance to win no matter who we're lined up against."

"Indeed," he said, turning to face the camera. "Dave King is currently averaging 272 yards a game passing. He's thrown for twelve touchdowns, against only three interceptions. And then there's his 319 yards rushing this season, a remarkable total considering that the Falcons employ a pro-set offense. Some football analysts, including this observer, believe that Mr. King is a legitimate Heisman candidate. But there are a lot of other weapons in the Western Iowa arsenal. Tailback Rich Bryant has already rushed for 703 yards. Preston Coleman and Sammy Jones are each averaging close to eighty yards a game receiving. And, of course, there is the offensive line led by Thor Heimlich and Tank Garber that has only allowed two sacks thus far this season."

His face flush, Slater swiveled toward me again. "Now, Dave, your success as Falcons quarterback has been most impressive. You've never lost as a starter. But this Saturday the team faces what may be its toughest test of the season when ninth-ranked Notre Dame comes to town. Are you and your teammates ready for this challenge?"

"I believe we are. We know that if we work hard in practice and then execute on the field, we'll have success." I looked straight at the camera. "Plus, we'll be playing at home, so I'm sure our fans will give us a big lift."

"Indeed. So, Dave, does Coach McNabb have a special game plan for Notre Dame? Any tricks up his sleeve?"

I pondered how to answer that potentially dangerous question. "Let's just say we'll be ready to play Saturday. It doesn't matter that we're facing one of the top programs in the nation. It doesn't matter that we lost in South Bend last year. We're just going to focus on playing Falcons football against the Irish, like we would against any opponent."

"Fair enough." He nodded while formulating another query. "As an independent often overshadowed by the Big Eight and Big Ten schools in the region, Western Iowa has not always received a lot of respect from the national media. Many Falcons fans believe the team should be ranked in the top ten right now. Do you think a victory over Notre Dame will finally earn your school the respect of the AP and UPI voters?"

"To tell you the truth, I don't worry about national rankings and the opinions of the so-called experts. I just want to honor Christ by playing to the best of my abilities." The corners of Slater's mouth drooped. "But, yeah," I continued, "I'm sure a victory over Notre Dame would get people's attention. The Irish have decades of tradition. They were national champions just two years ago. Beating them would really open some eyes."

"I know the coaches don't want you players thinking beyond the next game, but let's briefly discuss the remainder of the

Falcons' schedule. After Notre Dame, you play at Army, at Louisville, back home against Memphis and North Texas, and then down to South Carolina to close out the season against Coach McNabb's alma mater. The Falcons will likely be favored in each of their last five games. If you get past Notre Dame, is it time to starting thinking about an undefeated season? A major bowl game?" His eyes widened. "A national title, even?"

"Whoa, Bret," I said holding up both hands. "Don't talk like that. Not yet. Coach will have me running laps 'til midnight all month if I start talking about a national title in October."

"Okay, Dave," he said with a wink. "I understand. You've got to stay focused. But before we close, let me ask you one last question. What about the rumors that Coach McNabb will be retiring at the end of this season? Any truth to that? Is this it for the Coach?"

"I don't know. We players usually don't get too concerned about rumors."

Slater faced the camera. "After a successful coaching run at Northeast Texas State, Hugh McNabb took the reins of the Western Iowa football program in 1952. He had some strong teams in the sixties, but many experts believe this current group of Falcons is the best he's ever coached." Slater glanced at me. "How special would it be to go undefeated in Coach McNabb's final season?"

"It would be great to win all our games for Coach whether he retires or not. I personally hope he keeps at it for many years to come. Western Iowa just wouldn't be the same without Coach McNabb on the sideline."

"Indeed." Slater swiveled to face the camera, where a man with headphones slid his index finger across his throat. "Well that's all the time we have for this week's show. I'd like to thank our guest, senior quarterback Dave King. This Saturday, he leads your Falcons against the Fighting Irish of Notre Dame. Kickoff is at 2:00 p.m. You can watch the game right here on KETV, and then join us next Monday for another edition of *Falcons Football Wrap-Up*. I'm Bret Slater. Thanks for watching."

The red light on top of the camera went dark.

Tuesday evening at the training table, I loaded my tray with a cheeseburger, French fries, baby carrots, a slab of chocolate cake, and a protein drink. After exiting the line, I surveyed the athletes' cafeteria. Like usual, it resembled a crowded chessboard—white pieces on one side, black pieces on the other. Though racial issues were not a problem for the team, the football players generally self-segregated themselves when not in uniform.

At practice earlier that day, Coach Vanderlinden reiterated that I, as a co-captain, should be a leader both on and off the field. Considering his directive, I made a decision. Catapulting beyond my comfort zone, I steered over to the side of the room where the chess pieces were a darker shade than me.

As I approached a rectangular table populated by other members of the offense, seven ebony faces looked up at me. Their lively conversation slowed and then ceased. "Hey guys," I said, gesturing at an empty chair. "Mind if I join you?"

There was a moment of awkward silence. "Not at all, King," Preston Coleman finally said. "Grab yourself a handful of chair."

After I sat, the men at the table stared expectantly at me. Sammy Jones, sitting to my right, spoke first. "What's up, blood? Everything cool? Coach ask you to tell us something?"

"No." I shook my head. "Just thought I'd join my esteemed colleagues for some fine cuisine this evening." My teeth sank into a cheeseburger.

They exchanged confused glances. Preston, sitting directly across from me, grinned. "Well, alright. Glad you can join us, King." Disturbingly, the earlier conversations did not resume. Silverware clanking against plates and the occasional clearing of a throat were all I heard for the next minute.

"So, how are classes going with you guys? Aren't you taking photojournalism this fall?" I asked Rich Bryant.

"Uh, yeah, Dave," he replied. "It's great, man."

He looked down and scooped up a trio of ketchup-laden fries. I waited for more elaboration, but none came. I shifted to a new topic. "Who do you guys like in the Series? I'm thinking Pittsburgh. Pops Stargell and his family are looking hard to beat."

At the opposite end of the table, left tackle Reggie Lilly grunted in agreement. It was then that I noticed the Pirates T-shirt he wore over his expansive torso. Unfortunately, Lilly's offering marked the extent of our discussion about baseball.

As we continued eating, I decided to roll the dice one more time. "Anybody catch *The White Shadow* last night?" I asked. "I couldn't believe that Dwayne from *What's Happening!!* joined the team … and then died."

Second-string fullback Cliff Newsome snorted. "Yeah, can you imagine if it had been Rerun? Man, he'd have kicked it after the first layup drill." The ice broke. My teammates spent the next several minutes discussing the show, including an assessment of how fine Miss Buchanan looked and an evaluation of each cast member's basketball abilities. Sammy then decided to label each of us based on *The White Shadow* character we most closely resembled. Not surprisingly, I was the only Salami at the table.

After our lively discussion of the Carver High cagers died down, Preston peered at me through his black-framed glasses. His hair was close cropped and a thin moustache rested on his upper lip. A contemplative expression completed an intellectual mien that belied his on-field athleticism. "So King," he said in a smooth voice, "I see you procured some airtime for yourself last night."

"Yeah. Slater lassoed me into doing the *Wrap-Up*. I didn't watch. I'm sure it wasn't pretty."

"On the contrary. You accounted well for yourself. Not like Jones here who got all excited when he was on the show. Talked so fast during the interview, he sounded like a machine gun. A jive-talking, gibberish-shooting machine gun. Truly a disgrace."

"Forget you, man," Sammy shot back. "At least I looked good. The brother here don't know how to dress." He gestured at Preston. "What was that purple silk shirt and black bow tie you had on for Slater? Man, what was that?"

"That, my friend, was class. Something you know very little about. But I digress from the topic at hand, which is our quarterback's recent television appearance." Preston directed his attention back to me. "You handled the questions well. What's your major?"

"History. American History." I then started chattering about some of the topics I had studied this semester. A few of the other players added some sparing comments about their own classes.

Eventually, it was just Preston and me sitting at the table. He vacuumed up his remaining Jell-O cubes and touched his mouth with a napkin.

"Alright, Dave King," he said. "I must thank you for extending us the pleasure of your company tonight. You may be mayonnaise on white bread, but you're a cool cat."

"Uh, sure. Don't mention it."

"You always do well to promote team unity. I dig that. As captains, it's up to us to ensure a harmonious locker room environment."

"Do you foresee any problems there?"

"Not really. But after three centuries of slavery and segregation, you never know when racial tension could raise its ugly head. Especially since many of the brothers come to this team from impoverished backgrounds."

"Is it pretty bad for all of them back home?" I asked, glancing at the empty chairs.

"Not all of them. Some come from affluence. But most don't. For those gentlemen, the only time they see any real bread is when they sell their game tickets—usually to some rich white businessman."

My eyes dropped to my tray. "I hope I've never been insensitive about anything."

"Now, King, don't start that. Nothing will give you indigestion faster than white guilt. Like I said before, our team is pretty tight. You just keep focused on leading the offense. The only issue we brothers have with you is your wheels. A white boy clocking in at 4.4. That's just not right."

"Thanks." I smiled.

"The team is behind you. Myself, I personally have a great appreciation of your public testimony for our Lord Jesus Christ."

"That's what it's all about." I noticed the gold cross gleaming from the dark triangle formed by the open collar of his scarlet shirt.

"Amen. Alright King, I've got to fly. Thanks for dropping by the hood. That was cool. Do it again sometime." We shook, wrapping our hands around each other's thumbs.

"Okay, but you have to visit my table too."

"Maybe I will. Maybe I will." A slight grin crept across his face. "It won't be easy finding you though. You cats all look alike."

The team practiced with unprecedented fervor that week. To a man, we all focused on the task at hand. Even without the constant reminders from our coaches, we knew what was at stake. Defeating Notre Dame would announce to the world that the Falcons were for real.

After the usual short practice on Friday, the team bounded over to the training table for plate-sized Porterhouses. Levity filled the cafeteria. Even stupid jokes brought waves of laughter. The mood continued into the evening when, like every Friday before a home game, the coaches treated the first- and second-team players to a movie. *Rocky II* was the feature. I loved it. Judging by the raucous cheer at the end, most of my teammates did too.

Exiting the theater, we piled into a waiting bus. It carried us to the Ramada Inn at the edge of town. There, after visiting a snack table set up by the team trainers, we met with our position coaches. Ira Wilt, Abner's replacement as quarterback coach, grilled me on various plays and formations. Even though we had installed several new looks for Notre Dame, I had no trouble answering his questions. I had studied the playbook like it was scripture. When I shut my eyes at night, all I saw were Xs, Os, and arrows. Backup quarterback Jeremy Tuttle was also present at my meeting with Wilt, but the coach paid little attention to him.

Following Wilt's interrogation, Jeremy and I walked to our room. Once inside, I called Gail. We did not talk long. The coaches wanted us asleep as soon as possible. After hanging up, I turned off the lamp. My body responded quickly to the darkness. I started to fade.

"King, you asleep?" A voice called out in a budding dream. A few seconds later, it called out again. Startled awake, I realized that it was coming from the other bed.

"No, Tuttle. What is it?"

"You wound up? Man, I am. I can't get to sleep. Can you?"

"Oh, I think I could."

"Hey, were you talking to Gail just now?"

"Yep."

"Lucky dog. That chick is smokin'. I saw her in the library the other day. Had on these designer jeans. Man, she's got the sweetest ass."

"How about we don't talk about my girlfriend like that?" My voice conveyed irritation, though I totally agreed with his assessment.

"Sorry, King. You've got a fine woman. That's all I'm saying. Man, I can't wait 'til I'm starting quarterback next year. The girls will be lining up to get on the Tuttle train. You're gettin' some hot action from other chicks too, right? Probably all the time."

"No. Never."

"Really? You could though. You know that, don't you? There's this girl in my marketing class who's always asking about you. So-so face, but a niiiice bod."

"I don't want anybody else. I'm devoted to Gail. What we have is special."

"Wow. Okay then. She must be a tornado in bed, huh?"

"I wouldn't know," I mumbled.

"What!" I heard him spring up in his bed. "You mean you haven't … hey, you do like girls don't you?"

"Yes Tuttle, I like girls." I yawned. "I'm a Christian."

"Yeah, I know that, but—"

"And Gail and I are both committed to waiting until marriage." Memories of amorous encounters with her flashed through my head. Somehow we had always managed to avoid crossing the point of no return. To me it was a miracle no less impressive than the parting of the Red Sea.

"Man, whatever Kool-Aid you've been drinking, I don't want any."

"There's nothing wrong with obeying God's commands. He has blessed me with a beautiful, godly woman beyond my wildest dreams. How can I not seek to honor him with my relationship with her?"

"Uh, okay," he said, flopping down into his pillow. "Whatever floats your boat."

"It floats your boat too. You just don't know it yet. God is reaching out to you, Tuttle. He wants to bless you in this life and take you to heaven in the next."

"Hmpf. I bet you don't even let the tutors do your homework for you."

"Nope."

"Man, what a waste." He was quiet for a while. My mind started drifting until his voice again dragged me back. "Hey King, you got any family coming to the game?"

"Huh? What? Oh, family. Yeah, they're coming. My dad, four brothers, and a brother-in-law. Four nephews too. They'll all be in the stands. Had to trade away my entire set from the last two home games to get the extra tickets. It'll be the first time my dad has seen me play. How about you? Any family coming?"

"Nah. My folks live in Kentucky. Couldn't make the trip. Unless you get decapitated or something, I'm not gettin' into the game anyway. I sold my tickets. Got $500 for the set."

"Wow. That's a lot of money," I said through a heavy yawn.

"It's Notre Dame, baby. Bet you wish you'd have done the same."

"Nope. I never sell my tickets. I usually give two to my nephews in Omaha. Sometimes their mother will take one too. Give the rest to people at my church."

"Really? You just give them away? You are a rare bird, King. You know that?"

"Thanks Tuttle. Good night."

The piercing ring of the wake-up call jolted us to consciousness at 7:15. Shaking off the sleep cobwebs, my body buzzed with anticipation. After a light breakfast in the hotel restaurant, the team met with Coach McNabb in the main conference room. He reviewed assignments and plans of attack for offense and defense. In a calm voice he told us to keep our heads in the game and to execute, just like in practice. We then boarded the buses.

Near campus, we passed through flocks of green-clad fans. Several of them waved and cheered as we rolled by. The voltage within my body increased as we exited the bus and filed into the stadium. Fans who had gathered near the gate shouted encouragements and snapped pictures. Inside, my pregame ritual began with a visit to the training room. The fragrance of Tuff Skin adhesive spray filled my nostrils as Ned taped my ankles.

At my locker, I slid kneepads and thigh pads into my white game pants, which I then pulled on with much effort. Socks, shoes, and shoulder pads came next. The complete ensemble included an assortment of laces, straps, and strings; each was tugged and tightened just right. Finally, I donned my green jersey as a stereo vibrated the locker room walls with Pink Floyd's "Welcome to the Machine." Blocking out the music, I sat on a bench silently quoting Psalms.

A short time later, we took the field for pregame drills. After stretches and calisthenics, I warmed up my arm. Coach Wilt stood nearby, taking notes on a clipboard. Like usual, my first tosses were high. But after five or six throws, I was hitting the receivers right between the numbers. Back in the locker room, position coaches hovered over their players for final pregame instructions. After Coach Jackson prayed for us, the coaches left the room for the captains' speeches.

Linebacker Vince Hallohan went first. His face reddened and his neck veins bulged. None of us actually understood what he said, but his yelling and fist pumping fired up the team. Preston Coleman spoke next. A complete contrast to the previous speech, his discourse was smooth and elegant. Our confidence increased with every word. After Preston had finished talking, I rose to address the players.

"This week we've run, we've hit, we've sweat, and we've bled like never before. Now is when it all pays off." I paused to scan the faces staring back at me. "This room is filled with great athletes. I know that every man here will play to the best of his ability. More importantly, we will play as a team. Because when we do that, it doesn't matter who we're up against. When we play together, we're an unstoppable juggernaut. We've proved that week after week. Today, we face another battle." I raised my helmet. "Today, we vanquish another foe. It's time to take the field, men. It's time to CONQUER!!"

As the players cheered and shouted, the coaches threw open the doors to the tunnel. The team rumbled out of the locker room. While exiting, each player slapped Slayer, the green Falcon painted above the doorway. Upon reaching the end of the tunnel, the players stopped. There we waited, a pulsing mass bobbing up and down.

Coach McNabb, clad in his tweed jacket and gray fedora, moved to the front of the horde and led us onto the field. The crowd erupted. The band played. At the front of pack, I raced toward our sideline. Energy waves swirled around the stadium in a massive gyre. The electrical grid in my body was fully charged.

"Falcons! Falcons! Falcons!" thundered from the sea of green all around us. My teammates and I stomped about, slapping each other's shoulder pads. Several players waved their arms up and down to further exhort the crowd. In the midst of the mass excitement, I glanced over at the other side of the field where the Notre Dame players loomed large and confident. The sun gleaming off their gold helmets formed a nimbus of tradition and pride. Their leader, Coach Devine, paced before the team in a blue windbreaker.

Vince, Preston, and I marched out to midfield where we shook hands with the Notre Dame captains. A referee showed us both sides of a coin and then tossed it in the air. One of the Irish players called heads. The coin dropped to the earth. "Tails," the referee announced. I told him we wanted the ball. The crowd roared when he motioned that the Falcons would receive the kickoff.

Back on the sideline, I scanned the mass of humanity up in the stands. I spotted my father and brothers in Section 6. Brimming with pride, I slid my helmet over my head. Trotting onto the field after the kickoff, I felt a steely confidence spread throughout my body. After I told the men in the huddle the first play, they clapped in unison and shouted, "Break!" We approached the ball resting in the grass at the 27-yard line.

I lined up over Thor. The offensive linemen crouching in front of me formed a massive green wall. They snorted like stallions. Off to each side, Preston and Sammy stood poised and ready to bolt. Directly behind me, the running backs were similarly prepared to spring into action. I shouted the snap count so it could be heard above the roar of the crowd. "Hut-hut-HUT!" My hands gripped the ball. My soldiers charged into battle.

"Ohhh, I am sooo stuffed," Ozzie moaned, holding his stomach. "Why did I eat so much?" We exited Johnny's Cafe. After hobbling a few feet down the walkway in front of the restaurant, my brother turned and leaned back against the building. He unfastened the top button of his jeans. "That's better," he said with a long exhale.

A deep breath of cool autumn air refreshed my aching body. I limped over and propped myself against the restaurant wall next to Ozzie. "Yeah, it's hard to avoid eating too much in there. Best steakhouse in Omaha, I say." Though my ankle, knee, elbow, and ribcage throbbed, it was my gorged belly that registered the greatest pain at that moment.

"I think I ate half a cow," he said. "Say, how'd you get the banquet room in there reserved on the night of the Notre Dame game? Use your football clout to pull some strings?"

"Nah, I can't take credit. Zoe took care of the arrangements. Somebody at her company knows the restaurant manager or something."

"Cool. Whatever works. We gotta come back here again. How about after your next home game? I might be ready to eat again in a couple weeks." He then uncorked a monstrous belch that lasted longer than it takes to recite the Pledge of Allegiance. "Woo," he said, patting his distended abdomen. "How about that? I think I could eat some more."

"Forget it. We cleaned 'em out. There are no more cattle left in Nebraska or Iowa."

"Well, maybe we can get a pizza later."

I chuckled, though the thought of eating again brought a stab of nausea. Centered in the yellow glow of the ornate wall lamp above us, we stared out at the rows of cars in the dark parking lot. Ozzie inhaled from a cigarette he had just lit.

"Oz, did Dad say much during the game?"

"Huh?" Two streams of white smoke shot from his nostrils. "I don't know. I was too busy checking out the cheerleaders through my binoculars."

"Well, did he seem like he was having a good time?"

"Yeah, I guess. As much as he ever looks like he's having a good time. I'm sure he had a ball. You guys won your big game."

"Did he say anything to you about me?"

"Yeah. He said those three touchdown passes you threw were all luck." Ozzie snickered. "What's the deal? Didn't you talk to him in the restaurant?"

"No. Didn't get much chance. He was always busy talking to someone else."

"So you didn't get any praise from the old man? Boo-freaking-hoo. Geez Dave, don't be so needy. He's got a picture of you up at The Royal Court. What more do you want?"

"Forget it." I scanned the dark sky for a recognizable constellation.

"Aw, come on, man. There were thousands of drunken fans chanting your name this afternoon. You should feel pretty good about yourself, considering your past."

"Considering my past? I don't even want to know what that means."

He blew a ring of smoke from his open mouth. "See, I remember what you were like in high school. That wasn't so long ago. Back then you were a whiny annoying little hobbit, somewhat confused about his sexuality."

I squinted at him. "Have I ever told you how much I don't miss you?"

"When you think about how little you've changed since then, it's actually quite remarkable that so many people at college are able to tolerate you."

"Now would be a good time for you to *hush*."

"What, you think you've changed? Let's review the facts. You have grown in stature. I'll give you that. But what about the whiny part? I think your sniveling questions about the old man prove that hasn't changed. Annoying? Well, you still spout off about your silly religion all the time. So you've got that covered too." He returned the cigarette to his mouth for another drag.

Looking away, I pretended to ignore him.

After breathing out a thin current of smoke, he continued. "Now, about your uncertain sexuality. On one hand, you showed up at our family shindig tonight with a fine young female specimen. Assuming you two aren't sorority sisters, that tells me you may be straight. On the other hand, you do spend a lot of time playing a game that requires you bend over the rear end of another dude while reaching under his crotch. Plus, there are those frequent pats on the butt you strapping young lads give each other in those skintight pants."

I chuffed. "You're an idiot."

"This data suggests that you ARE still confused about your sexual identity," he said in his best attempt at a Freudian accent. "Therefore, it is my professional conclusion that, despite your physical growth, you are indeed still the same whiny annoying sexually ambiguous hobbit you always were. Your inner Bilbo is alive and well. Class dismissed." He waved his cigarette above his head in a gesture of triumph.

"Yeah, well it's taken you six years to finish college."

He frowned. "I'm graduating in December. That will be only five and a half years."

"*Only* five and a half years. You could've been done a year ago if you didn't start playing that stupid game."

"Dungeons and Dragons is cool, damn it. You should give it a try. I could roll up a character for you tonight." His eyes danced. "You could be a halfling cleric. That'd be right up your alley."

I shook my head. "Still don't have a girlfriend, huh?"

"Hey, I do alright." He thumped his chest.

"Really Oz? So what is it about you that attracts the ladies? Is it the complete lack of ambition? Or perhaps it's the noxious gasses you continually emit? Or is it your supercool expertise at Dungeons and Dragons? … Maybe it's everything combined. That's it, isn't it? It's the total package that makes you such a chick magnet."

"I've got your total package right here," he said, gesturing at his groin.

"I think that's just an empty box."

He bellowed a wave of fake laughter. "Aren't you funny? You're a funny guy, Dave. Say, where's the respect for your elders? Doesn't your Bible say something about that? You get a little fame on the football field and you think you can disrespect the

Wizard." He dropped the remnant of his cigarette and snuffed it out under his shoe.

I couldn't resist one more jab. "Don't feel bad about my fame, Oz." I put a hand on his shoulder. "It benefits you too, you know. Just think about it. You can be my Billy Carter. Got any ideas for a new beer?"

"The laughs just don't stop with you, do they? Bilbo the standup comedian, ladies and gentlemen. He'll be at the Comedy Club in the Shire all week."

I chuckled and leaned back against the restaurant wall. We both gazed beyond the parking lot to watch the traffic whiz by on the Kennedy Freeway. Off in the distance, a train whistle cut through the night. "Anthony and Joe seem better now," he said a while later.

"Yeah, I think they're gonna be alright."

"Did the police ever find out who paid that guy to set the fire?"

Abner's face flashed before my eyes, reviving long dormant feelings of unease. "No. The investigators never found anybody. Don't know if they ever will."

"Still think Joe is the evil criminal mastermind behind the hit?" he asked with a smirk.

"A guy died in that fire," I said with a hard look. "This isn't something to joke about. And no, I don't think that. I was just speculating when I told you that theory."

"But you still think our nephews *could've* been involved, don't you?"

I paced a few steps from the building. "I've never known what to think. After the police said they didn't have any suspects, I decided to treat Anthony and Joe as if they had nothing to do with it. That was the only fair thing to do."

"It does make you wonder," Ozzie said. "I mean, they do act kinda creepy sometimes."

"I try not to think about it anymore. I've given up playing amateur investigator. I know God is sovereign. He will deal with whoever's behind the fire. Whether it's our nephews or not."

"If you say so. Hey, it's too bad you gave up investigating. I was thinking you could team up with the Hardy Boys. I know you three geniuses could figure it out."

I glared at him. "Can it, Oswald."

"Yeah, you're right. It would never work. You'd just be hitting on Shaun and Parker all the time. It would totally disrupt their investigation."

"Shut up." I tried to punch his arm, but he darted away.

"You can't touch me, fool," he said, imitating Muhammad Ali. "I float like butterfly, remember?" He danced around throwing shadow punches.

"We should go back in. They're probably getting ready to leave." I turned toward the front entrance. "Hey, you remember how to get to my place?"

"Yep." He dropped his dukes. "Thanks for letting me stay with you tonight. Filling up the Ford for this trip left me without any dough for a hotel. And the old man cut me off, ya know."

"You can thank me by not teaching my housemates any of your disgusting habits. And no Dungeons and Dragons either, okay?"

"We'll see." The corners of his mouth curled ominously.

"Here's the spot," I said, gesturing at a grassy clearing near the water.

"Perfect," Gail replied. We spread a blanket over the ground and rummaged through the wicker basket for our food and drinks. "I love the view," she said, gazing at Lake Manawa. A couple sailboats loafed across the blue-green expanse. Golden rays fanned down through the clouds above.

Stretched out on the blanket, I leaned on one elbow while holding a sandwich in my other hand. "This past week was exciting and all that," I said, "but it's nice to finally get some time alone with you."

"Tell me about it." She sat cross-legged facing the lake. "This football mistress of yours is quite demanding. Sometimes I feel like I have to use my press credentials just to get a chance to talk to you."

"Notre Dame week was crazy. Coaches were all stressing out. Everybody wanting interviews. And then my family came out here. The rest of the games shouldn't be like that.... Hard to believe my college playing days will be over in a couple months."

"Well, it will be nice to get my boyfriend back. But I'll be sad too when it ends. This is a fun time with the team doing so well. People around here have football fever, and *you* are at the center of it all. That was so cool last night when everyone at the restaurant stood and clapped after you walked in."

"Yeah, I guess. I'm still not comfortable getting so much attention from strangers." I took a drink from my can of Dr. Pepper. "Did you have an okay time last night?"

"Yes! It was great. I always like spending time with your family."

"I'm glad you survived. It can be an adventure when the entire King clan gets together." I swallowed a bite of turkey and Swiss sandwich. "Sorry we got separated for most of the evening. My relatives didn't torment you too much did they?"

"Not at all. I talked to Abby for quite a while. Learned about Jerry's job and what little Andy has been getting into. Then she told me about their new kitchen. She wants us to stop over and see it the next time we're in Des Moines." Gail nibbled on a celery stick and scrunched her brow. "Let's see, who did I talk to next? Oh yeah, Shane and Pamela. They came over and let me hold Jolene, who promptly spit up on me."

"Oops."

"No, it wasn't a problem. Most of it stayed on her little blanket. Then I got to play charades with Betsy, Debbie, and Jane. Now, who do they belong to?"

"Betsy and Debbie are Eli and Katy's. Jane is Adam and Shannon's."

"That's right. After a couple more get-togethers, I'll have everybody straight."

"When you do, let me know," I said, chuckling. "I still have trouble with all the names."

She smiled and took another bite of celery. My heart bounded as she held me in her gaze. "That was nice of Zoe to invite everybody over to her house for the afternoon while the men were at the game."

"Yeah, she's cool," I said. "Get to talk to her much last night?"

"A little. She's smart." We munched on our food for a while. "So how are you feeling?"

"Fine. All the aches and pains are about gone." I stretched out my left leg.

"Good. You had me worried limping around last night. You took some nasty hits yesterday. I could feel them up in the press box."

"No big deal," I said with a dismissive wave. "I'm used to getting knocked around. I knew I'd be all right. Coach made me go see the trainer today, but it wasn't necessary."

She flicked a few stray locks of chestnut hair from her face. "How many games are left?"

"Five, plus a bowl game." I stroked the warm smooth skin on her arm. "Counting the days?"

"No. I love watching you play." Her eyebrows flashed up for an instant. "But I worry about you getting hurt."

"I'll be okay. God protects me. So does my line."

"And it will be nice when some of the female attention you've been getting subsides. You have a lot of lady fans, you know."

I dragged a napkin across my face and sat up next to her. "Silly girl, you know you have nothing to worry about. I don't want anybody else."

"Really? You're not going to trade me in for one of those bouncy football groupies?"

I laid my arm across her shoulders and pulled her close. "Absolutely not. How could I give up the most beautiful woman in the world? Especially when she's my best friend too. There's no way to count all the blessings you've brought to my life. Abigail Taylor, you've got my heart. I love you."

She tightened her arms around me. "I love you too, Dave King." She then shifted, pushed me down on my back, and pressed her mouth over mine. Off in the distance, the song "Babe" oozed from a radio on one of the sailboats.

We continued our unspoken interaction until the sun disappeared below the horizon.

Chapter 14 – January 1980

"Alright boys, now settle down," Coach McNabb said, patting the air in front of him with both hands. His wrinkly face was pale, but his countenance blazed. The locker room fell quiet.

"This afternoon the eyes of the world will be upon you. This is the biggest game I've ever coached and I'm purty sure this is the biggest game y'all have ever played. What happens over the next three hours will forever be part of yer lives. Now, I know that some of ya will go on ta do greater things than play in the Sugar Bowl. But you will *never* again have this opportunity right here, right now." Above us, stomping feet rumbled like distant thunder.

"Boys, I honestly can't tell ya if we're gonna win or lose," McNabb said, scanning our faces. "But I know that each and every one of ya will give everything he's got today. Gonna put it all out there on that field. I know that 'cause I know yer character and yer heart. But ya ain't gonna do it 'cause we got a shot at the national championship. And ya ain't gonna do it 'cause this is my last game. Gaining respect? That's not it either." He shook his head. "It don't matter that we're undefeated but only ranked fifth in the nation. It don't matter that we're a ten-and-a-half-point dawg. It don't matter that Dave was passed over for the Heisman." He gestured at me. "Or that Tank or Thor didn't win the Outland. Forget about all those individual trophies and awards ya didn't win. None of that matters now." His jaw jutted out in defiance.

"That's right," Preston said. A few other players murmured in agreement.

"Look around this room, boys," Coach continued. "Look at the man on either side of ya." He paused while we swiveled our heads.

"That's why you will go out there today and play the game of yer lives. You will scrap and fight and bleed for yer teammates. Because each of them is out there doing the same for you! This team is special. The best I've ever coached. I'll never forget any of ya boys. Now saddle up and ride one more time for the Big Green!"

After storming out of the tunnel with my teammates, I gaped in wonder at my surroundings. We had practiced in the Louisiana Superdome all week, but I had never seen the building packed to capacity. Flashbulbs exploded all around us. Sound waves from the roaring crowd bounced off the roof twenty-five stories above and undulated back to the AstroTurf. The bones in my feet vibrated.

Coach Wilt flitted about like a caffeinated moth. Since he was nearly a foot shorter than me, I had to lean down to hear his rapid-fire instructions. Though high-strung, he always knew his stuff. Today his stuff was the wishbone, an offense we had not used all season. McNabb wanted to surprise our opponents, so for the past month he and his assistants relentlessly drilled a new playbook into us. Our practices at home and here in New Orleans were shrouded in secrecy. I loved it. I loved the idea of surprising the other team and I loved that I would get to run the ball.

Looking around the dome, I estimated that about a third of the fans wore Falcons green. Nearly two-thirds of the fans wore dark red, the color of our opponents—the Alabama Crimson Tide. Regardless of allegiance, all 70,000 spectators were wound up and ready to go. Homemade banners appeared throughout the stadium. The largest sign draped from the top deck. It depicted Alabama coach Paul "Bear" Bryant pointing straight ahead like Uncle Sam in that famous World War I poster. "The Bear Wants You" was the caption.

Blaring horns sliced through the din of the crowd. Drums rattled away as cheerleaders performed and mascots strutted. ABC cameramen trained their lenses on the field. Riddled with frissons, my body levitated as Burhan sent the opening kickoff through the air. In white jerseys and green helmets, a wave of Falcons swept forward, crashing into crimson blockers. The Alabama return man sped upfield, cutting left to find daylight. The Rooster, fighting off a block, launched himself into the runner. The ball jarred loose. A white jersey fell on it. My teammates jumped up and down with wild enthusiasm.

The Bear, clad in a red plaid sports jacket and a houndstooth hat, paced in frustration on the other sideline. Our offense and their defense replaced the special teams units on the field. My mind, not fully grasping that we now had the ball, still pondered the movements of the Alabama coach.

"King, you imbecile!" Wilt screamed, his face the color of our opponents' uniforms. "You want an engraved invitation to play in this game? Put your helmet on and get out there!" Zapped by a cattle prod, I shot onto the field to join my teammates in the huddle.

The Bama defenders seemed confused when we lined up in a wishbone T formation, instead of the I. Their linebackers sidled one way and then the other as I called the snap count. Taking the football, I floated right. An unblocked defensive end charged at me. Just before impact, I pitched the ball to Rich Bryant. He darted forward while I got hammered into the hard AstroTurf. *Oh for the soft grassy field at Falcons Stadium.* Staggering to my feet, I saw Rich pushed out of bounds at the Bama 16. He had gained 27 yards.

Three plays later I handed off to fullback Garth Hickey, who burst into the end zone from two yards out. The fans in green roared. My ecstatic teammates bounced off the field. I thought some of them were about to start hyperventilating. Burhan's PAT split the uprights. Checking the scoreboard left my arms covered in goose bumps.

The Bear, however, had a surprise of his own in store for us. Taking possession of the ball at their 23, the Alabama offense lined up in a double wing wishbone set and put both backs in motion. Our defensive players struggled to adjust to the unexpected formation. True to its name, the Crimson Tide rolled down the field. A few minutes later the score was tied.

Mixing running plays with short passes, the Falcons offense again moved the ball. But the advances were hard fought. The crimson giants with the white numbers on their helmets were fast and smart. Our powerful line opened holes for the running backs and me, but the defenders closed in quickly. What would have been eight to ten yard gains against other teams, only netted three or four against Alabama.

And the men in red hit hard. On each play, they smashed into us like battering rams. The accompanying growls added to the ferocity of each impact. To make matters worse, it did not take long for Bama's top-ranked defense to adjust to our wishbone. After we drove to their 22, they stuffed two running plays and batted down a pass to stick us with a fourth and long. Our possession still ended happily though when Burhan hit a field goal to reclaim the lead.

Following the kickoff, Alabama's offense again went to work with methodical efficiency. Quarterback Steadman Shealy ran their wishbone to perfection. The long Bama drive culminated in a touchdown on the first play of the second quarter. Their fans erupted, shaking the dome. My teammates and I exhorted each other to keep fighting. Coach McNabb clinched his fists and coldly surveyed the field.

Penalties and a relentless Tide defense shut down our option in the second quarter. Fortunately, the Falcons D made effective adjustments to keep us in the game. Linebacker Vince Hallohan, jacked up on adrenaline and who knows what else, led an inspired defensive effort that allowed only three more points before halftime. Alabama was up 17-10 as both venerable coaches led their teams off the field.

Watching my battered teammates limp into the locker room reminded me of the Civil War field hospitals I had learned about in my military history class. Sammy Jones had a broken fibula and was done for the day. Thor winced with every step. Blood oozed from Tank's nose. My ears rang with a high-pitched whir; it sounded something like a band saw running inside my brain. The Falcons trainers worked their magic, treating dozens of injuries of varying degree. Meanwhile, our coaches reviewed assignments with us and made adjustments for the second half.

Though my body ached, my faith remained strong. Moving next to Thor, who sat grimacing on a bench, I began reciting Psalm 20 from memory. The locker room gradually quieted down. I raised my voice so more of my teammates could hear the verses. After I had finished, McNabb thanked me and added a few of his own words of encouragement. Buoyed and bandaged, we charged out for the second half.

Neither team could move the ball in the third quarter. The defenses on both sides seemed to know what was coming. On the first play of the fourth quarter, we faced a third and eleven from our own 36-yard line. I dropped back to pass. A blitzing linebacker knocked aside the hobbled Thor and drove me from the pocket. Darting left like a jackrabbit, I spotted a gap. Tucking the ball, I dashed across the line of scrimmage. Another linebacker moved over to block my advance. After a stutter step swerve that brought an "oooh" from the crowd, I blew past him into the secondary. Preston blocked a safety to create space up ahead. Meanwhile, a cornerback tripped trying to make a sharp cut into my path. My eyes at once beheld the promised land—no red jerseys stood between me and the distant goal line. My heart leapt as my legs hit the afterburners. Air whistled through the ear holes in my helmet. An instant later I was in the end zone.

Trying to catch my breath, I passed through a gauntlet of slaps, high fives, and hugs as I made my way to the sideline bench. My teammates bobbed with renewed energy. McNabb approached. "Great run, King," he drawled. "Way to get somethin' from a busted play." With the score tied again, the crowd stirred with restless anticipation.

After the return man struggled to get a handle on the kickoff, we pinned Alabama at their own 12. Undaunted, their offense started moving the ball. Twice the Falcons defense had them facing a third and long, but each time they got just enough for a first down. Like a machine, the Crimson Tide kept moving the chains. Their fullback rumbled over the goal line with just under eight minutes left in the game. Pushing aside the dejection, my teammates and I prepared to answer with a scoring drive of our own.

Following the return, we took over at the 31. A hitch pass and two Rich Bryant runs gave us a first down near midfield. The next play was an option. As I floated down the line, it seemed that the defenders were expecting the ball to go to the running back. Faking a pitch, I turned the corner and darted through a hole. Again seeing daylight, I hit the accelerator.

And then … IMPACT. The stadium capsized in a blinding flash of light. Something the size of a Mack truck had knocked me into another dimension. My bones rattled like bowling pins. Buried in the AstroTurf, I was barely cognizant that my helmet was gone. My body fell numb. Static filled my ears. I watched the Superdome roof swirl above me. The taste of vomit coated my throat. Then something horrible burned my nostrils. Instinctively, I swatted the objects—smelling salts I later realized—away from my face. My focus improved to the point where I recognized some of the people leaning over me. A voice asked if I wanted to sit up. I did. A while later, Tank and Ned, our head trainer, helped me to my feet. I tried to stagger over to where several Falcons players were huddled, but Ned guided me to the sideline.

"But me next play we run," I slurred.

"No Dave," he said. "That's our defense. Alabama has the ball."

My head throbbed as I trudged over to the bench. Ned, his face blurry, asked me a battery of questions. Slowly I provided the answers: my name, where we were, how many fingers he held up, the score of the game. I nearly collapsed as the realization that I had fumbled hit me.

"24 to 17, them," I said, answering Ned's last question. "Fourth quarter. They have the ball." I buried my head in my hands. A kaleidoscope of colors swirled inside my eyelids.

"It's okay, Dave," he said, patting my shoulder pads. "It's not your fault. No one could have hung onto the ball after that hit."

A couple minutes later, the crowd noise amplified. I opened my eyes and looked around. To my relief, people and objects were no longer fuzzy. "What happened?"

"They missed a field goal," Tank shouted. "We've got a chance!"

Peering over my shoulder, I saw Jeremy Tuttle throwing warm-up passes behind the bench. McNabb, Wilt, and Ned appeared, staring down at me with grim faces. "Son," McNabb said, "we got Tuttle ready. I don't think I can send you back out there."

I stood up. The ground was firm beneath my feet. The stadium had stopped moving. "I can do it, Coach. I am absolutely ready."

The three men traded glances. "You sure?" McNabb asked. I nodded and put on my helmet. He stared into my eyes for a few seconds and then gestured to the field. "Go get 'em."

We had the ball at our 29-yard line with 2:26 left in the game. I scanned the determined faces in the huddle. "This is it, men. Our last dance. Let's give 'em something to remember."

Coach called a pass for the first play. Taking the snap, I faked a handoff to Rich before fading back and firing a bullet that hit Preston between the numbers as he cut to the sideline. We gained 13 yards.

Having reestablished the aerial threat, Coach went back to the ground game for the next four plays. Rich and Garth ran like madmen, grinding out yards into Alabama territory. On the sixth play of the drive, I found tight end Rick Wilkerson on a crossing pattern. That gave us a first down at the Crimson Tide 21-yard line with 39 ticks remaining on the clock.

After an incompletion, we gained eight yards on a reverse to Preston. On third down, I dropped back three steps before planting and darting forward on a draw. Six yards later I met the Mack truck again. This time I was able to shift left to limit the impact of his hit to a mere fender bender. We had a first and goal at the 7-yard line with 12 seconds left.

One of my teammates called timeout. McNabb reminded us that we could not stop the clock again—we either had to score or get out of bounds. Beads of sweat dotted his creased forehead. After consulting with Vanderlinden up in the booth, McNabb called a play. As I trotted onto the field, my neurons crackled with electricity.

I took the snap and faded back. With his injured ankle, Thor could not stop the advance of a rushing linebacker. I scrambled to the right with the crimson rusher in hot pursuit. When another defender closed in, I fired a high spiral toward a Falcons receiver cutting across the back of the end zone. From out of nowhere, an Alabama safety jumped up and made a dazzling fingertip catch. My soul deflated. I bowed my head and unsnapped my chinstrap. But then I noticed the referee waving his arms back and forth to signal an incompletion. The safety had landed out of bounds after catching the ball. No interception. I exhaled in relief.

Five seconds remained. The play came in. The crowd turned up the volume. Blocking out the noise, my nerves, and the clock, I focused on the one thing I had to do. *Just throw the pass*. After the snap, I dropped back three steps and pump-faked right. Then, shifting my body, I lofted a high arc toward the back left corner of the end zone. Preston and the cornerback shadowing him both jumped, four hands reaching upward. The ball bounced off the tangled mass of fingers and floated away end over end. The two players landed off balance. While falling sideways out of bounds, Preston stretched out his hand just far enough to stop the descent of the ball. He scooped it into his belly and somehow managed to keep one foot in bounds before crashing to the turf. The referee's arms went vertical.

My teammates leapt about, hugging both Preston and me. The celebration was energetic, but brief. We still trailed by one point. After Preston and I congratulated each other, we jogged toward our sideline. "What do you think he'll do?" I asked.

"Probably kick the extra point. Get the sure thing. McNabb won't want to go out a loser after that comeback. Not when he could end his career tying the Bear."

Hoping Preston was wrong, I joined my offensive teammates gathered around the coach. His face held a reflective expression. "Boys, that was amazing. Ya proved to me that y'all are champions. Every last one of ya." The corners of his mouth then curved upward. "But those boys on the other sideline might still need some convincing. Go get two more points, alright?" We raised our helmets with a shout.

In the huddle, I saw steel in my teammates' eyes. Even Thor radiated determination, though tears of pain streaked down his cheeks. There was no way to keep him off the field for this play—our last one as Falcons. We lined up in the I formation. I silently thanked God for this moment. Although the crowd was louder than ever, the noise seemed to be miles away. I reviewed my warriors and then scanned the crimson monsters poised to defy us.

At the second hut, Thor put the ball in my hands. Huge bodies exploded into each other. I rolled to my left, looking for Preston. Defenders blocked him from my sight. Meanwhile two red jerseys burst through the Falcons line. I spun completely around as one of the rushers pawed at my back. He just missed grabbing a handful of uniform before I slid away. I scurried back toward the opposite goal line before cutting across the field. My retreat had taken me almost 20 yards behind the line of scrimmage.

My heart boomed like a howitzer. Nearing the right sideline, I slowed to a jog. My eyes searched the end zone for a target. Nobody was open. Sensing the pursuit closing in behind me, I bolted forward to the 10-yard line and cut left ninety degrees. The Falcons receivers were all now on the right side of the end zone. The Alabama secondary had followed them, leaving the left side of the end zone empty. *If I can just get around the corner*. Picking up speed, I darted straight across the field. A diving linebacker landed a hand on my foot. The contact caused me to stumble right into the path of the Mack truck. It was too late to change directions—all I could do was prepare to get spattered against his grille. Then suddenly, Thor flashed into my field of vision. With a piercing cry of anguish, he launched himself into the charging behemoth, knocking him away. The collision sounded like a hand grenade going off in my ear.

I continued racing across the field. Cutting toward the left end zone pylon, I saw daylight, freedom, victory. Accelerating beyond a full sprint, I crossed the goal line just before the Alabama secondary could cut me off. Whistles blew. Arms shot up.

An instant later, I was mobbed by joyous men in white bloodstained jerseys. Shouting incomprehensible words, they raised their helmets and index fingers. Jostled about by the frenzied throng, I glanced up at the scoreboard. Digital letters and numbers had never looked so beautiful: Western Iowa 25, Alabama 24.

We were a team of zombies on the bus ride to New Orleans International Airport the next morning. I had somehow squeezed in about two hours of sleep the night before. Many of my hungover teammates had never even made it to bed. Though not suffering from any alcohol-related maladies, my body still ached in most places and my skull vibrated with a faint hum. None of that mattered though. The joy welling within me far outweighed any physical discomfort I felt.

A gathering of fans greeted us at Eppley Airport in Omaha. We signed a few autographs before the coaches herded us to the team busses. My housemates and I stumbled into our shanty around 1:00 p.m. Unplugging the phone, we crashed for the rest of the afternoon. I ate some soup and watched a little television that evening before returning to bed by ten.

The next day was Thursday, January 3, the day the Associated Press and the United Press International released their final polls. The entire team gathered in the main lounge at the stadium field house to await the announcement of our final ranking from Martin Spanier, the university's sports information director. The room buzzed with anticipation. Three of the four teams ranked ahead of us—Ohio State, Alabama, and Florida State—lost their bowl games. Though the other higher-ranked team, the USC Trojans, won on New Year's Day, they had a tie from earlier in the season. Western Iowa was the only team in the nation with a perfect 12-0 record. We speculated about how much sway that would have with the voters. McNabb's retirement was another factor we hoped might work in our favor.

Finally, Spanier entered the crowded lounge with a paper in his hand. After he cleared his throat, the room became pin-drop quiet. "Gentlemen, the final AP and UPI results have been released. The margin between first and second place was close. Only four votes separated number one from number two in the AP poll. Five votes separated the top two UPI finishers. In both polls, the University of Southern California finished SECOND to the University of Western Iowa. Congratulations gentlemen, you are the national champions."

The room erupted. Our pains dissipated as we jumped up and hugged each other. McNabb's assistants swarmed around him, shaking his hand and patting his back. After about ten minutes of revelry, Coach made his way over to me. The beam on his face made him look twenty years younger. After an embrace, he gripped my hand. "Thank you, Dave. Thank you for an outstanding season. You're the best quarterback I've ever coached. If every player I had was like you, I don't think I'd ever retire. I'm gonna miss you, boy."

"Thanks, Coach. Thanks for taking a chance on me four years ago when no one else wanted me. I'm gonna miss you, too."

University officials organized a public celebration. It was held the following day at the Crowl Center, the 10,000-seat arena where the Western Iowa basketball team played its home games. With spring semester classes due to start the following Tuesday, many of the students were already back on campus. Their presence ensured an energetic audience for the occasion.

Green and white balloons, streamers, and banners filled the arena. Standing on the stage with my teammates, I soaked in the adulation. We all grinned from ear to ear—even Sammy and Thor, who both leaned on crutches. Fans bellowed and shrieked. I studied the mass of people gathered before us. If I squinted just right, the crowd looked like a giant swarming anthill. The scene was dizzying.

The program included a procession of speeches from the university president, the athletic director, and Coach McNabb, who broke down near the end of his talk. The crowd responded by chanting, "One more year." The team captains were next. Vince stomped up to the podium. Naturally, no one understood a word of his raging monologue, but the fans roared anyway every time he pumped his fist. Preston spoke next. His smooth delivery elicited a more refined response from the crowd.

It was then my turn. I gripped the podium with both hands and took a breath. "Thank you," I said into the microphone. "This national title would not have been possible without the hard work and tireless sacrifices of our coaches. I'm so thankful for all the effort they put into getting us ready for each game. I'm even thankful for all the torture they put us through in practice. I can say that now that I won't have to put up with them anymore." Laughter rolled through the arena. "Seriously, I really do appreciate all the time Coach McNabb, Coach Vanderlinden, and Coach Wilt devoted to helping me become a better quarterback. It was a privilege to play for each of them. The same goes for Abner Kishman. A lot of the credit for our championship goes to him, too." The crowd clapped respectfully as I paused for a moment of reflection.

"And how about these guys back here?" I pointed at the players behind me. "I couldn't have asked for a better group of teammates. The Falcons defense rose to the occasion time and time again this season. Their performance against Alabama was truly amazing. Then there's our offense. It's a quarterback's dream to play alongside receivers and running backs as talented as the ones we've got. I've seen the replays and I still don't know how Preston caught that last touchdown pass." Cheers flowed across the stage. Some of the fans started chanting his name.

"Of course, we can't forget the offensive line. Tank and those boys were steamrollers all season long. I wouldn't have completed a single pass or gained a single yard without them. And how about my friend Thor Heimlich? You guys know him as The Hammer. If you ever want to see the heart of a champion, just check out what he did in the Sugar Bowl. We didn't know it at the time, but he played the entire second half on a broken ankle. Somehow he overcame the pain to throw a block for the ages on that last play. You guys remember that one?" The crowd exploded into a cacophony of woofing and yelling that lasted over a minute. I turned to point at Thor. He nodded at me while fighting to keep his composure. Nearby teammates patted his back.

After the noise died down, I continued. "And I want to thank all you fans. You delivered the energy all season long. When we were down, you picked us up and kept us going. You inspired us to reach for greatness. This title is yours too." Another earsplitting roar ensued.

"Lastly, and above all else, I thank God, without whom none of this would be possible. He is my rock and my strength. Praise him forever!" The people responded with a polite cheer that was noticeably less exuberant than their earlier outbursts.

After a few more comments from the university president, we cleared off the stage. Several long-haired students began setting up speakers and musical equipment. The celebration was slated to close with a concert from Nebuchadnezzar's Oven Cleaners, a popular student rock group. A short time later, screeching guitars, a booming bass, thundering drums, and an electrifying keyboard shook the arena. The crowd gyrated. During the third song, some of my teammates jumped on stage and started dancing. They motioned for me to join them. By the next song I was up there too, dancing alongside them. Caught up in the moment, I didn't care about how moronic I looked. It was a great concert.

That night Gail and I went out for pizza and a movie. It was her turn to pick, so we ended up watching *Kramer vs. Kramer*. Since she had not complained about my last selection—*The Warriors*—I pretended to be engrossed in Dustin Hoffman and Meryl Streep's custody battle. Afterwards, we decided to call it an early night. I was still dragging from the hoopla of the past week, and we had to drive to Lincoln, Nebraska, the next morning.

I reached my front door a few minutes before eleven. The house was dark. Thor, Tank, and the Rooster had all decided to go home for the weekend. Tossing my letter jacket on the sofa, I trudged up the stairs. After a trip to the bathroom, I entered my room and flipped on the light.

"Beeyaaaaaahhh!!!!" The sound I emitted was a cross between the bleating of a lamb and the shrill scream of a little girl. My body recoiled in a violent flinch.

"That wasn't a very manly reaction for a big football hero," Michelle said with amusement. I stared at her in disbelief while my thumping heart slowly descended to its original location. She leaned back against the headboard with her legs stretched out in front of her on my bed. "Don't worry. I won't tell any of your adoring fans." A tight sapphire sweater and painted on jeans highlighted her curvy female form. The perfume in the air reminded me of high school.

"What are you … how did you …"

"Your roommate let me in. The weird-looking one. I got here just before he left. Nice guy, but if you ask me that red Mohawk doesn't work." She wiggled her argyle-clad feet.

I made a mental note to have a talk with the Rooster. "Michelle, you shouldn't be here. I mean, you could've called if you needed something."

Her face hardened. "Yes, I know I'm not welcome here. You made that perfectly clear last year when you rudely told me not to visit anymore. I remember."

"It wasn't like that. I didn't want to cause problems between you and Paul. Plus, I was starting to see Gail then. It wasn't fair to either of them for us to hang around each other so much."

"Ah, Gail. So how is your sweet princess?"

"She's great."

"I bet."

"Don't you care about what Paul will think? He is your fiancé now, isn't he?"

Her arm straight, she held up her left hand to gaze at the ring on her finger. "Yes, he is. But he can deal with you and me being friends. And if he can't, tough."

"The people we're with now shouldn't have to deal with us getting together … alone. We have a past, you know."

"Yes, I know we have a past. That's why I expected more compassion from you. Instead, you've ignored me for a whole year." Her eyes misted. "I lost my dad and my brother on the same day, remember?"

Her words stung my heart. Part of me wanted to go hold her, but an inner restraint kept my feet frozen in place. "I know," I said softly. "And I do care about you, but we have to do right by the people we're with now. Hurting Paul and Gail won't make anything any better."

She slid her body around so her legs dangled over the side of the bed. Her toes touched the hardwood floor below. "What Paul and Gail don't know won't hurt them." She flashed an inviting smile.

"Michelle, please." My face radiated with heat.

She stood, sizing me up with half-closed eyes. "Dave, we came sooo close so many times. Didn't you ever wonder what it would be like?" She spoke her last words in a breathy whisper.

My pulse raced, but not with anticipation. Instead, it was terror that seized me. I trembled at the thought of what I could lose. She held out her arms and stepped toward me.

"No!" I caught her wrists. "This can't happen. It would only hurt both of us." I stepped back. "I'm going to wait downstairs until you leave." Her face collapsed as I turned away.

"You haven't changed at all since high school," she snapped. "You always get scared and run away whenever we get close. You're a coward, Dave!"

Halfway down the stairs, I stopped. "Michelle, we're not right for each other. We never were."

"You bastard!" she screamed while I continued down the steps and into the living room. She pounded down the stairs behind me. I saw her father's rage flaming in her eyes as she unleashed a barrage of profanities at me. Her street vocabulary was much more extensive than I would have imagined. Her chest heaved when she finally stopped to breathe.

"Michelle, I just—"

"Shut up! I don't want to hear it. Do you know how stupid you looked today? You gave that shitty little speech and then you danced like a retard in front of everybody. You probably thought you were so cool. Well, you weren't. You looked like an idiot. You're a joke! That's all you are, Dave. A joke!"

"Maybe I did look stupid. Who cares? Up on that stage, my teammates were celebrating a national championship. Me? I was praising the Lord. It was the joy of my relationship with the living God that moved me to dance. My creator was with me. That's a feeling I hope you will experience yourself someday."

Her glare dripped with contempt. "You are such a little church mouse, with all those stupid Sunday School sayings. Pathetic. And your skinny newspaper bitch girlfriend is probably just like you. You two can have each other. I hope you both rot in hell together!"

She stormed to the front door, stepped into her shoes, and slid on her coat. My offer to drive her home was met with a middle finger. The whole house shook as she slammed the door and stalked off into the night.

I flipped the deadbolt and crawled into bed. Michelle's fragrance still hung in the air. I thought about the engagement ring I had bought for her resting at the bottom of the Des Moines River. *Good thing she never found out about that.* After praying a while for Michelle, and even longer for Paul, I fell asleep.

"That's everything?" Gail asked, staring straight ahead.

"That's it." I signaled and turned south on 27th Street in Lincoln.

"Okay. Thanks for telling me." She was quiet for a while.

"Are you mad?"

"No. Why would I be? You told me everything, right?" I nodded. "I have no reason to be mad," she said. "Actually, I think you handled it well."

"Thanks."

"Trust is vital to our relationship. We have to be able to tell each other stuff. I didn't freak out when you told me what happened with Amy when you were a freshman. And you didn't freak out when I told you about what I did with Caleb when we were together. It was difficult talking about the mistakes we made in the past, but our relationship is stronger now because we had those conversations. Right?"

My grip on the steering wheel tightened. "Yep."

"What happened with Michelle reminds me of last spring when Caleb sent me flowers and wanted to get back together. I nipped it in the bud and set him straight, just like you did with her last night. I'm glad these issues with our exes are finally settled."

"Me too."

After navigating a few more miles of Lincoln's streets, I pulled into the driveway of the Taylors' white and brick two-story house. It was the first time I had been able to drive all the way there without any directions from Gail.

After hugs and handshakes, we soon found ourselves sitting around the rectangular dining room table. Mr. and Mrs. Taylor each occupied an end. I sat next to Gail on one side of the table, her seventeen-year-old brother Mick sat across from us. After Mr. Taylor gave thanks for our food, he prayed for the safe return of the hostages from Iran and asked God to bless President Carter and the other leaders of our nation with wisdom.

"So Dave," Mrs. Taylor said, sliding a slab of lasagna onto my plate, "you certainly had an exciting week. Has it all sunk in yet?" Her strawberry blond hair had been recently permed. Warmth emanated from her green eyes.

"No, it really hasn't. This is still a bit overwhelming."

"That was the greatest bowl game ever," Mick said, his face lighting up. "People are never going to stop talking about that run you made for the two-point conversion."

"It was crazy." I took a roll and passed the basket to Gail. "I can't wait to watch a replay of the entire game."

"I don't think I'll join you in that," Gail said. "That hit you took scared me to death. I didn't know if you were ever going to get up."

"That was so cool," Mick said through a full mouth. "It looked like your head flew off!"

"Mickey." Mr. Taylor furrowed his brow.

"Sorry, but that was awesome," the teenager said, grinning at me. "After coming back from that, I bet you go in the first round."

Mrs. Taylor looked confused as she handed me a bowl of collard greens. "First round?"

"He means the NFL draft in April," I said. "I don't know if I'll get picked that high. There are a lot of talented seniors this year."

"Yeah, but you threw for 3,000 yards and 24 touchdowns. Plus all your rushing yards." Mick bobbed with enthusiasm. "And then there's the Sugar Bowl."

Mr. Taylor patted his mouth with a cloth napkin. "So, it's certain you'll be playing pro football next year?"

"I hope so. There are no guarantees, but I'll do my best to make the roster of the team that drafts me." I took a bite of lasagna, immediately wondering if it had been baked in heaven.

"Do you have any idea which team that will be?"

"No, not at this point. The scouts will be watching me at the Senior Bowl next Saturday and then there's a player evaluation camp at the end of February. After that, I should have a better idea about which teams are interested."

"I hope it's the Cowboys," Mick said. "Then I can tell my friends I know the guy who replaced Staubach."

"Texas would be warm," Mrs. Taylor added.

I swallowed a bite of roll. "I'd be thrilled to play on any of the NFL teams."

"I know that some college players quit school after their football eligibility is up," Mr. Taylor said, examining me over the top of his glasses. “Do you still plan to attend classes this semester?”

“Yes, sir. I’m taking fifteen credits this spring. Then I’ll be graduating in May, just like Gail. No spring practice should give me more time for classwork. Help raise that GPA.” I smiled.

“Oh man,” Mick exclaimed. “You don’t need to worry about grades. Leave that top three percent stuff for Miss Perfect here.” He pointed his fork at Gail. “Your future is on the football field.”

Mr. Taylor frowned at his son. “You’d do well to pick up some of your sister’s study habits. Otherwise your future will be on the detasseling field.”

Mrs. Taylor turned to her daughter. “You haven’t told us about New Orleans yet. Did you get to see much of the city?”

Gail’s face brightened. “Yes! It was beautiful and sooo warm. Dave had a couple of free nights the week before the game, so we got to see some of the sights. Visited the French Quarter. Strolled down Bourbon Street. Heard some great jazz. Ate at Antoine’s. We also went to a riverfront park to watch the Mississippi roll by. It was so much fun down there.” She elbowed me. “We’ve got to go back sometime. Does New Orleans have a pro team?”

With a mouth full of lasagna, I could not immediately answer. “Not really,” Mick said. “They have a team, but they stink.” He then launched into a lecture about the “cool” and “uncool” teams in the NFL. By the time he had finished, the rest of us were ready to discuss something other than football.

“Dave,” Mr. Taylor said with a raised brow, “as the only native Iowan present, do you have any insights about your state’s upcoming caucus?”

Having spent the last month immersed in the intricacies of the wishbone offense, I had not been following politics. I fidgeted with the edge of the white tablecloth and tried to recall the major candidates. “Well, um, Carter will probably hold off Kennedy for the Democratic nomination. On the Republican side, George Bush looks strong.”

“Interesting.” Mr. Taylor then presented a detailed argument about why Ronald Reagan was the best choice for our next president. I nodded whenever he seemed to hit a salient point.

That afternoon, Gail's parents took us on a tour of the University of Nebraska campus. Mick, electing to hang out with friends, did not come along. Mr. Taylor first showed us his office in Oldfather Hall, a tall building that overlooked the Cornhuskers' home field in Memorial Stadium. He next showed us the classroom where he taught sociology. We later visited the Nebraska Union and several other notable buildings on campus. Feeling conspicuous in my green UWI letter jacket, I was glad that classes were not yet in session.

Later that afternoon, we visited the towering capitol building, Lincoln's tallest structure. From the observation deck on the 14th floor, I surveyed the city in all four directions. The urban winter landscape stretched out before me with stark beauty. In the evening we ate Mexican food at Arturo's and watched *Cat on a Hot Tin Roof* at the Lincoln Community Playhouse.

Back at the Taylors' house, we talked and drank hot chocolate in the family room. Around 11:30, Gail and her mother said goodnight and went upstairs. Mr. Taylor led me into the den where he pulled out a bed from the sofa.

"Church is at nine. When do you want us to wake you?"

"I'll set my watch alarm for seven-thirty. Thank you anyway." I debated asking him about something, but decided to wait.

"Okay." He turned to leave but then stopped. "Say, Dave, we've never had much of a chance to talk one on one. Feel like staying up a little longer?"

"Sure. That would be great. I was hoping you and I could talk sometime this weekend." A twinge of anxiety ran through my gut.

He lowered himself into an upholstered chair beside his desk, while I claimed a seat at the foot of the pullout bed. Light from the lamp above gleamed off the vast expanse of forehead exposed by his receding hairline. "Now Dave, don't worry. This won't be an interrogation. We always save that for the church service so the entire congregation can grill Abigail's boyfriends."

I was ninety percent sure he was joking. "Uh-oh."

He laughed. "Kidding aside, Diane and I like you. We're thrilled that Abigail is dating a believer. Since she was a little girl, we've prayed that a godly man would come into her life."

I smiled. "I'm blessed to have a godly woman like her in my life."

He asked me how long I had been a Christian. I told him about my conversation with Pastor Samuels in the parking lot of my father's restaurant when I was fifteen. After I had finished describing the highlights of my walk with God over the past six years, his face took on a look of contemplation.

"Dave, listening to you talk about your faith as a Christian athlete reminds me of an issue I've often pondered in my own life." He pressed the tips of his fingers together in front of his chest. "See, I sometimes find myself ascribing my earthly successes and failures to my level of obedience to God. For example, when something positive happens, like getting a paper published, I subconsciously attribute that to God rewarding me because my walk with him is strong. When negative events happen, I tend to think that God is punishing me for something. Do you ever find yourself thinking that way with respect to your performance in football games?"

I reflected on his question for a few moments. "I guess I do. I've definitely been thinking that what happened in the Sugar Bowl was God's doing."

"But what if you'd have lost? What if on that last pass you threw, the ball would have deflected a foot farther away so your receiver couldn't catch it? Would that have meant that God was not blessing you? Or that he was displeased with you?"

"Well, I don't know."

"I wonder if the outcome of a sporting event is in any way a reflection of the participants' faith. Is the final score really an indication of how pleased God is with certain athletes at that given moment? Athletic ability is certainly a divine blessing, but does God intervene to help Christians win sporting events? Consider your opponents. There had to be strong Christians on that team. Does Western Iowa's victory mean the believers on your team had a stronger faith than the Christians playing for Alabama? Or that your collective walk was more devout than theirs?"

Convicted, I looked away. "Uh, maybe not."

"I'm not going to pretend like I know all the answers myself. But I do know that circumstances are constantly changing in life.

Whether you play in the NFL or pursue a career outside football, you will experience many victories and defeats. In either case, continue to humbly seek God every day. Your relationship with him is what's most important." He clinched his fist. "Don't lose sight of the path he has laid out for you, Dave. God has a purpose for your life, and I suspect that it is more profound than winning football games."

I paused to absorb his words. "Thank you, Mr. Taylor. That's good advice."

We sat in silence for a while. "Well, it's late," he said. "I guess I should head up to bed. Oh, wait, you said you wanted to talk to me about something. Is that right?"

Butterflies emerged from cocoons lodged in the lining of my stomach. "Uh, yeah, I did. It's um … see, Mr. Taylor, I wanted to ask … I um, was hoping to get your, uh …" I stopped to fill my tightening lungs with air. He looked confused for a few seconds, but then a smile spread across his face. I tried to continue. "I'm wondering if, uh …"

"Dave, I think I know where this is going. The answer is yes."

"Thank you, sir."

Monday morning, I called the sorority a little before 8:00. I drummed my fingers on the kitchen counter while the girl who had answered the phone summoned Gail.

"I just found out some bad news," I said. "There's major damage at the stadium."

"Damage? You mean like vandalism?"

"Yeah. I guess the field is messed up pretty bad."

"Oh that's terrible, Dave."

"Can you walk over there with me to check it out? From the sounds of it, you'll probably want to see this firsthand before sending any of your reporters."

"Well, I'm not really ready to go out yet. I haven't—"

"Please. I'm heading over there now. I'd really like you to be there with me when I see what happened. That was my home field for four years. It's not going to be easy."

She hesitated. "Yeah, okay. I'll just throw on a coat and a stocking cap."

“Thanks. See you soon.” Already wearing my letter jacket, I bounded out the front door.

Gail hung onto my arm as we walked toward Falcons Stadium. “I can’t believe someone would damage the field right after you guys won the national championship,” she said, her breath visible in the morning cold. “I wonder if it was Western Iowa students or some losers from another school.”

“I don’t know. Probably some fool who goes here.” We passed through an iron gate and saw Boomer, the head groundskeeper, standing in the main concourse of the stadium. His bald head hung low in dejection.

“Is it bad, Boomer?” I asked the burly black man.

“Dave, I just don’t understand. Man, I can’t talk about it now. You’d better go on and see for yourself.”

I patted his shoulder before Gail and I continued toward an entryway leading to the main deck. My nerves quaked as we climbed the concrete steps under the stands. Passing into the daylight, we surveyed the field below. Gasping, she put a hand over her mouth. Right in the middle of the green expanse were huge chalk letters surrounded by a giant heart. The letters formed the words, “GAIL, WILL YOU MARRY ME?”

Boomer and his crew made the message look even better than I had thought possible. Gail, standing paralyzed, did not notice that I was kneeling on one knee beside her. I popped open the lid to a small box. When I grabbed her hand, she jumped and looked down at me with shock in her eyes.

“‘A wife of noble character who can find?’ If you say yes, I believe I have found exactly that. Will you be my wife, Abigail Taylor?”

Her eyes glazed over and she started tipping to one side. “No!” she said sharply.

I dropped the box and rose to catch her. Regaining her strength, she grabbed hold of my jacket to stabilize herself. Meanwhile, a boulder crashed down upon me. “No,” I whispered, unable to contemplate what to do next.

“I said no,” she panted, still catching her breath, “to try to keep myself from fainting. I didn’t want to fall. My answer to you is yes. Yes!” She shouted the last word, causing it to echo across the football field. Cheers from the grounds crew rolled out from a distant corner of the stadium. Jumping up, she wrapped her arms and legs around me.

A few moments later, she lowered her feet to the ground. "Oh my gosh, the ring!"

"It's okay." I bent down to pick up the box while she pulled the mitten off her left hand. I plucked out the ring and slid it onto her finger. The round diamond blazed in the rays of the rising sun. The rock had completely wiped out my savings. But even though my money was gone, I now had everything.

"It's gorgeous," she said, locking me in another embrace. Oblivious to the winter chill around us, our bodies warmed with the promise of a shared future.

Chapter 15 – December 1981

"I hate you!" Gail yelled. Beads of sweat dotted her crimson face. I tried to think of a soothing reply, but came up with nothing. She squinted her scorching eyes at me and hissed, "Youuu … youuu …" She then shut her eyelids and howled something unintelligible. It probably wasn't a compliment. A moment later, she fired another round. "How could you do this to me? Get out!"

Heartbroken, I released her hand. "Okay, I'll go."

"No!" She reclaimed my hand with vice-like force. "Don't leave me!"

"Alright Gail," Doctor Foley said, the lower half of his face hidden behind a green mask. "We're almost done. Just give me a couple more big pushes. Can you do that?" A nurse wiped his brow as he focused on the life-form struggling to exit my wife's body. A large sheet blocked my view of the action down there. I was okay with that.

"Come on, Gail," I said. "You can do it." She grimaced through another mighty push. I recalled the time Zoe had told me that giving birth was like passing a bowling ball through a straw. I wondered what eloquence my wife would use to describe this experience.

After a few more heart-wrenching wails, the ordeal was over. Our son was born. He was slimy, wrinkled, upset, and beautiful. Gail closed her eyes. Her breaths came slow and heavy. I stroked her damp cheek with the back of my hand. Her lids slid open. Since a mask covered my mouth, I smiled at her with my eyes. "You did it."

"Thank God," she said through an extended exhale. "Dave, I don't hate you anymore."

"I love you too."

The rest of the morning was a blur. Nurses washed, weighed, and measured the baby. He tipped the scales at ten pounds, three ounces, and was twenty-two inches long. If he were any bigger, Gail would have altered my anatomy right there to make sure he was an only child.

A while later, my wife sat in her room holding our son. Though exhausted, she radiated joy. "Alright, sweetie, I'll be back in a while," said a rotund nurse named Mildred. She turned to me. "You tell your people in the waiting room the good news yet?"

"Actually, we don't have anyone in the waiting room," I said. "Both our families live in the Midwest. Plus, the baby surprised us this morning. He wasn't supposed to arrive for two more days. In the scramble to get to the hospital, I didn't get a chance to call anybody." An awareness swept into my head. "Oh no! I have to call the team. The coaches are probably freaking out that I missed practice."

"Practice?" Mildred's eyes lit up. "You play for the Tornadoes, don't you?" I nodded. "I thought I recognized your name."

"You'll have to excuse me," I said, backing toward the door. "If I don't call in soon, Coach will have a whole new set of names to call me."

Forgetting that there was a phone in Gail's room, I raced to the lobby. There, I found a payphone and called the team office of the Newark Tornadoes. All of the coaches were out on the practice field, so I left a message with Brandy, the receptionist. Upon hearing my news, she gushed with enthusiastic congratulations.

"Thanks, Brandy. Be sure to tell Coach Fish and the others how sorry I am. I'll definitely be at practice tomorrow."

"Oh, don't worry about it. The team can live without you for one day. It's not like your absence is going to disrupt their glorious march to last place."

Though I knew she did not speak for the coaches, her words removed some of my anxiety. I next called Nathan Rodriguez, the team chaplain. He wasn't home. His wife Jamie answered. She was

Gail's closest friend in New Jersey. "Oooh, a boy!" she exclaimed. "That is so exciting! I didn't think Gail was due until Friday."

"She wasn't. Guess the little guy got tired of waiting."

"Great. I'll leave Nathan a note and drive right over. You're at St. Barnabas, right?"

"Yep."

Gail was thrilled when her friend walked in the room, but an hour later she was fighting to stay awake. After my wife finally nodded off, Jamie went home and I ate supper in the hospital cafeteria. Later, I peered through the glass at the newborns in the maternity ward. I watched my son for nearly half an hour. My head spun as the reality of fatherhood descended upon me.

Our house in the suburb of Livingston was only two miles from the hospital. Entering the twenty-room colonial through the attached garage, I made a mental list of all the people I needed to call. Grabbing our address book, I sat at the desk in the study and wrote down the names. There was really no debate about whom I would call first. I paused to consider which day of the week it was—Wednesday. *Good, he should be home*. My fingers dialed.

"Hello."

"Hi Dad. It's Dave."

"Yes, Dave. Hello."

"Thought you might like to know you've got a new grandson."

"Very good. Everything go okay?"

"Yes. The baby's healthy. Gail's fine. It was a tough labor, but she's okay."

"What's the boy's name?"

"Kyle Daniel King."

"Kyle Daniel … I'll write that down."

"He's a big one. Ten pounds, three ounces."

"That poor wife of yours," he chuckled. "The boy sounds like a King all right."

"Yep. In a couple months I'll be taking him to the stadium to get measured for shoulder pads."

He grunted in amusement. "Well, I hope you're ready for this. Your life is never going to be the same. Once those kids come along, they keep you hopping."

"I've heard. Believe me, I've heard. So how did you end up with nine of us?"

"Well, I got married and Eli showed up about a year later. Zoe was next. Then I shipped out to France for two years. Once I got back, the kids kept coming. Your mother, she loved her children. Treasured every one of you. You probably don't remember her much."

"A little. I have some memories of her." I closed my eyes and recalled listening to Mom sing while I sat on the living room floor playing with my blocks. It was a familiar memory—one that brought warmth and sadness at the same time.

"Good woman," he said with a cough. "Wish she didn't have to go when she did. It was …" The phone was silent.

"Yeah, I know," I said softly. "Wonder what she'd have thought about all these grandkids. Got a dozen of 'em running around, plus Asa up in heaven with her." There was actually one more counting the boy Amy and I had placed for adoption, but Dad did not know about him.

"Oh, she'd have loved them. Every one. Knowing Rachel, she'd be bugging you all to have more. I bet she'd really be giving Ozzie the devil to get him to start a family."

"So how is Oz? I haven't talked to him in weeks."

"He doesn't know about your son yet?"

"No. I just got home from the hospital before I called you. Thought I'd try to catch him later this evening."

"Well, you know Ozzie. Never does anything more than necessary to get by."

"Still counting beans for Principal?" I popped open a can of Coke that I'd brought into the study.

"Yes. Thank heavens he finally got that job. I was dreading the thought of having to take him on at the restaurant."

"I'm sure Adam and Shane would've loved that too." I took a drink.

"Right. Say, do you know much about that gal he's living with?"

I sprayed a mouthful of pop across the desk. "What? Ozzie's living with a girl?"

"Yeah. Sherry or Sara. Something like that. I can't recall her last name."

"He didn't tell me about that. He didn't mention *any* girl last time I talked to him. That little rat." I pulled off a sock to sop up the mess I had made.

"Oh, they've been together for a while. I finally met her last week when he brought her to the restaurant for Thanksgiving dinner. Oriental gal. A little rough around the edges if you ask me."

"Ozzie likes 'em that way. Hope she has a sense of humor."

Dad was quiet for a moment. "You know, I never really understood that boy. The things that amuse him, I just don't get it."

"Yeah, Ozzie is … different. I'll leave it at that."

Dad paused again. "So how's the team? You keeping up okay?"

"Yeah, I'm finally getting a handle on the offensive schemes. I think I'd be ready if Billy went down and I had to start. Last year I couldn't say that." I flashed back to my rookie season. It was a nightmare: learning all the plays in the game plan—120 of them every week; trying to read the pro defenses; adjusting to the speed of the league. I was overwhelmed. Fortunately, I didn't have to take many snaps my first season in the NFL.

"Well, you were still learning the pro game back then. Has Hartman said anything about retiring? What is he now, thirty-seven?"

"Yeah, he'll be thirty-seven next month. I don't think Billy wants to retire, but it seems like the front office is encouraging it."

"The Tornadoes owners have to think about their investment. Hartman's not the quarterback he used to be. And the team used a first-round pick to get you. If the coaches think you're ready, the owners aren't going to want to pay his hefty salary for another year while you sit around doing nothing. He has to understand the business side of things."

"He does. We all do. I still hate the bad feelings this has created. I want to start next season, but I don't want to be known as the guy who forced Billy Hartman to leave before he was ready. He's a hero to a lot of people in New Jersey."

"Well, he's not getting the job done anymore. What's the team's record now?"

"Three and ten. Last place in the AFC Central. And with the Bengals up next, it looks like we'll soon be three and eleven. It gets depressing standing on the sideline watching the team lose week after week." I leaned back in my chair.

"Yes, but it could be worse. Look what happened to Thor. Blew out his knee and now he's done for the year."

"I know. I hated that. He had just made starter the week before it happened. I really miss him. He was the only center I knew in high school and college. I wish the Tornadoes would make a trade for him. The guy we got here isn't as good at snapping or blocking. And during scrimmages he likes to pass gas in my face when I'm calling the snap count."

Dad chuckled. "I bet being a backup quarterback in the NFL still beats waiting tables at The Royal Court."

"Maybe. But I wouldn't mind some of your Baked Alaska from time to time.... So how is the restaurant? You ever think about retiring?"

He paused. "Yes. I thought about it a couple years ago when I turned sixty-five, but I just couldn't do it."

"The restaurant would be fine with Adam and Shane. Didn't the doctor tell you to cut back and take it easy for your blood pressure?"

"Yes, those were the doctor's orders," he said with a sigh. "But your brothers might get some crazy ideas about changing the place. I'm not ready to see that happen to my restaurant. And I don't know what I'd do with myself if I didn't have somewhere to go every day."

"You could do whatever you wanted. You're set financially, right? You could come out to New Jersey and visit your new grandson. We could take you to New York. There's tons of stuff to do there. And if you come out next fall, you could go to a Tornadoes game. We may stink, but sometimes we play good teams."

"Hmm. Maybe I'll think about retiring next summer. We'll see how things go." The grandfather clock in his living room started chiming. The sound took me back home for an instant. "It's eight, already," he said. "That makes it nine there. I'd better let you go. I imagine you've got quite a few people yet to call."

"Yeah, okay."

"Thanks for calling, Dave. Congratulations. Give my best to Gail."

"Thanks, Dad. I will."

The next morning I visited Gail and Kyle at the hospital before driving to the Tornadoes' practice field at Kean College in Union, the township just southwest of Newark. The football facilities on campus were great for a Division III college program, but depressingly meager for a professional franchise. On the way in, I noticed a layer of smog hovering over Newark's skyline. It was a fitting visual representation of the cloud of defeat that hung over the city's football team.

Making peace with the head coach, Al Fish, and the quarterback coach, Dallas Raes, was easier than I thought it would be. Brandy was right—a second-string quarterback missing a day of practice with his last-place team was not an earth-shattering incident. Though relieved to avoid a tongue-lashing, my escape further underscored the stench of apathy that pervaded the Newark team psyche.

On Thursdays we practiced only in the morning, so I returned to the hospital after lunch. Though still exhausted, Gail was looking stronger. I finally had the opportunity to hold my son for an extended period of time. I gazed into his blue eyes wondering what he thought of this new world around him. His expression suggested he was still overwhelmed by the events of the past day and a half. He was not alone in that feeling.

Later that afternoon I drove to Newark International Airport to pick up Gail's mother, Diane. She would be staying with us for the next week. For that I was profoundly grateful. Diane and I arrived at St. Barnabas a little before six. The new grandma brimmed with anticipation as we strode through the hospital. My wife's face lit up at the sight of her mother. I had planned to stick around until visiting hours were over, but Gail reminded me about my Thursday evening Bible study. Knowing that she and her mother had a lot of catching up to do, I took off.

About twenty minutes later, I arrived at Nathan's modest house in Newark's Seventh Avenue neighborhood. He opened the door and greeted me in Spanish. The son of a Puerto Rican father and an Anglo mother, Nathan liked to test how much I remembered from my two semesters of college Spanish. I rarely passed. Eight of my teammates were crowded around his living room, open Bibles in their laps. They were discussing the book of Daniel.

At the end of the study, T.D. Franklin, a black battering ram of a fullback, closed in prayer. The rhythmic cadence of his supplication rang with energy. One never doubted if T.D. had the ear of God when he prayed. On this night his words were especially inspiring as he expressed thanks for the safe arrival of Kyle and prayed for God's hand of guidance to be upon Gail and me as we raised our son. A chorus of amens followed the final sentence of T.D.'s prayer.

Like usual, Nathan asked me to hang around afterwards for a while. He grabbed a couple of Dr. Peppers from the refrigerator and we sat on the front steps of his house. The December evening was cool but not cold. With several of the streetlamps shot out, the avenue before us was scantly illuminated. Santana's "Black Magic Woman" seeped out from the closed windows of the house next door.

"So how does it feel to be Papa King now?" The dark bushy eyebrows on his square face inched higher. The hair atop his head was also dark and bushy, though he kept the sides trimmed high and tight.

"Papa King? I thought that was your name for my dad?"

"It was. But now you're Papa King. He's Grandpapa King."

"Got it." I opened my can and took a swig of sweet flavorful soda.

"Not yet, you don't. When you change your first fully-loaded radioactive diaper, then you've got it. And believe me, you'll keep getting it over and over. With my boys spaced two years apart, I've been breathing the fallout for four straight years."

I laughed and started to reply when a faint siren grew disturbingly loud. A police car whizzed past Nathan's street a block away and continued west. The blaring softened as the siren moved farther and farther away. The process repeated a few seconds later when another cruiser followed the same route.

"Don't you ever worry about raising Jimmy and Cooper in this crazy world?" I asked. "Seems like things nowadays are out of control, especially here in the city with all the violence and drugs." Two gunshots echoed in the distance to punctuate my statement.

"Nothing new under the sun, bro," he said. "God's people have always lived in a dangerous and immoral world. Think it was easy raising children during the Babylonian captivity?"

"Yeah, I know. It just seems worse now." I glanced at him. "This city is swimming in crime and poverty."

"But you live in the 'burbs. You're in a safe place."

"Do you blame me for living in Livingston? I mean, Newark was ranked the most dangerous city in America."

"No, I don't blame you. You got a little guy to think about now, and who knows how many more down the road. You want to build a good life for your kids in a safe environment."

"That's the thing."

"And you got a six-figure income, so you can afford to live out there. Me? The Tornadoes don't pay me a dime. With just my associate pastor salary from our little church, I can't afford Livingston." We both spotted a tabby cat stalking down the sidewalk on the other side of the street. "But even if I could, I don't think we'd move. I feel like God wants me here, right in the middle of it all." He spread out his arms.

"Yeah?" A group of teenagers standing on the corner of the block caught my eye. I thought about asking Nathan if they were drug dealers, but decided against it.

"Yep." He nodded. "My ministry is urban. Just like Paul. Look at where he went … the cities. The places he hit during his missionary trips were just like Newark—crime-ridden, lost, and in desperate need of Jesus."

My eyes met his. "Now I feel guilty about where I live."

"I'm not saying *you* should move. We've all got to go where God calls us. Maybe for you that's the 'burbs. There's plenty of kingdom work to do in Livingston. But I believe God wants me right here in Newark, where I grew up. I have a heart for this place. You know I was thirteen when the riots broke out. That was insane. Since then, I've seen this city crumble. Businesses have closed. The middle class has gone away. People have lost hope. Man,

Newark needs revival. And it starts right here in this neighborhood."

"Yeah." I hung my head. Ever since moving to New Jersey, I had sought to avoid the city and all its problems. With my house in Livingston, our practice facility in Union, and our stadium in East Rutherford, I had largely succeeded in that goal. Aside from visiting Nathan, I rarely entered the city I represented on the football field.

We were both quiet for a while. After finishing my soda, I checked my watch. "Oh man, I've got to go. I told Diane I'd pick her up at the hospital at ten. Visiting hours are almost over."

We stood and shook hands. "All right, bro," he said. "I'll catch you tomorrow at the hospital. Got to see the little King again. Hey, sometime we've got to go back to Frank's. They put in this new video game—Pac Man. You seen that yet?"

"No. Haven't heard of it."

"Oh dude, it's awesome. Maybe next week we can grab a pizza and you can check it out. Bring lots of quarters."

"Okay, sounds good."

As he looked past me down the street, his face dropped. "Uh, King, did you have hubcaps on your car when you came over?"

"What?" My head spun around. Since I was a few minutes late to the study, I had to park a half block away from Nathan's house. Under a dark streetlamp sat my Mustang—my new 1982 black Mustang—with naked wheels. "Oh, come on!" I yelled. "That's just … crap!" A dog in a nearby yard started barking.

"What can I say? This is the hood, bro. Maybe if you guys start winning some games, this kind of thing won't happen."

"Funny, Nathan. Real funny." I stomped off toward my car, steam pouring from my ears.

Singing to the tune of a Tony Bennett classic, Nathan serenaded me as I walked away. "I left my caps in Newark city. Rolling down the street, they call to me."

Friday morning, my eyes popped open in darkness. Though it wasn't even 5:00 yet, I was wide-awake. *Great. The baby's not even home yet and my sleep schedule is already messed up.* As I lay in agitation, a thought came to me. I got dressed and left a note in the kitchen telling Diane that I would be home by eight to take her to the hospital.

After backing out of the driveway, my hubcapless car headed southeast. Several minutes later I crossed the Goethals Toll Bridge to Staten Island. My destination was Oakwood Beach on the island's eastern coastline. Gail and I had visited there a few times in the summer of 1980, just after we had moved to New Jersey. Finding a spot in the sand that was free of debris, I sat facing the Atlantic Ocean. The wind was cold at first, but I soon got used to its invigorating bite. The immense roar of the waves overwhelmed my auditory senses.

Alone in the darkness, I contemplated life. After an unknown duration, the horizon lit up with an orange glow. Minutes later a fiery orb emerged from the ocean. Its majestic radiance reflected off the surface of the water. Feeling the presence of the Lord, I began to pray.

"God, who am I that you have blessed me with so much? Sitting here amid your magnificent creation, my insignificance is so apparent. Yet, I am totally aware that your love surrounds me. You have given me so much more than I deserve. I thank you for my family. For Gail, a dream come true. For Kyle, who I pray will grow up to become a strong man of faith. Please help Gail and me to raise him according to your will. And Lord, I ask that you remember the son I've never met. He is four years old now with a name unknown to me. Guide his parents to bring him up in a godly home." I rose to my feet and scanned the brightening sky.

"Viewing this sunrise, God, I am overwhelmed by your awesome power. Thank you for your mercy and for hearing my prayers. I praise you for your Word and your promise of salvation. My soul rejoices in your presence, O Lord. May your blessing remain with your servant and his family forever." I stretched wide my arms as the dazzling rays warmed my face.

Later that day, Gail and I brought our son home from the hospital.

On Sunday the Cincinnati Bengals came to town. We played our home games at Giants Stadium in the Meadowlands Sports Complex, north of Newark. As the name suggested, it was a football home the Tornadoes rented from the New York Giants. Before our games, a crew repainted the end zone logos and hung orange and purple Tornadoes banners throughout the stadium. Newark players and fans still could not escape the depressing reality that our home field was in another team's stadium. It was little wonder that the stands were usually half empty when we played.

The Bengals showed us little mercy. They led 35-0 at the half and added another touchdown in the third quarter. Coach Fish sent me in to play the final fifteen minutes. I promptly threw an interception. Our next drive consisted of three plays and a punt. On our final possession, however, we moved the ball. My confidence soared during the drive, even though it came against disinterested second- and third-team defenders. With 1:40 left to play in the game, I threw my first touchdown pass in the NFL. Had there been any fans left in the seats, the event might have seemed more significant. Instead, my big moment passed with a few lackluster high fives. The final score was 49 to 7.

The following week Kyle kept busy with a full schedule of eating, sleeping, spitting up, and pooping. He also performed with great effectiveness his infant duty of ensuring that his mom and dad never had more than three uninterrupted hours of sleep. For our part, Gail and I groggily learned how to be parents. Though initially terrified when Diane returned to Nebraska, we did okay on our own.

The Tornadoes' next game was at Cleveland. It was Billy Hartman's best outing of the year. Recalling his glory days from a decade ago, he passed for 306 yards and three touchdowns against the Browns. Newark won the game 28-21 in a mild upset. My teammates celebrated like we had just made the playoffs.

Back home, Kyle's second week of existence was a lot like his first. Gail and I continued to catch on to the parent thing. We cherished every yawn, gurgle, burp, and smile our boy gave us. He even started sleeping for longer stretches at night.

Sunday, December 20th, marked the end of the season. Bud Grant brought his Minnesota Vikings to the Meadowlands for this final game. Like most of our opponents' quarterbacks, Tommy Kramer had a stellar day. From the sideline I watched his every move, dreaming that I too would someday fire spirals to open receivers all over the field. Newark had no answer for the Minnesota attack. Instead of living up to our name, we went out like a gentle breeze. I played the last seven minutes in a blowout loss that could not end soon enough for any of us.

Newark's final record was four and twelve, the same mark we had my rookie season. Our dismal finish was cause for mild optimism in the Tornadoes locker room. Only Baltimore and New England had a worse record than we did. That meant Newark would get the third pick in the draft next spring. Reviewing the stats of the top graduating college players generally brought more excitement to Tornadoes fans than anything the team did on the field.

Monday morning, I drove to Kean College for our last team meeting of the season. I was back home by noon. After decorating our Christmas tree, I played guitar and sang to Kyle as he rested in Gail's arms. After finishing "The Coloring Song" by Petra, I asked my wife what I should play next.

"How about 'Father's Eyes?'" she suggested, gently rocking in the La-Z-Boy.

"But that's sung by a girl."

"Don't be silly. It's a song about God. Plus, it was written by a man."

"I'm a football player. I don't sing chick songs."

She stared at me with the frown of a displeased schoolmarm. An instant later, I was singing like Amy Grant. I shuddered at the thought that my teammates would someday find out.

After I finished the song, Gail seemed disturbed. "Have you noticed anything unusual about Kyle?" she asked, looking down at our baby.

"No. What do you mean?"

"Well, he doesn't seem to respond to any sounds. Your guitar. My voice. Nothing."

"He's only three weeks old. Are babies supposed to respond that young?"

"I don't know. I thought so. I keep thinking he'll react to something … but he hasn't." The fear in her eyes sent a shiver down my spine.

"We'll take him to the doctor to get tested," I said. "I'll call right now. I don't know if we can get in before we leave for Iowa. Maybe they can see him next week, after we're back."

"As soon as possible."

"It'll be okay." Setting down the guitar, I walked over and kissed the top of her head. When I rubbed Kyle's belly, he looked up at me and squirmed. "It could be a lot of things," I said. "Maybe he has a little ear infection or something. Maybe some babies don't respond to sound until they're a few weeks older. That doesn't mean he's—" I couldn't say it. "We'll get him tested. Then we'll know he's okay."

She grabbed my hand. "I hope so."

Chapter 16 – October 1983

The locker room was a simmering cauldron of tension. Large men twitched, growled, and shook. Some sat on benches cracking their knuckles. Others paced, mumbling to themselves. All had the look of feral beasts locked in a cage. I sat staring at my hands. My right foot tapped the floor. As usual, the last moments before a game brought us all to a state of crazed restlessness.

Normally I tried to use those final minutes to mentally review the plays we would be running and the defensive alignments I was likely to see. But this time, a name kept bouncing into my head. *Dawn Lewis*. I'd push it away for a while, but it kept coming back.

Hal Nance, the Tornadoes' Director of Public Relations, had first mentioned the name to me a month earlier. It was no big deal. Fans occasionally called the team office asking to talk to the players. Calls for me had increased since I took over as starting quarterback in the 1982 preseason. Players, of course, were not expected to return any of the calls that came in for us.

Fans more commonly wrote letters. Most were from autograph-seeking children telling us how great we were. Other letters were from female fans, proposing marriage or a tryst the next time we were in their city. Sometimes they included a picture. I always destroyed the photos. The majority of my teammates had other ideas. The insides of their locker doors were covered with provocative images of "ladies" from around the country.

Not every letter, however, was filled with praise or propositions. Some people wrote to tell us how bad we were at our jobs. Michelle, for example, once sent a lovely note explaining how much I sucked as a quarterback and as a man. Now married to Paul and living in Denver, she apparently still held a grudge.

Dawn Lewis never wrote, but her calls kept coming. When I reached the stadium before the game, Hal informed me that she had called twice the previous week. Her persistence made me wonder if I once knew her or if she was a crazed stalker. As I sat in the locker room with the other caged animals, the name hovered just beyond my cerebral grasp. I had heard it before, but I couldn't place where or when.

Finally it was time to unleash the dogs of war. We rumbled down the tunnel like a barbarian horde charging into battle. Prior to this game, Newark's record was 4-3. That was cause for much excitement in New Jersey since the team had not had a winning record in over a decade. Our opponents, the Los Angeles Raiders, were 6-1 and leading the AFC West. As such, they were nine-point favorites. Upon reaching our sideline, I surveyed the crowd. The stands at Giants Stadium were filled to capacity. I had never before seen so many fans at a Tornadoes home game.

As the opening kickoff sailed through the air, all thoughts of the mysterious Dawn Lewis disappeared. My mind steeled to the task at hand. Rocket fuel coursed through my veins. Out on the field, I recognized the Raiders' formations and dissected their coverages. When they shifted during the snap count, I countered with an effective audible. Guided missiles flew from my hand toward open receivers. The ground game plowed forward with relentless efficiency. Newark kept the chains moving throughout the first half.

The key to our success was the offensive line. Offseason acquisition Thor Heimlich was having another great game at center. It had cost the Tornadoes a valuable second-round pick to pry him from the Lions, but it was worth it. The change of scenery was good for him too. Thor had struggled during his three years in Detroit, due to injuries and the death of his father. In Newark, he was once again a dominating presence on the football field. His intensity and on-field intelligence inspired the men blocking alongside him. The Tornadoes offensive line, mediocre only a season ago, was now among the best in the league.

We scored three touchdowns in the first two quarters. Unfortunately, Los Angeles matched our success. Jim Plunkett and Marcus Allen had little trouble moving the ball against the porous Tornadoes defense. At halftime the score was tied 21-21.

In the locker room, my adrenaline surge stopped and my body started to ache from a hit I took in the first quarter. Trying to pick up a couple extra yards on a bootleg, I did not notice the mammoth defensive tackle charging at me from the side. He nailed me at full speed, plowing me into the turf. It never ceased to amaze me how fast even the fat men in the NFL could move. While my body systems shut down during the halftime break, the throbbing from that violent encounter intensified.

Coach Fish addressed the players. "Today you've lined up with the best team in the conference. And guess what? You're still standing. You've matched them play for play. In the first half, the Raiders learned that you're just as tough as they are. In the second half, show those silver and black bastards that on this day, in this place, you're just a little better than them."

Quarterback coach Dallas Raes and offensive coordinator Troy Woods discussed strategies and adjustments with me. I downed a bottle of Gatorade while reviewing the different nuances from our playbook that we were going to throw at the Raiders in the second half. A few minutes later it was time to hit the field again. Marching through the tunnel, my teammates and I revved our engines for thirty more minutes of football. For most of the Tornadoes, including myself, this was the biggest game we had ever played as professionals.

The second half was a lot like the first. Both offenses racked up impressive yardage totals. The Raiders kept varying their defensive formations, but I consistently recognized how to counter. Midway through the fourth quarter, I threw my third touchdown pass of the day to give us the lead. Plunkett and his buddies quickly answered. He directed a scoring drive to put Los Angeles ahead 42-38 with just under four minutes left to play. On our next possession we started moving the ball again. But then, disaster struck. A fumble by Newark running back Biff Hawkins gave the Raiders the ball at their 35.

Dejection flooded our sideline as the realization set in that the game now rested on the backs of the Tornadoes defense. To our surprise, the orange and purple line held, stuffing Allen for no gain on a third and one play. Hope returned.

After the punt, we took over at our 21-yard line with 1:39 left in the game. On the first play of the drive I rolled out left and, spotting no one open, tucked the ball and raced ahead. Spinning past one silver helmet and sidestepping another, I scooted out of bounds after a 14-yard pickup. But the next two plays, an incompletion and a draw to Hawkins, netted only three yards.

On third down, I dropped back and scanned the secondary for orange jerseys. Unfortunately, my receivers were all accompanied by guys wearing white. The pocket collapsed around me. A hand clawed at my back. I stepped forward to break free from the hostile grasp and then darted through a narrow gap that had opened before me. Swerving past a defender, I raced into the secondary. After I had gained ten yards, a cornerback cuffed an ankle to trip me up. As I fell, a pursuing linebacker crashed down upon my back. The blow rattled my internal organs, but we had a first down.

Regaining my wind for the next snap, I found speedy wide receiver Jason Hackman near the sideline for 18 yards. After a screen pass to Hawkins, we had the ball at the 23-yard line with 16 seconds left. I called our last timeout and trotted over to Coach Fish. With his headset and large hooked nose, he looked like a hawk wearing earmuffs. After speaking a few words into the mouthpiece, he removed the headset and grabbed my shoulder pads. Unkempt copper hair flowed in all directions as his eyes zeroed in on mine. "Woods wants to hit 'em with a 19 Left Crescent Switch. You got that?"

I nodded. I was to take the snap and roll right with the line for a few steps before circling back around to the left on a naked bootleg. I would pass if a receiver was open, otherwise I would race toward the sideline picking up as much ground as possible. My nerve endings buzzed with anticipation.

Thor hiked me the ball. The ruse worked—the Raiders followed me to the right. Abruptly spinning around, I saw open field before me as I rolled left. Looking downfield, I spotted Hackman breaking free. In an instant my brain debated whether to run or throw. *If I run, I can get inside the 10-yard line before being forced out of bounds. We would then have time for one or two more plays.* The open receiver, on the other hand, was just beyond the goal line mirroring my movement to the left. Victory flashed before my eyes.

Shifting my torso, I drew back the ball and rifled it toward the end zone. The football spiraled forward on a rendezvous course with Hackman. His hands guided the ball into his body. My arms shot up. But the ball bounced off his chest, just between the purple numbers. In trying to regain control of the pass, he knocked the football up in the air with a flailing hand as a Raiders safety rammed into him. The ball floated upward end over end, then started its descent. Just before hitting the turf, it landed in the hands of a diving cornerback. Interception. Game over.

The Tornadoes locker room was a morgue. Coach Fish tried to console us with a cliché-laden speech about how we had just hung with the best team in the NFL. The reality of defeat nonetheless sunk in. I felt sick.

A pack of reporters surrounded my locker. After a few innocuous questions, they subtly crafted their queries to try to get me to assign blame for the loss. As a team leader, I had to watch my every word. Despite the interlocutors' best efforts, I refused to throw any of my teammates under the bus. Instead, I gave their tape recorders the usual canned responses. "We put forth a good effort today. Just came up a little short. The Raiders are a strong team. They played a great game. The Tornadoes can build on this for next week."

After showering and dressing, I walked with Thor out to the parking lot. Gail had long since gone home with the visiting members of my family who had attended the game. "Well, at least we had fun," I said.

"Yeah, that it was," he replied. "Nice pass there at the end."

"Thanks. Guess I should've run." We walked in silence for a while. The name bounced into my head again. "Thor, you ever heard of a Dawn Lewis?"

"Uh, no. Doesn't ring a bell. Why?"

"Some woman with that name keeps calling the team office wanting to meet with me. I don't know who she is."

"Did we go to school with her at Eastridge or Western Iowa?"

"I don't think so. I can't remember any classmates with that name."

"Hmm, me neither." We reached our vehicles. "If I think of anything, I'll let you know. Catch you tomorrow, King." He hoisted himself into the cab of his F-150.

"Alright, Hammer. See ya later." I crawled into my black Mustang and turned the key. The engine roared to life. Just then a spark flashed in my memory. I finally remembered a Dawn. "Yes! That has to be her," I said aloud.

When I got home, I called Hal and left a message on his machine. "Hal. This is Dave King. I remember Dawn Lewis. Tell her I'll meet with her. Arrange it as soon as possible, okay?"

That evening, Gail and I grilled rib eyes for our guests: Adam and Shannon, their two teenagers, Martin and Jane, and Ozzie. After supper we gathered in the living room as little Kyle entertained us by jumping and twirling around. Archibald Samuel King, his four-month-old baby brother, sat bouncing in Jane's lap. Gail eventually coaxed Kyle into demonstrating a few of the sign language words he had been learning.

When our food had settled, the men went outside to shoot some hoops on the cement half court beside the house. The game was horse. Since neither Adam nor I had any basketball ability, we both quickly picked up H-O-R-S. The abuse delivered unto me by the Los Angeles Raiders earlier in the day did nothing to help my woeful outside shooting. Ozzie, usually an even worse shooter than me, was having the night of his life. After he banked in a lucky 20-footer from the top of the key, I faced elimination.

I grabbed the ball and eyed the rim. "Alright, Chachi," Ozzie taunted, "let's see if Joanie still loves you after your second humiliating failure of the day."

"Oooooh," Martin and Adam chorused.

My middle finger flinched but did not extend. I bent my knees and brought the ball back above my head. Pain stabbed my ribs. Springing slightly off the ground, I lofted the orange sphere toward the rim. It looked good, right up until when it clanged off the back of the iron.

Ozzie pranced around in triumph. "One brother down, one brother and a nephew to go," he bellowed. His performance concluded with a sorry attempt at a moonwalk. A heavy coating of mousse kept his feathered hair locked in place through all his jerky motions.

I limped over to a lawn chair on the patio beside the court. A moment later, Martin, a starting forward at Eastridge High, eliminated his father with a hook shot. Adam grabbed a Coke from a cooler and pulled up a chair next to mine.

"Didn't you raise him any better than that?" I asked.

"He gets it from his mother," he said, popping open the red and white can. For the next few minutes, we watched Ozzie somehow match his nephew shot for shot. As dusk set in, moths fluttered around the pole-mounted lights above the court.

"So, how's the restaurant? You pried the reins from Dad's hands yet?"

"Nope. The old man's got quite a grip. He has cut back to thirty hours a week though. Says he'll retire when he turns seventy. I'll believe that when I see it." Adam wiped away the line of pop foam that had collected on his moustache. "Eli just lost his job. He's talking like he wants to co-manage the restaurant. Tell me *that* wouldn't be a disaster."

"Oh. Well, I'll be praying for that situation and for all of you."

"Thanks," he said, slouching back and stretching his legs out in front of him. "But I don't think that will help."

"Sure it will. With God all things are possible."

The corners of his mouth curled into a smirk. "You still think that God intervenes in your life, huh?"

"Of course I think that. Because he does. Just look at my football career."

"So if God intervenes in people's lives, then why doesn't he do something about all the suffering in the world? Consider what's happening in Ethiopia. Thousands are starving. With another year of drought, the country could be facing a full-scale famine. Is it too much to ask of your God to send a little rain over there?"

"It's not God's will that they suffer."

"Well, if it isn't," he said, shifting in his chair to face me, "then God must not have the power to help them. Your God is either malicious for allowing the innocent to suffer or he's weak—not really a god at all."

My body tensed. I hated his jabs at my faith, but saw this as an opportunity to defend what I knew to be true. "Adam, it's not like that. Man sinned, and that brought consequences. Because of the Fall, we live in a world in which evil exists. But Christ prevailed over sin. When he returns—"

"But why must evil continue to exist?" he interrupted. "If Christ won such a great victory, why do we have to wait for the results of that triumph? Why must humanity endure all this horrible misery century after century? Plagues, famine, cancer, and now this AIDS thing. Why can't Christ return today and spare us all this affliction?"

Out on the court, Martin attempted a free throw while standing on one foot. Bent over beneath the basket, Ozzie dropped his pants to moon him. "I don't know all the answers," I said. "But I know that God loves us and wants what's best for us. If we follow him and obey his commands, that brings blessings. But if we turn away and reject him, that brings trouble." Despite the distraction of his uncle's gleaming white buns, Martin sank the basket.

Adam scratched his head. His hair was short with a part on the side, a sharp contrast to the flowing brown mess he sported in his younger days. "Dave, ever since man invented the gods, the ruling classes have used the fear of divine wrath to preserve their power over the masses. Throughout history, organized religion in all its forms has existed as a means of social control. The different Christian denominations of today are basically doing the same thing—subjugating the proletariat to preserve the established hierarchy."

"So that's it? God is just a human invention. You can look at the world with all its complexities and deny that it was made by a creator? Look around you. The evidence of God is everywhere."

Adam's gaze remained on the court where Martin swished a 25-foot jumper. "Great shot, Marty!" he yelled. "A few years ago, I would have said no. Definitely no God. But now I can allow that there may be an intelligent designer. If that is the case, however, this God must have created the earth and let it go. She no longer has any knowledge of what's going on here. No divine interventions. No awareness of what we do. Because if God were aware, I think she would do something to stop all the terrible suffering that people endure in their lifetimes."

"But you're missing the bigger picture. The eternal picture."

"Shit!" Ozzie's disappointment at missing his shot echoed through the night.

"That's HORSE, old man," Martin said, starting a victory strut.

Ozzie grabbed the ball and punted it straight up in the air. "That punk son of your needs to learn some respect for his elders," he grumbled while approaching us.

"Don't blame me if you can't hang with the Bird," Adam said.

"Here's your bird." Ozzie raised the appropriate finger.

"Talk about your sinners." Adam gestured at our brother. "Look at this profane heathen. Even I wish this guy would get some religion."

"Whatchoo talkin' bout, Willis?" Ozzie asked. Martin, meanwhile, resumed shooting baskets.

"Oh, don't pick on Oz too much," I said. "At least he's not living in sin with Sherry anymore."

"That's right," Ozzie agreed, trying to look angelic.

Adam scoffed. "Yeah, but now he's living with another girl. What's her name? Colleen?" Ozzie pressed an index finger to his mouth in a shushing gesture.

"What?" I exclaimed. "You're living with *another* girl?"

"Damn it, Adam," Ozzie said. "I told you not to tell Charlie Church here about that. Now he's gonna get his goody-two-shoes buddy Pat Boone to come over and preach to me about changing my wicked ways."

"That wouldn't help," I said. "You're incorrigible. It's going to take years of fasting and prayer to get you set right. And don't make fun of Pat. I've met him. He's a nice guy."

"Yeah, you've mentioned that a few hundred times. It's really kind of sad, Dave. You're a starting quarterback in the NFL and the only famous person you've met is Pat Freakin' Boone. Like we give a rat's ass."

"Hey, I've met the guys in Bon Jovi."

"Who the hell's that?" Adam asked.

"Oh that's even less impressive." Ozzie rolled his eyes. "They're some local garage band that played a halftime show at one of Dave's games this year."

"They're pretty good," I said. "Haven't you heard 'Runaway?' The rock stations around here have been playing it all the time."

"No, I have not heard anything from those wannabes. Nobody outside of New Jersey ever has or ever will. Please Dave, if you're going impress us, you'll have to meet some real celebrities. Harrison Ford. Stallone. Mr. T. Even Pat Boone's daughter would be a step up. Her, I wouldn't mind taking to the Land of Oz." He added a couple of pelvic thrusts to illustrate his point. "It can't be wrong, cause it would feel soooo right."

I shot to my feet to defend Debby's honor. "It's time you learn some manners."

Ozzie stepped back and danced around like a boxer. "Now settle down, Ponyboy. I don't want to have to hurt you and get your coach mad at me. But if you force me, I'll unleash thunder and lightning on you." He kissed each of his fists.

Adam and I laughed at the bravado of our smaller brother. I wanted to lunge forward and tackle him, but my body still ached. "I hear ya, Sodapop. Enjoy your delusions."

"Hey," Martin yelled from the court. "Any of you geezers ready for some one on one?"

Adam checked his watch. "No. It's getting late. We'd better go in. Got to get up early in the morning." Martin groaned in protest.

"When's your flight?" I asked.

"Nine-fifteen."

"Good. That leaves time for pancakes. Gail makes them almost as good as Grandma."

"Sweet," Ozzie said. "That might make up for having to watch you blow the game today."

Aching body or not, that was the last straw. I nodded at Martin who was now standing beside my brother. When I sprang forward, my nephew clamped a bear hug on Ozzie. By the time he broke free, it was too late. Bending low to get a firm grip around his waist, I hoisted my brother's thin frame over my shoulder. I then rotated my body into an airplane spin.

"No!" Ozzie yelled as I spun him around, faster and faster. "Respect the Wizard! Reespeeeect thuuh Wiiiizzaarrrd youuuuu pieeeeeece uuuv shiiiiiiit."

After about a minute of twirling, I lowered him headfirst into an empty metal garbage can next to the garage. The impact knocked the can over. I gave it a push to start it rolling down the driveway. Clad in parachute pants, Ozzie's legs kicked about as they tumbled over and over each other. Upon rolling fifteen feet or so, the can veered off the driveway and came to a stop in the grass. Swearing up a storm, my brother shimmied backwards out of the can. He tried to stand, but was so dizzy he flopped face first into the ground. Adam, Martin, and I howled.

"That's right, laugh it up," Ozzie slurred, staggering to his feet. Taking a step, he lost his balance and toppled again. He rolled onto his back and spread his arms out on the ground. "I'm telling Dad. You're gonna get the belt, Dave. Then we'll see how funny this is.... Whoa, man, check out those stars spinning around up there. This is actually a good buzz."

Still chuckling, the rest of us went inside.

Despite the tough loss to the Raiders, the team was upbeat at practice Monday. Our coaches reiterated that we could play with any team in the NFL. And with a 4-4 record, the Tornadoes still had a chance to make the playoffs. We players drilled and scrimmaged with new levels of focus and intensity.

After supper that evening, the phone rang. It was Joe.

"I watched the game yesterday," he said. "You dominated."

"Thanks."

"Tornadoes should have won. Hackman let the team down."

"Jason is our best receiver. He's having a great year. He just lost the handle on that last pass. It happens to everybody."

"Can't drop the ball in that situation. The game was on the line."

I decided to change the subject. "So how's college? You still getting straight As?"

"Yes, sir."

"You're a poly sci major?"

"Correct again."

"Say, have you been keeping up with what happened in Beirut yesterday? I caught a little on the news tonight. I couldn't believe it."

"Yes, it's bad," he said grimly. "Looks like we lost at least a hundred Marines. Probably more. Plus the French casualties."

"Do they know who did it?"

"No. But I'm sure Iran is behind this in some way. The Ayatollah has been financing terrorist groups in Lebanon for years."

"What do you think we'll do in response?"

"We should just level the Beqaa Valley. Rain down hellfire and damnation over the whole area. Let God sort out the charred corpses. The administration can't go that far though. We can't risk offending our Arab allies in the region."

"First the Soviets shoot down that Korean airliner. Now this. Reagan has had a lot to deal with these past few weeks."

"Yes, but I trust him. He's got the right idea on foreign policy. Build up our military and our nukes. Stand up to the Evil Empire. Resist communism everywhere. Finally we have an administration with the guts to implement a strategy to win the Cold War."

"Wow. Sounds like you're ready to join the State Department."

"No. Although such work would be intriguing, Anthony and I are considering starting our own business. It's actually a venture that concerns you."

"Me?" I leaned back in my leather chair and placed my feet on my desk.

"Yes Dave, you." He cleared his throat. "Your current contract with Newark runs through the 1984 season. Correct?"

"Yes."

"And, according to my sources, the Tornadoes are paying you $130,000 this season and $140,000 in 1984. Yes?"

"Your sources? Do I even want to know what those are?"

"Probably not. But don't worry, Dave. I know the salaries of all the other NFL players, too."

"Great." I drummed my fingers on my desk.

"Actually, it's not great. Your salary is … crap."

"Excuse me."

"Yes. Montana is getting more than half a million. The Dolphins are paying Marino $150,000, and he's just a rookie. You know he'll be getting a huge raise next year. This is your fourth season. Plus, you're leading the resurgence of the Newark franchise. The team's future is built around you. You should be making three times your current amount. Maybe more."

"My agent will take care of that with my next contract."

"Charlie Maher," Joe scoffed. "I'm sorry, but you shouldn't trust him. He blew it with your current deal. I've read up on him. Nearly all his clients are underpaid. Teams don't respect him."

I recalled a recent conversation I'd heard in the Tornadoes locker room about how Charlie had lost his edge. "He's the only agent I've ever known, Joe. He seemed more trustworthy than the other sharks that swarmed around me my senior year at UWI."

"I agree. You shouldn't trust any of those other agents either. Fortunately, I've got a solution for you."

"You do?" I switched the receiver from one ear to the other.

"Yes. Anthony and I want to represent you."

His words stunned me into silence. If any of my other relatives had said such a thing I would have thought it was a joke. But there was nothing humorous in my nephew's voice. "Um, Joe, you're both still in college. What do you two know about being sports agents?"

"Plenty. We've both studied the field extensively. Next May, we graduate. Then, with degrees in hand, we'll be ready to open for business with you as our sole client. That's how we'll start out anyway."

"You're both graduating next year? But you're a year younger than Anthony."

"I graduated from high school a semester early, remember? And I've taken additional credits each term here at Grinnell. So I'm set to finish in May. The same time Anthony graduates from Nebraska."

"Oh. But I thought you were planning to get a law degree after your bachelor's."

"That *is* still my plan. I've been accepted at Harvard. I'll be pursing my J.D. and representing you, concurrently. The real world experience will be a great compliment to my legal studies."

"I don't know, Joe. That sounds like a lot to put on your plate. You're only twenty years old. You don't have to conquer the entire world right now."

"Your concern is understandable. But remember, Anthony and I are not your little nephews anymore. We're men. And we've had to grow up a lot faster than most guys our age."

A memory of Asa floated by, bringing a wave of sadness. "Yeah, I know."

"Dave, here's the plan. Next summer, Anthony and I will move to Boston to set up our office. After you sign with us, we can begin negotiations with the Tornadoes. This is a crucial time for you. You're just entering your prime. And with the USFL bidding for talented players, your value increases even more. You can't afford to miss this opportunity. Anthony and I know the football business. We know your value. We'll make sure you cash in. And if Newark does not compensate you adequately, we'll contact the New Jersey Generals. I'm quite certain Donald Trump would be willing to pay handsomely for a prize quarterback like you."

Conflicting thoughts swirled around my head. "You'd be able to do all this while in law school?"

"Remember, there will be two of us. Anthony will be in the office full time. He's an accounting major with a good mind for numbers. He'll handle the everyday affairs while we get established. I'll be in contact with him daily. And I'll head up the actual negotiations with the Tornadoes. Don't worry about my course load at Harvard. I don't want to sound arrogant, but I've yet to be seriously challenged at college. I can handle law school and representing you. You know I can."

The cold confidence in Joe's voice increased my interest.

He then played his final card. "Dave … Anthony and I are family. No other agent can say that. We'll go to the mat for you, just like you would for us. Remember what we've been through. Like Mother always told us, we've got to take care of each other. Everybody wins with this deal. You'll finally get paid what you're worth. The commission from your huge contract will help Anthony and me get started in the business world, along with covering my tuition at Harvard. I'll be facing some hefty expenses there. I can't burden Mother with that. Not after what she's already paid to put Anthony and me through college."

His words sunk in. Now I had a guilt trip to consider along with his promise to maximize my earnings. He knew I could not easily turn down a family member. "Well, Joe, you've made a lot of good points. I tell you what. I'll consider your proposal. Let's touch base after the season. Maybe you, me, and Anthony can get together in January sometime, when you're both still on break. Then I can hear more about the specifics of what you've got in mind."

"Excellent. Let's do that. I look forward to discussing this matter further with you."

I was not sharp at practice Wednesday. My mind was not on the field. I'd found it difficult to concentrate on anything since Hal told me that he had set up a meeting with Dawn Lewis. She was to arrive at 6:00 p.m. All day I wondered what she wanted to discuss with me.

We were to meet in a small office that the players and coaches often used for one-on-one interviews with reporters. While waiting, I sat behind a metal desk and tried to study the playbook. My mind wandered. I scanned the pictures of past Tornadoes owners and players that adorned the faded orange walls. A planter containing an oversized caladium hung from the ceiling in one of the corners. Two empty chairs stood in front of the desk.

At five after six, Hal entered. "She's here," he said, sliding one of the chairs off to the side of the room. He ignored my puzzled expression and walked out into the hall. Following his gesture, a blond woman stepped through the doorway. Her face bore a pedestrian beauty. A modest print dress clothed her slightly stout body. She would not have stood out in a crowd.

"Hello Dawn," I said, standing and extending a hand. "Nice to meet you." Hal then reentered the room pushing a young boy in a wheelchair. The child's eyes evoked the memory of a long-lost friend. I gasped and released Dawn's hand. My legs wobbly, I steadied myself against the desk. Hal exited, closing the door behind him. My gaze shifted between the two sets of eyes before me.

"Thanks for meeting me," Dawn said. "You probably don't remember who I am."

"I do, actually. We spoke briefly at the funeral. I'd planned to talk to you afterwards, but I took off. I just couldn't stay."

"I understand. I felt the same way that day."

The boy stared at me with large brown eyes. "And who is this young man?" I asked with a smile.

"That's Michael." She turned to the boy. "Say hello to Mr. King."

"Hello, Mr. King," he said shyly.

"Glad to meet you, Michael," I said, shaking his small hand. "You can call me Dave, okay?" He nodded and examined the room around him. "Do you like football?" I asked.

He nodded again. I opened a desk drawer and pulled out one of the toy Tornadoes footballs the team kept on hand for visiting children. I held it out to him across the desk. Eyes wide, he grabbed it with both hands. "Thanks, Dave King!" He spun it in his fingers.

"Please, have a seat," I said to Dawn.

After sitting, we shared an awkward glance. She took a breath. "Michael is John's son." Though I suspected as much, her words still had a shocking resonance. "John never knew. I didn't even know I was pregnant 'til weeks after his funeral. We were, uh, close the weekend before the accident. It only happened that one night." She looked down for a couple moments. "We both felt guilty afterwards. He knew how important my faith was to me. We went to church together the next morning. All through the sermon, he seemed restless. Like something was really on his mind. Then, at the end of the service, he went forward. I couldn't believe it, watching him walk to the front of the church. He gave his life to Christ right then and there."

My mouth dropped open. "Really? John was a Christian?"

She nodded. "Yes. He was so excited that day—he couldn't wait to tell you. But he wanted to see the look on your face, so he didn't tell you over the phone. He wanted to surprise you when he came back to Des Moines the next weekend."

"I remember now. The last time we talked to each other, he said he had something to tell me when he got back. With everything that happened, I forgot about that." A wave of joy passed through me at the thought of John's salvation.

"Yeah. Turned out that John had two surprises. He just didn't know about one of them." She looked over at her son. A shock of brown hair, the same color as his father's, covered the boy's head. Tossing the purple and orange football up in the air, he seemed to be paying little attention to our conversation.

"When was Michael born?" I asked, noticing that he wore a Tornadoes T-shirt.

"March 1977."

"March ninth," Michael announced with a grin. "I'm six and a half."

"Wow. You're so big," I said. "Before you know it, you'll be seven."

He laughed and tossed the ball up again. When it came down it deflected off his hands and bounced across the floor. He stretched out an arm in the direction of the football and let out a plaintive cry. "Mom!"

"It's okay, sweetie," Dawn said. She retrieved the ball and placed it in his hands.

"Where do you and Michael live now?" I asked, after order was restored.

"Indianapolis. Where I grew up. After what happened to John, I didn't go back to Iowa City. I never returned to school. I just couldn't. John's family still doesn't know about …" She glanced at her son.

"I understand. I was supposed to go to Iowa that fall, but I couldn't do it either." I blinked hard to keep my emotions in check.

Her mouth formed a melancholy smile. "He loved you, you know. Talked about you all the time. He was so looking forward to you coming out to Iowa City. I used to joke that he'd never have time for me once you got there." Her eyes misted over.

"John told me a lot about you, too," I said. "You were a great influence on him. I'm sure your faith played a big role in leading him to Christ."

She dabbed her eyes with a tissue. "I was so happy when he became a Christian. That removed my only hesitation about him. I could see our whole future. Thought we'd be together forever. And then he was gone. My faith wasn't so strong after that. It took a long time to get over losing him." Michael, now bored with the football, pretended to be a dog. He growled and barked several times before his mom shushed him.

"I know what you mean. My faith suffered too. It was quite a while before I got back on track." A brief silence followed.

"Dave, I don't know how to say this. I really don't want to ask, but …"

"Please, go ahead."

She trained her sad eyes on mine. "I'm a clerk in a fabric store. I don't make much, and we have special needs. The expenses add up, you know. My parents have helped out a lot, but Dad just retired. They can't spend as much anymore. And the bills just keep getting bigger. I'm concerned." She looked over at Michael, who was staring at his shoes.

My conscience was pricked. "Dawn, of course I want to help." I smiled at the boy. "Perhaps we can discuss the details later. Hey, can you and Michael come over for supper tonight? I know my wife would love to meet you both."

"Well, my father is with us. He drove the van. He's in the lobby right now."

"He's welcome too."

Dawn looked at Michael. "Would you like to have supper with Mr. King tonight?"

"Yeaaaah," he said, tossing the ball to me.

"If you'd like, you all could stay over with us tonight."

"Oh, we couldn't do that," she said. "We're staying with family in Philadelphia. We'll have to hit the road right after supper."

"Okay."

"You sure this is no trouble?"

"Not at all." After summoning Hal to give Michael, Dawn, and her father a brief tour of the complex, I called Gail to tell her we'd be having company for supper.

Following the departure of our guests, Gail went upstairs to feed Archie. I played with Kyle in the living room. Placing him on my shoulders, I galloped around the house like a horse. He laughed and screamed. I next took him on his other favorite ride: the pendulum. It started with me holding him low between my ankles and then swinging him high above my head. Down and up he went, over and over. Whenever I stopped to rest he immediately gestured for the ride to continue.

After a half hour of acrobatics, my son was finally exhausted. I carried him upstairs, slipped on his pajamas, and laid him in his crib. "I love you, little Kyle," I said, even though his eyes were shut. A moment later, Gail was at my side. "Archie asleep?" I asked. She nodded. Holding hands, we went downstairs.

A mountain of dirty dishes still awaited us in the kitchen. Though neither of us was enthused about the task, we got to work. After grabbing a towel, I turned on the radio for some news. The entire broadcast was devoted to the U.S. invasion of Grenada. I recalled Joe's words about Reagan standing up to communism.

Finally vanquishing the dishes, my wife and I sat together on the couch in the living room. She leaned into me, resting her head against my chest. The crackling fireplace provided the only light in the room. "Thank you for making supper for three extra people on such short notice," I said.

"Sure. It was good of you to invite them over."

"What did you think of Michael?"

"He's a sweet boy. Looks just like those pictures of John you showed me."

I paused. "Is it okay I told Dawn we would help her?"

Gail sat up so she could face me. "To be honest, I wish you would have discussed it with me first."

"You don't want to help them?"

"I didn't say that. It's just … we should make decisions like that together." The flames flickering from the hearth sent shadows dancing across her face.

"Sorry."

"Did you give her a number?"

"No. I didn't want to talk about it in front of Michael. I was thinking maybe four hundred a month."

"Every month?" Her eyes widened. "Are you serious?"

"I don't know. Dawn doesn't make much, and raising a handicapped boy costs a lot of money."

"Dave, we can't afford that. Trust me, I do our books."

I sighed. "John was my best friend. Losing him still hurts. It always will. But now with Michael, it's like I can still do something for John. Something to keep the memory of our friendship alive."

She grabbed my hand. "I understand, but we have to be realistic. Your income has limits. We're already stretched thin with all the money we give away. There's our church, the United Way, your foundation for the inner-city kids, that missionary family in Tanzania, the food bank … and Western Iowa always wants money. Then we have our own bills. The mortgage. The maid. And we've got two boys, one of whom is deaf. You do know there are going to be extra expenses as Kyle gets older?"

My eyes dropped. "You're right. I just feel like it's my responsibility to do something for Michael. Like God brought him into my life for a reason."

Her gaze softened. "You have such a heart for God and such a heart for people. That's one of the things I love most about you. But you can't help everybody who asks. You need to take care of your family first."

I nodded. "I know."

After staring at me for a few seconds, she smiled weakly. "I'll go over the numbers tomorrow. We can probably spare something for Dawn and Michael."

"Thank you," I said, wrapping my arms around her. She pressed her body into mine. Her female form felt heavenly. Minutes passed. A while later I asked, "So how tired are you?"

"I could stay up a little longer. What do you want to do?"

My response did not require words.

Chapter 17 – January 1987

I placed my folded slacks in the open suitcase. Surveying the remaining clothes on the bed, I plotted which items to pack next. Outside the window, tiny snowflakes floated down to the ground. The sun's rays reflected brightly off the already accumulated layer of snow. Bandit, a black Lab, lay half asleep on the carpet at the foot of the bed. A television provided background noise from a cherry armoire in the corner of the room. Hearing a familiar name, I grabbed the remote to turn up the volume.

A sports anchor addressed the camera. "The march to the Super Bowl was a slow, steady journey for the Newark Tornadoes," he said. "The franchise took its first step in April 1980 when it drafted Western Iowa quarterback Dave 'Long Live the' King in the first round. King took over as starting signal-caller for the Tornadoes in 1982. Though he struggled early, the young quarterback showed promise after the NFL players returned from their walkout. Newark finished with four wins and five losses in the strike-shortened season." The screen switched to a clip of me throwing a pass against the Rams.

The anchor continued to narrate. "In 1983 the Tornadoes acquired future All-Pro center, 'Hammer of' Thor Heimlich. Behind a rejuvenated offensive line, King turned in his first 3,000-yard season. But with a porous defense, Newark could finish no better than .500. The following year the Tornadoes improved to nine and seven, with King leading an offense that ranked fourth in the league in total yards. But once again the team failed to reach the playoffs." The television showed Houston scoring a late touchdown to stick us with a heartbreaking loss. The sight recalled unpleasant memories.

"In 1985 offensive guru Jack Depler replaced Al Fish as Tornadoes head coach. King thrived in the new system, passing for 3,400 yards and 27 touchdowns. Meanwhile, linebacker Braden 'Tennis' Schumaker and cornerback Levon 'Big Warren' Coolidge anchored an improving defense. Newark posted an eleven and five record to capture an AFC Wild Card spot. It was the team's first postseason appearance in fourteen years. However, the Tornadoes' stay in the playoffs was a short one. A concussion forced King out of the Wild Card game in the second quarter, and Newark fell to New England 27-14." The accompanying images showed me being carted off the field. Though I had seen the footage before, I still did not remember it happening.

"King and the Tornadoes bounced back in 1986. The team captured the AFC Central with a twelve and four record. Depler's variation of the 'Air Coryell' offense functioned with machine-like efficiency. King set personal bests with 3,872 yards passing and 32 touchdowns, while throwing only eight interceptions. Second-year running back Irvin 'Great' Scott added 1,513 yards on the ground. The Tornadoes defense improved to ninth best in the league in points allowed. Playoff victories over Cleveland and Denver earned Newark a trip to the Super Bowl and a chance to bring the city its first NFL championship."

The TV screen flashed with highlights from our triumph over the Broncos in the AFC title game a week ago. There I was at the Meadowlands jumping around on the field as the game ended. Reliving that moment sent ripples of excitement rolling through my body.

"And next week at the Rose Bowl in Pasadena, the Tornadoes will take on the New York Giants in Super Bowl XXI. The Newark offense will face its toughest test to date when it lines up against the top-ranked Giants defense. It may be a case of the irresistible force meeting the immovable object. Will the Tornadoes be able to move the ball against Lawrence Taylor and the Big Blue Wrecking Crew? Will Dave King be able to lead his team to victory on football's biggest stage? To break down the individual match-ups, we turn now to our football analyst—"

I clicked off the television. After watching endless hours of game film over the past week, I knew all about the Giants and how they matched up against us. And the Super Bowl was still a week away. That meant more film, more practices, and more meetings. I returned to my clothes.

Kyle entered the room. He pointed at my suitcase on the bed. "Uhh?"

I knelt down and looked into his concerned eyes. "Daddy is taking a trip. Play football." I said the words aloud while signing them simultaneously. Unfortunately, football had left me with little time to improve my meager American Sign Language vocabulary.

Kyle pouted and flopped his arms.

"It's okay," I said and signed with a smile. "Not gone long."

"Stay home with me," he signed.

"One more game. Then Daddy is back home."

He frowned. "No more football. You have too many games."

"Next weekend Grandma and Grandpa will stay with you." I rubbed his arm after completing the gestures.

"Maahmaah?" he said in a hollow voice.

"Mommy is going to the game. She'll be gone only three days. We'll come home after football."

Furrowing his brow, he plopped on the floor and crossed his arms.

"You have fun with Grandma and Grandpa," I signed. "You make cookies with Grandma." I tickled his side to coax a begrudging smile.

"Why do you have to go away again?"

"Super Bowl. You can watch Daddy on television."

"One game. No more."

"One game," I said, deciding that we did not need to discuss next season at this time.

Archie came running into the room. "Aaaaahhh, Kyle!" he yelled, jumping on his older brother. Bandit, wagging his tail, sat up to get a better view of the action.

"Noooaa, Archah," Kyle said, pushing him off.

I scooped up Archie and held him upside down. Bandit tilted his head. Gail walked into the room holding Tammy, our two-year-old daughter. "You're not done packing yet? The team's going to leave without you."

"I'm getting there. Only got a few more items to pack, but I don't know where *this* will fit." I dangled Archie above the open suitcase.

"Nooooo," he squealed through his laughter.

"Daahdee!" Kyle exclaimed, pointing up at Archie. "What doing? What saying?" He signed with quick motions.

I set his little brother beside him on the floor. "Playing." I positioned my face in front of his so he could read my lips. "Playing with Archie." Calm returned to Kyle's flushed face.

Gail leaned down to touch his shoulder. "Let's go downstairs," she said. "Daddy has to pack." The two boys sprang up and followed their mother out of the room. Bandit yawned and lay down on the carpet again.

I resumed transferring clothes from the bed to the suitcase. An hour later, I said goodbye to my family and was out the door.

Distracted by the warm weather and beautiful sights, the team plodded through its first practice in California. After adjusting to the new surroundings, we found our groove the next day. When we were executing well on the field, I did not mind the endless questions from the press so much. It would have been nice though, if the reporters had not been fixated on one particular topic. "Dave, does it worry you that you'll be facing the top defense in the league?" "Can the Tornadoes run the ball against the Giants?" "Will Lawrence Taylor get inside your head?" "Have you ever faced such a ferocious pass rush?"

Growing bored with giving the same responses over and over, I occasionally slipped in something facetious to make sure they were paying attention. "We're going to punt on first down the entire first half to lull them into complacency." "We'll be using our defensive players on offense for a quarter to see if we can confuse them." "All flea-flickers all the time, that's the game plan." Some of the reporters snickered at my nonsense. Others scribbled furiously in their notepads regardless of what I said.

Newark held its practices at the Raiders' training facility. That was also where we watched game film for hours on end. Following each film session, I attended meetings with Depler and the offensive coaches. Every day, they methodically reviewed and adjusted the Tornadoes game plan.

Wednesday evening, I met Joe and Anthony at Spago Hollywood on the Sunset Strip. Joe had made reservations in my name to take advantage of the Super Bowl hoopla. It worked. We were seated at one of the best tables in the restaurant—in the front room near the window. Joe somehow resisted talking business until well after we had placed our orders. Then, he opened his leather briefcase.

"Good news. Nike, Reebok, and Puma all want you onboard. Going strictly by the numbers, Puma's offer is the best. They want to issue a Kingmaker sneaker this summer. If the shoe sells, you're sitting pretty. If it flops, your image takes a hit. The Nike and Reebok deals are also attractive. They aren't offering as much money, but they are the top-selling athletic footwear companies. Less risk putting your name on one of their products. A case can be made for signing with any of the three."

He handed me a sheet with figures in three columns. The numbers jumped off the page. "Wow! Are these for real?"

Joe nodded with something resembling a smile. Anthony beamed like a little kid on his birthday. "Welcome to the big time, Dave. This Super Bowl gig is good for business. Bet you wish you'd thought of it sooner."

"I guess so." I took a drink of water.

"There are a few other endorsement offers to discuss," Joe said. Both he and Anthony sported hairstyles that reminded me of Duran Duran. Their wardrobes resembled Don Johnson's sartorial style on *Miami Vice*. "Some of these you might consider. Others are less appealing."

"I'm all ears."

"Well," he continued, "several beer companies are interested, but I know that's not your thing. Pepsi and Coke have both made inquiries. There's also the National Cattlemen's Foundation, Isotoner Gloves, 9 Lives …"

"9 Lives?"

"Yes. Cat food. They want you to appear in a commercial with Morris."

"But I don't even own a cat."

"We could get you one."

"No thanks."

"We don't need them anyway," Joe said. "There is one offer that I really like. Very lucrative." He exchanged a glance with Anthony who appeared to be suppressing a smile.

A waiter brought our food. "Let's hear it." I poked a fork into my seafood risotto.

"It's Hanes."

"Yeah? I wear Hanes. Are they thinking about a television commercial or something?"

"They want you for a series of magazine ads and billboards," Joe said.

"Okay. I could do that." The smile on Anthony's face widened. "What?" I asked.

"Hanes wants to shoot you wearing nothing but briefs," Joe replied.

Nearly choking on my food, I gulped down a swig of soda. "No," I coughed. "Absolutely not. I can't do that."

"Now, Dave, don't be so quick to dismiss this," Anthony said. "The compensation is very good. And you have to admit, it would increase your … exposure." Snorts of laughter shot from his nose. Joe glanced at the open kitchen, shaking his head.

"Very funny. Even if I did want to do it—which I don't—Gail would kill me. Oh, and can you imagine what Ozzie would say? I'd never hear the end of it."

"I know it's out of your comfort zone," Joe said, "but it would be a bold move. Could open some doors down the road. Look at what those Jockey ads did for Jim Palmer. And Namath wore pantyhose. People are still talking about him a decade after he retired."

"I can live with people not talking about me." I surveyed the room. A couple tables over sat Judge Reinhold. He smiled and nodded. I did the same.

"Your fans would love it," Anthony said. "Trust us, we're your agents."

"No, no, no." I wagged a finger at him.

"Oh, come on. Where's the love? Remember back in '84 when you were content to settle for $700,000 a year? We told you to hold out. Practically had to kidnap you to get you to do it. But guess what happened? That's right, Newark ponied up six million over five years." Anthony sat back with arms crossed.

"Yes. You've both done a great job representing me. But I'm not dancing around in public in my underwear. You've got other clients. Ask one of them."

"Most of them are linemen," Joe said. "I don't think Hanes is interested in the Thor Heimlich body type for its campaign. They want you."

"You'd look good," Anthony said. "With that Tom Cruise *Top Gun* haircut you got, the chicks would go crazy for you."

"I'm trying to be a Christian role model. Near nude photo spreads probably aren't the best way for me to promote God's kingdom."

"We respect that," Joe said. "But don't overdo the Christian thing. A little of it goes a long way. People can get skeptical." He devoured a bite of salmon.

"You talking about that stupid article in the *Times*?" I asked. "I don't care about that."

"I understand. But we don't want columnists portraying you as a prude, a puritan, a prig."

"A goody-two-shoes," Anthony added.

"Thank you Anthony, I get the point. I don't care what the world thinks. I'm a man of faith. I'm not ashamed of that." My face grew warm with irritation. I did not want to admit it, but the articles mocking my Christian beliefs did bother me.

"We just don't want you to appear weak," Joe said. "That guy called you 'a choirboy who lacks the machismo to lead an NFL team.' Granted he's a hack, but we can't let this opinion catch on with other writers. The public must think of you as an elite quarterback who commands the respect of his teammates."

I lowered my fork. "That's not a problem. The other guys know who runs the offense."

"Does Irvin Scott?" Joe raised a brow.

"What's that supposed to mean?"

"From what he said at Media Day, it sounds like he thinks he's the leader of the offense."

I glared at Joe. "Irvin likes to talk about himself. He likes to brag. But trust me, he knows his role on the field. Listen, just because I'm not struttin' around grabbing headlines like McMahon did last year, doesn't mean I'm soft. Look at my numbers. Look at our record. I get the job done when it counts. Period."

Anthony finished off his glass of wine. "That's absolutely right," he said. "We know you're the man. Forget that article. It's nothing. Written by some moron who never had the stones to play the game himself. How about we postpone all this business talk until after the Tornadoes win the Super Bowl? Then we can discuss endorsements."

I felt a hand on my shoulder. Turning and looking up, I blinked in disbelief at the dramatic presence of arching eyebrows, expansive forehead, and bared teeth.

"How ya doin' there, Dave?" the unmistakable voice said. "Just happened to see you sitting here and thought I'd say hello."

"Uh, thanks," I said, shaking his hand.

"You know, I'll be rootin' for you guys in the Super Bowl."

"I appreciate that." There was an awkward silence as the shark grin remained frozen on his face. I tried to think of something clever to say. "Uh, I loved you in *The Shining*."

His grin shifted from ominous to evil. "Heeeeerre's Johnny!"

"That's it." I smiled, though the famous look was even more unnerving in person.

"Well, I don't want to bother you and your associates. Enjoy your dinner, Dave. And good luck on Sunday."

"Thanks. We'll give it our best shot."

He ambled over to a nearby table where he joined an attractive woman with long dark hair. Anthony dropped his fork and stared at me, the look of shock still in his eyes. "Was that, uh?"

"Yep."

A smile crawled across his face. "You know, Dave, I'm really glad you hired Joe and me to be your agents." He looked over at his brother who nodded once in agreement.

"Yeah, I know. You boys thinking about some dessert?"

After the team meeting Saturday evening, Thor and I returned to our hotel room where we talked to our wives on the phone for a while. He then grabbed a Bible and sat at the table. I stretched out on my bed reviewing the playbook. After several minutes he asked, "Hey, you want to hear the Word?"

Since the play diagrams were starting to blur before my weary eyes, I welcomed his offer. He read the section in Joshua describing the fall of Jericho. Visualizing the Israelite victory stirred my soul. The passage concluded with, "So the Lord was with Joshua, and his fame spread throughout the land."

"Thanks, Hammer."

He shut the Bible and was quiet for a while. "You ever think we'd make it this far?"

I chuckled. "Hard to believe, isn't it? Not bad for a couple of Iowa boys, huh?"

"Yeah. Tomorrow we'll be playing in THE game. This is what I've been dreaming about since I was a little kid. I wish Pop was here to see it."

A memory of Neil handing me a silver aluminum bat flashed through my head. An instant later, I was a little boy riding a tricycle in the driveway at my parents' house. "I know what you mean. I wish my mom could see this game too."

A short silence followed. "You know there are going to be millions of people watching," Thor said, his eyes widening beneath his flattop. "Everybody. Movie stars, the president, maybe even Billy Graham. I usually don't get nervous before a game, but all this is gettin' me a little uptight."

"Yeah, I'm feeling it too. But I think once the game starts we'll forget about all the hype. We'll get down to business, just like always. We know our jobs."

"I wonder if Joshua felt like this before attacking Jericho. I bet he did." Thor tapped his Bible a couple times. Almost like an echo, there was a knock at the door.

I slid off the bed to see who it was. Nathan Rodriguez stood in the hall trying to maintain a serious expression. "Commissioner Rozelle just called," he said. "The Super Bowl has been cancelled. Pack your stuff. We're flying back to Newark."

"Good. I've got better things to do than play in some stupid football game." I waved him into the room.

"Hey, Hammer," Nathan said.

"What's up, Nathan."

"So, Depler gave the team chaplain the job of checking curfews?" I asked.

"Actually, he did ask me to help with that. I guess several of the coaches are out right now looking for Irvin. He and his posse slipped away."

Thor groaned. "That idiot," I said. "He's got all the talent in the world and not an ounce of common sense."

"He's young," Nathan said. "He'll learn. I wouldn't worry too much about it. Irvin wants to win tomorrow just as much as you do. He won't go far."

Simmering, I flopped down on my bed. "Hope the press doesn't get wind of this."

Nathan waved his hand dismissively before taking a seat in a stuffed chair. "So this is it. You farm hicks ready for primetime?"

"Primetime? Really? Is this game going to be on TV?"

"Yeah," Nathan said. "But I doubt if anybody will actually be watching the game. Most people just get together for the parties. Me, I'll be watching *This Old House* on PBS."

"Maybe I'll join you," Thor said with a chuckle.

"Man, your wife would kill you if you didn't play in this game," Nathan said.

"I guess Rebecca is a little excited."

"How about Gail?" Nathan asked me. "She into all this?"

"Yes, I think so. She was a little concerned about leaving the kids at home. But they're in good hands. Her parents flew out to New Jersey to watch them. Now that Gail's out here, I think she's having fun."

"Sweet."

"Say, Hot Rod, the Hammer and I have been fighting some jitters. Got any words of wisdom?"

Nathan sucked in a deep breath causing his cheeks to puff out like a chipmunk. He then exhaled and began reciting. "'Meaningless! Meaningless!' says the Teacher. 'Utterly meaningless! Everything is meaningless.'" He flashed a knowing grin at us.

Thor and I looked at each other. "Not exactly Knute Rockne," I said.

"No it isn't. It's Ecclesiastes. See, the world has built up this game as the most significant event in human history. But let's face it, what happens on the field tomorrow really ain't all that important in the grand scheme of things. Football games, even Super Bowls, all fade into memory. No matter who wins, next year there will be another big game. A new champion, new heroes, new goats. As the Bible says, 'Generations come and generations go.'"

"That's true," Thor said.

"Our lives on this planet are short," Nathan continued. "And we ain't taking nothin' with us when we leave. Don't get me wrong—I want you to kick some butt tomorrow. Just don't get caught up in the big production that's been made of this game. You both know that God has plans for you that are much bigger than football. Gotta keep an eternal perspective."

I briefly pondered his words. "Hmpf. I think that might actually help. Thanks, man."

"Glad to be of service. I'll send you a bill. Alright guys, bring it in for a quick word. Then I gots to go check on some of the other hooligans."

We stood and stacked our right hands while Nathan prayed. After he left, Thor and I crawled into our beds. Amazingly, I had little trouble falling asleep that night.

The ball rested on the Giants 44-yard line. It was fourth down. We needed nine yards for a first. With only 1:32 left in the game and New York ahead 21-16, Coach Depler decided to go for it. He had little choice. My teammates and I were all well aware that our chances to win Super Bowl XXI hung on the next play.

Ten sets of eyes stared at me in the huddle. The roar of the crowd—over 100,000 strong—thundered around us. I tuned out the noise, just as I had done since the opening kickoff. Nathan's words from the night before had helped me maintain my focus. Though I never thought of this game as meaningless, I was not freaked out to play in the enormous spectacle that was the Super Bowl. It almost seemed like just another game. I still had butterflies, but at least they stayed butterflies and did not morph into the dragons that had ravaged some of the other players' stomachs.

Peering through the facemasks around the huddle, I saw fire and exhaustion. The Giants defense had been as good as advertised. We had to fight for every yard. But we came ready to fight and we gained some yards. Our offense had thus far ground out drives resulting in a touchdown and three field goals. Late in the fourth quarter, confidence still burned in the eyes of my battle-worn comrades.

We approached the line of scrimmage and took our positions. Starting the snap count, I surveyed my protection. The Newark front five—their white jerseys and orange pants soaked with sweat and blood—were crouched down in three-point stances. The purple numbers on their backs matched the color of their helmets.

The Giants were arrayed before us as a hostile blue army. Three front linemen were poised to launch themselves into my blockers. Four menacing linebackers loomed just behind them. Taylor barked at me with a crazed look in his eye. Having already slammed me to the ground three times, he promised to make our fourth meeting even more memorable. I scanned the defense looking for signs of a blitz. Neither their eyes nor their body language indicated that they were coming. *But what coverage are they going to be in?* My mind raced through the possibilities.

The play Depler had called was a pass to wide receiver Ashton Alt over the middle about ten yards downfield. With only one catch and two drops thus far, Alt had not had a good game. He had even run the wrong route a couple times. Our coaches were hoping the Giants would not be expecting us to go to him at this crucial juncture.

My second option was to hit running back Irvin Scott coming out of the backfield. He would then hopefully be able to use his wheels to pick up a first down. Scott too had not played well today. At one point, I told him to pull his head out of his ass. Our teammates had to separate us during the heated argument that followed. As with Alt, Depler hoped the Giants would not be expecting Scott to see the ball on this play.

If all went according to plan, the defenders would be keying on wide receiver Jason Hackman and tight end Dan Barr. The pair already had 15 receptions and 147 yards between them. They seemed to be likely targets—or so we wanted the Giants to believe. After Barr went into motion, however, I noticed a problem. Outside linebacker Carl Banks had shifted away from his usual position to double cover Alt. The move surprised me. I had not seen anything like it in their game film. Suddenly, Plan A did not look so good.

To make matters worse, both inside linebackers appeared to be keying on Scott in our backfield. My confidence in Plan B dissipated too. Meanwhile, the play clock ticked down to five seconds. I frantically debated what to do. *Audible? Which one? Do we have the right people in?* Tick tick tick. *No time to change! We go with this play and hope for the best.*

"Hut-hut!" Thor placed the football in my hands. The lines exploded into each other in violent collisions that pounded my eardrums. My fingers found the laces on the ball as I completed my five-step drop. What I saw before me was disturbing. Alt had stumbled off the line and was now lost behind a defender. I looked to my right. Scott was open in the flat, but did not have enough room to run for a first down. As my head swiveled left to search for Barr, I sensed imminent danger. Taylor, snarling and yelling, had beaten his man and was closing rapidly. I stepped forward to avoid his initial charge, but that left me trapped in the pocket. With Giant rushers and my own linemen all around me, I had nowhere to run. My only option was to get rid of the ball.

Throwing a football properly requires the legs, hips, and shoulders to work together to generate enough momentum for the arm to deliver the ball to a moving target with power and accuracy. The close proximity of angry people flailing at you does not help with this task. As the hot breath of Giants steamed through the ear holes of my helmet, I estimated that I had about one second before the boom was lowered. Barr, running a straight pattern, was covered. Glancing downfield, I spotted Hackman racing along the left sideline. Two blue jerseys rode his back. Not a great prospect but I had no time to look for a better option.

Ignoring the impulse to curl up and brace for impact, I stepped forward and let the ball fly. If it went where I intended, it would land about fifty yards away—just beyond the goal line. That is where Hackman appeared to be heading. The ball spun off my fingertips and soared up into the Southern California sky.

CRUNCH! A massive iron wrecking ball slammed into my back. The ground rushed up to meet my face. An instant later all I could see were blades of grass poking through my facemask. After driving me into the turf, Taylor had me pinned. Someone fell on him, and then another body fell on that guy. I wanted to move, but was buried under nearly half a ton of sweaty, stinking football players.

At the bottom of the pile, I envisioned the ball sailing through the air. I imagined everybody in the stadium, plus the millions watching on television, following its trajectory. Eyes from around the world were locked on the flight of this little leather ball. My eyes, of course, were the exception. I was the one who had thrown the pass, yet I was blind to its fate.

I knew the reaction of the crowd would let me know when the football returned to Earth. Unfortunately, the sound would not tell me anything about the result that ensued. If Hackman caught the ball for a touchdown, Newark fans in the stadium would erupt in a loud raucous cheer. But the exact same noise would emanate from Giants fans if he did not catch the ball. Since it was fourth down, either an interception or an incompletion would give New York the ball and a Super Bowl victory.

Time seemed to slow as I waited for the explosion from the stands. My mind contemplated the significance of what was happening. Remembering Nathan's words from the night before, I pondered why so many people cared about who won this game. *Would one team's victory over the other end hunger, warfare, or disease? Will the outcome of this game cause people to love each other more? Does anybody's salvation depend upon who catches the ball?* Knowing that the answers were all no, I wondered if this epic contest was indeed meaningless. *Why should I care about this game?*

And yet, as I lay pinned to the ground with the taste of grass in my mouth, the honest realization was inescapable. I did care—a lot. In fact, at that instant, my entire being wanted nothing else than for Jason Hackman to catch the ball.

The roar of the crowd flooded the stadium.

I felt like I was in a funeral home. Somber faces and subdued conversations surrounded the long table. The children, for their part, remained oblivious to the mood of the adults. Seemingly unaware of the malaise clouding the room, they ran around and played like usual.

"Slow down, Archie!" I said to my young son racing behind me. He continued chasing his cousin Hannah. Gail held Tammy in her lap while talking to Zoe. That left it up to me to corral the boy. With pain radiating from my bruised ribs, I hobbled after him. Fortunately, he stopped running to jump up and down in some kind of dance. Slipping my hands under his arms, I scooped him up. "Gotcha, you little rascal." His legs kicked about in protest.

Abby, standing nearby, had just intercepted her daughter. "That's enough, young lady," my sister said to Hannah, before looking at me. "These kids have too much energy."

"Amen to that." I exhaled a heavy sigh.

"You still look bummed."

"I am. It's just a little hard to take."

"I feel the same way," Abby said. "I think we all do. But Dad had to retire sometime." Hannah slithered away from her mother's grasp. Archie squirmed in my arms trying to similarly escape, but his efforts were in vain.

"I know. I'd been encouraging him to do it for a long time. It's just, now that we're here for his farewell dinner, it's kinda sad." She nodded as we both looked around The Royal Court. The restaurant was closed to the public on this night. It was instead family members and a few of Dad's friends who populated the main dining room. A large banner congratulated my father on his retirement. "Well, this is good for Adam and Shane," I said. "They've waited a long time to take over."

"Did you hear that they're thinking about turning it into a sports bar?" she asked, brushing a few blond hairs from her face.

"What? No!"

"Yep. Adam thinks the change will bring in more customers."

"What does Dad think about this plan?"

"He about sh—" Glancing at three-year-old Archie, Abby caught herself. "Let's just say Dad was not pleased when he heard about the idea. But there's nothing he can do about it. Adam and Shane are the owners now."

"Dad was worried about that very thing. Maybe I can convince Adam to leave the restaurant like it is." I glanced at my father sitting at the head of the table talking to Eli. Dad's hair, what little remained, was entirely white. I had never before realized how much he looked like my grandfather.

Abby's husband Jerry joined us. "Hey Dave. Haven't had much of a chance to talk to you tonight."

"Yeah. You know what it's like when our family gets together."

A loopy smile crossed his face. "I know you're probably tired of talking about it, but I have to ask. How did you throw that last pass so accurately right before getting hammered by LT? The ball just barely cleared the safety's fingertips and dropped right into Hackman's hands. It's like you were threading a needle from fifty yards away."

Though I had described that play countless times over the past week, I still enjoyed talking about it. "Dropping back, I scanned the field. Both of my primary targets were covered. The rush came in like a ferocious blue tidal wave …"

A while later, people started saying their goodbyes. Ozzie asked if I wanted to take a ride in his new car. After helping Gail pack our three children into the minivan we had rented, I climbed into my brother's Corvette. The new car smell danced in my nostrils.

"How long you got?" he asked, pulling out of the parking lot.

"I told Gail you'd have me back at the hotel in an hour." I braced for a quip about being too old for a curfew, but nothing came. Aside from a few comments about the features of his car, Ozzie said little. Thinking back to earlier in the evening, I realized that he had not said much at the restaurant either.

"So, what's buggin' you?" I asked as he veered onto the freeway ramp. He grunted something incomprehensible. For the next couple minutes, I continued prying and he continued brushing aside my queries.

"You want to know what's bothering me?" he finally said. "The Super Bowl."

"Really? Why? We won."

"That's the problem. I had money on the Giants. That last pass you threw cost me two hundred bucks. I hope you're happy." The corner of his mouth curled slightly.

"Unbelievable," I said, shaking my head.

He accelerated past a rusty blue Datsun. "Actually, this whole week has really sucked."

"How so?"

"How do you think? Last Sunday I'm watching television and there's my little brother telling the world he's going to Disneyland."

"You can come with us."

"Damn it, Dave. That's not the point. I'm thirty years old and I haven't done shit with my life. I'm going nowhere with my job. All my old friends are now married with families. I haven't even had a date in seven months." He ran a hand over his receding hairline and down through his mullet. "And now I'm starting to lose my freakin' hair."

"Oh, stop it. You've got a lot going for you. Look at this sweet ride. You must be making some money, Mr. Underwriter."

"Not enough. I've still got fifty-nine payments before the car is actually mine. The things I do to impress the ladies. You wanna know how low I've sunk? Lately I've been telling girls I'm your brother to try to impress them. Oh God, what have I become?" He smacked his forehead with the palm of his hand.

"Oz, you're a King. You'll pull out of it."

"I'm a King in name only. I didn't get any of the family advantages. Look at everybody else, down the line from Eli to you. They all got something—size, athletic ability, looks, brains, musical talent. Everybody except me. I get to be the friggin' runt of the litter."

The tone of his rant made me snicker. "That's not true."

He scoffed. "Says the guy who got everything."

"I didn't get everything."

"You think you weren't born under a lucky star? You're the Super Bowl MVP. You have a hot wife. You can sing and play guitar." Having reached West Des Moines, he exited the freeway so he could turn the car around and head back to the east side.

"I'm not much of a musician."

He shot me a look. "Ever since you were a teenager you could listen to a song on the radio and then pick up a guitar and start playing it. You'd nail the song by the second or third try. That's not normal. Regular people can't do that. Hell, I can't even tune a damn guitar. You could have been a rock star if you wanted to, but instead you decided to be a quarterback in the NFL. That must have been a tough choice for you."

I paused to imagine myself as a rock star. "You have talent," I said. "All natural ability has to be developed. I wasn't successful at football until I worked at it. Hours and hours of practice. You could develop a skill if you …" A rancid smell drifted into my nose. "Oh man! Is that you?" I already knew the answer.

"Yeah, I ate a lot of sautéed onions tonight. That's going to get worse before it gets better, I'm afraid."

After another whiff started me coughing, I lowered the window. The winter chill bit my face, but it was still better than the alternative. "*That's* something you can do better than anyone else." I spoke louder to be heard over the rushing air. "Maybe the Army could use you in their chemical warfare division."

He replied with a middle finger and continued speeding down the freeway. At East 15th Street, he exited. After navigating a few side streets, he pulled into one of the lots at Eastridge High and parked. Fortunately, the car had been adequately fumigated by that point.

"Oz, being a star athlete doesn't bring happiness."

"Right. Your life must really suck."

"I'm not saying that. But the excitement of winning a football game always fades. And when it does, what's left is an empty feeling."

"Really," he said in a cynical tone. "What about your money, the big house, the fame? Does all that leave you feeling empty?"

I sorted through my thoughts. "Honestly, that's all pretty cool. Yeah. My money, my house, my cars, fans telling me how wonderful I am. It's hard not to love that stuff. But I know that none of it brings lasting fulfillment. In the end, wealth and fame are meaningless."

"I saw you celebrating with your teammates after the game. That didn't look meaningless."

"I admit, it's easy to get caught up in the exhilaration of a big victory. But my relationship with God is what matters most. And my wife and children, they matter far more to me than any wealth or fleeting glory I get from playing football. Being a star quarterback is not that big a deal to me."

Ozzie examined me with skepticism in his eyes. Pangs of guilt pricked my insides as I contemplated whether my life actually reflected what I had just told him. "You understand what I'm saying?" I continued nonetheless. "The things that matter most in my life are all things that you can have in your life too."

"I'd still like to trade places with you for a week. Man, I could score so much tail."

I stared at him, speechless.

He grinned. "I appreciate what you're trying to do, Dave. For as much shit as I give you, I'm happy for all your success. I really am. And I'm even glad that you seem to have found something meaningful in that religion of yours."

"Oz, do me a favor. You won't want to do it, but please, do it for me."

"Oh no."

"Dig out that Bible I gave you a few years ago and read the book of Mark. Then tell me what you think."

"You're right. I don't want to do it."

"Give me your honest thoughts about the book. If you don't like it or don't believe it, just say so. Either way, read Mark and then call me. It's not very long. You can get through it in an evening."

"Ugh. Okay, maybe. I've got a lot of TV to watch though. You ever seen *Alf?*"

"I'll take that as a yes. Don't worry, it won't hurt that much." I glanced at my watch. "Oh man, I'd better get back to the hotel. Gail's going to wonder what mischief you've gotten me into."

"Fine. But could we swing by Doc & Eddy's first? Walking into a bar with the Super Bowl MVP would really help the Wizard get laid."

I shook my head. "Unbelievable. You didn't hear a word I said tonight did you?"

"Yeah, yeah, I get it. Fame is no big deal. Money can't buy happiness. You don't care about being a big sports star. It's all meaningless. Blah, blah, blah."

"That's right, it all means nothing." After he had driven for a while, I looked over at him with a big shark grin. "Hey, you want to hear about the time I met Jack Nicholson?"

"Shut up, Bilbo."

Chapter 18 – July 1991

My feet pounded the asphalt track. With each step the fire in my left knee burned hotter. Joining the powerful sensation was an ache in my right ankle and a throbbing in my left hamstring. I pressed on toward the finish line with violent breaths. Passing the old man with the stopwatch, I let up on the gas. When finally able to stop, I bent over and tried to regain my wind. The hurt from my legs radiated throughout my body with nauseating effect.

The old man approached. He was Karl McGraw, the elder statesman of the Newark Tornadoes training staff. "Tell me … I made five," I panted, thinking I might vomit.

"I'm sorry, kid. Six-two."

"What?" His words slapped me across the face. "That can't be right."

He showed me the stopwatch. "I'm sure you felt like you were really movin' there," he said in a gravelly voice, "but I coulda balanced my checkbook waitin' for you to finish."

"Shit," I said. "I'm slower than my linemen."

He gestured to a bench near the sideline of the Kean College football field. I followed him there and sat down. Pain accompanied my every motion. "I'm going to need a shot before training camp, aren't I?"

Compassion filled his veteran eyes. "You ain't ready for training camp. You'd only hurt yourself worse."

"So where does that leave me?"

He gazed across the vacant field. "Kid, I know what you're going through. Went through it myself. Happens to every athlete eventually."

"But I'm only thirty-three. I'm too young to break down." I brushed the sweat from my forehead.

"Don't matter how old you are," he said. "Twenty-three. Thirty-three. Forty-three. Nobody's ready when it happens. But your body knows. It tells you when it's time."

My fists clenched. "I can still play this game."

"This game is killin' you. You've taken a beatin' out there. Five concussions. Broken ankle. Pulled hamstrings. And that ripped up knee. You played the game hard. Ran more than any pro quarterback I ever seen. Now the bill has come due."

"I can stop running. I'll be a drop-back quarterback."

"With that cardboard line the Tornadoes got, you'll get murdered."

"Our line isn't that bad."

"The hell they ain't. Ever since Heimlich had to hang it up in eighty-nine, the line's been going downhill. Lost Cardis, Samani, and Roeper to free agency. Then Witt retired last season. That was the last of the front five from the Super Bowl team. And the owners didn't get nobody to replace 'em. Tight-fisted bastards. They're probably glad you guys have been losing. Kills attendance. Gives 'em an excuse to move the team to Florida, like they been wantin' to do."

I scanned the empty bleachers across from us. "This year might be different," I said softly. "Maybe we can win again."

Karl gave me a rough stare. The lone tuft of hair atop his head danced in the wind like a white flame. "Kid, it's a war out there. Every play, 300-pound monsters trying to tear your head off. You used to have a line to protect you. That's gone now. You used to be able to run away from the blitz. Now you move like a grazing cow. Hell, I could catch you. Nothin' good can come from you trying to play this year." His mouth formed hard angles as he spoke.

I wanted to get angry, but all I felt was sadness. "I'm not ready to quit football."

He gripped my shoulder with surprising strength. "Listen to me. There's no shame in hanging it up at your age. Jim Brown, remember him? The best running back ever to play this game. He retired at thirty. So did Koufax. Best pitcher I ever seen, and I seen a bunch."

"He had arthritis."

"What you got's worse." His voice rose. "Your knee got ripped apart last season. Torn ligaments. Shredded meniscus. And that's on top of all the other stuff. Kid, you got to face facts. You ain't the athlete you once was."

I dropped my head into my hands.

He patted my back. "Your body may be too banged up to play football, but you're in good shape for the rest of your life. You get out now and you can still walk normal. Won't be crippled or nothing. The world is littered with broken-down, punch-drunk ex-ballplayers who didn't know when to quit. Don't become one more."

I raised my eyes to meet his gaze. "But …"

"But what? What you got to prove? For a decade you were one of the top quarterbacks in the game. You got a Super Bowl ring. You got money. And people love that mug of yours. If you don't mess it up, you can be a broadcaster or an actor or something."

I sighed. "I'll miss it, Karl. Ever since high school, football is what I've done. The crowd, the competition, the thrill of throwing a touchdown pass. Man, I'm going to miss that."

"You'll get over it faster than you think. The trick is to get something else in your life. With all that God stuff you're always spouting off about, maybe you could be a preacher. Whatever you do, it'll be a lot easier if you ain't got no permanent damage to your noggin."

"Think Buchacker can handle running the offense?" I asked, eying one of the goalposts.

"He's young, strong, got a hell of an arm. Coaches like him. We'll see."

"Reminds me of when I replaced Hartman after he got hurt."

"Except you was better than Hartman ever was, and you was better than Buchacker will ever be. In your prime, you could do it all … but nothing lasts forever." His voice trailed off.

"I just hate to abandon the guys. They were expecting me to play in the season opener."

"That was never a realistic option. Mid-season is the earliest you could get back. But even then you'd be a shell of your former self. Don't worry about the team. With that flimsy line and mediocre defense, they're lucky to win six games with or without you."

I squeezed my eyes shut. "So you really think I'm done?"

"Kid, your glory days on the gridiron are behind you. But you got your whole life ahead of you. It's time to go live it."

I pressed my palms into my thighs and slowly stood up. We left the empty stadium. As I walked to my car, the pain in my legs subsided to a dull ache. The emotional pain remained acute.

Standing calmly, I spotted my receiver breaking into the clear. Aiming several steps ahead of him, I lofted the football. He gathered it in and raced away from the pursuit. Stopping between the birch and the elm near the back of the yard, he turned around and spiked the ball.

"Great catch, Kyle," I signed, before raising my arms in the air. Archie, the would-be defender, flopped to the ground in disappointment. Bandit barked once and pounced on him.

"Noooo Bandit." Archie howled with laughter as the black dog licked his face.

Hearing my daughter giggling behind me on the deck, I turned around. Tammy had set cups and saucers on her kid-sized picnic table for a tea party. Her youngest brother, three-year-old Donnie, sat waiting for his imaginary tea. A pink bonnet covered his head.

"Tammy, don't make Donnie wear that. He's a boy. Boys don't wear bonnets."

She gazed up at me with deep almond eyes. "But I want a sister."

"I know you do, honey. But Donnie is your brother." I turned to him. "You don't want to wear that, do you Donnie?"

"It's okaaay," he said with a big grin.

"See, he's my sister," Tammy said triumphantly.

Oh, please no. Not today. I approached my son to remove the bonnet. "There, that's better. Where's your football helmet, little man?"

"Flowas," he said, pointing across the deck to where a toy Tornadoes helmet sat upside down filled with dirt. Pansies, relocated from the garden, peeked out of the makeshift planter.

"Tammy," I said with disgust. "Did you do that?"

"Nooooo." She shook her head causing brunette ringlets to flap against her face. A hint of a smile could be seen through the swirling hair.

"Daaaad," Kyle called in a nasal voice. Standing in the middle of the backyard, he held the football above his head. "More passes!"

"Later," I signed. "I'm going to help Mom with the dishes. Play with Archie." Turning to Tammy, I pointed at the helmet. "Replant those flowers in the garden and clean out that helmet, okay?"

"I'm busy," she said defiantly. "I'm having a tea party with my sister."

"Tammy!" I barked. "I told you to do something. You do not want to disobey me."

She paused to consider her next move.

"Now, Tammy."

Scrunching her face into a pout, she schlepped over to the helmet and took it to the garden. "And Donnie's your brother," I said, before passing through the sliding glass door into the kitchen. Gail stood at the sink, her forearms buried in suds. Batting her ponytail as I walked by, I noticed a couple gray strands peeking through the chestnut. Knowing better than to reveal my discovery, I silently grabbed a towel and started drying.

She sighed. "Tell me again why you sent Marie home early today?"

"After the day I had, I wanted to be alone with my family tonight. Just the six of us."

We both glanced out the window above the sink. Kyle and Archie were running around the vast green yard playing tag. Bandit raced alongside them. "So," Gail said, "what was it you wanted to talk to me about?"

"I thought we could talk about it later, after the kids go to bed."

"Might want to do it now," she said with a yawn. "Don't think I'll able to stay up that long."

I exhaled audibly. "Fine. Here it is. I met Karl at Cougars Field today. He put me through some light drills and timed me in the forty. It was a disaster. My body resisted everything. I couldn't even break six seconds."

"So you're not going to be ready to play as soon as you'd hoped?"

"No. The knee is killing me. The ankle and the hammy still hurt too. I just can't run. And the pain is throwing off my passes. I'm not even close."

"You'll get it back." She yawned again.

"This time, I don't know. My knee really got messed up in Pittsburgh last year. Hasn't healed liked I thought it would. Then there are the concussions and our crappy offensive line."

"What are you saying?" Her voice lacked the sympathy I was hoping to hear.

"Karl told me I should retire. I'm thinking he's right. I'm planning to tell Depler and the other coaches tomorrow."

"Really?" She stopped washing and looked at me.

"Yeah."

"Well, isn't this kind of sudden? Karl is just one guy. Have you talked to anybody else about this? Have you prayed about it? Did you ask your wife to pray about it?" Her eyes were firm.

"I'm talking to *you* about it right now. And yes, pray about it. Definitely."

"Why? It sounds like you've already made up your mind."

"Karl's been taping up football players for fifty years. I trust his opinion more than anyone else's in a matter like this.

"Apparently."

"Why are you giving me a hard time?" I asked with irritation. "I know my own body."

"I'm not giving you a hard time. It would just be nice to know when you're thinking about making a major life decision, rather than hearing about it afterwards."

"This is a medical issue that you're not familiar with. And I haven't made the official decision yet." I looked out the window. Tammy had returned the bonnet to Donnie's head and was teaching him how to shake his hips like Madonna. I gritted my teeth. *One crisis at a time.*

"You're planning to tell Depler tomorrow. Sounds like the official decision has already been made—without any input from me, I might add. And I do know something about your injuries, thank you very much. I read the literature the doctors sent home with you. Even more than you did, I bet. Plus, we're married. We're supposed to be partners. You should talk to me about things like this."

"I do."

"Not always."

"When haven't I?" My frustration grew.

"Well, there was that time you let Anthony invest your MVP bonus for us."

"The Microsoft shares? Those stocks are exploding. That was a great call he made. We're going to make a bunch of money from that."

"Maybe so, but I've been managing our finances since we got married. You should have consulted me before you let him do that. And that's not the only financial decision you've made without talking to me first. Remember when you increased the amount we send to Dawn each month for Michael? You didn't tell me about that until after the fact." Her tone grew surlier with each word.

A wave of guilt passed over me. "Sorry. I knew you were busy with the kids and church. I didn't want to bother you with business stuff."

"Business stuff? You mean important stuff. It's okay for me to take care of the kids and cart them around to the store or the dentist or wherever. And I can plan church socials and birthday parties. But financial investments, commercial deals, and your retirement from the only career you've ever known, well, there's no need to bother me about things like that. After all, I'm just your wife."

"Gail, I'm sorry. We can discuss it. I haven't told anyone else yet." A commotion directed our attention to the backyard. Kyle and Archie were rolling on the ground slugging each other. They were not playing. Tammy shouted and jumped up and down. Donnie, still in his pink bonnet, sat in the grass crying. Bandit barked at the two combatants.

"Great." I tossed the towel aside. "I'll take the big two. You want the others?"

"No," she said defensively. "You like to handle things by yourself. This will be a good opportunity for you to learn what it's like to deal with all four kids on your own. Then you can see how easy I've got it every day."

"Gail," I pleaded.

"You're the big football hero. You can handle it." She turned away.

Biting my tongue, I stormed out the sliding glass door and into the chaos.

The alarm clock's electric beeps jolted me awake at 7:30 the next morning. After pressing the button to restore silence, I rolled over and drifted off again. A few minutes later, Gail's voice brought me back to consciousness.

"You're not up yet? You're going to be late for prayer breakfast."

Annoyed, I cracked my eyelids. A shaft of light from the hallway cut through the dark bedroom. "I'm not going."

"You're not? Are you sick?" She stood as a silhouette in the bright doorway.

"No, I'm not sick. I just don't feel like going."

"Oh." She was quiet for a moment. "Hey, I'm sorry I was short with you last night. It was a long day for me too. If you want to retire, I'll support your decision. But maybe you could hold off telling the team until tomorrow. Then we could pray about it tonight as a couple."

"Training camp opens in five days. If I'm retiring, the coaches should know today so they can start evaluating other quarterbacks."

"Okay," she said softly. "We could still pray about it after you tell the coaches. We don't do that so much anymore. You know, pray together."

"Would you shut the door? I want to go back to sleep."

"Fine. I have to go finish my column anyway. Ed wants it on his desk by nine. Then I have to rush the kids over to the pool for swimming lessons. And I need to pick up some stuff at the grocery store. We probably won't be back 'til mid-afternoon."

I grunted.

She closed the door, leaving me in darkness. I tried to go back to sleep. My mind wandered. Memories of football triumphs floated through my head. Cheering crowds chanted my name. I rolled over, causing a stinging pain to erupt in my knee. My spirit deflated. The depression ignited a flicker of anger.

How could she treat me like that? I'm faced with the end of my career and she kicks me while I'm down. The coaches and players better not give me any crap after all I've done for them. They'd better appreciate me. The fans too. They will after I'm gone.

Minutes passed into hours. I could not quite go to sleep but did not want to get up. So I wallowed in bed, semi-consciousness and alone. Finally, I lifted my head to check the clock. Red digits glared back at me: 10:56. Not believing the display, I rubbed my eyes and looked again. The numbers were the same. "Son of a bitch."

Embarrassed by my sloth, I trudged down the long staircase. "Oh, Mr. King, you're still here," Marie said from the living room. She held a can of Pledge and a dust rag in her hands. "Would you like me to make you something for breakfast?"

"Okay. How about a couple eggs and some toast?" The phone rang. She moved to answer it. I figured it was Nathan wondering why I missed the team's weekly prayer breakfast. "Marie, I know who that is. Let's just let the answering machine take it."

A confused look spread across her plump face. "Really?"

I nodded to reassure her. "It's okay."

"I'll go make your breakfast then." The voice on the machine confirmed my prediction.

After skimming the paper and devouring my food, I settled in front of the computer in the study. Since I knew what I wanted to say, my letter did not take long to type. While the document printed, I glanced at the desk calendar: Wednesday, July 24. It was two years ago this week that my father had died. Memories flooded back—the phone call, the delay at the airport, running through the hospital to his room. But he was already gone. I had arrived an hour too late.

Reflecting on the enigma that was my father, I recalled hundreds of past conversations with him. But rarely did we talk. His distance frustrated me when I was young, especially since Mom wasn't around. But as an adult, I understood him better. I came to appreciate and admire the man for all he did to provide for his family after losing a wife and two sons. Two years after his death, I still missed my dad.

Pushing aside my gloom, I stuffed the letter into an envelope and hurried out to the car. I reached the team offices about ten minutes before one. I wanted to slip in and out while people were still at lunch. Brandy, sitting at the receptionist desk, was the only person who saw me as I slithered into the main office. After a quick hello, I slid my envelope into Coach Depler's mailbox. Exiting the building, I thought I had accomplished my mission without any unwanted conversations. I was wrong.

"King, what the hell are you doing here today?" The words lassoed me only a few paces from my car. Linebacker Braden Schumaker, all six and a half feet of him, approached. He must have been inside his Chevy Blazer when I scanned the parking lot before leaving the building.

"Uh, just had to drop off a note for Depler," I said, unable to think of a good lie.

He grinned. "Forget it. That little knee boo-boo of yours won't get you out of death camp."

I debated whether to tell him or not. *Might as well—he'll know soon enough*. "Actually, it will."

"Huh?" His tone matched the puzzled look on his scruffy face.

"I'm retiring, Braden. Just left my official notice in Depler's box."

His chiseled jaw dropped. "What the … are you kidding me?"

"I'm afraid not. The injuries have caught up with me."

"Damn. You sure about this? You put up some good numbers last year—before Pittsburgh. And that knee will heal. You could be back by midseason, I bet."

I lowered my head. "Yeah, I could probably take a few more snaps. But I don't think I'll ever be able to move and throw like I used to."

"Man, that sucks. We just lost Scott to free agency and now you're gone. Our offense is gonna bite it this year."

"Buchacker's coming around. He'll get the job done." I kept my eyes on the pavement.

"The Buck's got talent, but he's green. Besides, this is *your* team. You're the one who took us to the Super Bowl and you're the one who can take us back." He slapped my chest.

"That seems like ages ago," I said. "Two-thirds of the guys from that team are gone. This is a rebuilding year for Newark, with or without me. Might as well let Buchacker get some on-the-job training. He's the quarterback of the future."

"Maybe I can get traded." Braden looked just serious enough to make me feel bad. The sound of women laughing in the distance caused us both to turn our heads. "Cheerleading practice must have just ended," he said. "Oh … hell … yeah."

Though there were more than a dozen fit young women approaching the parking lot, I knew exactly which one inspired his last comment. Silently concurring, I took in the sight: flowing jet-black hair, orange crop T-shirt stretched taut over an abundant chest, exposed midriff, tight white shorts, and sculpted tan legs. "Who's that?" I asked.

"That, my friend, is Beth Schaeffer."

"She's new," I said, staring shamelessly.

"Yeah. She's married to Ryan Schaeffer, that safety from Illinois we drafted in the third round. Lucky bastard."

"Schaeffer, huh?" I tried to recall a face to match the name. "I thought cheerleaders and players weren't supposed to get together."

"They're not. But those two were already married. Got hitched in college. So the team made an exception. Can't blame 'em. Can you imagine telling that goddess she can't be on the squad? We get a few more like her on the sideline, people might start thinking Newark isn't such a hellhole."

The group of women drew closer. Most of them veered off to the other side of the lot. Beth, however, walked straight toward us. "She's coming over here," I said anxiously.

Braden chuckled. "Relax, King. You still in the sixth grade? That's probably her car right there." He gestured at an orange Volkswagen bug a few spaces away.

"Hey Beth," he said, flashing a toothy smile.

"Hi Braden."

"How was practice?"

"Hot. Wish Shelly would have cancelled it. If the temperature's a hundred degrees, we shouldn't have to be out there. Don't you think?"

Braden nodded. "I think you're on to something there. Maybe that can apply to the players too. I'll run that by Depler at camp next week." He glanced over at me. "So Beth, you met Dave yet?"

Her aqua eyes fixed on me. Perfect white teeth flashed from one round cheek to the other. The beauty radiating from her face sapped my strength, making me feel old and inadequate.

"Well, we haven't officially met. But I know who Dave King is. Who doesn't?"

I chuckled nervously. "Nice to meet you, Beth." The ensuing handshake sent a charge through my arm.

"Oh shit," Braden said, glancing at his watch. "I'm late. I was supposed to meet Karl at one. The old man's gonna tear me a new one. Sorry guys. Gotta run." A moment later he was gone, leaving me alone with Beth.

I tried to think of something witty to say, but her sultry aura jammed my ability to communicate. "My husband Ryan is your biggest fan," she said. "He was so psyched when Newark drafted him. He's like, 'Yes! I get to meet Dave King.'"

I felt my face redden. "Oh, wow. I've heard great things about him. He had quite a career at Illinois. I know the coaches here are excited to have him onboard." I had actually heard very little about Ryan, knew nothing about his college career, and had no idea what the Newark coaches thought of him.

"Oh, thank you," she said in a sweet voice. "He's sure been busting his ass this summer. Thinks he's got a shot at starting as a rookie. He's never been so focused. With all the time he spends at the gym, I hardly ever see him anymore."

"Yeah, I know how that goes. The first summer is rough." I stole a glimpse of her navel.

"Really? It was tough for you and Gail when you first got here?"

"Oh yeah. You have to get adjusted to a completely different environment. The city, the coaches … hey, wait a minute. You know Gail?"

"Well, not personally," she said with a laugh. "But I've read about you guys and seen you on TV with her in those United Way commercials. And when the Tornadoes were in the Super Bowl, the camera kept showing her in the stands. She's pretty."

"Uh, yeah. Thanks. You watched Newark in the Super Bowl, huh?"

"Of course. I was a senior in high school. Me and my girlfriends had such a big crush on you back then." She tilted her head, amplifying the magnetism of her smile. "I probably shouldn't have told you that."

"That's funny." I looked away like it was no big deal, but inside my spirits leapt with renewed energy. "I forget that I've been on TV so much. After back-to-back losing seasons, the networks don't broadcast many Tornadoes games anymore."

"You'll lead them back," she said, touching my arm.

"Well, I don't know. This knee injury might keep me out for a while." I could not tell her I was retiring. I wanted her to think I was young and strong, not old and broken-down.

"You might miss part of the season? That sucks. I was looking forward to cheering for you." For the next several minutes, she told me how great I was and how the team needed me. Fidgeting in embarrassment, I halfheartedly brushed aside her compliments. I then casually floated the idea that it might be time for me to think about something other than football.

"That would be such a bummer," she said. "But even if you never play another game, you're still the coolest quarterback Newark has ever had."

Though I doubted she could name any other Tornadoes quarterback, her statement pumped more air into my ballooning ego. "Thanks." Our eyes locked for a tantalizingly long time.

"Well, I guess I should get going," she finally said. "I've got to run to the store this afternoon. We're having a party Saturday. I have to get the booze and stuff."

"Cool. It was great talking to you."

"Hey, you guys should come. You and Gail. I know Ryan would love it if you'd stop by."

Excitement flickered. "Well, uh, okay. What can we bring?"

"It's actually a pool party. So bring your suits and towels. Don't worry about food or anything. We'll have plenty. Even got a big cake. It's kind of a birthday party for me." She grabbed my arm. "Do NOT bring a present. Nobody's bringing any presents. It's just a casual thing. Ryan thought it might be fun to get together with some of the other rookies before training camp next week. It would blow everybody's mind to have the star quarterback show up."

"Sounds like fun. We'll be there.... Oh, and happy birthday."

"Thank you. I'm going to hit the big two-three," she said with a giggle. "Here, let me give you our address and phone number." She scribbled the information on the back of a wrinkled supermarket receipt.

"Thanks, Beth. See ya this weekend."

"Bye Dave," she sang through a devastating smile.

My greedy eyes took in everything as she walked away. When she reached her car, I spun around and strode toward my purple 1990 Mustang. My aches and pains had diminished. Sliding into the driver's seat, I felt young and cool. Tesla's "Modern Day Cowboy" rang from the speakers. Cranking up the volume, I peeled out of the lot.

"Are you sure you can't make it tonight?" Gail asked. "It would mean a lot to Tammy."

"Sorry," I said, checking my hair in the bathroom mirror for the third time. "This is kind of a big deal for the team. I really should be there for the guys. I'll give Tammy a present tomorrow."

"This party or whatever you're going to, it came up all of a sudden, didn't it? I don't remember Jamie or any of the other wives mentioning a team function for this weekend."

"Yeah, I just found out about it." I tilted my head back to check my nostrils. "It's mainly a thing for the rookies. Coach wants me there as a veteran presence. Welcome the young guys to the team." The lie made my face grow hot. I wanted Gail to leave. She instead stood at the bathroom doorway, her stare boring into the side of my head. Finally, I turned to look at her.

"Well, it's good of you to be there for your teammates, especially since you're retiring. It will mean a lot to the younger players." There was understanding in her green eyes. It was a warm look, one I'd seen many times before. "Tammy has another recital in September. You can go to that one."

With no words to speak, all I could do was nod.

She moved to go, but then turned back. "The more I think about it, the more I like this retirement thing. I know you've prayed about it. This must be where God is leading you. It's actually kind of exciting you'll finally be free from the demands of football. There are so many things we'll be able to do that we couldn't before." Her smile widened.

Hammered by guilt, I could not meet her gaze. As my face dropped, I noticed she was wearing the pearls I had given her last year for our tenth anniversary. "Yeah, right. Well, I guess I should get going."

"Me too. It'll take me twenty minutes to round up the kids."

After a quick kiss, I said goodbye and slipped away. An instant later I was in the car speeding down the road. Gail's words pursued me. My guilt intensified when I realized that I did not wish Tammy good luck before leaving. As I drove on, the conflicting thoughts in my head coalesced into words of warning. *You should not be going to this party. You're married. You're a Christian. This isn't you. Turn around now. Before it's too late.*

Stopped at a red light, I saw a path of escape. All I had to do was turn right at the intersection. A couple blocks away was a residential street that would take me back to my neighborhood. I could be home in five minutes. My hand touched the turn signal.

But then a fiery collage of tight shorts, tan legs, bare midriff, alluring smile, and bewitching eyes flashed before me. I felt Beth's touch on my arm. Flames ignited within. The lustful excitement of the unknown charged my spirit. The thought of driving home, so appealing only a moment ago, suddenly seemed depressing.

The dialogue in my mind shifted towards rationalization. *Just go to the party. Nothing is going to happen. A bunch of people, including her husband, will be there. You're not doing anything wrong.* When the light turned green, I lowered my hand from the turn signal and hit the gas. My car sped straight ahead through the intersection.

I was impressed with Beth and Ryan's house. Nestled in a rich new subdivision, it was not much smaller than my own. I made a mental note to look up his signing bonus and salary. A sign on the front door directed guests to the back. After trekking around the all-brick custom colonial, I passed through a gate in the wooden privacy fence. A small crowd had already gathered on the patio behind the house. Everyone looked so young. Scanning the crowd for someone else over thirty, I saw only kids who appeared to be barely out of college. Some of the girls even looked like high school students. My first thought was to turn around and escape before anybody noticed me.

"Dave!" a voice yelled from somewhere. "You made it! Awesome!" A man I assumed to be Ryan Schaeffer emerged from a cluster standing near the pool. He was lean and athletic. His blond hair was cropped short with a ledge in back. An unbuttoned Hawaiian shirt revealed a smooth muscular chest. Like an insecure teenager, I started making mental comparisons. *He's got a better tan, but my pecs are bigger and I'm at least an inch taller.*

"Hey Ryan." We shook hands.

"Beth said you might be coming. Good to see ya, buddy."

"Thanks, man. Here, this is for you and Beth." I handed him a bottle of wine that I'd bought earlier in the day and hidden in my car.

He took the gift. "Wow. This is one of those expensive ones. You shouldn't have done that." He had a subtle smile that I was sure the girls just loved. "Awesome. I'll put this on ice." He disappeared into the house.

My solitude lasted only a few seconds. Two second-year defensive backs approached. It was a relief to see faces I recognized. They introduced me to a Newark draftee I had never heard of. Attractive young ladies accompanied all three men.

We talked for a while before Ryan returned. He pressed a plastic cup of beer into my hand and pointed out a few of the other rookie hopefuls. I soon found myself mingling with different collections of young people. The guys treated me like a star. I acted the part, sharing stories about throwing touchdowns, meeting celebrities, and shooting commercials. My Super Bowl tales drew the liveliest reactions.

Every so often, I caught a glimpse of Beth locked in conversation across the patio. She wore a purple and white bikini, the lower piece concealed by an orange sarong. I had been at the party nearly thirty minutes when she finally made her way over to me. "Dave!" She gave me a quick hug. "Thanks for coming. I'm so glad you're here."

"Happy birthday."

"Thank you. Where's Gail?"

"She had to stay home. One of the boys is sick."

"Oh, that's too bad. Hope he gets better soon."

"Uh, thanks. I'm sure he'll be fine."

She checked out my polo shirt, khaki shorts, and sandals. "Didn't you bring anything to swim in?"

"No. I have to avoid stressing the knee for a while."

She furrowed her brow into an expression of playful disappointment. "Oh Dave, it's not like we were going to make you swim laps. The water would have been good for you."

I smiled. "Well, maybe next time."

"Okay. I'm going to hold you to that, mister." She stuck a finger in my chest. "I'll remember." The look she flashed left me unable to move or speak.

A loud voice shattered my trance. "Time to dunk the birthday girl!" Ryan shouted. Now wearing only his swim trunks, he grabbed his wife from behind and tossed her, sarong and all, into the pool. She hit the water with a scream. The partygoers cheered. I did too, though I was not pleased with this turn of events.

Ryan jumped into the pool after his wife. A wave of other players and their dates followed. Standing alone, I scanned my remaining conversation prospects. Nothing looked too promising among the few guests left on land. I drifted over to the grill and watched the frivolity in the pool. Beth, now free of her sarong, bounced around splashing her friends. I eyed her body as it moved about under the shimmering surface of the water. I felt dirty, like some leering old drunk at a strip club. Yet, I couldn't stop looking.

Finally, a stout young man dressed entirely in black came over and introduced himself. His name was Evan. He hoped to make the team as a left tackle. I tried not to dwell on his shaved head, nose ring, and skull tattoos. His pink-haired girlfriend displayed a similar assortment of piercings and body art. They were a welcome sight. I was no longer standing alone like a geek. I did not even mind that Jeffery Dahmer was their preferred topic of conversation.

While Evan and Pink Hair regaled me with their considerable knowledge of serial killers, I continued to glance at Beth in the pool. At one point she and her husband kissed, punching me in the gut. *Why did that bother me? They're married. That's what they're supposed to do. You've known her for three days. You have a wife and four children. Quit acting like an idiot. Leave now and go to your daughter's dance recital, where you belong.*

I plotted my escape. First, I would need an excuse to get away from my current companions—something like wanting to get another beer. If I dawdled long enough at the keg, Evan and Pink Hair might join another conversation. Then I could slip through the gate. Since Beth, Ryan, and most of the guests still frolicked in the pool, no one would notice my exit. I could then put this moronic episode behind me.

My plan seemed to be working. Near the keg was an ice-filled cooler. I feigned interest in the bottles of imported beer within. After a minute or so, a quick glance over my shoulder revealed the tattooed duo talking to another couple. I moved along the back of the house toward a flowerbed near the gate. Pretending to be fascinated with the roses and begonias, I slid closer to the wooden exit. My hand grasped the latch.

"You are so busted, Dave King!" The female voice sent me airborne. I spun around to behold Beth approaching. Water dripped from her dark hair.

"Busted?" I stammered.

"Yes, busted. Ryan told me what you brought. That's a three hundred dollar bottle!"

Actually, it was closer to four hundred. "Oh, it's no big deal. Just a little something for your birthday."

"I told you not to bring anything. You are so bad." Her face then brightened. "Well, thank you. That was sweet. Hey, have a seat and I'll pour us a couple glasses." She gestured to an empty deck table on the other side of the patio.

I still could have left. All I had to do was say something about my child with the fake illness. My eyes glimpsed her smooth stomach. "Okay," I said.

"Great." She walked toward the house. Even wrapped in a towel, her swaying hips destroyed me.

Sitting under the umbrella at the deck table, I surveyed the scene. Most people still played in the pool or sat on the edge, talking. "Mmmm, this is so good," Beth said, savoring a sip of wine. She handed me a stemmed glass and claimed the chair next to mine.

"Glad you like it." I took a sip and forced a smile as the liquid slid down my throat.

"I love it. But you are still a bad boy for disobeying me. Now, how should I punish you?" She bit her lower lip.

A thousand fantasies exploded in my head. "Uh-oh," was all I could say.

"I know. You're not going to Ithaca with the team, right?"

"No, I won't be going."

"With Ryan gone at training camp, I'll be here alone with nothing to do. I think you should have to take me out for dinner one night and show me some of the sights around here. He still hasn't taken me to the city yet. So you can be my tour guide. Think you could handle that?"

I nearly fell backwards out of my chair. A red light switched on in my head. An instant later it turned green. Bright green. Almost blinding. "Well, I suppose that could be arranged." I tried to sound nonchalant.

We continued talking. Our conversation transported me to another world. I felt like a college student. I was the star athlete flirting with the prettiest girl on campus. Nobody was married. Nobody had kids. Nobody had responsibilities. I soaked in the freedom. She flitted from topic to topic. No matter what she discussed, my ears echoed with her invitation to go out—just the two of us.

Eventually two of Beth's friends summoned her back to the pool. Not interested in mingling with anybody else, I told her I had to get going. She looked disappointed, but quickly relented. She walked me to the gate. "I'm going to hold you to our agreement, tour buddy."

"We'll see."

"Don't even think you're going to get out of this." She laughed. "I'll track you down."

We said goodbye. She moved in for a hug. My hands sizzled touching her bare back. I held her just a little tighter and a fraction of a second longer than I would have for a normal friendly hug. We parted with a smile.

Escaping the 'burbs, I hopped on the interstate and sped west into the northern New Jersey countryside. I did not want to lose the high I felt. That evening, I was twenty-three again. Life seemed filled with possibilities.

The next morning, I went to church with Gail and the kids. My mind, however, did not accompany my body to the pew. The choir sang and the pastor preached. I did not hear any of it—not the songs, not the sermon, not even Gail's piano solo during the offertory. My state of detachment continued the rest of the day. Physically I was home with my family, but mentally I was somewhere else.

On Monday, the Tornadoes opened training camp in Ithaca, New York. Ryan Schaeffer was there. I was not. It was the first time in eleven years that I did not accompany the team to camp. Though a little sad, I was quite pleased to avoid the torturous practices in oppressive heat. My children were also happy I stayed home. That afternoon, I took them to the zoo at the Newark Museum while Gail worked on her weekly column for *The Star-Ledger*. Throughout the outing, my mind kept wandering.

Tuesday morning, I told Gail I needed to go to the team offices to fill out some paperwork related to my retirement. With the coaches, players, and training staff away, much of the building was empty. The only people I saw were Brandy the receptionist and Luther the custodian. Since neither seemed overly curious about why I was there, I had the run of the place.

Taking the stairs up to the third floor, I found a vacant office overlooking the small field where the cheerleaders practiced. I sat at the window and watched. Beth wore a purple sports bra and black spandex shorts. It was close to an hour before I could pull myself away.

Driving home, my senses slowly returned. My guilty conscience produced a litany of questions: *What am I doing? What is happening to me? How did I get like this? Why don't I pray anymore?* Pulling into the garage, I resolved to stop playing with fire. No more adolescent behavior. No more obsessing about Beth.

That evening I tossed the football around with Kyle and Archie in the backyard. After the fifth pass, I felt a twinge in my knee. Two throws later, the ache spread to my entire left leg. The realization that my football career was over hit me with full force. Before, I had been entertaining thoughts about maybe trying to come back after a year off. The persisting pain in my knee, however, exposed the fallacy of such thinking. Karl was right. I was done. A dark cloud settled over me. But then Beth flashed into my head. The cloud dissipated. My energy returned.

And so went the next couple of days. One minute I would realize the insanity of pursuing a married woman and drive every thought of Beth from my mind. Then something would happen to bother me: a tiff with Gail, a tantrum from one of the kids, a TV ad for an upcoming NFL game. Each occurrence added to my sense of discontentment—until images of Beth arrived to invigorate me. I could not let go of the rush that came from thinking about her.

Thursday morning I watched cheerleading practice again. This time I conveniently left the building the same time the girls walked out to their cars. Beth's greeting was warm. I worried that she might ask what I was doing there, but the issue never came up. I "accidentally" mentioned something about me owing her an evening out. We laughed. We made plans for Friday evening. The next day.

My body buzzed with nervous excitement all day Friday. A lie about meeting Joe that night to discuss an endorsement deal paved the way for my absence. It was a plausible excuse, as long as Joe or Anthony did not call the house while I was gone. My first thought was to pray that did not happen. The irony hit me a moment later. I quickly started thinking about something else.

The afternoon could not pass by fast enough. My wife and children were like ghosts, barely visible. After a workout and a shower, it took me almost an hour to pick out which clothes to wear. Gail, busy downstairs, did not notice. When she kissed my cheek and told me goodbye, I nearly crumbled. One last crisis of conscience blocked the road. But then my mind churned out a justification to push me out the door. *You and Beth are just going out as friends. Nothing is actually going to happen.* Sliding into the car, I reached under the seat where I had hidden a bottle of my best cologne. I slapped some on and started the ignition.

Driving over to Beth's, I rehearsed my lines. Goldfish flopped about in my stomach as I pulled into her driveway. I gasped when she opened the door. Her red dress was tight and revealing. Her perfume smelled of youthful fantasies.

For about a half hour I drove around Newark, showing her a few points of interest. I then headed east across the Newark Bay Bridge and took the Holland Tunnel into lower Manhattan. After parking in a garage, I led her to our dinner destination: Chanterelle on Harrison Street. I had met the restaurant's manager a few years earlier at a team party. I signed a bunch of jerseys, footballs, and pictures for his kids. That favor allowed me to get a reservation with only a day's notice.

I was concerned that the elegant atmosphere of Chanterelle might come off as inappropriate. Beth did not seem to mind. In fact, she mentioned more than once how nice it was to finally get the chance to eat at a fancy New York restaurant.

Our dinner conversation was lively and flirty. When I made a joke, she laughed. Though careful not to talk too much about myself, I occasionally mentioned my football career. She seemed impressed and asked several questions about what it was like to play in the Super Bowl.

She drank wine. I did too, but at a slower pace. I wanted to learn all I could. She talked about Ryan and his hyperdedication to earning a starting spot on the team. Reading between the lines, I could tell that his endless workouts had left her lonely. Ever since junior high, males had vied for her favor. She was not used to competing with anyone or anything for a boy's attention. A cold opportunist, I made her the center of the universe. When she talked, I listened as if whatever she described was the most fascinating topic in the world. In a subtle and unspoken way, I reassured her that she was a beautiful, amazing woman. An illicit connection strengthened as we locked eyes across the table. She owned me, and I plotted to possess her.

After dinner, we strolled around lower Manhattan. Slightly tipsy, she gripped my arm. Walking with Beth amid the bright lights of the city sent me into a dream. My old life was a thousand miles away. On the drive back, my heart pounded as we neared her neighborhood. By the time I pulled into her driveway, I trembled like a fifteen-year-old on his first date.

"Thanks for taking me out tonight," she said. "I hope you didn't feel like you had to babysit me because of what I said at the party."

"No, not at all. I wanted to do this. It was fun."

"Yeah. It was a blast." Held motionless by her gaze, I awaited my fate. "Hey, I'm not sleepy yet," she said. "Would you have time to come in for a quick drink?"

I thought I might lose consciousness. "Sure."

We went inside. It was a few minutes before midnight. She opened a bottle of wine. We talked for a while, each word inching us closer to a forbidden destination. Then, like a tempest, fantasy became reality. It was nearly 3:00 a.m. when I finally left.

Traversing the empty streets, I stared through the windshield in a daze. Even though I had contrived this whole evening, my guilt-wracked brain could not grasp what I had done. *That wasn't me back there. If you just wake up from this dream, none of this will have happened.* But it was not a dream. What had happened was forever real.

There was a light on downstairs at my house. My stomach knotted at the thought that Gail might still be up. I felt like a thief as I snuck into my own home. The sight of an empty living room brought temporary relief. Creeping down to the shower in the basement, I washed away the olfactory evidence. Physically clean, I tiptoed upstairs and slid into bed next to Gail without a sound.

Lying in the darkness, I descended into a pit of fear and shame. *How could I have been so stupid? What if Gail finds out? What if someone recognized me tonight? What if Beth tells somebody?* I wanted it all to go away, but reality remained unrelenting. Sleep never came to rescue me from my tormenting thoughts.

Hours later the soft glow of sunrise crept past the edges of the curtains. I left our bed and plodded to the kitchen. Shortly thereafter, Gail came downstairs and started making waffles. She was cheerful and chatty—just another normal Saturday morning. She asked about my meeting with Joe. I told her it went fine. Not interested in the details, she quickly moved on to other topics: meeting the new couple at church, taking the kids to Central Park, planning a getaway for the two of us. Each sentence she spoke drove a spike into my head. I barely had the strength to lift my fork.

That afternoon, Gail took Tammy and Donnie to the mall. Needing to make a phone call, I sent Kyle and Archie outside to play in the backyard. I had to find out Beth's state of mind. *Is she wallowing in guilt? Is she hysterical? Does she blame me for what happened?*

Taking a deep breath, I dialed the number. She sounded tired, but happy to hear from me. After some tentative small talk, we returned to the previous evening. "Ryan doesn't need to know," she said. "It would just hurt him." Her words eradicated any thoughts I had about telling Gail. The bullet dodged, I saw a light at the end of the tunnel. She then blindsided me.

"Dave, last night was amazing. When can I see you again?"

Minutes earlier, I was ravaged by guilt. All I wanted to do was to sweep this episode under the rug and move on with my life. But her last question unleashed a flood of images and sensations. The night before replayed in my head with vivid detail. The high I had felt from being with her intoxicated my senses. Evicting all contrary thoughts, I started plotting my next rendezvous with Beth Schaeffer.

Chapter 19 – January 1992

I drew a card from the deck. "Molasses Swamp." I moved my blue plastic gingerbread piece to the appropriate spot on the board.

"Oh no, Daddy," Tammy said. "Now you're stuck there until you get a red." She drew a card. "Double purple!" She moved her piece ahead on the track. "Your turn."

I grabbed a card. Since it was green, I remained mired in place. My daughter giggled. She sat cross-legged on the floor across the board from me. A few feet away Gail was on the sofa reading to Donnie. Kyle and Archie played downstairs with the train set they had received for Christmas. The faint buzzing of the toy locomotive seeped into the living room through the floor register.

Tammy reminded me to pick a card. I did. It was red, freeing me from the swamp. *If only it were that easy.* Glancing up, I saw how enthralled Donnie was by the story his mother read. A feeling of nausea returned. It was not the sight that made me sick, but the thought that someone was hurting that loving woman and innocent child. Someone close to them. But they had no idea.

"Daddy!" Tammy exclaimed, holding her pigtails straight above her head. "Pay attention! It's your turn." The image of that sweet little girl, similarly betrayed, was too much for me to handle.

"I'm sorry, honey," I said, springing to my feet. "Daddy has to go to the bathroom." I bounded up the stairs.

"Hurry back," she called. I rushed through the master bedroom and into the adjoining bathroom. A tear escaped from each eye as I stared into the mirror. The face I saw was both familiar and strange. "How can you keep doing this?" I asked aloud. A monster glared back at me. My insides churned. The dam broke.

"Dad! Come see the train!" Kyle's yell startled me. I had not heard him climb the stairs. Since he was already in the bedroom, there was no time to shut the bathroom door. I hurriedly turned on the water.

"Dad! Come see—" He froze in the doorway.

I splashed my face and wiped away the water with a towel. My eyes glowed red. Looking down at my son, I saw fear contort his freckled face.

"What's wrong?" he signed.

"Nothing," I signed in reply. "I'm okay."

"You're crying." Shock remained in his eyes. My reaction would have been the same had I seen my own father crying when I was ten years old.

"No. I'm getting a cold. My eyes are irritated. That's all."

After several moments of silence, sympathy replaced the distress on his face. Taking me by surprise, he lunged forward and hugged me as tightly as he could. Returning the embrace, I needed every fiber of my strength to keep from breaking down again. Determination coursed through my veins. *You are going to end it. You have to.*

When finally sure I could maintain my composure, I pulled back to look at my son. Forcing a smile, I tousled the auburn mop atop his head. Youthful green eyes stared back at me. "I want you to get better," he said aloud.

"I will. Let's go see your train."

The next morning I holed up in the study, presumably to review financial reports from my charity foundation. In actuality, I was planning what to say in an impending conversation. I wanted to be compassionate, yet decisive. There could be no doubt in her mind. Though resolute, I struggled to find the right words. Images from the past clouded my thinking. After lunch, I returned to the study for more rumination. Hours passed. The phone rang.

"Dave, we need to talk." Beth's voice sent a cold shiver up my spine.

"I told you never to call here," I hissed.

"Chill. I would have hung up if Gail answered."

"She's home right now," I whispered. "I can't talk. I was going to call you later."

"When? Ryan will be home in an hour. Can you do it before then?"

Gail appeared at the doorway to the study, nearly sending me into cardiac arrest. "Who called?" she asked.

I covered the mouthpiece. "Joe."

"Oh. Tell him I said 'hi.' I'm going to pick up the kids from school. I won't be long."

"Dave?" Beth asked. "Are you still there? What's wrong?"

"O—Okay," I stammered.

"Love you," Gail said, blowing a kiss.

I waved a trembling hand at my wife. "Alright Joe," I said into the phone, "tell me more about this idea."

"Can you talk?" Beth asked.

"Hang on a minute." I paused until I heard Gail exit the house. "That was close. See why you can't call here?"

"Sorry. You want me to hang up?"

"No. She's gone now. The house is empty."

"Dave, I have to tell you something." Her voice sounded strained.

"I have something to tell you, too."

"Oh. Well, maybe you should go first."

I took a deep breath. "Beth, this isn't right. We have to break it off for good this time. We're hurting too many people, including ourselves."

She was quiet for a few moments. "You didn't seem like you were in too much pain when we met at the hotel last weekend."

"That should not have happened," I said, irritated. "We can't see each other anymore."

"So just like that, it's over? After everything we've shared. I thought you loved me."

"We're both married. I have four children. We have to end it."

"I wish you would quit being so immature."

"What?"

"You keep doing this same thing over and over. Ever since last summer. When Ryan was at training camp, you wanted to see me all the time. Then he comes back and you want to cool it. A couple weeks later you want to get together again. Then after a while, you tell me we have to stop. We don't see each other for almost two months. But in December, we're back together. So we're on again and off again. And then there's last weekend."

Exposed by her words, I hung my head. "I'm sorry. You're an amazing woman. It's not easy to let you go. What we had was special, but we can't do it anymore."

"Actually, it's not that simple," she said with defiance.

"What do you mean?"

"I'm pregnant."

Her two-word punch to the solar plexus sent me reeling. My frantic mind groped for an escape hatch. "You're married. Married women get pregnant."

"It's your baby, Dave. I'm six weeks pregnant. Ryan hasn't touched me since Thanksgiving. Before my last period."

"Are you kidding me? Not even once?"

"He suspects something. He's never said anything, but I could tell he was getting suspicious when you and I started seeing each other again in December. He's been cold and distant ever since. Kinda depressed too."

"Does he know it's me?"

"I don't know what he knows."

I slammed my fist into the desk. "Great! You're pregnant and I'm the father."

"It's not the first time this has happened."

"What?" I shouted. "What's that supposed to mean?"

"At the end of September, I found out I was pregnant. The doctor said the date of conception was sometime during the first week of August. Ryan was in Ithaca then."

"And you didn't tell me?"

"I found out right after you told me we had to break up. I didn't know if I'd ever see you again." She sighed. "Ryan and I were together right before he left for training camp. That was close enough. He was so happy when I told him he was going to be a father."

"Oh." I rested my aching head in my hand.

"At the end of October I miscarried. I hadn't heard from you in nearly a month. And it would be another month before we talked again. So I didn't tell you that I lost our first child."

Her disclosure about the miscarriage brought a sharp pang of sadness. The room started spinning. I placed my free hand on the desk to steady myself. Gail and my children smiled at me from a family portrait. A frightening guilt shook my body. "You've got to get back with Ryan." The words shot out of my mouth like machine gun bullets. "Do whatever it takes. If you two get together now, you can still tell him it's his baby. You're only six weeks along. When the baby's born, say it came early."

"But Dave," she said in a hurt voice.

"What?"

"What about us? This is the second child we've made together. I lied to Ryan about it once. It was because of that lie that I lost our first baby. I was being punished. I'm not going to let that happen again."

My dizziness intensified. I tried to speak, but could not.

"Dave, I love you. I've tried to deny my feelings for you, but I can't do it anymore. We both have to realize we're meant to be together."

"What about Ryan and Gail?"

"I know it won't be easy to tell them, but we have to. It's gone too far. My heart is with you now, and your heart is with me. You're just too scared to realize it. We're starting a family, Dave. You and me. We have to let Ryan and Gail go, so they can find other people. It's not fair for us to stay in our marriages when you and I belong together."

My arms quivered. Even after all my dalliances with Beth, the thought of actually leaving my wife and kids terrified me. The devastation I envisioned etched across their faces was unbearable. But with Beth's revelation, a noose tightened around my neck. If there was a way out of this predicament, I could not see it.

I heard a noise from the garage. "I think someone is coming home," I said. "I have to go. Don't do anything yet. We'll talk about this later, alright?"

"Well, okay. But the sooner we tell them, the better."

"I'll call you soon."

After hanging up, I checked the garage. The Mustang and the Cadillac were there, but the Explorer was still gone. It must have been the wind that I had heard. Back in the living room, I fell to my knees and pounded the floor. *Why is this happening to me? Just when I was going to end it!*

Ten minutes later my car raced toward the Newark Tornadoes office and training facility in Union. It was a desperate gamble for a desperate situation. Barely acknowledging Brandy, I hurried down the hallway to the north end of the building. After scrambling down the stairs, I reached my destination: the team weight room. It was 3:50 p.m. Ryan Schaeffer usually worked out on Friday afternoons until 4:00.

Upon entering, I saw only three men. One hulking lineman spotted while another completed a set of bench presses. Both were former teammates of mine. Several feet away, Ryan sat in a leg press machine. I greeted the linemen. They responded in kind. One of them asked what brought me to the weight room.

"Came to talk to the rook," I said, gesturing at Ryan. The eyes on his exhausted face widened. I could not tell if he suspected me or not. "Coach asked me to poll some of the new guys. Get their take on their first season as a Tornado."

"Really?" the lineman asked.

"Yes, indeed," I lied, walking toward Ryan. "Whaddya say, Schaeffer?" I asked with a grin. "You ready for an interrogation?"

Rivulets of sweat rolled down his face. "Well, I'd like to do a little more here. Can I have another ten to finish up?"

"No problem. I'll head up to the lounge. Meet me there when you're done."

He nodded. Since the Tornadoes' season had ended weeks ago, I assumed there would be nobody hanging around the players' lounge. I was right. After plopping onto an orange leather couch, I stared at the clock on the wall. Watching the second hand move round and round reminded me of my life slowly circling a drain. I started making up questions for the fake interview.

Ryan arrived fifteen minutes later with wet hair. He wore a gray T-shirt and stonewashed jeans. "Sorry I took a little longer," he said. "Thought I should shower first." He dropped his gym bag on the floor and claimed a spot on the purple couch that formed a ninety-degree angle with the orange one.

"Much appreciated," I said. For the next several seconds, the hum of the clock was the only sound in the room. Drawing a breath, I finally launched into my interview. I asked about the highlights of his rookie season, how he liked playing for Newark, his goals for next season, and which college players he thought the team should draft. I closed by asking him who he thought would win the Super Bowl.

His responses were mainly positive. He was especially pleased about making starter by game five and helping the team finish 7-9, exceeding most preseason forecasts. Nonetheless, his voice carried little emotion. It may have been exhaustion from his workout—I still could not tell if he suspected anything between his wife and me.

After he answered my final question by picking the Redskins 28-10, I strategized on how to subtly shift the topic to Beth. His next statement brought an abrupt end to my deliberation.

"Dave," he said as a grim look furrowed his smooth face, "I heard something about you last summer."

My body tensed. "You did?"

"Yeah." He paused. "I heard you were going to become a pastor after retiring from football. Some of the guys at training camp said that."

I exhaled. "Actually I was thinking about applying for the position of musical director at our church. I didn't end up doing that."

"Oh." His eyes fell to his shoes.

"You seem disappointed."

He stared at me for a few seconds. "I don't go to church so I don't know any priests or pastors. And I don't know Nathan Rodriguez all that well. But there's this thing that's been driving me crazy. I know we don't hang out much, but you're a religious guy, right? … I really need to talk to somebody I can trust."

"What's wrong, Schaeffer?" I could barely speak the words.

He shook his head and looked past me out the window. "It's Beth. I think she's been messing around on me. It's tearing me up, man."

I swallowed. "Are you sure?"

"No. But something's up. She's been acting different the past few months. Like she's somewhere else. More than once she's quickly hung up the phone when I've walked in the room. And when the team traveled, she hardly ever wanted to go. That was really weird—she never missed any of my road games in college. Then I'd call home from the hotel and she wouldn't pick up. Late at night even. Her explanations were so weak. She's a terrible liar."

At first I wondered if this was his way of pricking my conscience. Looking into his eyes, however, I saw genuine anguish. He was a tormented kid looking for advice from an older man he thought he could trust. I felt like I might vomit. But despite my self-revulsion, I remained determined to hide the affair.

"Sometimes things are not what they seem," I said. "Maybe Beth had some trouble adjusting to life in a new city. It can get tough for the wives, you know. And then there's all the media coverage, especially on starters like yourself. Maybe it's just stress that's been bothering her. Now that the season is over, make an extra effort to reconnect with her. You could grab some flowers on the way home. Maybe take her out to a nice restaurant tonight. Have some wine. See where things go."

"I don't know, Dave."

"All marriages hit ruts. It might just take a little romantic push to get yours back on track."

He thought for a few moments before shaking his head. "I appreciate the advice, but I can't do that. Something's not right between me and Beth. Something big. There are too many unanswered questions. It's not right for me to pretend like everything's okay so I can get her into bed. I'd feel like I was using her."

His verbal haymaker nearly knocked me to the ground. He had unknowingly shined a light on me, and what it revealed was not pretty. "I understand," I said weakly.

A short time later we parted with a handshake. Walking out to my car, I felt coated in layers of slime. But my brain still focused on finding a way to cover up all I had done. After returning home, I picked up the phone. It was a call I did not want to make, but time was running out.

I arose early the next day. After a hurried breakfast of Wheaties and grape juice, I took off. I raced east on I-280 through the Newark metropolitan area. Crossing the Hackensack put me in Jersey City, where I reached the Newport Tower at precisely 8:00 a.m. The clouds in my mind darkened during the long elevator ride. The bell rang and the doors opened. My feet hesitated. *I have to do this. There's no other way.*

Following a short walk down the hallway, I stood before a glass door, upon which "Krieger Brothers, Inc." was printed in bold black lettering. After entering, I passed a receptionist desk and a bank of cubicles. The computers were off and the chairs were empty. Light filtered into the dim room from an open door along the side wall. As I approached, Joe appeared in the doorway. "Hello Dave." He wore gray slacks and a white button-down shirt. His red hair was slicked back with mousse, gel, or some such substance.

"Thanks for meeting me here on a Saturday," I said, following him into his office.

"Of course." He settled into the high-back leather chair behind his desk. "I've always got time to talk to my most important client, especially when he has an urgent issue to discuss." A man of average height and build, Joe kept his chair adjusted a few inches higher than normal.

Taking a seat in front of his desk, I looked up at the framed degrees on the wall behind him. Since I had never told anyone about Beth, the words did not come easily. "I don't know how to begin," I mumbled. My eyes squeezed shut for one final internal debate on whether I actually wanted to do this. Moments later, I unloaded.

My nephew stared at me with a stone face the whole time I spoke. "Is that everything?" he asked, after I had stopped talking.

I nodded. "Yeah, that's it.... Joe, what am I going to do?"

"Does anyone else know?"

"I don't think so. Like I said, Ryan didn't seem to suspect me when we talked yesterday. Unless he's an incredible actor."

Joe's brow wrinkled in concentration. He leaned back and clasped his fingers behind his head. After about a minute, he shifted forward and squinted at me. "Okay. Our best option is a continuation of what you tried yesterday."

"But Ryan was adamant. He won't touch his wife with this issue hanging over him."

"Perhaps we can lessen his resolve."

"What do you have in mind?"

"As you know, Mr. Schaeffer is also my client. I'll give him a call this morning. Tell him I have an endorsement deal I'd like to discuss with him. We'll meet tonight at a gentlemen's club, somewhere in Newark or maybe West Orange. I think I know just the place." The corners of his mouth curled. "After drinking and watching the buxom ladies for a few hours, he'll be inebriated and ready for an amorous encounter. Then I take him home to the lovely Mrs. Schaeffer. Before sunrise, her baby has a daddy and you're in the clear." A look of confidence spread across his face.

"But Beth is talking like she loves me. She might refuse her husband's advances."

"That's where you come in. While I'm out with Ryan, you call Beth. Tell her in no uncertain terms that it's over between you two. You've decided to stay with your wife, and that's final. But don't be too hard on her. Can't push her over the edge. Just make it clear that you're out of the picture. Leave her with no options other than returning to Ryan. When I drop him off, she'll be more than ready to seek comfort in her husband's arms."

I rubbed my temples. I did not feel good about the plan, but saw no better alternative. "Alright, let's give it a try. I hope this works."

"It will. But if not, we have other options." The coldness of his tone disturbed me.

"Like what?"

"We need not worry about that now, Dave. I'm confident that Plan A will work."

The uneasiness grew in my stomach. "Joe, don't do anything crazy. I don't want this thing to get out of hand."

"Don't worry. Whatever we do, no one will get hurt."

"Good. Say, could you not tell Anthony? I don't want anyone else to know about this."

"Of course. In matters relating to my clients' behavior, I do not judge nor do I gossip. It's bad for business. My job is to increase their earnings, and that's what I do."

"Thanks." I stood and walked over to the window. Across the Hudson River the twin monoliths of the World Trade Center towered majestically above the lower Manhattan skyline.

"Relax, Dave. You've come to the right person. We'll fix this. I have as much interest in defusing this crisis as you do."

"You do?" I turned around.

"Absolutely," he said, his eyes widening. "Remember a few months ago when we talked politics?"

"Yes, but does that matter now? I'm on the brink of a scandal that could destroy my political career before it ever gets started."

"Do NOT talk like that." He pointed a finger at me, glaring. "This mess WILL be cleared up." His look softened. "People love you. And they will vote for you if you run. Think about the difference you could make once you're in office. You do still want that, don't you?"

"Well, yeah. But lately I haven't been able to think much about any long-term plans."

"A month from now this Beth thing will be a distant memory. You'll be free of her with your reputation intact. Then, we get to work. I'm thinking it's best if you move back to Iowa. We can start planning for a run at a House seat in '94."

"You think I should move?" The idea of relocating my life far away did sound appealing.

"Yes. I know you're a hero in New Jersey, but you're even more popular in Iowa. It's that whole local boy made good thing. Iowans consider you one of their own. You move back there and you'll have a strong base already in place."

"Yeah?"

"Absolutely. Next week I'll get to work on a preliminary plan. Throw some ideas and numbers together. Then you can get a basic idea of what I'm thinking. First though, I need to know your party. You're a Republican, right?"

"Actually, I'm registered as an independent."

He frowned. "No. That's no good. We need to get you into a party. Which one do you like?"

"I don't know," I said, still distracted by the crisis at hand.

"Well, what's your position on abortion?"

"I'm pro-life, though the thought of asking Beth to get an abortion did briefly cross my mind." I snorted with disgust. "Look at what a hypocrite I've become."

"Don't worry about it," Joe said. "This is politics. You don't need to practice or even believe your own rhetoric. I just need something to start crafting your official position on various issues. How about Israel? Does Dave King favor more or less support for Israel?"

"More."

"Government? Larger and more activist or smaller and laissez-faire?"

"I don't know. Can we talk about this some other time?"

"Of course," he said. "You're looking like a Republican to me. I'll start planning in that direction. We can always change later if necessary."

"You really want to do this? Politics? What about your agency? You and Anthony just moved into this great office here in Jersey City. You guys have dozens of clients."

He leaned back in his chair and sighed. "The agency is about money. That's all. Granted, the money has been good. But politics is about power." He clinched his fists. "*That* is what excites me. And you my beloved uncle, with your looks, intelligence, and name recognition, are the perfect candidate. With the right campaign manager you can win a House seat in '94. And that's just the beginning." A rare smile beamed across his face.

I left Joe's office a short time later. By the time I reached my car, I had already forgotten about politics. My mind could focus on only one thing—getting Ryan together with his wife. Joe called an hour after I got home. Ryan had agreed to meet with him that night. Everything was set.

After supper that evening I made up a story about wanting to bring home a dessert surprise for the kids. Racing to a nearby convenience store, I called Beth from a payphone. Our conversation was gut-wrenching. She cried. She yelled. She swore. Over and over she reminded me about the child she carried. Our child. I urged her to rebuild her marriage and raise the child with Ryan. "He's a good man," I said. "He'll be a good father."

Sometime after I deposited a second quarter in the phone, Beth calmed down. I could not tell if she was less upset or just tired of arguing. Either way, I was relieved that the assault upon my eardrum had subsided. I told her repeatedly that I had to go. She pleaded with me to stay on the line. Finally, I said goodbye and hung up.

My head rang with the aftereffects of the horrible conversation. I hoped that the call accomplished its intended purpose. The rest of the plan was out of my hands. Remembering my fake reason for being out, I sped over to a nearby Baskin-Robbins to buy an ice cream cake. Back home I explained my delay by saying I had to help an old lady change a flat tire. After six months of covering my tracks, the lies flowed easily off my tongue.

My body roiled with trepidation the rest of the evening. Even after going to bed, I remained tense. Nearly three hours passed before I fell asleep. The phone's piercing ring jolted me awake early the next morning. Dreading that it was Beth, I grabbed the receiver.

"Dave," Joe said, "there was a problem."

"Oh no." I felt my soul deflate.

"Sometime after I dropped off Ryan at his house last night, he shot himself.... He's dead."

"What did you do?" I gasped.

"I didn't do anything. I got him drunk and we watched some strippers. That's it. I didn't know about his condition."

"Condition? He had a condition? They're going to trace this back to ..." Hearing Gail roll over, I stopped myself. "There could be some trouble for somebody."

"No. Not at all. I just talked to the police. Since I was out with Ryan last night, an officer stopped by to ask me some questions. I told him that all we did was drink vodka and a few beers, which is the truth. They've already ruled it a suicide. You're not linked in any way."

"What about his wife?"

"Don't worry about her. The officer who talked to me is the same one who took her statement. Beth told him that Ryan was manic-depressive. She said he would sometimes stop taking his medication without telling her. He didn't like the side effects. So that's what everybody is going to think happened. Ryan stopped taking his drugs and got depressed. End of story. Listen, Beth is not going to drag your name into this. She'll want to keep the affair quiet just as much as you do. Think she wants people to know her husband killed himself because she was cheating on him?"

"Where is she?"

"The police took her to a friend's house. We'll contact her later. I'm guessing she'll want to terminate the pregnancy. You'll have to pay some money for that—and a little extra just to be safe—but then you'll be in the clear."

Feeling sick, I had to end the conversation. After I hung up, Gail asked who had called.

"Joe. One of my teammates killed himself." I ran to the bathroom and threw up.

Returning, I told Gail I did not feel well enough to go to church. She lay next to me in bed and held me in her arms. She thought I was upset because I had lost a friend. My guilt multiplied. I told her I would be okay while she and the kids went to church. A while later they left, and I was alone. A vision of Coach Kishman sitting dead in his office flashed through my head. My mind then conjured grotesque images of Ryan's lifeless body. Darkness surrounded my soul. A thick feeling of dread caused me to shake and sweat.

Around noon, I pulled myself out of bed and slunk downstairs. Kyle and Archie were watching a pregame show in the living room. I had forgotten that it was Super Bowl Sunday. There was going to be a party at our church. Members were encouraged to bring their non-Christian friends for a night of food, fun, football, and fellowship. Super Bowl MVP Dave King was to be one of the hosts. Gail let the head pastor know I was sick and could not attend.

By game time, word of Ryan Schaeffer's suicide had reached the major news outlets. There was a moment of silence for him prior to the kickoff. Thousands of heads bowed throughout the

Metrodome. I imagined each of them condemning me for the death of an innocent young man.

I remained slumped in my recliner while the Redskins battled the Bills on the television screen before me. My eyes were open, but I saw very little of the action. My sons occasionally shouted at the TV, rousing me from my haze. But each time, I sunk back into the fog a few seconds later. When the game ended, I did not know who won. Nor did I care.

Following the Super Bowl, *60 Minutes* aired a special interview with Bill and Hillary Clinton. The topic was infidelity. I clicked off the television and crawled back to bed. The phone rang. Gail came upstairs and said it was for me. It was Nathan. He wanted to get together—said it had been a while. We agreed to meet the next morning at an IHOP on the west side of Newark.

Before leaving the house Monday morning, I put on a Newark Eagles baseball cap to avoid being recognized. Nathan was already at the restaurant when I arrived. He said little while we waited for the hostess to seat us. No antics or goofy jokes this time. Later, at our booth, we shared a few words of distracted small talk. After the waitress brought our food, he prayed. He then stared at me. "Dave, I want to tell you about these two guys I once knew. One of them was rich. The other, poor."

"You know about the affair, don't you?"

"Oh man. There goes my story. It was a good one, too. I stayed up all night working on it." The restrained smile on his face faded away.

"When did you find out?"

"I heard rumors about something going on last August, when the team was at training camp. A couple of the players' wives were talking. One of them said she saw you and Beth Schaeffer out at some restaurant. I dismissed it as idle gossip. I thought, 'No way, not Dave King.' So I told her to stifle it. But the rumors continued. Every time, I defended you. 'That's impossible,' I said. But yesterday, Ryan Schaeffer kills himself. Man, I couldn't believe it. That guy had everything going for him. Then it hit me, why he might do that. My heart sank, amigo."

I looked down to escape his gaze. "It's bad, Nathan. It's really bad."

"I should have known something was up when you stopped coming to prayer breakfast and Bible study. Didn't return my calls either. But I figured with this retirement thing, maybe you wanted some space. I never dreamed you'd be messing around with a teammate's wife.... And now Ryan is gone." Nathan raised his bushy brows. "I heard he was out with your nephew the night before."

"Joe was just supposed to get him drunk, which is all he did. We didn't know Ryan had a problem with depression. All we wanted to do was get him to sleep with his wife."

"Huh?" He frowned in confusion.

Speaking in a low voice, I told him the whole story. Near the end, I struggled to blink back my tears.

His face paled. "Man, we go back eleven years. Why didn't you call me? Last summer, back when you were first tempted. I would've helped you. Together we could have stopped this thing before it ever got started."

"I know I should have called you." I poked at my eggs. "When I first met Beth, it was so exciting. This gorgeous young woman, she made me feel alive just by talking to me. Everything else in my life seemed dull by comparison, especially since I didn't have football anymore. Maybe I was feeling trapped. Still, I told myself nothing would ever happen. She was just a harmless fantasy. Then after something did happen, I thought I could break it off. And I did. We quit seeing each other for a while. But I weakened. I couldn't stop myself from going back."

Nathan took a drink of orange juice. "Yeah. When it comes to the senoritas, we dudes are stupid. Trying to resist that temptation by yourself, forget about it. You need your bros. 'Though one may be overpowered, two can defend themselves. A cord of three strands is not quickly broken.'"

I lowered my forehead into the palm of my hand. "I've really messed up. What am I going to do?"

"You need to repent. Get on your knees and confess everything to God."

"What I've done is unforgivable."

"No," he said, thrusting a finger at me. "What you did was bad, but not unforgivable. Don't underestimate God's compassion and mercy. And don't ever place limits on the redemptive power of Christ's blood. If you repent of your sin, God will take it away. 'As far as the east is from the west.' Remember?"

I nodded. "I know what I've read, but a man is dead because of me. And a woman who is not my wife is carrying my baby. Look at the lives I've ruined."

He sighed. "Yes, there will be fallout from all this. Actions always have consequences. But God will blot out your sin and start healing those who have been hurt."

"I'm scared about what's going to happen next." I looked out the window at the overcast sky.

"What's going to happen next is you're going to go home and tell Gail. Everything." Nathan's unyielding stare brought a paralyzing dread.

"Oh no."

"You have to, Dave. You have to face the music. Gail may not know it yet, but you've wronged her. You've damaged your marriage. Confessing to her is the first step toward repairing that damage."

I glanced down at my barely-touched food. My stomach twisting, I pushed the plate away. "What am I going to do about Beth?"

"Don't even think about contacting Beth. Jamie and I will visit her today. I won't tell her that we've talked. I'll just be there as the team chaplain."

"Pray for me, Nathan."

"I will bro. After we're through here, we'll go pray in the car. Then you go home and talk to Gail. Start making things right at home."

Back at my house, the nervous ache in my stomach intensified. Not ready to talk to Gail, I decided to wait until evening, after the kids were asleep. Seeking solitude, I retreated to the garage. My official reason for being out there was to fix a door opener that had stopped working. Cold and distracted, I had little success with that project. I eventually found myself sitting on the concrete floor, my arms wrapped around my knees.

Later that afternoon, Gail called me into the house. Nathan was on the phone. I took the call in the study. After hearing Gail hang up, he asked me how the talk went. "I haven't done it yet," I said. "I'll do it later tonight. How's Beth?"

"She's hurting, like you'd expect. This has been terrible for her."

Imagining Beth's grief crushed me even more.

"She didn't say anything about you," Nathan continued. "I don't think she knows the real reason why Joe asked her husband to go out Saturday night. All she told me was that Ryan met his agent to talk about some business deal."

"Is anybody still with her?"

"Yes, Jamie is. A couple friends are there too. Ryan's funeral will be Thursday in Illinois. Beth will be flying out there tomorrow morning. A bunch of the players and their wives are going. Beth may try to call you before she leaves. Hard to know what she's thinking. But you can be sure she's gonna want to talk to you sometime. That's why you've got to tell Gail as soon as possible. She needs to hear about this from you instead of the other woman."

After hanging up, I pulled the receiver off the cradle and buried it in my stomach until the beeping stopped and the line went dead.

I stewed in agony as the evening hours passed. By 10:30 the kids were in bed. I asked Gail to come to the basement with me. We sat on the overstuffed green sofa in the game room. She knew something was bothering me. With sympathy in her eyes, she grabbed my hand. I wanted to run away, but knew I had to do this. Jumping off the cliff, I began talking. Hearing my voice speak such terrible words caused my composure to break. Trembling, I continued onward.

Watching Gail's expression collapse tore me apart inside. Shock and anguish covered her face as the realization of what I had done crashed down upon her. She pulled her hand away from mine to wipe her welling eyes. She said nothing the whole time I talked.

"Gail, I'm sorry. I—"

She held up a hand to cut me off. Her mouth opened in an attempt to speak but no words came out. She then rose from the sofa and walked upstairs. Seconds later, I did the same. She stood in the living room facing the large bay window. Beyond the glass, white flurries swirled in the wind.

I approached. "Gail."

"I want you to go," she said, without turning around.

"Please, can't we talk about this?"

"I need you to be out of this house. Pack a suitcase and leave. I don't care where you go." Though spoken barely above a whisper, her words hit with sledgehammer force.

"Gail, I just—"

"Now, Dave. Go."

I treaded up the stairs. Passing the rooms of my sleeping children sent tears streaming from my eyes. After throwing some clothes and toiletries in a bag, I returned to the living room. With one hand covering her mouth, my wife stood like a statue facing the window. Moments later I was starting my car, trying to process how this had all come about. The tears flowed harder as I drove away from my home, banished to the darkness of the cold winter night.

Chapter 20 – February 1992

An Arctic blast slapped my body as I opened the door. Nathan stood before me wrapped in a purple Tornadoes parka. "You look like crap," he said, brushing past me into the room. "When's the last time you shaved, slacker?" I glanced out at the dark parking lot. Nathan's blue Escort was parked a few feet from the door. My Mustang, buried under a layer of snow, occupied the adjacent stall. I pulled the door shut as he draped his coat over a chair at the round table near the window.

"Looks like you're cramming for midterms." He gestured at the books strewn over the bed.

"Just doing some reading," I said. "Trying to figure out some stuff."

"Well in that case, I hope you got the right books." He examined the cover of one of the tomes before tossing it back on the bed.

"Any messages?"

"Yeah, here." He pulled a piece of paper from the back pocket of his jeans and handed it to me.

I read aloud. "Thor called – Wednesday. Ozzie called – Thursday."

"Thor? It's been forever since I talked to that farm boy. How's he doing?"

"Okay, I guess. Haven't talked to him for a couple months. He's living in Des Moines selling home security systems. Last fall he started teaching Sunday School—his youngest boy's class. Can you imagine that big oaf surrounded by a bunch of six-year-olds?"

Nathan chuckled before his expression turned serious. "You gonna tell him?"

"No. Just don't feel like having that conversation. I finally told Anthony last week. Hated to do it, but it was getting too hard to keep it from him. He'd been calling the house wanting various documents so he could get started on our taxes. I finally had to tell him, 'I'm living in a motel, Anthony. Want to know why?'"

"Hmpf. How about your brothers and sisters? You tell any of them?"

"No. Aside from Ozzie, I'm not really that close to any of 'em. Oh no! What day is it?"

"The ninth."

"Crap. Zoe's birthday was yesterday. Now I have to run out and get her a belated card."

"Bummer. So you gonna tell Ozzie?"

"If I keep living in this damn motel I'm going to have to. He's planning on visiting us in March for a few days. I'd rather he didn't know. I've been witnessing to him for years. Trying to get him to read the Bible. He just makes fun of me. Calls me the Church Lady. Imagine what he'd say if I told him I had an affair."

"You never know," Nathan said, lowering his stout body into the chair that held his parka. "Maybe God will use your experience to speak to his heart. You've been larger than life for a long time. This shows that you need God's forgiveness and mercy, just like everyone else."

I pushed aside some books and sat on the bed. "Nathan, I've been rotting here for two weeks. Gail won't even talk to me. How much longer is she going to keep me in limbo?"

He shrugged his shoulders. "Don't know, dog. She let you see the kids, didn't she?"

"Yeah, once. She had Marie call here to tell me when I could come over. Gail didn't even want to be in the same house with me. She stayed away the whole time I was there."

"How were the tadpoles?"

"It was rough, man. They don't understand why I'm gone. And why Mommy is so sad all the time. They're too young for this. Archie asked me if he did something to make me go away. Then, when I was leaving, Donnie started crying and asked if I was ever coming back. I about lost it." Unable to remain on Nathan, my blinking eyes moved to the drawn saffron flower-print drapes.

Moments of silence followed. "You didn't hear this from me," he said. "Jamie's been meeting with Gail about every day. Word is, your wife's about ready to talk to you."

"Really?" I looked at him again. "Is she going to let me come back home?"

"Don't know, man. Jamie don't either. But at least talking would be progress."

Frustration knotted my stomach. "Or she might tell me she wants a divorce. Man, I hate not knowing anything. Why is she letting me twist in the wind like this?"

"Listen, this is a time for you to work on yourself. Can't control what Gail does. So what you need to do is get in the Word. Pray. Start going to church again. Trust God. He's in control of this situation."

"I don't know anymore." I glanced at the television. It was on, but muted. On the screen raged an argument between the four people inside Herman's head.

"What? You doubting God now? Is that what this is all about?" He plucked two books off the bed. "Dominic Crossan. Marcus Borg. These are the Jesus Seminar guys, right?"

"They raise some interesting points," I said. "Haven't you ever wondered about Christianity? Did the stories in the Gospels actually happen?" The skepticism of my brother Adam echoed in my head. "Is the Bible really the inspired Word of God? Millions of people believe the Koran is the Word of God. Why don't we? Why is one book the Word of God and the other not?"

"Every believer has doubts at some point," Nathan said. "It's good to ask these questions and examine your faith. You wonder about the reliability of the Bible? Fine. A bunch of Christian scholars have addressed that issue. Norman Geisler, C.S. Lewis, F.F. Bruce. There are others. But forget about them for a second. Just look at history. People have been attacking the Bible for centuries. Trying to disprove it. The book always survives."

"Everybody's looking for something to believe, Nathan. Just because a book has survived doesn't mean it's inspired. The Koran is still here. So are the Vedas. Does that mean they're all from God?"

His gaze lingered on the floor for a few seconds. "I think the big issue with any scripture is, does it reflect reality or not. You know, the reality of the human condition. The reality of the world we live in. Based on those standards, the Bible looks true to me."

"If everything in the Bible is true, then why am I in this mess?" I asked with a flash of anger. "You say that the God of the Bible is in control. If that's the case, then why is Beth pregnant? Why did Ryan die? Why did God let that happen?"

His eyebrows rose. "You sound like a guy who shoots a man while robbing his house, and then blames God when the man dies. The Bible clearly states that we have choices. And we are responsible for every decision we make. God doesn't stop us from making mistakes."

I stared at him silently.

"Your experience over the past six months proves my point," he continued. "You're living the Bible. You turned away from God and now you're paying the price. You're reaping what you sowed, just like it says in Galatians. If you want to investigate Christianity and the Bible, that's okay. God isn't threatened by people searching for the truth. But don't use your own mistakes to question his sovereignty or the truth of his Word."

"I don't know what to think."

"That's because your thinking is still clouded, Dave. You've got to completely repent of your sin."

"I have repented," I said, walking to the sink to grab a piece of ice from a bucket.

"You still seeing Beth?"

"No. She wants to see me, but I haven't told her where I'm staying."

"You're still talking to her then?"

I nodded as my teeth crunched a frozen cube. "I use a payphone so she can't trace the call."

"You're thinking of getting together with her if Gail wants a divorce, aren't you?"

"Maybe. We would both be single."

"Man!" He slapped the table. "How is that repentance? You're a married man. You're married to Gail. Your focus should be on her, the woman you betrayed. You should be figuring out what you can do to fix your marriage, not making plans to be with someone else."

"Beth is part of this too, like it or not. I can't just ignore her. Not after everything she's been through."

Nathan stood. "Be careful with that. Don't let her talk you into getting together. Your wife is your first priority. If you meet Beth and Gail finds out. Shwooo, that would be bad."

"I know. I'm not going to meet her."

After a few more admonitions, Nathan shifted the conversation to the antics of his teenage boys. I was relieved to move on to a lighter topic. He left around 9:30. I cleared the snow off my car and drove to a 7-Eleven to buy a card for Zoe. After making the purchase, I found myself outside at a payphone on the front of the building.

She answered on the second ring. Her voice, once an igniter of fiery anticipation, now pricked me with sadness.

"Beth."

"Dave! I was hoping you would call."

"Are you alone?"

"I am now. Jamie Rodriguez stopped by earlier. She left about an hour ago."

"You okay?"

"I'd be better if I could see you. Why won't you tell me where you're staying?"

"I've told you, us seeing each other would only make things more complicated."

She was quiet. "You're going back to your wife, aren't you?"

"That might not be an option."

"Why don't you tell her that your feelings for me are too strong? I know that would be hard, but then we could finally start our new life together."

I waited for an elderly man to walk past me toward his car. "I've already betrayed my wife and children. I can't just abandon them now and go off and be happy with someone else."

"I know what we did was wrong, but what's done is done. I have feelings for you now, and you have feelings for me. We fell in love. We can't ignore that, Dave. You have to tell her you want to be with me."

My stomach churned. "I love my family. I can't cast them aside like that."

"That's great, Dave. Where was this love for your family when you were with me all those times? I thought you cared about me. But I guess you were just having a little fun."

"I *do* care about you, but our relationship hurt people. And if I tell my family I want to leave them, it would cause even more hurt."

"Guilt is not a good reason to go back to them." Her words came faster. "It would be worse for you to stay with Gail when your heart belongs to me. She'll get over you. She'll find someone new. And you won't be abandoning your children. You'll still be their father. You'll get joint custody. Eventually, they'll accept me as their stepmother. I'll win them over."

"Don't push, okay? It's not that easy. I've got a lot of shit in my head to sort through."

"Yeah, it must be rough for you," she sobbed. "Too bad you don't have it easy like me. My husband just killed himself and I'm carrying the child of a man who's going to abandon me if his wife takes him back. So I'm either a second choice or a castoff. But that's no big deal, because you've got a lot of shit to sort through."

Staggered by that blow, I leaned against the cold brick of the convenience store. "You know how devastated I am about Ryan. I never would have done any of this if I had known what was going to happen."

"It's a little late for that now." She sniffled and blew her nose.

"I'm sorry, Beth." I couldn't think of anything else to say.

There was silence before she started talking again. "About a year ago he started taking a new drug." Her voice was distant. "It worked wonders. It was like a miracle. No mood swings. No depression. I thought everything was going to be okay. After a few months, I pretty much forgot he had a condition. He did too. He forgot how dark things could get.... Sometime during the season, he stopped taking the pills. He thought they made him slower, sluggish. He didn't want to lose his starting spot."

"When was that?"

"I don't know exactly. He didn't tell me at the time. In December I found some unopened pill bottles. When I asked him about it, he said he didn't need them anymore. Said he played better without them. I begged him to take his medication, but he ignored me. Things between us were strained by then, so I couldn't push it. He told me he'd start taking them again after the season ended. He never did."

Memories of Ryan's youthful face flashed by. "Beth, you don't have to talk about this."

"When he came home that last night, I didn't think anything was wrong. He was drunk, but calm. He just came into the bedroom and stared at me. I was in bed watching TV. I asked him if everything was okay. He nodded. Then he smiled at me and walked out. I thought he was going to the kitchen to get something to eat. After about ten minutes he didn't come back, so I went to look for him. I was in the living room when I heard a gunshot in the basement. I was terrified … but I had to go down there."

Her words trailed off into crying. The sound drove a hundred nails into my skull.

"I—I found him," she finally said, her voice shuddering. "He was on the floor in the storage room next to a trunk where we kept a bunch of college stuff. One of our yearbooks was in his lap. It was opened to a picture of us as Homecoming king and queen."

My body shivered as she continued weeping. "Beth, I would do anything to bring him back. I wish I could change all this."

"Dave, don't leave me. Please don't leave me now."

My grief-stricken thoughts stumbled over each other. "I can't rush any decisions. I don't want to make a bad situation worse."

"I'm going to have our baby. I'm not getting an abortion."

"I don't want you to get an abortion."

"We should raise our child together. He or she will be an angel—something beautiful to rise above all this horrible stuff." A dreamy hope replaced the sobbing in her voice.

"Whatever happens, I'll help you. I'll take care of you and the baby. Whatever you need."

"I need YOU. Our baby needs a father. Please don't abandon us."

My heart ripped in two. I wanted to throw down the phone receiver and run away. "Both of you will be taken care of. I promise."

"Come over and hold me. Please." Her last word came as a whisper.

"I can't. I have to go. I'll call again soon."

She would not let me hang up. It took another ten minutes and another quarter before the conversation finally ended. Back at the motel, I buried my face in a pillow and lamented the horrible reality confronting me. *No matter what I do, I am betraying someone.*

The sound of a shower running in an adjacent room woke me up the next morning. Upon reading 11:04 on the clock, I rolled over and groaned. Minutes later I grabbed the remote and clicked on the TV. *The Price is Right* provided a welcome distraction. Just as the Showcase Showdown began, the phone rang.

"Dave, I'd like to talk to you." The sound of Gail's voice shocked me from my lethargy. I sat up and hit the mute button on the remote.

"Okay. When, uh, when would you like to meet?"

"Marie just took Donnie to the library. Can you come over here now?"

"Yes," I said, not wanting her to know I was still in bed. "I'll be right over."

"Fine."

Bolting into action, I hurriedly shaved, showered, and dressed. Ignoring speed limits cut my drive time to less than ten minutes. Fortunately, no police officers observed my race through Livingston.

An eerie feeling came over me as I walked up the sidewalk to the front door of my house. Though I had lived there for over a decade, I felt like a stranger—especially after ringing the doorbell. It had been two weeks since I had seen Gail. It felt like two years. Upon opening the door, she looked at me with the somber countenance of a widow.

Following her gesture, I sat on the burgundy leather sofa in the living room. She chose the matching armchair along the opposite wall. Her movements were stiff and formal. With the fireplace dormant and no lights turned on, the room was pale and gloomy.

"A few nights ago I had a dream," she began. "I was wandering through a field. The fog was thick and I was lost and scared. Then the fog thinned and I saw you standing in front of me. I was so happy. My fear went away because you were there. I ran to you and tried to hug you … but you hit me." She spoke in a vacant tone. The pain in her gaze caused me to regret my very existence. "I stumbled backwards and you hit me again. The blood from my face was everywhere. I begged you to stop, but you kept hitting me. You had this wild, angry look—like a beast."

"You know I wouldn't do that," I said, my voice cracking.

"Then I woke up. I was so relieved. It was just a dream. For an instant, life was normal again. I got out of bed and started thinking about what I would make the kids for breakfast. I tried to remember if any of them had a field trip or something special going on at school. I thought about asking if you wanted to meet me for lunch. Then it dawned on me. It was real. The nightmare. I'm living it every day. The terrible dream is my life now."

"I am so sorry, Gail."

"I'm still trying to figure it out. What I could've done differently. I just don't understand."

I closed my eyes as excuses and explanations swirled around my head. Nothing coalesced into a coherent reply.

"What happened is so far beyond the realm of possibility," she said. "I can't process it. How could the man I shared my life with for so long do this? I thought he was my best friend, but did I ever really know him? Or maybe it was me. Did I do something to make him turn against me?"

Unable to bear any more, I blurted out an explanation. "It wasn't you. It wasn't anything you did. I was dealing with a bunch of stuff. Injuries. The end of my football career. I had been a star quarterback since high school. I liked the attention—people treating me like I was a big deal. And then it was over. Suddenly, I was nothing. I felt like less of a man."

"Dave, I NEVER felt that way." She shook her head. "You were never less of a man to me. And our children didn't think any less of you either. You have always been their hero. We loved you more than ever. It didn't matter that you weren't in the NFL anymore. Yes, it was nice that you were a big success and made a lot of money. But football was never really that important. I would have loved you just as much if you were a menial laborer making minimum wage. Who you were on the inside was the man I loved. And my love for you has always been unconditional.... I'm just sorry you didn't feel the same way about me."

My heart shattered. "I never stopped loving you."

She stood and walked to the bay window. I recalled the night two weeks earlier when she cast me from the house. "Dave ... why? Was it because she's prettier than me?"

"No."

"Then what was it? What drew you to her, and away from me?"

"I don't know."

She spun around with truculent eyes. "There has to be a reason you chose her over me. What was it? Is she better in bed?"

Panicking at the force of her words, I scrambled for a response. "She's younger, I guess."

"Oh, that's great," Gail scoffed. "You just had to have a hot young babe, huh? Well, I'm sorry I keep getting older every year. I should have known better."

Paralyzed by shame, I said nothing. A deathly silence filled the room.

"You know, Tammy woke up bawling this morning," she said. "Then that got Donnie started. 'I want Daddy. When's he coming home?' No matter how many times it happens, I can never get used to it. The crying always tears me up inside." After wiping her eyes, she gripped me with an icy stare. "I hope it was good, Dave. I hope you and Beth had the best sex any two people ever had, because it came with one hell of a price tag."

"Gail, please."

"To think of all those hours I spent in aerobics class. I've busted my ass trying to stay in shape. I know I'm not a size four anymore, but I still look pretty damn good for someone who's given you four kids. Guess I can't compete with some cheerleader just out of college."

"It wasn't about sex," I said, reeling.

"It wasn't? So what exactly did you do with her all those times? What kept you going back for six months, all the while lying to your children and me? Was it her brownies? The stimulating conversation? Or maybe you two played Monopoly." She glared at me for a couple breaths. "Don't tell me it wasn't about sex! I'm not an idiot! Or maybe I am. For six months you pulled the wool over my eyes. I knew something was different, but I figured you were a little down about not playing football. Just needed some time for yourself. But no, you needed time to spend with your new girlfriend."

"It wasn't six months. I broke it off several times. We didn't see each other at all in October and November."

"But she was so damn good you just had to go back, right? Whenever you got into bed with me you were wishing it was her, weren't you?"

"No," I pleaded. "It wasn't like that. I wasn't in my right mind. It was like a drug addiction."

"I wish it would've been drugs. At least that I could understand. And you wouldn't be having a child with another woman." She wiped her eyes again and chuckled bitterly. "You know what's funny? I'm still on the Tornadoes party committee. Since Beth is the girlfriend of one of the players, I get to help plan her baby shower. How far along is she? Eight weeks? Guess I should get going on that."

"You don't have to—"

"No, it'll be fun. Since I know the player who happens to be the father, I can consult him. What theme do you think we should go with? Rainbows? Ponies? Adultery?"

"Gail, please." I stood. "Just stop."

Crossing her arms, she turned again to face the window.

"Gail, what can I do?" My voice quavered. "What should I do to …"

"I used to know this wonderful man," she said without turning around. "He had such a heart for God. And he seemed to really love me too. I fell in love with that man, but he left me. Now I'm faced with raising four children by myself. You want to do something? Go look for that man. I don't know why he left or where he went. Maybe he never even existed. All I know is that he's gone."

I slunk away to continue my life of exile.

Back in my cave at the motel, I spent the afternoon buried under the covers. A vending machine inside the motel office provided my supper that evening. Afterward, I tried to read a book about the historical origins of Christianity. Words and concepts jumbled incoherently. I flipped on the television, watching nothing in particular. Hours passed. Around midnight, I shut off the TV.

Sleep eluded me as I lay in darkness. Gail's stinging words echoed inside my head. Beth's plaintive cries joined in to form an anguishing chorus. Flailing about, I pushed the sheets away and then pulled them back. Beyond the drapes, a terrible noise cut through the night. It sounded something like the howl of an animal.

Creeping over to the window, I pushed open a small gap between the curtain panels. My room faced a parking strip that ran along the rear of the motel building. Beyond the strip was a field. Tangled stalks of dormant grass and flora poked through the layer of snow on the ground. Amid the moonlit desolation, three dark shapes appeared to be moving across the field. After I rubbed my eyes, the shapes were gone.

Moments later, I was back in bed fading from consciousness when I heard growling and scratching at the door. Springing up, I trained my ears in that direction. Silence. *Was that real or part of a dream?* Flopping back into my pillow, I again tried to drift off to sleep. The sound repeated to startle me awake once more. I clutched the covers to my body as my wide-open eyes fixed on the door. I prayed for daylight, but the night refused to pass. A tormenting voice spoke in my head. *You are completely alone now.*

Eons later, morning light seeped into the room. Peering through the curtains, I saw nothing but a few cars and an empty field. I opened the door. Several nicks and scratches marred the red paint on the outside, but I couldn't tell if they were preexisting or new. Slipping into my street clothes, I crossed the narrow parking lot to check the field. Hours of brisk wind had stirred the white powder, erasing any tracks that might have been made during the night. Back in the room, my unease grew stronger. The four walls seemed to inch closer. *Am I losing my mind?* Impulsively, I darted to my car and took off.

Driving without destination, I soon found myself heading west on I-78. The Mustang covered mile after mile of highway, eventually crossing the toll bridge over the Delaware River. Not far into Pennsylvania, a road sign informed me of Bethlehem's proximity. For some reason, I exited. As I rolled through town, my eyes were drawn to the older structures, especially the churches with tall steeples and the stately halls at Moravian College. A few of the aged stone buildings looked as if they could have been around during the Revolutionary War. I ate lunch downtown at Casa Mia Pizzeria.

Back on I-78, my car sped west through the mountains. I entered Harrisburg an hour and a half later. There, another sign beckoned me. This one drew me down Highway 15 until I reached the town of Gettysburg. South of the town was a vast military park that encompassed a huge battlefield. At the Visitor Center I learned that one could tour the area by car, an eighteen-mile circuit. Following the route designated on the tour map, I drove south along the ridges and woods where General Lee's men had long ago formed their line. Soon after rounding the southern tip of the loop, I came upon a wooded hill called Little Round Top. It was there that the men of the 20th Maine under Joshua Chamberlain endured fierce Confederate assaults to save the Union position, and maybe even the Union itself. I parked the car and got out.

My feet crunching the snow below, I ascended the rocky slope. Upon reaching the summit, I looked around in all directions. To the north and west, sun gleamed off the white layer covering the fields once contested by two mighty armies. Shutting my eyes, I heard the sounds of July 1863—cracking muskets, thundering cannons, shouts of charging infantry, groans of the mortally wounded. Overwhelmed, I found a nearby rock on which to sit.

I gazed up through skeletal trees. Words I had heard long ago rang though my head—*a man's character is his fate*. Sitting among the ghosts of those who had died with honor, I realized the depth of my own dishonor. A new understanding slowly pervaded my being. The separation from my creator became fully evident, leaving me with a hollow feeling inside. My soul ached for restoration, but I feared that my sin was too terrible for that to happen. I fell to my knees. Ignoring the chill of the wet snow soaking through my jeans, I began to pray.

"God, though unworthy to ask anything of you, I beg for your forgiveness. I confess my sin against you. I have done evil in your sight. Any punishment I receive is just. My only hope is that through your grace and mercy, you will remove my transgressions. I know that your love is unfailing and your compassion is great. Please cleanse me of my sin with the redemptive blood of Christ. Blot out my iniquity so that my heart will be pure and my spirit restored. Renew my strength so that I may tell others of your mercy and forever declare your praise. My heart is broken before you, God. I want to come back. I want to follow you again."

All became still among the barren trees surrounding me. With closed eyes, I let the quietness suffuse my being. After a time, my soul discerned something—an ethereal resonance just beyond my ability to comprehend. At last it became clear. There, kneeling on hallowed ground, I heard the forgiving whisper of God.

At the motel that evening, I prayed again—this time for Gail and my children, as well as for Beth and the child she carried. I then wrote a song for my wife, not knowing if I would ever have the chance to sing it to her. Despite the continuing uncertainty, peace buttressed my soul. Lying in the same bed where I was so tortured a night earlier, I no longer felt alone.

The next morning I called Nathan. I told him about my trip and asked if he thought it would be okay for me to call Gail. "Not yet," he said. "You may have found your path, but she might still need some time to find her own way through this. Give it a few days."

I hated to wait, but I knew he was right. She was so angry and had every right to be. She also had every right to divorce me. If God wanted her to take me back, I needed to give her plenty of time to hear the message. I spent the day praying and reading the Bible. I hoped the phone would ring. It did not.

The following day was Thursday. It was nearly a carbon copy of Wednesday. More praying. More Scripture. No calls. Friday morning, I rose early and called Joe at his office. He then added Anthony for a conference call, and the three of us talked business for half an hour. After hanging up, I realized that it was February 14th. I made a decision and picked up the phone again. Dialing the number, I was nervous but hopeful. She agreed to meet me.

Along the way, I stopped to buy a card, a box of chocolates, and a dozen red roses. I then drove to the house that was once my home. Gail opened the door. My heart stirred with longing. She, on the other hand, showed no emotion. Once inside, I handed the Valentine's gifts to her. She laid them on the coffee table. A moment later, I was sitting on the sofa. She sat in the chair across the room. These were the same spots we had occupied during our last talk. It was not a promising start.

Speaking first, I recounted what had happened on my trip to Pennsylvania. "You told me about a man you once knew who had a heart for God," I said. "I've found him. He wants to come home."

Her stare remained firm.

"Gail, I love you. More than ever. I fully realize now how much you mean to me. My life is empty without you. I'm sorry I hurt you and our children. I have no excuse for my actions. I hate what I did. I wish I could go back and take it all away. I know that's not possible, but I promise you nothing like that will ever happen again.... I have no right to expect you to take me back. If you don't, I'll understand. But you're the greatest earthly blessing God has ever given me. I'll do whatever it takes for us to be together again."

She stood and gathered up the roses from the coffee table. I prepared to duck. After smelling the flowers, she laid them back down. "I've been on a journey too," she said, sitting beside me on the sofa. "Doing a lot of what you did. Praying. Reading the Bible. I didn't make it to any Civil War battlefields, but I did take some walks. And I spent hours talking to my mother and Jamie. They both told me to take you back—that it was God's will. But I couldn't. I was still in shock. What happened was so overwhelming. It turned everything I thought I knew about life upside down. I didn't know if I could ever trust anyone again. I mean, I loved you with all my heart and you became someone else—a person I never imagined you would be. It even caused me to question my faith."

My spirit recoiled in shame.

"But last night, something happened." She paused to take a breath. "Lying in bed, I sensed that God was speaking to me. I felt he wanted me to know that he was working in your life and that you still belonged to him. I woke up this morning with a hope that our marriage would be restored. And then you called."

I wiped my welling eyes.

"I forgive you," she said. "And I still love you with all my heart. I want you to come home. I want us to be a family again."

I leaned into her arms. Her powerful hug sent currents of joy flowing through my body.

We spent the afternoon sitting together on the sofa eating chocolates and talking. Gail's face brightened when describing how excited the kids would be to find out I was home. We then discussed the future. Both of us liked the idea of moving back to the Midwest. That would place us closer to our families and farther from swirling rumors and painful memories. Eventually the subject of the unborn baby came up. "You'll have to pay child support," she said.

"Yeah, I've discussed a payment plan with Joe and Anthony. They're going to draw up some documents. If it's okay with you, I'm planning to be generous to her. She's been through hell, you know. And it will be another blow when I tell her I'm back home." The thought of one more heartrending conversation with Beth brought a wave of sadness.

"She has been through a lot," Gail said grimly.

Not wanting to lose the mood, I changed the subject back to something we had discussed earlier that afternoon. "So what do you think about that idea for my next career? If it works out, it could be a way for me to help a lot of people."

"Well, yes. It is exciting to think about, but also kind of scary."

"I won't do it if you don't want me to."

"I didn't say I don't want you to do it." She smiled. "It's just … it would be a quite an adjustment for us."

"Yes, it definitely would."

Chapter 21 – November 1994

The wind tousled my hair. The bottom of my coat flapped against my shins and calves. I was among old friends—some I hardly recognized, others had hardly changed. We stood waiting for our names to be called. Though pink from the chill, our faces glowed with pride.

"You seen the Rooster?" Tank asked.

"Yeah," I said with a chuckle. "He's been plucked."

"Clean as a cue ball."

I positioned myself so that Tank's girth shielded me from the wind. Several moments later my name echoed through the stadium. A surround sound cheer emanated from the stands. I walked across the grass to join the line that had formed on the field. A few more names boomed from the PA system. A few more men joined the line.

"There they are, ladies and gentlemen," the echoing voice announced. "Your 1979 national champion Western Iowa Falcons." The roar and standing ovation lasted at least three minutes. We, the honored, looked around the stadium, nodding and waving. The nostalgic aroma of Saturday afternoon football filled my nostrils. My heart yearned for the past.

The university president, a lively gray-haired sprite, bounded to the microphone stand several feet in front of us. In a high voice, he said something about being proud of all the esteemed alumni standing behind him. After recounting a few of the highlights from our undefeated season, he told the crowd that he had asked the quarterback to say a few words. I approached and shook his hand.

The eruption from the stands swarmed my ears. I scanned the crowd to find Gail and our children. Like everyone else, they stood cheering. I wondered what this was like for Kyle—experiencing the frenzied roar of 50,000 fans in total silence. Raising both hands, I motioned for the people to sit. They finally did. The stadium fell quiet.

"Thank you." I paused to listen to the reverberation of my amplified voice. "Thank you. It's a great thrill for all of us to be part of the Homecoming festivities this year. We appreciate all that you've done to celebrate the fifteenth anniversary of our national championship season." Bursts of applause rained down from above. "It's hard to believe that so many years have passed since we donned the green and white and stormed across this very field. In many ways, it seems like yesterday. Talking to that great group of guys behind me has brought back a lot of memories. I think all of us wish we could suit up for just one more game here at the stadium." As the crowd cheered, I glanced behind me. Nearly all the men in the line nodded their heads.

"We were proud to call ourselves Falcons—to be part of the great Western Iowa tradition. What an honor it was to play for a legend like Coach McNabb." I raised my eyes to the azure sky. "I wish he could be here today. But I know he's up there in heaven, probably still ribbing his buddy Bear Bryant about the Sugar Bowl." More applause. "Western Iowa will always occupy a special place in my heart. Attending the rally last night, walking across the beautiful campus, watching this game today—it's all been so wonderful." Though he clapped with everyone else, the university president repeatedly shifted his weight from one foot to the other. I recalled his request to keep my talk short so as not to delay the start of the third quarter.

"When we played, the fans were a big part of our success. We couldn't have done it without them. It's no different for those young men in the locker room right now. So when they come out here to take the field for the second half, let 'em hear your spirit! Keep it noisy in here for thirty more minutes of football and help these Falcons soar to victory!" Another ovation followed as the band started playing the school fight song. My former teammates and I waved at the cheering throng.

A short time later, I settled into my seat in the stands. Kyle gave me a crisp high five. Archie, Tammy, and Donnie followed suit. We had a great view of the action. The section reserved for the 1979 Falcons was front and center at the 50-yard line.

"Most of the other guys are sitting with only their wives," Gail said, her breath faintly visible. "Not many children in this section. How did you get six tickets?"

"We gotta get something for all the money we've contributed to this fine institution."

"Is that why the university president let you give the halftime speech?"

"Nope," I said, grinning. "That's because I was such an awesome quarterback."

She rolled her eyes and smacked me with the free end of her green scarf. The nostalgia thickened as I watched the rest of the game. Memories of long ago plays floated through my head. I could almost feel the leather ball in my hand, which ached to throw one more pass. Out on the field, Western Iowa rallied in the fourth quarter to take a 27-20 lead over Kent State. With a minute left to play, I felt a tap on my shoulder.

"We better get out there," Thor said, leaning over my shoulder. "Otherwise you'll get stuck in the crowd."

I nodded. Stepping over the feet of the people in my row, I made my way to the aisle. After exiting the stadium, we advanced halfway down a wide cement walkway that led to one of the main parking lots. There, we met two students holding placards. Jon, the stocky one with the blond crew cut, was the son of my brother Shane. Todd, the tall skinny guy, was one of Jon's frat brothers. Both were juniors at Western Iowa. I greeted them with a handshake. My nephew reminded me to affix my red, white, and blue elephant pin to my coat lapel.

A cheer rose skyward from the stadium. "Sounds like it's over," Thor said.

"You ready, Mr. Head of Security?" I asked him.

"Yes sir, boss."

Moments later a middle-aged couple exited from the stadium gate. Two young men wearing flannel followed. Four UWI coeds were not far behind. After them came a wave of excited fans. As always, my adrenaline surged before first contact. The middle-aged couple approached. Smiling, I extended a hand.

"Hello! I'm Dave King, candidate to be your representative in Congress."

That evening, the university held a banquet honoring the 1979 team in the main ballroom of the Student Union. The guest list included university officials, players and coaches—both former and current—and wealthy alumni known for their generosity to the football program. Adding spouses made for a crowded room. After devouring Omaha Steaks, guests were treated to a narrated slide show recapping our season and, of course, a cavalcade of speeches. The university president led off, followed by Coaches Vanderlinden, Jackson, and Wilt. The captains of the '79 team were next. Preston Coleman, a minister at an inner-city church in Chicago, spoke with eloquence about the importance of teamwork. Vince Hallohan, the bald and buff owner of a gym in Tucson, barked out some enthusiastic, but unintelligible, remarks. I was up next.

The university president had asked me not to mention politics during my speech. Even without his admonition, I had no intention of using the opportunity to promote my campaign. It was a relief to give a speech and not have to explain why I should be elected. My talk was all about the '79 Falcons, our splendid season, and how great it was to see everybody again.

The event nonetheless promised to benefit my campaign. Two large pictures of me in uniform were among the photos adorning the walls. A television screen showed clips from our championship season, including several of my best plays. And nearly all of the speakers, aside from myself, praised my leadership skills. Since reporters from three different newspapers covered the event, the accolades directed at me were certain to reach a wide audience. With the election only three days away, I could not have planned the timing of UWI's Homecoming celebration any better.

Sometime around eleven, the mingling and nostalgic reflections started to subside. After posing for a picture with a moneyed alumnus and his wife, I spotted Jon approaching. He was one of the student volunteers helping with the event.

"Dave, there's this woman outside in the commons area. She asked if it would be possible to get a word with you."

"Really? Is she a reporter?"

"I don't think so. She looks harmless enough. Kinda old. You know, like fifty. Hair's all done up. Got a nice dress and all that. Probably some rich lady wantin' to discuss a campaign contribution."

"Alright," I said with a sigh, "I'll meet her."

My nephew led me out of the ballroom and down a hallway. Thor followed about ten paces behind. Ever since I had hired him as my campaign bodyguard, he rarely let me out of his sight at public functions. He usually tried to remain inconspicuous by blending into the background. However, at six-three, 320 pounds, subterfuge was not his strong suit. His efforts sometimes reminded me of a rhinoceros trying to hide behind a sapling. Nonetheless, I always felt safer meeting the masses with a trusted friend watching my back.

Upon descending a flight of stairs, we entered the Union lobby. A woman rose from one of the upholstered chairs. She stood with her shoulders back in a dignified stance. Her lips formed a smile that was restrained and formal. I had never seen her before. We introduced ourselves. She was Lilly Nelson from Kenosha, Wisconsin.

"You've come a long way," I said. "Were you a student here?"

"Oh no. I did not attend Western Iowa."

"Oh." We stared at each other in awkward silence for a few moments.

"Actually, I'm here for my son," she said.

"I see. Is he thinking about enrolling here?"

"Well, he has enjoyed visiting the campus."

"Great. Would he start next fall?"

"No. He's a junior in high school."

"Ah, planning ahead. Excellent. Have you met with someone in the Admissions Office yet?"

"No." She looked pensive. "We came here so he could meet you."

"Oh," I said, assuming her son was a football fan. "Sure. I'd love to meet him. Is he here?"

Lilly nodded and then motioned to someone behind me. "His name is Tom."

I turned to spot a gangly teenager emerging from an alcove just off the lobby. He shuffled his feet while approaching. I stepped towards him with hand extended. "Hi Tom. I'm Dave King. It's nice to …" The features of his face became clearer as he neared. My head spun in sudden dizziness. "… meet you." I shook hands with him. Standing as tall as me, he met my eyes for only a second before looking away. It was long enough. I knew who he was.

Lilly stood next to her son. "Tom's father, my husband, passed away about a year ago. After that, Tom became curious about …"

"His birth parents," I said, studying Tom's face.

Lilly's eyes widened briefly. "Yes. It took some digging, but my lawyer found the names. We located his birth mother last month. She confirmed that you were …"

"Tom's birth father."

"Yes. I'm not a football fan, so I must confess that I had not heard of you. But Tom was quite excited." Her voice trailed off. The boy looked up and smiled. A camera flashed to my right. My brain was too overwhelmed to tell my eyes to find out who had snapped the picture.

"Wow. This is, uh, quite a surprise." Memories of Amy swirled through my head as I stared at Tom. "Guess we have some things to talk about," I said to him.

I waved to Jon, who was across the room talking to Thor. After I explained to my nephew that Tom and I needed a private place to talk, he led us to the College Republicans office in the basement of the Union. "No one will bother you in here," Jon said, unlocking the door. Lilly remained with us for a few minutes before leaving Tom and me alone. The features of his face—aside from the acne and thin vertical scar below his right temple—reminded me of what I saw when I looked in a mirror. His wavy hair, cut short and parted on the side, was a shade lighter than mine; his blue eyes were slightly darker than my own.

"So," I said, clearing my throat, "how's Amy? I mean, your mother, your birth mother?"

"Okay, I guess. Married. Got two kids."

"Where is she living now?"

"Outside of Chicago. Downers Grove."

"She doing okay?"

"Yeah." He nodded. "Guess so. Got a big house. Her husband's some kind of doctor or something. She's a volleyball coach at the college there." Tom's eyes sparked with curiosity when he looked at me.

"So you live in Kenosha?" Cool beads of sweat streaked down my sides.

"Yeah."

"Your mom said you're a junior this year. Do you play any sports?"

He paused. "I play basketball. Starting forward. I'm the best player on the team. Coach told me so in practice last week."

"Great. So you're liking school?"

"It's okay, I guess. I'm gettin' straight As." He glanced over at a bulletin board, which featured several anti-Clinton cartoons, a pair of George Will columns, and a large photo of Bo Derek in a swimsuit.

"Wow. That's outstanding. Do you have a girlfriend?"

"Oh yeah," he said, looking back at me. "Sure."

"What's her name?"

"Um ... Shirl, Shannon." He smiled and started wiggling his legs back and forth. "Actually, I don't have a girlfriend right now. Broke up with her. But I'll have several options once basketball season starts."

"I see." After a few more questions, I learned about his Honda Civic, his part-time job at a video rental store, and his Amiga 1200. He then asked me about playing in the NFL. When we had talked for about a half hour, I decided it was time to address *the* issue.

"Tom, did Amy tell you about the adoption?"

"A little. We didn't talk for very long. I don't think she was too psyched to see me."

"I'm sure she was just surprised. It certainly is a surprise for me. But I'm glad you're here. It's great to meet you. You know, I started praying for you even before you were born, and have been ever since."

"Thanks," he said, again looking at the bulletin board.

"Amy and I were freshmen here at Western Iowa when she got pregnant. Weren't much older than you are now. And we were breaking up. It wasn't really possible for us to raise you. We very much wanted a good life for you; we just couldn't provide it ourselves. I'm so thankful that a loving couple adopted you."

He nodded as his face reddened.

"Your mother mentioned that your father was a metallurgical engineer."

"Yeah."

"Wish I could have met him. Do you have any brothers or sisters?"

He shook his head.

"How long will you and your mom be staying in Iowa?"

"We're flying back home tomorrow night."

"I see. You probably heard that I'm running for office," I said with a smile. "With the election Tuesday, these next few days are going to be crazy. My campaign manager has got me racing all over the place. I've got to hit the road in the morning. So unfortunately, I won't be able to hang out with you tomorrow. But I'd like to spend more time with you. If it's okay with your mother, maybe you could fly down for a weekend later this month. I'd buy your ticket. We live in Johnston, not far from Des Moines. How does that sound?"

"Yeah, okay."

"For the rest of this weekend, you might like to hang out with my nephew Jon. He's a student here at Western Iowa. I think you met him. I'm sure he'd love to show you around campus tomorrow. Shoot, I bet you could even crash at his fraternity tonight—if your mom doesn't mind. Then you could get a taste of the college life."

He grinned. "Yeah. I'm sure Mom would be cool with that. After all, it would be like hanging out with my cousin."

"I guess it would," I said with a chuckle.

Shortly thereafter, we emerged from the office. Thor was pacing at the end of the hallway. I introduced him to Tom. "Thor here was my center in high school, college, and the pros. Wouldn't have won half as many games without him." I turned to Thor. "Does Gail know where I've been?" He nodded.

"Would you like to meet my wife?" I asked Tom.

He shrugged. "Okay."

Without a hint of awkwardness, Gail chatted pleasantly with my firstborn. Afterwards, Tom talked to his mother about staying at Jon's fraternity. She did not object. Jon, on the other hand, was reluctant to spend time with a high school kid he had never met before. He quickly warmed to the idea after I slipped him a fifty-dollar bill.

"You okay?" Gail asked when we were alone later that evening.

"Yeah. Didn't see that coming."

"I bet. So, what's going to happen now? Think he'll stay in contact?"

"I don't know."

The next morning I did not want to get out of bed at the hotel. Unfortunately, skipping church the Sunday before the election was not an option. Someone would notice and make it an issue. So my family and I attended the Council Bluffs Church of Christ. The sermon was encouraging and I met several nice people, though my presence seemed to elicit a few whispers and strange looks.

After the service, Gail and the kids piled into the Explorer and headed for home. Thor, standing next to a Buick, spoke to someone on a mobile phone while he waited for me to say goodbye to my family. He was to drive me to a campaign luncheon in Atlantic, a town halfway between Council Bluffs and Des Moines. I crawled into the passenger seat. "Joe just called," he said. "There's been a change of plans. The deal in Atlantic is cancelled." He started the ignition. "He wants you back at campaign headquarters ASAP."

"Huh? Why?"

He gestured at a newspaper lying in the backseat. I reached back and grabbed it. The front-page headline blared like a trumpet: "KING'S SECRET PRINCE." Below was a picture of Tom and me just after we had first met in the Union lobby. I was so shocked at the time, it did not occur to me that reporters were picking up on the story. The guy who wrote the article had interviewed Lilly while I talked to Tom in the College Republicans office. Now the world knew that Dave King had fathered a child with a woman who was not his wife.

After I finished the article, my face burned hot. "I'm ruined. Why did this have to happen now?" I flung the paper into the backseat. "Damn it!"

"Take it easy," Thor said. "Joe said he's got a plan. Didn't say what it was, but he sounded confident."

"I don't know what he can do about *this*," I grumbled. After a couple fretful hours on I-80, we reached my campaign headquarters on Grand Avenue in downtown Des Moines. I entered the conference room at the rear of the main office area. Joe, Anthony, and a man named Levi Zadok sat at a rectangular table waiting for me. Zadok, rotund and earthy, sported a salt and pepper beard that fully covered the lower half of his face. Republican Party officials had recommended him to me a year earlier when I announced my candidacy. Joe, agreeing that my campaign could use an outside professional, hired him to be our chief advisor.

Slamming the door behind me, I collapsed into a chair at the end of the table. "It's over," I announced. "We were so close, finally even in the polls. But we just can't overcome this."

"Oh ye of little faith," Zadok said in his characteristic baritone. Grinning, he exchanged a knowing glance with my nephews. "We've got a plan."

"Actually, this barely even requires a plan," Joe said. "All we have to do is go with it."

"Go with it," I said in disbelief. "Two days before the election, a story breaks that I fathered a child out of wedlock. You do remember I'm supposed to be the candidate of family values?"

"I can't believe you don't see it." Joe's lips curved to resemble a cat's mouth. "This fits perfectly with your message. For months we've hammered Smith as an out-of-control abortion-on-demand liberal. You, on the other hand, are the candidate who values life. The protector of the unborn. What Tom proves is that you not only talk the talk, you walk the walk."

"It proves I had sex outside of marriage. Not the best revelation for a Christian candidate. The opposition will be all over this."

"You were eighteen. A lot of kids are sexually active at that age, Christian or not."

"And those who aren't," Zadok added, "wish they were." He shoved a footlong sub into his mouth and ripped off a hefty chunk.

"Exactly," Joe continued. "Trust me on this, Dave. People are going to understand. Very few voters cast stones at you on the premarital sex issue. More important is what you did after you found out about the pregnancy."

I leaned back in my chair. "Adoption."

"Yes!" Joe slapped the table. "There you were, a freshman in college. Your girlfriend tells you she's pregnant. No way the two of you can raise a child. So what do you do? Abortion? Absolutely not. You gave that baby the opportunity to live—to be raised by parents who loved him. This shows that even as a teenager, you were a man of conviction. Just by showing up, young Tom has strengthened your pro-life credentials."

"You really think voters will see it that way?"

"They will after you explain it to them. I've scheduled a press conference for three o'clock. Here are your notes." Joe slid a couple sheets of paper across the table to me. "Basic stuff. You confirm that Tom is indeed your child. You are thrilled to learn that he was placed with an upstanding couple who gave him a good life. Something you could not do back in college. Mention that you told Gail about the baby long before you two were married. It was nobody else's business. Then, conclude by hammering home your pro-life message."

"And be sure to rip your opponent a new one for being a godless baby killer," Anthony added. Zadok, his mouth full of sandwich, chuckled.

"No," Joe said, "don't go that far. This press conference is all about being positive. Tom is a fine young man. You are looking forward to getting to know him better. Lilly and her late husband were wonderful parents. Amy is an admirable woman who joined you in making a noble decision. Get the point? Take the high road here and you come out smelling like a rose."

I skimmed the notes. "Hmm … maybe this will be okay."

"Better than that, my friend," Zadok said, after swallowing a gulp of pop. "This kid's really going to help us. Once we provide people with the proper interpretation, you're going to race ahead in the polls." He jabbed his half-eaten sandwich at me. "You've already got a lot going for you—the Contract with America, dissatisfaction with the Clintons, the advanced age of your opponent, demands for change. The people want new blood. They want Dave King."

"That reminds me," Joe said to Anthony. "Did you send those 'VOTE, Do It Now' T-shirts to Jon?"

"Yep, he got 'em. Said they'll be all over campus on Tuesday."

"Excellent. We need to get the MTV crowd to the polls."

Zadok chuckled. "Speaking of that, I loved the way you sent Dave around town in that '58 Chevy pickup to remind people of when Smith was first elected to office."

"The age thing works both ways," I said. "The Democrats have really pounded me about my lack of experience."

"That's nothing," Zadok responded, finishing off his sandwich. "Your celebrity status more than compensates for your inexperience. Plus, you've got a big advantage with how this district was redrawn in '92. This area is perfect for you. It includes the city where you grew up and the city where you starred as a college quarterback. I couldn't have drawn the Fourth District any better myself." He punctuated his statement with a vigorous eructation. Anthony snickered.

"Celebrity will only take me so far. It's the message that counts."

"That's true. And you've got a great message: protecting the rights of the unborn, strong national defense, lower taxes, smaller government. But don't sell this celebrity thing short. Look at Oklahoma. There you got two football players who are going to make it to the House. And right here in Iowa, who's the representative from the Fifth District?"

"Fred Grandy."

"That's right." Zadok wadded his yellow sandwich wrapper into a ball. "If Iowans will vote for a Gopher, they'll definitely vote for a Super Bowl MVP."

"Don't make fun of Fred," I said. "He and his people have been good to us. Gave us a lot of helpful advice when we were just getting started."

"Sure, sure." Zadok tossed his wrapper into a wastebasket in the corner. "I'm just saying the people dig you. Crowds go crazy when you show up. You're a handsome guy, you know how to give a decent speech, and you connect with people. Voters are listening to your message. There's an electricity about this campaign. I felt the energy months ago when you beat that doctor in the primary. Your volunteers are excited, especially the young ones out there canvassing and distributing fliers. And look at the contributions that have been rolling in. People want to be on your team, Mr. NFL."

"Don't forget all the work these two guys have done," I said gesturing at Joe, who nodded, and Anthony, who smiled.

"Indeed. These boys have run a fine campaign. Not bad for a couple of rookies."

"Let's not congratulate ourselves yet," Joe said in a stern tone. "The election is two days away and there is much work to be done."

"Ah, Joe Krieger, the master tactician," Zadok said, rising from his chair. "That calculating brain of yours never shuts off, huh? Oh, that reminds me, I just saw your latest TV ad—the *Mr. Smith Goes to Washington* parody. Funny and memorable, with a subtle punch. Classic stuff."

"Yeah," I said, "I have to watch these guys all the time. I've told them not to go negative."

"But that was the beauty of it." Zadok grinned, causing a few sandwich crumbs to fall from his beard. "It wasn't negative. Not on the surface. The jabs were camouflaged and that Jimmy Stewart impersonation for the voiceover was perfect. I tell you, I'm glad this boy wonder nephew of yours is on our side."

Joe remained serious. "After your afternoon press conference, you've got a rally at Living History Farms. Here's your speech." He slid the stapled sheets to me. "Then we head over to Valley Junction. Later tonight, we've got that deal with the governor at the Convention Center."

I sighed. "You know, it's funny. I retired from football because my body couldn't take the pounding anymore. Yet, somehow, I've ended up doing something that's even more grueling."

"At least with politics you're not getting physically knocked to the ground," Zadok quipped, sliding over to slap my back.

"That's some consolation, I guess. And here if I win, I can make a real difference in people's lives." I heard voices out front. "Sounds like the volunteers are starting to file in. I should go thank them for all their hard work. Give them some encouragement before they hit the phones."

"Amazing," Zadok said. "I've been in this game for almost thirty years. I can count on one hand the number of candidates who actually got into politics because they genuinely wanted to help people. They all say they do, mind you, but most of them don't really mean it. Dave King, you are a true believer. It's inspiring, even to a cold-hearted cynic like me."

"Thanks, Levi." I opened the door to leave the room.

"We'll see how long that lasts." The big man unleashed a boisterous laugh.

It was nearly eleven that night when I rolled down the long driveway to my acreage just outside Johnston. Ozzie's black Corvette was parked near the house. After pulling into the garage, I contemplated taking a nap right there in the driver's seat. But curiosity barely won out over fatigue. Feeling like my suit was made of concrete, I trudged through the kitchen and into the living room. Ozzie thrashed about on the floor wrestling with my three sons, their faces crimson with laughter. Tammy stood nearby pretending to be a schoolmarm admonishing her unruly students. Gail sat on the sofa surveying the scene with a slight smile. Noticing my presence, she shrugged her shoulders at the frivolity before us.

"Daaaaaad," Donnie yelled as he escaped the pile and ran over to hug my waist. "Guess what Uncle Ozzie taught me?"

I knelt down and looked into his mirthful eyes. "Donnie, my precious son, I think that's the scariest thing I've ever heard you say."

He was confused for a moment. "No, it's funny. Sounds just like the real thing." He slid his left hand to his right armpit and started flapping his arm.

"Okay sport, that's enough," I said, after his efforts had produced a succession of squeaks. "Actually, it's time for all of you to go to bed. You've got school tomorrow." The four children, five counting Ozzie, groaned in protest. "Come on, let's go." I snapped my fingers. "Give Uncle Ozzie a hug and head up to bed."

My brother complimented his goodbyes with a series of noogies. Gail then corralled our offspring and herded them toward the stairs. "See you soon," Ozzie signed when Kyle turned around for one last wave.

"So Oz, aside from corrupting my children, to what do I owe this honor?" I shed my suit jacket and tossed it on the sofa.

"Got to ask you something," he said, still lying on the floor.

"Alright. Hey, let's talk downstairs. My back's killing me. I need my comfortable chair.... You want any pop?"

He nodded. I grabbed two Wild Cherry Pepsis from the refrigerator and we descended to the basement. Bandit, who had been resting by the fireplace, followed along. His tags jangled with each step. After flipping on the florescent lights in the game room, I settled into the sweet relief of my leather recliner. Ozzie grabbed a small round Nerf ball from the toy box. Bandit curled up on the white fur rug under the pool table.

"So, Citizen King," Ozzie said, "rough day on the campaign trail?"

"Ugh. They're all rough."

"Yeah, I hate it when one of my secret sons shows up." He lofted the soft orange ball at a plastic hoop on the wall. "Especially when the press is around."

"Yes. Things like that can make for an interesting day." I appraised the ever-expanding bald spot crowning his head.

"Gotta say, you kept that one quiet. I never would have dreamed you were getting some action in college." He shot another basket. "Were you ever going to tell me about this kid?"

"No. Long ago, I decided it was best to keep this as quiet as possible on my end."

"You've never told anybody?"

"Just Gail, back when we were dating. And I told Joe at the start of the campaign. He wanted to know if I had any skeletons in my closet so he could be ready with damage control. I never told anyone else."

Mouth agape, Ozzie stopped shooting. "Wait a minute. You told our creepy nephew and you didn't tell me. I'm hurt, Dave. I've always treated you like a brother and this is how you repay me."

"I had to tell Joe. In politics you never know what your opponents are going to dig up about you. It's a good thing I did tell him about the adoption. You have to admit, he came up with an effective response. The press conference today went great. I think this will turn out okay. Won't know for sure until Tuesday though."

"Hmpf. You think you know somebody." Ozzie lobbed another shot at the basket. "So, you got any other secret kids out there running around?"

Thanks to months of training from Joe and Zadok, I had learned to keep a poker face when questioned about difficult subjects. But after an exhausting day, the cobwebs filled my head. I momentarily dropped my guard. My brother, glancing at me right after his last question, saw it—the fearful wide-eyed expression of someone with something to hide. It flashed across my face for no more than an instant, but that's all it took.

"Oh, no way!" he exclaimed. "You ARE hiding something else. Man, who are you?" He leaned over me with his hands on his hips. "Are you telling me that this nerdy Christian thing was just an act? All these years you've been partying and getting laid by different women, haven't you? Dude, the Wizard could have been your wingman."

Squeezing my eyelids shut, I debated how much to reveal. "It's not like that, Oz. But there is something else. It's big." I gestured at the recliner across from mine. "Have a seat."

Sitting on the edge of the chair, he leaned forward, his face frozen with anticipation.

"You have to swear not to tell anyone."

"Of course. If there's anybody who knows how to keep stuff quiet, it's me."

"Alright." I took a deep breath. "It started three years ago when we were still in New Jersey. It was summer, about the time I announced my retirement. I met this girl. She was married to one of the other players—a rookie."

And so I told Ozzie about Beth Schaeffer and me. With eyes wide, he absorbed every word. "She took it hard when I went back to Gail. It tore my heart out. Several months after having the baby, she moved back to Illinois. Cairo, her hometown. I'm not in contact with her anymore, but she sends letters to my campaign office to keep me updated about the child. Sends pictures of him, too. Cute little guy. He just turned two. She wants me to be part of his life. I can't, you know."

Ozzie was speechless, a rare phenomenon. "Wow," he finally said, flopping back in the recliner. "I mean … wow … it's … whoa."

"Yeah, I know."

"Aren't you worried that Beth will tell someone? You're running for public office now. People are just aching to find dirt on you. Giving up a kid for adoption in college is one thing. But adultery, a dude offing himself, another baby—that could wreck your campaign." He rubbed his fuzzy goatee.

"I think about that every day, Oz. It almost kept me from running. After Gail took me back, I prayed about what to do with my life. It seemed like God was leading me into politics. It was a risky move given all that had happened, but I moved forward in faith. I'm trusting God. It's in his hands."

"But man! Beth could go forward anytime—pull a Gennifer Flowers on you. She could be waiting for just the right moment to bring you down."

"I know. That possibility is always there. But I am paying her a hefty chunk of change in child support. Even more than the courts would've awarded her. Anthony sends the checks. He and Joe consider it hush money. I don't know if that's it. Whatever the reason, she's kept quiet."

"For now," he said, raising his eyebrows.

"Yeah, for now. But I don't think she's too excited about publicizing the affair either. She doesn't want people to know her husband killed himself while she was cheating on him. So as far as anyone knows, Ryan is the father of that boy she's raising."

"You don't think anyone else found out? Other players? People who knew you guys? I bet somebody suspected something."

"Yeah, there were rumors. But I don't think anybody has any hard evidence. I did tell Nathan Rodriguez, the team chaplain. He and his wife are the only people in New Jersey who know the whole story…. I hope."

"But somebody who suspected could come here and feed rumors to your opponent."

"As long as Beth doesn't talk, there is no story. And if anybody prints anything unsubstantiated, Joe will hit back with a libel suit."

Ozzie was quiet for a while. "Damn. When you said you had something big to tell me, I never would have guessed this. I just figured you were finally coming out of the closet."

"Shut up. Jerk."

He snickered. "I'm just giving you shit."

"You think I'm a big hypocrite now, don't you?"

"Not really. You're a man. You're made of the same stuff as me. I always thought it would be difficult trying to resist the nubile vixens who throw themselves at football players. I myself wouldn't know what that's like," he said through gritted teeth. "But I can imagine it would be really tough. So, no judgment here."

"Thanks."

"Sounds like you might think of yourself as a hypocrite though."

I leaned back in reflection. "Sometimes. Especially when I'm asked to speak at Christian functions. You know, Promise Keeper rallies, youth groups, church events—stuff like that."

"Don't be too hard on yourself. We dudes are programmed to admire the ladies. It's not like you went out looking for trouble. Trouble found you at a time when you were vulnerable. You tripped up. That happens to guys—a lot. At least you did the right thing afterwards. Many dudes don't. You're still a decent person."

"Thanks, Oz. That's actually one of the coolest things you've ever said to me."

He paused. "Of course, you gotta admit, you're not the sharpest tool in the shed."

I sighed. "You could have just left it at what you said earlier."

"Well, it's like you've never even heard of birth control. I can understand giving in to temptation, but you don't need knock up every woman you're with. That's not smart. Kinda reminds me of one of those inbred yokels on *Springer*."

"That's enough, Oswald."

"Seriously Dave, do you know how to use a condom? I mean, it's like you're the poster boy for why sex education should be mandatory in school."

An angry surge of adrenaline shot through my weary limbs. I lunged toward him. Anticipating my charge, he slithered out of his chair. Unable to stop my momentum, my face slammed into the padded leather where his back had rested a moment earlier. I growled as stars appeared before my eyes. The pain, along with my brother's laughter, added to my fury. "I'm going to wring your bony neck," I said, bounding up. He sought refuge behind the pool table. I faced him on the opposite side.

"This isn't very dignified behavior for a congressional candidate," he snorted.

I leaned across the table to swipe at him, but he backed away like a crab. "That's right, laugh it up now," I said. "When I catch you, I'm going to shove a pool stick up your ass."

"My, my. What would Jesus say about such talk? Don't forget what the Bible says in First John: 'Whoever loves God must also love his brother.' I gotta say, Dave, I'm not feeling much love from you right now."

"YOU are quoting scripture to me?" I stalked around the table. He moved in the opposite direction to keep the barrier between us. Bandit continued snoring on the rug below.

"After hearing you whine about the Bible for the past two decades, I figured I should check it out. See what the big deal is."

"Well?"

"It's a little preachy and long-winded in places, but I like some of the stories. Especially all the smiting and ass-kicking in the Old Testament."

I stopped my fruitless trek around the table.

"How about this," he said. "If I promise to read one of the Gospels all the way through, will you stop this childish behavior? I mean really, you're just embarrassing yourself."

"Fine." I leaned forward on the green surface of the pool table.

"Good.... Want to shoot a game?"

I glanced at the colored balls in the corner pocket. "Yeah, why not?"

After Ozzie shot the break, he looked over at me and said, "Hey, I almost forgot. I wanted to ask you something."

"Wonderful." Assessing the angles for my first shot, I braced for another smart-aleck comment. "This better not have anything to do with gay hobbits." Sliding the cue stick through my fingers, I aimed at the center of the white ball. Slowly, I drew back.

"I was wondering if you'd be my best man."

My arm lurched forward in spasmodic reaction. The cue sent the ball sailing off the table. The hard white sphere flew across the room and brained a three-foot-tall Snoopy standing by the wall. "What the, huh?" I stammered, as the stuffed dog toppled over. Bandit, awakening with a snort, sauntered over to investigate the commotion.

"Yep, I'm finally gettin' hitched. You know Sandy, that chick in HR I've been seeing the past year? I popped the question Friday night and the dumb girl said yes."

"That's great!"

Ozzie shuffled over to retrieve the cue ball before Bandit could snatch it up. The black Lab then sniffed Snoopy's motionless corpse. "Well?" my brother asked, setting the ball on the table.

"Of course. Yes. I'd be honored." I stepped forward and hugged him.

After a couple seconds, he pulled away. "Okay Dave, let's not make this Hallmark Moment any gayer than it already is."

"I'm so happy for you, Oz." A grin stretched across my face. "When's the big day?"

"July fifteenth. If she doesn't wise up before then." He eyed his next shot. "Oh, you don't need to go overboard for the bachelor's party. Two strippers will be fine. But would you make sure they start out looking like Judy Garland? You know, the Dorothy look? With that blue checkered jumper, the white blouse, and the long pigtails. The ruby slippers too. Gotta have those."

Uh yeah, Oz, I'll get right on that."

My long and winding campaign trail finally ended Tuesday night in the second floor ballroom of Adventureland Inn in Altoona, a suburb northeast of Des Moines. The tension was thick, almost as thick as the jungle of red, white, and blue decorations cluttering the room. Piranhas gnawed away at the walls of my stomach. It reminded me of what I used to feel before a big football game. This was actually worse though, because I could not burn away the nervous energy on the field. Encased in a dark blue suit, all I could do was roam about mingling with supporters.

Gail floated gracefully through the crowd in a stunning scarlet gown. Her bright smile spread optimism among the anxious gathering. Stone-faced Thor patrolled the perimeter of the room, looking like a bear ready to pounce. My six brothers and sisters were also in attendance. Ozzie's fiancée Sandy, normally a shy and somewhat mousy girl, showed off her new rock with pride. Her intended remained close by, grinning awkwardly. The domestication process had already begun. Zoe, her hair recently colored for the occasion, beamed as she subtly reminded people that she was the mother of my campaign manager and finance chair. Counting Joe and Anthony, eleven of my nieces and nephews populated the ballroom. Since eight of them were of voting age, more than one staff worker had joked that the votes of just my relatives could carry me to victory. Adam, however, made little secret that he did not cast a ballot for me. "I can never vote for a Republican," he said, "even if he is my brother." He nonetheless promised not to groan too loudly if I won.

My nerves tightened as the first returns flashed across the television screen. With one percent of the precincts reporting, I trailed by 287 votes. The mood in the room deflated. "Not to worry," Zadok bellowed. "Those are from a Democratic district. We'll pull ahead when the Republican counties are counted." His prediction proved prescient when a half hour later I had 51 percent of the tallies. A huge cheer erupted in the ballroom. In next returns, however, I trailed by two points with ten percent of the vote counted. My gut clenched.

As the tension-filled minutes passed, TV reporters and their cameramen hovered nearby to ensure they could capture my reaction when news of victory or defeat became evident. Joe stalked to and fro talking on a mobile phone. He looked like a constipated lawyer holding a gray brick to the side of his head. At one point, he decided that I should be sitting with Gail and my children watching the coverage. "It will be good for your 'family values' image," he said. I collected my wife and, with the help of my teenage nieces Jolene and Hannah, rounded up our roaming offspring.

Finally the six of us sat as one big happy family in front of a large TV screen in the corner of the ballroom. Viewers at home had no idea that we had to promise our dressed-up little angels copious amounts of pizza and ice cream to get them to sit still. Before the cameras lit up, Zadok asked a lady to adjust the makeup around Archie's eye. He had received a shiner during a fight at school the day before. Some classmates had been taunting him about having a "secret" brother, so he started swinging. It broke my heart when I found out what had happened. Not wanting to punish him for my past, I let him off with a short lecture about keeping his cool.

The cameras started rolling when word arrived that the next returns were imminent. Moments later, the numbers appeared on the screen before us. I had 52 percent of the vote, a lead of more than 1,600 ballots. Gail and I smiled with restraint. Kyle and Archie leapt to their feet and high-fived. Tammy and Donnie jumped up and down. Shouts filled the room. A reporter asked me how I felt. I said something about feeling optimistic. Twenty minutes later, I had a 53-47 lead with thirty percent of the precincts reporting. Fifteen minutes after that, CBS declared me the winner. Gail threw her arms around me as we sprang from our seats.

A massive celebration broke out in the ballroom. The scene reminded me of the postgame parties after the Sugar Bowl and the Super Bowl. Like those victories, this was a team effort. But this time the team was named Dave King. That made the victory even more exciting for me.

The rest of the evening was a storm of happy chaos that included more interviews, an avalanche of hugs, and my opponent calling to congratulate me. In my victory speech I thanked him for his many years of distinguished service to the state of Iowa and the nation. I then thanked Joe, Anthony, and Zadok for running a successful campaign. I also praised the rest of my staff, my supporters, and the legions of volunteers who had worked so hard to get me elected. I concluded by expressing my thanks to Gail for supporting my decision to run and for keeping me sane through the arduous journey.

The party raged for several hours. The Republican sweep of the House and the Senate added to our elation. Just after 3:00 a.m., Gail and I found ourselves slumped in chairs at a table strewn with empty glasses and other debris. Only a few stragglers remained in the ballroom, which resembled a patriotic garbage dump. My ears rang. My temples throbbed. My stomach ached. Gail appeared to be in a similar state. Fortunately, my sister Abby had volunteered hours earlier to take our exhausted children home and put them to bed.

"Well, the fun part is over," Gail said.

"That was the fun part? I think I'm dead. Don't wake me up until Christmas."

"Uh-uh. Your work has just begun. I've made a list. You have to find a place in Washington, assemble a staff, meet your 434 colleagues—and now you have a half million new bosses here in Iowa. They might have something for you to do, too. What do you think about that, Congressman King?"

"Uhhhhhhh," I moaned. "What have I gotten myself into?"

Chapter 22 – August 1999

"Fifteen-forty," I announced, tossing the yellow ball above my head. As it reached the top of its ascent, I swung my racket in a sweeping arc. With a deep PONG the tight strings drove the ball over the net. It landed just inside the service box. Like a cat, Gail sprang to her left and met the serve with a crisp backhand. The ball rocketed back across the court to my right. Fighting the ancient pain in my knee, I sidled down the baseline and with a lunge sent a return arcing back in the opposite direction. My wife waited for the ball to bounce into her sights. She then stepped forward and unleashed a ferocious forehand. A yellow laser blazed over the net. I watched helplessly as it hit about six inches inside the far corner of my backcourt.

"That's game and set," Gail announced, waving her racket above her head. "You've been getting soft sitting in that office in Washington." She skipped up to the net.

I trudged forward to meet her. "Yeah, I've really got to spend less time trying to help govern this country. Say, where'd you learn to hit like that?"

"Kyle and I have been playing this summer."

"Great. While I'm rotting away in the House chamber listening to the endless droning of my colleagues, you're out here playing in the sun learning how to kick my butt."

"It's called spending quality time with our son," she said with smile. We walked off the court toward a round deck table shaded under a large green umbrella.

"Well, I've got a month before I have to go back to D.C. Maybe that'll give me time to brush up on my game so I can give you a challenge."

"Don't bet on it. I barely broke a sweat mopping up the court with you this afternoon."

"That's enough out of you, woman." As she patted her face with a towel, I wrapped my arms around her from behind. "And what's the deal with these little shorts? They could be considered an unfair distraction, don't you think?"

"No," she said, breaking free and pecking my cheek. "I'm just wearing comfortable sporting attire. But next time, just to give you a chance, I'll wear an ankle-length dress buttoned up to my neck. I don't know if that will help though. You looked really slow out there today." She tapped my rear end with her racket and slid into a chair at the table.

"Is that any way to talk to your congressman?" I wiped my face and sat down.

She grinned. "I've heard people say much worse about you."

"Yeah, but those were Democrats. They don't count." I stretched out my legs before me. "Where are Kyle and Archie? Maybe they'd like to play some doubles. I get Kyle though."

"They took off. Said they were going to the Fair with some friends."

Gazing across a section of lawn, my eyes settled on the pool beside our house. Tom and my nephew Jon were having a cannonball contest. "How about those two jokers?" I asked.

Gail craned her neck and squinted at the pool. "Don't think so. The boys tried to get Tom to play doubles with them last week. No go. He still doesn't do much with our kids." She looked back at me. "He's either hanging out with Jon or on our computer surfing the Web."

"I guess that's to be expected. It's still kind of an awkward situation for him."

My wife frowned. "It's a little weird though. He always accepts your invite to come stay with us for a couple weeks in August, but then he virtually ignores us when he's here."

"He and I do things together."

She tightened her lips. "Yes, but when you two are doing something, he doesn't want anyone else around. You have to admit, there's an aloofness about him."

"Well, he is going to the lake with all of us Saturday. But I know what you mean. I've seen it too. I really thought he'd be getting along better with our boys by now. Still, I'm glad he's here. I feel like we can make a difference in his life. I think he benefits from being around his father and a godly family."

"I know you have good intentions, and I support what you're trying to do. But regardless of the biology, you're not really his father. His real dad died years ago. You can't ignore that."

I continued watching Tom and Jon splash about the pool. "I guess we should be thankful he connects with someone in our family."

Gail paused. "What *is* the deal with Jon?" she asked, lowering her voice though no one was close enough to hear us. "It's been two years since he graduated college and he's still never had a real job. Archie told me that he usually just plays video games at his apartment all day. Except when Tom is visiting us, of course. Then he's over here hanging out in our pool all afternoon."

"Really? Jon still doesn't have a job? Shane told me he had some good prospects."

"Guess they fell through. Unless his boss lets him take a really long lunch."

"Well, it won't be long before Tom heads back to Wisconsin for college. Then neither of them will be around here to bother you."

"They don't *bother* me," she protested. "It's just … odd. I don't know."

"Hey, you two." A young female voice called our attention to the tennis court gate. Tammy sauntered toward us. "Done playing already?"

"Yes," Gail said. "Your geriatric father doesn't put up much of a fight anymore."

"Hey! I'm ONLY forty-one," I said. "Just like you, my love."

"But with all those years playing football, you've got the body of a much older man."

They both giggled. "Now I forgot what I was going to say," Tammy said, her summer-tanned face beaming with levity. "Oh, I remember. Kim just called. She has a piano solo at the recital tomorrow. She's like really freaking out. I kinda told her I'd help her practice. Could I get a ride over there tonight?" My daughter's green eyes brightened with hope.

"Of course, honey," Gail said. "One of us will take you. Or one of your brothers will if they're back by then."

"Weren't you going to cook for us tonight?" I asked.

"Yeah, I'm still cooking," Tammy said. "I won't leave 'til after supper."

"What's on the menu?"

"Yankee pot roast, mashed potatoes, bean salad, corn." She tapped her fingers as she listed the items. "Oh, and a surprise dessert. It's homemade."

"Sounds great," I said, as my stomach awakened. "Your grandfather would be impressed. I couldn't begin to do all that. The King cooking gene must have passed by me and went straight to you."

"I love to cook. It's fun."

"Well, thank you for doing that for us. I can't wait." I patted my belly.

"I should go," Tammy said as a gusty breeze set her brunette hair dancing atop her shoulders. "I want to get some sun this afternoon."

"Oh?" A red light flashed in my head. "You're going over to the pool?" Though still a girl, my daughter was developing the curves of a woman. I did not want her lying out in a swimsuit in front of Tom and Jon, relatives or not.

"No, Daddy. I'm going to the deck out back."

"Ah," I said, trying to cloak my relief. "Sounds good." Tammy scooted away, her flip-flops clomping on the court below. "Doesn't seem that long ago we had this sweet baby girl running around the house in a diaper."

"Yes," Gail said with a sigh, "that was last week. Then you blinked and now you have a teenager who thinks she's ready to drive."

I shook my head. "I'm not ready for this. I'm not ready for her to become a woman. The boys can grow up. That's fine. But not my little girl."

"Ready or not, it's happening. She starts high school in two weeks."

"Ugh, don't say that. She knows she can't date 'til she's thirty, right?"

"Wouldn't that be nice," Gail said. "Actually, she already has a couple admirers."

"What? Where's the shotgun?"

"It's nothing. She told me all about them. Harmless crushes. She's not interested."

"Yeah, but that could change if the wrong boy comes along."

"I'm not worried about Tammy. She's an intelligent girl. And she still talks to her mother. She'll make the right decisions in high school."

"It's not *Tammy's* decision-making skills I'm worried about," I said. "Teenage boys are not known for their wisdom and restraint, you know."

"Don't worry. The girl's going to be smarter than all of us. She gets straight As and she's good at everything she tries. A few silly boys won't be a problem for her."

"Yeah … I'm still going to dig out the shotgun."

The next day around noon, I drove to King's Stadium, the eating establishment formerly known as The Royal Court. Though still in its same location on Hubbell Avenue, the restaurant bore little resemblance to my father's place. Years ago the exterior castle facade had been altered to resemble a modern football stadium. Inside, mounted television screens surrounded the dining room. Pennants, uniforms, team pictures, and other memorabilia covered every remaining square inch of wall space. Several prominent portraits, jerseys, and framed sports pages celebrated my career at Western Iowa and Newark. The demise of my father's legacy was bad enough, but knowing that my face and name had contributed to the dismantling was especially galling.

The man I was meeting for lunch was well aware of my feelings. That is why he insisted that we eat nowhere else but King's Stadium. I would have held out for another location, but Adam and Shane continually bugged me to support the family business. As much as I hated what they had done to the place, I still did not like hurting their feelings. So inside I went.

The hostess greeted me with a smile. “Hello, Mr. King. We’re so glad to see you again.” She led me through the half-full dining room toward a booth in a secluded corner. As I passed by a table, a portly young man in a Hawkeyes jersey did a double take. He then bolted from his chair, extended a hand, and started a conversation. Not wanting to disappoint a potential voter, I had to oblige. Like most strangers who recognized me in public, he wanted to talk sports with a former quarterback, not politics with a current congressman. He asked if I was bummed that my old team had moved to Jacksonville a few years ago. I replied that I was sad when the Tornadoes left Newark, though I understood the economic reasons behind the decision.

After signing a few autographs for the Hawkeye fan and his friends, I was safely ensconced in a corner booth scanning the menu. Minutes later, I heard a familiar voice.

“If it isn’t my congressman,” Ozzie said, feigning surprise. “Fancy meeting you here.”

“Sit your skinny butt down,” I said. “Of all the places you could have picked …”

“Tsk tsk. Whatever happened to family values? This is the FAMILY restaurant, you know.” He slid into the opposite side of the booth. The top three buttons of his white shirt were undone.

“Where’s your tie, slacker? This casual Friday thing has gone too far if you ask me.”

“I took it off,” he said. “I’m not going back in today. Got a tee time at 2:00. My weekend officially begins right now.”

“Hmpf, I may need to have a word with your boss at Principal.”

“Yeah, well I’m a registered voter. That means I’m *your* boss. So you can just suck it.” He opened his menu.

“You being the boss of anybody is a terrifying thought.”

“So, Mr. King,” he said, clearing his throat to project a deeper voice, “how is everything in Washington? Have you been cleaning those toilets like I asked you to do?”

“I tried, but the Democrats keep plugging them up. I’m going to need a bigger plunger.”

"I'll call Bubba to see if he has a spare lying around the White House. Say," he continued in his normal voice, "did you ever get me his autograph?"

"Sorry Oz. The president's been a little busy lately."

"He should have time for you though. You were one of what, five Republicans to vote against impeachment?"

"He did call to thank me afterwards, but I wasn't able to work an autograph for my brother into the conversation."

"Man, I love that guy," he said, grinning. "He gets a hummer from an intern. Gets totally busted after lying about it. So what does he do? He starts a national debate on the meaning of the word, *is*. Pure genius. That hound dog is the best president ever."

"I'm glad you're finally taking an interest in politics, sort of." A waitress came over to take our order. We both selected the Kingburger. Ozzie ordered extra onions.

"Check out Adam over there." He gestured at our older brother standing at the bar talking to a patron. "Looks like somebody's ready to go protest the Vietnam War."

"He really is letting his hair grow," I said. "The beard too. Guess he heard about that Woodstock reunion and got nostalgic for the sixties."

"I think he's just trying to rub it in that I'm going bald. Me and Eli. If the two of us leaned our heads together, from above it would look like a giant ass. But Eli's almost sixty—he's got an excuse. I'm still young, damn it. What's up with that?" He patted his nearly barren pate. "Stupid Adam over there pretending to be Cat Stevens. Shane's got hair too. And your hair is friggin' perfect. Makes me sick. You look like James Bond or something."

"Well, I was planning to go bald, but my advisers talked me out of it."

"Shut up, Double-O-Seven."

I surveyed the restaurant. Most of the diners were males in their twenties or thirties. "So how's Sandy?" I asked, turning back to Ozzie. "Life at home going okay?"

"Oh my home life is just a warm fuzzy cocoon of domestic bliss. The old lady? Lately she's been on a crusade to buy every shoe at every mall in the city. The woman's gonna bankrupt me, I tell you. Hey, you're on the Appropriations Committee, right?

Can't you pass a bill appropriating some funds for dudes whose wives are shopping freaks?"

"Wish I could help with that, Oz. But it takes a miracle to get anything out of committee. Even good bills." My thoughts drifted back to the conference rooms of Washington. "It sucks."

"Oh, come on. You've got a sweet gig and you know it. Doesn't that Frank guy pay all your postage?"

"Funny. It isn't so sweet having to pore over reams of information about public policy. Or listening to the endless chatter of lobbyists. Then I get phone call after phone call from everybody and their dog telling me how to vote. Plus, I have to spend hours in subcommittee meetings debating minute details of countless subsections of flawed legislation. And then I watch helplessly as the good bills get clogged with pork."

The waitress brought our food. I paused as she set the plates before us.

"Don't get me wrong," I continued. "I'm proud of what we've accomplished since '95. And I'm gratified to have had the opportunity to use my office to help so many people here in Iowa. But the big changes I dreamed of spearheading, forget about it. Can't punch through the gridlock. Even that education bill I sponsored. Joe and I worked forever writing and rewriting that thing. Teachers loved it. It would have brought about some much-needed reforms. So what happens? It dies in committee." Memories returned of stone-faced colleagues dismissing my impassioned pleas.

Ozzie, similarly, looked unsympathetic. "Fine. I'll vote against you in the next election. Put you out of your misery."

"Not yet. I'm still naive enough to think I can change the system." I grabbed the saltshaker and tilted it above my fries. The silver lid flipped off and plopped onto my food. An avalanche of salt followed, burying the plate. My brother unleashed a barrage of snorting laughter. "You are a jerk," I growled. "You're forty-three, Oswald. Aren't you a little old for this crap?"

"I can't help myself," he said, still cracking up. "You're such an easy mark."

Adam showed up at our table as I started excavating fries from the white mountain on my plate. He wore an orange polo shirt with the restaurant logo emblazoned over his left breast. "Look at that wasteful allocation of resources," he said, shaking his head. "Typical politician. Guess that's what happens when we let Republicans in here."

"Are you the manager?" I asked. "I'd like to lodge a complaint about this idiot right here." I pointed across the table.

"We've had complaints about him before," Adam said. "I throw him out, but he keeps coming back."

"I had to do something," Ozzie said. "Congressman Bilbo here was whining about how tough he has it in Washington. He just wouldn't shut up."

A smirk peeked through Adam's facial hair. "Well, maybe we can cut our dear baby brother a little slack. I must admit he hasn't been the brainless tool of the right wing that I thought he'd be."

"Thanks, I guess." I dusted off a fry and shoved it in my mouth.

"It's a good thing too," Adam continued. "If you'd have turned out to be one of those Rush Limbaugh–Pat Buchanan freaks, I would have had to remove all your pictures."

"You still could." I downed a quaff of soda to rid my mouth of the salty taste.

"No, no. I'll deny this on record, but I'm actually somewhat proud of you. Though a member of the Dark Side, you usually vote your conscience, regardless of the consequences. I dig that."

"Sometimes those consequences can get nasty," I said. "Like when I voted against impeachment. Newt and his minions were furious. For a while I thought I was going to be burned on Capitol Hill as a witch. Joe had a fit. He almost quit over that."

"Wish he would have," Adam said. "You could use a different chief of staff. Replace that little Machiavelli with uh … Ann Richards or James Carville."

"Uh-huh, either of them would be a perfect fit."

Adam smiled. "So, you officially on vacation now?"

"Almost. After lunch I'm heading over to the office to type up my newsletter. Then one of the techies on my staff is going to help me update my Web site. After that, I'm off for two weeks. Tomorrow, I'm taking the family to Lake Panorama. Abby and Jerry invited us out to their lake house."

"Cool."

"You have a Web site?" Ozzie asked.

"Yeah. I've had it for three years now. You mean you've never seen it?"

"Why would I go to your Web site? Maybe if it had some naked chicks. You know, like a naughty interns gallery."

"Someday you should try growing up."

Before he could respond, the crash of breaking dishes rang out from behind the metal doors to the kitchen. It was followed by the obligatory moment of stunned silence. "Son of a bitch," Adam said. "I better go deal with that." He stalked away.

Ozzie and I ate quietly for a while. "So has that Beth woman given you any trouble?" he asked after swallowing a gulp of beer.

I looked around to make sure nobody was nearby. "No, not really. She still sends an occasional letter to my office asking me to meet her and the boy. I always have Anthony send a reply telling her that can't happen."

"She's never threatened to go public?"

"No, thankfully."

"You ever wonder what that kid's like? I mean, he is your son."

"Of course I wonder about him. I've debated whether I should meet him or not. Spent a lot of time on my knees praying about it. The answer is always the same: 'Stay away. The situation is too volatile.' So I've stayed away. Haven't seen Beth in seven years. I just send her a check every month."

"Hmph." He brushed a crumb from his goatee. "Say, you getting any dessert?"

We concluded our dining experience with a confection called the Chocolate Bomb. It was, as described on the menu, destructively delicious.

After the waitress took my credit card, Ozzie's expression turned contemplative. "Did Beth ever tell you the boy's name?"

"Sure. Why do you ask?"

He scrunched his brow. "I dunno. Just curious about my mystery nephew, I guess."

"Yep, she told me.… His name is Solomon."

The house buzzed with activity Saturday morning. My kids darted about gathering towels, sunglasses, flip-flops, sunblock lotion, and assorted other paraphernalia that a young person might deem necessary for a day at the lake. After corralling the crew into the kitchen, I counted heads. There were four children and one wife, but no Tom. A quick interrogation revealed that no one had seen him yet this morning. I went upstairs and stood outside the door to his room.

"Tom. You about ready? We're going to be taking off soon."

No answer. I rapped the door a couple times and turned the knob. It took my eyes a few seconds to adjust to the darkness inside the room. The shaft of hallway light allowed me to barely discern the human-sized lump buried under the covers of the bed. "Tom," I said quietly, "you okay?"

There was a faint moan followed by a pained voice. "I don't know … stomach's all messed up. Must have ate somethin' bad."

"Are you in pain? Want me to call the doctor?"

"Mainly queasy. I don't need a doctor. I'll be fine. But I better not go with you guys today.… Sorry."

I stepped closer to the bed. Tom's head lay on its side, sunk deep into a pillow. His hair splayed out in all directions. "It's okay," I said. "It's not your fault. You sure you're going to be all right though? Maybe we should stay home with you."

"Don't ruin the big day because of me," he groaned. "You don't all need to stay."

"I can't leave you here alone like this. What if you need help? What's Jon doing today?"

"He's got some deal he's going to. Don't worry about me. I'll be … urrgh … fine."

"I'm going to stay with you. Now get some rest."

"No. The boys have really been looking forward to spending this day with you. You shouldn't stay. Maybe …" His voice trailed off.

"Well, someone should stay here with you."

Down in the kitchen, I explained the situation to my family. "You guys will have to go without me. I need to stay with Tom. He says he'll be okay, but I don't think he should be alone."

Looks of disappointment covered all five faces. “I’ll stay,” Gail said, grabbing my arm. “You haven’t had a vacation with the kids in over a year. You need to go.”

“No,” Tammy interjected. “I’ll stay. You’ve all been talking about this for a month. And I’m not that into waterskiing, you know. Plus, I need to practice with Comet. The barrel racing competition is only three days away and he’s not ready yet. I had been thinking I should stay home today anyway.”

“Oh sweetie, no,” Gail said. “You go have fun at the lake.”

“If one of us has to stay, Mom, it should be me. I can use the time. Working with my horse today will really help. Then I won’t be so stressed.”

Gail and I looked at each other. I was proud of my daughter for her willingness to give up her day at the lake, yet felt guilty at the thought of leaving without her. After a few more assurances from Tammy, we agreed to let her stay.

“Our cell number is on speed dial,” Gail said. “So is the number for the lake house. You call us if anything comes up, okay?”

“Yes, Mom. And I know Ozzie and Sandy’s number, and Adam and Shannon’s number, and Shane and Pam’s number, and Eli and Katy’s number. And believe it or not, I know the number for 911. I’ll be fifteen in three months. I think I can handle a day here on my own.”

After thanking Tammy again, Gail and I climbed into the Ford Explorer. The three boys piled into Kyle and Archie’s Dodge Charger. I backed out of the garage and swung the car around to head down the long driveway. Glancing over at the house, I saw our daughter standing on the front stoop. She smiled and waved. We waved back and drove away.

After a forty-mile drive due west, we reached Jerry and Abby’s place at Lake Panorama a little after 9:00 a.m. Their son Andy, a senior at Central College, greeted us at the door. Short and wiry, he sported a mop of dark hair and a thin beard. My boys loved his many impressions. I did too, except when he imitated me. Petite and demure Hannah, Andy’s sister, was also there. A sophomore at Central, she was disappointed by the absence of her female cousin.

Jerry started off the day with a whirlwind tour of the lake in his speedboat. Then, after a light lunch, we took turns waterskiing and riding inner tubes behind the boat. Feeling the wind in my face as I hurtled over the water brought a major rush. Gail and the boys seemed to feel the same exhilaration. Whenever someone spilled into the lake, Andy provided commentary in a celebrity's voice. For example, it was Jerry Seinfeld who described the action when Congressman Dave King flopped onto his face several times trying to get up on the water skis. My boys laughed so hard, I thought they were going to fall out of the boat.

For supper we stuffed ourselves with grilled burgers and hot dogs. Gail called home just before we ate. Tammy was upbeat after a productive day of practicing with her horse. She also said that Tom had been up for a while during the day and seemed to be feeling better. The news was a relief.

The adults passed the rest of the evening out on the deck talking. The kids fished from a nearby dock. After dark, Andy, Archie, and Donnie went inside to play video games, while Kyle taught Hannah a few words in ASL. Around ten, Gail and I said our goodbyes. Our sons remained in front of the television, promising to take off after finishing just one more PlayStation game.

On the drive home, my head still buzzed from the hours of exposure to speed and water. Thoughts of the lake disappeared, however, when we pulled into the driveway at our acreage to find a dark house looming before us. "That's odd," I said. "Tom could be back in bed, but Tammy's always up at this hour."

"Maybe she's watching a movie," Gail said.

A knot of anxiety formed in my stomach after I noticed that one of the garage doors was open. The knot tightened when I drove closer and saw that the stall inside was empty. "My Mustang is gone."

"Maybe Tom went to meet Jon somewhere. You did tell him he could borrow your car if he ever needed it. Tammy will tell us where he went."

I pulled the Explorer into its usual spot. After shutting off the ignition, I prayed a quick silent prayer. The door to the house was ajar. I slipped into the kitchen with Gail right behind me. She hit the light. Everything seemed to be in place—except for the spare keys to my car that usually dangled from a hook near the door.

I moved into the living room and turned on a lamp. Nothing unusual stood out. Gail, standing at the base of the stairs, called our daughter's name. Silence. She started up the stairs.

"Wait," I said. "Let me go first." But she reached the top before I could pass her. She called Tammy's name again. No reply. My wife darted down the hallway with me a step behind. Our daughter's door was shut. Gail twisted the knob and pushed open the door. Darkness.

"Tammy, honey, are you okay?" A faint noise returned from somewhere inside. Gail flipped on the light. My adjusting eyes roamed the room. The initial sights I took in—pastel green walls, walnut vanity, jade lamp, portrait of Jesus—were familiar details. But the mattress was bare. Then I saw Tammy. She was sitting on the floor between the bed and the far wall. Wrapped in a sheet and bedspread, she had pushed her face down into her knees. Only her hair, tangled and strewn, was visible. A wave of dread chilled my soul.

Gail flashed across the room. Leaning into her mother's embrace, Tammy cried out with hard sobs that shook her body. Her pink face was streaked with tears. Gail stroked her hair. "What happened, sweetheart?"

My little girl, still shaking, tried to speak. Only anguished sounds came out. The pain in her voice slashed through me. Finally there were words. "He raped me." She pressed her face into Gail's chest.

The room quaked as my brain refused to process information that could not be true. I turned away and braced myself against the dresser. *This isn't happening*. But when I looked again, the painful image was still there. Gail and Tammy remained huddled on the floor next to the bed.

My daughter drew several stuttered breaths and spoke again. "It was Tom." Trembling, I stepped forward and knelt beside them. Tears flowed down both of their faces. Struggling with every sentence, Tammy recounted what had happened.

When she first checked on Tom at noon, he appeared to be sleeping. A couple hours later, she saw him outside on the deck watching her as she rode Comet. By the time she went back in the house, he was in front of the television. He complimented her about how good she looked riding. A while later, he said he wanted to rest and went back to his room. In the evening, she checked on him for supper. He asked her to bring him a sandwich. When she set the bed tray over him, he grabbed her arm and started kissing her. She begged him to let go. He pushed her down on the bed. She pleaded with him to stop. He didn't.

Afterwards, he cursed at her. He blamed her for what he had done and ordered her not to tell anyone about it. He then threw her out into the hallway. She hid in her room. Moments later, she heard him run down the stairs and out of the house.

While Tammy spoke, my mind continued to deny what I was hearing. *This did not happen to my daughter. This did not happen in my house.* I heard a noise behind me. Rising to my feet, I saw our sons standing at the door to the room. Archie was signing to Kyle. I did not know how long they had been there, but the tears in their eyes told me that they had heard enough.

"Come on, boys. Let's go." I herded them into the hallway and shut the door to Tammy's room. "Go downstairs. I'll be down in a minute." After they left, I went to Tom's room and flipped on the light. On the floor was a sandwich drenched in a puddle of splattered milk. Nearby was an overturned bed tray. The bed itself was unmade and in disarray. My stomach twisted as if to vomit. I bent over gagging. After several deep breaths, I regained my composure and went downstairs.

The boys were whispering among themselves when I entered the living room. "Dad," Archie said, "we have to call the police. You're going to call aren't you?"

An icy fear gripped me. I did not want anyone to know, especially strangers. The more people knew, the more real it became. At that moment, I reasoned that keeping it quiet would somehow shield Tammy from more pain. "No, not yet."

"Why?" he demanded.

"I'm a public figure, Archie. We have to be careful how we handle things. I don't want the press all over this. I need to call Joe first."

My son glared at me with cold blue eyes. His face, normally handsome and strong, contorted with fury. I retreated to the den to dial Joe's cell phone. I told him the situation. "Don't do anything," he said. "Don't call anyone. I'll be right over."

When I returned to the living room, Archie was pacing like a caged tiger. Kyle sat on the couch with his head in his hands. Donnie, looking scared, sat next to him. "Dad, we have to do something," Archie said, blocking my path with his muscular frame. "We can't let him get away with this." Though only sixteen, he was nearly as tall as me.

"Calm down, Archie. He won't get away with anything. But we have to be smart. We have to handle this the right way. I'm a congressman."

"What's there to handle? That son of a bitch raped my sister!"

"That's enough! Joe is on his way over here. I'll talk to him. Then we'll decide what to do."

"Unbelievable," Archie growled as he turned to the built-in shelves beside the fireplace. "Why did you leave her here alone with that freak?" He grabbed a framed photo of Tom—his senior picture—and spiked it onto the hearth. Shards of broken glass rattled across the bricks.

Kyle moved across the room. "Archie," he said aloud, putting a hand on his brother's shoulder. Kyle signed something, but with his back to me I could not tell what he said.

Archie nodded and started pacing again. Kyle walked over to me. "What can we do for Tammy?" he asked. His thin build and clean-cut cherubic appearance was a stark contrast to Archie's brawn, stubble, and dark shoulder-length hair. Nearly every stranger who saw the boys together incorrectly assumed that Archie was the older of the two.

"Right now, pray for her," I said. "We'll all help her through this. We need to stick together. You boys remember that. We're going to take care of her." The four of us waited in silence.

Joe's Jaguar skidded to a halt outside the house barely ten minutes after I had called him. Once inside, he hustled me into the den and shut the door. His Armani suit and persuasive cologne indicated that he had been out with a lady friend. He asked for the complete story. I gave it to him.

"Do you know where Tom is now?" He stood facing me with arms crossed.

I shook my head. "All I know is that he took my car."

"Do you have any idea where he might have gone? A friend's house maybe?"

"The only person he hangs out with here is Jon. You know, Shane's kid."

"Yeah." Joe chewed a thumbnail. "Dave, this is poison. You know that. If this gets out, it's over for you. The public will overlook a lot of things, but rape and incest within your immediate family—people won't forget something that messy."

"What should we do?"

"We need to find Tom, now. And then get him the hell out of here. Tonight. Get his ass back to Wisconsin. Tell him he never breathes a word of this to anyone. And he never sets foot in Iowa again. We make it clear he goes to prison forever if he comes back here."

"That's it? We just send him home?"

"It's our only play, Dave. This is *your* son who did this. People will identify him with you. Putting him on trial will erode your public image. It will end your career."

"My son ..." Memories of time spent with Tom passed through head. "I thought I knew him. I thought he was a good kid."

"Well, he's not. And we've got to get him out of here. Bury this thing."

An image of Tammy struggling vainly against Tom flashed before my eyes. "How could he do that to her?" With blind fury, I shoved everything off my desk. The lamp, phone, family portrait, and a host of other objects clattered to the floor. "That damned kid! Why did he have to track me down? I welcomed him into my life and this is how he thanks me."

"Dave, you need to focus. We have a mess. We need to clean it up."

There was a commotion somewhere in the house. I darted out of the den and hurried into the empty living room. After hearing the low rumble of a garage door opening, I ran to the kitchen. Kyle was stooped on one knee rubbing the back of his head. Donnie stood over him looking like he did not know what to do.

"What happened?" I asked.

Kyle continued rubbing his head. Donnie turned to me with fearful eyes.

"Answer me!" I heard a car screech out of the garage and race away.

"Archie said he was going to find Tom," Donnie blurted. "Kyle tried to stop him but Archie pushed him into the wall."

"Damn it," Joe said. "We have to stop him. Did he say where he was going?"

Donnie shook his head. "He'll probably start with Jon's place," I said. "That's where I would go first."

"We've got to get over there," Joe said. "I'll drive."

I helped Kyle to his feet. "Archie was listening at the door," he signed. "He said you were going to let Tom get away with it." Then he spoke. "That's not true is it?"

My eyes lowered to the floor for a moment. "We have to find Archie," I said. "Do you know where Jon's apartment is?"

Kyle stared silently at me. I repeated the question.

"I've only been there once," he said. "It's somewhere on the south side. I don't remember the address."

Joe swore. "Where's your phonebook?"

Tearing through the white pages, I found Jon's address. After Joe scribbled it down, we took off. The Jaguar engine roared as we raced into Des Moines. Headlights and streetlights passed by in a blur. My heart rate accelerated as Joe weaved through traffic, running yellow and red lights. Left in our wake were horn blasts and curses from drivers who had to slam on their brakes to avoid a collision. Adding to my fear was the thought that Archie was probably driving the same way in his rage to find Tom.

Still flying as we neared Jon's neighborhood, Joe missed a turn. Doubling back to the intersection, he finally found the apartments and screeched into the parking lot. Unfortunately, the complex included a dozen buildings that covered almost an entire block. While trying to read address numbers in the dark, we heard the wail of tires from the far end of the complex. Joe weaved through the buildings toward the direction of the sound. Looking down a backstreet, we saw the shrinking taillights of a car speeding away from the apartments. I shuddered at the sight of my Mustang parked in front of the building now closest to us.

"The address matches," Joe said, stopping his car.

I bounded out of the Jaguar and burst into the building. I took the stairs two at a time and ran down the hallway looking for unit 213. Upon reaching the door, my body tensed with a sick foreboding. The doorknob hung askew next to a jagged indentation in the wood. I ran my fingers over the damaged area. Footsteps echoed down the hallway. Joe was sprinting towards me. I pushed open the door.

Not ten feet inside Jon knelt on the floor. With one hand he steadied himself against a chair at the dining room table. His other hand covered a spurting gash above his left eye. Crimson blotches mottled his face and blond crew cut. Disoriented, he did not notice my presence. I stepped forward. Beyond the table, something else came into view. It was a man lying face down on the floor. He wore white tennis shoes, denim jeans, and a black T-shirt. I then saw his head. The sight sucked all my wind into a horrified gasp. Coated in red-blue ooze, the skull had been smashed into an unnatural shape. A dark stain several feet in diameter covered the beige carpet below. With a violent convulsion, I turned away.

Joe was now standing beside me. "My God … is that Tom?"

The room spun. I fell against the wall near the doorway. Too shocked to shut my eyes, I viewed the rest of the apartment. Blurry details came into focus—a broken beer bottle, an overturned chair, an old sofa shoved out of place, a toppled lamp with a torn green shade. My roaming gaze stopped at the aluminum bat on the floor. The once silver barrel was now coated red. I recognized the black handle. Earlier that summer, I had seen Archie use that very bat to hit a monstrous home run to lead the Johnston High baseball team to victory. Now it lay dented and discolored, never to hit a baseball again.

Joe helped Jon to his feet. They spoke to each other but my brain could not comprehend the words. My emotions seared, I slid down the wall to the floor. Images from the evening returned. I saw the anguish in Tammy's eyes, her innocence shattered. I saw Gail stricken with grief as she desperately tried to protect her daughter from an evil already committed. I saw Archie's rage as he doubted his father's resolve. And I saw Tom, his head smashed, his life gone.

The pain shook my soul. I barely had the strength to breathe. One child was dead. Another, violated and traumatized. A third, guilty of murder, racing away into the darkness. I struggled to my knees and pressed my burning face into my hands. Trapped in the throes of a nightmare, I pleaded with God to make it all go away.

Chapter 23 – April 2002

My fingers pressed the frets. My pick hit the strings. The electric emanations of my Fender Stratocaster harmonized with the Nirvana bleeding from the stereo speakers. I sang along with Kurt Cobain. As the music and lyrics of "All Apologies" blended into a melody of haunting resonance, a familiar ache spawned in my heart. The hurt brought a strange comfort.

Gail entered the room—a carpeted bedroom-sized space in the basement that we had designated for the family's musical pursuits. She waited until the end of the song to speak. "You about ready to come upstairs for supper?"

I unslung my guitar and set the instrument in a stand. "Yeah."

"Are you planning to spend some time with the kids tonight?"

"Well, I need to check in with Joe at some point. Go over the schedule for this week."

She frowned. "I still don't understand why there has to be a schedule for this week. You're on Easter recess."

"Could be a tough election this fall. When I'm in Iowa I need to make the most of my opportunities to connect with the voters."

"When you're in Iowa you need to make the most of your opportunities to be with us."

My eyes moved away from hers. "I know."

"Like this afternoon. Ever since we got back from church, you've been down here alone playing your guitar. Why didn't you ask Tammy and Donnie to listen? They hardly ever get to hear you play."

"They were busy. Donnie was on the Xbox and Tammy was in her room doing homework or something." I straightened a stack of CDs next to the stereo.

"Maybe they thought *you* were busy. You could have asked. At least then they'd know you're interested in them."

"Sorry. I've got a lot on my mind. I just wanted to unwind by myself for a while. I didn't realize I'd been down here so long. Time got away from me."

Her expression softened as she stepped closer. "So what's on your mind?"

"Oh, the usual. Washington crap. And then there's the stuff scheduled for while I'm here. That Habitat for Humanity thing goes all week. Plus, I've got evening speaking engagements Tuesday, Wednesday, and Friday. Not much of a vacation, huh?"

"Don't you have any control over your schedule?"

"Yes, but it's an even-numbered year. You know what that means."

She sighed. "Yeah."

I grabbed her hand. "How about this? Right after supper I'll call Joe and get that out of the way. I should touch base with my press secretary too. But neither of those calls should take very long. Then we can do something as a family."

As it turned out, the calls took longer than I expected.

The next morning I sat at the kitchen table reading *The Des Moines Register*. I had just finished off a bowl of Honey Nut Cheerios when Donnie walked into the room.

"There he is," I said. "Up at a quarter to seven. I'm impressed."

"Well, I like to surprise you every once in a while."

"Sports or comics?"

"Comics," he said through a yawn. I handed him the appropriate section. After reading for about a minute, he cleared his throat. "Dad? Any chance I can go with you today?"

"I don't think your mother would like that."

"But you're gonna build a house, right? That could be like my shop class. Eighth graders at school get to take shop."

"I know," I said, lowering the paper to look at him. Mussed auburn hair swooped down below his ears. His face bore my eyes and Gail's cheeks and nose. "But your mother works hard on those lesson plans for you. She doesn't like it when anything throws off her schedule."

"What you're doing helps people," he protested. "I'd like to get out there and help people. You're always saying in your speeches that we should do stuff like that."

"Using my words against me, huh?"

"Ooh, how about this? Building houses is carpentry. Jesus was a carpenter. If you let me go, I'll be more like Jesus."

His goofy grin coaxed a snicker out of me. "I know you wish you could get out more during the day. And I know you miss seeing your friends at school." I sighed. "It was cool of you to agree to be homeschooled. Your mother and I really appreciate that. And Tammy does too, even if she doesn't say it. I think it would really bug her if she had to do it alone."

He looked down and nodded.

"Here's the deal. Your mom takes her job as your teacher very seriously. It might hurt her feelings if she thought you were bored and wanted to skip out."

"It's not that I'm bored," he said in a high voice. "It's just, I wanna do something different."

"I understand, Donnie. But the construction site is a dangerous place for someone your age. Neither of us wants you to get hurt."

His expression deflated. "But you're gone in D.C. all the time. I was thinking it would be fun to do something with you while you're back. Just you and me."

His words sent a spear of guilt through my abdomen. "I'm sorry, sport. How about if we shoot some hoops when I get home tonight?"

"Fine," was his faint reply. He walked over to the counter and dropped a Pop Tart in the toaster. Little more than a minute later he was back at the table with his food and a glass of grape juice. "Dad? You know that distance learning thing Tammy is in?"

"Yeah."

"When she's done, will her diploma count? You know, like from a real high school?"

"Of course it will. The Independent Study High School *is* a real high school. It's accredited and everything. Why do you ask?"

"I was thinking, I'm gonna be starting ninth grade this fall. Tammy will be a senior. And we've been homeschooled for a long time—almost three years now. I was wondering if I could maybe …"

"You want to go to Johnston High this fall."

"Kinda. I don't think Tammy would mind doing school here alone for just a year."

"Well maybe." I rubbed my chin. "It's something we can—"

"I was gonna ask you and Mom if I could go to tenth grade at Johnston anyway, after Tammy had graduated. Then I got to thinking, it would be a shame to miss my freshman year there."

"You've got a point. You really want to do that instead of taking classes at home?"

"Yeah."

"Tell you what. Let's float the idea past your mom. Give her time to think about it. Then we'll go from there."

"Okay." He crammed the remainder of his Pop Tart into his mouth.

"I think she'll be okay with the idea. If you want to go to high school, I think you should." A printer sprang to action in another part of the house. "Sounds like she's finished with her column. We'll take this up later, okay?"

He nodded. After another minute, Gail appeared. "Tammy's not up yet?" she asked.

"I heard a faucet running upstairs a while ago," I said. "She'll be down soon."

Gail looked over at the stairs and frowned. "Are you ready for your algebra test today?" she asked Donnie. He grunted, not moving his eyes from the comics page.

"You have an algebra test today, huh?" I asked with raised brows.

"Yeah," he said, looking flustered. "But that's not why … never mind."

My wife, standing at the sink, glanced at us with a curious expression. Tammy then drifted into the kitchen. She wore a floor-length pastel robe. A curtain of brunette hair hid most of her face. "Good morning," I said.

"Morning," she mumbled, slumping into a chair at the table.

"What do you want for breakfast, sweetheart?" Gail asked in a pleasant voice. "I can make you some waffles."

"I don't care."

Gail poured a glass of juice for her and grabbed a box of waffle mix. "So do you have a test today too?" I asked Tammy.

"Yeah." She leaned over the main section of *The Register*.

"What subject?"

"English."

"Good luck."

No response. After a few more questions and a few more one-word replies, I checked the clock. It was time for me to go.

About fifteen minutes later, I pulled into a driveway in the Beaverdale neighborhood of northwest Des Moines. Thor lumbered out of a brick bungalow and settled into the passenger seat of my silver '99 Mustang. The car chassis groaned under the added weight. "Hammer time!" I said, as he pulled the door shut.

"It's Monday morning, dawg." He yawned. "That's more like coffee time."

"You sure you're up for this?" I asked, noticing the bags under his half-closed eyes.

"Yes, sir. I told the guys I'd be there this morning."

"Yeah, but you're coming off an eight-hour night shift patrolling the mall. Nobody expects you there now. Why don't you catch some Zs and then show up in the afternoon? Or tomorrow even. We'll be there all week."

"Just drive, brother. I'll be alright."

I backed out of the driveway. "It's good to see you, man. How long has it been?"

"Just after Christmas, wasn't it?"

"Yeah, that's right. So what's new on the home front?"

He unleashed another yawn. "Well, Neil's all wound up about baseball. The boy thinks he's gonna make varsity this year. And, let's see … got an email from J.J. He doesn't seem to be gettin' into too much trouble at Western Iowa this semester. Lookin' forward to two-a-days this summer. The nut."

"Sounds like his dad."

"Yeah," Thor said, adding a restrained woof. "How are your kids? Kyle still likin' ISU?"

"Oh yeah. He's doing great up there. Got a girlfriend now.... Hard to believe we both have a son in college."

"I hate to say it, King, but we're gettin' old." His expression reminded me a sleepy lion.

"We're not that old." I turned onto Hickman Avenue and headed east.

"Yeah we are." He patted his expansive belly. "And I'm getting soooo fat."

I snickered. "You can take it off whenever you want."

"We both know that's not true," he said. "You know, it'd be nice if you'd add a few more pounds. You're making some of us look bad."

"Well, I would, but I have to stay in shape for my big comeback in the NFL. Know any teams in need of a 44-year-old quarterback with a bad knee?"

"The Cardinals might be interested." We both laughed as I drove farther into the heart of the city. "So how's Donnie-boy doing?" he asked.

"He's good. Wants to come to the work site with us."

"Yeah? You gonna let him?"

"Nah. He's still a bit too young for this."

"Gotcha."

"Gail would really worry," I added, not actually knowing my wife's opinion on the subject.

"How's Tammy?"

"She's about the same. Gets good grades. Doesn't say much. I'd like to think it's just normal adolescent detachment, but she seems so sullen at times. I'm afraid the pain is still right there, just below the surface."

Thor sighed. "Tough thing what that girl went through."

I waited for a traffic light to turn green. "It's like she's lived two different lives. One before. One after. I would do anything to go back to that day. Stay home in her place."

"Yeah, but we can't go back. Just gotta press on. Do the best we can … and pray. Rebecca and I pray for your kids every night."

"Thanks, man.... He still won't see me, you know." An empty feeling returned.

"Really?" Thor shifted in his seat. "Well, Archie's a tough kid. A little hardheaded maybe, but I'm sure he still loves you. And he knows you love him. He'll come around one of these days. He still talks to Gail and your other kids, right?"

"Yeah. Gail and Donnie went down to visit him last week. Tammy still can't go to the prison. She wants to, but it scares her. And she can't bear to see Archie locked up. But she writes to him all the time. They trade letters every week."

"When's he eligible for parole?"

"Couple more years. I pray he makes it 'til then, and that he forgives me." A rush of emotion hit. I fought it hard, but my face shuddered and a tear escaped.

Though looking straight ahead at the street, I could sense Thor's eyes fixed on me. "Dave, we've been over this. It wasn't your fault. You've got to stop blaming yourself. Trust God. He'll bring healing." He put a hand on my shoulder. "He'll bring you and Archie together again. Your family will be restored."

"I hope so, Hammer. I hope so."

My Mustang wound through the streets of the River Bend neighborhood about a mile north of downtown. After I found a parking spot a few houses away from the construction site, we got out and walked toward a sign that read, "Greater Des Moines Habitat for Humanity." The morning chill nipped at our faces. Several men were already there, talking, moving boards, and looking over plans.

"Congressman, ya made it!" A white-haired man in a CAT cap and a plaid flannel shirt approached. He was lean and wiry, with a face leathered by a lifetime of working outside. "I can't thank you enough for taking time out of your busy schedule to help us this week. We really appreciate it." He looked at Thor. "And you brought some extra muscle with ya. Outstanding! Ya boys will have this house up by noon, right?"

"Better make it one, Murray. We've got to give those news crews a chance to catch us in action."

The foreman laughed. "One it is. Alright boys, grab a hammer. I've got you over with Munson's group."

"Sounds good," I said. A few minutes later we were hard at work.

Thursday evening I drove downtown to Sec Taylor Stadium, home of the Iowa Cubs. Taking the elevator to the upper level, I reached the skyboxes. Anthony leaned against the wall by one of the doors. He wore a breezy smile that matched his casual attire.

"Hey Dave, come on in." After a handshake, we entered the empty skybox. He shut the door behind us. "What can I get you?"

"Mountain Dew sounds good, if you got any."

"Sure do," he said, pulling a green can from the mini-fridge. "Whaddya think of the place?" He tossed the soda to me.

The cold aluminum soothed my calloused hands as I scanned the room and its amenities. "Nice." Rubbing the frigid can over my aching right arm, I stepped forward to gaze through the glass at the diamond below. "Great view. My compliments to your buddy at McGladrey."

"Who says accountants aren't cool?" he said with a grin.

"So none of your friends will be joining us tonight?"

"That's right. We've got the run of the place."

After the National Anthem, we each claimed a chair at a pub table near the front of the box. Not long after the first pitch, Anthony started to fidget. The Cubs sent the New Orleans Zephyrs down in the first inning with only a harmless single. "How about if we relocate outside?" I asked, gesturing at the seats just beyond the front glass of the skybox.

Anthony checked his watch. "Um, maybe later. I'd like to talk to you about something first, in private."

"You're not just here to share your deep abiding love for minor league baseball with your favorite uncle?"

"Yes, there is that." He smiled. "But we also need to talk business."

"So are you here as my office manager or my personal financial advisor?"

"The latter. Here's the deal, Dave. You're losing money."

"I know." I took a drink of Dew. "We've got reserves though."

"Not so much anymore. Your financial ship is sinking."

"What?" I shifted my torso to face him. "What do you mean? What about my savings and my stocks? You're supposed to be managing my money. What happened?"

"Now Dave, relax," he said, holding up a palm like a traffic cop. "I AM managing your money. That's why we're having this conversation. You're not in trouble yet, but you're heading in the wrong direction. Faster than you might think."

I slouched back in my chair and looked out the large skybox window. Beyond the blue centerfield wall, the gold-domed capitol building gleamed in the setting sun. "I thought I had a lot left. You made all those great investments for me."

"The thing is, this market downturn has ravaged many a portfolio. The value of your stocks has shriveled. And paying that big settlement to Tom's mother wiped out a huge chunk of your savings."

"That's just great," I murmured. Out on the field, a drive from Cubs third basemen Ivanon Coffie hit the Hy-Vee billboard on the right field wall. The crowd roared as he motored into second base.

"We have to come up with something. I don't want you to lose your house."

"My house? I'm not that bad off, am I?"

He pressed back his shoulders and rotated his head. A couple vertebrae cracked in response. "At your current pace, I estimate you're about a year away from bankruptcy."

"That soon?" An anvil sunk into my stomach. "But I stopped sending payments to Dawn Lewis when Michael graduated college. That helped didn't it?"

"It helped." Anthony's face tightened into a grim expression. "See, your salary from Congress is decent, but it's not enough. You're not bringing in NFL money anymore. The seven-figure days are over. Then came those brutal legal fees from Archie's trial and the civil suit from Lilly Nelson. And now Kyle is in college. Plus, there are those hefty payments you send to Beth every month."

"What do you think I should do?" I mumbled, staring at the green outfield.

"Cut expenses. Increase income. Let's talk about the latter first. What do you think about memorabilia? A lot of former athletes have cashed in on that."

I groaned. "I hate the idea of charging people for my signature. It's not me and it wouldn't look good for an elected official to be involved in that."

"Okay, how about a book? I think there are a few publishers that would be interested in your autobiography."

The gears turned in my head. "That's a possibility, but not now. Not with Archie still in prison. Maybe someday."

"I understand." Anthony left his chair and moved somewhere behind me. The Cubs scored a run, bringing another roar from the crowd. When the noise died down, I heard my nephew draw a deep breath. "Dave, I've come up with something that will help you."

The gravity in his voice caused me to turn around. He stood a few feet away with his hands thrust into the pockets of his khakis. "Oh? Will I approve?"

Nervousness spread across his face. "No, you won't."

"Really? You're worrying me, Anthony."

He paced to the door at the rear of the skybox. "I've made a deal for you. It's a good one. It will save you a bundle. But you're not going to like it … at first."

"A deal? What kind of a deal?"

"I told Beth you would meet her and the boy. In exchange, she agreed to accept half of what you're currently sending her each month. I guess she's doing okay for herself financially."

"Anthony!" I stood. "No! I can't meet her. You had no right to make that agreement."

"You're heading toward financial ruin. I had to do something to protect you."

Anger blazed inside me. "I'd expect a stunt like this from Joe, but not you. I thought you were a Christian."

"I AM a Christian," he shot back. "And I've got a family too. I would never shirk my responsibility to provide for my children. You shouldn't either, Dave. This is just ONE meeting. That's it! Do you know how many thousands of dollars this will save you each year?"

"That's not the point. I had an affair with that woman. It's not right that I see her."

"That boy is your son. You should meet him."

"I won't do it!" I yelled.

"Actually Dave, you will." He checked his watch and then turned to open the door. In a flash he was gone and she was there, standing in the doorway.

"Beth," I gasped.

She stared at me with aqua eyes. Her dark billowy hair flowed down below her shoulders. She wore a skirted navy business suit that accentuated her curvy figure. A familiar beauty radiated from her face, which had barely been touched by the passing years. Her lips formed a wan smile as she held me in a knowing gaze—a look that bore a hint of warmth and a hint of sadness.

Standing before her, I felt small and horrible. I awaited her words like a prisoner before a judge. Seconds passed. Then, as suddenly as she appeared, she was gone. My eyes blinked in shock after she disappeared into the concourse. Moments later, a boy entered and closed the door.

Wearing a white shirt, tie, and gray dress slacks, he stood with perfect posture. His short brown hair was parted on the side, not a lock out of place. Curious blue eyes examined me through rimless glasses. His round face, though reflecting many of his mother's striking features, reminded me of pictures of myself when I was his age.

"Hello, Mr. King," he said. Although he spoke with a child's voice, I detected in his words a mature timbre rarely heard on the playground.

A wave of unexpected feelings swept over me. Though I had never before met the boy, love for him filled my heart. "Solomon."

"It is an honor to meet you, sir."

I stepped toward the rear of the skybox. My mind calculated the passage of time. "You must be nine now. Does that mean you're in the third grade?"

"I'm in fourth grade, sir. I skipped a grade."

I moved closer. "You skipped a grade? Wow. Your mother wrote in her letters that you were smart." He smiled slightly, returning my gaze. I knelt so our eyes were at the same level.

"Solomon, I'm sorry that I haven't come to see you. It's uh, difficult to … it's complicated."

"I understand, sir. Mom explained the situation to me. You have a family here."

I wondered what exactly Beth had told him. "Solomon, please, you don't need to call me sir. I'm not much for formalities."

"Very well. Everybody calls me Sol."

"Fair enough. Would you like something to drink, Sol?"

"Yes, please."

After he selected a 7-Up from the mini-fridge, we moved to the front of the skybox. "Your mother," I said, "we shouldn't leave her alone outside."

"She's not alone. She and Mr. Krieger are watching the game elsewhere in the stadium. She won't be coming back. She wants me to stay here with you. Unless you want me to leave."

"No. Of course not."

We sat at a pub table and drank our sodas as the game played on. Responding to my questions, Sol told me about school, Boy Scouts, and Science Club. Responding to his questions, I told him about Congress, the NFL, and building houses. By the fifth inning, any awkwardness between us had dissipated. When the concession cart came to our door, I bought us each a hot dog. We continued talking about a myriad of other subjects. He especially enjoyed hearing about how my high school baseball team won the state title on the very field below us nearly three decades ago. For a fleeting couple of hours, we were like a typical father and son out at the ballpark. The end of the game came as an unwelcome interruption.

"Thank you, Mr. King," he said following the last out. "I had a nice time."

I wanted to tell him to call me Dad, but felt that would not be fair to my family. "Me too, Sol."

We walked to the rear of the box. Extending a hand, he looked like a lilliputian business executive at the end of a meeting. After the handshake, I knelt down and wrapped him in a hug. He smiled briefly as I stood again. "Perhaps we could keep in contact," he said.

"Yes. I would like that."

He retrieved a card from his pocket and handed it to me. "This has my email address. I have my own account now. Maybe you could send me a message, when you have time."

"Of course, definitely. Then you'll have my email too." I stared at him a while longer, not wanting him to go. The commotion of fans passing through the concourse increased in volume. "I should take you down to your mother. Do you know which section she's in?"

"Actually, I'm supposed to wait here until Mr. Krieger returns for me."

"Oh." An image of Beth appeared in my mind. I felt sad that Sol could not see his parents together, but I knew it had to be this way. A few seconds later, Anthony entered. After I said goodbye to my son, they left. I drifted to the front of the room and faced the baseball field.

Anthony returned a while later. He stood behind me in silence for about a minute. "Dave, please understand I had good intentions. I just wanted to help you." He paused. "Am I fired?"

"No," I said, still mentally reviewing my conversation with Sol. "It was good that I met him."

He exhaled audibly. "That's great. And this will really ease the strain on your finances. Trust me. Maybe we can get together next week and talk more about income options."

"Fine." Moving to the back of the skybox, I put him in a headlock. "If you ever do anything like this again, I'll wring your neck. Got it Tony-O?"

"Okay, okay," he said, squirming in vain to escape my grip. "Uncle!"

Back home, Gail was reading an Anne Lamott novel when I walked into the bedroom. While changing clothes, I considered waiting until the next morning to tell her what had happened. After I slid under the sheets next to her, she asked about the game. Waiting was not an option. When I got to the part about the surprise visitors, she shut the book and removed her reading glasses.

"You didn't know anything about this?" she asked curtly.

"Not at all. Anthony never even mentioned that he was considering the idea."

"And she just walked out after she saw you? Didn't say anything?"

"Not a word."

"Were you attracted to her?"

"No," I lied. "I was more shocked than anything."

Gail chewed her lip. "You and the boy watched the whole game together, alone?"

"Yes."

"What's he like?"

"Smart. Really sharp for his age. He handled the situation well."

"You like him?"

"I do. He's a good kid."

Gail stiffened her back and crossed her arms. "I hope you're not planning to bring him over here. We can't do that to our children. Not after what happened before. They don't even know about this kid. I can't imagine what they'd do if they found out."

"That's not going to happen," I said, adjusting my pillow so I could sit up against the headboard. "I wouldn't do that to them. I told Sol I would email him, that's all. I thought I should at least do that much. He is my son."

"Don't say that," Gail snapped. "It reminds me of before. Turns my stomach."

"Sorry."

"I don't like you having contact with that boy. It's too easy for *her* to get involved."

My body tensed at her truculent tone. "You don't trust me?"

"Yes, I trust you. But I don't like the idea of this type of thing returning to our lives again. It could dredge up a lot of hurt. Your own family comes first."

"None of what happened was Sol's fault. He's just a child."

"So is Archie," she said bitterly, before rolling away from me onto her side. "And he's in prison."

"Gail, our kids won't know about Sol. I'll only send him an occasional email. You can read them first." I paused for a reply that did not come. "I didn't ask for this to happen tonight. But it did happen. Sol knows we won't be visiting each other. I just thought I should do something so he doesn't feel rejected."

"Fine. Do what you have to do, Dave. But this better not end up hurting my children." She turned off the nightstand lamp, bringing sudden darkness upon the room. I did not sleep well that night.

The next morning at the job site I barely had the strength to swing a hammer. The day crawled by at a snail's pace. It took three bottles of Mountain Dew to carry me through to quitting time. That evening I was to be the keynote speaker at a charity fundraiser for the Boys and Girls Clubs of Central Iowa. I did not know how I was going to do it with an exhausted body and a caffeine-fried brain. Gail's frosty silence on the drive over did nothing to energize me to the task.

Fortunately, my mouth was able to deliver the speech without much guidance from my brain. Upon returning home, I realized that I had left my cell phone off all evening. Checking my voicemail revealed that Joe had left three messages asking me to call him back ASAP. Though it was nearly midnight, I dialed his number. He wanted to meet, but would not say why.

The following morning I drove downtown to the Federal Building on Walnut Avenue. My congressional suite was on the seventh floor. Since it was a Saturday, the place was nearly deserted. I entered Joe's office, an impressive chamber of mahogany and political opulence. Along the side walls, volumes on policy and law filled bookshelves from floor to ceiling. Centered in front of the back window was a polished executive desk. Behind it sat my nephew wearing a white silk shirt and red suspenders. On the near side sat Levi Zadok, his corpulent form clad in wrinkly office casual. After the handshakes, I claimed the other chair in front of the desk.

"Dave, I'm not going to lie to you," Joe began. "Anthony told me about your meeting with him at the ballpark the other night. As your top two staffers, we function as a team."

"I know how you two operate," I said.

"I must say, I am impressed with my brother. Thanks to him, you're not facing bankruptcy anymore. And about that agreement, let me add, I had nothing to do with it. That was all Anthony."

"This must be a proud moment for you," I grumbled. Zadok's chuckles drew my eyes over to him. He stroked his beard with a look of amusement. I wondered why he was in Des Moines.

"Alright, let's get to the real reason we're all here," Joe said, no doubt detecting my curiosity. "Levi just flew in from Washington. He has some news for us. Levi?"

"Party leaders had a bunch of powwows last week," Zadok said in his usual baritone. "Long-range planning. National strategies. Stuff like that. Long story short, the party wants you to run for the Senate in '04."

"The Senate?" I said, shifting in my chair to face him. "Well, I'm flattered. But I haven't even been a congressman for that long. Plus, I've got to defend my House seat this fall. I might not be in office by '04."

"Dave, Dave, Dave," he said chuckling. "You're going to win this fall. Everybody knows that. And that will be your fifth term as a representative. Plenty of preparation for the jump to the Senate."

"But I'm comfortable in the House."

"Your party needs you in the Senate. The world is a different place. Nine-eleven changed everything, my friend. This nation is at war and the front lines are everywhere, including Iowa. Now, more than ever, America needs strong leadership. Men of character. Men of integrity. Men who will make the tough choices necessary to win this fight."

"I appreciate that, Levi. But surely the Republican Party has someone more experienced to run for Senate here. A career politician."

"Nobody in this state has your name recognition. You're about to get inducted into the pro football Hall of Fame, for Pete's sake. See, Dave, Iowa is losing a longtime Republican senator to retirement in 2004. We need to keep that seat in the fold. We can't afford to let the Democrats increase their strength in the Senate. Not now. Not while we're fighting a war against terrorism. The liberals lack the will to fight our nation's enemies. Your country *needs* you to run."

"Me?" I shook my head. "After what happened with my family three years ago, I've got liabilities. I'm just lucky my hometown support in Des Moines and Council Bluffs is so strong. If those two cities weren't in my district, I might have lost in 2000. I don't think I'm electable to a more competitive statewide office."

"Nonsense! The public doesn't blame you for that tragedy. You did nothing wrong. People sympathize with you. Especially the ones who've got kids. They understand the pain you endured. And they know you've got a good heart. They see you on TV using your recess time to build houses for the less fortunate. They've read articles about you working in the soup kitchen serving the homeless. Iowans know that you're willing to sacrifice for them."

"I don't know if that's enough to overcome my baggage, Levi. A run at the Senate might just be asking for a beating."

"Dave ..." Zadok lowered his voice and leaned closer as if to tell me a secret. "The president himself wants you to run. He knows what's at stake here in Iowa. He needs good men like you in the Senate to support his campaign against global terror. It's a patriotic cause. A holy cause."

"The president mentioned me?"

"Asked for you by name. Heard it with my own ears. The party bosses like you too. You've served in the House with distinction. You've got the legislative experience. You've got the trust and respect of the people. You're the perfect candidate."

Both men stared at me with expectant eyes. Sighing, I looked out the window behind Joe. The downtown buildings stood in relief against the cloudy blue sky. Conflicting thoughts rolled through my head. My seat in the House was relatively safe. Running for the Senate, on the other hand, was risky. I would not have the advantage of being an incumbent and would likely have to face an experienced well-connected Democratic opponent. Moreover, if I ran and lost, I would be out of a job at time when I could ill-afford to be unemployed. Since I had spent more years of my life playing football than serving in public office, the idea of me running for the Senate seemed like a long shot. *Or was it?* Zadok's words stoked my competitive fires. I visualized myself in the Senate chamber. *More power. More prestige. Six-year terms.* Excitement coursed through my veins.

"What Levi says is true," Joe said. "I've done some preliminary research on this. The data is positive. I think we would have a shot. I really do."

I looked at one set of eyes and then the other. "Alright gentlemen, I'll pray about it."

Chapter 24 – October 2004

"Working together," I said, scanning the legion of faces before me, "we can build a stronger Iowa. We can build, uh …" *Oh crap!* The moment I had been dreading for months finally arrived—my mind went completely blank during a speech. I was near the end, but just could not pull in the closing sentences. Since this was an after-dinner talk I'd given a dozen times, I did not have any notes to bail me out. The silence grew more awkward with each passing second. I looked down, away from the hundred sets of eyes boring into my skull. *Say something! Anything!* "… we can build a stronger tomorrow for the children and, uh, for our families, and friendship for every citizen. To America and beyond!" I punched my fist for emphasis.

Looks of confusion spread throughout the audience. But then someone started a trickle of clapping. Slowly the applause gained momentum. Like a wave rolling across the dining hall, the well-dressed crowd rose to its feet. Leaving the podium, I glided over to shake hands with people at the nearest table. Thor soon appeared at my side to shepherd me toward the side exit. Passing through the door, we entered a hallway where Joe and a couple campaign staffers awaited.

"To America and beyond?" Joe asked, with a raised brow. "What the hell was that?"

"I don't want to hear it," I said as we strode through the corridor with Thor and the staffers trailing behind. "You got me going to too many of these things. I could have used a night off."

"A night off? You know how much cash this event brought in?"

"No." We exited the Bettendorf VFW Post to a sparsely-lit back parking lot. The breeze blowing in off the Mississippi brought cool relief to my burning face.

"Well, you saw how many were in the crowd. Take that number times a hundred dollars, plus extra contributions. Not a bad haul for one night's work."

We reached a black limousine. Joe gave some instructions to the staffers before he and I climbed into the back of the vehicle. Thor occupied the passenger seat in front. As the driver steered the limo out of the parking lot, Joe flipped a button raising the privacy divider.

"Your campaign has attracted big money," he said. "But we're spending it almost as fast as it's coming in. You can't pass up prime fundraising opportunities like we had tonight."

"Yeah, yeah." I slouched back in my seat, which faced the rear of the car.

Sitting across from me, Joe eyed the mini-bar to his left. "We're on a roll," he said. "Have been since the last debate. We're ahead twelve points in the latest poll, but there are four weeks to go." He poured himself a glass of brandy. "Your lead could vanish overnight."

"I know." I loosened the knot in my tie. "So, what's next?"

He checked his Rolex. "We should hit Iowa City around eleven. Then, you go to bed. You need to be sharp tomorrow. At eight, you're meeting the firefighters. At ten, there's a rally on campus. And noon is the Kiwanis luncheon. Then we head for Des Moines."

"Good. I told Gail I'd be home by four tomorrow afternoon. We'll make that won't we?"

"Yes, I think so." He took a drink. "What's the hurry?"

"Archie's home. Remember? It'll be the first time I've seen him since the trial."

He wrinkled his brow. "Oh yes, I knew that."

"He got out Friday. Gail had a big welcome home party for him Saturday night. Kyle drove down from Minneapolis. Gail's parents came in from Lincoln. Ozzie, Adam, and Abby were there. A bunch of family showed up. But not me … his dad."

Joe's look became condescending. "Dave, this swing through the eastern counties was scheduled weeks ago. Building support in this part of the state is crucial for your campaign. I'm sorry you had to miss Archie's party, but you have to make sacrifices. A seat in the U.S. Senate is at stake. Your opponent is a wily politician. He's not going to give you this election. You have to TAKE it." He clinched his fist. "To do that, you have to campaign your ass off. Because you know Ben Shea is out there campaigning *his* ass off trying to beat you."

I pressed my head back against the seat. "I know this trip is important. I just feel bad."

"Archie should understand what's at stake. He knows you have responsibilities. And you're going to see him only three days after the party."

"It's just, I've worked so hard to repair my relationship with him. This summer he answered one of my letters. It was the first time he'd ever done that. His response was brief, but positive. I think he finally stopped blaming me for what happened. I don't want to do anything to drive him away."

"You haven't done anything to drive him away." Joe lowered his glass into a holder. "You two will have plenty of time to talk tomorrow when we get back. Everything will be fine."

I shut my eyes. "I hope so." The limo sped west toward Iowa City.

The next day was Tuesday. I arrived home a few minutes before four. Gail greeted me as I entered the kitchen. "Is Archie here?" I asked, anxiety roiling my stomach.

"He had a meeting with his parole officer," she replied. "He said he'd be home around four."

"How about Tammy and Donnie? Will they be here for supper tonight?"

"No. Donnie is at a friend's house. He's going to eat over there. And Tammy has a big English test tomorrow. She'll be at her dorm studying all night."

"Oh." My spirits sank. "It's been so long, I was hoping we could all be together tonight. I don't get too many evenings at home anymore."

"Guess it's just not going to work out this time," she said with some bite.

"Is something wrong?"

"Nope." Turning to the refrigerator dispenser, she filled a glass with water.

"Something's wrong. What is it?"

After a drink, she set the glass on the counter and studied me for a few seconds. "They're a little disappointed you didn't come home for Archie's party."

Her words stung. "I had campaign engagements. I thought they understood."

"It was kind of a big deal to them. They thought you could have cancelled something to make it here. It was just one night." Her crow's feet darkened as she squinted with disappointment. It was a look I had seen before.

"Sounds like you agree with them."

"It doesn't matter now." She plucked a set of keys from her purse.

"You're leaving? But I just got here. Where are you going?"

"Valley West. Archie said he wanted to talk to you alone, so I'll be at the mall for a while. My phone will be on."

I contemplated her words. "He wants to talk … alone. That's good, right? Or is he mad at me too?"

"No, he didn't act like it. I think he just wants to spend some time with you, especially since he hasn't seen you for so long. You two have a lot to talk about." After a peck on the cheek, she left.

I lugged my suitcase up to the bedroom before returning downstairs to review the pile of mail on my desk in the den. As I settled into the comfort of my lumbar support leather chair, the fatigue of campaigning caught up with me. I intended to shut my eyes for only a couple seconds, but I dozed off for a few minutes. From somewhere in the house, a calling voice startled me awake. "Anybody home?"

"In the den," I answered, shaking off the cobwebs.

An instant later, a man stood in the doorway. "Archie," I said, rising to my feet. With broad shoulders, bulging pectorals, and thick arms, he looked even more impressive than the robust teenage athlete I remembered from five years ago. Dark hair slid down in waves to his shoulders. His stubbly jaw set, he eyed me with a trace of a smile.

"Hello Dad," he said in a voice deeper than I expected.

"It's good to see you." I paused as my voice momentarily choked with emotion. "Man, look at those guns. You look great."

"Thanks." He advanced into the room. "I've had plenty of time to work out, you know."

I moved around the desk to stand before him. He was at least an inch taller than me now. I wanted to hug him, but an unseen barrier stood between us. "I don't know where to begin. It's been …"

"A long time. I know."

"I'm sorry I missed the party Saturday. This campaign schedule your cousin has me on is so crazy."

"Not a problem, Dad. More cake for me," he said with a wink.

I stared into his blue eyes searching for the son I once played football with in the backyard; the son I once taught how to hit a curveball; the son who once called me his hero. I longed for that boy to return to me. "Archie, not a day went by that I didn't think about you. I prayed constantly for God to watch over you. I'm so sorry for what happened. Do you forgive me?"

His face softened. "Dad … of course I do." He wrapped me in a tight embrace. After a few seconds, he stepped back. "It's good to be home."

"Amen. Gosh, there's so much to catch up on, I don't know where to begin." I realized that I was repeating myself.

He scrunched his forehead into a look of contemplation. "I've got an idea."

"Sure." I gestured for him to proceed.

"How about if you tell me about a kid named Sol Schaeffer?"

His words jarred the wind from my lungs. "Huh?" I stammered. "Where did you hear that name?"

"Well, I was on the computer in here the other day. Thought I'd do some surfing. Not always easy to keep up on current events in the big house, you know. Then I saw the Outlook Express icon and I just couldn't resist clicking it. Next thing I knew I was taking a peek at your emails."

"You read my personal correspondence?" I asked incredulously.

"You know us convicts." He shrugged his shoulders.

"But my email account is password protected. How did you get in?"

"It's *amazing* what you can learn in prison," he said with a catlike smirk. "Not everybody there is a dumb murderer like me. Some of the dudes are smart computer geeks. Not much they can't hack into. Taught me a lot of neat tricks, they did. I'll show you later. But we're strayin' here. About this Sol kid, you were saying?"

I tried to recall the content of my recent email exchanges with Sol. "He's a boy I know," I said quietly. "Lives in Cairo, Illinois."

Archie's face lit up. "Wow, Dad! You really are a politician. 'A boy I know.' That's a good one…. Sol is your son! At least, that's what you call him your emails. Or is that a little nickname you have for all the boys you know?"

"Archie, please." I raised my hands in a gesture of pleading. "Yes, he's my son."

"Now let me remember." He turned and paced away. "In one of his messages, the boy mentioned being in seventh grade. Hmmm, that means he was born in … oh shit, I'm not good with numbers." Archie tapped the side of his head. "Somewhere around '91 or '92, right? Wait a minute." He spun around to face me. "Weren't you married to Mom back then? Yes, I think you were." A look of mock surprise covered his face.

My eyes dropped. "I had an affair when we were living in New Jersey. It only lasted a few months. I told your mother about it. She forgave me and we moved on. I haven't had contact with the other woman in twelve years."

"Oh, well at least it was all wrapped up neat and tidy. Except for the boy, of course. You've sure had contact with him, haven't you?" His face hardened. "Unbelievable, Dad. First you sired Tom, and what a delightful kid he turned out to be. Now we've got little Sol. How many other bastards you got running around out there?"

"That's enough, Archie," I said with a spark of anger. "I'm your father. You watch how you talk to me."

Sarcasm oozed from his chuckle. "My father, huh? Actually, I don't know who the hell you are. When I was growing up you lectured us over and over about Christian values and the importance of family. But the whole time, you're out screwing all the whores you could find. What was it like when you were away from Mom in Washington? Did you and Clinton have a competition about who could score the most interns?"

My face tightening with fury, I could not speak for several seconds. "There were NO others," I hissed. "I only strayed from my marriage once. That's it. Never before. Never since."

"Ooooh," he mocked, waving his fingers at me. "You say that with such pride. Like you expect some sort of medal for limiting yourself to just one affair."

"Okay, I get it. I sinned. It was a terrible mistake, but I repented. What more can I do now?"

"Nothing, Dad. It doesn't matter what you do now."

"What's that supposed to mean?"

He stepped closer to me. "What I mean, Dad, is that you've already done enough damage with your selfishness. Maybe you're not cheating on Mom anymore. It doesn't matter. You're still the same person who always put his own interests before his family. When I was a little kid, football came first. Then you won a seat in Congress and that came first. Now it's this big Senate race. Meanwhile, Mom had to raise four kids pretty much by herself."

His words hit like a sucker punch. "That's not fair and you know it. Your mother didn't raise you alone. I was a father to all you kids."

"You were gone a lot," he said, "especially after you got into politics. We knew your career was more important than us. But if that wasn't bad enough, when Tom showed up you bent over backwards fawning over him." He pointed a finger in my face. "You brought him into our house and you let that bastard rape Tammy. Then you were going to let him get away with it to avoid any embarrassment to yourself."

"That's not true," I said, raising my voice. "Joe suggested it, yes. But I wasn't going to go along with his plan."

"Don't give me that bullshit." His face twitched. "You'd do anything to protect your public image. If that meant letting the guy who raped your daughter get away with it, that's okay. Whatever it takes."

"How can you say that?" The blood in my face burned hot.

"What, am I wrong? You want the world to think you're the perfect Christian husband and father, but look at what you've done to your own family. You betrayed Mom. You betrayed Tammy. And you betrayed me. I spent FIVE years locked up because of you."

"I love my wife!" I shouted. "And I love my children! I may have made some mistakes, but there was NEVER a time I wouldn't have done anything for any of you."

"You're pathetic." Sneering, he turned toward the door.

"We're not through here," I said. In a flash, he whirled back around. Before I could blink, a massive fist crashed into my face. For an instant, the room went dark. Then bright jagged bolts of pain shot through my head as my body flew backwards over the desk. Against the backdrop of the wood-paneled ceiling, I saw the unfamiliar sight of my feet floating above my body. While falling, my back crashed into the arm of the chair. It tipped over on me as I hit the floor, shoulder first and head second.

Dangling on the edge of consciousness, I heard my son's continuing vitriol. I could not discern everything he said, but a few words stood out: "adulterer," "hypocrite," "fraud." A hefty expectoration splattered upon my cheek. Though numb, I could feel it trickle down my neck. After a slamming door rattled the windows, the only remaining sound was a sharp ringing in my ears. With my brain feeling like it had been caught in a paint shaker, I lay crumpled on the floor beneath my toppled desk chair.

The next day, Joe cancelled my campaign appearances for the rest of the week. He issued a press release stating that I fallen ill and needed a few days to recover. Close enough. My head throbbing, I moped around the house all day Wednesday. By evening the physical pain started to abate. Emotionally, I still bled profusely.

Archie, meanwhile, had moved to his cousin Andy's apartment in Ankeny, a town just north of Des Moines. I was heartbroken that my son felt such hostility for me. Before his arrest, I had always thought that we had a special connection. Since he was the most athletic of my children, we forged a bond over sports. He even vowed to follow in my footsteps as a pro quarterback. But his raging accusations cast doubt that we had ever shared anything real. My boy had become a stranger to me. His hateful words replayed in my head, lacerating my soul. *Does he really think I'm a hypocrite? Does he really hate me?* I did not think I could sink any lower. The next day, I found out differently.

Gail woke me up a little after eight Thursday morning. She said Joe and Levi were downstairs waiting to talk to me. I asked why they were here so early. She knew, but would not tell me. I threw on a robe and traipsed down to the living room. The rotund Zadok, unkempt as ever, slouched on the couch. Joe, having shed his suit jacket, paced in front of the fireplace. A bolus of dread grew in my stomach. My nephew stomped across the room and thrust the morning newspaper in my face. "We've got a problem," he said.

Taking the paper, my eyes scanned the front-page headline. "Congressman's Adultery Exposed." I read with horror the article below. Archie had given reporters copies of my email correspondence with Sol. The press then moved quickly to expose the skeleton that had been hiding in my closet for more than a decade. Though Beth declined comment, a picture of her accompanied the article, which also mentioned her husband's suicide. I collapsed into the couch.

"Dave, this is a mess," Joe said. "That kid of yours really let you have it. But we're going to fight back. Our campaign is NOT going to end like this. Not after everything we've worked for."

"We're going to have to respond immediately," Zadok added.

Joe stood before me, his eyes blazing. "Dave, are you still in this? Are you willing to fight to save your campaign?"

My eyes rose to meet his, but I was unable to focus. The realization that the world now knew about my affair plunged my spirit into an abyss of shame. I said nothing.

"Dave! There are thousands of people who have supported this campaign. They have donated their time and money. They are counting on you. Don't quit on them. We can still win this. Don't let a rebellious son destroy all your plans to help this state. I need to know right now, will you continue the fight?"

His words sparked a flicker. I nodded. "Yes, I'll fight."

Joe, Zadok, and I spent the rest of the morning drafting a statement. Calling a press conference was not necessary. By noon, an army of reporters was camped on my front lawn. I showered, shaved, and dressed. Then, after a prayer, I walked out onto my porch to address the media. Gail stood by my side.

"I had an affair thirteen years ago," I began, glancing at the horde. "It lasted a few months and then it ended, for good. There is a child from that relationship. I have paid the boy's mother child support every month since his birth. I will continue to do so. I confessed the affair to my wife at the time it happened. I profoundly regret hurting her. I am thankful every day for her forgiveness and determination to save our marriage. I have knelt at the foot of the cross and repented of my sin. Having experienced God's mercy, I truly understand the need we all have for a Savior." I paused to take a breath as tapes rolled, lenses zoomed, and shutters clicked.

"To my supporters, I apologize for the embarrassment my actions have caused. I ask for your forgiveness as I continue my campaign to be your representative in the U.S. Senate. Please give me the opportunity to regain your trust. To the media, I implore you to respect the privacy of the mother and her son. Let them live their lives in peace. They have suffered enough already. Finally, I wish to tell my son Archie that I love him. It breaks my heart that something has come between us. My door remains open for you. Please come home."

A barrage of questions followed. Did I have any other illegitimate children? Will I be dropping out of the race? Did Ryan Schaeffer kill himself because of the affair? What caused the swelling on my face? Do I have any right to claim to be the candidate of family values? Am I qualified to be a senator? To avoid a feeding frenzy, Joe stepped up to announce that I would not be answering questions at this time. Zadok then hustled Gail and me back into the house. The experience was humiliating, but I knew I had brought it upon myself.

From inside, I heard Joe talking to the press. Shifting into lawyer-speak, he fended off their questions for twenty minutes before they finally dispersed. A half hour later, Nathan called from New Jersey. He had read about the story on the CNN Web site. He spoke words of encouragement and prayed with me over the phone. Later that afternoon, Thor and my pastor from Faith Community Church, Geoff Ittai, showed up to offer their support. Ozzie and Anthony came over that night. The presence of each of them helped keep the dark clouds from overwhelming me.

Unfortunately, the news went from bad to worse over the following week. Archie continued giving interviews attacking me as a hypocrite and a horrible father. He even started appearing at campaign functions for my opponent. Blaming me for his imprisonment, my son told the world that I had plotted to let Tom escape punishment for raping Tammy.

Archie's efforts produced the results he desired. My poll numbers plummeted. In only a few days, I dropped from twelve points ahead to ten points behind. Contributions slowed to a trickle. One of my best advisors, Phil Atkins, resigned. Volunteers quit. I was heckled at speaking engagements. In Boone, an old man threw rocks at me and called me a scoundrel. At Waldorf College, a student pelted me square in the chest with a tomato. As officers dragged her away, she shouted that I would always bear the red stain of adultery.

The harassment extended to my children. Students at the University of Minnesota mocked Kyle, a grad student in biology, when they saw him on campus. Tammy, a sophomore literature major at Drake University, stopped going to classes after receiving prank phone calls. Donnie, a junior at Johnston High, found his car covered with egg in the school parking lot. Sol emailed that his mom was pulling him out of school so they could go away for a couple weeks.

Racked with guilt, I thought about quitting the race. Joe talked me out of it. He said if I dropped out, my children would face even more scorn and persecution. So I pressed on. All along the campaign trail, I owned up to my past mistakes. I spoke of repenting and receiving God's forgiveness. I asked the people of Iowa for understanding. Gail, though heartsick over the rift in our family, joined me on stage at several rallies. Her presence always brought a friendlier reaction from the crowds.

Joe, meanwhile, worked overtime to find a way to turn the tide back in my favor. He wanted me to press charges against Archie for assault. I refused. Though my son's continuing attacks threatened the survival of my campaign, I could not send him back to jail. He was still my boy, and I loved him. Longing for reconciliation, I prayed that our relationship would be restored.

Thursday morning, a week after the story broke, I woke up at five with my stomach aching from stress. Unable to fall asleep again, I went to the den and read a few chapters from the book of Job. Around six-thirty, I trudged down our long driveway to retrieve *The Des Moines Register* from the newspaper receptacle below the mailbox. The tranquil country morning brought a rare sense of peace to my embattled psyche. After I reached the kitchen table, the phone rang. It was the Des Moines Police Department. My peace was shattered.

An officer relayed the bleak details to me. Around midnight, police observed a Mercury Topaz at a stoplight on Martin Luther King Jr. Parkway. The vehicle sat unmoving through several green light cycles, prompting officers to investigate. They found the car in neutral and Archie passed out at the wheel. They also found a meth pipe in his jacket and three bags of crystal meth in the passenger seat of the Topaz, which was registered to a man named Tony Huscher. At the police station, Archie tested positive for amphetamines.

Gail entered the kitchen and asked who had called. When I told her the news, she shrieked in anguish. "Oh no, not Archie! They're going to send him back to prison." I tried to embrace her trembling body, but she flinched and backed away.

Having heard his mother's cry, Donnie bounded down the stairs. After I told him what had happened, he asked if he could skip school to go visit Archie. He and Gail took off for the Polk County Jail a short time later. Without discussion, we all knew that my accompanying them was not an option. I roamed the empty house as my stomach lining eroded away.

Finally, Gail called. "How is he?" I asked. "Did you see him?"

"Yes, they let us see him. He looks terrible. He's so scared."

"What happened? Who is this Tony Huscher?"

"A guy he knew in prison. I guess they were friends before Tony got out last year. Archie said Tony contacted him a few days ago. Wanted to go out and catch up. Last night Archie was hanging out at Tony's apartment. There were some other people there he didn't know."

"Were they doing drugs?"

"Yes," she said in a pained voice. "But Archie wasn't. He said all he did was drink a couple beers. Then at some point he blanked out. The next thing he remembered was waking up in the backseat of a police car."

"How could that have happened?"

"Dave, our son was set up. They drugged him at the party and drove him out to that intersection to be found by the cops with all that meth."

"He thinks Huscher did this?"

"Of course it was Huscher!" Her voice rose. "The jerk even had the nerve to tell police that Archie had stolen his car."

"But why would Huscher do this? I thought you said they were friends. Did he have a grudge against Archie?"

"I don't think it was Tony's idea. Someone paid him to do this to Archie."

A chill swept over me as I grasped her implication. "Oh."

"Dave, did you authorize this? Did you tell Joe to get our son arrested?" Her accusation drew blood.

"How can you ask that? I would never do that to our son. Never!"

Her sobs poured through the phone. "They're going to hold him until the parole board meets for a revocation hearing. They might send him back to prison."

"We'll get a lawyer. We'll help him."

"They've got evidence.... Dave, he was crying when I left him. He's terrified of going back." Overcome with emotion, Gail had to hang up.

I stepped into the living room where the family portrait on the fireplace mantel caught my eye. It was taken in the spring of 1999, before the disasters hit. Archie looked so happy. Young and strong, he had his whole life ahead of him. My heart wept. Then, in the midst of my grief, a rage ignited. I dialed Joe's number. He said we could meet at his office.

On the drive downtown, I turned on the radio for a distraction. "Distant Early Warning" by Rush was playing on KGGO. After the song ended, one of my campaign ads aired. I recognized the opening, but then an ominous voice started castigating my opponent. It was dirty and cheap—the exact type of attack ad I had promised not to run. At the end of the commercial, I heard my own voice. "I'm Dave King and I approved this message." My fingers tightened around the steering wheel.

After reaching the seventh floor of the Federal Building, I barged into Joe's office and slammed the door shut. He stood facing the back window. Hands clasped behind his waist, he surveyed the city blocks stretching out before him. Silently, I advanced.

"It's a gorgeous morning," he declared. "I love autumn, don't you? The leaves changing … it's just so beautiful."

Without a word, I glared at the back of his head where the tips of his coiffed hair met and curved down toward his neck.

"Not as beautiful as New England, mind you." He turned to reveal a vulpine countenance. "I do miss Cambridge this time of year. But this is still nice. Care to take a look?"

"What did you do to my son?"

"What do you mean? Did something happen to Donnie?"

"You know damn well who I'm talking about," I said, clenching my fists. "What did you do to Archie?"

"Ah yes, Archie. The young man doing everything in his power to destroy you. Now that you mention it, I did hear something about him. Had a little run-in with the law, did he?"

"They're probably going to send him back to prison."

"Well, crime has consequences." The corners of his mouth curled slightly.

"You set him up. How much did you pay Tony Huscher?"

His expression fell serious. "Careful. Throwing around wild accusations is never wise. Especially for a man in your position."

"Cut the bullshit, Joe! I know this was your doing."

He returned my stare for several seconds. "You know nothing."

"You had no right to frame my son." I circled around his desk.

"Why are you so upset? What happened is a great victory for you. If I did what you're insinuating, then I have served you well."

I put my face only a couple of inches from his. "Archie's just a kid. He didn't deserve that."

"He's twenty-one. That's well past the age of accountability."

With both hands I grabbed his shirt collar and shoved him into the side of a bookcase. He grunted as his head and body slammed into the hard mahogany. "He was on parole!" I yelled. "They're going to send him back to prison. We may never see him again."

His eyes flashed fear for an instant, before transforming into a hard glare. "Dave, what is the matter with you? Don't you know what's at stake? Don't you know how many people have pinned their hopes to you? Good people across this state are counting on you to represent them." His mouth sneered as he spoke. "But you don't give a shit about your supporters. The only person you care about is that psychotic son who's trying to wreck your career."

I released my grip as Joe continued haranguing me. "Remember that widow with the five children you mentioned during the debate? You looked straight into the camera and told the world how you wanted to help her build a better life. And remember those disabled veterans you met at the VA hospital two weeks ago? You said you wouldn't forget the sacrifices they had made for their country. Said the same thing about our troops serving in Iraq. And what about all the Christians in this state? You promised to be their voice in the Senate. Tell me, Dave, did you lie to *all* those people?"

Disgusted by his presence, I turned away and stalked toward the door.

"Your campaign has raised more than five million dollars," he said, his voice amplified. "Over half of that is from individual donations. Money from hardworking Iowans. Some of them barely getting by. But they tightened their belts and wrote you a check. Why? Because they believe in you. Are you going to tell them all to go to hell because you don't have the stomach to fight for your campaign?"

Spinning around, I glowered at him. "You went too far with what you did to Archie."

"What's the great moral tragedy here?" he asked, throwing up his arms. "A convicted murderer goes back to prison. He'll be eligible for parole again in two or three years. It was a sacrifice that had to be made for the survival of your campaign."

"You think I still have a campaign?" I scoffed.

"Yes!" He slapped his desk. "What you did thirteen years ago is not a big deal. You had an affair in a past life, so what? You paid child support and took responsibility for your actions. Sure the revelations shocked some people, but they're already starting to forgive you. The public has overlooked far worse from its leaders. Without Archie out there reminding them, most voters won't even care about your past indiscretions by Election Day."

I stepped forward. "So that's why you had to do something to shut him up."

"You don't know that I did anything."

"What about the attack ads against Shea? I just heard one of them on the radio. My own campaign commercial. One that I did not authorize. You going to deny doing that too?"

Joe shook his head. "Dave King the white knight, always trying to take the high road."

"I've told you, I will not tolerate negative campaigning."

"Given all the success I've brought you, I'd think twice before you question my methods."

I advanced to the front of his desk. "Are you trying to take credit for my career?"

A smirk crept across his face. "No, not all of it. But you've been much more successful with me than you ever would have been without me. Plus, I've afforded you certain luxuries."

"Luxuries? What luxuries?"

"You've cultivated this image of yourself as the upright Christian family man. In the NFL and in politics, you always wanted people to think you were the good guy. And you were able to pull it off because you had me and my minions doing all your dirty work for you."

"I never asked you to do anything dirty."

"Maybe not directly, but you didn't have any problem with reaping the benefits of my labors. You think that negotiating your salary with Newark's tightfisted owners was a friendly chat? It was long ugly process filled with lies, bluffs, and threats from both sides. But Anthony and I got you your money. And then there are those House elections you won." His eyes narrowed to squint. "Politics is a nasty game, Dave. It involves a lot of whoring. How do you think your campaigns always raised so much money? How do you think you won the support of so many special interests? It sure was convenient that you had people willing to roll around in the mud for you, so you didn't have to."

An ill feeling crawled up my esophagus as I contemplated his words.

"For the past twenty years, dear Uncle, you've had an angel looking out for you. Call him a dark angel if you must, but don't pretend like you didn't benefit from his protection."

"What exactly did you do?"

"I did what was necessary. Let's just leave it at that. Our relationship works best when you don't ask too many questions."

Staggered, I broke away from his gaze and moved over to the rows of law books covering the side wall of his office. A forgotten memory returned, causing an icy dread to coil around my spine. A long-buried question arose. Before I could stop myself, the words left my mouth. "Joe, did you have anything to do with Abner Kishman's death?"

Looking askance, I saw his face pale. "What the hell are you talking about?" he asked just above a whisper.

"When I was in college, his house burned down. Did you pay the arsonist to set the fire?"

"Are you out of your mind? That case has been closed for decades."

"Answer the question."

Joe turned away to face the window. "We don't have time for this nonsense, Dave."

"After the rally in Council Bluffs last month, I went to Omaha to visit your mother. Somehow we got on the subject of crime rates. She said the only time she was ever robbed was back in the '70s. I didn't think much about it at the time, but now I remember when that happened. I was a junior at UWI. It was about a month after Asa died and about a month before the fire." I paused as my nephew continued staring silently out the window.

"Joe, I think it was you who robbed your mother. And then you used the money to pay somebody to burn down Abner's house." I shuddered upon hearing my voice speak those words.

He turned around, his crimson face contorted with rage. "You weren't there when Asa died," he said, jabbing a finger at me. "You weren't driving the car that crashed. You didn't hear his last breaths, how he cried in agony. You didn't see the blood all over his broken body.... AND YOU WEREN'T HOLDING HIS HAND AS HIS GRIP FADED TO NOTHING!" He slammed his fist into the computer keyboard on his desk. Blood dripped from his knuckles onto the shattered plastic below.

I said his name. He said nothing. I approached to put a hand on his shoulder. Recoiling with an angry horror in his eyes, he stepped away to the other side of the office. For more than a minute, his quaking breaths were the only sounds in the room. He then faced me again.

"Anthony is involved in this too. It was my idea, but he helped. Nobody was supposed to die. We told that lowlife thug to make sure nobody was home when he set the fire. The miscreant just took our money and did it the first chance he got. My brother panicked when we found out about Abner the next day. He almost called the police to confess, until I told him it was all part of God's plan. His divine justice. An eye for an eye, just like it says in the Bible. Abner killed Asa, so Abner had to die."

"But you were chasing Abner on the freeway. He was just trying to get away from you. Abner didn't kill Asa. He didn't mean for anybody to die."

"Well, I didn't either," Joe said bitterly.

Overwhelmed, I sank into one of the chairs in front of the desk and stared out at the sky. Joe dropped quietly into his own chair. We sat in silence. "Dave," he finally said, "I don't know what you're planning to do, but let me say this. If you go to the police, they still won't have enough to arrest me. It's been almost thirty years. There's no evidence. Daggar is long dead. And to protect

Anthony, I will admit to nothing. He has a wife and two children. I'm not going to let him go to prison."

Meeting his gaze, I gave him no reply.

"And the race," he continued, "you're probably planning to drop out. But forget for a moment all the evil you see in me and think about what *you* could gain. With my help you can still win this election. Then you, not Joe Krieger, will be a U.S. senator. That is a powerful position. You'd be able to do so much good for so many people. This state and this nation are better off with Dave King in office."

I sighed wearily. "I don't know, Joe."

"You remember when my father died? I was only seven. Then I lost Asa when I was still just a kid. My soul was corrupted long ago. Please, let me at least do this one good thing by helping you win. I need this, Dave." His pleading eyes matched the tone of his voice. "Listen, Archie's final revocation hearing won't be until after the election. If you stay in the race, I'll make sure a couple of Huscher's friends testify that it was all a setup. Archie will go free. His time in jail will only last a few weeks. That's a much better prospect than what he's facing now."

"If you get those people to reveal the setup, won't that bring you down too?"

"Of course not. There's a network in place for these types of operations. Nothing can be traced to the source. Huscher and his cronies have no idea who really paid them."

My mind swirled with anger, sympathy, revulsion, sadness, guilt, and ambition. I did not know what to say.

"Dave, a man has to choose his battles in life. Sometimes you have to tolerate a little evil to bring about a greater good. If you drop out now, you will never again have this opportunity. Your political career will be finished. I really believe this Senate race is a battle you *must* fight."

Before leaving Joe's office, I agreed to stay in the race and let him remain as my campaign manager. It seemed like a small price to pay to keep Archie from returning to prison. Plus, deep inside, I wanted to win. So I continued campaigning. For three more weeks I crisscrossed Iowa, selling myself to the people. It was actually a relief to be on the road so much, away from a wife who still seemed to believe I was indirectly responsible for her son's arrest. When I was home, our conversations were short and chilly. It was no different with Tammy and Donnie, who were still reeling from the news that I had cheated on their mother. And Kyle, hundreds of miles away, never returned my emails anymore.

Losing myself in the campaign routine kept me sane. Over time, interest in the adultery story faded. I crept closer to Shea in the polls. He responded with a barrage of attack ads questioning my morals. They were cheap shots, so I allowed Joe to fight fire with fire. The ugliness escalated on both sides. Not surprisingly, my nephew and his "minions" were better at slinging mud than my opponent's guys. By the end of October I had closed the gap. Election Day brought one of the tightest electoral contests in Iowa history. A winner was not declared until well after midnight. When the last ballot was counted, I had a slim 755-vote victory.

In January I returned to Washington to be sworn in as a U.S. senator. Though they were no longer thrilled about my political career, or me for that matter, Gail, Kyle, Tammy, and Donnie attended the ceremony. They all flew back to Iowa the next day. While in D.C., I lived very much alone in a Capitol Hill apartment.

Archie's parole revocation hearing was scheduled for the following week. Joe had pulled strings to postpone it until then so as not to disrupt my swearing-in ceremony. Just as he had promised, Joe found two witnesses whose testimony would exonerate my son.

Three days before the hearing was to be held, Donnie called a few minutes after midnight. "Dad?" His voice was grave. In the background, I heard what sounded like wailing. But it was too loud and unremitting to be a person crying, I thought. "Mom wanted to talk to you, but she can't. She asked me to call."

"What is it, Donnie?"

"There was a big fight at the jail. Archie got caught in the middle of it. He was stabbed. They took him to the hospital, but they couldn't save him …"

After hanging up, a terrifying restlessness came over me. I had to get out of the apartment. I climbed the access stairs to the roof of my building. Standing at the ledge, the nocturnal lights of the nation's capital glowed before me. I was a U.S. senator at the peak of my professional success. But I felt nothing but soul-choking misery. Gail was drifting away from me. So were my children. *And Archie is dead.* The words repeated over and over into a shattering crescendo. My body shook at the realization that my son was gone. *At the end, he still hated you.* I was forty-six years old and for the first time in my life, I wanted to die. I eyed the sidewalk ten stories below.

Chapter 25 – January 2008

“Is this straight?” Thor asked.

Looking below his bottom chin, I examined the tie knot he had just tightened. “Yeah, it’s fine.” After briefly dwelling on the roll of neck skin bowed out over the sides of his stiff white collar, I returned my face to the window. Lights blurred as we sped down the freeway toward downtown.

“Hey Dave, this is great,” he said. “Thanks for letting me ride with you in back this time.” His eyes darted about the luxurious rear cabin of the limousine.

“Sure, no problem.”

“I really appreciate it. It’s an honor. Not that I mind riding in front. It’s just, this is such a huge night for you, I figured you’d be wanting to ride in with the top guys on your staff.”

I gazed at 801 Grand, the Ruan Center, and the other illuminated structures of the Des Moines skyline. “It’s nice to ride with a friend,” I said. “My conversations back here are usually so stressed and hectic. ‘Do this, don’t do that. Say this, don’t say that.’ Gets old, you know.”

“I bet.”

Recollections stirred uneasily in my head. “Thor, you know how insane things have been for the past … well, pretty much since I was first elected to Congress?”

“Yeah,” he chuckled. “If you think things were crazy before, just wait ’til after tonight. Your life is going to hit a whole new level of insanity.”

“Don’t remind me. Anyway, I just want to thank you for everything you’ve done for me. My life got so chaotic that I sometimes took you for granted. I’m sorry for that. I should have treated you better. Invited you to more of the social occasions as a friend rather than an employee."

His eyes dropped to his wingtips. "You treated me fine, Dave. You've paid me more than I deserve. I know you could find someone better to head your security detail here. Someone who's not so fat and hobbled by bum knees."

"You're the best man for the job, period. I wish I had you with me in the other states too."

"You need younger guys," he said, shaking his head. "Professionals who can react quicker. From now on you're going to be in a lot more dangerous situations. Larger crowds."

"No, you're The Hammer. I know I can count on you. You've always had my back. I never would have made it as a quarterback if it weren't for you. Not even in high school." A painful memory returned. "I might not even be alive if it weren't for you. That night Archie died, my head was a mess. Things could've turned out a lot differently if you hadn't called when you did." Dark thoughts lurked at the edge of my consciousness. "I'm just lucky I had my cell phone with me when I was up on that roof."

"That was God. You know that. Just like it was God who moved me to call you at that moment."

"Yeah.... Thank you for your friendship, brother. You've really helped me through some tough times. I'm glad you're still on my team after all these years."

He nodded and looked away. After a few moments of silence, uneasiness wrinkled his face. "Hey, you got your vest on?" he asked, gesturing at my chest.

"Yeah. I don't like it though. It's uncomfortable. Distracts me when I'm making a speech."

He frowned. "Is it more distracting than taking a bullet? Think about it. What if Anthony didn't happen to be standing next to that guy when he pulled his gun?" Thor's eyes turned grave. "He would have had a clean shot at you."

My thoughts careened back to that terrifying event in New Hampshire three months earlier. During a speech, a commotion drew my eye to the front of the crowd where Anthony was wrestling a duster-clad man to the ground. A woman screamed as the two men struggled over a gun. Bystanders assisted my nephew in subduing the would-be assassin. It was a frantic scene. "That was out of state. I've got you and J.J. leading my security detail tonight. There's nothing to worry about." I tried to believe my own words.

"Dave, the crowd at the hotel is going to be insane. Didn't you see the movie *Bobby*? It's impossible for us to watch everybody in that type of situation. You need that vest." He crossed his arms and stared at me with an anxious mien.

I turned to the window again as the limo rolled down an exit ramp and came to a stop at a red light. "Thor," I said, preparing to change the subject, "what did you think when I hired Joe back as my chief of staff?"

His eyes widened slightly before breaking away from my gaze. "Oh, uh." He fidgeted with his watch. "That was your call. You know I don't get involved with your policy decisions and stuff like that."

"Yes, but you had to have some opinion. Did you think less of me?"

"I wouldn't say that," he mumbled. "You were in a tough spot. The other guy wasn't working out. Couldn't handle the job. That was limiting your effectiveness as a senator."

"Joe told me he'd found God. He was a new person, so he promised."

"Really? Well, maybe he is. The Lord knows a man's heart."

"Yeah," I sighed, wondering what Thor would say if he knew about Joe's role in Abner's death and Archie's framing.

"You can't argue with the results," he said, scratching the top of his head. "Things really took off after you brought him back. You landed that spot on the Agriculture Committee. Your education bill passed. Then you went to Israel and gave that speech everybody liked. And now, here you are tonight." My thoughts skipped ahead to what was to happen later in the evening. My anticipation swelled, though it came with a twinge of fear.

The limo stopped at a downtown intersection. Pedestrians on the sidewalk shouted and waved, even though they could not see us through the tinted glass. "We're about there," Thor said, shifting his body to peer out the window. In so doing, his blazer opened wide enough to reveal the handle of his gun protruding from a shoulder holster. I knew he carried a piece, but actually seeing the weapon on the breast of such a kind-hearted man struck me as a harsh incongruity. "Any of your kids going to be with you at the podium?" he asked. "I'll make sure there's space for them."

"No, none of them will be there. I'll be lucky if Gail joins me on the stage."

He nodded, holding a finger to his earpiece. "How's she feeling?"

"Physically, fine."

"It's been about a month since the surgery, hasn't it?"

"Yeah, a month."

"I told Rebecca to stay close to her tonight, so don't worry if the two of you get separated after your speech."

"She still might divorce me, you know."

His face dropped. "I thought you two were seeing a counselor."

"We are. But the pain of losing Archie has not gone away. It's still right there between us." I glanced at the crowd outside the car. "I think the only reason she's stayed with me this long is because she doesn't want to disappoint all the Christians who are supporting me."

Distracted by a voice in his earpiece, Thor raised a hand to cut me off. "Sorry to interrupt, Dave, but we're here." The limo stopped at the front entrance of the Renaissance Savery Hotel. "The monarch is preparing to enter the castle," he said into his wrist microphone. "Okay, copy." He slid his ample frame across the leather seat in anticipation of the car door opening for us. "You know the drill," he said, looking over his shoulder. "Stay on my tail and The Hammer will knock a path through the crowd."

"Just like in the Sugar Bowl," I said. He woofed in reply.

Already waiting at the curb, Thor's son J.J. and Levi Zadok's son Maz helped keep the cheering horde at bay as I emerged from the limousine. With Thor at vanguard and the young men at my flanks, I moved toward the hotel entrance. The gauntlet of hands extended for me to shake slowed progress to a snail's pace. My ubiquitous campaign smile in place, we finally passed through the front doors. The heat of the crowded lobby provided a welcome contrast from the chilly outdoors. A chandelier glistened above, adding to the room's bright atmosphere. Like a bottle on a conveyer belt, I jostled forward through the throng. Minutes later we reached the hotel boardroom on the second floor, where closed doors shut out the chaos.

Standing around the long conference table, my staff clapped upon my entrance. I motioned for them to sit. Moving to the head of the table, I addressed the beaming faces, thanking them for their hard work. Then I sat and Joe stood. He reviewed the schedule for the evening and our itinerary for the week. By this time tomorrow, most of us were to be in New Hampshire. After dispensing specific instructions to the different staff members, he asked for questions. There were only two—one from Tracey Hiddard, my pollster, and one from Ben Jeffries, my press secretary. After answering the queries, Joe dismissed everybody from the room. I stood to shake each person's hand as they left. Zadok, wrapped in an ill-fitting suit, threw a beefy arm around me. A whiff of Old Spice invaded my nostrils. "Congratulations, kid. We may just pull this off." He exited with a round of boisterous laughter.

"Alright," Joe said, after the room included only him, his brother, and me. "We got what we wanted tonight." He punched some keys on his BlackBerry. "Latest numbers have you with 86 percent."

"Gotta love it," Anthony said.

I slid into a chair across from them. "But does this really mean anything? An Iowan winning the Iowa Caucus hardly locks up the nomination. Look at Harkin in '92."

Anthony's smile disappeared. Joe, still perusing the information on his device, nodded. "That is true," he said. "We've got a long road ahead of us. But you're not Harkin. He was way behind in New Hampshire when he won here. According to Tracey's latest numbers, you're now even with McCain and Romney there."

"Plus," Anthony added, "you're in much better financial shape than Harkin was back then. And after tonight's mandate, the cash is just going to keep rolling in. Face it, Dave, people are excited about your campaign."

"Yeah, but after tonight I'm going to have a big target on my back. The attacks are going to get more intense—not enough experience, not a true conservative, questionable past, family problems, took one too many hits on the football field.

"Nobody thinks of you as a dumb jock," Anthony said. "Especially after your showing in the last two debates."

"And those other attacks have been refuted as well," Joe said. "We've been over this. Counting your ten years in the House, you've got more legislative experience than either of the two Democratic frontrunners. Moreover, your record in the Senate is strong. You've advocated a sensible Iraq strategy, your pro-life family agenda appeals to the Christian Right, and your positions on immigration, the environment, and health care for children have won support from moderates and even a few liberals."

"More importantly," Anthony chimed in, "the ladies still think you're hot. They just can't resist those distinguished gray temples."

"Oh please," I groaned, rubbing my forehead.

"He's right," Joe said. "The numbers from Tracey are conclusive. Your looks are an asset with female voters … and gay men."

"Wonderful." I shook my head as Anthony snickered.

"Okay." Joe's tone indicated the shifting of gears. "Here's the revised version of your speech. There's only a slight change in the opening and a couple new lines near the end." He slid the papers across the table to me.

"Thanks." I scanned the top page.

"Don't linger in the crowd too long afterwards. Ben scheduled you for the late edition of *Larry King Live*. You go on sometime after eleven. Stick with the talking points and try to keep it short. Your flight tomorrow departs at 9:32 a.m. You need the sleep."

"Sleep? Is that still allowed?"

"Only after victories," Anthony replied with a grin.

I finished skimming the speech. "Any questions?" Joe asked.

I shook my head.

"Alright, good." He checked his watch. "It's a quarter 'til. Anthony and I should hit the ballroom and make sure everything is in order. Plan on taking the podium in a half hour. I'll send Thor to your room to escort you down. We've checked you and Gail into the penthouse suite under the name Vince Zahn, so people shouldn't be bothering you there." He slid the room keycard to me.

"Thanks. I know about the suite. Gail's already up there. She called when she arrived with Rebecca about an hour ago. Said she had a headache and wanted to lie down for a while."

"Okay. We'll see you on the stage." We rose from our chairs.

"Joe, Anthony," I said, looking at each of them. "Thank you. Whatever happens, I want you to know I appreciate the amazing work you've done for this campaign."

"You bet," Anthony said, smiling. "We're an unbeatable team."

Joe and I exchanged a knowing glance. Though the wounds from three years ago had not fully healed, I harbored hope that somewhere inside him was a good person. I wanted to believe that he had done nothing worse than the people working for my opponents. I told myself that he had never meant for anybody to die. I really hoped all that was true, because no one could get results for me like Joe Krieger.

We walked to the door, where I shook hands with my nephews. "See you on the other side," Anthony said.

"Remember," Joe added, "the entire nation will be watching you tonight. This speech could make or break your campaign. You have to project confidence. Show them what the next president of the United States looks like."

My body flinched with nervous excitement. "I'll see what I can do."

Illuminated by only the dim bulb of a small corner lamp, the penthouse suite resembled a cavern. Shadows concealed most of the room's lavish comforts. Gail lay on the covers of the vast bed, one arm draped over her eyes. I eased the door shut, muting the sound to a soft click.

"I'm awake," she said.

"Oh, I didn't know."

"My head still hurts."

"I'm sorry." I stepped lightly to the foot of the bed.

"Nice room, huh?"

"Yeah," I said with a quick glance around the bleakly lit chamber. "Swanky."

She lowered her arm from her face. “Is it time?” she asked, peering at me through narrow slits.

“Not yet. We’ve got about a half hour.” I sank into a plush chair a few feet from the bed.

“Mmpf. Guess I should get up. Check my hair.”

“You don’t have to go down there if you don’t want to.”

“That wouldn’t look very good.” She swung her legs over the edge of the bed and sat up. “The wife of the Iowa Caucus winner not showing at her husband’s victory speech. The press would be all over that.”

“Don’t worry about the press.”

She clucked. “Yeah, sure. Besides, I just had my hair colored. I think they finally got it right. Who knew my original shade would be so hard to match?” Yawning, she slipped her feet into the pumps on the floor below.

“Gail, if you don’t feel up to it, you don’t have to go. It’s just one speech.”

She eyed me with annoyance. “Why do you keep treating me like this?”

“Like what?”

“Like I’m an invalid.”

“You just had major surgery a month ago.”

“I had a mastectomy. And I’m fine. I can do everything now that I used to do.”

“I just don’t want you to exert yourself, especially so soon after—”

“I’m not going to break.” She stepped forward and turned around. “How’s the back of my dress. Is it wrinkly?”

I slid my hand over the teal fabric to smooth out the furrows. “Looks fine.”

“Good. The magazines have ripped my sartorial choices enough during this campaign. Don’t want to give them any more fodder by showing up with wrinkles.” She moved toward the bathroom. “On my clothes anyway. The wrinkles on my face I can’t do much about.”

“Your face isn’t wrinkly.” I stood. Through the open door, I watched as she adjusted her makeup in front of the bathroom mirror.

"There." She snapped shut a compact. "Now those fashion witches won't have as much to criticize about my appearance."

"They're critical of everybody's appearance," I said. "Don't pay attention to those idiots. Look at all the ridicule I take. The moron who plays me on *Saturday Night Live* wears denim overalls and a football helmet. Then he dances around like a hillbilly.... I haven't worn overalls since I was a kid."

She turned off the bathroom light and walked over to face me. "You're the one who wants to be president."

"Yeah." Our eyes met in the dimness. Her countenance fell solemn. I tried to recall when such an expression was not so common.

She glanced at her watch. "I should go. I told Rebecca I'd meet her in the ballroom about twenty minutes before your speech."

I nodded. "I'll see you at the podium then."

After Gail left, I clicked on the television to check CNN. Since my Republican opponents had long ago surrendered Iowa to me, the network focused its coverage on Barack Obama's victory in the Democratic caucus. Flipping channels, I found a report on Fox News about my triumph. "As expected, Iowa Senator Dave King wins big in his home state. But the race for the Republican nomination doesn't really begin until the New Hampshire primary on Tuesday ..."

A short time later, I turned off the TV. Alone in the nearly dark room, my being filled with uneasiness. I knelt at the side of the bed. "Lord, thank you for this great victory today. Please be with me as I speak to the nation." My disquiet continued to grow. *What if I blow it? What if I fail?* I quoted a favorite Psalm. "Hear my prayer, O Lord; listen to my cry for mercy. In the day of my trouble I will call to you, for you will answer me." I closed my eyes, yearning to hear God's voice.

A deep thumping shattered the silence. I shot to my feet and stared at the ceiling in confusion. "Senator Dave King," a voice bellowed. "Are you there?"

As the pounding continued, I realized that the sound was not coming from above. My pulse racing, I approached the door. "Who's there?"

"It's Britney, bitch. Open up before I tell the world that you're real father of Sean Preston and Jayden James."

I opened the door to behold a bald head and a smirking goatee. "Ozzie."

"What the hell are you doing in the dark?" he asked, brushing past me. "On second thought, maybe I don't want to know the disgusting things you do when you're by yourself." He flipped a wall switch, adding more light to the room. "I bet the press would though. For a couple grand, I'll keep your nasty little habits a secret."

"What are you doing here?" I shut the door.

"Thor told me you were up here. So I just had to check out your accommodations. Make sure they're up to my high standards." He wandered to the small refrigerator. "Oh, hell yeah. Check out these imported beers." He filched a bottle. "Gimme gimme."

I drifted over to the window. Car horns and shouts emanated from the street ten stories below. "Do you think they really like me?"

"Who?" Ozzie asked, removing the cap from his lager.

"All the people who voted for me," I said, still watching the pedestrians and vehicles below. "Do they really think I can be the next president?"

"I don't know. Maybe they're just used to having a clueless dimwit in the White House. People must figure you're the next best thing to what we got now."

I turned to glare at my brother, who was sitting in the plush chair I had occupied earlier. "Just because you resemble Howie Mandel doesn't mean you're funny."

He took a swig. "Oh come on. I'm a little funny. Remember when I Photoshopped your head onto a Teletubby's body and blew it up into a poster? *That* was friggin' hilarious." He snorted with laughter. "At least everybody driving by your campaign headquarters that afternoon thought so."

"Yeah, that was a riot. Especially when it made the evening news. Jerk."

"Getting back to your question," he said, still chuckling. "Maybe it's not that people like you, per se. Maybe it's that they don't like your opponents. I mean, even you have to admit there's a weak crop of Republicans this year. You've got Rudy the drag queen. McCain the grumpy old man. Then there's Mitt the flip-flopper. Who else? Oh yeah, that crusty fart from *Law and Order* and that Huckleberry Finn guy from Arkansas. Not much presidential timber there. I can see why a washed-up quarterback from Iowa is getting some votes."

"Forget it." A spasm of anxiety flared in my stomach.

Aside from the sound of Ozzie swishing beer around in his bottle, the room was quiet for a while. "Alright Dave, what's wrong with you? Are you really surprised that you won tonight? Why shouldn't voters like you?"

"I'm scared," I mumbled.

"Hope you're not planning to open with that in your big victory speech."

"This is supposed to be a huge night for me and I can't escape the feeling that something terrible is going to happen."

"Huh? You just won. Why would something bad happen?"

"It's because of my sin. Look at all the wreckage I've caused. I cheated on Gail and left Beth a pregnant widow. Two of my sons were killed. Kyle lives a thousand miles away and wants nothing to do with me. Tammy doesn't talk to me either. She lives alone in that apartment and hardly has any friends. And Donnie, he's back in rehab. All of that happened because of me."

"Come on, man. You can't blame yourself for—"

"Gail and I used to be best friends. Now she wants to leave me." I looked down at the floor. "It's my fault. The affair. Ryan's suicide. What happened to my children. It's all my fault."

Ozzie sprang to his feet and stepped toward me. "Dave, you've got to stop this. You're going on national television in five minutes."

"It's the same with our brothers and sisters," I said, continuing my gloomy descent. "Abby won't talk to me because I didn't stop Joe from firing Andy from my staff. And Zoe still hasn't forgiven me for dismissing Joe after I won in '04—even though I brought him back. Adam and Shane are upset I didn't do more to save the restaurant. Eli, when he died we hadn't spoken to each other in years."

"Eli was an ass. A bitter chain-smoking ass who couldn't hold a job."

"I should have done more to reach out to him."

"Dave, what is the point of all this? Huh?" His voice rose as his eyes narrowed. "There's no reason to dwell on any of that stuff now. This is the biggest night of your life and you're acting like a scared little kid. Don't you want to win?"

"Of course I want to win." I walked away from him. "But I'm afraid God is not through punishing me." I stopped in front of the mirror, where I saw a tremulous face. "The people are going to turn against me."

"You're the frontrunner for the Republican nomination," he said. "Start acting like it. Leave that other stuff in the past. It's not like you're hiding anything from the voters. Your indiscretions were well documented. If people want to forget about your past misdeeds, let them. You're not that person anymore."

"I know all that," I said, turning to face him. "But something's still not right. All I want to do is serve God and put him first." My eyes blinked hard to stave off a rush of tears. "But I feel like he's so distant from me now."

Ozzie stared at me for a few seconds. "To be honest with you, I've never believed anybody who says he puts God first. Especially a politician. It strikes me as a bunch of sanctimonious fluff. And I'm afraid it's no different with you."

"What?" I asked with irritation. "You're doubting my faith?"

"I know you believe in God. I just wonder about the purpose of all your religious blather."

"What do you know about Christianity?"

"Not much, admittedly. But from what I've observed, you worship something like a PEZ dispenser god."

"You're crazy."

"Oh really? Look at how you always talk about how God has blessed you with this and that. Football championships. Wealth. The Senate. Popularity. You praise Jesus so much for your success, it seems to me that your faith is nothing more than a means to that end. I really can't see how your religion is any different from a kid asking Santa Claus for presents."

I gaped at my brother as he continued talking.

"You pray to God to give you blessings and stuff, and then you act all righteous so he'll comply. Because if you're naughty, then you won't get what you want." His mouth formed a smirk. "You've been career focused ever since college. I can understand that. Gotta put bread on the table. But sometime after you got to Congress, it seemed like your career became *all* you cared about in life. So of course it became the focal point of your faith too."

"That's not true. It can't be."

"Okay. Whatever."

My BlackBerry rang. It was Joe informing me that Thor was on his way up to escort me to the ballroom. I slid the device back into my jacket pocket. "I have to go."

Just as I turned, a hand gripped my shoulder. "Dave," Ozzie said with earnestness in his voice. "I didn't mean to unload on you like that. Just forget everything I said. I think I had too much wine over at Splash earlier tonight. I'm actually proud of you."

Still reeling, I did not know what to say. "Okay, Oz."

"Give 'em hell, little brother. Show the world what a King is made of."

I tried to focus on my speech as the elevator descended, but Ozzie's words would not go away. Next thing I knew, I was standing just outside the doors to the ballroom awaiting my introduction. Inside, a chant grew louder: "Dave King, Dave King, Dave King."

The voice of Cal Tjaden, my publicist, boomed through a microphone. His enthusiasm exhorted the crowd to even higher levels of frenzy.

"Keep your eyes open," Thor said, anxiety lacing his voice.

"It'll be alright, buddy." I clapped his shoulder.

From inside the ballroom Tjaden bellowed, "Please welcome the next president of the United States, DAVE KIIIING!!"

I passed through the doors and strode toward the podium. As I waved to the people, they responded with an earsplitting roar. Cameras flashed with blinding intensity. Crowded onto the stage behind where I was to speak stood a gathering of supporters—prominent Iowa Republicans, former teammates, and assorted members of my campaign staff, including Joe, Anthony, and

Zadok. Gail was there too, dutifully stationed near the podium. Though she looked lovely in her teal dress, her face bore a forced smile and apprehensive eyes. After a perfunctory kiss, I took my position at the microphone.

Smiling and nodding, I surveyed the throng before me. Some of the faces were familiar, particularly those of volunteers, staffers, and contributors. Many others I did not recognize. As the wild cheering continued, time seemed to slow. I gripped the podium and took deep breaths to steady my senses. "King for President" signs bobbed above the crowd. Television camera lenses reminded me that the world was my audience. I raised my hands to call for silence. While waiting for the din to decline, I girded my mind to speak.

"Today, Iowa made a statement. The people of this great state have indicated loud and clear that this campaign is on the move." Shouts and claps rang in my ears. "We have taken a major step in our journey. Together we will march forward from this victory and prepare ourselves for the next battle in New Hampshire. And we will win there, too." During the following burst of applause, a stray thought bounced into my head. *What do I care most about in life?*

"Nobody gave us much of a chance when I first announced my candidacy. But look what we've accomplished."

Is it really my career?

"Working as a team, we gained momentum."

Is my own success all I care about anymore?

"And now, the goal we have set our sights on is within reach."

Is the focus of my faith to get God to grant me my selfish desires?

I looked over my shoulder at Gail. Our eyes locked. For a moment we were back in college, when our love bloomed and forever wasn't long enough to be together. But an instant later the loneliness in her gaze brought me back to the present reality. My body shuddered with a cold pain. I turned to the cameras. "The goal this campaign has been pressing toward …"

… is not the goal God has for my life.

"… is not the goal God has for my life." The audience stirred with murmurs and shocked expressions. Unable to continue, I squeezed my eyes shut. A titanic struggle raged within. The voice of the Lord thundered through my head with flashes of lightning. In a decisive moment, my soul yielded to the power of the divine. I felt a cleansing shower wash away layers of iniquitous residue.

Regaining an awareness of my surroundings, I opened my eyes and looked out at the confused faces. "I used to think that I was right with God—that I walked the path of righteousness. But something happened. Things changed." Mouths agape, the crowd stood transfixed in eerie silence.

"Throughout my career in public office, I have talked a lot about faith and honor and helping others. Over the past several years, however, my primary motivations have been to win votes and to stay in office. You've all heard my professions of faith, but the truth is, somewhere along the way, I lost the fellowship I once had with my Lord. And I turned away from the people who were closest to me. I let down those who loved me and counted on me to be there for them. My personal ambition took precedence over that which was truly important. I became a person I do not want to be."

Bolstered by a calm surge of power, I realized what I had to do. "Among my opponents there are several fine choices to be your next president. But it has become clear to me now that God has not called me to serve in that capacity. Therefore, I officially withdraw my candidacy for the Republican nomination. I also announce my official resignation from the U.S. Senate." Gasps and groans escaped from the audience.

"To my staff and volunteers, thank you for your service. I could not have asked for a better group. To all those in Iowa and across America who have supported me, you have my gratitude. You deserve a president who will be fully committed to that high office. I'm sorry that I cannot be that person, but I am confident you will find such a leader among the honorable candidates still in this race. God bless you all. Good night."

The masses remained paralyzed as I turned, grabbed Gail's hand, and led her to the exit. Thor stood near the doors, a smile creeping through his surprised expression. We exchanged nods as my wife and I left the ballroom. Moving at a brisk pace, we passed by several wide-eyed people still gripped by shock. The mass astonishment gave way to pandemonium as Gail and I entered the elevator. The doors closed, shutting out the mayhem exploding from the ballroom. We started to ascend.

Gail was silent as bells marked our upward movement. "That went well," I said, still holding her hand. "Don't you think?"

Her head bobbed with a hard swallow. "What just happened? Are you okay?"

"Never better."

She stared straight ahead, offering no response. We exited the elevator and reached the door to our suite. After entering, I felt a hand grab my arm. I turned to face her. She beheld me with gleaming green eyes. "Dave?"

"I know I haven't been the man I promised you I would be. When you and our children needed me most, I wasn't there. I didn't know how to handle what we were facing with Tammy and Archie. It was like the family tragedies from my childhood were replaying. I couldn't bear to go through that again. I got scared and withdrew. My career in Washington became my escape.... I'm sorry."

Her gaze remained locked on mine.

"I know you may not like the person standing before you right now, but please, be patient. God is not finished with me. He's working to change me, and I'm finally going to stop resisting him."

"Dave," she whispered.

"Do we still have a chance?"

A tear escaped from her eye. "I never stopped praying for that."

"Things are going to be different," I said, taking hold of both her hands. "With us. With our children. We'll be a family again."

We stayed up talking for two more hours. Though at times painful, it was a conversation that was long overdue. Through the tears, a budding hope emerged.

When I rolled over to check the time, the display read 2:45 a.m. The rhythmic sawing of Gail's soft snores floated through the surrounding darkness. Still wired from the evening's events, I had yet to fall asleep. I slipped out of bed, grabbed my BlackBerry and went into the bathroom. As expected, I had dozens of new messages—voice, text, and email. Joe had sent about half of them.

The first ones went something like, "Don't worry, we'll fix this. Tomorrow we'll hold a press conference and say that you were sick." The next set of messages contained profanity-laced tirades about how stupid I was to throw it all away. In the most recent set of missives, he begged me to reconsider and promised to make whatever changes I wanted. I was impressed. In only a few hours, he had already progressed through three of the Five Stages of Grief.

While scrolling through my emails, I found a new message from Sol. "We just watched your speech. Mom said she's proud of you. I am too. BTW, I had a strange dream last night. I'll explain later."

Ozzie had also sent an email. "Thanks a lot, moron. Way to rob me of my chance to get laid in the Lincoln Bedroom."

I dialed his number. "What the hell?" he grunted into the phone.

"Hey Oz. It's me."

"Figures. My fruit loop little brother."

"You want to go ride around for a while?"

"What? It's almost three and I've got a big meeting at work tomorrow morning. So … yeah, okay. You got wheels?"

"No. I arrived here by limo."

"Alright, I'll pick you up. You still at the hotel?"

"Yep. I'll wait for you at the Locust entrance."

Fifteen minutes later, I was in Ozzie's Corvette heading east on Locust Avenue toward the capitol building. "So," he said through a yawn, "what exactly happened to you back there?"

"Believe it or not, it was something you said."

"Oh, hell to the no! You are NOT going to pin that on me. I'm not taking the blame for your meltdown."

"It's true, Oz. You actually helped me realize something very important. Go figure, spiritual insights from my heathen brother."

"Great," he said. "You *are* going to blame me for your insanity."

"I'm not insane. I've never been thinking more clearly."

"Right. You had a chance to become the president of the United States, and in one rash decision you flushed it all down the toilet. I didn't think anybody could lay a bigger egg at the Iowa

Caucus than Howard Dean. But by golly, you topped him. The only thing missing from your speech was a big 'yeeeaaaahh' at the end." He punched the air for emphasis.

I chuckled. "You were right in what you said earlier about my career. I'd become so self-centered. You helped me remember that relationship with God and family should be the top priorities of my life, not personal gain and material success."

Now on Grand Avenue, Ozzie continued driving east. "You weren't supposed to take it that seriously, Dave. I was just trying to get you to quit peeing your pants over the divine wrath you thought was going to zap you. I mean, please, God doesn't even exist. At least not the one you Bible thumpers are always spouting off about."

"But God does exist, Oz. And he loves you. Someday you will realize that."

He drove on in silence for a while. "It's just as well you dropped out of the race. Hillary would have kicked your ass in November."

"You don't know that."

"Yeah I do," he snorted. "She would have slapped a collar on you and made you her bitch."

"Your confidence in me has always been a great inspiration."

The Corvette rolled past the dark shell that was once my father's restaurant. Graffiti covered the boarded-up windows and cracks marred the surface of the barren parking lot. I felt a twinge of melancholy as a collage of memories returned.

"So what are you going to do now?" Ozzie asked, driving through the University intersection past the Anderson Erickson cows. "Jobless slacker."

"I may have a lead. Remember Shawn Sanders from high school?"

"Graduated in your class, right?"

"Yep. Ran into him at a rally last month. He's the principal at Eastridge now. Said they needed a baseball coach. Offered me the job as a joke. Playing along, I said I'd consider it if I lost the election."

"And now you're serious." He eyed me with raised brows.

"Yeah, why not? I've got some experience in competitive athletics. I'm going to call him tomorrow. Tell him I'm interested."

"So you gave up a career as one of the most powerful politicians in America to be a high school baseball coach? Makes sense to me."

"The coaching position had nothing to do with my decision tonight. But I do need a job now. One that will allow me to stay close to home. Plus, coaching my old team sounds like fun."

"Back to your roots, huh? Guess you'd be taking over Sal Kishman's old kingdom."

"Yeah. I hadn't thought about it like that." My mind drifted back to a baseball game more than three decades earlier. I tossed the ball to John to start an inning-ending double play. His freckly face beamed as we jogged to the dugout.

"I gotta ask, Dave. Did you really have to burn all your bridges? Couldn't you have at least kept your Senate seat?" Alone on the road, my brother's car continued its leisurely pace up the long incline of Hubbell Avenue. After cresting the hill, we coasted past the Grand View Golf Course.

"No, I had to resign. The job kept me away from home all the time. Living in D.C. and traveling so much took a toll on my marriage. I want to be here with Gail to rebuild our relationship. I've let her down in the past. Never again. Same with my children. Kyle, Tammy, Donnie—they've all taken a backseat to my political ambitions. No more. I'm going to visit each of them and ask for their forgiveness. I'll do everything I can to restore my relationship with them. They've lived without a dad long enough."

"I don't want to rain on your parade," Ozzie said, "but what if it doesn't work out with them? What if you can't get the magic back with Gail? Sandy and I tried for nearly a year to work things out. It just didn't happen. And what if your kids don't want you back in their lives? Young people can be stubborn, you know."

"I know it won't be easy," I said, noticing that he was turning onto our old street. "But I'm trusting God to strengthen me for the challenges ahead."

He slowed the car to a crawl as we neared the house where we grew up. Both of us gawked at the familiar two-story structure. "Who would have guessed that the drippy little nerd who once lived there actually had a shot at being president?" he asked. "Man, I don't think I could have done what you did tonight. Passed up an opportunity to be the leader of the free world."

I turned to him. "You're right. By the world's standards, I completely wrecked my future. But in actuality, nothing compares to what I gained tonight. Not wealth. Not fame. Not even the presidency. The Lord is again my shepherd. I shall not want."

Ozzie drove on down the street. "Yeah," he sighed, "I'm sure things will turn out fine for you."

"You really believe that?"

"Absolutely. I bet someone even makes a statue of you someday."

"And David became more and more powerful, because the Lord Almighty was with him."

1 Chronicles 11:9

Character Guide

Characters are listed in order of appearance in the novel.

Novel Character	Biblical Figure
Dave King	King David
Ozzie King	Ozem, brother of David
Obadiah King	Obed, grandfather of David
Sal Kishman	King Saul
Jesse King	Jesse, father of David
Anthony Krieger	Abishai, nephew of David
Joe Krieger	Joab, nephew of David
Asa Krieger	Asahel, nephew of David
Zoe Krieger	Zeruiah, sister of David
Abby King	Abigail, sister of David
Eli King	Eliab, brother of David
Adam King	Abinadab, brother of David
Shane King	Shimea, brother of David
Reverend Samuels	Samuel the prophet
John Kishman	Jonathan, son of Saul
Phil Galbraith	Goliath
Coach Acheson	King Achish
Doug Edmonds	Doeg the Edomite
Neil Heimlich	Ahimelech the priest
Michelle Kishman	Michal, daughter of Saul
Boz Kishman	Ish-Bosheth, son of Saul
Anne Kishman	Ahinoam, wife of Saul
Abner Kishman	Abner, cousin of Saul
Thor Heimlich	Abiathar the priest
Coach Keeler	citizens of Keilah
Calvin Ziph	the Ziphites
Perry Arbuckle	Paarai the Arbite
Amy Martin	Ahinoam, wife of David
Caleb Nagel	Nabal the Calebite
Gail Taylor	Abigail, wife of David
Tank Garber	Gareb the Ithrite

Character Guide, continued

Novel Character	Biblical Figure
Paul Lasch	Paltiel, husband of Michal
Kyle King	Kileab, son of David
Nathan Rodriguez	Nathan the prophet
Jason Hackman	Jashobeam the Hacmonite
Archie King	Absalom, son of David
Michael Lewis	Mephibosheth, son of Jonathan
Tammy King	Tamar, daughter of David
Jerry Irving	Jether, brother-in-law of David
Donnie King	Adonijah, son of David
Beth Schaeffer	Bathsheba, wife of Uriah
Ryan Schaeffer	Uriah the Hittite
Jon King	Jonadab, nephew of David
Tom Nelson	Amnon, son of David
Levi Zadok	Zadok the priest
Andy Irving	Amasa, nephew of David
Sol Schaeffer	Solomon, son of David
Ben Shea	Sheba the Benjamite
Geoff Ittai	Ittai the Gittite
Phil Atkins	Ahitophel the Gilonite
Tony Huscher	Hushai the Arkite
J.J. Heimlich	Jonathan, son of Abiathar
Maz Zadok	Ahimaaz, son of Zadok
Ben Jeffries	Benaiah, son of Jehoiada

Chapter Guide

Novel Chapter	Biblical Passage
Chapter 1 – September 1973	1 Chronicles 2: 13-17; 1 Samuel 17: 34-36
Chapter 2 – November 1973	1 Samuel 16: 1-13
Chapter 3 – May 1974	1 Samuel 16: 14-23
Chapter 4 – July 1974	1 Samuel 17
Chapter 5 – October 1974	1 Samuel 18
Chapter 6 – May 1975	1 Samuel 19-22
Chapter 7 – October 1975	1 Samuel 23
Chapter 8 – April 1976	1 Samuel 24, 26-27
Chapter 9 – June 1976	1 Samuel 28-31; 2 Samuel 1
Chapter 10 – March 1977	1 Samuel 25: 43; 2 Samuel 3: 2
Chapter 11 – September 1978	1 Samuel 25: 1-35; 2 Samuel 2
Chapter 12 – November 1978	1 Samuel 25: 36-44; 2 Samuel 3-4
Chapter 13 – October 1979	2 Samuel 5
Chapter 14 – January 1980	2 Samuel 6; Psalm 20
Chapter 15 – December 1981	2 Samuel 3: 3; 2 Samuel 7
Chapter 16 – October 1983	2 Samuel 9
Chapter 17 – January 1987	2 Samuel 8, 10
Chapter 18 – July 1991	2 Samuel 11: 1-4
Chapter 19 – January 1992	2 Samuel 11: 5-27; 2 Samuel 12: 1-23
Chapter 20 – February 1992	2 Samuel 12: 13; Psalm 51
Chapter 21 – November 1994	2 Samuel 12: 26-31
Chapter 22 – August 1999	2 Samuel 13: 1-34
Chapter 23 – April 2002	2 Samuel 12: 24-25 2 Samuel 13: 35-38
Chapter 24 – October 2004	2 Samuel 14-20
Chapter 25 – January 2008	2 Samuel 21-22; 1 Kings 3: 5-6; Psalm 29

Discussion Questions

1. Did you recognize any events from the Biblical story of King David in the novel? If so, which ones?

2. Did the novel's connection to King David influence your reading of this book? If so, how?

3. Which phase of Dave's life did you find most interesting? (high school, college, NFL, politics)

4. Did you identify with Dave or any of the other characters in the book? If so, how?

5. Have you faced any decisions similar to those Dave had to make? Did you respond in a similar way?

6. How would you describe Dave's faith throughout the book?

7. What does the story of Dave King say about repentance and forgiveness?

8. Describe the role each of the following characters played in Dave's life: Ozzie, Michelle, John, Thor, Joe, Nathan, Gail.

9. Do you agree with the choices Gail made regarding her husband?

10. How do you feel about the decision Dave made in the final chapter?

11. What was the biggest surprise in the book?

12. What do you think is the central message of *The All-American King*? Does this message apply to your life?

About the Author

Kent Krause writes content for online high school history courses and social studies textbooks. He holds bachelor's and master's degrees from Iowa State University, and a doctorate from the University of Nebraska-Lincoln. In addition to his three novels, he has published articles in *Great Plains Quarterly* and *The International Journal of the History of Sport*. USA Book News selected *The All-American King* as a category finalist for the National Best Books 2009 Awards. Kent lives in Nebraska with his wife Jill.

Visit Kent online at: **kentkrause.com**

www.ingramcontent.com/pod-product-compliance
Lightning Source LLC
LaVergne TN
LVHW020516100826
845148LV00010B/1250

* 9 7 8 0 6 1 5 8 7 8 5 6 0 *